A blow to the face and chest knocked her back onto the moss.

She lay there, her forehead throbbing, tasting blood; she had bitten her lip. She sat up and probed forward along a mossy mound, and up. She had run into the trunk of a tree.

Sulien felt her way around it and tried to regain her bearings, but she could see nothing save an occasional luminous mushroom. Using her sensitive's gift, which she did not understand, she sought the unnerving presence of the Whelm and found it some distance to her left.

She stretched out her arms, turned until the presence was directly behind her, in the west, then, her head aching and her heart as icy as her feet, headed east towards the unseen frozen mountains.

By Ian Irvine

THE THREE WORLDS SERIES

The View from the Mirror quartet
A Shadow on the Glass
The Tower on the Rift
Dark Is the Moon
The Way Between the Worlds

THE WELL OF ECHOES QUARTET

Geomancer
Tetrarch
Alchymist
Chimaera

SONG OF THE TEARS TRILOGY

The Fate of the Fallen
The Curse on the Chosen
The Destiny of the Dead

THE GATES OF GOOD AND EVIL

The Summon Stone
The Fatal Gate

Related Fantasy

THE TAINTED REALM

Vengeance
Rebellion
Justice

THE FATAL GATE

WITHDRAWN

BOOK TWO OF THE GATES OF GOOD AND EVIL

IAN IRVINE

www.orbitbooks.net

Copyright © 2017 by Ian Irvine
Excerpt from *The Shadow of What Was Lost* copyright © 2016 by James Islington
Excerpt from *Soul of the World* copyright © 2017 by David Mealing

Cover design by Jack Smyth—LBBG
Cover images by Shutterstock
Cover copyright © 2017 by Hachette Book Group, Inc.

Orbit
Hachette Book Group
1290 Avenue of the Americas
New York, NY 10104
orbitbooks.net

Simultaneously published in Great Britain and in the U.S. by Orbit in 2017
First Edition: June 2017

Orbit is an imprint of Hachette Book Group.
The Orbit name and logo are trademarks of Little, Brown Book Group Limited.

The publisher is not responsible for websites (or their content) that are not owned by the publisher.

The Hachette Speakers Bureau provides a wide range of authors for speaking events. To find out more, go to www.hachettespeakersbureau.com or call (866) 376-6591.

Library of Congress Control Number: 2017934972

ISBNs: 978-0-316-38690-6 (trade paperback), 978-0-316-38691-3 (ebook)

Printed in the United States of America

LSC-C

10 9 8 7 6 5 4 3 2 1

To Simon

CONTENTS

MAP OF MELDORIN ISLAND
IX

MAP OF THE CONTINENT OF LAURALIN
X

MAP OF WESTERN LAURALIN
XI

PART ONE:
PURSUIT
1

PART TWO:
ALCHEMY
153

PART THREE:
BATTLE
355

PART FOUR:
REVELATION
479

GLOSSARY OF CHARACTERS, NAMES AND PLACES
560

GUIDE TO PRONUNCIATION
572

MELDORIN ISLAND

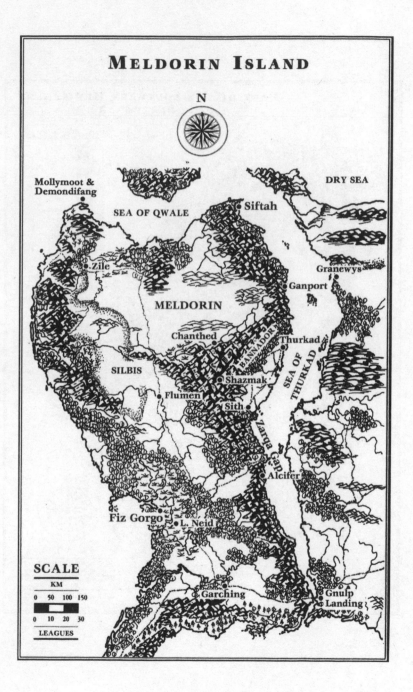

N

Mollymoot &
Demondifang

DRY SEA

SEA OF QWALE

Siftah

Zile

Granewys

Ganport

MELDORIN

Chanthed

Thurkad

SILBIS

Shazmak

SEA OF
THURKAD

Flumen

Sith

Zarqa Gap

Alcifer

Fiz Gorgo

L. Neid

SCALE

KM

0   50   100 150

0   10   20   30

LEAGUES

Garching

Gnulp
Landing

PART OF THE SOUTHERN HEMISPHERE
OF SANTHENAR

Gwine

Banthey

LEGEND

Mountains
Hills
Desert
Salt Lake
Marsh, Swamp
Conifer Forest
Broadleaf Forest
Tropical Forest
Grassland
Reef
Main Road

Fankster
Gendrigore
Huccadory
Bel Torance
Nys
Taranta
FARANDA
Strinklet
Tar Gaarn &
Havissard
Roros
Twissel
THE
DRY SEA
Mistmurk Mountain
Jepperand
Guffeons
Katazza
Gosport
Flude
Maksmord
Nithmak
Ashmode
CARENDOR
KALAR
QWALE
STASSOR
Tifferfyte
Zile
MELDORIN
Morrelune
Fadd
Thurkad
Great Mountains
Nennifer
Burning
Mountain
Tirthrax
Tiksi
Fiz Gorgo
LAURALIN
MIRRILLADELL
KARAMA MALAMA
(Sea of Mists)
OOLO
HA-DROW
Ogur
LUUMA NARTA
SALLIBAN
Hessular
SHAZABBA
Steppe
KARA AGEL
(Frozen Sea)
Noom
Grinding

20°
30°
40°
50°
60°
70°

N
W E
S

SCALE
KILOMETRES
0 100 200 300 400 500 600 700 800 900 1000
0 40 80 120 160 200
LEAGUES

Maps by the author

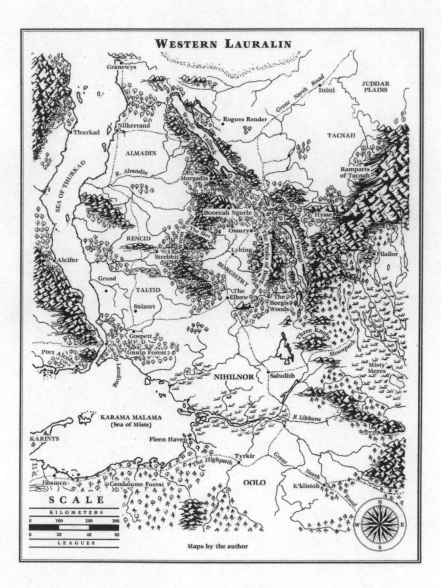

WESTERN LAURALIN

Granewys

JUDDAR
PLAINS

Great North Road

Ittiti

Rogues Render

Nilkerrand

Thurkad

TACNAH

ALMADIN

Wyrde

Yellicca

R. Almadin

Ramparts
of Tacnah

SEA OF THURKAD

Morgadis

Booreah Ngurle

Hysse

The Slot

Ossury

RENCID

Peaks of Bexer

Alcifer

Strebbit

Lybing

FilaBor

Grund

BORGISTRY

Parnett

TALTID

Snizort

The
Elbow

The
Borgis
Woods

Gospett

Three Knot

Moonpath

Port Ajcoba

Gnulp Forest

NIHILNOR

Saludith

Misty
Meres

KARAMA MALAMA
(Sea of Mists)

R Libbens

KARINTS

Fleen Haven

Tyrkir

The Highpath

Great

OOLO

North

Jibstorn

Candalume Forest

K'klistoh

Road

SCALE

KILOMETERS

0   100   200   300

0   20   40   60

LEAGUES

Maps by the author

N
W   E
S

PART ONE

PURSUIT

1

NO ONE COULD HELP HER

"Gergrig wants the child," said Yetchah, the weathered boards creaking as she moved around the circle of Whelm. Her dark eyes, touched by the firelight, blazed with longing. "If we give her to him, he will surely agree to be our master."

Every hair stood up on Sulien's head, and her throat went so tight that she could scarcely draw breath. The Whelm were going to betray her!

"Gergrig wants her *dead*!" grated Idlis. "And we swore to protect her with our lives."

"*You* swore to protect her," said Yetchah. "The rest of us vowed, after our incomparable master Rulke was slain, that we would do whatever it took to gain a master his equal."

"Oh perfect master!" sighed the other eleven Whelm in the circle, and they raised their bony arms to the sky.

"The life of a nine-year-old girl is a small price to pay to gain such a master," said Yetchah.

"We made Sulien into a little Whelm," choked Idlis. "Would you send one of us, a *child*, to a cruel death by torture?"

For a moment Yetchah looked uneasy, then the ecstasy flooded back. "No outsider can ever be one of us," she cried. "No one matters more than our new master."

Sulien, crouching in the shadows, clenched her fists helplessly as they shuffled sideways in a ring around the fire. The crude stone fireplace was set on the boards of a long-abandoned village built on stilts at the centre of a chilly coastal lake. The flames roared shoulder high, the sole source of light on this winter night, but no warmth reached her. What could she do? Where could she go? The Whelm knew this cold southern land, which they called Salliban, and she did not.

She had lived in fear for months now; every day and every hour she kept watch for an enemy determined to see her dead. The attack could come through a mental link to burn out her mind, a blow from a stranger or poison slipped into her mug, and now from those who had sworn to protect her. Terror was crushing her; every day she felt smaller and weaker and a step closer to death.

"Yes, yes, *yes!*" they chanted.

Sulien had attempted a link to Karan many times, but it was as if her mother no longer existed. Had the Merdrun's evil old magiz *killed* her? She choked back a sob. If she had, no one could help Sulien now. Not even Idlis, the strangest of all the Whelm, could defy their collective will.

He stood outside the circle, licking his flaking lips. He was trembling; he desperately wanted to join his people. How long before he betrayed her too?

Idlis and Yetchah had been at Sulien's traumatic birth, and without them both mother and baby would have died. Sulien had often seen Yetchah gazing at her yearningly, as if she longed for a child of her own. Sulien had felt closer to her than any of the other Whelm, but this Yetchah was a cold, obsessed stranger.

Sulien backed away across the rough-sawn boards, which were weathered to a splintery grey. Everything was grey in this awful place: the wet sky, the crumbling huts and even the Whelm themselves. Their lips were the colour of dirty snow, their eyes as dead and dark as soot.

"Yes, yes, *yes!*" Yetchah cried ecstatically.

On the long journey south they had kept up the chanting for hours at a time, dully and listlessly. But two days ago, when Sulien made a despairing link to the magiz on the little world of Cinnabar, attacking her to try to save Karan's life, everything had changed.

The magiz, a hideous enchanter, drank innocent lives to give herself the power to open the ancient Crimson Gate that would finally bring the Merdrun to Santhenar, the beautiful world they had long coveted.

Sulien's world. The mighty Merdrun army was unconquered in ten thousand years of warfare aimed at a single purpose—to escape the void and seize one of the real worlds for their own.

But Sulien's link had revealed Gergrig, the greatest warrior and most ruthless leader in the void, to the Whelm. And they knew on sight that he was the perfect master they craved so desperately. They would do whatever it took to get him.

Now he was somewhere on Santhenar, for just minutes ago the magiz had succeeded in opening the Crimson Gate. *This is the hour!* Gergrig had roared as his army stormed the gate. And the Whelm had cried out their ecstasy.

Mummy? Sulien had sent desperately, over and again. *Help!*

But Karan had not answered. Sulien's only chance was to run, though Salliban was a cold, wet wilderness and winter was underway. Without food, shelter or anyone to help her, how could she survive it?

"Yes, yes, *yes!*" cried the Whelm.

Sulien slipped away to the hut she shared with Idlis and Yetchah, and tied her bedroll to her pack. She stuffed in half a dozen bags of the gritty grey cereal the Whelm used to make their daily gruel and added her knife, metal cup and wooden spoon.

They were still chanting like a flock of evil crows. Some distance away, Idlis, a gaunt, tormented loner, shifted his weight from one bony foot to another and twisted his fingers together. His skin was so rough that Sulien could hear it rasping, and the breath hissed in and out of his tunnel-like nostrils.

As she slipped out through the door he turned her way and the fire-light touched his eyes until they blazed red-black. She froze. He was looking right at her; even in the dimness of the abandoned village he must have seen her.

Sulien stared back at him, her small body rigid. *You gave your word,* she sent. *You swore to protect me.* She did not know if he could hear sendings; few people could. But the plea in her eyes was clear enough.

"Yes, yes, *yes!*" chanted the Whelm.

After an endless few seconds Idlis's left hand gave a tiny jerk. Sulien interpreted it to mean that he would not stop her. She crept around the hut then, keeping to the band of shadow behind it, darted across the deck towards the walkway that led to the shore a quarter of a mile away.

Then stopped. If she used the walkway the Whelm would know where to look for her tracks. She turned and, heart pounding, felt her way across the southern side of the deck to the rickety ladder down to the lake.

As she went down the ice-crusted rungs, the cold came up through the soles of her worn boots. The surface of the lake had been frozen three inches thick when they arrived a week ago, though there had been a thaw since then and the ice was cracked and dotted with the Whelm's square fishing holes. If she fell through she would freeze to death before she could get out.

Sulien slid one foot forwards, then the other, *rasp, rasp*, testing the ice with each step. The night was still. If the Whelm stopped chanting they would hear her.

She gained the shore, reached out, and her fingertips touched a steep moss-covered bank. It rained most days here, and the Whelm, who were brilliant, relentless hunters, would easily track her across the soft ground.

The lake, one of hundreds in this rain-drenched land, was surrounded by a coniferous rainforest of vast old trees, widely separated and hung with grey-green streamers of a plant Sulien had never seen before. Karan's geography lessons had covered the frozen interior of the south, which was called Shazabba, but Sulien knew nothing about Salliban save that it was home to many kinds of beasts that would enjoy eating her.

She stepped up off the ice onto moss that sank two inches under her slight weight, though when she lifted her foot the moss sprang back again. Endless forest lay ahead but it was too dark to see the way. Arms outstretched, she turned her back on the gaunt figures encircling the fire and their cawing cries of "Yes, yes, *yes!*" and headed east towards the range of mountains she had seen from the ship on the way here. It felt safer than heading north along the coast, which was so indented with fjords that it might take ten miles of walking east and west to get one mile further north, closer to home.

Gergrig wanted her dead because, in her first nightmare about him, she had seen the Merdrun's one fatal weakness, and as long as it lay buried in her mind they would kill her to protect it. The only way to save herself was to recover the nightmare and tell as many people as possible, but it had vanished like a dream on waking. She could not remember a thing and neither Karan nor anyone else had been able to recover it.

The ground was all hollows and humps here, and fallen trees often blocked her way. She kept stumbling into them in the darkness.

She reached the top of a small ridge and was standing there, icy hands in her pockets, wondering which way to go, when she heard a collective roar behind her. Her heart lurched; the Whelm knew she had bolted.

Sulien darted down the slope away from the lake. They were slow and awkward; she could outrun them for a little while. But the Whelm never gave up and they would get her in the end.

Thump!

A blow to the face and chest knocked her back onto the moss. She lay there, her forehead throbbing, tasting blood; she had bitten her lip. She sat up and probed forward along a mossy mound, and up. She had run into the trunk of a tree.

Sulien felt her way around it and tried to regain her bearings, but she could see nothing save an occasional luminous mushroom. Using her sensitive's gift, which she did not understand, she sought the unnerving presence of the Whelm and found it some distance to her left.

She stretched out her arms, turned until the presence was directly behind her, in the west, then, her head aching and her heart as icy as her feet, headed east towards the unseen frozen mountains.

2

HE WANTS HER DEAD, KARAN

Karan looked down at her furious Aachim friends, forty feet below in the semi-dark clearing, and knew they would never forgive her.

"Stop!" Malien said in cold fury.

"Yggur, go!" Karan said hoarsely.

Yggur, who was seated behind a mushroom-shaped bulge rising from the floor of the sky ship, did not move. A crescent carved into the bulge at the height of his waist held three small levers, the left one topped with a knob of red, granular porphyry. The middle knob was the oily green of malachite, and the right one was black obsidian. Behind them a small rod, ending in a crystal of golden beryl, could be raised to add the buoyant and highly explosive gas, protium, to the airbag, or lowered to release it.

The cabin of the sky ship, which was twenty feet long and eight wide, was shaped like a dolphin. The inside walls were of honey-yellow resin, an oval window three feet across allowed a restricted view ahead, and there were three small oval windows on each side. Six rows of seats, two to each row, filled most of the cabin. The Aachim had fitted dozens of compartments into the remaining spaces, high and low. All were beautifully finished and every surface was decorated with intricate engravings of the strange plants, beasts and landscapes of their lost homeland, Aachan.

"The Merdrun have opened the Crimson Gate," yelled Malien. "They're invading and we don't know where. We—need—my—sky ship!"

"Yggur, hurry!" said Karan.

Sickening guilt churned in her belly. It was the first aerial craft ever made and it would make a big difference to the war—but her need was desperate. She kept seeing the last image Sulien had sent—Yetchah's eyes alight with longing.

Gergrig wants the child. If we give her to him, he will surely agree to be our master. Take her!

Karan had seen no more and could not contact Sulien. When Malien had unblocked Karan's gift for the Secret Art, several hours earlier, she had not realised that it would cost her the ability to make links and sendings.

"Come down!" snapped Malien.

"The Whelm have seen the Merdrun," said Karan. "They want Gergrig for their master and they're planning to betray Sulien to seal the deal. And the moment he gets Sulien, he'll kill her!"

Malien's breast heaved. "I'm sorry. I love her with all my heart . . . but this isn't the answer. She's too far away."

A sickening dread overwhelmed Karan. What was taking Yggur so long? She could hardly breathe; she felt as though she was choking. "Hurry!" she gasped.

The western side of Shazabba, where she believed the Whelm had taken Sulien, was seven hundred and fifty miles away and even at the fastest pace of this unreliable craft it would take at least three days to fly there. In three days—maybe even three *hours*—the Whelm could have contacted Gergrig and betrayed Sulien to him.

Shand pelted into the glade, followed by Nadiril, his ancient bones clicking. He carried a storm lantern and Lilis was beside him. She looked bitterly disappointed in Karan. Join the queue.

"Karan," called Nadiril. "Without the sky ship we'll never find the Merdrun in time."

"And if we don't, Santhenar is lost," said Shand, reaching up with both hands. "Millions will die because of your selfish choice."

"How dare you lecture me," cried Karan, "after you betrayed us."

"You can't put Sulien before the lives of all my people," said Malien, "and all the others on this world."

"Sulien and Llian and I gave everything we had to keep the enemy out of Santhenar, and all we've got for it is abuse and demands for more sacrifice. Damn you!"

Nadiril raised a long, fleshless arm and fear shivered through her. Was he trying to stop them? Could he?

He conferred with Malien and Shand and they pointed at the rear of the sky ship. The wooden rotors, powered by subtle aspects of the Secret Art, went still. The nose of the sky ship dipped and drifted downwards.

Karan looked over her shoulder. "You said you could fly the damned thing," she screeched. "Do something!"

Yggur turned frosty grey eyes onto her, unblinking, and she shivered. He was a strange, dangerous man who had recently suffered another mental breakdown, and he had never been her friend. His big hands moved the three levers gently, as if sensing out the purpose of each via his enigmatic arts.

"Shouldn't I understand what I'm doing first?" he said mildly.

The nose of the sky ship dipped until the floor of the cabin sloped too steeply to stand on. "They're pulling us down!" Karan's sweaty hand slipped on the vertical rail beside the cabin door; she lurched forward and almost fell out.

"Shut the door and sit down!" he snapped. "You're distracting me."

She pulled it closed, hauled herself up to a seat and clung to it, panting. The rotors were making a ticking sound.

"Sulien's got no money, no food, nowhere to go. And the Whelm—"

"Your whining isn't helping." Yggur pulled on the right-hand lever and the nose of the sky ship jerked upwards until it was level again. "Ah!" He thrust forward the stubby lever on the left, with the red knob; the sound of the rotors rose to a roar and the craft surged forwards.

"I'll make you pay for this, Karan!" raged Malien.

Karan sank back in the seat and closed her eyes. Malien was kin, and an old friend, and Karan had betrayed her trust.

The sky ship headed into the darkness, south-west, and Yggur's jaw was knotted as he sensed out the workings of the craft. It was not something she could comprehend. Karan's gift for the Secret Art, blocked at the age of twelve, had recently been rewoken, but after more than half her life without it, it was unlikely ever to be much use to her. The basics of mancery had to be learned before the mind was fully formed.

It reminded her of a more immediate problem—Sulien's powerful gift for the Secret Art. Since first seeing Gergrig far across the void, which was astounding in itself, her gift had grown in all kinds of ways. But where had it come from? No one knew.

Karan did not understand Sulien's gift and had no idea what to do about it. She could not block it; never would she do to her daughter what had been done to her, but neither could she tutor Sulien in it.

But she dared not give the job to anyone else—could anyone be trusted to guide and protect Sulien in so deadly an art while the Merdrun were hunting her with all their strength and cunning and mancery, determined to see her dead before the secret could be extracted?

Karan could not ignore Sulien's gift either. She was too clever and determined a child; she would explore it on her own, and that would be like giving a dagger to a baby. An untrained gift was a danger to its owner and everyone around her, and it would draw all manner of unsavoury people towards her—to say nothing of the Merdrun's mancers.

Sick terror overwhelmed Karan, that there was nothing she could do to help Sulien; that it was already too late. She fought an overwhelming urge to scream—being a sensitive, she felt things far more deeply than other people. It built up in her, and up; she rose from her seat, her mouth opening, eyes wide, fists clenched—

Whack! The back of Yggur's hand struck her across the face and she fell and hit the floor on both knees.

"Pull yourself together," he said coldly. "Do you want to save your daughter or not?"

3

I . . . HAD . . . A . . . BREAKDOWN!

Karan fought an urge to thump Yggur over the head. She rubbed her throbbing cheek, glowering.

"Think about how we can get her away from the thrice-cursed Whelm," he said.

They had served him for many years though they had never given him the respect owed to their true master—the Whelm had not thought him ruthless enough, and perhaps they had despised him for his past breakdowns. When Rulke contacted them twelve years ago the Whelm had abandoned Yggur and never looked back.

"But by the time we get there . . ." She could not say it, dared not think it.

He squinted through the front window into the darkness. "How high are the mountains directly behind Alcifer?"

"Maybe five thousand feet."

He thrust the left-hand lever forwards, hard, and jerked on the black knob; the rotors howled and the sky ship shot up. Karan clung to the edges of her seat. With a gesture he extinguished the lightglasses on the front and side walls, leaving the cabin illuminated only by one small glass at the rear.

"As I understand it," said Yggur, "the Whelm can't contact Gergrig directly. They can only do so via your daughter's ability to make sendings and mental links."

"I think so," said Karan.

"Then they'll have to force her to link to Gergrig before they ask him to become their master. What are the dimensions and limitations of Sulien's gift?"

"I don't know; it's still growing in unusual ways."

"What can she do?" he said impatiently.

"There are two parts, physical and psychic. With her physical gift I've seen her do things like boil a carafe of wine at a touch, and burn someone who was trying to hurt her. But she may be able to do much more—"

Yggur grunted. "And the psychic?"

"The far-seeing and far-sensing you know about. She's also a sensitive, much stronger than I am, and sometimes she senses when people are about to do dangerous things."

"Such as?"

"When Llian—" She choked; she felt sure he was dead. "When Llian was overwhelmed by the summon stone in Carcharon, and drawn into the mad fantasy that he could destroy it, Sulien cried out to him from hundreds of miles away, *No, Daddy!*"

Yggur frowned. "Llian hasn't got a sensitive bone in his body, yet she sensed what he was about to do and made a sending to *him*?"

"Yes," Karan said softly.

It was painful to think about him too. She had chosen to go after Sulien rather than Llian, but had a sick feeling that she'd made the wrong choice and now it was too late for him.

"That's *powerful*." said Yggur. "What else has she done that I should know about?"

"The second last time I went to Cinnabar, a couple of days ago, the magiz caught me. She was forcing a link to form between me and Sulien, so she could kill her *and drink her life*, and there was nothing I could do." Karan's voice sounded harsh in her ears. "But then . . ."

In the dim light Yggur's long head was just a shadow as he turned towards her. A stray ray touched his grey eyes, making them shine like moonbeams on frosty leaves, then they faded. "What?"

"Sulien cried, *Leave . . . my . . . mother . . . alone!* I *sent* to her to stop but the magiz yelled, *I've found the brat, Gergrig!* And then . . ."

"What?" said Yggur.

"Sulien exploded with fury and a searing light burst right in front of the magiz's eyes. They turned blood-red and she was blinded for a while. It saved my life."

After a very long pause, the sky ship rocking in the mountain air, Yggur said, "How could Sulien, a girl of only nine, attack the Merdrun's mightiest mancer from so far away?"

"I have no idea."

"Has she been trained in the Secret Art?"

"No."

"*Why not?*"

"Until six or seven weeks ago," Karan said slowly, "we didn't know she had a gift for it."

"But there must have been signs," Yggur said accusingly, as though Karan had been negligent in her parenting. "After all, she's a triune like you. Why didn't you check?"

"Before she was born, Llian and I had suffered two bloody, terrible years. The Time of the Mirror scarred us both; I still have nightmares and flashbacks, and he gets panic attacks. We just wanted Sulien to live the life of a normal little girl."

He grunted. "Gifts like hers are dangerous, especially if they're untrained. When you get her back—"

"I'm never going to get her back," Karan cried, the agony exploding in her. "Gergrig will order her killed."

"Don't be stupid. He won't tell the Whelm to kill her."

"Why not?"

"How could he trust them to carry out such a vital task? Once he has a new magiz—which could take time—he'll order her to drink Sulien's life."

"She might be doing it already." Karan strangled a sob.

"For pity's sake stop whining," he snapped. "I've had enough of it to last me a lifetime."

Karan had had enough. "And you've done enough whining to last *me* a lifetime," she snarled.

"How dare you!" he cried, abandoning the controls and standing up to tower head and shoulders over her.

"You've spent most of the last two months wallowing in self-pity, criticising everyone and offering nothing, yet it was your reckless abdication last year that gave Cumulus Snoat the opportunity to tear Meldorin apart."

"I . . . had . . . a . . . breakdown!" he said through clenched teeth. "I'm still suffering from when Rulke broke into my mind—possessed me, drove me out of my wits . . ."

"That was *a thousand years ago*! Get over it."

"The mind is its own master, you little fool! You can't tell yourself to snap out of it." He thrust his face so close to hers that, as he roared, drops of spittle spattered her.

He was so powerful and intimidating that Karan felt the urge to run up the back and hide under the hammocks. She wiped her face and forced herself to meet his eyes.

"Do you think I don't know that?" she said softly. "My father was killed when I was eight, and that very day I saw my mother's mind break. I lived with it for four years, until she took her life and left me all alone. I circled the pit of madness myself once, while I carried the cursed Mirror of Aachan; circled it and fell in and was lucky to escape. But I did, and it strengthened me, and I will never go there again."

Karan softened. A trauma that made one person stronger could break another, and it had nothing to do with size or physical strength or intellect—it simply happened. Yggur was still in great pain.

"I'm sorry," she added. "If there's any way I can help you, I will."

His head jerked back and she saw his yearning, that someone could lift the burden from him. Rulke had ransacked Yggur's mind from the inside, the most terrible violation anyone could experience, and Yggur had borne the burden of it for a thousand years.

He turned away and took the controls. "I've tried everything," he said harshly. "No one has ever been able to help me." He looked through the oval window into the dark, jaw clenched, then said, "We've got days to fill before we get there. Tell me the rest."

Karan's mind was a blank. "The rest of what?"

"What happened when you went to Cinnabar a few hours ago."

Had it only been a few hours? It felt like months. She realised that no one knew what had happened there; after she'd been flung back to Alcifer there had not been time to tell anyone. She gathered her thoughts.

"Malien made a spell to send me to Cinnabar, to stop the magiz from opening the Crimson Gate, but before I could trigger the spell the magiz dragged me back there, to the icy plateau at the top of the mountain where the gate stood, intending to drink my life and Sulien's.

"The Merdrun broke through the defenders' ring fortress and were about to take the gate when I discovered that two gates had once stood there side by side—the Gates of Good and Evil crafted by Stermin in ancient times. But the Azure Gate, the *good* gate, had been toppled and buried long ago.

"Before I could move, the enemy captured the Crimson Gate, caught me, and the magiz used the power of all the lives she'd drunk to open the gate. Gergrig stormed it with his greatest warriors, leading the charge, but they all went mad and hacked each other to pieces. He retreated back to Cinnabar, the only survivor."

"Why?" said Yggur.

"The gate was a trap; the Charon must have set it up nine thousand years ago when they gave Cinnabar to the defenders. The Charon had toppled the Crimson Gate and buried it, then disguised the Azure Gate with a permanent illusion, making it appear crimson. But the Azure Gate had been the *ennobling* gate, changing the people who chose it, just as the Crimson Gate had corrupted those who passed through it.

"The conflict between the ennobling gate and the Merdrun's own corruption had been too great for the troops who entered the gate; it drove them insane. And since their entire lives had been devoted to killing, in their madness all they could do was kill."

"But the gate *was* opened," said Yggur.

"Gergrig was furious that they had been duped. He cast down the false gate and raised the true Crimson Gate, but the magiz had exhausted her power, and the only way she could get more was by drinking powerful lives—mine and Sulien's. But first she had to beat me in physical combat . . . and she nearly did."

Karan shivered. It was frigid at this altitude and it reminded her of the unbearable cold as the magiz had cast her down onto the ice, tore her clothes open from breast to belly and prepared to gut her.

"I shoved my fingers into her open mouth and cast the one spell I was confident would work, a simple freezing charm I'd used as a little girl before Tensor blocked my mancery. At any other place the spell would probably have failed, but it was easy there. And the magiz had no way to block it because it had been cast inside her defences. It froze her from the inside out, but unfortunately . . ."

"Enormous power is released on the death of a great mancer," Yggur said thoughtfully, "and she contrived to open the gate with it."

"How did you know?"

"Nothing else could have done it," said Yggur. Then added, "And our allies don't know any of this?"

"I only had time to tell them that the enemy were coming through the gate somewhere, and that Shand was the magiz's unwitting spy."

"I overheard. That was badly done, Karan."

"After the way he abused me and Llian the past six weeks," she muttered, her cheeks glowing, "how else was I supposed to tell them?"

"Without malice! He's long been your friend, and he's also going through a difficult patch."

"The moment I mentioned the spy in our midst, he looked at you."

To her surprise, Yggur laughed. "I'd expect no less."

"The Merdrun are somewhere on Santhenar and we have no idea where," she said bitterly. "It's all been for nothing."

Yggur shrugged, one shoulder rising higher than the other. "Maybe, maybe not. How many Merdrun are there?"

"I don't know."

"Guess."

"Ten thousand. Maybe more."

"I don't see how ten thousand can threaten Santhenar."

"They're tougher than Charon, and a *hundred* Charon took Aachan."

"Special circumstances. It would never work here."

"On Cinnabar, over and again I saw single Merdrun soldiers take on three, five and once *ten* of the enemy, and cut them down. They're . . . superhuman."

"I doubt that, but they're bred and trained for a single purpose—war. And no doubt reinforced by mancery to make them seem even more terrible." He pushed the red porphyry knob forward until the sky ship was racing, the air whistling around it. "And how many thousands more of them are waiting their turn, back wherever they come from?"

"We've been invaded by the most vicious army the void has ever seen," Karan said in a dead voice, "an army so powerful that even the mighty Charon were terrified of them, and we don't have a clue where they are."

"But we do know they want Sulien dead," Yggur said softly.

4

SHE'S OUR BARGAINING PIECE

Where is she, Idlis? What have you done with her, traitor?

For Sulien to detect the Whelm's mind-speech, they had to be close. She did not hear any reply, but Idlis's anguish, as they battered him mercilessly, was like a spike digging into her back. She did not like him, for he was a hard, creepy, unknowable man. Yet he had been a faithful friend to Karan and always kept his word, and Sulien felt his pain.

All night she had groped her way through the cold rainforest, struggling through knee-deep moss, clinging ferns and masses of slimy toadstools that squelched underfoot and stank of rotting meat. She was desperate for sleep but had not dared to stop. The Whelm hunting her would not rest.

Now a dismal grey light was creeping between the gigantic trees. Were the Whelm close enough to sense her? If a sensitive broadcast her emotions it could be used to locate her. Karan had told Sulien about this flaw when she was a little girl and taught her how to prevent it, by rigidly controlling her feelings. Sulien wished she had practised more, because little snippets of terror kept escaping.

Mine is a life thrice-owed, said Idlis in mind-speech, *and because I owed Karan, I swore to protect her daughter with my life. I cannot allow you to harm her.*

The Whelm were skilled at inflicting pain. They tortured him until Idlis, the most stoical of them all, shrieked.

No obligation to an outsider can supersede your duty to your own kind, said the Whelm who had spoken earlier. *Besides, Karan could be dead.*

Makes . . . no . . . difference, gasped Idlis.

Your oath was to the mother; it ceases on the mother's death.

Should it be proven that Karan is dead, I will review my oath.

She will come after her daughter by the fastest means possible.

Sulien's heart leapt. Karan would come after her, whatever the cost.

When she does, the Whelm continued, *I'll cut her throat and end the obligation once and for all. And then, Comrade Idlis, you will finally do your duty to your own kind.*

Sulien could not move, could not speak, could hardly breathe. She felt like a frozen lump with a desperately pounding heart in its middle. She huddled under the overhang of a moss-carpeted rock, looking out at the teeming rain and praying that Karan did not come. Though she knew she would.

My obligation cannot be ended in such a way, said Idlis.

But he sounded less convincing now; he was weakening. Sulien hugged herself desperately, trying to think what to do. He would break soon, then the Whelm would catch her and betray her to Gergrig, and he would kill her as slowly and cruelly as only he knew how.

Let's just hunt the little brat down and kill her, said a second Whelm, one who had not mind-spoken before. *Then we can show her head to Gergrig and—*

In the first place, the first Whelm said coldly, *we have no way of contacting Gergrig save through the child. We have to take her alive so we can force her to link with him. Second, she's our bargaining piece. If Gergrig knows the child is dead, why would he agree to be our master?*

They were definitely closer now. But how close? She peered out from her hiding place. The rain was heavier than before; little streams of water poured over the lip of the overhanging rock and down in front of her like silvery ribbons.

Judging by the depth of the moss, it rained most of the time here. Sulien felt a pang of longing for dusty old Gothryme, where they were constantly praying for rain and hardly ever got any, and for dear old Rachis. He must be so lonely and sad, and he didn't even have Piffle for company—Maigraith's evil son Julken had strangled Sulien's beloved puppy.

She wept, then realised she was broadcasting her emotions again, leading the Whelm to her. She choked her feelings down and squinted across the hummocky ground. They were close now; she could smell their sweat and the rank herbs they used to flavour their food.

It was still gloomy and patches of mist kept the visibility low. She slipped out, treading carefully so she did not break through the moss. Ahead, the tangled branches of three fallen trees blocked her way. To the right the ground rose steeply and her dark clothing would stand out against the green moss.

On her left it plunged into a valley, dark at this early hour, with more fallen trees and hundreds of moss-covered boulders. It offered better cover though it looked dark and wet, and was bound to be full of leeches, centipedes and other creeping horrors.

But it would be easier to hide there and more difficult to search. She headed into the valley, then upstream, checking over her shoulder every couple of minutes. She was in the deep shade between the boulders dotted along a little stream, and feeling safe for the first time since the Whelm had seen Gergrig, when the biggest Whelm of all, lanky Bervi, stepped out from behind a boulder only yards away and lunged at her.

Sulien squealed, threw herself sideways and evaded his clawing fingers by half an inch. But Bervi wasn't as clumsy as the other Whelm; he kicked out and the toe of his iron-shod boot caught her in the right ankle, knocking her off her feet into the shallow water.

The bottom was littered with pebbles. Sulien, desperate now, flung a handful at his face. Most of the pebbles missed but one glanced off his blade-sharp nose and hit him in the left eye. And in the gloom of the forest he wasn't wearing his eye covers.

Bervi reeled backwards, caught a heel and landed hard, striking the back of his head on a stone. Sulien scrambled to her feet, her ankle throbbing, splashed across the stream and darted into the gloom on the other side. From there she scrambled over boulders and fallen trees, then hobbled down the valley until the shade was so dense that she could barely see at all.

The trees here were the biggest she had ever seen; they must have been three hundred feet tall and their trunks were many yards through the middle. But was she safe here? Could she ever be safe when the Whelm were hunting her? No, never.

She sat down, gasping. Her ankle was swelling, hideously painful and bore a purple bruise the shape of the toe of Bervi's boot. But she had to keep going and find a hiding place where she could sleep, somewhere that the Whelm could not get to. A hideout with several exits.

This was basalt country, and it was unlikely that there were any caves. The big trees were widely spaced, there were no branches for the first hundred feet, and the straight trunks were impossible to climb without claws. But she noted cracks in the trunks here and there at ground level, where the heartwood had rotted away leaving cavities inside. Sulien checked dozens of trees and found many with cavities, though some were too narrow for her to squeeze into and she was afraid of what she would find inside. Safe holes were probably inhabited by creatures she would not want to sleep with.

But the sooner she was out of sight the safer she would be. The biggest tree of all was a hoary old giant that might have been a thousand years old, and its buttressed base, which was at least twenty yards around, was cracked and fissured in many places.

Only two of the cracks were wide enough for her to squeeze inside. She slipped into the wider one, careful not to leave scrape marks on the moss, clambered down a narrow conduit like a flattened piece of pipe, then down for at least another twenty feet into the rotted-out subterranean heart of the monster tree. Here, she discovered by feeling around, the conduit flared out like a door knob into a space seven or eight feet wide. Other cavities led off in three directions but she did not probe them to their limits. She was too exhausted.

When her eyes had adjusted to the dim light filtering down, she saw that the floor was rotten wood, and horribly damp and mouldy, though it was soft and a lot warmer than outside. It was teeming with cockroaches, wood beetles and woodlice, and the thought of them crawling on her made her shudder, but at least they didn't want to eat her.

Her ankle was more swollen than before and painful to touch, but there was nothing she could do about it. She ate some tasteless Whelm gruel mixed with water, rolled herself in her damp coat and lay down.

But the moment Sulien closed her eyes she saw her beloved father again, as she had in a nightmare a couple of months ago. Llian lay in the middle of an expanse of grey stones, as still as death.

Her fondest memories were of being cradled in his arm as a little girl, listening to him telling tales great and small, or making stories up just for her. She had felt loved and safe, and his stories had taught her more than all her lessons. She whimpered and wrapped her arms around herself. He could not be gone!

Finally she dozed. She woke a couple of times, startled by sounds in the forest above, then slept soundly until hunger and thirst woke her. She yawned, stretched and was reaching for her mug when the hairs rose on the back of her neck.

She turned and gasped. Idlis was sitting on a mound of rotted wood on the other side of the little cavern, his black eyes fixed on her unblinkingly. Before she could move his bony fingers clamped around her wrist.

"You will come with me now. Don't struggle or it will go very badly."

5

HE FELT NO HEARTBEAT

Wilm clung desperately to Aviel as the second of the shadow gates, the azure one, enveloped them and spun faster and faster. She gasped and doubled up, clutching her middle, then everything around him blurred into streaks of colour.

His eyes watered so badly that his whole face grew wet. Something burned the inside of his nose and down the back of his throat. Then, with a swoop that left his stomach behind, the gate plunged down through solid rock into darkness. It became so cold that the tip of his nose and his left ear burned. His throbbing right ear, what remained of it after the summon stone had consumed the top half, went blessedly numb.

Aviel stiffened in his arms, gave a little sigh and went limp.

Panic struck him. Was she dead? Wilm cried out her name, then shrieked it. *"Aviel, Aviel?"*

The empty silence mocked him: how insignificant he was, how helpless to do anything for her. She must not be dead! Yet again he saw that festering brute, Unick, pointing his Command device at Dajaes. The black crystal on its tip had flashed and Wilm's wonderful, loyal, loving Dajaes fell dead. The memory would haunt his nightmares, sleeping and waking, for all his days.

He dared not relax his grip to check on Aviel for fear she would be torn away from him in the wildly spinning gate, and lost for ever. Wilm hugged her more tightly, trying to protect her with his long, lean body.

The streaks of colour faded to black until the darkness was absolute. The temperature rose sharply and the air grew thick and heavy; it smelled like hot rock and each breath burned all the way down to his lungs—the gate must be taking them deep underground. Wilm's claustrophobia swelled; solid rock was closing in on them from all sides;

what if the gate vanished and left them here to die? He'd often had nightmares about being trapped underground, unable to breathe and battering bloody knuckles on the walls as he slowly suffocated.

The gate was spinning ever more slowly now. Was it fading out? He squeezed Aviel's body more tightly against himself, trying to understand what had happened. As the Merdrun opened the Crimson Gate on Cinnabar the summon stone had projected a shadow gate on the cavern wall. Aviel, in a desperate attempt to stop the enemy, had hurled the flask of quicksilver from the Origin device at the summon stone, poisoning it, and the shadow gate had split in two.

Why? And what had happened to the Crimson Gate? It had spun upwards and vanished from sight, though he did not think it had closed. Had it brought the invading Merdrun to Santhenar? He had to find out, fast, and send out a warning.

"*Aviel?*" Wilm said softly. He still could not see a thing.

He squeezed her small frame, but she was limp and did not react. Had she struck something in the whirling gate and been knocked out?

It was still utterly black around him. He enclosed her with his left arm, holding her tightly against him, then, self-consciously, felt her head and neck. His face grew hot. Aviel was a very private person and did not like to be touched, but if she was injured he had to know.

He probed her back and her right arm. Nothing was broken or torn, nor could he smell any blood. He felt down her left arm and the muscles were taut. She was holding a metal tube, Unick's Origin device, which was designed to locate sources of power, though without the flask of quicksilver it was probably useless. Certainly useless to him, since he had no gift for the Secret Art.

The two sections of the tube were still partly open and a faint blue glow came from the needle-like crystals on the end. Inside, something reflected silvery blue—a few drops of quicksilver. Wilm inspected Aviel's face but gained no comfort. Her eyes were closed and she was as still as death, then the glow went out.

He felt her throat but his callused fingers sensed no heartbeat. He licked a finger and put it under her nose, though if she was breathing it was too faint to feel. In his distress he clapped a hand to the hilt of the black sword on his hip, the enchanted blade that had once belonged to the great Magister, Mendark, and was now his. Wilm had saved Aviel's life with it, avenged Dajaes with it, and it was the only precious thing he owned. But as he touched the hilt, the gate began to spin again, dizzyingly fast.

It jumped sideways with such a lurch that the blood drained from his head and he almost fainted. He clung desperately to Aviel. Once more the gate seemed to be skipping through solid rock. It rushed through him, dragging on his bones and teeth and organs, though how could that be? Each skip was longer than the one before though Wilm could not tell whether they were travelling yards at a time, or miles.

Then his head struck something hard and the world around him faded away . . .

A bright light shone on his face and his head throbbed. He was lying on warm wet grass, the air was warm and sticky, and distantly he could hear shouting and screaming. He opened his eyes and the rising sun dazzled him.

Aviel was no longer in his arms. Had he lost her? He staggered to his feet, hearing the roars of soldiers hurling themselves into battle, the clash of steel on steel and the shrieks of the dying, only a few hundred yards away.

"Get down!" she hissed. "They'll see you."

He felt a great swelling in the centre of his chest. "You're alive!"

"Down!"

He fell to his knees, wiped his eyes and at last he could see. He was on a small hilltop in full view of anyone who should look his way. The ground was covered in short springy grass of the most brilliant green, unlike any green he had seen in his hometown of Casyme, or during the past six weeks of travel. The flowers in the grass were large and brightly coloured, and the humid air was thickly scented from myriad blossoms, overlain with the smell of wood smoke. Even the birds in the sky were different—their plumage shouted in glowing yellows and reds and blues. Wherever the gate had taken them, it was a long way from home.

The gate was only ten feet away. It was shaped like a trilithon and was sky-blue, and still. It had shrunk and faded since carrying them away from Carcharon; it was not much taller than Wilm now. Aviel stood in front of it, staring at him.

She was a small, slender girl, almost sixteen. Her heart-shaped face was elfin; tendrils of her fine silvery hair drifted up and down in the warm breeze. Her twisted right ankle and angled foot were partly concealed behind her left leg. Even with Wilm, her oldest friend, she kept them hidden.

"I was terrified you'd died," he said. "What—"

"The Merdrun are here!" she hissed. "Come back into the gate."

Wilm felt confused. "But where are we?"

Aviel's voice, which was naturally high, became shrill. "I don't know. Come on."

"We've got to find out as much as we can. It's vital information, Aviel."

She hesitated. "All right, but be quick."

To his left, half a mile away, stood a forest of gigantic trees that extended over hills and valleys for miles. To the right a broad brown river wound across a plain towards the sea. A large town on its further bank had streets running in sinuous curves, and dozens of boats were tied up at its wharves.

"Merdrun, to me!" The battle cry soared above all the other shouts and screams.

Wilm could not see the fighting; a ridge of rock fifty yards down the hill blocked his view. He crouched down and scurried that way.

"Wilm, come back!"

He had to know what was happening. He crept down to the ridge, climbed it, peered over and saw a smaller town only a quarter of a mile away. Many of the buildings were aflame, and its dark-skinned inhabitants were fighting from behind hastily erected barricades.

Aviel limped down. "What are you doing here?" he whispered. "Go up."

"Not without you."

The inhabitants of the town were doomed. Squads of armoured

Merdrun were advancing from all sides, cutting down everyone they came across, just as they had done on Cinnabar. Over and again he saw groups of locals attack single Merdrun soldiers. And over and again, with methodical savagery, the soldiers killed all their attackers. The Merdrun were supernaturally strong and violent, almost magically so. Clearly the rumours about them were true—they were the most deadly fighters in the void, and each the equal of at least five ordinary troops.

Buildings were also burning in the town on the far side of the river, and smoke rose from other parts of the landscape. He could not tell how many Merdrun there were, though they were everywhere.

"Wilm?" hissed Aviel. "We can't stay any longer." She scrambled back down the ridge and headed up the hill.

He was still staring at the besieged town. "The Crimson Gate must have got here a long time before ours. Looks like the Merdrun have been here all night."

She stopped. "If they have, they must have seen our gate open. *Come on!*"

The gate flared bright blue, lighting up the hilltop, faded then flared again.

"Wilm, hurry!" wailed Aviel.

He was running up the slope, bent low, when a band of Merdrun came storming up the hill, fifty yards to his left. They had the black glyph burned into their foreheads and were led by a lean, hard-faced fellow with a close-cropped black beard and a completely bald head. Gergrig!

They had not seen Wilm; their eyes were fixed on the glowing gate and on Aviel, who was still twenty yards from it.

"The little bitch who poisoned our gate," said Gergrig. "Cut her down!"

A spasm of terror shot through Wilm. Why hadn't he listened to her? The Merdrun were ten yards closer to the gate; he would never reach them in time.

"Aviel!" he bellowed. "Go!"

The Merdrun turned and it was clear from Gergrig's grim smile that he had recognised Wilm too. Wilm wrenched out the black sword. He had no hope of beating any of the Merdrun but he might delay them long enough for Aviel to get away.

"Run for it!" he screamed, putting on a burst of speed.

Aviel hobbled to the gate. As she entered it, it flared again, but that was all.

"Aviel, go!"

"I don't know how to make it go," she screamed.

Gergrig let out a bark of laughter. "Kill her," he said to the two soldiers on his left. "I'll deal with the *boy*."

Wilm had been put down all his life and the insult slid off him. He raised the enchanted black sword but it resisted him. No, it was being pulled to his right, towards the gate. Why? Was it trying to tell him something?

There was no time to think about it; the Merdrun were between him and the gate, there was no way he could get to it, and Aviel would be dead in seconds. He sheathed the sword, unbuckled the copper sheath then ran to Gergrig's right and hurled sword and sheath into the gate.

"Draw it!" he roared. "I can't get there."

Aviel's pretty face twisted in agony. She drew the black sword, raised it in the gate and it flared so brightly that for an instant it outshone the sun. When Wilm could see again the gate was gone. He had done one thing right, at least.

And now he would pay for it.

Gergrig cursed. "Lebbix, run to the triplets. They've got to drag that gate back."

Lebbix, a slab-faced bull of a man whose arms and hands were covered in tightly curled black hairs, froze, his eyes wide and terrified. "The . . . *triplets*?"

"You heard. Go!"

"That gate's a diminutive of the true Azure Gate. We can't touch it."

"Find a way! The girl knows too much; she has to die."

Lebbix pounded down the hill. The other four Merdrun came at Wilm from all sides.

His heart was trying to hammer a hole through his ribcage. He tried to run, but one of the soldiers tossed a loop of rope over his head and yanked him off his feet.

"Beat him to within an inch of his life," said Gergrig. "But don't kill him. That pleasure is reserved for me, when you're finished."

The Merdrun began, slowly and savagely. They were masters at inflicting pain, and Wilm, who had thought he had suffered in his brief, poverty-stricken life, now realised that he had not suffered at all.

6

OUR EFFORTS WILL ULTIMATELY BE FUTILE

"You swore to protect me!" Sulien hissed.

"And so I am," said Idlis, "despite how dearly it is costing me." His voice was thick and gluggy, as if he spoke through a mouthful of gruel. He tried to smile but only managed a ferocious grimace. His ugly face was battered and bruised, one top front tooth and two lower ones had been knocked out, and there was fresh blood on his grey lips. "Quiet, or we will both die. If you broadcast your feelings, they will find us."

"But my feelings make me what I am."

His black eyes blinked, three times. "You're a little Whelm now, and to be Whelm is to be in control of your emotions at all times. *Never* let them control you."

"I'm not Whelm in here," said Sulien, touching her chest. "And I never will be."

"Listen carefully, little one. My people are hunting you."

"All eleven of them. I know!"

His bark of laughter was arid, mirthless, and raised her hackles. He caught her wrist, and her skin crawled from his touch, for it was cold and rubbery and somehow inhuman. "Child, you don't know anything! Yetchah called for help and she has been answered. The entire Whelm nation is on the move, *twenty-five thousand people*, and they're coming this way from the north, the south and most of all from the east, Shazabba. Every Whelm wants Gergrig for their master."

"Including you," she whispered, shocked and shaken.

"Yes, little one," he said gently. "Even me. But my oath is everything to me. Gather your gear, we're going."

With twenty-five thousand after her there was no hope. "How?"

"Yetchah's band is searching along the stream and will be here in minutes. We have to go out the . . . back way."

"How do you know it?"

"Salliban is my homeland; it's why I led my people to the village on the lake in the first place. As a child I used to know every tree in this forest, and many of the secret pathways still exist. Come."

Idlis wriggled into one of the conduits Sulien had been too tired to investigate. She hesitated. Could she trust him? She had no choice.

The conduit, a hollowed-out root of the great tree, ran down gently for ten feet or more, then out horizontally. It was not much wider than her shoulders, and Idlis had to hunch his own to get through. He did not seem bothered by the confined space but Sulien could not stop thinking about being stuck here, unable to move forward or back, while small creatures with slimy bodies and sharp teeth lunged and tore bits off her.

He reached a wider section of the tunnel, turned, then touched a small dumbbell-shaped lightglass on his belt until it glowed muddy brown. "Calm yourself! You're broadcasting again."

She tried to clamp a lid on her feelings, but she was too afraid.

Idlis knelt, his rough joints clicking, and stared at her. "How you've changed these past days," he whispered, his thick voice awed yet troubled.

"What do you mean?"

"Your gift is growing. It's so strong now, even I can sense it. There's a power in you I never saw before, a very troubling power."

Sulien did not know what to make of that. Her gift for the Secret Art was just there when she needed it or, more often, not. "I don't know anything about it."

"You've got to master your gift or it will lead your enemies straight to you."

"I don't know how."

He looked disturbed. "But . . . surely Karan taught you how to use it."

"No."

His black eyes flashed and he thrust his hideous face at her until his battered nose touched hers. "*Why not?*" he hissed. "Stupid woman!"

She recoiled from the contact. "Mummy's not stupid!" she said hotly.

"Then she's wilfully negligent. How can she not see?" Idlis looked down into the muddy brown depths of his lightglass. "You *must* find a teacher, little one, or you will not survive."

"I don't know where to look for one."

"Find out!"

He turned and scrabbled on. Sulien followed on hands and knees, thinking about what she knew of her gift. It had two parts, physical and mental. With the physical side she had blistered Julken's fingers when he'd tried to crush her hand. It was her best means of defence though she had no idea how she had done those things. The gift sometimes rose of its own accord when she was angry, or desperate. Though more often it didn't come at all.

The other side of her gift had to do with *far-seeing and far-sensing*. She had *seen* the magiz preparing to attack Karan on Cinnabar, and Llian about to do something incredibly foolish in Carcharon. Sulien had cried out to him, *No, Daddy!* but she had no idea how she had done it. Since he lacked the gift, she should not have been able to reach him mentally at all.

And then there was Gergrig. Why had she seen him in a nightmare in the first place? How could she have seen anyone from so far away across the void? Why had she seen him at exactly the time when he'd been talking about the Merdrun's one weakness? Pure luck? She did not think so. There had to be a reason, but what was it?

Her head was throbbing and her ankle worse. Sulien abandoned the useless thoughts, wiped tears from her eyes and crawled on, enduring the pain as best she could.

After ten minutes Idlis turned into a square hole cut in the side of the conduit and passed into the hollow roots under another tree. This cavity was smaller than the one she had hidden in and much darker.

"How much further—" said Sulien. She was starving and very thirsty.

Idlis's iron fingers crushed her shoulder. "Shh!" His head was cocked to one side, listening.

Sulien made out distant, echoing sounds that might have been people shouting.

"They know where you hid," he said. "They'll hack into the base of the great tree within an hour, and follow us."

His lightglass outlined a high, narrow tunnel through red earth. They scrambled in. The sides were reinforced with stone here and there, but it must have been made a long time ago as some of the walls had collapsed and roots came though the sides and top of the passage in many places.

It was high enough for Idlis to walk with a stoop and Sulien to stand upright, and after half an hour she thought they must have gone a mile, though she had no idea of the direction.

He stopped, rubbing the back of his neck, then gestured to her to go past. The roof here was supported by thick boards furred with patches of white mould. When she was in front he heaved out some of the boards and the tunnel collapsed behind him.

"I'm not the only one who knows these pathways," he said. "They were vital to our ancestors' survival in the centuries when we were hunted like dogs—before we took a master who could protect us in exchange for our service. We've maintained them ever since, in case of need."

This must have reminded Idlis of some terrible memory for he stood there, staring at the wall, his jaw tight. *Who hunted you like dogs?* she wondered. *And why?* She felt for him; the revelation made him seem more human.

She laid a hand on his knobbly wrist. "I'm sorry; I can feel your pain."

Idlis looked at her in astonishment. She withdrew her hand, wondering. Had no one ever been kind to him before?

They continued for hours along a series of earthen passages, a short
tunnel through solid basalt that climbed at a steep angle, and then a
longer tunnel, lined with yellow sandstone blocks, that curved ever
upwards. It was followed by more earth tunnels, miles and miles of
them, all climbing.

The trek was exhausting and tedious, and now every passage looked
the same. Sulien was always hungry, always thirsty, always exhausted.
Did Idlis even know where he was going? Or were they trapped in a
maze from which there was no escape?

It reminded her of Karan, far away. Why did she never answer? *Don't
you want me any more?* Sulien needed the comfort desperately. Surely a
tiny link couldn't hurt.

She tensed, preparing herself, then stopped. The Merdrun's evil old
magiz had used Sulien's link to find her and attack her, and she had
attacked Karan through it too. But the magiz was dead; Karan had
killed her on Cinnabar yesterday.

Sulien looked up. Idlis was almost out of sight ahead, the lightglass
a tiny swinging point of brown light in his hand. She stumbled after
him. Her ankle throbbed and her back hurt.

"Is . . . far to go?" she gasped.

"Very far," said Idlis.

"Can we rest for a while?"

"No."

"I'm starving."

He did not reply.

"I . . . I've got to do a wee."

"Hold it in."

It was all too hard. The link to Karan beckoned, and Sulien was
about to make one when it occurred to her that the Whelm wanted her
to do just that. They wanted to lure Karan here so they could kill her
to please their future master. To save her mother, Sulien had to keep
her as far away as possible.

She was standing head down and eyes closed, aching with fear and
misery, when Idlis clouted her over the top of the head. "You're *broadcasting* again! Curb your feelings! Deny them completely."

Tears welled. She tried to hold them back and be a good little Whelm who never showed emotion. Not once had she wept in front of them, though she had shed tears every night in her hard bed after the daily punishment the Whelm gave all their children, good or bad.

But nothing could hold back Sulien's tears now. She let out a sob, which led to another, and then she was crouched down on the floor, rocking back and forth on her haunches and howling as if it was the end of her world.

Light approached, pink through her scrunched-up eyelids. She choked back her tears, expecting another blow, but it did not come. The light moved away a little.

She wiped her eyes on her arm, then her nose, and looked up. Idlis, one of the ugliest men she had ever seen, was gazing at her with an expression she was unable to fathom. It was almost as though he *cared*—though that seemed impossible. The Whelm were bound together by bonds of duty and iron-hard discipline, and their aeons-old yearning for a master to complete them, but Sulien had never known them to show any positive emotion towards each other, much less to an outsider who was only there under sufferance.

"Are you in great pain, little one?" said Idlis.

She nodded, afraid to speak.

"What would your mother do?"

"She would hug me and stroke my hair, and tell me that everything was going to be all right . . . and after a while, everything would be."

Idlis considered that. "I can't do any of those things for you."

Sulien wiped her stinging eyes. The thought of him hugging her was preposterous, not to mention repellent. "I'm . . . not asking you to."

"I would never lie to you. Things are *not* going to be all right. Life is privation and torment, bitter endurance and failure—and then we die."

"Thanks!" The Whelm were prone to such statements; they seemed incapable of taking joy from anything.

"I'm pleased to be able to help you," said Idlis. Levity of any kind being anathema to the Whelm, they did not recognise sarcasm. "I have always found comfort in knowing that, no matter how hard we strive, our efforts will ultimately be futile."

Sulien gaped at him. "How can you take comfort in *that*?"

"It takes us out of our petty selves. It reinforces our need and yearning to serve one who is far greater than us—a master who sees what we cannot. A master who can shape life, the world and even the future to his will."

"A cruel master."

"Life is cruel. All that matters is strength, and survival, for the alternative is the oblivion our ancestors faced."

"You said 'to *his* will'," said Sulien. "Must your master be a man?"

Idlis stared at the floor of the tunnel for a long time. "The question has never come up."

"I'm asking it," she said boldly.

"I can't speak for my people, only myself. I yearn to follow the orders of a master who has the vision to see what I cannot, and the strength to fight for it and never yield. I followed Rulke, but I could also have followed Yalkara."

"It must be hard for you to go against your own kind, then. To rob them of—"

"It's very hard." He looked both ways along the tunnel, then back at her. "You've stopped crying. You feel better."

"Mmn," said Sulien.

"I think my way was more help than your mother's." He headed on.

Stupid man! Nothing could ever substitute for the lovely warm feeling of having her mother's arms around her and knowing she was *safe*.

But his people were hunting her, and she could sense the rest of the Whelm nation too, twenty-five thousand of them, flooding towards this place from the north, the south and the east. She was the key to contacting their hoped-for master, and gaining him. They had to find her.

The terror was back, worse than ever. Sulien limped after Idlis. He was just one man, and he wanted a master as much as any of the Whelm. How long could he hold out before he cracked, and betrayed her?

Life is privation and torment, bitter endurance and failure—and then we die.

What if he was right?

7

SABOTAGE!

"What the hell is the matter now?" cried Yggur, heaving hard on the black-knobbed lever. The front of the sky ship had pitched down so steeply that Karan was falling out of her seat.

The craft shook, then dropped so sharply that she tasted the smoked fish she'd had for lunch. She choked back a scream. "What's—happening?"

Yggur did not reply, though it was clear that the controls were not answering. She clung to the sides of her seat, her heart racing, assessing their chances of surviving a crash. They weren't good.

The sky ship was high above the long southern panhandle of Meldorin. The Sea of Mists was on their left and the endless southern ocean to their right. The range below them wasn't high but the peaks were sheathed in snow and ice and cut by glaciers. If they crashed there, they would die. Even if Yggur landed safely but could not take off again they would probably freeze to death. At this latitude, fifty degrees south, the land was well into its five-month winter.

"Come here!" said Yggur, rising from the pilot's seat. "Take over."

"Me?" Karan squeaked.

She swung from seat to seat down the steeply sloping cabin, strapped herself into Yggur's chair and took hold of the levers. Panic flooded her. Flying a sky ship required a gift for mancery, so as to channel power to the rotors, but her gift was small, untaught and unpractised.

"You know how they work?" Yggur was hauling himself up towards the rear hatch.

"The left lever controls the speed of the rotors, the middle lever turns left or right, and the right-hand lever controls climb or descent. What are you doing?"

"Feels like something's come apart. Got to fix it or . . ."

As he heaved the hatch open, a long metal object fell through, crack-ing him hard across the forehead and nose, then tumbled the length of the cabin and thudded into the front wall below the oval window. Yggur slipped but managed to hook his left arm around the seat at the rear. He clung there for a few seconds, blood pouring from his left nostril, then heaved himself up through the hatch. His long legs kicked and he disappeared.

The metal object was a hexagonal rod, threaded at one end and with a hole in the other. Karan prayed that it was not something vital. She tried to pull the right-hand lever back so the sky ship would level out but the lever was jammed in the dive position. Why?

Two and a half days had passed since they had stolen the sky ship and fled Alcifer, heading for Salliban, and the craft had been plagued by inexplicable breakdowns all that time.

"Any luck, Yggur?" she called over her shoulder.

He did not reply, though she heard metal clanking and clicking from beyond the hatch. A minute went by, and their plunge to doom was unabated. The mountains appeared to be thrusting up at her—in another minute or two they would slam at high speed into the ice-sheathed rocks. Why was the sky ship diving so rapidly? The Aachim had built it in great haste and it was the first of its kind; did it have some fundamental flaw?

Fifty seconds. None of the levers were working now and the rotors were still. Karan's heart was beating a tattoo against her breastbone—they had to survive, for Sulien's sake. She tried to sense out the problem but got nothing.

Forty seconds. But how could the sky ship be flawed? The Aachim were brilliant designers and builders, the best in the world, and this vessel had brought Malien all the way from Mount Tirthrax, a distance of fifteen hundred miles. Why had had it gone wrong now?

Thirty seconds until the sky ship slammed into the rocky peak between two heavily crevassed glaciers.

"Heave the right-hand lever back hard," Yggur bellowed through the hatch. "Then shove the left lever forwards as far as it'll go."

Karan heaved on the black knob and the sky ship's dive shallowed, but not quickly enough to save them. She thrust the red knob forward; the rotors roared and the nose of the sky ship lifted towards the horizontal, but the grey, jagged rocks were no more than a hundred feet below, and less ahead; it seemed impossible that the craft could rise in time to clear them. She hauled back on the black knob with all her strength; the craft was in level flight now; now it lifted and they shot over the little peak, so close that the landing skids scraped on ice.

Yggur emerged from the hatch. There was blood all over his face, a long bruise across his forehead and his swollen nose still oozed blood.

Karan slumped in her seat, exhausted. "That was too close. What was wrong? Did something break?"

"Not exactly," Yggur said grimly. He held out several lengths of metal rod and pointed to scratches on them. "See those."

"What about them?"

"Sabotage!"

"Why would the Aachim sabotage their own craft?"

A wild gust sent the sky ship skidding sideways. Karan turned back to the controls; there were cliffs and mountain peaks on three sides. Yggur came down to her, swaying on his feet. "They wouldn't."

"Then who?" An awful possibility struck her. "Not Shand, surely?"

"He was under the control of the magiz. Maybe he still is. Go down!"

She eyed the crevassed ice of the glacier below and ahead. "Here?"

"Land on the first flat bit of ground you come to."

"Me?" she squeaked.

"You've got to. Not feeling too good." Yggur slumped into a seat and sat there, head lowered, eyes closed, breathing shallowly. "I'm still channelling power to the rotors. All you have to do is work the levers."

Landing was tricky enough in good conditions. In this gusting wind, on a bumpy, crevassed glacier, one small mistake was liable to damage the sky ship beyond repair. She circled a relatively flat section of the glacier, trying to work out the best approach.

"Hurry up!" said Yggur thickly. "Don't know how long my repair will last."

She turned, lined the sky ship up with the flat section and slowed the rotors. A gust heaved the sky ship sideways, then up fifty feet in a stomach-churning instant. Karan panicked and yanked the middle lever to the right.

"Steady," said Yggur. Then, "A little faster."

She regained control, lined the sky ship up again, descended sharply and the skids hit the ice with an impact that twisted the frame of the cabin. Timber groaned and creaked; compartment doors flew open and mugs and cutlery rained down. She cut the rotors.

The wind howled. Yggur wiped his bloody face on his sleeve, staggered to the doorway, slipped on his own blood and fell out onto the ice.

Karan rose, her knees shaky. She hung on as a gust skidded the sky ship sideways, then clambered down the ladder to Yggur, who was on his knees, gasping. "You all right?"

"No," said Yggur. "Get it tied down."

He headed towards the cowling behind the rear of the cabin. It protected the mechanisms that powered the rotors and let protium in and out of the airbag.

A series of canvas eyelets, reinforced with metal rings, ran along the outside of the cabin, and one of the compartments held spider-silk ropes, light but strong, plus pegs with hooked ends. She climbed down, hammered some pegs into the ice, tied the craft down, then went gingerly to the edge of the nearest crevasse.

It went down an awfully long way, and low, grinding sounds issued from the blue depths.

Crack!

The ice quivered under her feet, then a triangular piece of the edge broke off and crashed down the crevasse. Karan cried out and leaped back, her heart pounding, then froze. She was on the edge of another crevasse, three feet across; it was partly concealed by a bridge of crusted snow that could collapse at any time. She had walked across it without realising it was there.

She sprang across and, checking that the ice ahead of her was sound, headed towards the rear of the sky ship. Yggur's feet and lower legs could be seen below the partly lifted cowling, and banging sounds came from inside.

Thump. He roared, "You!" then scrambled out backwards, hauling something—no, someone—out on the ice.

"Hingis!" Karan exclaimed. "What were you doing in there?"

The master illusionist was one of the sorriest sights she had ever seen. He had been kicked repeatedly by a mule as a boy, smashing the bones of his face, caving in the left side of his chest and withering a lung. He had always been ugly, yet when she had seen him with Ussarine at Alcifer he had been so animated, because she saw him as a normal man worthy of her love, that his looks had seemed irrelevant.

But at the worst possible moment, when Llian had needed their help to attack Snoat in the pavilion on the island and seize the Command device, Hingis's obsessive twin sister Esea had forced him to choose between her and Ussarine. Hingis had chosen Ussarine, and Esea, unable to accept the rejection, had blasted the pavilion down onto them, breaking both Ussarine's legs and several ribs. Then, apparently believing that she had killed them, Esea had fled in the darkness.

Hingis, evidently, had stowed away in the sky ship. His face was bruised and badly swollen, his blood-red eyes looked as though every vein had burst, and the tip of his nose was frostbitten.

"The little bastard has been sabotaging us for days," said Yggur. He drew back a huge fist as if planning to punch Hingis in the face, but thought better of it and dropped his hand to his side. "Why?"

"Destroyed my sister, and Ussarine," said Hingis in a breathless voice. Having only one good lung, and it not very good, even speaking was an effort. "Want to die."

"You could have jumped in the lake and drowned yourself," Yggur said coldly. "Why try to kill us too?"

"Why not? We're all going to die soon enough."

"You whimpering little shit!" Yggur heaved Hingis bodily into the air and turned towards the nearest crevasse. "Your wish is about to come true."

Karan sprang at him and caught hold of his right arm. "Yggur, no!" He raised it higher, lifting her as well. He was immensely strong. She pulled herself up and roared into his face, *"Put him down!"*

He shook her off. She caught him around the ankles and hung on. For a moment she thought he was going to send her skidding across the ice towards the crevasse, then he stopped and looked down at her.

"Why not?" said Yggur. "It's what he wants."

"Why should he escape the consequences of his crimes so easily?"

Yggur dropped Hingis to the ice. "What use is he?"

Hingis bit back a cry of agony as he landed, then doubled up and put his arms over his face.

"He's a brilliant illusionist. He could be very useful in the war."

Yggur curled his lip. Karan looked down at the wretched little man and, despite all he had done to them, felt a trace of pity. "Ussarine isn't dead. She's just got broken bones and bruises."

Hingis's hideous face crumbled. "Makes no difference. I can never look at her again."

"Why not?"

"She begged me not to choose her over my sister, but like a fool I did. I can never forgive myself. I can never be with Ussarine."

8

BLACK LIPS AND RED TEETH

In the middle of the night Karan jerked awake in her hammock, realising that she had cried out. It was miserably cold, for the flimsy walls of the sky ship did not retain heat and the cabin was no warmer than the glacier it rested on so precariously.

"Something the matter?" said Yggur, who was lying up the front, wrapped in a heavy coat. Hingis was swathed in blankets in a hammock at the rear, his hands and feet tied, and his teeth chattering.

As Karan sat up, the hammock swung gently. "Bad dream. About Sulien."

The wind shook the sky ship, and if it strengthened they would have to take off. Hazardous as it would be in the air in such weather, it was even more dangerous on the ground. Should the wind tear the pegs free, the fragile craft would be bowled across the glacier and tumbled down a crevasse, or smashed against the ragged little peak on the other side.

"How bad?"

"She's on the run."

"Better than being in the Whelm's hands." He went to the tiny galley at the rear, boiled water in a pot by closing his big hands around it, and made two mugs of chard. He handed her one and perched on the pilot's seat.

Karan warmed her half-frozen fingers on the mug. "They're hunting her."

"Any idea where?"

"In the far south, the west coast. Salliban."

"I used to know that land," said Yggur.

Karan had never been anywhere near it. "What's it like?"

"Rain-sodden. The coastal range is covered in trees as tall as any you saw in the jungles of Crandor, and the moss comes up to your knees."

"I thought it'd be a frozen wasteland."

"The interior is—Shazabba—but a warm ocean current runs along the west coast and keeps Salliban mild. It rains three hundred days a year and only snows twenty."

"Sounds miserable."

"Good place to hide if you know the land."

"Sulien doesn't." Karan choked. The thought of her gentle daughter running for her life through such a hostile place was unbearable.

"If she got away, the Whelm might never find her. There's only a dozen of them, isn't there?"

Karan started, rocking the hammock wildly.

"What?" said Yggur.

"There was something else in my dream. Something bad." She struggled to recall it.

"About?"

The dream flooded back. *"Mummy, Yetchah has called the Whelm, all of them. Idlis said the whole Whelm nation is hunting me."*

Yggur stood up abruptly, cracking his head on the low ceiling at the front. The cabin rocked. He paced, rubbing his head, then whirled. "And if they catch her—if they use her to contact the Merdrun—if they join forces . . ."

Karan hugged herself and rocked back and forth. "Yes," she whispered. "Sulien's the key."

"To our survival. You've got to find her."

"I—*can't!*" she wailed.

"Why not?"

"When Malien unblocked my gift for mancery, I lost the ability to make mind-links."

"Or are you *afraid* to?"

Karan had not considered that. "Um . . . Well, I had to close the link to Sulien weeks ago; the magiz was using it to hunt her down."

"The magiz is dead. Reopen the link."

Karan tried to but kept shying away; the fear was too ingrained.

"Focus," Yggur said softly. He pressed his big hands to the sides of her head, fingers touching at the top of her skull where the magiz had attacked.

The world around Karan slipped away—sight and sound and every sense save the touch of his fingers—and then the world within. Nothing mattered; for the first time in years she was at peace. Warmth spread through her and her mind opened out in all directions—she sensed the world spinning on its axis, forests shrinking and expanding over the centuries, ocean currents swirling, glaciers grinding rock to paste—

Yggur's voice broke through. "Focus on *Sulien.*"

Pain speared from the top of Karan's skull to her chin, jagged around the sides of her lower jaw and stabbed at the base of her skull. A sequence of blurred colours flooded her: vivid greens, angry flashes of red, areas of silvery grey rippling in the wind, then a sweltering heat that felt so wrong in the frigid cabin.

"Aah!" Karan hurled herself out of the hammock and lurched to the front of the cabin. Sweat was running off her; she sat down with a thump and felt so weak she had to support herself with her arms.

"What was that?" Yggur said sharply.

Karan's voice seemed to come from far away. "I saw somewhere *tropical.*"

"Where?"

"Don't know." Another pain speared into the base of her skull, then a vivid image flashed through her mind. "Gergrig!" she said thickly. "Directing a group of acolytes."

"Doing what?"

"They're gathered around three women ... like identical triplets. Big, strong women ... Black hair. Skin the colour of treacle. Long, handsome faces. Why did I see them?"

Yggur did not reply.

"The acolytes are chanting, painting the triplets' faces, blackening their lips ... *staining their teeth red.*" She shuddered. "What do you think it means?"

"I'm very much afraid," said Yggur, "that he's creating a new magiz."

"From one of the triplets?"

"No, from *all* of them."

Shivers rippled down Karan's backbone. "How could that work?" she said hoarsely.

"Identical triplets understand one another in ways, and to a depth, that no other group of people can. If Gergrig succeeds, his new magiz could be far more dangerous than the one you killed."

How long would it take to create a new magiz? The Secret Art was difficult and long in the learning; even if the triplets were already skilled mancers, she did not see how a magiz could be made overnight.

She stretched her mind out, very carefully, to the place, a hill topped with enormous round boulders, the spaces between them carpeted with velvety grass. Below the crest springs gushed from a dozen places, forming rills that networked the lower slope. It was a verdant land, as unlike Cinnabar as she could have imagined. She could almost smell it.

But where was it? There was no way of telling.

Sulien? Sul-ien! Suulieennn?

"The triplets are whispering Sulien's name," said Karan. "They're after her."

"You've got to find her first."

The sweltering heat vanished and with it her sense of Gergrig and the triplets; Karan started to shiver. She swathed herself in blankets and Yggur extinguished the lightglasses. Starlight filtered in through the small round windows and reflected up from the ice, dimly illuminating the cabin in shades of blue and grey.

As she closed her eyes and tried to sense Sulien, a savage gust heaved the sky ship sideways. Hingis jerked upright, staring wildly around him, then scrunched up again and pulled a blanket over his head.

"We can't stay here," said Yggur, thrusting the red knob forwards to engage the rotors. "Take the controls; I'll undo the stays."

He heaved the door open and leaped down. Karan scrambled across to his seat and took hold of the levers. Another gust struck the sky ship, heeling it over and spinning it around by ninety degrees. Some of the pegs must have torn out of the ice and the airbag above the cabin was now acting like a sail.

Yggur hurled a handful of pegs and ropes in through the door. She heard him yelling but could not make out what he was saying over the wind and dared not leave the controls for a second; it was taking all her efforts to keep the sky ship head-on into the shifting wind.

A stronger gust sent it skidding back towards the crevasse she had looked into earlier. Again Yggur roared.

"What?" Karan yelled.

"What's going on?" shrieked Hingis.

She turned the nose into the wind, revved the rotors and stood up, but could not see Yggur through the clouds of powdery snow. What if he'd fallen into a crevasse, or walked into one of the whirling rotors in the darkness?

Another gust whirled the sky ship around again. Yggur let out a roar of pain, then the left side of the craft dropped several feet with an almighty crash. There was a thump behind her, a groan, then silence.

Her heart missed several beats; one of the skids had slid into a crevasse. She checked on Hingis, who had been hurled head-first out of his hammock and lay in a crumpled heap. Had he broken his neck? There was no time to check.

She darted to the door but could not see through the wind-driven snow. The airbag was a lot wider than the crevasse, though if she could not free the skid the back and forth movement would eventually break the cables that held the airbag to the cabin. The bag would hurtle skywards and the cabin would plummet to the base of the crevasse and smash to bits.

She yanked on the beryl-topped rod that allowed more protium into the airbag, then pushed the red knob that controlled the speed of the rotors. They spun up to a roar and the vessel shuddered but did not move.

Yggur's head and shoulders appeared in the doorway. He had sprung up and caught hold of the rail beside the door.

"More power!" he bellowed. "And more lift."

"Doing all I can." The power he channelled through her to the controls came at a cost; her head was throbbing and nausea churned in her stomach. Aftersickness was rising and it would only get worse. "Get in!"

"One of the skids is caught. I'll try and heave it out."

"It's too dangerous! You could be crushed."

He leapt back and disappeared.

There was nothing she could do to help; she had to keep the sky ship head on and the airbag buoyant enough to lift them the moment the skid was freed, but not so buoyant that it would hurtle up, leaving him behind.

Yggur let out a roar and the left side of the cabin lifted a foot, the skids scraping on the ice, but fell back with a crash that sprang half a dozen compartment doors and tumbled blankets, cutlery and packets of food down onto her head and shoulders.

He roared again and heaved again, with the same result. Karan waited for the next heave but it did not come. A minute passed, then two, and three. Fear clamped around her heart like frozen tongs.

Had he fallen into the crevasse? If he had, there was no way to rescue him.

No way for her to get out either. If he died or was knocked unconscious, the flow of power would stop and the sky ship would fly no more.

9

I DIDN'T *LET* HIM ESCAPE!

Tallia hurtled into the clearing as the sky ship disappeared over the treetops. Half a dozen furious Aachim were clustered there, waving their fists. Malien was silent but her face wore a very ugly look.

"What's going on?" said Tallia.

"Karan stole the sky ship," said Nadiril. "And Yggur helped her."

"Yggur!" Tallia said incredulously.

"It seems he's *better* now."

"About bloody time!" said Lilis with uncharacteristic venom.

"Why did she take it?" said Tallia. Nothing made sense any more.

"The Whelm saw Gergrig coming through the gate," said Malien in a drear voice. "They want him for their master . . . and they're prepared to betray Sulien to seal the deal."

"And Gergrig will kill her to protect their secret. Kill that gentle little girl . . ." Tallia felt the pain in her own heart. She had always wanted a daughter and, fearing that she would never have a child, had focused her own hopes and dreams and burning love on the girl she knew better than any other. "I suppose . . . if Sulien were my child . . . I might have stolen the sky ship too . . ."

"It's futile!" Malien choked. "Sulien will be dead before Karan goes a hundred miles. And without my sky ship we can't do anything to stop the Merdrun."

"Making matters worse," Nadiril said quietly, "it's Shand who's been betraying our plans to the Merdrun."

"What?" bellowed Malien.

"I don't believe it," said Tallia. "Where did this come from?"

"Karan," said Nadiril, "when she came back from Cinnabar after killing the magiz. She said the magiz was boasting about her pet traitor and how she put a link into him when he went to Carcharon a *month* ago."

He looked around at their shocked faces. "It's been clear for a long time that Shand was susceptible to the emanations from the summon stone. They changed him, weakened him and set off those rages we all saw. It's also been clear that someone was betraying our plans to the Merdrun—plans only known to me, Yggur, Tallia, Shand and Lilis. But only one of us was at Carcharon a month ago: Shand, when he was looking for Maigraith, fearing that she was dead. Then, when he was at his weakest emotionally, and the effects of the drumming were strongest, the magiz got to him."

"But Karan killed her," said Lilis. "Surely—"

"The link to Shand may have survived," said Malien. "And when the Merdrun create a new magiz she or he may be able to reactivate the link."

"Can't you remove it?"

"It's unknown mancery; I wouldn't know where to begin." She swung around to Tallia, eyes glinting. "Since the drumming began, you old humans have been a squabbling rabble, and it can't go on. Sort yourselves out or—"

"Or what?" said Nadiril coldly.

"Or we go our own way," said Malien.

Tallia's heart gave a painful thud. How could things have fallen to pieces so badly, so quickly? "Malien, we've got to work together. It's our only hope."

Malien folded her arms across her chest. "If you can put your own house in order, I'll consider it." She stalked back to her own people and they headed down a path through the forest.

"She's right," said Nadiril wearily. "You've got to deal with Shand right now."

But *how?* He had once been one of the greats, and though he had renounced most of his powers after the bitter rejection by his lover, Yalkara, Tallia was sure he could get them back if he needed to. He had long been a friend and she quailed at the thought of taking him on. What if he attacked her? Could she strike to hurt, even kill, if it came to that? And what if he beat her? The allies' position would be desperate.

She headed through the forest, overwhelmed.

"What are you going to do?" said Lilis, falling in beside her.

"After I 'deal with' Shand?"

"Yes."

"Lead!" Tallia said firmly. "Though I'm not a commander of armies . . ." She mentally ran through a list of generals, discarding them one by one until only one remained. "To fight the Merdrun we need the best, and the best is Janck."

"Dedulus Janck?" said Nadiril. "Isn't he a bit of a piss pot?"

"He's a *lot* of a piss pot," she conceded, "but he's a brilliant tactician and an inspirational leader."

Nadiril frowned. "Never trust a fat general."

"Or a scrawny old librarian!" she flashed back.

"Touché!" Nadiril grinned.

She stopped. "Might be an idea if you two stayed back while I talk to Shand."

He waved her on. Tallia crept up the path, agonising about the coming confrontation. Shand had supported her ever since Mendark had taken her on as his assistant at the age of eighteen, and she had been utterly out of her depth.

It was a cool night yet, as she entered the dimly lit clearing, she was drenched in sweat. Ussarine lay on the ground on the far left, a blanket wrapped around her upper body. Her long legs, both broken below the knee when a marble column had fallen across her, were encased in wooden splints, Aachim work. She was asleep, probably sedated against the pain.

A compact figure sat slumped on a log under the trees to her right, pack on his back, head in hands, stray gleams of firelight reflecting off the top of his sparsely-haired head. He was swaying from side to side;

had he had some kind of a turn? Tallia stopped on the other side of the campfire.

"Shand, are you all right?"

He raised his head. His face was blotchy and a large flask lay on the ground beside him.

"Been expecting you," he said thickly.

Smoke stung her eyes. "I'm really sorry," said Tallia. "I would have given anything—"

His eyes glinted. "Get on with it."

"I'm taking you into custody until we can free you from the magiz's link. It's not that we don't trust you . . ." She sounded weak and cursed herself for it. She had to harden herself.

"It *is* that you don't trust me," grated Shand. "I'd have thought you, of all people, would have had faith in me after all the times I propped you up when you weren't up to the job. How can you do this to me, on *her* word?"

Clearly he was going to make it as hard as possible. "Karan has got nothing to do with it."

"Maigraith was trying to help Karan," said Shand. "And Karan betrayed her! She dosed Maigraith with hrux, which is perilous to people of Charon descent; it drove her out of her mind for weeks. Then Karan and Llian met Maigraith in Alcifer, and Maigraith vanished. What did they do to her?"

"That's not the issue, Shand. You've been betraying our secrets— unwittingly I'm sure—but—"

Shand stood up abruptly. "*Karan* is the issue! She's the traitor; she proved it by stealing Malien's sky ship, the one hope we had of rallying an army to defend ourselves. *And you take her word against mine?*"

Tallia's resolve wavered. What if he was right? But she knew Karan even better than she did Shand. He was a moody, unpredictable man and over the past month she had seen at first hand his rages, his irrational accusations and the results of betrayals that could only have been perpetrated by him, witting or unwitting. Karan was honest and straightforward; it was inconceivable that she would make up a false accusation against anyone, least of all Shand.

"Your silence is eloquent," said Shand, raising his right hand. "Take me, *if you dare.*"

She was running towards him when the campfire exploded like a barrel of fireworks and multicoloured sparks struck her in the face and body. She staggered back, beating out the sparks on her clothing, so dazzled that she could not see.

Ussarine woke with a cry, thrashed, then screamed from the pain.

Someone hurtled into the clearing. "Bend over!" cried Lilis. "Your hair is smoking."

Tallia could feel the heat on the top of her head. She fell to her knees and Lilis's little hands whacked at her hair.

"Allow me," panted Nadiril. *"Douse!"*

A deluge of cold water struck the top of Tallia's head, drenching her. She stood up, coughing and dripping. Lilis knelt beside Ussarine, stroking her forehead and trying to soothe her back to sleep.

"Where's Shand?" said Tallia.

"Gone," Nadiril intoned.

"He just . . . vanished," said Lilis in an awed voice. "One minute he was there, the next . . . not."

"How could he make a gate so quickly, so easily?" said Tallia.

"I don't think it was a gate," said Nadiril.

"Then how did he escape?"

He shrugged. "There's a lot about Shand we don't know. Like what he did in the long gaps in his life where he dropped out of sight. And most of all, what gifts of mancery Yalkara, one of the greatest Charon of all, gave him when she terminated their relationship."

"She gave him an extra-long life," said Lilis.

"And secret Charon mancery no one else knows," said Nadiril. "Or will ever know, now they're extinct. Mancery that would greatly aid us if he could be brought back into the fold—"

Malien appeared silently from the trees on the other side of the clearing, her Aachim ranked behind her. "Or utterly ruin us if his treachery isn't curbed. You were supposed to deal with Shand, but you let him escape."

"I didn't *let* him escape!" snapped Tallia. "He used mancery that—"

"That you, the great Magister, could not counter, *or were afraid to.*"

10

THEY WOULD CEASE TO EXIST

Nadiril drew himself up to his full beanpole height. His withered flesh thickened, his chest filled out and his clouded eyes smoked in his wrath.

"Enough!" he said in a roar that made Malien take a step backwards. "We're at war, Malien, with a merciless enemy that will be the end of Santhenar unless we stand united against them. Shake hands with Tallia and apologise."

The Aachim were a proud and imperious people, quick to take offence and quick to anger, and for a long moment Tallia thought that Malien would storm away.

Then she said stiffly, "Magister, please accept my apologies—it's been a troubling day . . ." She bowed to Tallia, though not very low, extended her hand and they shook, Malien's extraordinarily long Aachim fingers wrapping right around Tallia's own hand.

"Malien?" said the yellow-haired Aachim Xarah, who was carrying her scrying board, a device with concentric brass rings, and brass pointers that could be slid around them, mounted on a circular wooden base a foot across. "Shand didn't use a gate."

Tallia frowned. "What are you saying?"

"He disappeared, but he's still in the area."

The hairs rose on the back of Tallia's neck. "He's gone after the Command device, and then he'll head for our boat!"

She bolted down through the trees towards the triangular island in the little lake. The quickest path to the cove ran across the westernmost of the island's three bridges, around the southern shore and across the eastern bridge.

The island had been a beautiful, tranquil place, but now, lit by fires here and there, it was ruined and littered with the bodies of Snoat's personal guard. From here she could see the shoreline of the cove a quarter of a mile away. Something was burning there too; firelight reflected off the water and the sails of Snoat's huge flagship, anchored offshore. The anchor chain was rattling. He was preparing to leave.

Tallia hurtled across the eastern bridge and down onto a broad expanse of paving, then froze, staring around her in the semi-darkness. Shortly Malien skidded to a stop beside her. Four Aachim men were behind her, and Lilis, scarlet in the face, then more Aachim.

"What's . . . the . . . matter?" panted Lilis.

"Something's very wrong." Tallia could feel radiant heat on her face, coming up from the stones, and smell charred flesh. "Malien, send your strongest people down to the jetty. Stop Snoat's ship any way you can."

Malien issued quiet orders and four men ran for the jetty. Tallia created light with a fingertip and walked towards the source of the heat. A bloody body lay across it, on its belly, its arms wrapped around something. She took a closer look, and flinched.

"Snoat." His head and legs were intact but his torso was a bloody ruin.

"His middle has been turned inside out," said Malien.

Tallia had seen many violent deaths in her time as Mendark's assistant, then as Magister herself, but this was one of the more unpleasant ones. "What's he trying to protect?"

She prised one of the bloody, scorched pages out of his hand and held it up to the light. "Beautiful calligraphy."

Lilis crept forward, trying not to look at Snoat's gruesome corpse. "It's Llian's manuscript for the *Tale of the Mirror*—what's left of it." She gathered the pages.

There were two more bodies. Tallia headed towards the closest, dreading that it would be Llian's, but it turned out to be a one-armed man with a narrow face, rather larger on the left side than the right, a bulbous jaw and sagging, wrinkled ears. "Snoat's mancer-for-hire, Scorbic Vyl. He's no loss."

His snake-headed staff lay some distance away. She picked it up; it was a dangerous object and could not be left lying around. Not far away was a leather bag full of old books. She drew one out, then another. They were the manuscripts of the first twenty-two Great Tales, all but one of Snoat's once-perfect collection.

"I'll take charge of them," said Lilis, putting what was left of Llian's Great Tale in and heaving the heavy bag over her shoulder. "They must go back to the college."

"Not while Snoat's lackey Basible Norp is running it," said Tallia.

"They'd better go to the Great Library then."

Tallia headed to the third body, a young woman with blonde hair, Esea. Her throat and chest were peppered with small, bloody wounds though she was otherwise unmarked, and her lovely face had a serenity that Tallia had never seen while she was alive.

Tallia probed several of the wounds, which had been made by jagged shards of brass.

"Where's the Command device?" said Nadiril, who had just tottered up.

Mutely, Tallia held out several bloody shards.

"It's dangerous," said Nadiril. "Gather up every piece."

Malien gave an order and her Aachim formed a line, moving slowly forward across the paving stones and picking up every object they found. Tallia crouched beside Esea's body and picked out the rest of the shards. What a waste!

Xarah was walking back and forth, moving the little brass pointers on her scrying board and making notes on a slate. Malien conferred with her, then said, "I'd say Esea attacked Snoat and Vyl, perhaps trying to make up for her failure up at the pavilion. She used a reshaping spell to transform the Command device—"

"Or destroy it," said Tallia. "And them."

"Perhaps. But the spell killed them and the device exploded, killing her."

"But where are Llian and Hingis?" said Tallia. "And Ifoli, for that matter?"

"On Snoat's boat?"

"Ifoli loved books with a passion," said Nadiril. He choked. "She would never have left them behind."

Tallia stared at him. "How do you know? Out with it, old man."

"Ifoli is my great-granddaughter and she's been my spy in Snoat's camp for the past year and a half."

"*Your great-granddaughter?*"

"I did my damnedest to dissuade her . . . but she seemed to have something to prove—"

There was shouting from the jetty. The Aachim had failed to stop Snoat's flagship, which was a hundred yards out in the cove and moving swiftly away under full sail.

"The captain must have got wind of what happened here," said Malien.

Tallia swore fluently. "Snoat's fabulous war chest will be aboard—and we need it desperately. Can anything else possibly go wrong?"

Wordlessly, Lilis pointed to the little inlet half a mile north of the cove, where flames had suddenly leaped as high as the treetops. "That's our boat."

The beautiful little yacht that had brought them here from Vilikshathûr, successfully racing Snoat's flagship all the way, would be ashes within minutes.

"How the hell are we going to get home?" said Nadiril.

Tallia could not speak; the loss was too crushing. Vilikshathûr, where they had a small army, was a hundred and fifty miles to the north by ship, though a lot further on foot. The coast road was rough, winding and hilly; they would be lucky to reach Vilikshathûr in ten long days. And in ten days, with no opposition, the Merdrun might have taken Santhenar.

She jammed Vyl's snake-headed staff into a crack between the stones and conjured bright light from it. "What have you got?"

The Aachim put their fragments down on the pale stones. Tallia laid down the bloody pieces of brass she had taken from Esea's wounds. Malien squatted and, after a few seconds' thought, began to put the pieces together as if she were assembling a puzzle. The brass casing of the Command device took shape. It had been roughly the size of a large beer tankard, though the metal was curved now as if it had been forced into a sphere then had partly sprung back, and a third of the casing was missing.

"Is that all?" she said.

"All we could find on the paving stones," said the young Aachim man called Nimil, who had a metal slit in his neck and spoke with an odd whistle. "The rest of the casing will be in the grass beyond."

"Search the grass for thirty yards in all directions."

The Aachim resumed the search. "What are you looking for?" said Tallia.

"The black crystal from the end," said Malien, "and whatever was inside the casing."

Xarah was still pacing back and forth with her scrying board, moving in a series of parallel lines across the paved area. She conferred with Malien again, then walked outwards in a tight spiral centred on a patch of paving stones that bore red scorch marks. Suddenly she stopped, turned and spiralled back in to the point she had started from.

Tallia headed across to her, and Nadiril and Lilis followed. "What have you found?" said Tallia.

"Evidence of a gate," said Xarah, "but unlike any gate I've sensed."

"Did Snoat made it?"

"Making gates takes powerful mancery, way beyond anything he or Vyl could have done."

"Then how did it get here? *Was it Shand?*"

"No, I know his gates." Xarah rubbed her short yellow hair, making it stand up. "I ... I think the destruction of the Command device linked this spot to the Merdrun's gate just as it was opening, via the summon stone. I think that created a kind of ... bastard gate—an appendix of the true gate—and it unbalanced the Crimson Gate. And in the backlash the bastard gate was flung away like a speck of mud off a spinning wheel, who knows where." She fell silent, colouring a little. It was a long speech for her.

"Taking Llian, Ifoli and Hingis with it?" said Nadiril.

"There's no evidence Hingis was here," said Malien.

"What about Llian and Ifoli?" said Lilis.

"The bastard gate might have taken them," said Xarah. "But it was very unstable; it wasn't meant to exist. And I'm afraid ..."

"What?"

"That without any source of power to maintain it, it couldn't last long before it collapsed."

"Into what?"

"Nothing."

"And if Llian or Ifoli were inside?"

"If the gate collapsed on them, they would cease to exist."

11

THEY'RE KILLING EVERYONE

"Is there a chance the bastard gate could still be in existence?" said Nadiril, glancing up at the stars. "Must be hours since it formed."

Malien shrugged. "Unlikely."

"Can Xarah have a look?" said Tallia.

Xarah was moving her pointers around the brass rings. She looked up from her scrying board for a second and her eyes flashed green, then looked down again without speaking.

She seemed excited. What about? Tallia considered what she knew about Xarah. Her twin, Shalah, had been killed many years ago by a flailing stay cable when the great tower of Katazza collapsed, not long after Rulke escaped from the prison of the Nightland. It had taken Xarah many years to come to terms with her grief—if indeed she had.

Since the accident she had devoted her time, her craft and her gift to the development of scrying devices like the one she had here, and no other Aachim had a tenth of her skill at it.

"This place is saturated with waste mancery," said Malien. "We'll go back to the campsite. Xarah can work better there."

A rare smile utterly transformed Xarah's sad face. By the time they were back in the clearing it was well after midnight. She sat back in the trees, well away from the glow of the campfire, and set to work with the scrying board. "This could take a while."

Tallia slumped onto a log, struggling to digest the reversals of the night: the Merdrun invading through the gate, the disastrous failure of the attack on Snoat, Sulien's mortal danger and Karan stealing the sky ship, Shand's treachery and mysterious disappearance, the loss of Snoat's flagship and war chest, and the fate of Llian and Ifoli. Every way forward was littered with unknowns and, with the best will in the world, how could they have any hope? Was she leading this sad collection of allies to their doom? Would the doom of Santhenar follow? Had the last ten years of her life been an utter failure? It seemed so.

The Aachim prepared supper, and she ate it without knowing what it was, or caring. Afterwards she sat watching the deft movements of Xarah's long fingers, though her own thoughts were far away. The failed confrontation with Shand had shaken her; it had brought home the realisation she had been avoiding for years now—that she wasn't hard enough or single-minded enough to be a good Magister.

Why had she wasted half her life in an occupation that required control and domination of others? An occupation that, clever and hardworking though she was, she was utterly unsuited for. Because Crandor, and the prospect of a life learning the management of her family's cocoa plantations, had utterly bored her. She ached for it now.

But she had taken on the job and no one else could do it. Could she learn domination? Perhaps in this situation the end did justify the means.

"Ahh!" sighed Xarah.

"What is it?" said Malien.

Xarah lifted off the long, curving brass pointers, then added a third graduated ring inside the two mounted on the board, and a milky, opaline half sphere at the centre, replaced the two pointers on the outer ring and extended them so their tips hovered above the half sphere. She added a third pointer to the middle ring, and a fourth to the inner ring, nodded, then, eyes closed, slowly moved the pointers around their circles.

Tallia wrapped a blanket around her and dozed. Whenever she woke, Xarah was bent over her scrying board. From where Tallia sat it was just a blur of graduated brass circles, pointers, the opaline half sphere in the centre, now glowing bluish-grey, and a little orange crystal inset into the upper rim that was winking, winking . . .

"I've found a gate!" cried Xarah. "And there's someone in it."

Decrepit old Nadiril, a collection of brittle bones held together by skin as wrinkled as boiled parchment, leaped out of his blankets. "Is it *Ifoli?*" There were tears in his cloudy eyes.

Tallia scrambled up. It was well after dawn—the sun was slanting through the trees. She ran to Xarah.

"I can't even tell where it is." Xarah pointed to a bright blue spot on the half sphere. "It's too far from the centre."

"The general direction?" said Malien.

"North-north-west."

"The Great Library is north-north-west from here," Lilis said excitedly.

"So is the great island of Faranda," said Nadiril, "and a thousand other places near and far."

"It's further than the Great Library," said Xarah. "More than that, I can't say."

"What's the gate doing?" said Tallia.

"Sitting there—as if it's waiting."

"Can we take it?" Nadiril said quietly.

Malien caught his arm. "What are you talking about?"

"Snoat's mancers tried to take control of the gate Shand and Ussarine escaped from Carcharon in. And nearly succeeded before Shand directed it to us in Vilikshathûr."

"How did he do that?"

"I was using a bit of mancery," said Nadiril obscurely, "and it allowed him to locate us." He thought for a moment. "What if we tried . . ." He put his lips to Malien's ear.

She nodded. "It can only fail."

He shook his head. "If it goes wrong—" He looked to Tallia.

Tallia wrestled with her long-held fear of making the wrong decision. *No*, she thought. *If ever there's a time for boldness, it's now.* "Do it!"

Malien and Nadiril set to work, conferring with Xarah all the while. Tallia gnawed her knuckles until they bled. Why was it taking so long? Was this the most reckless decision she'd ever made? What if Merdrun held the gate? They might burst forth into the clearing, in which case they would finish their only opposition in a few seconds of violence.

The gate appeared as a hurtling, howling, blue-streaked cyclone. It struck the ground on the far side of the clearing, flinging dirt and fallen leaves everywhere, bounced, touched down again on the fire, hurling red-hot coals high and sending up a mushroom cloud of ash, shot towards Xarah, then all the violence drained out of it and it shuddered to a stop a yard in front of her.

The whirling blue streaks went still and Tallia saw someone inside the gate, holding a stick or staff. She drew her sword. Beside her, Malien's long fingers were extended towards the gate.

"Ifoli?" cried Nadiril.

The wall of the gate became transparent. The figure wasn't Ifoli, or Llian. A slender silver-haired girl stood there, supporting herself on a black sword Tallia knew all too well.

"I've seen the enemy," gasped Aviel. "They're killing everyone. And they've got Wilm!" She hobbled forward, her ankle turned under her and she fell. Tallia sprang and caught her. "They ... they're going to kill him."

Aviel told them what had happened at the summon stone, and that the Merdrun were in a hot, humid land where the grass was thick and a brilliant green, the forest trees were gigantic, and the people were even darker than Tallia.

"Most of the far north is like that," said Tallia, "from Nys in Faranda to Roros in southern Crandor, and thousands of islands scattered near and far."

"Note all your settings," Malien said to Xarah. "Try to locate the place."

"The gate can't last," Nadiril rapped out. "Is there anything we can do?"

Xarah moved the pointers on her scrying board, looked up sharply, then whispered to Malien.

Malien, clearly startled, said, "Really?"

"If you do it *right away*."

The gate was colourless now, and smaller. Malien shouted to her people, who heaved their packs on and drew their weapons.

"What's going on?" said Tallia.

"We think we can take control of the gate."

Malien went into a huddle with Nadiril and Xarah, then Nadiril put his right hand on Xarah's left shoulder and Malien put her left hand on Xarah's right shoulder. Xarah's jaw muscles stood out, her fingers moved the pointers delicately, then the gate brightened and began to rotate.

"Direct it to Vilikshathûr," said Malien.

"No, Sith!" said Nadiril.

No, thought Tallia. *We need coin more than anything.* "No! Xarah, we're taking Snoat's flagship—and his war chest."

No one moved. Was this the stupidest decision she'd ever made? But there was no time to think about it; the gate was shrinking by the minute. Xarah nodded. Tallia drew her sword and leapt in. "Come on!"

The world vanished. She felt a thump in the lower belly, a whirling dizziness that robbed her of sight for a few seconds, a whiff of salt spray, then she landed on a wildly rocking deck lit only by a pair of lanterns behind her. It was windy, the ship wallowing in heavy seas, and every time the bow plunged into the swell cold spray was flung into her face.

"We're under attack!" bellowed someone from behind her. "Guards!"

Boots thundered along the deck. Tallia cursed. Snoat's troops and sailors were well trained, and she was alone. Where was the gate? Had Xarah lost control of it?

A pair of soldiers wearing the uniform of Snoat's personal guard hurled themselves at her. She thrust at the man on the left but he parried, thrust and almost got through. She fought back desperately, knowing that the fellow on the right was waiting for the chance to put his blade into her belly.

He saw his opportunity and hacked at her. She ducked, and his sword struck the mast and wedged there. Instantly she thrust into his heart. He died without a sound though there was an awful lot of blood; it flooded the deck around him, and the soldier on the left slipped in it and lurched backwards. Tallia struck him hard on the kneecap. He shrieked and fell on his back, howling and holding his ruined knee.

But now guards were coming from everywhere, dozens of them, and if she had to fight them alone she would soon be killed. Behind her, four steps led up. She scrambled up onto a deck with the wheelhouse in the middle.

The captain, a very fat, bald man, was half turned away from her, roaring for more guards. His purple sagging jowls were covered in a week's growth of stubble and he wore a vulgar but expensive coat of crimson velvet with gold buttons over a lurid green waistcoat whose buttons were under near-fatal strain.

He was swaying on swollen, stubby feet crammed into shoes that no longer fitted. Tallia leaped behind him, grabbed him with her left arm and thrust her blade against his throat.

"Back!" she roared to the half-dozen troops who had reached the foot of the steps. "Or your captain dies."

The leading soldier, a lantern-jawed fellow in a lieutenant's uniform, sneered. "Think we give a damn if the fat fool lives or dies? Cut his throat and be damned."

Without help she would soon die, but she had to keep fighting; she had to take control. "I'm the Magister! Snoat's dead and we're at war. If you steal this ship, you're mutineers. Wherever you go, you'll be hunted down and hanged."

"No one can stop the Merdrun. It's every man for himself now—and a fast ship to the end of the world is our best hope."

The captain whined, "They're dangerous waters and no one knows them but me. You need me, Lieutenant!"

Clearly he was a greedy man with his eye on a fortune. Snoat had plundered the wealth of Iagador for his personal collections, and to support his army of fifty thousand men he would have needed a colossal war chest. Most of it would be on this ship—perhaps the greatest treasure ship in the history of Santhenar. What soldier, or captain, wouldn't kill for a share of it?

She needed it desperately. For the past two months the allies' efforts to raise an army had been hindered by lack of coin; thus far they had only been able to recruit and arm five thousand men. This treasure ship could change all that, and Snoat's well trained army was there for the taking, if she acted fast. But she had to get to it before his generals heard that he was dead and the army broke up into militias bent on plundering while they could.

The lieutenant was climbing the steps, grinning. Where the hell were the Aachim? Had the dying gate faded out before they could get into it? She fought the fear; she had to keep going.

The captain gasped and clutched at his chest. Was he having a heart attack? She shoved him aside and sprang forward as the lieutenant stormed up the last three steps and thrust up at her. She swept his blade aside then swung hers horizontally at his exposed throat. The tip carved a red line across it though the wound did not stop him.

"You'll have to do better than that," he grinned and leaped at her. "Die, bitch!"

But on the last word his bloody throat frothed and gurgled, and the breath whistled out of it. She had nicked his windpipe. He stumbled and fell to one knee, looking up at her, and she saw the moment he realised that he was doomed. Terror contorted his face. He tried to shrug it off, to go at her and take her with him, but as he came to his feet she slid her sword into his heart and with her left foot thrust him down the steps into his men.

"There's only one of her!" yelled a squat, muscular fellow. "Cut her down and we're rich beyond our dreams."

The sun broke through the clouds, lighting up the deck and the mass of soldiers advancing towards her, at least a hundred of them.

Tallia was fighting hopelessly when the gate reappeared near the foot of the mainmast with a *boom* that shook the flagship, and a dozen Aachim stormed out of it, followed by Malien, Nadiril and Lilis, and finally Xarah. Soon there was fighting everywhere but the Aachim troops, outnumbered eight to one, were being driven back. The ship was miles offshore and if they were forced into the sea they would drown.

From the corner of an eye Tallia saw Nadiril swaying on his feet, trying to shelter Lilis and Aviel behind him. He had a sword in one hand and, for an ancient, was wielding it competently, though there was no hope of him beating an experienced soldier. Her reckless gamble had failed and Santhenar's hopes would founder here.

"Sorry about losing the gate," called Xarah, who was hunched against the side, still working her scrying board. "But this may pay for it."

She stood up, moved all her pointers to the centre, and the gate whirled across the deck and into the mass of enemy soldiers. There were wild cries as it passed between them, tossing everyone it touched off their feet and tearing down spars and rigging, then it exploded with a reverberating *thud* that blasted soldiers, ropes and splinters of wood in all directions, and vanished.

At least fifteen troops had been hurled over the side into the roaring seas. Their cries soared above the whistle of the wind in the rigging, then stopped.

"Surrender!" shouted Xarah, brandishing her scrying board. "Or next time I'll take the rest of you."

Their officers tried to rally the soldiers for another attack but the heart had gone out of them.

"Those who surrender will be treated fairly," said Tallia, stepping across the bloody deck. "Those who continue to fight will be hanged as mutineers, there." She indicated the lowest boom of the foremast.

Every eye turned to it. The moment was poised, then a sergeant came forward onto the open deck between his comrades and Tallia, and tossed down a sword and a pair of knives. Another man followed him, then another and another, and it was over. The Aachim collected the weapons, then marched the troops below decks and locked them in.

"How did you do that?" Tallia heard Malien say to Xarah.

Xarah began an explanation that Tallia, for all her mastery of the Secret Art, could not follow. Her knees had gone weak and she could not think straight. The short fight should not have taken so much out of her, but over the last couple of months, dogged by an infected wound that had only recently healed, she had lost battle fitness. She had better get it back, quick.

"Could you have attacked them?" she said to Xarah.

Xarah shook her head. "The gate's gone to nothing."

"We've got to race back to Vilikshathûr and take command of Snoat's armies before word gets out that he's dead." Tallia looked around. "Where's the captain?"

"Hiding!" Malien said contemptuously. "I never trusted the fellow and clearly he's got a lot worse over the past decade."

"What do you mean?"

Malien indicated the coast of Meldorin, only a few miles to their west. Jagged black mountains, covered in forest, ran right down to the sea. "That's Point Porp, and it's the best part of a hundred miles *south* of Alcifer. If Xarah hadn't acted so quickly the captain would have got away with the greatest theft in history."

"He has to face trial," said Nadiril. "And the senior army officers."

Tallia heaved a great sigh. Finally something had gone right and, though it was only partly her doing, she felt better about herself than she had in months.

Shortly the captain was dragged up from his hiding place, whining and blustering. He was a miserable-looking fellow; his stubbly jowls were covered in salt spray and mucus from a running nose, his skin was blotchy and the buttons of his waistcoat had burst open under the strain of his enormous belly.

"Tallia!" he cried, reaching out to her with both arms. "For pity's sake, help me."

Tallia stared at him. "Do I know you?"

"It's Pender," Lilis said softly. "Pender, why did you do it?"

Only now did Tallia recognise, beneath the ruined skin and sagging blubber, the brilliant sailor who had carried her and Mendark halfway around Lauralin a dozen years ago. She had briefly been an investor in his first ship, though within a year she had withdrawn her coin. They were too different to be in partnership, and he had always been a greedy, self-justifying man.

"Haven't done no harm," he muttered. "You can forget about all this, can't you?"

"We're at war!" she said incredulously. "Our very existence is under threat, yet you stole Snoat's flagship and war chest and ran for it."

"Haven't touched a grint of his treasures," he whined. "You've got the lot."

"But had you got away, you would have been the richest man in Meldorin, and the loss would have crippled us in the war. You've committed a capital crime, Pender, and I can't protect you."

"Please," he said piteously, his nose oozing all over his upper lip.

"You've really let yourself go," Tallia said coldly.

Pender wiped his nose on his velvet sleeve and burst into tears. "But I've got children to support—you can't do this . . ."

Tallia assembled a jury of ten from the sailors on the deck. "You know the facts. What do you say?"

They only took a minute to judge him guilty.

"You've got no choice now," Nadiril said quietly.

Pender had been a decent man once, in his greedy and self-serving way, and he had done Mendark and herself good service. But that had been long ago, and there was nothing left of the man he had been. It was hard but it had to be done.

"Take a stout rope," said Tallia, "and hang him from the boom."

12

I'M ASHAMED OF YOU, GIRL

The image of that far-off, dreadful scene had burned itself into Llian's mind—the Merdrun army charging the red gate on that ice-sheathed plateau on Cinnabar.

"They're coming through!" he cried to Ifoli. "We've failed; we've lost."

"Ugh!" Ifoli clutched at her back and fell.

They were trapped in a shimmering force-bubble near the shore at Alcifer, in darkness. Before he could catch her the bubble hurtled away so rapidly that the world blurred around him. His lungs felt as though they weighed a hundred pounds; each breath was a fifty-foot climb.

The bubble plummeted from a height, bounced and bounced again, tossing him down, rolled across a bumpy surface and came to rest. He ached all over and something hard was jammed against his right hip—the top of Ifoli's head. She groaned.

He sat up and checked himself. He was covering in bruises but nothing was broken. The inside of the bubble had lost its shimmer and much of its colour; it was only faintly pink now. As he stood up it evaporated and he dropped six inches onto muddy sand that smelled of salt and rotting seaweed. They were on a beach or a tidal flat.

It was still dark, though the bubble must have carried them a long way because it was considerably warmer than Alcifer. A few stars speckled the sky to his left. Ahead a black, irregular outline marked rising ground. To the right, a small mountain blocked a third of the sky. Behind him a series of low, scalloped shapes might have been hills. But there were no lights; no signs of life in any direction.

Llian took stock. If his vision of the Merdrun storming the gate was true, and he felt sure it was, Karan's reckless mission to Cinnabar had failed. He choked and fell to his knees, clawing his fingers through the sand. She had taken one risk too many and it had been the end of her. No Karan ever more. The pain rose until it was unbearable; he wanted to scream, to punch something, to batter his head against the ground until he fell senseless and could no longer feel.

But Sulien was in more danger than ever. He had to find her.

Ifoli groaned, and Llian remembered, through the mental haze, that she had been injured. His eyes were adjusting to the dimness now. She lay on her side on the wet sand, knees drawn up to her chest and her arms wrapped around them, and her teeth were bared.

"Where are you hurt?" he said.

"My back. Below the left shoulder blade."

He pulled up her coat and blouse and probed the area with his fingertips. She winced.

"It's swollen but there's no wound. I'd say a fragment of the Command device hit you. We were lucky. It killed Scorbic Vyl and

Esea ... and Snoat." That image would haunt his nightmares. "We don't have to worry about him any more."

She sat up painfully, the starlight catching her eyes. "Why did you throw your *Tale of the Mirror* onto the fire?"

It had been an impulse, quickly regretted. "I suppose ... I just wanted to hurt Snoat. He'd done so much damage, ruined so many lives. I couldn't let him die knowing that his perfect collection was back together."

"I could never burn a book."

"Books are my life, but they're not worth the lives of good people." He scanned the horizon again. "Any idea where we are?"

"Near Mollymoot," said Ifoli.

"Never heard of it."

"It's a little island at the north-western tip of Meldorin. Six hundred miles from Alcifer."

Llian could not see the sea, but he could hear it, a distant hissing. "We'd better move."

Ifoli tried to get up, but sank down again. "Another minute."

What was the matter with her? She was one of the cleverest people he had ever met, seemingly good at everything, and had always been decisive and quick to act in an emergency. She had saved his life in Pem-Y-Rum when Unick had tried to kill him, and saved him from making a fool of himself with the Command device half an hour ago. Something was badly wrong with her.

The hissing sound grew louder. "How do you know where we are?"

"I grew up here. It's familiar, even in the dark. Perhaps that's why the bubble brought us here."

"I assumed—from your name and accent—that you came from the far east."

"I was born in the east, but my great-grandfather has a place just over there." She indicated a shadowy hill, then took three rasping breaths. "My aunt manages the estate—Nadiril seldom gets the chance to come home these days ..."

"Nadiril is your great-grandfather?" said Llian in astonishment. He had never thought of the Librarian as having a family.

"That's how I ended up being a spy in Snoat's household. When I was younger I was . . . constantly seeking new challenges."

"But not any more?"

"Took too many risks." She was panting now. "Lucky to be alive. Half my friends—brilliant, determined spies—tortured to death. What a waste!"

Llian could identify with that. He had wasted much of the past ten years trying to be what he was not and satisfying nobody, least of all himself.

"Played the role . . . too well," said Ifoli, now stopping for breath after every few words. "Without me . . . Snoat might have done . . . far less damage."

Llian had often wondered why she'd served him so faithfully. She had seemed too perfect, and now she was paying for it. The rushing grew louder. "What's that noise?"

"The tide!" cried Ifoli. "They're huge here—thirty feet low to high." She looked around. "Only cross to Mollymoot at low tide. Comes in . . . fast."

Llian could see it now, a distant line of white, foaming towards them. He heaved her to her feet and gave her his shoulder. "Which way?"

She turned to face the black shape of the mountain. "There."

They headed off, sometimes on hard sand, sometimes on smelly mud that sucked at their boots; it was slow and exhausting and he had to heave Ifoli along. Every time he looked back the white line of water was closer and the rushing sound louder; it was almost a roar now.

"Won't make it," she said listlessly. "We're way off causeway."

What causeway? He saw a faint line thirty yards to the right. The ground would be harder there and they could go faster.

"Leave me," said Ifoli.

"Put your arm around my neck."

"What? *No!*"

He swept her up in his arms and ran. She was neither big nor heavy, but her weight pushed him an inch deeper into the mud with each stride. He could not have done this a couple of months ago, but all his time on the road, climbing ridges and mountains and towers with thousands of steps, had given him stamina he had not had in a decade.

He needed all of it. By the time he reached the causeway the foaming tide-front was racing towards them. He clambered onto the paved surface, which was potholed and slippery.

"Put me down," said Ifoli.

He ignored her and set off towards the island. The shore was a hundred and fifty yards away, as near as he could judge. The tide was now a breaking wave, crashing and roaring behind them. He made ten yards, then twenty, but the wave was moving at twice his speed and there was no hope of outrunning it.

His left foot plunged into a pothole and he fell, dropping Ifoli and landing on top of her. She shrieked. Before he could get up the water struck him, bowling him over her and along the causeway.

Llian thrashed around in the boiling whiteness. A second wave struck him in the back and he went under, scraping his hands and knees on barnacle-covered stone and cracking his head on something hard, then the wave passed on. He stood up in hip-deep water, head throbbing, wiping gritty seawater out of his eyes.

He was veering off the causeway and there was no sign of Ifoli. He fixed on the high peak of the shadowy mountain and, as the water surged the other way, thrashed towards the shore. He made another twenty yards and stumbled again, this time over something much softer. Ifoli, floating face down.

Drowned? He heaved her upright, turned her and thrust his clenched fists in under her ribcage. Water gushed from her mouth; she gave a great choking gasp and began to retch. He threw her over his shoulder and staggered up the causeway, making it to the shoreline just as a bigger wave broke behind him, driving him forward. He used its momentum to heave her up five or six feet, above the high-water mark, and dropped her there.

He crawled further up, hanging onto tussocks of wiry grass, and fell on a bed of shells and gravel, gasping.

"Ifoli?" he said after a couple of minutes.

Nothing. A rocky fist closed around his heart. Was she dead? He felt her face, neck and throat, and she was cold. He put his ear to her chest and she was breathing, though he heard a faint crackling, as if there was still water in her lungs.

There were no lights along the foreshore. If she were to be saved, he had to do it. He turned her on her side and felt inside her mouth in case her airway was blocked.

She retched again, water and mucus dribbled out and she breathed a little more easily. A minute passed, then she let out a feeble croak.

He heaved her upright. "Where's the nearest house?"

"Aunt Dilly's place." She dipped her head to the left.

He carried her up the track from the causeway, then off to the left along a narrow path between tussocks of coarse grass that sawed at his weary legs as he passed. Dry sand squeaked underfoot. He staggered over a little hill where the shrubs smelled like lavender, then up a winding path of lime-washed flagstones to a high, narrow stone house with a shingle roof, the shingles shining silver in the starlight.

Llian could barely stand up. He banged his head on the front door and shortly a stern-faced woman opened the door.

"Who are you?" She thrust a six-sided lantern into his face. "What do you want at this hour?". Then she looked down and cried, "Ifoli?"

"Dilly," Ifoli whispered.

Dilly took Ifoli from Llian's arms, effortlessly, and carried her down a hall and around a corner to the left. Llian's knees gave way and he subsided onto the grey-green hall rug. It rasped against his cheek and smelled as if it had been woven from dried seagrass.

The lighted room at the other end, when he finally reached it, was a large old fashioned kitchen: small cast iron stove, wide fireplace with an iron bar across the middle and a large pot, black as char, suspended over the coals. A table, covered in a blue cloth embroidered with white flowers, sat under a small window that looked out over a steep, bushy slope down to the sea.

Aunt Dilly, who could have been any age from thirty-five to sixty, was tall and lean, with a beaky nose, deep blue eyes and thin fingers. She bore a distinct resemblance to Nadiril, though she was not an unhandsome woman. She had settled Ifoli on a chair and was cleaning blood and mud off her face with a brown sponge. Ifoli had gone a pale green; a fist-shaped bruise marred her high forehead and she was breathing raggedly.

She looked up as Llian entered, wobbly on his feet. "Saved my life," she croaked. "Don't know why I'm so weak."

"Guilt!" said Dilly. "From serving that monster, Snoat. Acting as his right-hand woman! And who knows what else you did for him," she said with a judgemental sniff. "I'm ashamed of you, girl."

Ifoli went a delicate shade of red.

"I can't think what possessed Nadiril to let you be his spy," Dilly said crossly. "I'm giving the old fool a piece of my mind. How dare he!"

"I pestered him until he agreed, Aunt Dilly. If anyone's at fault—"

"He had no right agreeing!" Dilly thundered. "And I'll be having stern words with you too, young lady, the moment you're better."

"Yes, Aunt Dilly," Ifoli said meekly, though she seemed pleased to be fussed over.

"You're not going back to that vile man. I won't hear of it."

"Snoat's dead," said Llian.

Dilly turned to him. "I'm delighted to hear it—if you're sure?"

"We saw him die. It was . . . ugly."

"And who are you?" she said. "Apart from the hero who saved my beautiful niece."

"He's Llian," said Ifoli. "The Llian who told the Great—"

"The *Tale of the Mirror*," sighed Dilly. Goose pimples rose along her lean forearms and her blue eyes took on a liquid shine. "We're bookish folk in this family. We love the Great Tales, and there's none greater."

"Thank you," said Llian, moved by her quiet passion. It was a wonderful thing to have a Great Tale to his name, but the look in the eyes of those people who loved his stories was greater still.

"What were you doing out on the mudflats with the tide coming in?" Dilly frowned at Ifoli. "I'm surprised at you, girl; you know better."

"A gate," said Ifoli. "It hurled us all the way from Alcifer in an instant."

"Are the stories true, then? About a terrible enemy gathering in the void to attack us?" She turned to Llian. "News comes slowly to our forgotten end of the world."

"They're true. The Merdrun have invaded, and we don't know where."

Dilly shivered. "You need tea." She went to the black pot over the fire but swung back. "No, wine. Have you eaten?"

Llian shook his head. "Not since lunch time . . . couldn't stomach anything."

He sat at the far end of the table, out of the way. Dilly propped Ifoli up with cushions, for she was looking wan again, went out the back door and returned bearing a glass jug of pale green wine. She poured Llian a generous glass and Ifoli a little one.

Ifoli managed a smile. "How come he gets more than I do?"

"You're ill. Besides," she gave Llian a keen sideways look, "tellers are legendary drinkers."

"Indeed we are," said Llian, and raised his glass to them both.

The wine, though weak, was welcome. Llian would have preferred the glorious Driftmere brandy that he had pilfered from Pem-Y-Rum, but the decanter lay forgotten in Alcifer.

The only other occupant of Dilly's house was her fifteen-year-old nephew Reggeley, who had gone to bed hours ago. By the time they finished supper and washed the mud and salt off, it was two in the morning. Dilly showed Llian to a long, narrow room under the roof, up three flights of creaking stairs. A boarded ceiling followed the roof line, the low walls were olive green and there was a small bed at the far end, under a white window.

"Can't remember when I last slept in a proper bed," he said, yawning.

"You've got the best views in Mollymoot. The south window looks down the west coast of Meldorin. And to the north," she gestured to the window by the bed, "our twin island and its great mountain, Demondifang."

"Twin island?" he said wearily.

"Mollymoot and Demondifang are like two peas, linked at low tide by a two-mile-long spit of gravel, but the rest of the time they're separate islands."

"Does anyone live on Demondifang?"

"Not any more. After the last raid ... the survivors would not go back."

There was a haunted look in her eyes. He looked out the north window but the mountain was just a tall, pointed shadow. Beyond it, far out to sea, lightning turned the insides of a towering thunderstorm milky. He sat on the bed, overcome by exhaustion and hopelessness.

Dilly went to the door but stopped, her hand on the knob. "What will you do now?"

"Try to find out what happened to Karan. I don't even know if she's alive. Though, realistically—"

"You mustn't give up hope," said Dilly.

The past day had battered him down; he couldn't think, couldn't plan. "If she is alive, she'll be heading for Sith with our allies."

"Sith is a month's ride from here, if you had a horse. Or several weeks sailing."

"By the time I got there the war might be over. And then there's Sulien, somewhere in Shazabba with the awful Whelm ..."

"You might wait weeks for a ship going that far south. And it'll cost a fortune."

Llian's pockets were empty; Snoat's guards had taken everything when they had searched him last night. He groaned.

"If you need fresh air," said Dilly, "there's a roof platform up the stairs to the right. In olden times they kept watch there for the return of the fishing fleet. Hungry times if it came late—or never came back," she said with a little shiver. "Good night."

A chill crept into Llian's bones and he threw off his clothes and climbed into bed.

A distant rumbling roused him and he saw that the storm had moved closer. He slept again, only to be woken by a brilliant flare of lightning and an almighty crash of thunder. The storm was approaching Demondifang, which he now saw to be a fang of yellow rock rearing up for a couple of thousand feet out of forest.

His grim thoughts turned back to Karan. How could she have

survived that mad attack on the magiz? The lightning flashed, the thunder boomed—*she's dead, dead, dead!*

His eyes stung, but he had to face the unbearable truth—dead or alive, there was nothing he could do for her. All the more reason to take Sulien back from the Whelm, who would beat her, crush her spirit and turn her into a little Whelm like their own miserable children. But how, in that frozen wilderness, was he supposed to find her when he had no coin and no way to get any?

The lightning was now so frequent and the thunder so loud that there was no hope of sleep. He dressed and went up the stairs, then climbed a short wooden ladder through a circular hole in the floor of the lookout platform. It was only a couple of yards square, with a low wooden rail around it on all sides, and the wind was strong enough to shake the timbers.

To his surprise, Ifoli stood at the rail, looking north at the mountain. "I've never seen a storm as fierce as this. And it's heading right for *our* mountain."

The storm crept closer until it was directly above the peak and lightning struck at the highest point, over and over. The wind strengthened and it started to rain.

He was about to go down when something occurred to him. "You were Nadiril's spy for more than a year."

She did not reply.

"You would have needed a safe way to contact him."

"Mmn," she said.

"In the olden days, Nadiril used to make quaint little devices for talking to people from afar. If you've still got one, can you find out if there's any news of Karan?"

After a long hesitation she said, "I'll try, though they don't work well over such long distances."

He turned back to the mountain. "What's up there?"

"I don't know; I've never climbed Demondifang. But young couples still do if the weather is good; it's considered lucky."

It did not look lucky now; it looked as though the storm was trying to hammer the tip of the peak to pieces.

13

I'LL DISPOSE OF THE SURPLUS

The Merdrun warrior who had been beating Wilm for the past ten minutes struck him a final savage blow in the belly that sent jags of pain in all directions, then let him go. Wilm crumpled to the ground, writhing. There was no part of him that did not hurt. But it would soon be over. Gergrig was coming down the slope, raising his sword as if to split Wilm's head in two.

Someone called from further around the hill, out of sight. Wilm did not hear what was said, but Gergrig stopped and lowered the blade.

"Garlugg's right," he said quietly to the man beside him. "The magiz mentioned this youth. He's close to some of their most important people; he may be more use to us alive." He kicked Wilm in the head, almost reflectively. "Besides, we need all the strong young slaves we can get. Bring him."

"Get up!" snapped the warrior. He was as muscular as a weightlifter; there were even knots of muscle along his jawline.

Wilm lurched to his feet, trying not to cry out, for he ached all over. He raised his hands to his face, which felt hot and bloated. His fingers came back bloody. His nose was dripping blood, both lips were split, and his left eye was so swollen that he could not see out of it.

His hands were bound behind his back and he was driven at sword point down the hill. He was staggering by the time he got to the bottom, and felt like throwing up, but fought to hold it in—the Merdrun gloried in killing and, if they saw the slightest weakness, might cut him down. He had to survive. The invasion must not succeed.

After an exhausting march across undulating green countryside he was shoved through the guarded gates of a large walled estate. To the left there were orchards and vegetable gardens. On the right stood a

cream-coloured manor, even larger and grander than Snoat's villa of
Pem-Y-Rum, into which Wilm and Dajaes had tunnelled less than a
month ago to rescue Llian. And where Dajaes had been murdered by
Unick.

Wilm choked at the memories. But he had made Unick pay; the
summon stone had consumed the brute and he would never hurt
anyone again.

Wilm put the past aside. For the moment only one thing mattered:
he had to survive, learn as many of the enemy's secrets as he could, then
escape and help to defeat them.

He was driven past the colonnaded front of the house, across a terrace
which stood a yard higher than the lawn and was paved with polished
slabs of the same cream-coloured stone. Ribbons of blood ran down
the broad steps, and dozens of bodies, all dark-skinned and with black
hair, strewed the paving, the steps and the lawn.

Some of the dead wore brightly coloured silks—sleeveless shirts or
blouses and knee-length pantaloons. Wilm assumed them to be the
family who'd owned the estate, slaughtered as they tried to escape.
Others, servants, wore simple white garments. A group of men, apparently slain as they ran to the defence of the owners, were only clad in
loincloths, farm labourers perhaps.

They rounded a corner and ahead milled a throng of dark-skinned
folk, mostly men though with a few women. All looked young and
strong, though many bore the marks of savage beatings. Their hands
were tied and they were watched by Merdrun guards.

"Form lines of ten," grated a red-handed guard. "No talking."

They formed into lines. Anyone who was too slow, or did not line
up precisely behind the person in front, was beaten.

"You all right?" the man next to Wilm said quietly. "Take it easy."

He was a big handsome young fellow, and the sympathy in his eyes
was evident. Wilm gave an almost imperceptible nod.

"In line, you!" snarled the red-handed guard, smacking Wilm over
the head with the flat of his sword. The blow made his ears ring.

The handsome young man said, "He's going as fast as he can."

The guard swung his curved blade in a horizontal arc faster than

Wilm's eye could follow and beheaded the kindly man before he could blink. Blood went everywhere.

Wilm froze, staring down at the body and the severed head, which had come to rest with those soft eyes looking blankly into his.

"No . . . talking!" grated the guard.

Wilm could not have spoken even if he had wanted to; his breath had congealed in his throat in horror. More guards appeared and tied each line together.

"Don't move," said the killer. "Look straight ahead. Don't speak."

The tropical sun pounded on Wilm's aching head. He was drenched in sweat in his winter clothes but his mouth was dry as paper. He had drunk nothing since leaving the freezing little hut last night with Aviel, heading down to Carcharon and the summon stone. Dizziness overcame him and he swayed, but the dark woman next to him elbowed him in the ribs. Horror stabbed through Wilm—if he'd fallen it would have cost him his head.

An officer appeared, a burly fellow whose right eye socket was empty. The top of his flat bald head was a mass of lumpy red scars, as if he had been scalped. He was accompanied by a muscular woman with a close-cropped skull. The Merdrun glyph was tattooed on her broad forehead in blue, and a different glyph on her right cheek in black. She carried a rolled map in one hand and a roll of buff leather in the other.

She looked down at the beheaded man without interest, then gestured to the end of the colonnade, five yards away. She unrolled the map on the paving stones and they studied it for several minutes, the officer pointing out hills, rivers and bridges and other features of interest. Wilm watched from the corners of his eyes.

"Here?" The woman prodded the map with a stubby finger.

"Vulnerable here and here," said the officer, leaning over the map.

"What about here?"

"Poor water supply."

"Here?"

After a minute's consideration he said, "Not ideal, but we can make it work. It doesn't have to last." He lowered his voice until Wilm had to strain his ears to hear. "We've got to work fast, before the enemy—"

She let out a hiss and he broke off, then added, "How long to draw up the plans?"

The woman, whom Wilm assumed to be an architect or builder, glanced at the cloudless sky. "I'll have them sketched by noon, enough to make a start."

The officer nodded. "How long will the fortress take to build?"

"Depends on how many slave masons we can find."

"What about our own masons?"

"We've only got fourteen."

He scowled. "Why so few?"

"We lost more than half in the assault on the ring fortress on Cinnabar."

"Then our fourteen must supervise the slave masons. How many slaves do you need?"

The architect did a series of calculations on the side of the map and added the numbers, her thick lips moving. "If we tear down the town nearby and reuse the stone, we can get by with four thousand."

"We have five thousand—"

"We don't have the masons to direct that many slaves."

"Then I'll dispose of the surplus. No point feeding the swine if we don't need them."

The back of Wilm's neck throbbed as if a sword was swinging at it. If they were killing surplus slaves he would be one of the first.

The architect shook her head. "Working flat out, we'll lose dozens of slaves a day. We'll need at least a thousand in reserve."

"How long will it take?"

"It'll be defendable after . . . twenty days."

The officer grunted. "It'd better be."

He walked off. The architect carried a table out of the manor onto the colonnade and stood at it, working on her drawings. The sun pounded down on Wilm's unprotected head and it took all the self-control he could muster to stay upright.

A group of slaves appeared, heaving barrels on hand carts, and half a dozen wooden troughs that, judging by the smell and the crusted stains, had been taken from a pigsty.

Two of the troughs were filled with water, the others with a foul-smelling swill that might have come from the same sty. The slaves were led forward in their lines, one line to each trough, and each slave allowed a minute for drinking and two for eating before being kicked out of the way. Clearly the Merdrun considered their captives to be little more than beasts.

Wilm, who had grown up in the poorest family in Casyme, was so hungry that he was salivating—and disgusted with himself for doing so. He had no father and had lived with his mother in the meanest of huts, but she had been a proud woman. The hut had been scrubbed until it shone, and his clothes, though made of the cheapest homespun, had been beautifully sewn and were always scrupulously clean. He was proud too. How could he bear to eat swill from a pig's trough?

No, he thought. *The only way we can beat the Merdrun is if every one of us, in big ways or small, does whatever it takes.* If he had to eat swill he would do it, but not like a pig. And with every mouthful he would screw his determination a little higher.

While his line of slaves waited their turn, he looked along the colonnade at the murdered owners and their servants, then down at the fly-covered corpse beside him, a kindly young man cut down solely to teach the other slaves obedience. The Merdrun had to be stopped before they destroyed the world the way they had ruined this pretty place. But what could he, an untrained youth, do?

After Dajaes' murder, Wilm had taught himself the basics of sword fighting, using a pamphlet Llian had written out for him, and as an antidote to his grief he had practised with such iron determination that he had subsequently bested Snoat's master assassin, Jundelix Rasper. After that, Wilm had set out to rescue Aviel from Unick, and had done so.

With dogged determination and a little bit of luck an untrained youth could do a lot. Wilm was going to play his part in bringing the Merdrun down . . . though first he had to survive.

The guards drove Wilm's line of slaves to the troughs. He drank his fill of the foul brown water then knelt before the stinking feeding trough. The muck smelled disgusting, but it was food and he needed it. He choked down as much as he could in his two minutes, then stood up.

He would bend his knee to the Merdrun and do whatever they required of him, but all the while he would be studying their defences, their arts of war, their strengths and weaknesses, and the way they managed their slaves, and he would prepare himself in every possible way for the moment a chance came. He would *never* give in.

Wilm was going to study himself just as diligently. He would analyse his strengths and work out how to foster them, assess his weaknesses and how to eradicate or hide them. He would make himself into a warrior as determined as any Merdrun. No, more determined, for he was fighting for the world he loved.

And when a chance did come, he would strike.

14

I'M AFRAID OF BEING CORRUPTED

Kill him! Kill him! Kill him!

Gergrig's order kept echoing through Aviel's mind. It was like being stabbed in the same place again and again; she could not rid herself of the memory. "Wilm, Wilm?" she whispered, as if the endless repetition of his name could keep him alive . . .

But how could he be alive? Hours had passed since the gate, captured by Malien and Nadiril and dragged to Alcifer, had been diverted. When it reopened Aviel had been tossed out onto the bloody deck of Snoat's flagship, into the middle of a ghastly battle; she'd had to scramble over red-ruined bodies to reach a cluster of water barrels. Cowering there, shivering, she had seen more horrors in five minutes than in her previous life, and every death had reminded her that Wilm was a prisoner of the vicious Merdrun. What if they strung him up like that poor, pathetic captain, Pender?

Aviel groaned.

Now the flagship was racing north for Vilikshathûr, and she lay huddled under a smelly blanket in the tiny cabin that Tallia, seeing her distress, had made over to her. It was no bigger than a cupboard, with a narrow bunk that her small frame barely fitted into. The cramped cabin was mouldy and dank, but it suited Aviel; it felt like a protecting cocoon.

Wilm's black sword stood in the corner in its gleaming copper sheath. She did not like swords but it was all she had left of him now. She reached out to it, then stopped. What would he think of her, huddled here in filth and apathy?

Aviel could not bear to be unclean; it reminded her of her drunken father, her six slatternly half-sisters and the filthy ruin, once a grand old house, they lived in back in Casyme. She undressed, scrubbed off the blood and grime with a rag and water from a jug clamped to the cabin wall, and dressed in clean, crumpled garments from her little pack.

She got out the deadly scent potion grimoire she had borrowed from Shand while he was away. She had planned to give it back and humbly beg his forgiveness, but Shand had fled, accused of being a traitor. Had the world gone mad?

Someone rapped at the door. Aviel shoved the grimoire under the blanket, her heart pounding, but did not answer. She did not like meeting new people. She just wanted to be back in her little perfumery workshop, alone with her grief and her misery. The repetitive tasks of scent making—harvesting herbs and flowers, distilling, purifying and cleaning, cleaning, cleaning—were comforting, and she missed them desperately.

The door opened and a thin, long-faced young woman stood there, carrying a basket. Her hair, cut short, was pale. Aviel could not remember her name.

"Lilis," said the young woman. "I'm Nadiril's assistant at the Great Library. I thought you might be hungry."

Go away! Leave me alone.

Lilis held out the basket and Aviel smelled hot soup. She salivated; she'd been on starvation rations for weeks.

"Thank you," she said hoarsely.

The basket contained a huge mug whose silver cap was engraved with a single rosebud, a slab of hard, dense cake full of nuts and seeds, a salt shaker and a spoon. She lifted the cap. The mug was full of a thick, meaty soup. She smelled pepper, yellow peas, and parsnip.

"Would you like some?" she said politely to Lilis.

"No, thanks."

Then clear out.

Lilis settled herself on the end of the bed as if she planned a long visit. Aviel sighed, but the odour of the soup was irresistible. She ate most of it and a small piece of the cake, then leaned back and closed her eyes.

Kill him! Kill him! Kill him! She choked.

"What is it?" said Lilis.

"Wilm's dead! Gergrig killed him!"

Lilis caught Aviel's right hand between her own hands. "You poor thing. Right in front of you?"

"No, the gate carried me away. But Gergrig ordered him to be killed."

"He might have changed his mind."

"The Merdrun love killing. Why would they spare Wilm?"

Lilis looked down at the square bulge under the covers. "Is that the grimoire you pinched from Shand?"

Aviel flushed. "I only borrowed it. Are you going to take it?"

"You've done more good with it than he ever did."

"It's a terrible book, but a great book too. When Shand comes back . . . When he proves himself innocent . . ." Aviel stroked the cover through the blanket. "I've never owned a proper book. The only book I have is a little one on scent-making I copied out."

"Any book you copied yourself is a very proper book."

"Are there grimoires in the Great Library?"

"Quite a few, though they're locked away and no one can see them without permission from Nadiril. They're very dangerous books."

"What about grimoires on scent potions?"

"Why do you ask? You already have one."

"Most of Radizer's scent potions are for unpleasant purposes," said Aviel, "and some are . . . evil. I think he was a very bad man."

"A dark potion can still be used for a good purpose. As you proved by using the Eureka Graveolence to find the summon stone."

"I'm afraid of being corrupted."

Lilis laughed aloud. "In the *Register of Wickedness*, which I've read three times, your deeds wouldn't rate a mention."

Aviel felt her cheeks growing hot. She hesitated, but she needed to tell someone and she felt sure Lilis could be trusted. "I'm attracted to the dark potions. I'm scared that one day I'll do something really bad."

"We all have bad thoughts from time to time."

"I'm sure you don't. You're so respectable."

"Can I tell you an embarrassing secret?"

"Of course," said Aviel, leaning forward eagerly.

"All the important librarians are old and, except for Nadiril, very boring. And as an assistant librarian, I'm becoming more like them every day. I love my work, yet sometimes I feel a mad urge to burst into their meeting room, throw off my clothes and run the length of the table, kicking off all their papers and whooping like a mad thing."

Aviel smiled for the first time. "Do you think you ever will?"

"Of course not," said Lilis, a trifle wistfully. "But that's why I came east with Nadiril. It takes me back to my childhood, when life was hard and painful and dangerous—but every day I knew I was alive." She stood up. "Nadiril wants to talk to you as soon as you've finished."

"Oh!" Aviel said with a sharp intake of breath. She took the cap off her mug of soup and ate the rest slowly, then the cake.

"Don't be afraid," said Lilis. "He's hard on people who don't meet his expectations, but he's a kind man . . . deep down."

It did not help. What expectations would he have of her, and how could she, an uneducated girl from an insignificant town miles from anywhere, possibly fulfil them?

Lilis rose. "He said to bring the sword and the grimoire . . . and anything else that's important."

Was he talking about the remains of the Origin device?

Aviel limped after Lilis along a series of narrow companionways that stank of grime, pee and the putrid bilges, then up again into a large and luxurious cabin which, judging by the treasures in it, must have belonged to Cumulus Snoat. A little brass incense burner clipped to the far wall emitted trails of blue smoke and a thick, cloying scent that did not completely disguise the reek of bilgewater.

Nadiril sat at the end of a large table. Tallia was to his right and Malien his left, and there were three Aachim men at the nearer end.

"Ah, Aviel," said Nadiril. "Sit down." He indicated the seat across the table from Malien. "We need to know what happened at the stone before the gate carried you and Wilm away."

Aviel perched on the front edge of the chair, the copper sheath in her lap, and stared at her fingers. "Wilm was down, paralysed," she said quietly, "and Unick was going to kill him. And then we saw the Crimson Gate."

"Leave out no detail," said Malien.

"It was like a red shadow on the wall of the cavern. I could see the Merdrun army through it and I knew they were about to invade. Unick went for me, and Wilm, um, ran him through." Aviel held up the black sword. "Unick crashed into the summon stone and . . . it . . . consumed him."

"And then?" said Tallia.

"The shadow gate was turning into a real gate and the Merdrun were racing towards it. There wasn't time to think—but I realised that if the gate was alive it might be poisoned, and I took the flask of quicksilver out of the Origin device and hurled it at the summon stone, and it smashed and ran down it."

"Ahh!" sighed Malien. "And then?"

"The enemy were shouting and yelling; they seemed afraid. Then the summon stone split into a crimson one and a blue one. The crimson one carried the Merdrun up and away, and the blue one closed around me and Wilm and took us with it. I must have been unconscious all night; the next thing I knew the blue gate had opened in a hot green land, and it was dawn."

"Could you see the other gate?" said Malien.

"No," said Aviel.

"You ended up in the same place as the enemy, somewhere in the tropics, but eight or nine hours later," said Tallia. "The gates must have been linked; we'll need to ask Karan about that."

"If she ever comes back," said Malien, tight-lipped.

"That was very well done, Aviel," said Nadiril. "By poisoning the stone, you made the enemy's gate open far from where they planned the invasion. And from Xarah's observations, I think it closed after they got there, and they don't have the power to reopen it."

"You mean they're stuck there?" said Nadiril.

"Until they can draw enough power from the summon stone to reopen their gate."

"The summon stone is gone from Carcharon," said Xarah.

"What?" cried Malien. "Where to?"

"I can't find it. But it seems more powerful now, more dangerous, and more warped."

"How naïve we were," said Malien, "to think it could be destroyed so easily."

"Well," said Nadiril, "it's two days' hard sailing from here to Vilikshathûr. By the time we get there we've got to have a plan to find the stone, locate the Merdrun and attack them before they can reopen the gate."

"We've got the bulk of Snoat's war chest," said Tallia, "and if we're quick we can take over some of his armies. If only we had the sky ship . . ."

"I have more on the way," said Malien, "though it may be another fortnight before they get here."

"We may have lost the war by then."

Malien knotted her knotted fingers as if wrestling with a dilemma, then said, "There are shipyards in Sith, are there not?"

"The best in Meldorin."

"As an iron rule, we do not share our secret craft with outsiders. But the Merdrun threaten us all and—for the duration of the war—I'm prepared to assist your people to make your own sky ships. We have a small supply of the vital crystals, and my people are skilled artificers. We will begin the moment we reach Sith."

The Aachim at the other end of the table scowled and stood

up. Malien held up a hand and they sat again. They did not look pleased.

"Thank you," said Nadiril, who looked astounded.

"Just for the duration of the war," said Malien. "Then we will have our crystals back."

Aviel, sure they needed nothing more from her, slipped away. She longed to go home but Casyme was hundreds of miles away and with no money she had no way of getting there. Indeed, with Shand on the run, wanted for treason, it wasn't clear that she had a home any more. Shand, who had taken her in, protected her from those who wanted to enslave her, and had given her her beloved workshop, might be put to death as a traitor and have all his possessions confiscated.

If that happened, what would become of her?

15

THERE THEY ARE! TAKE THEM!

Karan was steeling herself to go out into the howling darkness when Yggur let out a savage roar and the stern of the cabin lifted by a couple of feet, swung sideways in the wind and crashed down again, snapping her teeth together. He had freed the trapped skid from the crevasse.

The sky ship started to drift across the ice, lifting and crashing down on every bump and rut. A cupboard door at the back sprang open and dozens of carefully packed boxes crashed to the floor. Small metal parts went everywhere.

"Yggur?" she yelled, but he did not reply.

She sat down and took hold of the levers, gnawing her lip. She could not risk the sky ship sliding into a bigger crevasse, but if she moved it and Yggur was trapped she ran the risk of killing him. She ran to the door, looking left and right. There was no sign of him.

"Yggur!" she screamed into the darkness.

A groan. He was directly below her, clinging one-handed to the ladder. His left arm hung limply and clearly he did not have the strength to climb in.

She crouched in the doorway, hanging on to the rail with her left hand, and reached down. "Take my hand."

He bared his teeth in a rictus of pain. "Never . . . lift me."

"Hand! *Now!*"

His huge hand caught her small one and tightened into a crushing grip. Karan winced. There was no possibility of lifting him with one arm; she did not have the strength. But if she could take some of his weight . . . She tried to straighten her legs but the gusting wind heaved the sky ship left, then flung it to the right. She hung on until the wind died and tried again.

But Yggur was too heavy; her leg muscles were burning and she could feel the strain in the thigh bones she had shattered twelve years ago. He grunted, groaned, heaved again and so did she, and he made it up another rung, then another, then doubled over at the waist, pressing his long body flat against the floor. She forced herself backwards, heaving his arm, and after a tortured couple of minutes he raised his dangling legs and she dragged him in.

"Get us gone!" Yggur rolled over, kicked the door shut and lay on his back, panting.

Karan's right arm felt as though it had been wrenched out of its socket. She pulled herself up into the pilot's seat, jerked up the golden beryl knob to let more protium into the airbag, heaved back the black obsidian lever and thrust the red porphyry lever forward. The sky ship shot into the air, tossing him against the side wall.

"Steady on," he murmured. He braced himself between two seats, closed his eyes and lay there, holding his shoulder and grimacing.

She climbed until the sky ship was higher than any of the mountain peaks, turned south for the rain-drenched western coast of Salliban, and looked back. Hingis had not stirred. Yggur's pain-clenched face had relaxed and he was breathing steadily. He was asleep.

Karan wished she was too, but that wasn't going to happen. She was concentrating on keeping the sky ship steady in the unpredictable winds when pain flowered behind her forehead, and a link was forced open.

Karan! roared Malien, and her rage would have cracked rocks. *Answer me!*

The contents of Karan's stomach curdled. She was tempted to break the link and block Malien, but that was no way to treat a kinswoman who had gone out of her way to help her.

I—I haven't been able to link since Cinnabar. How did you get through?

With great pain and labour, Malien said furiously, *neither of which I could afford, I found what was blocking you and lifted it . . . temporarily. Where are you?*

Approaching Salliban.

Have you found Sulien?

Karan was tempted to lie and say she had, but could not do that either. *Not yet.*

Come back at once. I need my sky ship.

Karan did not respond.

Karan?

No!

I . . . need . . . my . . . ship . . . now.

As you once told me, a mother must do what it takes to protect her child— whatever the cost. Tell me that you would not do the same.

Karan could sense Malien's anguish, for she had only ever had one child. Rael had been Karan's dearest friend when she lived in Shazmak after her parents died, and Malien had thought they would wed. But later Karan had fled in anger and confusion, and when she returned, years later, it was with Llian.

Twelve years ago Rael had drowned helping them escape from Shazmak with the stolen Mirror of Aachan, and Malien had never come to terms with his death. It was one of the great tragedies of Karan's own life.

I'm so sorry, she sent.

Sorry doesn't begin to compensate!

I meant about Rael. I should never have involved him.

Oh! Karan sensed Malien's shock and wonder but said no more.

A minute ticked by, then Malien said, *You're not coming.*

I am, the moment I get Sulien back.

Don't link to her!

What?

The link between you and Sulien is fatally compromised. Use it at your peril, for it can be used to find you both and attack—

Malien? Karan cried when she did not continue. *What have you found? Is there any news of Llian?*

No answer.

What about the Merdrun? Where are they?

But the link was gone and she could not get it back.

The sky ship was nearing the southern tip of the peninsula now and there was enough starlight for Karan to see the rugged coastline curving around and into the narrow entrance to the Karama Malama, the landlocked Sea of Mists. Beyond, the coast of Salliban, a series of long deep fjords, curved away to the south for hundreds of miles. Between the coast and the mountains ran the shadow of vast untouched forests.

Sulien was in there somewhere, but where? She could not see any signs of civilisation: no roads or cities or towns, not even the lights of a solitary manor or campsite. How could she find Sulien in such a wilderness?

Karan leaned back in the pilot's seat, overcome by a sense of futility. She felt so very tired. She had been tired for months now, ever since the drumming began and Sulien had seen the Merdrun army in her nightmare.

"I'll take over," said Yggur, sitting up with a groan. He rubbed his shoulder and winced. "You're about to fall asleep."

Karan was glad to relinquish the responsibility for flying a craft whose workings she barely understood. She tried to stand up and nearly fell; her hands and feet were icy lumps.

She lurched down to the tiny galley at the rear, stumbling over Hingis in the darkness, though he did not stir. She felt his throat; he was breathing, either unconscious or asleep, so she tucked his blanket around him and left him there.

The galley was less chilly than the rest of the sky ship since a pipe

ran through it from the rotors, providing hot water. She filled a pot
with water and dried needles of *gulid*, a pungent plant the Aachim used
for making a spicy tea, found two mugs and carried everything back.

"Tea isn't very hot, I'm afraid," she said.

Yggur clamped a big hand around the pot, strained, and the water
boiled. "It is now."

Karan poured two mugs of blue-grey tea and handed him one.
While she warmed her hands on the other, she told him about Malien's
brief link, and her warning.

Yggur sipped his tea. "What are the enemy up to?"

"I don't know. What am I going to do, Yggur?"

"About what?"

"Locating Sulien." Karan took off her boots and socks and attempted
to warm her icy toes with her hands. It made no difference so she put
her boots on again. "I don't see that I have any choice but to link to
her, dangerous though it is."

He looked out the window at the dark landscape. "You've got to link
to her—there's no other way to find her. Do it soon, before the triplets
come into their full power."

Uncharacteristically, Yggur shivered, and that was disturbing: he
was one of the most experienced old-human mancers of all. He had
lived for eleven hundred years, fought some of the greatest figures in
the Histories and survived when most of them had not. If the triplets
scared him, Karan should be very afraid.

"But if I link to Sulien, the triplets will locate her—and attack."

"They may not yet have the strength. But the longer you leave
it, the stronger they'll be—and then they *will* find her." He looked
away, evidently thinking, then added, "You'd better include me in
the link."

Karan drank her tea in a scalding gulp, then sat on a blanket with
her back to the wall and closed her eyes, trying to sense out Sulien's
distant presence. The sky ship jerked in an updraught, knocking her
empty mug over with a clatter. The rotors went *ticker-tick*; wind whined
around the taut airbag cables.

The top of her head throbbed, an echo of the pain she had felt when the magiz had attacked her previously, though Karan did not sense any connection to the triplets. She prayed that they were still weak.

In the past it had been relatively easy to make a link to Sulien, but now Karan's sense of her was gone and she had to create a link from scratch. But when it guttered into feeble life, like a candle flame in the wind, she did not sense Sulien at all. She caught a sour, sweaty odour underlain by the foul reek of a herb the Whelm fed to their cadaverous horses and chewed to numb pain or give themselves extra endurance on long journeys.

"That's Idlis!" she said aloud. "Why am I sensing *him?*"

It had to be because Sulien was smelling him, but why could she not detect her? Karan probed deeper and caught a series of glimpses, each accompanied by its own odour: a cramped passage smelling of wet, rotting wood; part of a tunnel collapsing with a thump and a strong earthy odour; another tunnel made of cut stones with brown, peaty water trickling through the gaps, and the gaggingly foul reek of cat dung.

"Idlis is taking her somewhere," she said. "They're underground."

The cut stones faded into blackness, and all Karan could sense as Yggur flew south, and hour followed hour, was a desperate, plodding weariness and Idlis's stale sweat. Yggur turned and headed north again, along the western edge of a snowy range. It was miserably cold.

Then suddenly she picked up what Sulien was feeling—plod, plod, her belly empty and her feet aching, her legs so weary that it was all she could do to keep moving up this eternal, slippery slope. Her back hurt low down and her head was throbbing.

Sulien? sent Karan, but the sending failed.

Now Sulien was above ground and Karan saw what she was seeing. It was raining heavily and the sweaty odour of Idlis was gone. They were in the ruins of a once-great city, though clearly it had been abandoned for centuries. Every surface was inches deep in moss, the roofs and many of the walls had fallen long ago and the roots of gigantic trees had thrust the paving and building stones apart and piled them in great, overgrown heaps.

Sulien limped up a broad ramp. Idlis's gaunt, awkward figure was a few yards ahead, walking more slowly and jerkily than usual.

"She doesn't seem to be his prisoner," said Karan. "But where is he taking her?"

Yggur did not reply.

Sulien and Idlis went up steps that might have formed one side of a flat-topped pyramid, climbing until they were as high as the surrounding treetops. The wind was strong there, driving the rain before it in hissing sheets.

Sulien plodded across the flat top, a distance of about forty yards. Karan sensed her utter exhaustion. Some distance ahead, beyond the pyramid, a series of large public buildings were still partly roofed. Idlis led Sulien that way. But had he taken her there to protect her, or betray her? To left and right there were no trees now, for this part of the city was partly flooded, just broken walls and crumbling towers rising above still green waters.

They were trudging down the other side when a harsh cry rang out far to their left. *There they are! On the pyramid! Take them!*

"Yggur, the Whelm have found her!" cried Karan. "We're too late."

16

AND CARRIED HER AWAY

Sulien looked around dazedly. How had she ended up here?

Their trek through the tunnels had lasted for days, and it had been so exhausting that she had slipped into a state where she took nothing in, just plodded after Idlis through the endless dark, drinking when he said, "Drink!" eating when he said, "Eat!" and scurrying away from the light of his fading lightglass when he allowed her the briefest of toilet stops. He did not seem in need of food and only drank water once a day. He was more emaciated than ever; she could not imagine what drove him so relentlessly.

Occasionally he had stopped, crouched down and studied her, and said, "Sleep!"

Sulien had crumpled to the floor of the tunnel and slept at once, but when he shook her awake it felt as though only a few minutes had passed. She could not guess how far they had gone. It might have been twenty miles or a hundred, though they had laboured uphill most of that time and must be in the mountains by now.

Finally, when her old boots were falling apart, the soles of her feet were covered in blisters and her weary legs could take no more, Idlis stopped, cocked his bony head and said, "We're here!"

Sulien lacked the strength to ask where *here* was or what was going to happen now. She stood in the stony tunnel, rocking on the soles of her feet to ease the pain, her stomach cramped in terror. Was he going to betray her to the Whelm? Or sacrifice her to some hideous deity only they would worship? Why else would he have brought her all this way?

He climbed a crumbling stair that ended at a stone ceiling only four feet above the top step. Idlis used the point of his knife to clean the accumulated dirt out of the joins around a small square slab then put his palms flat on it, straightened his legs and heaved. With a grunt he raised the slab and slid it to the right.

Sulien saw grey daylight, then muddy water poured in on Idlis's head, drenching him and splashing her. It was icy. He wiped his eyes, climbed up through the hole and reached down for her.

Sulien shook her head. "I can manage." After staring at her for a moment—he was always staring; he did not seem to know that it was bad manners—Idlis moved away.

After much scrabbling and gasping she found herself on an expanse of moss-covered paving. They were in the overgrown ruins of a city whose broken buildings extended further than she could see. The icy rain was unrelenting here. Pools of water lay everywhere, and the ruins had a sodden, stagnant smell.

"Where are we?" she said hoarsely. She scooped water from the nearest pool and drank it from her hand. It made her teeth ache and the cold burned all the way down her throat.

Though the light was dim, Idlis put on his slitted-bone eye covers and checked all around, his prominent larynx bobbing. He looked agitated.

"Are your people here already?" whispered Sulien.

He looked down at her. "Not yet, little one. But they will come, and I don't know what to do."

"What is this place?"

He opened his mouth, shuddered, closed it again and said forlornly, "Hessular."

"I haven't heard of it," said Sulien.

"It died a very long time ago." His larynx oscillated wildly. "No, Hessular was *murdered*."

Clearly it was painful to talk about. But for the past month she had been at the Whelm's mercy, taken where they wanted, told nothing, forced to be "a good little Whelm" and, save for the past days on the run with Idlis, given a daily thrashing to teach her to be a better Whelm. She needed to know.

Her teeth chattered. After days in the mild underground it was miserably cold here. Her hair was sodden and water was running down her neck and chest and back. "How can a city be murdered?"

He led her to a small circular stone building, no bigger than a cottage, with a stone dome for a roof. The doors and windows had rotted away but the roof was sound. He gestured to a crumbling bench inside the door, protected from the rain. Sulien sat.

Idlis stalked back and forth, his joints click-clacking.

"My people were a peaceful folk when they dwelt here, thousands of years ago. Salliban was vast, they were few and there was plenty of room for all. No one else wanted our land, for it was too wet and cold to farm ... until a spice trader from wicked Thurkad discovered that a miraculous healing potion could be brewed from growths found on certain trees in Tardigraal."

"Where's that?" said Sulien.

"It was a small upland forest in the centre of Salliban, fifty miles south of here. The potion was worth a fortune, though only if he could keep the source secret. If everyone knew, it would be grown in other cold wet places and his monopoly would be lost.

"He tried to buy Tardigraal, but our people would not sell. The land belongs to everyone; no one has the right to *sell* it." He spat out the word as though it was offensive.

"What was his name?" said Sulien.

"Skunder Krespin!" Idlis hissed. "And he was determined to have his prize, for it could make him the richest man in the world. He mortgaged everything he owned and borrowed every grint he could, enough to hire a mercenary army to attack Salliban and seize Tardigraal. Our ancestors fought back, but we were a peaceful folk then and it takes many years to master the arts of war.

"Because my people looked different to other old humans, Krespin declared they were subhuman aliens who wanted to take over the world, and ordered them exterminated. His mercenaries poisoned the water cisterns of Hessular, our only city, and in two days half the Whelm were dead. Then the enemy blocked the exits and attacked from all sides, killing everyone they saw. Of the twenty thousand who had dwelt here, less than a dozen escaped."

"But, that's evil!" cried Sulien, shaking with outrage.

"And not the worst. Krespin's mercenaries brought in corpses riddled with northern diseases Salliban had never known, and left them throughout the land. Uncounted thousands of my people died, but no one else cared—he had hired chroniclers and tellers to spread false stories about us."

"I don't believe it!" Sulien said stoutly. "No chronicler or teller would do such a thing. The Histories are truth!"

"Chroniclers and tellers can be bought like anyone else."

"Not *anyone*!" cried Sulien. "Daddy can't be bought. The Histories are his life!"

"One of Krespin's paid stories became a Great Tale, one of the Twenty-Three!" Idlis said, choking in his fury. "*Downfall of the Beasts*, it's called. Do you know it?"

"No," whispered Sulien. This went against everything Llian had taught her and everything she believed in, but in her heart she knew Idlis was telling the truth.

"Every word of that tale is a lie!" he choked. "And it did us more damage than the ruin of Hessular; it destroyed us in the eyes of the world." He took a long, rasping breath and continued.

"By then Krespin was sickeningly rich but he wanted Salliban for himself, so his family could control Tardigraal for ever. His mercenaries hunted my people like dogs until they could take no more. They fled east over the mountains into the miserable frozen steppes of Shazabba, a land so cold no one else cared to live there."

"I'm sorry," said Sulien. "Does his family still control Tardigraal?"

Idlis let out a harsh bark; no one would have described it as laughter. "He brought in one disease too many—his workers unwittingly spread a fungus that transformed the healing growths into poisonous ones. Hundreds died from his healing potions before he was arrested, his wealth confiscated, and he was put to a cruel death." He bared his teeth in a vindictive rictus.

"Oh," Sulien said softly.

"But it was too late for us." He stared blankly at her. "Krespin taught my people a cruel lesson in power and powerlessness. The survivors vowed they would never be powerless again, but they were so reviled that no one would deal with them. They saw only one remedy—to take a mighty master to protect them. In return they would obey his every command, without ever questioning."

"Even if he ordered them to do terrible things?"

"What could my people do that was more terrible than what was done to them? But their search was long and painful until, at the time of the Zain rebellion two thousand years ago, a chance came to do the great Charon, Rulke, a favour. My ancestors did it gladly, and in the heat of his gratitude they offered their undying service, and he accepted. They changed their name to Ghâshâd and—"

"My father is Zain," said Sulien frostily. Llian was a great teller and she loved him dearly, but he was also hopelessly impractical and constantly getting into trouble. She sensed that he was in peril now, with no one to help him.

"And the Zain broke their word to our master," Idlis said with a curl of his scarred grey lip.

"That was two thousand years ago."

"It would not matter if it was two *million* years. Whelm do not forget or forgive. My people see your father as another treacherous, lying teller like the one who wrote *Downfall of the Beasts*—"

"Daddy's not treacherous and he's not a liar!" cried Sulien, leaping to her feet and thumping him in the ribs with her little fists. "Take that back."

Idlis took a step back. "I didn't say he was, little one; I said that's how my people see him. Since our betrayal we see all chroniclers and tellers the same way."

"You Whelm have done terrible things. Things just as bad as Krespin did to you."

"But never out of greed, lust, hunger for power or any other human failing. We have only ever done bad things because our master, who is greater and more far-seeing than us, ordered them done."

"That's a coward's excuse! If your *perfect master* ordered you to kill me, would you do it, even though you swore to protect me with your life?"

After a very long pause, Idlis said, "If I had sworn to serve my master before I swore to protect you, then yes, I would have to kill you."

"Then you're a hypocrite and an oath-breaker!"

"I would not do it gladly. But an oath is an oath."

"What if you'd sworn to protect me first?"

His grey face went even greyer. He lurched to the bench and sat down hard, each breath like coarse paper being torn to shreds. "I . . . I would have to repudiate my oath to my master and become an outcast for what little remained of my miserable life."

His agony burned into her soul. She took a slow step towards him, saying softly, "Why *little*?"

"My people would hunt me down, flay me alive then torture me to death for scorning my master."

"Oh!" said Sulien. "Have you sworn to a master?"

"You know I have; it's in your father's Great Tale. I swore to obey Rulke."

"But he's dead."

"And I am masterless. Bereft. Less than a man. As pathetic a creature as the least of my miserable ancestors."

"You used to serve Yggur. Did you rep-repudiate your oath to him?"

"Not exactly," said Idlis.

"Aha!" cried Sulien. "You broke your oath!"

"I did not!" he said hoarsely. "My ancestors' original oath to Rulke bound every Whelm, or Ghâshâd, for as long as he lived. It superseded our oath to Yggur, and when Rulke returned from imprisonment in the Nightland we had to cleave to our oath and resume serving him. We did so gladly."

Sulien sensed something high up that made her shudder. She looked out through the doorway. Idlis had been right: her gift *was* growing.

"What is the matter?" said Idlis.

"It felt like something was watching us."

"Some *thing*? Not my people?"

"What I *felt* wasn't Whelm. And it was up in the sky."

"A bird? An eagle?"

"Much bigger than any bird."

"Nothing *much* bigger than a large bird can fly."

"It's got mancery." Sulien did not know how she knew that; she had just sensed it.

"I'm not troubled by any creature in the sky," said Idlis.

"I am. Shouldn't we go underground?"

"All the tunnels here are flooded. We'll cross the drowned part of the city using the broken walls, then go underground again. Be careful. The moss is very slippery."

She followed him along a series of uneven mossy walls, then up to the top of a stepped pyramid. Then stopped, shivering in her sodden clothes. "The Whelm are coming!"

"And I don't think we can escape." Idlis was breathing heavily, the air tearing in and out of his ragged throat. He lowered his voice, "But if you do, you must find a teacher and master your gift *before it's too late*."

There was no time to ask what he meant, for she sensed them all around now. The Whelm nation was closing in on Hessular from all directions and, despite all Idlis had said about holding to his oath, he was cracking under the strain.

She eyed him surreptitiously. His movements were even more jerky than before, and he was unsteady on his feet. Was he signalling to the other Whelm? The breath clotted in her throat and she felt a stabbing pain in the middle of her chest. He was about to betray her.

Yetchah's scratchy voice soared. "There they are! On the pyramid! Take them!"

There was nothing Sulien could do. The Whelm had encircled Hessular just as Skunder Krespin's mercenaries had long ago. They would force her to link to the Merdrun, then Gergrig would order them to kill her, and they would.

She turned, ran down the pyramid and bolted along the ragged top of a wall that ran off to the right. At the corner she stopped, teetering, her arms windmilling, then raced on. If she could reach the next corner before Idlis came after her she could run along the wall that branched off it, then up and across the great arch of stone beyond and down the other side, and out of the drowned part of the ruined city into the forest.

A trio of Whelm, led by Yetchah, were scrambling along a mossy wall to her left. They weren't as fast as Sulien but they were closer to the corner. She hurtled on, leaping from one slippery block of stone to another, and gained the corner only a couple of yards in the lead.

Ahead was a gap of five feet to the next section of wall, and a fall of twenty feet onto rubble if she missed it. If she fell she would certainly break bones, and possibly die. She sprang the gap, landed hard and off balance, fell forwards and struck hard stone with both knees. The pain was awful; for a few seconds she could not stand up. She clung desperately to the top of the wall, her heart crashing from one side of her chest to the other. It had been too close!

The three Whelm were approaching from the left and another man, a stocky Whelm with little black eyes, was closing in from the right. He and Yetchah would arrive at almost the same time, each desperate to claim her as their prize.

Sulien got up, gasping from the pain in her knees. Yetchah and the stocky man hurtled towards the corner and one another. Sulien prayed that they would collide.

Yetchah slowed, allowing the stocky Whelm to reach the corner first. But he was going too fast; he could neither stop nor turn the corner, for the crumbly stone was loose and his iron-shod boots slipped on it. He tried to recover, failed and pitched over the side.

The other Whelm stopped, staring down at him. Sulien, twenty yards further on, did too. He had landed on his back on the tumbled stone and could not move. It looked as though he had broken his back, and that was a death sentence. She bent double, gasping for air, shocked at how quickly the life of a living, breathing person had been ended. It could have been hers.

She was still bone-weary from the days-long trek. Ahead was the stone arch, a hundred yards across and rising to a height of fifty feet. Could she cross it? She had to.

By the time she began the climb her calf muscles were burning and she was going slower and slower. The tireless Whelm were gaining; before she was halfway up, Yetchah had reached the bottom of the arch. She would catch Sulien before she scrambled down the other side.

Sulien staggered to the top of the arch. It was a yard and a half wide, but she was weaving from side to side, in danger of sliding off the edge. She was watching Yetchah's head and shoulders coming up the slope when again Sulien had the shuddery feeling that something high in the air was watching her. No, stalking her.

What could it be? Where could it be? She was looking all around when Yetchah froze, her mouth hanging open and a look of naked terror on her gaunt face.

"Aiieeee!" she shrieked, backing away.

Sulien checked the walls around but saw only the trees, the teeming rain and dozens of Whelm on the walls behind her, howling and holding their bony arms up as if to defend themselves against some monstrous foe. Then they turned and ran for the nearest shelter.

"Run, little one!" screamed Idlis from fifty yards away.

Shudders rippled down her back. "What is it?" she choked, her blood thickening and freezing in her veins.

"I don't know."

"Where is it?"

"There!" He pointed up, then bolted.

And then she saw it: a winged beast with an enormous toothy mouth that could have bitten her head off. Its body was more or less human, though much bigger and more heavily muscled than any human—it had to be eight feet tall.

Sulien ran for the far side of the arch but the creature was diving far too quickly. Her only hope was her gift for the Secret Art and she had never needed it more; surely it would come this time. She raised her arm, pointed with fingers and thumb, and prepared to give the beast such a blistering blast that it would be knocked out of the air.

Down it plunged, down, down, the wind whistling around the tips of its wings and the extended claws, as long as daggers, on its fingers and toes. Sulien quailed. How could she hope to stop such a beast? It would tear her apart.

The winged beast swooped. She thrust up her shaking arm, trying to create a blast bigger than anything she had ever made. It hurtled in, her forefinger touched the middle claw of its left foot and . . . nothing! Her gift had failed her and she was going to die.

The beast caught her around the waist with its huge toe claws and carried her away, swinging wildly beneath it.

Mummeeeee! she sent involuntarily. *Mummy, Daddy, it's got me. Help!*

But no one could help her now. Sulien knew, without any shadow of a doubt, that the creature was going to eat her.

17

FROZEN IN A RED RICTUS

There they are! On the pyramid! Take them!

"That was Sulien!" cried Karan. *Sulien, where are you?*

Her heart was thundering, the backs of her hands tingling, her belly throbbing as if she had been kicked there. Who were "they"? Where was Sulien? Panic flooded Karan—she had to find her but could not think of a thing that would help.

"I heard her too," said Yggur. "Link! *Now!*"

He clamped his hands around her head as he had done before, and
it calmed her. Karan focused on Sulien, on the *sense* of her, the *feeling*
of her, on her wavy red hair streaming out in the wind, her love for her
little puppy Piffle and the sad, faraway gaze that was her trademark, as
if Sulien were seeing a future where she had been robbed of everything
dear to her.

Thump! A psychic blow drove the wind out of Karan. She bit her
tongue, tasted blood and all went dark. She tried to call out to Yggur
but could not speak.

Then she saw a curving line of dark red stones, surrounded by
blackness.

Unbuly! Unbuly?

The voice in her head was soft, insistent, cajoling, and sent shudders
through her. The blackness closed over the red stones, blocking them
out.

Unbuly? Jaguly? Help me!

The line of red stones slowly reappeared, followed by another curving
line of stones below them. Karan let out an involuntary groan—they
weren't stones, they were teeth! Blood-red teeth framed by black lips.
Another sickening psychic blow struck her; she was seeing into the
mouth of one of the triplets.

Drink! said a hard voice, not one of them. *Eat!*

The red teeth vanished and she saw a weathered forehead with the
jagged Merdrun glyph deeply etched into it. Dark deep-set eyes, in
shadow save for stray indigo gleams. A high domed head, devoid of a
single hair; a short, dense beard, thick and char-black.

"Gergrig!" Karan whispered.

Where? Yggur said into her mind.

Karan could not see or hear him; she had lost her surroundings, sight
and sound. All she could sense was his hands around her head and the
sky ship rocking in the wind. Why was she seeing this now? And why
could she not sense Sulien at all?

I can't tell.

What's he doing?

I can't see. Ah, now I can.

Karan relayed what she was seeing to Yggur. Gergrig stood on a bare round hill where all the grass had been burned to ash. At its centre a large triangular slab of white limestone lay on three round black rocks like a plate resting on three marbles. Grey-robed acolytes were gathered around the broad base and lower sides of the triangle, singing in high voices. Gergrig stood at its apex.

Karan's viewpoint rose and she saw the top of the slab; she started and let out a small cry.

Steady! said Yggur. *Don't give yourself away.*

The triplets sat side by side on the slab, their outstretched legs bound with ropes tied to iron stakes driven into the stone at thighs and shins. Their hair, formerly long, black and silky, had been hacked short. A red torus a handspan across, made from polished stone, sat upright on a gold stand at their bare feet, at the centre of the slab.

A powder-blue bowl, the same shape as the slab, stood at its apex in front of Gergrig. It held several dozen small red tablets, as red as the rocks on the world of Cinnabar. As red as the triplets' teeth.

What's going on? said Karan.

Shh!

Gergrig offered the blue bowl to the head acolyte, a pretty, round-faced young woman a foot shorter than himself; her pixie-cut hair was palest amber. Using forefinger and thumb, she took a red tablet from the bowl and held it up while he pointed the tip of his black iron staff at it. There was a small white flash, and a silvery drop formed at the bottom of the tablet and hung there. The acolytes brought their song to a final high note, almost a shriek, and held it, unwavering.

The high note was like a barbed wire drawn in one of Karan's ears and out the other. She did not know what the ritual was for but she knew it was bad; bad for Sulien and bad for the world.

"Jaguly!" said Gergrig.

The head acolyte popped the tablet into the open mouth of the triplet on the left. Jaguly bared her blood-red teeth and licked her black lips, then leaned forward, glaring at the head acolyte, who took a sharp breath and a small step back.

Gergrig shook the bowl at her. The head acolyte took a second tablet. Gergrig performed the same ritual, then said, "Unbuly!"

The head acolyte gave the tablet to the middle triplet. Unbuly did not react; she just sat there, staring straight ahead.

The head acolyte took a third red tablet from the bowl. Gergrig touched it with his staff and a third silver metal drop formed.

"Empuly!"

The singers still held that screeching note, though it was wavering now.

As the head acolyte knelt and reached out towards the third triplet, the one on the right, Empuly convulsed, straining at the ropes that bound her until they tore into her thighs and shins, crumpling the skin like rubber. She made an awful sound in her throat, a screechy, whining howl that raised Karan's hackles even further.

"Hold her!" snapped Gergrig.

The acolytes on the right side of the slab took hold of Empuly's head, body, arms and legs. She was immensely strong, and it took six of them to keep her still, and another to prise her mouth open. Empuly snapped at that acolyte's fingers with her red teeth.

The head acolyte forced the tablet in and worked Empuly's jaw up and down, then held her nose until, with a despairing moan, she swallowed. She stopped struggling; her breast rose and fell; her eyes were open but empty.

"Blood torus," said Gergrig.

Karan sensed Yggur's hiss of shock. He was alarmed, and that made her even more afraid. This was a powerful ritual intended for some terrible purpose.

Can we stop it? she said.

No! If we tried they'd find us in an instant.

The head acolyte lifted the red torus from its gold stand. It was only a handspan across but appeared to be extremely heavy. She carried it to Gergrig and held it out before her at shoulder height, her arms trembling under the strain. Gergrig clenched his jaw, raised the iron staff and thrust it through the hole in the torus. White, crackling discharges zigzagged out in all directions; the torus went the colour of quicksilver then slowly turned red again, though a darker red than before and webbed with black.

Gergrig gestured to the head acolyte. Fear shivered across her pretty face but she carried the blood torus to Jaguly, knelt and touched it to the centre of her forehead. Jaguly fell back to the stone with a thud, black lips bared to display red teeth. Her fixed grin was sickening.

The head acolyte touched the blood torus to Unbuly's forehead, but she did not react. She seemed indifferent, though her mouth slowly distended until she wore the same fixed red grin as Jaguly.

The head acolyte touched Empuly with the blood torus, and she howled and shrieked and ground her knuckles against the white marble until they bled. Her black mouth stretched into a rictus, and froze.

The head acolyte climbed down off the white slab and presented the blood torus to Gergrig, who fixed it to an iron chain whose links were shaped like the jagged Merdrun glyph. Holding it by the chain, he carried it to Empuly, whose mouth pouted like a vampire sipping from a throat as she licked the bright red stone. He frowned, then after a short pause reached across to Unbuly, who lay unmoving; he had to prise her mouth open and pull out her tongue until it touched the blood torus. He walked around the base of the slab to Jaguly, who made a screeching sound in the back of her throat, then licked the blood torus slyly, sat up and looked sideways at the acolytes.

Gergrig slipped the chain over Jaguly's head and laid the blood torus between her breasts. White discharges cracked out from it to surround her, then jumped to Unbuly, who shot upright, then to Empuly, who did the same.

Empuly let out a cracked howl, tore her right arm free of the stone, pointed a long finger at the head acolyte and made the pouting movements with her black lips again. The head acolyte's amber hair stood up. Her eyes were staring; she backed away.

Empuly, with immense and remorseless strength, tore the iron stakes out of the slab and stood up, the ropes dangling from her heavily muscled legs. With a gesture she freed her sisters and they rose too, twitching and trembling. They pointed at the head acolyte, who whimpered and turned to run.

Gergrig blocked her path with his staff. She made to dart past him but Empuly clapped her big hands and the head acolyte could not move. She could still scream, though, and it was heart-rending.

Empuly's black lips pouted, and pale shimmering threads formed on the head acolyte's face and chest. They were drawn to Empuly, who gobbled them down like a glutton, so fast that little bits of ethereal matter remained clinging to her chin and caught on the front of her robes.

Karan fought to hold back her own scream; Yggur's hands tightened crushingly around her head and she could feel him shuddering.

The more the head acolyte screamed, the more Empuly fed on her pain until, as the last of the shimmering plasma was torn from her victim, the head acolyte's eyes went blank and she crumpled to the ashy hilltop. Her flesh seemed to be eaten away from the inside, leaving her skin sagging off her slender bones.

The triplets were steady on their feet now and looked much stronger. Gergrig was smiling grimly, as if he had not expected the ritual to work so well or so quickly. His gaze swept across the other acolytes and Karan saw their horror turn to terror. They bolted in a mass but Gergrig gestured lazily towards them with the iron staff and froze them in place.

"Drink their lives," he said to the triplets.

When they had done so, and the baggy remains of the acolytes lay on the grass as empty as their former leader, Gergrig turned away.

"Dispose of them after we're done," he ordered a squad of wild-eyed soldiers twenty yards away. "Magiz," he said, speaking to the triplets as though they were now one, "You have the power. Find the brat and the mother, and suck their lives out of them."

Fury surged through Karan, then she was hurled backwards against the side wall of the sky ship. She gasped. Could the triplets have found her so quickly? Were they attacking?

Bright light dazzled her, and she was lifted and put in a seat.

"What happened?" she whispered.

"Had to stop you," said Yggur, lowering his hand and dimming the light streaming from his fingertips. "You can't take them on, Karan— they're already stronger than the old magiz."

"Then they'll soon find me, and Sulien."

"I'm afraid so. What did you see of her?"

"She was running through the ruins of a great city, a place abandoned so long ago that forest had almost reclaimed it." She told him what she had seen.

"Doesn't help much," said Yggur. He rubbed his jaw, his stubble rasping. "You'll have to risk a link to her."

"What if the triplets detect it?"

"What if they locate Sulien before we do?"

Karan relived the deaths of the acolytes and the sick glee on the faces of the triplets. It could not be endured.

"The longer you leave it, the stronger they'll become," said Yggur.

She readied herself for another attempt at linking. It would not be easy; her head felt fuzzy and her belly was heaving—aftersickness, the bane of all sensitives, was tightening its grip.

Karan fought it; Sulien's life depended on her. She was reaching out, very carefully, for her sense of Sulien, when Sulien shrieked into her mind loud enough to wake the dead.

Mummeeeee! Mummy, Daddy, it's got me. Help!

Karan saw a soaring arch, a crumbling pyramid in the background and dozens of terrified Whelm, some perched precariously on the tops of mossy walls, others running for their lives.

The image changed. Sulien was looking up at a monstrous winged creature that had her in its claws. In its belt it had a spike-tipped flail and a heavy hammer.

"Was that ... a *thranx*?" Karan whispered, almost fainting with dread.

Many savage creatures from the void had invaded Santhenar during the Time of the Mirror, especially when the Way between the Worlds was opened ten years ago. Most of them had been hunted down and exterminated, but some had survived and bred in the wilderness. Thranx were incredibly strong and tough. She had seen one crash straight through a stone wall at Carcharon, unharmed.

"There are no thranx left," said Yggur. "They were wiped out by creatures very like them, but cleverer and far better mancers."

Karan felt sick. "What are they called?"

"Lyrinx," said Yggur. "They're called lyrinx. And that was one of them."

18

WHAT IF I REFUSE?

Aviel was limping down the broad hall of the mansion Tallia had commandeered for their headquarters when she sensed someone watching her. She crouched and, pretending to tie her bootlace, checked behind her.

Ten yards away in a doorway, Tallia was arguing with a plump, uniformed officer who wore two rows of medals on his chest. But he wasn't looking at her; he was staring at Aviel as if they had been talking about her. But why would they? She was no more use to anyone.

Two servants in orange and black emerged from a side hall, wheeling a steaming tureen. Aviel could smell the spicy chowder called bimbull, one of the staple dishes of Sith, though to her keen nose it had a faint foul odour as if the fish was going off. It felt like a sign.

They had disembarked in Vilikshathûr a day and a half ago and sailed upriver in a smaller boat. She limped on, clutching her copy of the laws of Sith. Everyone who entered the city had to make their personal rubbing of the laws, which were inscribed on brass posts on every street corner, and anyone could be examined on their knowledge of the laws at any time. In Sith you could be fined for being ignorant of the laws.

As she turned the corner a hard hand caught her by the shoulder. Aviel whirled. There was no one within ten yards but the hand kept squeezing; an *invisible* hand.

"In there," said a low, familiar voice. Shand thrust her towards an open door, jarring her ankle.

He wasn't the stern yet kindly Shand of old; he was a traitor with a price on his head. What was he going to do to her? She stumbled through, the door closed and she heard the lock click.

"Move away from the door," grated Shand. "Stop that infernal squeaking."

She was making a keening sound; she had not realised she was doing it. Aviel cast a swift glance around her. A large high-ceilinged meeting room with intricate plaster cornices outlined in gilt and painted in many colours, a pair of tall windows with green velvet curtains, a long white table in the middle, so polished that it reflected the ceiling, surrounded by hard rectangular chairs. Bookcases on the walls were filled with more books than she had seen in her life.

She limped to the other side of the table and supported herself on it. The pain was always worse when she was afraid, and she was very afraid now. Why had he come to Sith? Was he still spying for the enemy? What could he want from her?

Aviel felt a tingling in the palms of her hands, heard a grunt, and ever so slowly Shand materialised, feet first, then his pack, his legs and arms and body, and his head last. It was unnerving.

His leathery old face was flushed and his eyes were hard. "You owe me, girl," he grated, advancing around the table towards her.

More than she could ever repay. On Aviel's thirteenth birthday her dissolute father, Gybb, had been planning to indenture her for seven years to evil old Magsie Murg, who would have forced her to do hard labour fourteen hours a day in her stinking tannery. Aviel had run away, but her six older half-sisters, who were all far bigger than her and even meaner than Gybb, had hunted her down and dumped her into the hollow inside of the vast old Sacrifice Tree, knowing she would not be able to get out.

The following morning Shand had heard her desperate cries, released her and later, for reasons known only to himself, paid the indenture price to Gybb and allowed Aviel to use the abandoned workshop in his back garden to make and blend the perfumes that were her life's passion. No one could have given her a greater gift; his generosity still brought tears to her eyes.

"You took advantage of my good nature," he raged. "You abused my hospitality. *You stole my grimoire!*"

Guilt scorched her; she had betrayed his trust and now she was going to pay. She edged away, trying to keep the table between himself and her.

"I didn't *steal* it," she said, and knew how feeble she sounded. "I just—"

"*Where is it?*" he hissed.

"Here." She fumbled in the bag she carried everywhere with her, pulled out the heavy square package in its canvas covering tied with green cord, and laid it on the table.

"It had better be undamaged. Unwrap it!"

Her normally nimble fingers fumbled with the wrappings. He pushed her aside and tore them open to expose a heavy book eleven inches square with covers of polished pink rosewood inlaid with camphor laurel, sandalwood, incense cedar and other scented timbers. The original owner's name, Radizer, was embossed in red gold on the front cover. Below it in black silver was the title, *Scent Potions*.

"You took it without permission," Shand said through his teeth. "You removed it from my house and you've carried it with you ever since. How is that *not* stealing?"

"M-Malien's second letter c-came, s-saying that the summon stone had to be destroyed urgently, and you were a h-hundred miles away—"

"You're a fifteen-year-old girl! It wasn't up to you to do anything except send the letter on."

"I'm sixteen," she whispered.

"Since when?"

"Y-yesterday." No one had known; this important day had gone uncelebrated.

"It makes no bloody difference. You knew Radizer died making one of the scent potions. It splattered him across the walls and ceiling of his workshop in smoking chunks and oozing gobbets." Shand's eyes bored into her. "And he had twenty years' experience; he was a *master*. You're not even an apprentice, but you took my grimoire and recklessly used it—"

"I . . . I meant well."

"Are you saying that it's all right to commit a crime," he hissed, "as long as it's with good intentions?"

She hung her head. "I . . . don't . . . know."

All along she had been terrified that this would happen. He would cast her out, and she could not blame him. But in a world at war, how could a little cripple with no money and no skills except scent-making survive?

"You owe me and you have to pay," said Shand.

Aviel's heart gave a convulsive thud. "I don't have any money."

"You don't have *anything*," he said nastily, "except what I've given you."

Why was he so changed, so mean? She knew that the drumming— the corrupting emanations from the summon stone—had badly affected Shand, turning him cold and angry and allowing the old magiz on Cinnabar to get to him. But the magiz was dead and the drumming had not been heard since Aviel poisoned the stone.

She hung her head. Whatever he was going to demand of her, she had no way of paying it. Avoiding his blazing eyes, she rewrapped the grimoire. Her hands were shaking so badly she could not tie the knots in the green cord.

"Yet despite the theft," said Shand, his eyes still piercing her, "and your criminally reckless stupidity in using the grimoire to make a scent potion to locate the summon stone, despite choosing a dark and deadly Great Potion, the Eureka Graveolence . . . somehow you succeeded in making the potion, finding the summon stone and, most astonishing of all, poisoning it with quicksilver at the moment it was linked to the newly opened Crimson Gate."

Aviel could think of nothing to say. She made another fumbling attempt at the knot.

"Leave it!" Shand snapped.

She choked. He was going to cast her out.

Shand sighed. "You did well, girl," he said gently. "Better than all of us put together, despite us being old and experienced and, in our own ways, a thousand times more powerful."

"I don't understand," she whispered.

"I, who have always done my very best for my country and my world, am now despised as a traitor." Shand's voice shook. He sat at the table and dropped his head into his hands. "And *I am* a traitor! I was used."

"How?"

"The magiz got to me when I was weak and vulnerable, and embedded a secret link in me, and via that link I unwittingly betrayed our plans to her." He snapped his teeth. "How could I have allowed it to happen? How did I not realise? The shame is unbearable! Had it not been for you and Wilm, and Karan and Llian and Sulien, Santhenar would have fallen by now."

"But," she said quietly, "what do you want from me?"

"If I'm caught I'll be taken, tried and imprisoned, then hanged like that sad villain Pender."

Aviel could never forget his bloated body hanging from one of the spars of the flagship. "They wouldn't!" she whispered. "Not *you.*"

"In wartime there can be no tolerance for traitors. But I can't be caught! I've got to make amends and help to stop the Merdrun," he said passionately. "And, though it matters not to anyone else, I have to restore my good name."

She understood those needs, but why he was telling her?

"I must be free, but the only way I can stay free is with an exhausting spell of invisibility."

"Where did you get it?"

"Long ago my former consort, Yalkara, gifted me with some aspects of her own Secret Art, unknown even to her own people. She warned me of the dangers of using them, and the cost—"

"What cost?"

"Never you mind. But I only dare use the spell for a few hours a day; the rest of the time I have to hide. That's why I need you."

"What for?" Aviel said warily.

Shand took off his pack and withdrew the device called Identity—a brass tube the length of her forearm with paired red crystals in one end. Gurgito Unick, a drunken brute but a genius at making enchanted devices, had invented it.

"Where did you get that?" said Aviel.

"Carcharon. And I understand that you have another of Unick's devices—the one Wilm hid from me," Shand's eyes flashed and his jaw tightened, "and Unick took back."

"Not all of it," she said. "I don't suppose it's any use without the quicksilver." She gave the device to him. "Is that all you wanted me for?" she said hopefully.

He laughed mirthlessly. "It's only the smallest part."

"What's the rest?"

"I need the resources to make a very dark scent potion."

She let out a squawk. "W-what for?"

He hesitated as if unwilling to speak it out aloud, then said, "The summon stone is an evil artefact, created by the Merdrun aeons ago with mancery we cannot understand. Tallia and Malien are making plans to destroy it—plans that will soon involve you."

"Me?" she croaked. "What use am I? And how do you know?"

Shand smiled thinly. "They will fail. I also believe Malien is wrong to say mancery must never be used on the summon stone. The only way it can be destroyed *is with mancery.*"

Aviel shivered. "But she's old and wise."

"And she suffers from flaws that characterise most of the Aachim. It takes them for ever to come to a decision, and sometimes their courage fails at the sticking point. That's how the Hundred, led by Rulke, took their world from them."

"What if you're wrong?"

"The Merdrun are already here," he said harshly. "How can I make things worse?"

"What does the scent potion do?"

Again he hesitated. Was he telling the truth or making things up?

"If it works I'll be able to recover brilliant spells, long lost, and make them even more powerful."

But what will you do with them? "Why does that require a dark scent potion?"

"To do so, I'll have to go to forbidden places. Terrible places."

"I don't want anything to do with dark potions," said Aviel quietly.
His eyes flashed. "Why the hell not?"

"I've already done too many bad things. To make the Eureka
Graveolence, I had to rob a grave of someone's skull bone. I'm on a
slippery slope, Shand."

"What a load of rot," said Shand. "You're one of the most moral
people I know."

"But . . . I'm attracted to the dark side, more and more, and if I have
to—"

"Too bad! You owe me, and I need to use your workshop and
equipment."

"I don't have either."

"You will. I need to make the Afflatus Effluvium."

Her knees gave; she clutched desperately at the table for support.
"But that's one of the forbidden scent potions."

According to Radizer's book, the Forbidden Scent Potions had been
copied from a proscribed grimoire written more than 1500 years ago,
but no one had ever successfully made any of them; they were considered to be impossible.

"What if I refuse?" she said, her voice going squeaky.

Shand bared his crooked teeth. "You won't!" He vanished and the
door opened and closed.

Was that a threat? But there was nothing she could do about it, short
of betraying him, because her debt to him was too great. Yet if she did
not, she would be betraying her world and herself.

19

SHE LOOKS QUITE USELESS TO ME

As Aviel emerged, still trembling, Lilis caught her arm. "Where have
you been? We've been looking everywhere for you."

Aviel started. "W-why?"

She felt sure Lilis could read her face. Lilis would have to tell Tallia and Malien about Shand, and then Aviel would be condemned . . . and hanged.

"Are you all right?" said Lilis. "You're trembling all over."

"Yes," Aviel croaked. "Is something the matter?"

"Tallia wants you at her council of war."

Aviel clutched her chest. "Why would she want me?"

Lilis shrugged. "I wasn't told."

"Why not?"

"The more people know our secrets, the more likely they'll be revealed."

Aviel felt her cheeks growing hot.

"You've gone all red," said Lilis gaily. "If I didn't know you better I'd think you had a *guilty* secret."

Aviel was almost throwing up with terror. If Lilis could read her so easily, how could she pass muster with Tallia, Malien and Nadiril? The moment she entered the room they would know she was up to something bad.

Lilis led her down the hall to a chamber guarded by a huge fierce-looking man with grey hair and very dark skin.

"Osseion," said Lilis, "this is Aviel. Aviel, Osseion is Ussarine's father, and in the olden days he was personal bodyguard to the great Magister, Mendark."

Aviel dared not look him in the eye. He would read her like a scrap of parchment.

Osseion reached down and shook her hand. His hand was gigantic, greatly scarred and callused, and missing the middle finger. "Thank you," he rumbled.

"What for?" Aviel said dazedly.

"For all you've done. You're braver than any of us."

Without thinking, she said, "I have Mendark's black sword."

"Do you really?" said Osseion, astonished. Then he smiled. "Do you use it much?"

Aviel found herself laughing, and liking him. "No, I'm minding it

for my friend Wilm." She felt a spasm of fear for him, but buried it.
"It's his now."

"I hope you find him again," he said and opened the door.

Lilis said, "Good luck!"

What did she mean by that? Did Aviel need good luck here? If she
did, she was in trouble. Where she came from, being a twist-foot, a
silver-hair or a seventh sister were each considered bad luck, and the
combination made her one of the unluckiest people of all. She had been
plagued by ill luck most of her life.

"Don't stand there gaping like an imbecile," snapped a little old man
at the end of the table.

He was dressed in extravagant mancer's robes, the cream linen gor-
geously embroidered in gold, deep blue and emerald thread, though
they only highlighted his own meagreness. He was stooped and
scrawny, with a bulbous nose, a pale face and bald head, both covered
in brown moles and age spots, and a mean little mouth flecked with
papery shreds of dry skin. Oddly, and undermining his expensive robes,
the long stringy hair on the back of his head was tied in a queue with
a scarlet ribbon.

"We're busy people. Sit!" He pointed to the chair on his right with
a knobbly yellow-stained forefinger.

Aviel crept across and slipped into the chair, trying to look invisible.
Tallia, her head bent over a pile of papers, sat at the far end. Malien,
to her left, was writing on a long yellow scroll curled at the top and
bottom. To Tallia's right, Nadiril was slurping at a cup of tea the size of
a small saucepan. Next to him sat a stout middle-aged man with short
white hair and a round sunburned face marked with small red veins.
It was the beribboned officer Aviel had seen talking to Tallia earlier.
His fingers were covered in black ink smudges and he was studying a
tattered map a yard square.

"Ah, Aviel," said Tallia after a long interval. She gestured to the
stout man. "This is General Dedulus Janck, our commander-in-chief.
He wanted to meet you."

Janck looked up from his map and inspected her thoughtfully. His
white eyebrows twitched and he bent over the map again.

"And this is Grand Master Torsion Tule." Tallia indicated the angry old man beside Aviel. "Your new master."

Aviel let out a squeak of alarm.

"Assuming she passes muster," Tule said coldly. He swallowed noisily, leaned close and studied her as if she were a blowfly on his dinner. His flaky lips curled and the stained forefinger rose, pointing at her face, her throat, her chest. His arm had a tremor; no, his whole body was quivering, more on the right than the left. He swallowed again, with some difficulty. "Which seems very dubious. How old is the runt? Twelve?"

"I'm sixteen," she whispered. He couldn't be her master, he just couldn't.

"Little liar!" With a series of twitches and tremors, Tule turned to face Tallia. "She won't do at all. She looks quite useless to me."

"Aviel has a rare gift," said Tallia coldly. "She made the Eureka Graveolence on the first attempt, *and* used it successfully. Without it—"

"Scent potions!" sneered Tule. "A bastard art practised by frauds and incompetents. Not part of the true Secret Art. I won't take her on. I won't take any *girl* on—they don't have the aptitude for it."

"You will! Aviel has to learn the art as quickly as possible, and you're the only master who can teach her."

Aviel looked from Tule to Tallia, back to Tule. What was he supposed to teach her?

"Find me a lad with breeding," said Tule, "one who's completed a five-year apprenticeship with distinction, and I'll consider it." He rose unsteadily and turned towards the door.

"What's breeding got to do with learning the art?" Janck said in a steely voice.

"Everything! She's a little bastard, I hear—a cuckoo in the family nest—and I won't take on a moral degenerate. Can't trust them; can't rely on them."

"Since when do we blame a child for the faults of the parent?"

"Only for the past five thousand years," sneered Tule and wavered off. Janck bounced to his feet. "Sit!" he said softly.

"Damned if I will."

Janck's voice hardened. "I'm your commanding officer, Grand Master."

"I'm not in your miserable little army, fatso."

Nadiril looked up from his papers. "When a State of War has been declared our commander-in-chief commands every man, woman and child in the land. Disobey his order, Grand Master Tule, and you can be charged with mutiny."

"Which is a hanging offence," said Tallia. "Sit down, Tule."

Tule lurched back to his chair, rotated to face Aviel and gave her such a look of contempt that she quailed. He hated her and she had no idea why, but she knew she did not want him for her master.

"You *will* take on Aviel Foyl as your apprentice," said Janck in a voice like chilled steel. "You will teach her all you know about *the project*. Is that clear?"

Tule's response was indecipherable.

"An alchemical workshop has been set up, but other things may be needed." Janck scribbled on a piece of paper and held it out. "Your warrant to draw on the necessary resources."

Tule rose, snatched the paper and wavered his way across the room. "Get the door, twist-foot!" he said through his teeth, which were as yellow and crooked as his forefinger.

"Aviel stays," said Janck. "We have matters to discuss."

"Such discussions are always held with the master."

"Private matters. Off you trot, Grand Master."

Tule gave Aviel another look of utter loathing and went.

Aviel shrank down in her chair while Nadiril, Malien, Tallia and Janck discussed something in low voices. What else did they want? She knotted her fingers in her lap. Were they going to interrogate her about Shand?

And why had they made Tule her master when he held the art of scent potion making in such contempt? How could she work with him? He was the most unpleasant man she had ever met.

"Ah, Aviel," said Tallia, looking up. "We have a job for you. The summon stone has gone from Carcharon and we don't know where."

"I suppose you want me to make the Eureka Graveolence again," she said dully, wondering why she now needed a master for it.

Malien shook her head. "That scent potion can only be used to find things that are lost or hidden, and the summon stone isn't either. It has simply moved."

"Then . . . how am I supposed to find it?"

Tallia and Malien exchanged glances. "That's not what we need you for," said Tallia. "This job doesn't involve scent potions."

"But perfume-making is all I know."

"Have you ever heard of nyphalle?" said Nadiril, leaning forward and fixing his cloudy eyes on her. "Also known as nivol?"

"No," said Aviel.

"It's an alchemical fluid first mentioned in ancient times. And several times in Mendark's secret papers, which we've retrieved from the council's spell vault."

"I don't understand."

"Nivol is also known as the Universal Dissoluent. It consumes everything it touches—flesh, paper, metal, rock . . ."

"And you want it so you can destroy the summon stone."

Malien rocked back in her chair, staring at Aviel.

"Told you she was quick," said Tallia. "Yes, we believe nivol is the only substance in the world that can consume so powerful and alien an object as the summon stone."

"And you want me to find it?"

"It doesn't occur naturally." Tallia paused, then said in a rush, "We want you to *make* some nivol."

This knocked the breath out of Aviel. "But . . . that's alchemy, isn't it?"

"Yes," said Nadiril, his eyes now fixed on the painted ceiling.

"I don't know anything about alchemy."

"Hardly anyone does these days," said Tallia. "It's a forgotten art."

"Is Torsion Tule—"

"Grand Master Tule to you," said Nadiril. "He was a brilliant alchemist in his day, the very last alchemist in the west. But his day was a long time ago and none of his apprentices became masters . . . ah . . ."

Because he's so obnoxious, thought Aviel. "Why can't he make some nivol?"

"The man quivers like a hummingbird in a hurricane," said Janck. "He can't hold a cup of tea without spilling it."

"But there must be hundreds of people better suited to the job than me."

"As I said," said Tallia with a touch of impatience, "Grand Master Tule is the last alchemist in the west."

"What about the east?" Aviel said desperately.

"We can't get one here in time."

"How bare our cupboard is," said Nadiril, "that we have to rely on an untrained girl."

"Aviel," said Janck forbiddingly, "nivol is top secret. You cannot talk to *anyone* about it save the people in this room and your master. Not a hint to your friends."

"I don't have any friends." With Wilm probably dead, all Aviel had were a few acquaintances like Lilis who, if they could see into her heart, would have to inform on her.

"This work is urgent," said Malien. "We believe the Crimson Gate closed quickly, leaving the Merdrun far from their destination, and they won't be able to reopen it until they find the summon stone and install a new magiz strong enough to draw great power from it. If we can destroy it first, it'll rob them of much of their power and they'll be stuck where they are. It'll give us a chance."

"Why me?" said Aviel.

"Many of the techniques you've used in scent-potion-making are alchemical ones," said Tallia.

"Lots of people know alchemical techniques. Apothecaries, and people who make healing potions, and—"

"Plodders all!" snapped Malien. "People with little if any under-standing of the Secret Art and no creative insight. You made one of the Great Potions on your first attempt, and survived. And it worked! You have a great gift, an intuitive grasp of some of the techniques required and the drive to succeed. We need you."

Aviel could not refuse such a plea. "I'll do my very best," she said, gulping. "But . . . if nivol dissolves everything it touches, how can it be made at all?"

"It's only formed in the final blending. Once you've found, made and purified all the necessary ingredients, you will do the final blending in the one substance in the world that can contain nivol—a phial cut from a single unflawed diamond."

Aviel swallowed. They were going to cut the middle out of a precious diamond just for her work? "It'd have to be a big diamond."

"A perfect diamond suitable for the tiara of the greatest lady in the land," said Janck, his eyes fixed on her. "And that's probably where we'll get it. That's how much your work matters, Aviel."

Aviel sat back, stunned and overburdened. To put such faith in her untrained abilities, they must be desperate indeed, but she knew it could not be done. Alchemy was a great art, very difficult to master, and far more than a collection of workshop techniques. You had to have a gift for it and she did not.

Tallia handed her a sheaf of papers and parchments. "Copies of all the documents that mention the preparation of nivol. Keep them safe and don't read them in Grand Master Tule's presence."

"Why not?"

"He has . . . old-fashioned views on the relationship between master and pupil. He will want to dole out the information grudgingly, and we don't have time for that."

"Are you saying I should disobey my master?"

Tallia hesitated. "Certainly not. He has much to teach you."

"Making nivol is *your* job, not his," interrupted Nadiril. "It's the most important job in the world right now, and the most urgent. You have to find a way to learn everything you need to know from Tule and prevent him from hindering you in any way."

Aviel's heart sank to her frayed bootlaces. "How long do I have?"

"At best, a few weeks."

She let out a squawk of dismay. It was impossible.

Tallia stood up. "A workshop has been equipped for you, however to collect certain rare ingredients you may need to travel to distant lands. If so, a sky ship will be put at your disposal."

"But Karan and Yggur stole it."

"Sith is famed for its artisans and boat builders. Under the guidance and supervision of the Aachim, we're building more sky ships. That's top secret too."

A sky ship just for her! Aviel rose dazedly. "I'll get started. Though—"

"Tule is a very difficult man," said Janck. He rose, heaved his trousers up over his big round belly and came round to her end of the table. "It may be that your greatest task is not the creation of nivol, but learning how to work with your master. But you must, for all our sakes." He held out a meaty hand.

Aviel shook it and felt her spirits lift. There was something about Janck that inspired confidence, and as she went out she was hardly limping at all.

20

GNASHING THEIR FANGS

Llian woke late, aching down to the bones, to a howling wind lashing rain at the windowpanes. He was tying his bootlaces when he heard a crack of thunder, then another. The storm had not moved, and the lightning was still striking the eastern tip of Demondifang. It now seemed ominous.

That island was a few miles across, conical in shape and covered in forest, with a broad band of mangroves ringing the shoreline. Waves broke across the two-mile-long gravel spit connecting Demondifang to Mollymoot.

Finding the kitchen empty, he helped himself from a pot of gruel on the blackened hob of the fireplace and made tea from some herbs he could not identify. He carried his tea into the next room, a small living room with two ancient settees and a pair of armchairs facing a small fireplace.

Dilly was in the left-hand armchair by the fire, darning a thick fisherman's sock by feel with green thread and studying a book of accounts.

Ifoli, pale and barefoot, her short hair tousled, was perched on a curving window seat looking out at the wild sea.

"Morning," said Dilly without looking up.

"Nice day for ducks," said Llian.

"And librarians. You won't be heading south today or tomorrow."

"Why not?"

"Take a look at the causeway," said Ifoli.

He went to the window. A big sea was driving breakers right across the mile-long gap between Mollymoot and the mainland.

"Not even at low tide?" said Llian.

"This is low tide."

"Are you saying there's no way to get off the island?"

"Would you take a boat out in these conditions?"

Llian had been out in worse, though only in vessels sailed by master seamen. The gnawing feeling in his belly sharpened.

"Gives me time to think, I suppose," he said, trying to make the best of it.

"What about?" Ifoli said listlessly.

"Why we ended up here and why that storm is still there."

"Demondifang attracts storms," said Dilly, turning the page of her book of accounts and frowning. "I've seen them hang there from mid-afternoon until midnight. Though I've never known one to still be there in the morning. It's unnatural."

"Did you have any luck contacting Nadiril?" he said quietly to Ifoli.

"Not exactly . . ." She was still staring out the window, jaw clenched. "I heard a couple of snatches of talk, all bad. But I couldn't speak to him and he couldn't hear me."

"All bad?" he repeated.

"The Merdrun have invaded but no one knows where."

"Anything about Karan or Sulien?" he croaked.

"No."

A tall well-built youth came in, carrying a fishing rod and a basket containing half a dozen fat fish, each the length of Llian's forearm. His thick brown hair was windblown, his handsome face crusted with salt. He set his basket down, propped the rod against the wall, looked around and saw Ifoli on the window seat.

"Cousin Ifoli!" He ran to embrace her. "I didn't know you were coming."

She stood up, smiling. "I didn't know myself. We got here in the middle of the night. I was wondering where you were."

"Went out at dawn," he said. "It's the best time." He looked round as Llian rose, and studied him for a few seconds before saying, "Hello, I'm Reggeley."

"This is Llian," said Ifoli. "He's a teller."

Llian shook hands with Reggeley, who seemed overawed and said hastily, "Better clean my fish."

Four days later Llian was still trapped on Mollymoot and the ominous storm was still coiled above Demondifang like a striking snake. He had written up the climactic events at Alcifer in his salt-stained journal, and now, with nothing to occupy him, he was chafing to head south and look for Sulien, hopeless though the search was likely to be. Unfortunately a strong westerly had been blowing for days and the causeway was still underwater.

"How do you stand it without any news?" he said to Dilly that night in the kitchen. "The world outside could be falling to pieces and we'd never know."

She was hanging bunches of marjoram from ceiling hooks. The whole house was scented with it. "How would it help you to know when you can do nothing about it?"

"Everyone I care about is in danger. I've got to do something."

"The wind's turning; you'll be able to cross to Demondifang at low tide tomorrow morning. But if you decide to climb the mountain be prepared to stay the night—you can't climb the peak and get back to the spit before the tide comes in."

The following morning, Llian's unease grew with every step they took towards Demondifang. The unnatural thunderhead was still there, a black, rotating coil centred on the tip of the mountain.

Ifoli was labouring through the wet gravel. Though not fully recovered, she had insisted on accompanying him and so had Regg, who knew the island well. He was a hundred yards ahead, carrying a long fishing rod in one hand. Llian wondered what it would be like to be fifteen again and have his whole life ahead of him, but there was no profit in that train of thought.

"What's *that*?" called Regg.

The sun had finally broken through the clouds and it was the first time Llian had seen Demondifang clearly. The yellow toothed peak thrust up out of the forest though it was not, as he had first thought, sheer all around. The cliffs at the western end were broken by ledges covered in shrubbery.

"What?" Llian jogged across to him, the gravel rattling underfoot.

"There."

On the right side of the tooth a brown shadow crept down the yellow rock into the forest like a trickle of sludge down the side of a column. But it wasn't a shadow; the eastern side of the peak was in direct sunlight.

The hairs rose on the top of Llian's head. "Is that new?"

"I've never seen it before."

Ifoli reached them, panting. "I don't like that at all."

"Is it safe to go up?"

"The lightning's only striking at the eastern end; as long as we stay well away from it we'll be all right."

They continued across to the mangroves, which stood on clusters of stilt roots a good fifteen feet high. It was a warm day and Llian was glad to pass under the leaf canopy, though they had not gone far before the humidity became oppressive. The stilt roots were covered in huge jagged barnacles and razor-sharp oysters the size of the palm of his hand, and the air was full of mosquitoes and gnats determined to suck his blood, and sand-flies that burrowed through his hair and left stinging lumps on the top of his head.

Beyond the mangroves, Regg led them along a faint path through fifty yards of barren salt flats, then a band of salt marsh, and then into forest that grew taller and darker with every step inland. The soft ground rose steadily and was covered in ferns and scattered boulders of hard yellow stone.

Regg took them to a suitable campsite beside a rivulet, where they left the tent and sleeping pouches and headed on. They had been climbing the slope for about twenty minutes, heading towards the point below the cliff where Llian had seen the creeping brown stain, when Regg, who was a few yards ahead, froze with one foot in the air. He turned slowly, his face blanched. "I . . . *felt* . . . something."

"What?" said Ifoli, stopping dead.

"A . . . a screeching sound, like someone dragging the tip of a knife down a window, but it was in my head."

Llian had not heard anything but he was notoriously insensitive to arcane phenomena. "Stay here. I'll go ahead."

Fifty yards on, the misty green light under the forest canopy suddenly changed to yellow, and further on it was an unpleasant mud-brown. The ground underfoot felt spongy now and the air had a pungent smell he could not identify, though it stung his nasal passages and made his eyes water. He crept forwards into the brown gloom, keeping a wary lookout. What could have caused such a change?

The ground was even softer here and the ferns were distinctly odd—their stems had side stems growing in places where there should have been none, and the fronds formed unnatural wavy patterns. There were toadstools everywhere: red-capped ones spotted with white, blue and sometimes black, bright yellow toadstools and big white ones with broad caps that were a pale oily green in places—he knew that kind were deadly.

He was walking across a half-buried slab of yellow rock when it gave under him. Llian looked down, thinking he must have stepped in a mossy hollow, and saw his boots sinking into what should have been solid stone.

"Stop!" he roared to Ifoli and Regg.

He tried to step off but the stone clung to his boots like toffee. He twisted free, hurled himself backwards onto the spongy earth, then stood there, his throat so dry that it was a struggle to draw breath, staring at the rock. The twin depressions his boots had made were slowly rising back to a level surface. His knees were shaking, his breath coming in gasps. He picked up a fallen branch and prodded the rock where he had stood. It was quite solid.

Regg was gasping and Ifoli looked unnerved, but not as unnerved as Llian felt. If he'd hesitated, the quick-rock would have held him. What was wrong with this place? From the corner of an eye he saw more luridly coloured toadstools thrusting up out of the ground, growing in seconds to a height that should have taken them days.

Suddenly Regg let out a screech and whacked at his trouser legs. "Get off!" he shrieked. "Off, *off!*"

He spun around, smacking his legs furiously, and every spiral took him closer to the treacherous rock and the furiously growing toadstools.

Llian caught him by the arm and pulled him away. "Back!"

Regg continued to thump his legs until Llian had hauled him thirty yards back the way they had come, when he stopped as suddenly as he had begun.

"Sorry," he said sheepishly. "There were huge hairy spiders crawling up my legs." He shuddered. "I could *hear* them gnashing their fangs."

"Stay here," said Llian. He drew Ifoli aside, saying quietly, "You know a lot more about the uncanny than I do. What was that?"

She was trembling. "I've read about places called unreality zones," she said slowly. "Though I didn't think they actually existed."

"What causes them?"

"You know how there are places in the world where mancery just seems to be stronger, and it's easier to work?"

"I've been to some of them. Carcharon and Shazmak, and Katazza at the middle of the Dry Sea."

"It's said that if very dark mancery is done at such places, and too much power is drawn from them, the waste power can create an unreality zone."

"But what *is* it?"

"A magically polluted wasteland. A place where toxic waste left over from the uncontrolled use of powerful dark magic contaminates the land, sometimes for miles around."

"And causes plants to grow wild."

"Animals too. Physically and mentally."

"You mean they can go insane?"

"You saw how quickly Regg was affected by hallucinations—if that's what they were. He saw, felt and *heard* spiders crawling on him, yet he was at the very edge of the unreality zone. What must it be like in the middle?"

"The rock softened under my feet, then started to close around them," said Llian, shuddering. "If I hadn't leapt out, I would have been trapped in it."

"But what's causing it?"

He looked up at the yellow peak, just visible through the forest canopy. "Who's using dark magic up there? And what for?"

"Let's go home," said Ifoli, and rubbed her arms as if spiders were crawling on her.

Llian wanted to, more than anything. "It's no accident that the gate brought us here at the same time as the storm struck. And I'll bet the unreality zone wasn't created long ago either. I've got to know what's up there."

21

COME CLOSER

"Not long now," said Regg an hour later. "Just another hundred yards."

The moment they reached the western side of the island he had reverted to his normal, cheerful self. Llian wished he shared the lad's uncomplicated view of the world, for his unease had grown with every upwards step. Ifoli was trailing behind again, holding her back and staring at the ground beneath her feet as if afraid to look up.

They were climbing the steep western face of the peak via a series of zigzagging ledges. The yellow rock formed a ragged wall to their right and fell away for hundreds of feet to their left.

It was darker here, since they were directly under the black thunderhead, a slowly whirling cylinder towering miles above the peak. It was spitting rain and wisps of mist trailed up here and there.

"Can't come too soon," muttered Llian.

The ledge was narrow here and the drop to his left was hundreds of feet. This was far from the biggest cliff climb he had done, or the most dangerous, but the sooner it was over the happier he would be. There was no sign of the unreality zone here but something was definitely wrong. The prickles down his arms grew stronger with every step.

Lightning sizzled down to the far side of the mountain top, the ground quivered underfoot and there came a shattering clap of thunder. Small rocks and loose earth tumbled down at him in a miniature landslide. Llian let out an involuntary yelp, skidded on loose gravel, his arms flailing, then caught a knob of rock protruding from the cliff and clung on desperately as the slide rumbled past and over the edge.

"It's all right," said Ifoli, who had merely stepped to her right to allow it to pass.

"Must be nice to have no fear," he said sourly.

"I have many fears," she said quietly, "and the time I spent serving Snoat reinforced all of them."

There were three more lightning strikes before they made it to the top, each louder and brighter than the one before, and Llian's nerves were shredded by the time they got there. What would they find? Did he really want to know?

He rounded a head-high wall of ochre rock covered in clusters of little ferns sprouting from every crevice, and the path petered out on bare yellow rock. Ahead, their view to the east was blocked by a large rock outcrop with a cleft running through it.

"Stay low," said Ifoli, eyeing the great thunderhead.

Llian crept through the cleft for fifteen feet, and peered out. There were no trees here, though wiry bushes, bent inwards by prevailing updraughts, encircled the rim of the peak like thick hair around the edges of a bald head, and its uneven centre was covered in ferns and grey lichen. A patch of fog obscured the eastern end of the peak, apart from a small scarp of orange rock on the far right, with a ribbon of silver cutting through it from top to bottom.

Regg, who was standing behind Llian, let out his breath in a whistle. "Wow!"

"Stay back," said Ifoli sharply.

Lightning struck the silver ribbon, sending smoking chunks of rock arcing through the air. The thunder blast knocked Llian off his feet. He came to his knees, rubbing his aching ears. The blast had dispersed the fog and there it was—the thing he had been dreading since the morning he had woken to see the storm still hanging above Demondifang.

The summon stone.

Though not as Shand and Ussarine had described it when he'd met them outside Alcifer. They had seen a trilithon of dark red rock as smooth as polished marble. The two upright stones had been seven feet high and the third had been laid across their tops.

This summon stone was a good twelve feet tall, though the uprights leaned dangerously to the right. It had gone the muddy brown of bad meat, with veins of sickly yellow and bile green, and parts of each stone were eaten away like rotten teeth. Yet it seemed stronger than ever; it squatted on the peak like a malicious demon, warping everything it touched.

The air had a pungent tang due to lightning striking close by, though it was underlain by the offensive stench of rotting flesh and blood, as if a corpse was slowly decaying inside the summon stone. Festering brown sludge oozed from its twin bases, pooling around them then trickling down channels in the rock and over the eastern edge of the peak—the source of the unreality zone now spreading through the forest below.

Another lightning bolt struck the silver ribbon cutting through the scarp and Llian saw what he had missed the first time: a surge of liquid silver flowing across the yellow rock to congeal between the uprights as, clearly, it had done many times before. The brown sludge sizzled and surged over the edge, and the summon stone grew a little taller, a little wider.

"Is the lightning empowering it?" said Llian. "Is that why it moved here?

"I've never heard of such a thing," said Ifoli.

Nothing grew within thirty feet of it—every fern and patch of moss or lichen had been charred down to bare rock in an oval around the stone. No, on the edges of the brown deluge the ferns were distorted and perverted like the plants in the unreality zone.

A whisper in his head. *Come closer.*

"Let's go," said Ifoli, pulling him away. She had gone pale and was clutching her back again with her other hand. "I've got to get a message to Nadiril and I daren't do it here."

"We'll never have a better chance to find out about it," said Llian.

"It's too dangerous. We've got to go down."

Come closer.

The urge was almost irresistible. He took a half step towards it.

Lightning struck again, sending another pulse of liquid silver down to congeal between the uprights. Somewhere to his left a rock struck another—*click.*

Ifoli thumped him across the side of the head. "It's trying to get at us! Remember how madly you acted when you held the Command device?"

Llian stopped, rubbing his eyes as if roused from a dream. Each time he'd held Unick's Command device he had felt delusions that he could use it, and before that its drumming had got to him. On several occasions when he'd heard it in Pem-Y-Rum he'd been tempted to sneak off to Thandiwe's willing arms. Heat flooded his face at the memories. Was he really that easily corrupted?

He turned his back to the stone and helped her along the cleft, but before they reached the western end she doubled over and threw up.

"Don't feel well," she mumbled, wiping her mouth.

He turned. "Where's Regg?"

Ifoli stumbled back to the eastern end of the cleft and her beautiful face twisted in horror. "Regg, no, *stop*!"

Regg was only twenty yards from the summon stone, his arms reaching out to it. If he touched it, it would annihilate him in an instant, and feed and grow.

Ifoli let out a little moan and started towards him. Llian caught her by the arm. "It'll get you too."

She struck at him in desperation. "He's my *cousin*, Llian! He's just a kid, and I brought him up here. I've got to get him down." She gasped, doubled over and fell to her knees. "What's . . . happening . . . to me?"

"Stay here!" he said, pushing her back into the shelter of the cleft. "Keep low."

What he was about to do was utterly reckless but Llian could not afford to think about that. He slipped across into the wind-twisted shrubbery. He had no idea what he was going to do when he reached Regg but he had to keep out of sight of the stone.

Lightning flashed and thunder crashed as he scrambled through the scrub, only feet from the precipice. Now Regg was only five yards ahead, at the outer edge of the charred oval around the summon stone, and Llian's entrails throbbed at the thought of exposing himself to it. He did not think he could resist it.

Come closer, closer, closer.

"What are you?" said Regg in a high, breathless voice. His whole body was quivering.

Everything you've ever wanted.

Regg gave a little trembling shudder, took a step towards the stone but stopped.

"Regg!" Llian hissed. "The enemy sent it here to open the way for them. It's corrupt!"

Regg looked over his shoulder. "Why are you lying to me? It can give me everything I've ever dreamed of."

"Nothing can *give* you anything. Only you can make your life, Regg."

Regg made a dismissive gesture with his right hand and took another step towards it.

"It wants to kill you, Regg. To *feed* on you."

Regg took another step.

From the cleft, Ifoli let out a despairing cry, "Regg, come back!" then staggered across the open ground towards him. Llian groaned; they were all going to die here. He burst out of the shrubbery and hurled himself at Regg, bringing him down.

Good. Come closer.

Lightning struck the silver vein with shattering force. Llian, blinded and deafened, clung on as Regg struck at him wildly. Regg was desperate to get to the stone now; he was in a kind of mad ecstasy.

Closer, closer.

Llian's sight came back and he knew he had only one chance. He freed his arms and swung at Regg, an uppercut that caught him under the chin, snapping his head back and knocking him senseless. Llian caught him as he fell and dragged him away.

Come back!

"Damn you!" Llian ground out. "I won't."

He had fought this battle many times before, and won it most of the time, but the power of the stone this close was overwhelming. He felt himself slowing, turning, a vacuous smile stretching his mouth.

But he could not let it beat him. Sulien was in the hands of the pitiless Whelm far away and he had to save her.

It took every ounce of willpower Llian had to deny the voice in his head and the compulsion that was trying to take control of his limbs, but he did it. He turned his back to the stone and was heaving Regg along when the boy stumbled on a loose rock and Llian lost his grip.

Regg moaned and clutched at his right ankle. His eyes were still closed, as if he were not fully conscious, then he shouldered Llian aside and scrabbled blindly across the yellow rock, heading straight back towards the stone.

22

YOU WILL LEARN RESPECT

"You stupid little girl!" roared Torsion Tule, thrusting his blotchy red face against Aviel's. His breath was so foul that she could see it; the oozing exhalations from his crusted mouth were an oily green. "Don't you know *anything*? Do it all again, twist-foot."

She gagged and backed away. He glared at her, his sludgy brown eyes glittering, then headed for the door.

Aviel had only been his apprentice for a day but she knew it was not going to work. He had refused to discuss the making of nivol or indeed even the most basic techniques of practical alchemy.

"You won't be ready for the first lesson for at least a month, twist-foot," he had snarled first thing this morning. "Until you learn cleanliness. Wash *everything*!"

Aviel had looked at the array of equipment in dismay. There were hundreds of flasks, beakers, stills, retorts, crucibles, mortars and pestles, bowls, scrapers and other pieces of equipment she did not know the names of. Washing everything had taken her all morning and her back was aching by the time the job was done to her own high standards.

Tule had returned at midday, taken a perfunctory look, cuffed her over the head and said, "Do it all again, *properly*."

She had scrubbed, rinsed and dried everything again; it had taken most of the afternoon. Every piece of glassware or metal shone, and even the stone mortars and pestles gleamed; there was nothing he could find fault with.

But he had. Without inspecting a single item of equipment he had ordered her to clean everything again, but by now her ankle was so excruciatingly painful that she lost control.

"All right!" she snapped as he reached the door. "But this is the last time."

Tule rotated, slowly and awkwardly, and lurched back to her. His right side was shaking more than before. "What ... did ... you ... say, twist-foot?"

"I said I'll do it again," she said, more politely though still with an edge of sarcasm.

He struck her across the left cheek with his swollen knuckles, knocking her head sideways. "You will call me Grand Master Tule. You ... will ... learn ... respect."

He went out.

Aviel slumped onto a stool, rubbing her stinging cheek and thinking impotent thoughts of revenge. Why did he hate her so? And what was she to do? Making nivol grew more important every hour. The future of Santhenar might depend on her succeeding, but with Tule for a master she never would. He was determined to crush her spirit, then force her to re-learn the basics the way the dullest of apprentices might, working on each elementary task for a month before being allowed to begin the next.

It did not matter that she had mastered many basic techniques, and some advanced ones, in the three years she had spent making perfumes and scent potions. She had to begin at the beginning, *his* way.

The latch clicked. Aviel hastily slid off her stool, expecting another blow, but there was no one there. She plodded to the nearest bench and gathered up the flasks.

"How are you doing?" said Shand, materialising in front of her.

She started. "On the um . . . project?" She had almost mentioned nivol. If she'd told such a vital secret to a traitor she would be hanged as one.

"Making nivol," he said with a grim smile, as if to emphasise that he knew everything. "Any progress?"

"I can't talk about my work."

"What's so secret about washing-up?" He let out a sour chuckle. "Tule doesn't want you to succeed, Aviel. He'll do everything in his power to block you."

She propped herself up on the bench, uncomprehending. "But it's his job to teach me."

"He doesn't believe nivol can ever be made, and he's probably right. In times long past some great alchemists attempted it. None got close."

"How do you know?"

"I dabbled in the art myself, in my youth."

"You seem to have dabbled in a lot of arts," she said sarcastically. "Did you actually master any?"

She leaned away from him, knowing she'd gone too far, but he favoured her with another grim smile. "About time you showed some spirit, girl."

"But . . . why is Tule blocking me?" She had to understand.

Shand locked the door and perched on the stool opposite hers. "As a young alchemist he was a great genius, but he burnt out early. By the time Tule was thirty people were calling him a has-been and he knew it to be true, and it embittered him.

"From that day onward he was a plodder; he knew alchemy backwards but was utterly incapable of doing anything new with it. And the more embittered he became, the more he held back his knowledge from his apprentices; he could not bear for them to surpass him. The clever ones, knowing they were wasting their time, left without completing their apprenticeships. Only the dullest remained."

"Why haven't you told Tallia?"

Shand smiled thinly.

"Then what am I to do?" said Aviel. "The . . . project is urgent."

He took the sheaf of papers and parchments from her pack and scanned them.

"Hey!" cried Aviel, limping at him. "They're secret."

"Are you going to stop me?" he said coolly.

She stopped, all the weight on her left foot, feeling powerless. Where should her greatest loyalty lie—with the man who had changed her life, or the allies who were struggling to deal with an overwhelming enemy? Tallia, Malien and Janck would expect her to inform on Shand but if she did they would set a trap for him, and hang him. Aviel could not do it.

He was sorting the nivol papers into a small pile on the left and a larger one on the right. "Shand?" she said timidly. "How am I going to get the job done?"

"You've got to find a way to deal with Tule."

"What do you mean?"

"You're a resourceful girl," Shand said blandly. "I'll leave that up to you."

He finished sorting the papers. "The big pile on the right is worthless. The papers on the left can help you, especially the one on the bottom; it's a tricky method, but by far the quickest."

She nodded, still anxious about trusting him. "You said you wanted my help. What for?"

"Nothing yet. For the time being I'll work here after you've gone to bed." He climbed off the stool, rubbed his back and vanished.

Deal with Tule? What did he mean by that? Aviel began to carry the glassware to the big sink, then stopped. Damn Tule! Since he hadn't bothered to look at her work before, he wouldn't know if she'd cleaned the equipment again or not.

Mindful of Tallia's injunction to keep the papers secret, she hid the thicker bundle and started on the small pile of methods Shand had said would be some use. And immediately encountered a major problem. Radizer's grimoire was written in relatively clear language, with a minimum of abbreviations, arcane words and symbols; it had not been hard for her to follow. But the first method for making nivol seemed deliberately obscure. The first paragraph contained ten words she had never heard before, plus many abbreviations and references to unexplained techniques.

She checked the papyrus below it. It began with a list of formulae made up almost entirely of symbols, none of which were familiar to her. The rest of the papers, papyri, scrolls, parchments and tablets were much the same.

After hours of reading that left her with aching eyes, Aviel gleaned that nivol required either thirty-seven basic ingredients, forty-six, fifty-one or, from the faded purple writing on a sheet made from beaten silver, eighty-nine.

Some ingredients were animal, some vegetable, some mineral, and some were impossible to classify; however it wasn't simply a case of obtaining them, extracting their vital essences and blending them, as she had when making the Eureka Graveolence. To create nivol she first had to transform many of the ingredients using alchemical techniques she had never used before—ones that Tule wasn't planning to teach her in the next year, if ever.

Aviel's head was throbbing. She had tried to cram too much into it. She rubbed her eyes and looked down at the pile again, but the words and symbols were blurred; just looking at them made her feel ill.

She stumbled to an old cracked-leather settee at the far end of the workshop, but when she lay down the whole room started rocking. She rose and made a mug of very strong ginger tea. It burned as it went down but did not clear her head.

As a distraction she unwrapped Radizer's grimoire, which oddly Shand had not taken earlier, and slowly turned the pages. What kind of a man had Radizer been? Not a good one!

Three quarters of the scent potions in the grimoire were dark ones: there were potions to weaken, to exhaust, to confuse and to control another person; potions to make an enemy ill, potions to blind and to spread disease, and potions to turn a wound septic or even gangrenous. There were scent potions to rob enemies of their wits or drive them insane; potions to turn good people to the dark side and potions that could utterly corrupt them. Potions to poison an enemy in all manner of unpleasant ways.

And potions to kill, slowly and agonisingly or in a blinding instant. The grimoire contained thirteen death potions, all different, and some were so perilous that they could only be tested on the intended victim.

Aviel clapped the book shut, shuddering. Why was she reading about such wicked things? She limped to the cast-iron cauldron in the corner, which was full of boiling water, ladled out a bucket, carried it to the sink and began to wash the equipment again. But it could not ease her agitation; it was as much as waste of time as before.

Returning to the settee, she took up the grimoire again, scanning the titles and avoiding any that seemed the least bit dark. There was a small section on love potions, just three, and she hesitated, smiling sadly. Had anyone ever loved her? Certainly not her father or her six horrible sisters. Perhaps her mother had, for a while, though since she had run away when Aviel was only a year old, her mother could not have loved her much.

But love potions were also dark mancery—they were used to manipulate or coerce another person. Aviel wrapped the grimoire and had just slipped it under a cushion, out of sight, when the door was flung open and Tule stalked in. When he saw her on the settee such a look of fury crossed his age-spotted face that she quailed and scrambled to her feet.

He lurched across and backhanded her across the face. "You lazy slattern!" He struck her again. "You haven't done a lick of work since I left." And again. "You just moved everything around, thinking I wouldn't notice."

Tule slammed his bony knuckles into her left ear, knocking her sideways. "I . . . notice . . . *everything,* twist-foot. You're a useless, slovenly little rat." *Thump.* "You're not capable of anything worthwhile." *Thump.* "You've fooled the Magister and the commander but you . . . can't . . . fool . . . me." *Thump, thump,* so hard that it knocked her to her knees. "Clean the equipment, *properly*!"

Aviel's head was ringing. She tried to stand up but could not. She crawled across to the sink, hauled herself up on it and stood there swaying. Tears filled her eyes. She wiped them on her sleeve but they kept flowing.

"You will acknowledge my orders, girl, or suffer."

"Yes, Grand Master Tule," she whispered.

Tule came up behind her. "*Now!*" he roared.

She put half a dozen sparkling clean beakers in the sink, tipped in some of the liquid soap she had made earlier and scrubbed them furiously, the beakers clattering, though it wasn't until the water went red that she realised she had broken one and cut her right palm badly. She raised her hand, staring at the flowing blood.

Tule let out a bellow of fury, caught her head from behind and forced it down into the sink. Aviel fought desperately, fearing he was planning to impale her on the broken beaker, or drown her. The hot soapy water went up her nose, stinging and burning, and down her windpipe, half choking her.

Her forehead cracked against glass though fortunately it was not the broken beaker. Tule was holding her head under but she could feel his arms shaking. She twisted sideways, he lost his grip and she went up on tiptoes and slammed her head back and up. *Crunch*! He let out a gurgling cry.

The soap stung Aviel's eyes, water dribbled from her nose and her hand dripped blood on the floor.

Bloody, slimy bubbles foamed from Tule's nose, staining his beautifully embroidered mancer's robes. He wiped his nose on the back of his hand, spat blood onto the floor and wobbled round to face her. "How dare you lay a finger on your master!" he choked.

"I didn't."

"You will refer to me by my title!" He raised a hand as if to strike her again, but lowered it.

"I didn't lay a finger on you, *Grand Master* Tule," she said with as much sarcasm as she could muster.

"Don't mince words with me, twist-foot."

Aviel clenched her fist to staunch the blood flowing from her palm. "*Never* touch me again, *Grand Master*," she said, amazed at her boldness yet knowing she would pay for it.

"By law and custom, I can treat my apprentices how I damn well like," he hissed.

"Not if you want me to finish the project."

"I couldn't give a damn about it. Nivol is a fool's errand; it can't be done."

Blood was still running from his nose, which was swelling visibly and probably broken. He wavered his way to the door, then turned. "Clean this mess up. And when I come back . . ."

An evil smile twisted Tule's thin mouth, then he went out.

Aviel shuddered. He was a decrepit old man, but he was also a powerful mancer and what he said was true: by law an apprentice was her master's property and, short of actually killing her, he could do whatever he wanted to her. When he recovered, he would make her pay.

But she had to make some nivol; therefore she had to deal with him first. Aviel let the bloody water out of the sink, rinsed the beakers, threw out the broken one and bandaged her hand. Then she headed back to the settee and the grimoire.

There was only one way to deal with a powerful mancer like Tule—with one of Radizer's scent potions. The dark ones.

23

THE SAME DISPLAY OF PERFECTION

The power of the summon stone scalded Llian. It was flowing into him and through him, trying to corrupt him.

Bring them and you will have everything you ever dreamed about.

Ifoli caught Regg around the waist, but he was far stronger and he kept going, dragging her towards the stone.

You know you want to—

Llian had to act now or they would all die. He faced the stone, drew on the iron will he had developed over months of fighting the drumming, and roared, "*I defy you!*"

He pulled Ifoli away. "Go back! I'll deal with this."

She took one look at his face and nodded. Llian darted around in front of Regg, who looked dazed, uncomprehending. Llian slapped him across the face, left cheek then right. Regg's eyes cleared and Llian used the moment.

Using all the authority of his teller's *voice*, the almost magical power a great teller had to move people by the sheer power of his words, he said, "*Go down, now!*"

Llian turned him and pointed him towards the cleft, and to his surprise Regg meekly hobbled that way. Still consumed by fury, Llian shook his fist at the summon stone.

He was about to use his *voice* on it when Ifoli said, "Not a good idea. Come on."

She yanked on his hand. The spell broke, and he ran with her back to the cleft. Ifoli was staggering and gasping by the time they got there. Regg was staring at the summon stone and the yearning was back in his eyes.

Come back, come back!

He was falling under its spell again, and Llian could feel it undermining his own resolve. If he could not get Regg away at once, they were lost. Llian had used the best of his strength and could not do it again.

"Thank you," Ifoli said limply.

She was on the verge of collapse, and he did not see how he was going to get her down either, though at least she could resist the call of the stone. He hesitated. If he helped her, Regg would probably break free and run back.

He stepped out of the cleft. His weight came down on his twisted ankle and tears of pain formed in his eyes, but his eyes had taken on that fervid shine again. Soon he would walk on bloody stumps to get to the stone. Llian had to get him beyond its reach.

"Ifoli, take this."

Regg handed her the leather manuscript bag he had stolen from Snoat at Pem-Y-Rum; it held his journal which he carried at all times. She slung it over her shoulder and the heavy bag thumped into her back. Ifoli gasped.

"We're going down," Llian said to Regg, using just a hint of the *voice*, and gave him his shoulder. "Lean on me."

"Yes, Llian." Regg went with him, trembling with every step.

They passed through the cleft, headed down the steep path and Llian felt the will of the summon stone, which had been beating at him all this time, ease.

"I'm all right now," said Regg, pulling away.

Llian held on to him. He did not believe in miracles.

"I feel better too," said Ifoli, then added hopefully, "Do you think, by defying it, that you've broken its power over us?"

Spiders crawled down Llian's back. "Not for a second."

"Its power was really strong on the way up; it was all I could do to keep going. But it's gone now and I don't feel ill any more."

"It's a trick to lure us back. Go down, quick as you can."

"I'm all right," said Regg. "Really I am." He poked around in the trees and found a forked branch that made a rude crutch. He led the way down the cliff path.

Llian watched him warily, but Regg showed no signs of the compulsion. He was his normal cheerful self again, hopping along on his crutch and making light of his injury.

Towards the bottom, Llian realised that Ifoli still had his manuscript bag. He took it from her.

"Any chance we can cross the spit? I don't want to spend the night here."

Ifoli headed up a long ramp of rock to a knoll which formed a small lookout with a view south to Mollymoot. Her shoulders sagged. "Not even if we ran all the way down."

Llian came up beside her. The tide was racing in, surging over the long band of gravel. "How long until it's low again?"

"There's a low tide tonight, but it won't be low enough," said Regg. "Next chance is tomorrow morning."

Ifoli rubbed her back. She had gone pale again. They continued to their camping place, put up the tent and gathered firewood. Regg took his fishing rod and headed down to a rock platform on the eastern side, where large waves were breaking. The wind was rising and the swell seemed bigger than before. It was not a good sign; they could be trapped here for days and if they were he did not think any of them could resist the call of the stone.

Llian lit the fire and Ifoli perched beside it, shivering. He opened the food bag Dilly had prepared for them. It contained several kinds of local root vegetables, unfamiliar to him, a bag of flour, a packet of mixed spices and a small jar of lard.

"What are these?" He held up a long hairy yellow root, thick in the middle and tapering on either end.

"Ghurd," said Ifoli. "It tastes like turnip, though more bitter. The round orange ones are noolies—they're best baked—and the red knobbly roots are tiblets." She grimaced. "They're supposed to be very healthy but you have to peel them; the skin's poisonous."

"Do you want to cook them? I dare say you know more about it than me."

"I've never cooked a meal in my life."

"I thought you were brilliant at everything."

Her eyes flashed. "I'm good at a few things because I never do any-thing else."

Did she regret the way she had lived her life? Llian supposed she

must. He peeled the tiblets. He was an experienced camp cook, though
not a particularly good one.

He dug a hole in the ashes and put the vegetables in to bake. The
sky clouded over and the wind grew chilly. He climbed a small rise
that looked down on the rock platform, to check on Regg. The call of
the stone was weak here but it had already put its mark on him and
would be trying to lure him back.

But Regg was at the edge of the rock platform, casting his lure into
the heaving waters. There was no sign that the summon stone had
ever got to him. Llian returned to the camp and sat by the fire. The
top of Demondifang was not visible from here, though every time the
lightning flashed it lit up the thunderhead. It was still striking at the
peak, empowering the summon stone.

He wrote up the day's events in his journal until the light faded. Ifoli
lay on her sleeping pouch, staring at the fire. Every so often her hand
crept to her back and she winced.

"What's the matter with your back?" said Llian. He had probed it
on the mudflat on the first night, though only in darkness.

"I don't know. The lump disappeared four days ago, but now it's
back."

"I'd better take a look."

"Dilly checked it the first night and couldn't see anything."

"Roll over."

She turned onto her face. Llian pulled up her blouse. Six inches below
her left collarbone there was a shiny plum-sized lump, as if something
had bitten her. He pressed down on it, gently. It was firm and hot.

"Aaahh!" she cried.

"Why did it go away and come back?" he wondered.

"Sometimes it gets hot and inflamed, and I feel weak and feverish.
Other times I hardly know it's there."

An ugly suspicion surfaced. "Is there a pattern?"

"When the stone was trying to get at us the lump felt twice as big
as it does now. But on the way down it almost disappeared."

"I've seen all kinds of poisoned wounds and bites and stings,"
said Llian, who had spent years travelling across the western world,

"and I've never come across anything like this. Is there a healer on Mollymoot?"

"Just a midwife." Ifoli pulled her blouse down and her coat around her, and sat up.

"Can you have another go at contacting Nadiril?"

"I don't think so."

"Tallia's got to know the summon stone is here."

"Do you think I don't know that?" she snapped.

"You've really changed since we came here. You used to be—"

"So calm and controlled and clever at everything," she said waspishly. "Yes."

"I had to seem perfect in every way or Snoat would have got rid of me, the way he disposed of every other *possession* that wasn't good enough. My life was in danger every day I served him, Llian—every *hour*—and when I was alone I was hard put not to scream in terror. So now I'm free," she said sarcastically, "forgive me for not putting on the same display of perfection for you."

He flushed. "I'm sorry. But our news is vital, and—"

"Using Nadiril's farspeaker over such a distance takes a lot out of me," she said quietly, "and what if the stone attacks while I'm doing it?"

Nonetheless, she took off the small pearl and gold earring in her left ear, pressed and twisted the pearl so it rotated in its mount and held it up to her ear. She pressed and twisted a slightly larger pearl on a chain that had been hidden under her blouse and held the pearl close to her mouth. In the dancing firelight, her face, one the most beautiful Llian had ever seen, was haggard.

She exerted her famous self-control, the drawn look disappeared, and she was the perfect Ifoli again. Was she putting on a show for her great-grandfather or for herself?

"Ifoli?" The voice issuing from the earring was faint, but it was unquestionably Nadiril's. "Where are you? Is everything—?"

A distant thumping began, not unlike the drumming that had so troubled Llian previously, and it grew faster and louder.

"I've seen the stone—"

Crack!

The pearl earring shattered in her fingers and she cried out and dropped it. She picked out a curving shard from her middle finger, stared at the welling drop of blood, then her eyes rolled up and she fell backwards.

24

USING IT TO ATTACK US

Ifoli was trembling fitfully, and every so often she gave a convulsive jerk and a whimper escaped her. Had he pushed her too hard?

Regg climbed the slope from the rock platform, whistling a merry tune. He had abandoned his crutch and only had a slight limp. He stepped into the firelight, stopped and cried, "What's happened? *Ifoli?*"

He dropped his rod and basket. Four fat golden fish spilled out.

"She was trying to contact Nadiril," said Llian. "I think the stone attacked her."

Regg lifted Ifoli to a sitting position. She shuddered and her eyes came open.

"Get off the island," she said. "Now."

"There's no way off until tomorrow morning," said Regg.

Her eyelids fluttered. "But *it's coming.*"

"What do you mean?" said Llian.

"Tried to take control of me." She spoke slowly, exhaustedly. "It's much more powerful than it was before." A mighty lightning strike lit up the forest above them. "And every bolt's making it stronger."

"How are you feeling?" said Regg.

"Scorched . . . in the head." She noticed the yellow fish scattered across the ground. "I'm starving."

Regg put a pan on the fire, collected the fish and started scaling and gutting them. They only took a few minutes to cook. Llian dug out the roots he had buried in the coals, picked the ash and charcoal off and divided them into three portions. The fish were perfectly cooked, the roots overcooked and dried out, but no one noticed the good or the bad. Regg and Ifoli kept looking up at the mountain. Llian felt sure the stone would strike again.

By the time they'd finished and Regg had taken their plates and cutlery down to the water to wash them, Ifoli's head was drooping.

"Get some sleep," said Llian, putting more wood on the fire. "I'll take the first watch."

She pulled her sleeping pouch up to her neck and lay down, her head pillowed on her arms. "Not sure I can sleep," she murmured, "with it watching us."

"Can it actually see us, down here?"

"It's got a kind of *presence* now," said Ifoli. "It's tap-tapping on my skull, trying to get at me." Her eyes were huge, wet and staring. She jerked the sleeping pouch up over her head and lay there, rigid as a log.

Regg returned and went to his own sleeping pouch. Even more troubled now, Llian circled the campsite, knife in hand, then circled again beyond the reach of the firelight. Apart from the sound of waves breaking on the rocks and the regular crack of thunder, the night was still.

After three hours he woke Regg for the next watch, but Llian was too on edge to sleep. He dozed a couple of times but each time snapped awake to see that the stars had hardly moved. After an hour or two he got up. Ifoli was trembling in her sleep and Regg's head was drooping.

"Get some sleep, lad," Llian said. "I can't."

He was pacing in the semi-dark when he heard a distant crackling, like a heavy object rolling over dry leaves. The sound was ever so slowly moving down the mountain.

A cold breeze on the back of his neck made him shiver. He crept up the rise behind the campsite, trying to make no sound, and looked up at the mountain. The top two-thirds of the forest was glowing!

The yellow-green radiance was creeping down on all sides, and it was brightest on the eastern side of the mountain where they had encountered the unreality zone. It was coming for them and it was only a few hours after midnight. Six or seven hours until they could cross the gravel spit to Mollymoot.

Llian hurtled back, crashing through tall ferns that whipped at his face and stumbling over unseen rocks and logs. Ifoli was still twitching in her sleep. Regg was perched on a stone, head pillowed on his arms, and woke with a start as Llian skidded into the campsite.

"Get up!" he gasped.

Ifoli jerked upright. "What . . ."

"Unreality zone is spreading down the mountain. Got to go, *now*!"

She rose shakily, holding her back.

"Is the lump——?" said Llian.

She grimaced. "Worse than ever."

Llian heaved his pack on and led them down to the scalded ground of the salt flats. "The glow's moving fast."

"But what *is* it?" said Regg, bewildered.

He was an ordinary country boy who might never have seen any kind of mancery. How could he hope to understand what was happening here?

"Magical pollution from the summon stone," said Ifoli. "Dark waste that corrupts everything it touches."

"And the stone's using it to lure us back," said Llian.

"Then where can we go?" Regg said hoarsely.

"Down to the shore. Quick!"

By the time they reached the inner edge of the mangroves the glowing unreality zone had developed three fast-moving lobes. The middle lobe was rumbling straight at them, the others heading out to either side as if to hem them in.

"It's trying to stop us getting to the gravel spit," panted Llian.

"We can't cross it anyway," Regg said gloomily. "It'll be underwater for hours."

Ifoli doubled over, gasping. Llian could feel the heat radiating from the lump in her back, yet she was shivering violently.

"If we stay here we'll be trapped," he said. "If we can reach the end of the spit, we might be able to fight it off until we can cross . . ." But he could not lie to himself—in his heart he knew it was almost hopeless.

"How—fight off—unreality zone?" said Ifoli.

Suddenly the left- and right-hand lobes extended like drops of glowing honey hanging from a spoon. "It's accelerating," cried Regg. "Can it read minds?"

"Down to the water!" said Llian.

As they squelched through sucking mud into the mangroves they lost sight of the lobes, which was worse than seeing them. He went ahead, feeling his way. In the tall, stilt-rooted mangroves, all he could hear was the lapping of waves on the distant shore, the whine of mosquitoes and his own heavy breathing.

They ploughed their way to the shore. Llian looked right and a yellow glow was creeping from tree to tree, no more than a hundred yards away. Fear struck him a series of hammer blows, beating him down.

"Left!" he rapped. "Faster!"

But it was impossible to hurry here; the sticky mud clung in layers to their boots and the best they could manage was a zombie walk. Regg, despite his sore ankle, was fastest. Ifoli was blanched of face and stumbling. Llian glanced over his shoulder; the unreality zone was moving faster than they were. At this rate they'd never make it to the gravel spit.

"Regg, carry her."

Regg, ignoring Ifoli's protests, heaved her over his shoulder and they laboured on, but before they had gone another hundred yards the lurid yellow light brightened ahead of them and a second lobe swept down through the mangroves. They were trapped.

Llian's bowels spasmed painfully. What would the unreality zone do to them? Would it drive them insane, or turn them into monstrosities like the forest plants they had seen yesterday? As far as the summon stone was concerned, the more corrupt the better—before it fed on them.

Regg put Ifoli down. "What now?" she said, sagging against him.

"Into the water," said Llian.

"But we'll be trapped," Regg said wildly. The glow had turned his grey eyes a sickly yellow.

"Most kinds of mancery don't work in water."

"This is alien mancery; it may follow different rules." Ifoli looked around wildly. "But it's our only chance."

She held onto Regg's shoulder and they waded out until the sea was waist deep on her, then walked slowly to their left, parallel to the shore. The water drew the warmth from Llian's body and Ifoli was already in bad shape. How much longer could she keep going?

The two glowing lobes converged in the mangroves, only thirty yards away. Dark knobs formed all over the stilt roots and twisted out in all directions, coiling and writhing and battering at everything they touched, including each other.

The oyster shells were also growing madly, doubling and redoubling in size and forming spikes and razor-sharp blades, deadly to anything that came within range of the writhing roots. They were trapped in the sea . . . and what if the unreality zone followed them in?

"What's it doing?" Regg said shrilly.

At the shoreline, the unreality zone formed little yellow-green bulges that extended across the seabed for several feet, only to be broken up by the waves and fade out.

"If we stay out here," said Llian, "I don't think it can get to us."

"But the tide's rising," cried Regg, holding Ifoli up. "It'll drive us into the mangroves and we'll be hacked to death."

"We'll have to swim around to the spit. There's a break in the mangroves there."

"Ifoli can barely stand up."

"Have to manage," she gasped.

Llian led them out until the water was up to her shoulders then turned parallel to the shore. The waves weren't breaking here but the surge was troublesome and it was hard going, especially for Regg who, despite living by the sea, was a poor swimmer and had refused to discard his precious fishing rod.

Ifoli's teeth were chattering. "Are you up to swimming?" said Llian.

She nodded. "Lump's gone down a bit. The cold water helps."

It was less than a mile to the spit and the narrow break in the mangroves, but it took them an hour to swim it. They had to stop every couple of minutes so Regg could stand up and catch his breath, and by the time they got there he was gasping and grey-faced.

The shoreline was gravel here, and the beach about thirty yards wide, heaps of flat oval pebbles and cobbles piled up by storm waves. Nothing grew in it and the unreality zone was struggling to cross it, though wisps of glowing yellow clung to the pebbles here and there and Llian, not knowing what power they had, was reluctant to go ashore.

But they might have no choice. They were exposed to the wind here, the water had leached the warmth from their bodies long ago and Ifoli was in a bad way. Llian did not see how she could last.

They stood in hip-deep water, pressed together for warmth, eyeing the glow that now covered the mangroves to east and west for as far as they could see. Only the oval gravel bank resisted its progress, but for how long?

The next two hours, until the winter sun finally rose sometime after seven, were eternal. "Th-three hours to go," said Ifoli, her teeth chattering so hard that Llian was afraid they would crack. "Only three more hours."

It was a clear day, and the sunlight warmed them a little, though it created another problem—they could no longer make out the glow on the shoreline. They had no choice but to go into deeper water, cling together and pray.

Finally, around nine, the falling tide began to expose the shoreward ends of the gravel spit to Mollymoot, though it would be three-quarters of an hour before the central part would be above water. Llian, Regg and Ifoli were moving down the spit when every hair on his body stood up and he heard, in his inner ear, a shriek of terror that would live with him all his days.

Mummeeeee! Mummy, Daddy, it's got me. Help!

Through Sulien's eyes he saw a gigantic winged beast with six-inch talons, a myriad of bone-crushing teeth, and saliva dripping from its leathery lips. It was hundreds of feet in the air and carrying her away.

"Hold on!" he screamed, witless with panic. "I'm coming!"

He tore free of Ifoli, knocking her down, and splashed out along the submerged spit. He could think of nothing save getting to Sulien as quickly as possible, and nothing could be allowed to stop him.

"Stop!" shrieked Ifoli. "Regg, grab him."

Llian evaded him, waded out from the end of the bar until the water was up to his shoulders, then thrashed towards Mollymoot. But he had only gone ten yards when a powerful current dragged him to the left, off the submerged gravel and into deep water. He turned towards Mollymoot and swam harder, but now he was fighting a current that was moving faster than he could swim, and it was rapidly exhausting him.

He was being swept east towards the Sea of Qwale, and there was nothing out there for more than a hundred miles.

PART TWO

ALCHEMY

25

SUCCUMBING TO THE DARK SIDE

After the brutal confrontation with Grand Master Tule, Aviel could not sleep. What if the scent potion to deal with him went wrong? She was a novice working on an art she did not understand, and just because the Eureka Graveolence had gone well, this did not mean any other potion would.

She went back to the workshop, lit a candle and turned the pages of Radizer's grimoire. Even the minor dark potions were dangerous to make and more dangerous to use, and they did not always work the way they were supposed to. She did not want to harm Tule. She might have turned to the dark side but she wasn't that far gone. She had to find the simplest, easiest and safest way of disabling him for a few weeks.

Was a few weeks enough time to make some nivol? It seemed most unlikely, even assuming she could decipher the instructions and obtain all the ingredients, but if she failed it was unlikely humanity would survive. Even so, why had Tallia, Malien and Commander Janck put their faith in *her*? They must be desperate.

She settled on Essence of Ague, one of the mild dark potions she had read about back home in Casyme. It caused fits of shivering and shaking that rendered the recipient unable to speak or stand up, and was accompanied by profuse sweating and very unpleasant body odour. The grimoire noted, wryly, that victims had to be isolated until the effects of the scent potion wore off, though they normally made a full recovery.

She could blend Essence of Ague from half a dozen of the phials in her scent belt, plus the aromas she could extract from common garden herbs, and three mild stenches easily found in Sith. Aviel reread the method until she knew it by heart, then hid the grimoire. No one must ever know that she had used it on her master.

Not long ago she had been an innocent girl who worked hard, was polite to everyone and never made a fuss. Now look at her. Aviel item-ised her crimes since beginning the study of scent potions less than two months ago: stealing the grimoire; sneaking into Magsie Murg's tannery and knocking the wicked old woman into a muck-filled de-hairing pit; robbing a grave of a skull bone and burning it; failing to inform on a known traitor; collaborating with that traitor; and now planning to attack her legitimate master.

You don't have to worry about succumbing to the dark side, she thought hysterically. *You already have!*

Suddenly the workshop felt airless and confining. She hid the grimoire and the papers on nivol and went out, locking the door behind her. It was after midnight and the halls of the vast old mansion were empty. Though Sith was said to be a safe place, she feared to go out onto the streets at this time of night, however the mansion occupied a whole city block and had a rectangular courtyard in the middle. She went up to the top level, where a series of large semi-circular balconies served as viewing areas and watch posts.

A couple sat on a bench on the first balcony, their bodies entwined. She continued to the second, which was empty and faced east. Aviel sat on the bench, looking over the low stone rail at the great River Garr. It enclosed Sith in its two protecting arms then wound away east to Vilikshathûr and the coast of the Sea of Thurkad like a fat silver snake in the moonlight.

It was windy here, and chilly, and Aviel pulled her coat around her-self and scrunched up on the seat. Her bruised face was hot and ached down to the cheekbones. Could she do this wicked thing to her master? And if she did, would it be one step too far down the dark path?

A heavy tread made the balcony quiver. A huge shape was pacing along, limping a little. Just a guard. She resumed her mournful con-templation of the dark city, the shining river and her sadly stained little soul.

The footsteps stopped, then came towards her. "Aviel?"

She jumped and spun round, crying out, "W-who are you?"

"Didn't mean to alarm you," he said, stopping several yards away. "I'm Osseion. We met yesterday."

Relief flooded her, then her troubles overwhelmed her and, to her mortification, she began to cry. Osseion sat beside her, the bench creaking under his weight, and put an arm around her shoulders. For such a huge man he was remarkably gentle. He said nothing until she had finished and wiped her eyes.

"What happened to your face?"

She did not want to say. "I was taught not to tell tales."

"I've kept Mendark's secrets, even ten years after his death," said Osseion. "I can keep yours."

"Grand Master Tule beat me," she said in a low voice. "He hates me because I make scent potions. And because I'm a girl."

"Tule hates everyone because he's been a failure for the past fifty years."

"He says he can do whatever he wants to me. He ... he held my head under the hot washing water; I thought he was going to drown me. I ... I think I broke his nose."

Osseion gave her a squeeze. "You're entitled to defend yourself."

"But he won't teach me *anything* about alchemy," she wailed. "He just tells me to wash the equipment, over and over. And my work—" *Not a hint to your friends. Not even a whisper.*

"Don't tell me about it," Osseion said quietly. "It's urgent, and our survival relies on it; that's all I need to know."

"But I can't—"

"You have to find the quickest way to get it done. Nothing else matters—not the law, nor friendship, nor loyalty. Just your work."

He rose and paced off. Aviel remained there, thinking hard. Everyone was telling her the same thing. *It's the most important job in the world right now, and the most urgent,* Nadiril had said. *You have to find a way to learn everything you need to know from Tule ... and prevent him from hindering you.* Even Shand had told her to deal with her master.

She would make Essence of Ague right away, even if it took all night.

And in the morning, unless Grand Master Torsion Tule had miraculously become reasonable, she would use it on him.

At ten past nine in the morning the workshop door was thrust open, and Tule stood in the entrance, swaying. The right side of his body had a slight tremor, his nose was red and swollen, and the rage in his eyes topped even that which she had seen the previous day.

After studying her bruised face, his mouth twisted into a malicious rictus. His gaze swept the bench, the glassware and equipment, which was all where it had been when he left yesterday.

"You haven't done a thing!" he cried, stalking towards her. "Wash ... everything ... again ... now!" He raised a trembling fist and swung.

Aviel ducked but not quickly enough. His knuckles caught her left ear, where he had hit her yesterday, and she felt the swollen flesh tear. She scrambled backwards, her bad ankle twisted under her and she fell on her back. Tule, his face twisted in maniacal rage, raised a foot as if to stamp on her face. She rolled across the floor, but he came lurching after her.

Do it, now!

She felt in her pocket for the phial of Essence of Ague, levered the wooden stopper out with her thumbnail and, as he raised his foot again, flicked the scent potion up into his face, all ten drops of it.

Tule froze, staring at her. The drops were spattered across his chin and upper lip and she caught the dominant scents—mouldy, rotting lemons and a very old, desiccated mouse corpse.

"What ... you ... done?" choked Tule. "Dare ... attack ... your *master*?"

The scent potion did not seem to be working. Had she made a mistake? If he was unaffected, she was doomed. She came to her feet, staring at him, the warm blood from her torn ear trickling down the left side of her neck.

He let out an ear-piercing screech, went so still that she feared he had been paralysed, then shuddered wildly and toppled sideways. Instantly, and with scalp-crawling horror, Aviel knew that she had gone too far. Scent potions were only supposed to be sniffed, but it was on the skin under his nose and on his mouth. He was getting a far greater dose than she had intended. What if it killed him?

When Tule let out another screech and began to convulse on the floor, terror flooded her. People would come to investigate and discover what she'd done. She wet a rag and wiped his face again and again until all the scent potion was gone, then tossed the rag onto the hot coals under the water cauldron, at the back where it would quickly burn away.

She was shaking; she had smelled the scent potion and it was affecting her too. She tried to think—what else must she do to cover up her crime? The phial! She found the stopper, tossed it and the phial into the fire and raked the coals over them. Her hands were shaking badly now.

The grimoire! She closed it and hid it and scanned the bench where she had made the scent potion. She had washed up all her eye droppers but the phials containing eleven scented oils, the ingredients for the potion, still stood in a line. She put them in her scent box with all the other phials then hobbled back to Tule, stomach acid burning a track up to her throat, wondering what to do.

If he died, Tallia's forensic mancers would work out how Aviel had attacked him, and she would hang for murder. But if Tule recovered quickly he would inform on her and she would also be done for.

He grunted and gasped, then began shuddering so wildly that his brown teeth were clacking together. There was blood on his lower lip; he must have bitten his tongue. She was forcing a wooden spatula between his teeth when Tallia ran in, followed by Commander Janck.

Aviel stood up, feeling sick. Tallia studied her swollen and bruised face, her bleeding ear, then looked down at Tule.

"Speak," said Tallia.

Aviel told them how he had refused to teach her anything and kept hitting her.

Tallia's face hardened. "Are you telling me that, after all this time, you've made no progress whatsoever?"

"Yes," Aviel whispered.

"But you know how urgent this work is."

"He won't tell me anything. He doesn't believe nivol can ever be made."

"It's your job to convince him."

"With respect, Magister, that's *our* job," said Janck. "How can a kid be expected to deal with a fellow like Tule?"

"I rather suspect she *has* dealt with him," said Tallia, walking around his shuddering body. "What happened, Aviel? Leave nothing out."

She told them, up to the point where she had been lying on the floor and he had been about to stamp on her face. "Then he went all funny," she lied, "as if he'd had a seizure."

"Wouldn't surprise me," observed Janck. "He's a choleric man." He gave Aviel a sympathetic glance.

Tallia, who had always been friendly to Aviel, looked more forbidding than ever. She crouched and inspected Tule's face, sniffed and wrinkled her nose. Her head shot round and she stared at Aviel. *She knows!* Aviel thought. Her face grew hot; she prayed that the bruises would conceal it.

"Peculiar smell," said Tallia.

"Tule's breath stinks like a drain," said Janck dismissively. "Magister, our meeting grows urgent."

"Yes," Tallia said absently. "Would you call for a healer?"

Janck went out.

"We've long been friends, you and I," said Tallia, then paused.

Aviel had once done Tallia a great service, though the idea that she, an inexperienced girl, could ever be friends with the great Magister was preposterous.

"If we can't work as a team the enemy will soon overwhelm us," Tallia added. "Individuals are no use to me, Aviel, no matter how gifted. They cause more trouble than they're worth . . . if you take my meaning."

Aviel took it to mean that if Tallia discovered how Tule had been attacked, it would be the end for herself.

"Yes, Magister," she said. "But what am I to do?"

"Tule is a difficult man, but he's the only master alchemist we have. You've got to work with him."

"But he refuses to tell me anything I need to know."

Tallia frowned. "What do you need to know, precisely?"

Aviel showed her the key papers and parchments. "All the methods are full of obscure words and symbols, and abbreviations. I can't follow the instructions."

Tallia frowned. "A pity that Shand . . ." She broke off, shooting Aviel another keen glance.

Aviel's heart gave a convulsive thud and the blood that had surged to her face drained from it. Did Tallia suspect that she had spoken to Shand and was protecting his secret? Was that why she was being so hard?

"I'll send you an adviser," said Tallia. "He doesn't know anything about practical alchemy, but he's read all the books and he knows the words and symbols. He can help you until the grand master . . . gets better."

She gave Aviel another cold stare and went out. Shortly a healer ran in, followed by his assistants. They lifted Tule onto a stretcher and carried him away. He looked bad. And what if he died? What if she had *killed* her master?

It would add manslaughter to the list of crimes she had committed in the past two months. Or was it murder? If he died she might well be accused of murder. How quickly she had descended to the dark side.

26

WHAT DID THE LIFE OF A CRIPPLED GIRL MATTER?

"Earnis," the young man said, offering Aviel a large, solid hand.

She looked up at him. Being barely sixteen and a late developer, she had given little thought to the merits of the other sex, though she had to concede that he was worthy of further study. Earnis was a very handsome young man, taller than average, with twinkling cocoa-brown eyes, wavy chestnut hair and a square jaw along which the shadow of a heavy brown beard could be seen. His muscular arms were hairy, though not unattractively so, his voice was deep, and he looked altogether strong and solid and friendly—the very opposite of Grand Master Torsion Tule.

But a life of adversity had taught her to be wary. "What do you want?" Her voice sounded high and squeaky.

Earnis smiled. "Tallia sent me. I'm to teach you the language and symbols of alchemy."

"Oh!"

He was still holding out his hand. She extended her own. His palm was hard but his handshake gentle.

"What do you know about it?" she added. Tallia had said there were no alchemists in the west any more.

He looked around the crowded workshop with its shelves of bottles and jars, racks of tubes, beakers and phials, and the benches full of incredibly clean equipment. "About the practical side—about actually *doing* alchemy—I know nothing at all," he said cheerfully. "But I know the language and symbols, and the philosophy behind it."

She frowned. "You look more like a soldier to me."

He laughed. "I've just done a month of army training; I'll be sent to fight the enemy before too long."

And unless I can make some nivol, quick, you'll be killed with everyone else, she thought with a shiver.

"I have to make . . . something, urgently," she said. "I don't have time to learn the philosophy of alchemy."

"And I don't have time to teach you, because it takes many years to master and I'm far from a master myself. What do you need to know?"

Aviel folded over her papers and parchments so he could not see the titles. "Er . . ."

He glanced over his shoulder, checking that no one could see into the workshop. "Tallia said you're trying to make the alchemical fluid called nivol. Without knowing that, I'd be little help to you."

"Oh! Well, I'm used to reading recipes for scent potions but the methods are all like this." On the top parchment she indicated a large symbol consisting of several concentric circles with smaller symbols around the outside. "It's gibberish."

The smile left his face; she had offended him. "Alchemy is an ancient discipline, powerful and dangerous," he said stiffly. "And its adepts have often been persecuted; in some countries it's forbidden on pain of a most unpleasant death. Long ago, the grand masters of alchemy developed its language and symbols for three reasons: to protect dangerous secrets from the reckless, greedy and ignorant; to protect their art from those who would debase or destroy it; and to protect themselves."

He paused, then, before she could speak, went on in a slow voice, now devoid of colour. "For the same reason, it is forbidden for adepts to teach the language and symbols of alchemy to outsiders, *under any circumstances*."

"Are you saying you'll be punished for telling me?"

"I'll be ostracised, cast out and for ever cut off from my colleagues all over the world. And there's no way back." Earnis forced a smile. "But Santhenar stands in peril and we have to make sacrifices." He looked her up and down. "Extraordinary," he said softly. "But still impossible."

"What do you mean?" said Aviel, though she understood all too well.

"Alchemy is an aspect of the Secret Art, and using it involves far more than getting the techniques right. It's also a mental disciple where understanding the use of power, and controlling it, is vital. Even for those who have the gift, and they are few, alchemy is an art long in the learning—and *fraught*."

She stared at him. "You're saying I'm a deluded fool with no hope of succeeding and every chance of being killed by forces I can't understand."

"I don't think *you're* deluded," he said quietly.

"But you think Tallia is, for giving me the job?"

His cheeks coloured, then he looked away. "That's not for me to say. We're desperate and . . . maybe our leaders think it's worth the risk."

Aviel swallowed. So Tallia, Malien and Nadiril had little hope that she could succeed, but it was worth the gamble. What did the life of a crippled girl matter when the whole world was in danger?

She slumped on the couch, her heart thumping leadenly. If they had so little faith in her, how could she believe in herself? "Then what's the point?"

Earnis came across at once, looking chagrined, and lifted her to her feet. "Don't take any notice of my silly maunderings. Tallia chose you because of your strength, your courage and the great gift you've already proven. No one can argue with those things, and if anyone can do it, you can."

Aviel scowled and looked away. Did he think she was that easy to get round? He had said it right the first time.

"Shall we begin?" he said with fake cheer. "What do you need to know?"

She forced herself to focus. "I need the full list of ingredients and how each one has to be collected, prepared or purified. Then I've got to have the recipe for making nivol."

"That you call it a recipe shows how little you understand about alchemy."

"Or want to know," Aviel said tartly.

He frowned. "Then why——"

"I'm doing as I've been ordered as best I can, and it's already cost me more than you can know."

"It's cost Grand Master Tule too," he said quietly.

"Is he . . . all right?"

His look was frosty now. "Very far from it. Let's get to work."

By the end of the day Earnis had gone through the papers and parchments Shand had said were useful and had helped Aviel compile two lists. The first contained the thirty-seven ingredients that the simplest and quickest formula for making nivol required, and the second the step-by-step methods for purifying and refining certain key ingredients.

She ticked items off the first list. Sixteen were common alchemical substances she had in the workshop, such as Koboldt, Spiritus Fumans and the highly corrosive Oil of Vitriol, though others, such as Colcothar, Butter of Antimony and Fulminating Gold she would have to make.

"It's going to take ages to make all these," said Aviel, studying the other ingredients on the list in dismay. "I'd have to learn the techniques, and some of them can take weeks."

"Many of them can be bought if you know where to shop," said Earnis.

"I was told alchemy was almost unknown in the west these days."

"It is, but many alchemical substances are imported and used in healing, tanning, for making blasting powders . . . and a hundred other purposes, not necessarily legal. I know all the apothecaries and chymical suppliers in Sith." Again he glanced over his shoulder, then lowered his voice. "And there are other sources. Less . . . *official.*"

"I'm not buying stuff from bad people," said Aviel. "How would I know if it's what they say it is?"

"I wouldn't purchase from criminals," Earnis said hastily. "But not all the laws of Sith are . . . um, conducive to certain lines of business. There are reliable suppliers, people with a reputation for quality, who just skirt the rules a little."

"I don't like the idea."

"It's the only way. If you had to make every chymical you need, to the required purity, you wouldn't get the job done inside two years." He glanced down at his list. "All these chymicals can be bought." He ticked off another thirteen items. "That's twenty-nine. And these five—" he circled them "—you will have to prepare fresh, immediately before use."

Aviel studied the methods for preparing the five items. "I think I can do that."

"That's the easy part," said Earnis.

"What do you mean?"

He tapped the parchment. "The last two ingredients are very rare and can't be obtained in Sith. They must be collected from where they occur, far away."

"What are they?"

"A perfect golden brimstone, the length of the palm of the alchemist's hand."

Aviel studied her small hand, then indicated a jar on the highest shelf. "That's full of brimstones, though most are broken."

"They won't do at all. Brimstone is common but rarely found in perfect crystals, however the only place *golden brimstones* can be found is Grund."

"Where's that?" Aviel's knowledge of geography was feeble.

"In the arid land called Taltid, a hundred leagues south-west of Sith across the Sea of Thurkad. Grund is a bitumen seep, one of many in that land. It's been used since ancient times, and around the edges there are veins containing golden brimstones, though it won't be easy to obtain one."

"Why not?"

"The people who own and profit from the seep consider them to be unlucky. Cursed, in fact."

She laughed hollowly. "So am I." She peered at the last item on the page. "Colophony from a bubble-bark pine. What's colophony?"

"Rosin—the hard stuff that remains after distilling off the volatile oils from tree resin. But a bubble-bark pine?" He shook his head. "They're thought to be extinct."

"Can I use any other kind of colophony?"

"No," said Earnis.

"Why not? There are lots of different kinds of pine trees."

"Nivol is an incredibly potent substance, and to make such things every ingredient must be exactly as the formula states. The alchemical power of colophony from the bubble-bark pine undoubtedly comes from its incredible rarity."

"But if it's extinct, nivol can never be made," said Aviel.

"*Thought* to be extinct, I said. I'll ask old Hammibas, the apothecary. No one knows more than he does about such things." He headed for the door.

"Wait," said Aviel. "That's only thirty-six." She turned the page. On the other side she had written down the last ingredient, used in the final step that created nivol. "Three drams of Archeus of Eidolon, whatever that is."

Earnis's thick hair stood up and he took a step backwards, eyes wide. "No!" he gasped. "That's . . . too much. I can't help you any more."

He turned and reeled towards the door.

Without thinking, and at great cost to her bad ankle, Aviel grabbed him by the arm. "Wait! You've got to tell me what it is."

He caught her wrists in his big hands and for a moment she thought he was going to fling her from him. He was gasping, fighting for air. He bent double, his throat rasping, put his head between his knees for a while, then slowly straightened up, his tanned face drained of all colour.

"Archeus . . . of Eidolon," he panted, "isn't an alchemical substance at all. It's a *necromantic* one."

The dark side crept a little closer, and Aviel imagined the floor had tilted beneath her feet as if to slide her down into an abyss from which there would be no escaping. "What is it?" she whispered.

"Spectral blood distilled from a ghost vampire, and it's one of the darkest substances of all. Perhaps *the* darkest."

Aviel shivered. Why did her work keep leading her away from the scent work she loved and down this terrible path? "Are vampires *real*, then?"

"Very uncommon but very real. And sometimes, very rarely, when a vampire that feeds on the blood of the recently dead is itself killed, a ghost vampire will form. They're exceedingly dangerous—far more so than any living vampire."

"Are you saying that to get Archeus of Eidolon, I'd have to catch a ghost vampire, kill it and distil the spectral blood from its spirit essence?"

"No. It has to be distilled while the ghost vampire is 'alive' . . . but that's unthinkable."

"As unthinkable as allowing the Merdrun to wipe us out and take Santhenar for themselves?"

He was sweating so profusely that it was trickling down his face. He staggered to the settee and collapsed onto it, his chest heaving.

"If I'm distilling the spirit essence of a ghost vampire," she added, "what will that do to it?"

"Assuming you could, conceivably, do such a thing—" everything about Earnis's manner said that it was impossible "—because it will fight you with all its terrible power, it will die very horribly." He gave her another assessing glance, then looked away, shaking his head.

Cockroaches scuttled up and down her spine. "Where can ghost vampires be found?"

He looked evasive. "How would I know? I'm not a necromancer."

"I think you do know. You've got to tell me."

"It's said ... where lots of people have been killed. Battlefields, massacre sites, cities shattered by earthquakes or tidal waves, plague pits—that sort of place. Ghost vampires are incredibly rare though ..." He trailed off, swallowing hard.

He knows, she thought, *but he's afraid to say*. "This is really important, Earnis. Do you know of any place where there *is* a ghost vampire?"

"Only one." Shudders racked him. "Rogues Render."

"Where's that?"

"I don't know," he said almost inaudibly, though Aviel was sure he was lying.

"What do you know about the ghost vampire there?"

"His name ... is Lumillal. He's very, very dangerous. And that's all I'm going to say."

She perched on a stool, rubbed her throbbing ankle, then studied the circled items on the list of ingredients. "Even if you can buy all these from your unlawful sources, how can you be sure each chymical is what they say it is?"

"I know who's reputable and who's not. I'll get them straight away." He rose.

"Wait. I've got to see Tallia."

"What for?"

Aviel could not bear to work here an hour longer; the workshop was tainted by Tule's brutality, and what she had done to him. She had to get as far away as possible. If she succeeded in making nivol her crimes might be forgiven. And if she failed, perhaps she would not come back.

She took a deep breath. "Tallia is getting more sky ships made in the shipyards. I need one big enough to carry all my equipment. Urgently."

"Why?" said Earnis.

"Even if you can buy those thirteen chymicals, the only way I can hope to make nivol in time is to work on it while we're looking for the last three ingredients. Everything has to be ready by the time we get the final ingredient, the Archeus of Eidolon, from ..."

His hair was standing on end again. "A desperate and deadly ghost vampire."

27

IDIOT! IMBECILE!

Dimly, over the roaring in Llian's ears, he heard Ifoli shouting and Regg bellowing, but he could not make out what they were saying. Was there any way to save himself? If he went with the current, maybe he could get to shore further around the island. He turned but the current was sweeping him east, while the band of mangrove trees curved away to the north.

Regg and Ifoli were still shouting. "There! There!" Regg bellowed.

Llian kicked himself up in the water until his head and shoulders were exposed and made out a reef of dark rock that ran out from the shoreline for fifty yards or so. The falling tide had just exposed its top. Could he reach it if he angled across the current? Possibly, though it would be an exhausting swim.

He headed for the reef. The rock was jagged and no doubt covered in sharp shells and barnacles. If a wave drove him into it he might break bones and would certainly gash himself badly, but it was his only hope. Llian put his head down and swam as hard as he could, but soon saw that the current would sweep him past a few yards from the end of the reef.

He swam harder but did not have the strength to maintain it; swimming against the current a few minutes ago had exhausted him. There was nothing he could do to save himself.

He was regretting his stupidity when Regg hurtled along the broken reef, slipping and skidding and risking going in himself, still carrying his fishing rod.

If the reef extended out beneath the water there was a faint possibility that Llian could grab it and haul himself out, but as the current swept him closer he saw that there was no rough water past the end—it fell sheer into deep water.

He made a last desperate effort, which did not even gain him a foot. Regg had reached the end of the reef and was standing there, rod outstretched, but it was not nearly long enough. Llian was carried past four yards away and the current took him east towards the Sea of Qwale.

Thwack! Something cracked him hard on the back of the head. Then he was jerked backwards, the current spun him around and he felt the coat pulling off his shoulders. Regg had done a perfect cast—the sinker had bounced off Llian's head and the big hook had caught in his coat. He wrapped his arms around himself to hold his coat on so Regg could pull him in.

But neither the line nor the rod was designed for such a heavy catch. The line was wire-taut and the rod bent to breaking point. If either snapped . . .

"Swim!" yelled Ifoli, who had come up beside Regg. "Take the weight off the line."

The current was a little slower here, in the lee of the reef. With the last of his strength he swam for his life. The tension on the line eased a little, Regg hauled him to the edge of the reef, Ifoli crouched and stretched down her arm and between the two of them they got him onto the rocks with no more damage than half a dozen barnacle gouges down his arms and legs.

"Idiot!" she yelled. "Imbecile!" She threw her arms around Llian and burst into tears.

"Thank you," he gasped. "Thank you both." Too weak to stand up, he slumped onto the wet rock, shuddering.

"What the hell was that all about?" said Ifoli.

"Sulien! A great beast had her in its claws. I just . . . panicked."

His teller's gift could not stop imagining her fate—Sulien mauled by that thranx-like creature, eaten by it—but it was unbearable to talk about it. He choked out what he had seen. Ifoli crouched down with her arms over her face, rocking back and forth. Regg smashed a length of driftwood against the rocks until he had reduced it to splinters.

"She's a thousand miles away," Llian said wretchedly. "There's nothing I can do." It was his job to protect her and he could not.

He had to try and find her, hopeless though it was, but how? The unreality zone covered the shoreline here too and a pale bulge was creeping down the wet rock towards them, far slower than it moved across dry land. There must be something about water, or salt water, that was inimical to it.

But the reef was drying in the sun and soon the unreality zone would have a clear passage. He checked the gravel spit—the middle was still underwater though its location was clearly outlined by a line of breakers. They went back up the reef until the water to either side was only waist deep, jumped in and waded towards the spit.

"Tide's falling rapidly," said Ifoli. "Another twenty minutes . . ."

"I can't wait that long," Llian choked.

The sun went behind a cloud and in the shadows he saw that the shallow water next to them was glowing. The unreality zone was almost on them.

"Come on!" said Regg.

They swam to the spit, which was now exposed for several hundred yards and glowing pale yellow for half that distance, but as they approached it the yellow crept their way—the unreality zone was determined to get them.

"Stay in the water," said Ifoli.

They waded along beside the spit, towards Mollymoot. The current tugged at Llian's legs as if it yearned to take him again, but he had to get across. The tide was running out rapidly now. To the west a hundred yards of mudflat was exposed outside the band of mangroves. The water shoaled in front of him and he went another ten yards, then ten more. Come on, *come on*!

Suddenly the waters parted, the whole spit was exposed, and he took off without looking back. Regg and Ifoli could look after each other; he had to get to the mainland. He ran in a weak-kneed stagger for Mollymoot, thinking to borrow money from Dilly then head to the nearest town to look for passage south, but by the time he reached her house it was too late; the tide was already creeping across the causeway to Meldorin. He slumped on the steps outside her front door and watched as the sea robbed him of his last hope.

"I could not have helped you anyway," said Dilly, after he, Ifoli and Regg had told their stories. "The mayor turned up yesterday, collecting for the war fund, and I gave her every coin I could spare."

On a little stone-flagged terrace at the rear of the house they lunched on bowls of clam soup and fresh bread dipped in oil. Llian's journal, which had been soaked, was drying in the sun. The soup smelled delicious but he ate mechanically, unable to taste anything.

"It's hopeless," he said dully. "Even if I could get to Shazabba, and had the coin to mount a search in the middle of winter—"

"You could spend the rest of your life searching and find nothing," said Dilly. "But you've got powerful friends, Llian. Ask them for help."

"I've got no way to contact them," he said, feeling utterly helpless.

"Ifoli does."

"I'm afraid to try again," said Ifoli.

"Shame on you, girl! Do your duty by your friend."

Judging by the look on Ifoli's face she had never thought of Llian as a friend, but she took off her remaining earring, gave it a twist and sat there, shuddering.

He was putting the journal into its bag when he noticed that the leather spine was scratched and scored near the bottom, as if it had been rubbing against something. He felt along the thick leather base of the bag. Something sharp was embedded there and he dug it out with his knife and laid it on the table. It was a little brass cone, about an inch high, with a flat brass base.

"Where did that come from?"

Llian weighed it in his hand; it wasn't heavy enough to be solid brass, and he saw that the base was designed to be removed. He was about to lever it open with the point of his knife when Ifoli said sharply, "Put it down!"

He laid it on the table. "What's the matter?"

"Move away from the table, everyone."

Dilly, Regg and Llian rose and moved to the other side of the terrace. Ifoli studied the little object, lifted it carefully and put it down again, then picked up Llian's bag and poked her little finger into a small tear he had not noticed in the base.

"What is it?" said Regg.

"It's the core of the Command device," said Ifoli. "When the device burst, killing Esea, the core must have embedded itself in the base of the bag."

"Is it dangerous?" said Llian.

"Unick sometimes booby-trapped his devices. But Tallia may be able to do something with it."

They returned to the table. Rather gingerly Llian wrapped the cone and put it in one of the pockets of his bag.

Ifoli picked up her earring but put it down again. "I'm scared."

"We're miles from the stone," said Dilly. "Get on with it."

Ifoli took off her necklace and twisted the pearl. Her eyes lost focus and the tendons in her neck stood out, then she mastered herself and said softly, "Great-grandfather?"

Ten seconds went by, then twenty, then his wheezy old voice came from the earring. "Where are you?"

"Mollymoot, with Llian. Great-grandfather, we've seen the summon stone. It's on top of Demondifang and it's huge."

"Say no more!" It was Tallia's voice. "We're coming."

The earring went dead. Ifoli twisted each pearl back the other way, then clapped a hand to her back.

Dilly inspected the lump, which looked as it had when Llian had checked it at the campsite, though it was larger and hotter. "I don't like that at all. I should call the midwife to cut it open."

"No!" Ifoli said sharply.

"If it gets any bigger—"

"It's reacting to mancery. I need a healer who understands the Secret Art."

The following day the lump had disappeared and Ifoli was almost her normal self again. The weather turned, the westerly wind died away and the causeway was open every day at low tide, though Llian did not cross it. Without a copper grint to his name he had no way to get to Shazabba and no hope of finding Sulien if he did. She was probably dead, and Karan too, and he struggled to find a reason for going on. Not even his journal could console him any more.

A week later, at dawn, he was woken by a colossal racket outside his window. A ramshackle sky ship was hovering not thirty yards away, though it was nothing like Malien's sleek craft. The cabin was an ugly rectangular box with strips of canvas hanging off it, the airbag was made of a variety of different-coloured fabrics, and the rotors had an alarming rattle. But with Nadiril and Lilis waving from the doorway, it was a most welcome sight.

"Can you take me to Shazabba?" he said the moment the craft landed on a small flat patch at the back of Dilly's vegetable garden, and Nadiril, Lilis and Tallia had alighted.

"To join your partner in crime?" Tallia said coldly. "Not a chance."

"What are you talking about?"

"Karan and Yggur stole Malien's sky ship," she snapped, "and it's put our defences back by weeks."

"Karan's all right?" he cried, embracing her.

Tallia pushed him away, though she managed a small smile. "She killed the magiz on Cinnabar but couldn't stop her from opening the gate. Karan was well the last time Malien got through to her, about a week ago."

"She might have found Sulien," he said desperately. "I have to keep hoping."

Nadiril looked up. "Uh-oh!"

Dilly came storming down the yard, swinging a straw broom menacingly, as if she planned to swat him over the side of the hill with it. "How dare you involve Ifoli in your deadly schemes!" she hissed. "Never again, you old fool!"

"I tried to talk her out of it," he said feebly.

"Not hard enough!"

"No. It was very wrong of me."

"Excuse me!" said Ifoli. "Being a double agent was my idea."

"And I should have refused you. But we'll talk about it later," he said to Dilly. "We need their news and everyone needs ours."

Nadiril filled them in, briefly, on the war situation, and that Shand had fled and was a traitor.

"Shand!" Llian couldn't take it in. "I don't believe it."

"He as good as admitted it."

"What are you going to do now?"

"We're moving our headquarters to the Great Library," said Tallia.

"It's only an eight-hour flight from here. And a lot closer to the enemy."

"Where are they?"

"A long way north, somewhere in the western tropics. With the Aachim's help we're building more sky ships, and we're sailing part of our army north to Framan, the port at the mouth of the River Zur."

"How many troops do you have?"

"Twenty-four thousand, and the numbers are growing fast. Though few have combat experience."

"Are you planning on attacking the Merdrun, wherever they are?"

"Sending an army thousands of miles by sea isn't practical," said Tallia. "Besides, if the enemy can reopen their gate they could turn up in Thurkad or some other vital place without notice."

"Then what are you going to do?"

"Find a way to destroy the summon stone, of course."

"Is this any help?" Llian put the core of the Command device on the table.

Tallia started. "Where did you get that?"

"I found it in the base of my manuscript bag." He explained. "Can the device be remade?"

"I'll send for our best practical mancers," said Tallia. "Ifoli, you can advise them based on what you know of Unick's original design."

"You'll also need a black crystal," said Ifoli.

"What kind? There are lots of black minerals."

"I have no idea."

28

IF YOU'RE NOT GOING TO EAT ME

As the flying beast carried her away Sulien was sure she was going to wet herself—or worse. Her hammering heart was threatening to tear itself in two, the backs of her hands were tingling and there was no strength in her arms or legs. The monster was going to eat her.

They were hundreds of feet in the air now and it was still climbing, though cold rain was battering her face and she could not tell where the beast was taking her. She dared not struggle in case it dropped her. And yet, falling to her death would be better than being torn to pieces and fed to its young ... No! Karan had taught her that while you were alive there was hope. And from Llian, *never* give up!

"Where ... you taking me?" she croaked.

The creature looked down as if surprised that she knew how to talk, then flew faster, sinews creaking and leathery wing membranes flapping. The rain was lighter here, and colder, and there were snowy peaks in the distance. It was taking her into the high mountains.

Its talons had closed around her waist so tightly that she could not draw a full breath, and several of the points had torn through her skin, very painfully. It touched her on the forehead with the tip of a claw, said, "Sleep!" and she sank into a well of darkness.

When Sulien woke, it felt as though a long time had passed. It was dark; she lay on rough rock, and the smoky air reeked of the monster that had carried her away. A fire burning in the distance shed just enough light to reveal a rocky roof high above. She was in a huge cave.

Bulky winged shadows shifted around the fire—more of the beasts. They seemed to be talking. What did they want her for? She would hardly make a meal for the smallest of them, but perhaps they fed their young on live prey ...

Sulien swallowed, and her throat was so dry that it rasped. She was unhurt save for three very painful claw punctures in her middle, though her leg muscles were aching and the blistered soles of her feet throbbed. She was trying to see a way out when all the beasts rose at once and her captor strode her way, his toe claws making scratching sounds on the rock. She tried to run but her legs refused to move.

"Going somewhere?" His rumbling voice was so deep that she could feel it in her bones. He caught her around the waist with one hand, carried her to the other beasts and put her down in the middle of their ragged circle.

Waves of colour shimmered across their scaly skin, camouflaging them. There were thirteen of them, six males and seven females, and the females were just as big and deadly as the males.

"Are you . . . going to eat me?" she quavered.

Several of the beasts laughed. "We prefer our meat mature," said a massive female with red-gold eyes the size of oranges and a green crystal on a thong around her neck. "You wouldn't have any flavour."

"We could smoke her," said a small male with half a dozen teeth missing from his lower jaw and a large chunk out of his right nostril.

"Don't toy with the child," said the male who had carried her here. "Old-human girl, my name is Ghyll and I lead—"

"Equally with I!" the massive female said sharply. Her red-gold eyes steamed and violent jags of yellow and purple raced across her skin.

Waves of gentle, calming pastel colours ebbed and flowed across Ghyll's yard-wide chest. It had to be some kind of skin speech. "We, that is Taitt and I, jointly lead this clan of lyrinx. We—"

"If—if you're not going to eat me, why have you brought me here?" said Sulien, very politely.

"How dare you interrupt!" hissed Taitt, her skin colours clashing violently. "Be silent, grub, or I will feed you to my pups!"

Sulien envisaged that gory fate as only a sensitive could. Would Taitt divide her up first, or toss her to the pups and let them fight over her? She choked.

Ghyll scowled at Taitt before turning back to Sulien. "You're an important little girl," he said. "Well connected. We invited you here because we can help each other."

"You didn't invite me, you kidnapped me," she snapped.

"I saved you from your hunters."

The word *saved* was debatable. "How did you find me?"

"I homed in on your gift. It's the strongest I've ever sensed in an old human."

A gift she did not understand, but needed to. "How can we help each other?"

Ghyll exchanged glances with Taitt. She did not speak, but waves of orange and black washed across her front.

"The Merdrun are our ancient enemies from the void," said Ghyll. "We fought them many a time—"

"Gergrig said they've never been beaten, in ten thousand years of war," said Sulien.

The lyrinx rose as one, their great wings cracking and their teeth bared, and their skin colours flared so brightly that they lit up the cavern for fifty yards. Sulien let out a squeak and cowered against the floor.

"They never beat us!" hissed Taitt. "Not once!"

"And the last time we fought," said Ghyll, "the Merdrun broke and ran."

Sulien slowly came to her feet, staring at Ghyll and Taitt. Were they offering to help? The aid of such mighty creatures could win the war— if they were telling the truth. She thought they were, for she could always tell if people were good or bad inside, but did that sense apply to the lyrinx as well? But what if it was a trick? "What are you saying?"

"If we joined forces . . ." said Ghyll.

"As equals!" snapped Taitt.

"Will you give your people our message—that we offer our friendship and aid in the greatest battle of all?" said Ghyll.

"Why would you help us?" Sulien said carefully. "It's not your fight."

"It will be if you lose," he said gravely.

"Um . . . But what do you want in return?"

"The gift of a small part of Santhenar. And a treaty guaranteeing our lands, for ever."

It seemed a small price to pay for their aid, though even a nine-year-old girl could see the conflicts that would create. "I can't offer—"

"Treaties take patient negotiation between equals, compromise, and benefits to both sides. But you know the greatest people in the west. Will you speak for us?"

Sulien looked down at her ruined boots. An alliance with the lyrinx, who knew the enemy and had never been beaten by them, seemed like the answer to a prayer. But could they be trusted? They looked bad, yet her gift did not detect anything evil about them, just a desperate hunger for a safe home.

"And in return, you'll help us fight the Merdrun?" she said.

"Once the treaty is signed," said Ghyll.

29

LIKE ALL OUR OTHER ENEMIES

Karan's clung desperately to her seat in the sky ship. A lyrinx was going to eat Sulien. "She's dead," she moaned. She wanted to hurl herself out the door.

"Not yet," Yggur said coldly. "Pull yourself together! Track her."

"I don't know where to begin."

That was the brat, calling to its mother! It was Gergrig's voice. *Can you find her?*

Someone let out a high, nerve-rasping giggle. Empuly, Karan thought.

She's in the land called Salliban, said Jaguly.

And it's hundreds of miles long.

Narrowing, said Jaguly. A long pause. *A hundred miles.* Another pause of several minutes. *Sixty miles . . . twenty-five.*

Still too big an area, said Gergrig.

Then the voices were gone.

"I think I know that city," said Yggur, clamping his hands around his head and closing his eyes. "A square, stepped pyramid, and a dome collapsed to a broad arch. It's Hessular!"

"Can you find it on the map?" said Karan.

"I have it on this map." Yggur tapped his forehead. "It's forty miles south-south-east."

"But Sulien isn't there any more."

"The lyrinx's lair won't be far away. Find her!"

He drove the sky ship south at a furious pace. Karan was struggling to regain her sense of Sulien when she heard Gergrig again.

I'm troubled by the brat's cry. What did it mean?

Who cares? The listless voice had to be the apathetic Unbuly. *Something's got her and she'll soon be dead.*

Before she dies, said Gergrig, *we've got to know the names of everyone she's told about our weakness. We've got to hunt them down as well. Empuly, link to the brat and find out why she cried for help.*

Karan heard no more for the best part of an hour, then Empuly moaned.

What is it? cried Gergrig. *What do you see?*

Karan sensed Empuly thrashing her arms and legs in a fit, then an image flashed into her own mind so clearly that she could see the detail of the lyrinx's scales, the patterns in its great, intelligent eyes, and a thread of white sinew caught between its rows of teeth. She cried, "No!"

Yggur cut the rotors and the sky ship slowed and stopped, wallowing in the bumpy air.

What's a lyrinx doing on Santhenar? hissed Gergrig.

He sounded alarmed. There was a long pause in which Karan could sense the triplets' inner turmoil.

What did your predecessor magiz know about this? said Gergrig.

After some minutes of silence Jaguly spoke. *The lyrinx reached Santhenar . . . ten years ago*, she said slowly, as if struggling to read the clouded memories of the dead. *When the Way Between the Worlds was opened and we first saw this world. Why does it matter?*

We fought the lyrinx an aeon ago and they were fierce, clever enemies, our greatest.

But . . . why were they not exterminated like all our other foes?

They were based in a place that could not be taken without losing over half our number, and our ancestors had other enemies to fight. Now I wish they had taken those casualties and extinguished the lyrinx for ever. What if they join forces with Santhenar?

Jaguly giggled. *What can a handful of lyrinx do?*

Gergrig did not reply. Karan glanced at Yggur, who shrugged.

Lord Gergrig, said Empuly. *I've caught a very strange call.*

Who from?

One of the base-born scum the brat was travelling with. Whelm, they call

themselves. A woman, Yetchah, used the child's cry to contact our previous
magiz, not knowing she was dead, and the call came to me.

Karan sat bolt upright, knowing what was coming. Twelve years ago
her own gift had been used as a bridge between the Whelm and their
master, Rulke, and look at the ruin that had caused.

Yes? Gergrig said impatiently.

The Whelm want you for their master. They swear you will have no more
perfect servants.

Gergrig let out a derisive bark of laughter. *Merdrun have no need of*
servants—only slaves.

They promise to obey your every order, without question. Yetchah says they
know where the lyrinx's lair is—a cave near a nearby glacier. They offer to
take back the child, force her to link so you can interrogate her, then kill her.

That pleasure is reserved to me, said Gergrig.

Yetchah says the whole Whelm nation, twenty-five thousand, is hunting the
brat. And once she's dead they will fight on your behalf. They are relentless.

Why not? he mused. *Let them serve—for as long as we need them.*

And then?

We will treat them like all our other enemies. Then Gergrig and the
triplets were gone.

"What are we going to do?" said Karan, so afraid that every nerve
stung. If the lyrinx didn't eat Sulien the Whelm would kill her—if the
triplets didn't get to her first.

"Find Hessular, then get to the lyrinx before they do."

Half an hour later the sky ship was over the ruins of the half-
drowned city. "No sign of the Whelm," said Yggur. "They've gone
after her."

"How are we going to find her?"

He hovered over the arch and slowly rotated the sky ship. "Stop me
when you know which direction the lyrinx was heading."

"There," said Karan, pointing towards three peaks that stood rather
higher than the rest of the range.

He climbed to the base of the clouds and headed for the peaks. A
quarter of an hour later they were flying low over a pair of glaciers that
ground their way down between walls of broken grey rock.

"Keep a sharp lookout," said Yggur. "Lyrinx are heavy creatures; where they've gone to ground there will be signs."

"If they're so heavy, how can they fly?"

"Via the Secret Art, though few can use it for any other purpose."

"Lucky there's only a handful of them," said Karan. "But once they breed . . . If there were thousands of lyrinx, what chance would we have?"

"We've got more than enough real threats to worry about."

"I can't see any sign of the Whelm."

"It'll take them hours to get here. Any lyrinx tracks?"

"Yes, there, running down towards the glacier."

Yggur set the sky ship down several miles away, hidden behind upthrust slabs of ice. They donned heavy coats, gloves and hoods, made sure their weapons were ready for use, and tied the vessel down.

"Out!" said Yggur, tipping Hingis out of his hammock with one foot.

"Are you sure?" said Karan.

"I'm not leaving him here to sabotage the sky ship again, or steal it."

Hingis studied Yggur with empty eyes but said nothing.

They headed down the glacier, then onto the broken wall of the valley. Below them the lyrinx tracks plunged into a gap at a point where the side of the glacier had pulled away from the rock.

Down they went for more than a hundred yards, the ice now looming precariously above them. She eyed it uneasily. The glacier, which was in slow but relentless motion, creaked and groaned as it moved, opening crevasses with reverberating cracking sounds only to slam them shut again. Ahead, a rectangular tunnel had been cut into the base of the ice.

"It's not safe," said Hingis, who was gasping and blue around the lips.

"What do you care?" Yggur said coldly. "You want to die anyway."

"Not crushed under a million tons of ice."

"You were happy to see us smashed and burned if the sky ship crashed," Karan said coldly. There was no room in her heart for anything but finding Sulien—if it was not too late. "Stop whining."

"I'll go first," said Yggur. "There may be traps."

He headed in and, after a moment's hesitation, Karan followed.

"How can they live down here?" said Hingis from behind her. "No one can know when the ice is sound or when it's going to collapse."

The tunnel became a triangular passage lit by pallid grey-blue light that leached all colour from their faces. It looked like a crevasse that had been opened out, and Karan did not like it at all. The cracked ice creaked and groaned all around them and jagged lumps kept falling from the roof and walls. The forces down here must be immense—perhaps enough to snap the crevasse shut and smear them against the iron-hard ice.

Had the lyrinx brought Sulien this way? Or had it already eaten her? There were no marks on the floor and the air had no smell; it was too cold.

After a mile or so the passage passed from the ice into banded grey and white rock and sloped upwards. Yggur studied the walls. "This is freshly cut. Can't be more than a year old. Can you smell anything? Your senses are keener than mine."

"There's a faint rank odour, not one I've ever smelled before," said Karan.

"Go and have a look. We'll make a plan."

What about traps? Karan gulped, then felt her way up into absolute darkness.

The further she went the milder the temperature became, and the stronger the rank odour. Suddenly she caught another, horrifyingly familiar smell—meat hanging in a coolroom. She stifled a shriek and fought the sickening terror that threatened to overwhelm her. It was well-aged meat and must have been hung for weeks. Not a freshly killed girl.

She passed along a sinuous passage, still climbing, then another, and a faint orange light appeared in the distance—some form of mage light—and beyond it a log fire. She stopped, her heart thudding slowly. Dare she go on? If there were guards out, they would see her before she made them out against the light. But Sulien could be up there; she had to keep going.

With every step she expected to be discovered, caught, killed! Another corner. The light was brighter ahead and the passage wider and higher.

And then she saw her. Sulien was alive, but surrounded by lyrinx. Karan's knees gave, relief warring with terror. They hadn't harmed her yet, but they were monsters; they might do anything.

She backed away, sick with dread. Yggur was a great mancer but not even he could free Sulien away from so many lyrinx.

"She's up there," she croaked when she reached Yggur and Hingis. "In a broad cavern with several passages leading off the far side. Couldn't see how far they went."

"How many lyrinx?" said Hingis, speaking for the first time in hours.

"Thirteen, and all staring at Sulien as if they can't wait to eat her. I don't see what we can do, Yggur. I couldn't even take on a *baby* lyrinx."

"I don't know." He rubbed his eyes. "But we'll go up."

Karan led the way, knowing it was hopeless. She had a knife and knew how to use it, but it would be no use against an armoured lyrinx. And she had no faith in Hingis. No one could rely on a man who just wanted to die.

As she rounded the last corner and the orange-lit cavern opened up before her the lyrinx rose together, blocking her view of Sulien. Most headed towards one of the shaded passages but a big female came the other way, towards Karan. She wore a heavy blade on her right hip but did not need it; the retractable talons on her hands were six inches long.

Yggur retreated around the corner into the dark. "Should've expected they'd guard the way in."

"Have you got any kind of a plan?" said Karan.

"Hingis will confuse the guard with an illusion. I'll take care of her, silently, and we'll go up. Hingis will craft another illusion and I'll attack the lyrinx with my most powerful mancery, giving you the chance to get Sulien away. If we're pursued, I'll bring the tunnel down behind us and we run for it."

"Not much of a plan," muttered Hingis.

"Got a better one?" Yggur said in a frigid voice.

"How long to prepare the illusion?" said Karan.

"It's ready," said Hingis. "All I have to do is release it. But there's only so much power I can draw from this—" he looked down at his meagre, twisted body, "—and when it's gone the illusion will fail. Ready?"

No, thought Karan. They crept to the corner. The guard stood at the entrance to the cavern, forty yards away. There came a tiny thud, an exhaled sigh, and she toppled and fell, half blocking the entrance.

"That's one hell of an illusion," Yggur said softly.

"I haven't used it yet," said Hingis.

"Then what . . . ?"

There came a chorus of chilling howls from the cavern.

"Whelm!" cried Karan. "How did they get here so quickly?"

"There must be another entrance," said Yggur. "Hingis, work your illusion!"

The orange mage light flared then broke into a dozen orbs, half casting bright light and the other half beaming out impenetrable shadows. They shot in all directions, bouncing off the walls, bursting and forming more bright and dark orbs, until the maze of light and shadow utterly confused Karan's senses.

But not Yggur's, for he drew his sword and raced up. Karan leapt over the body of the dead guard, who had been struck in the back of the head with the bolt from a heavy crossbow, and ran after Yggur. How was she supposed to find Sulien in all this?

Someone bellowed, "Dismiss!"

The illusions vanished; Hingis cried out in pain and the cavern was plunged into a smoky gloom lit only by the distant fire. A group of lyrinx raced out of one of the tunnels but a dozen Whelm, concealed behind a low rock shelf, rose and fired at them. The lyrinx shrieked and clawed at the bolts embedded under their armoured skin. Evidently they had been dipped in some corrosive substance, for the lyrinx were in such agony that they could not defend themselves.

The Whelm—who appeared to be killing out of pure loathing— slew the lyrinx where they lay, thrashing and helpless. Karan felt sick at the sight.

"Stop!" Sulien screamed. "They're our friends."

Karan crept from rock to rock, trying to see her. Why would she say such a thing?

A lanky female Whelm darted forward, then lunged. Sulien shot out to one side and bolted towards the nearest cavern, the Whelm after her.

"Sulien!" Karan screamed, but Sulien kept going.

Karan followed, weaving between the dead and the dying. To her right a big lyrinx in heavy armour was fighting a band of Whelm. They had shot many bolts at him but none had penetrated his armour and now he hurled himself at them, swinging a great hammer in his left hand and a spike-tipped flail in his right.

It was no ordinary flail—green lightning radiated from each of the spikes, sizzling and crackling and striking down everyone it touched. Already four Whelm lay dead and the rest were backing away, though more had massed further down the passage. On the far side of the chamber Yggur was fighting to get to Sulien. The Whelm were after him too, firing poisoned bolts which he turned away with magical flicks of his long blade.

Karan's knife was useless here so she heaved the crossbow out from under a dead Whelm and loaded it with a three-inch bolt. She was no expert with the weapon but at this range all one had to do was point and shoot. She crouched in the low-hanging smoke, saw a tall, scrawny Whelm creeping after Yggur, and fired.

The Whelm went down, screaming and clawing at his shoulder. She gathered a handful of bolts and shot a second Whelm, a woman. She fell too. But where was Sulien? The light was dimmer, the smoke thicker, and it was hard to tell friend from foe.

Mummy?

A Whelm had Sulien bundled under his arm and was creeping towards the tunnel where they had massed earlier. Karan aimed carefully, intending to disable, but her shot went astray and hit him in the back of the neck. He slid to the floor, kicking and screaming and tearing at the wound, then went still. She had killed him.

"Sulien, this way!" she yelled, reloading the crossbow.

Sulien kicked free, looked around wildly but did not see Karan, then ran towards Yggur, crying out his name. He was locked in battle with a pair of Whelm, and when Sulien was still ten yards away another Whelm raced towards her and scooped her up.

Karan was about to fire when she realised that the Whelm was Yetchah, who had once helped Idlis save Karan's and Sulien's lives. Karan hesitated too long; Yetchah ran into a patch of low-hanging smoke and vanished, taking Sulien with her.

30

THE LAST BREATH
OF AN UNDEAD KILLER

Within seconds of the sky ship taking off, Aviel wished she was back on solid ground. The pilot seemed dangerously incompetent, her head was spinning and her stomach was churning, and she was sure they were going to crash and die.

The allies' need for nivol was so urgent that Commander Janck had made available the first vessel their teams of artificers had built—with much help from Malien's Aachim—in one of the riverside shipyards of Sith.

At least, *almost* built. The cabin, which was not an elegant ovoid like Malien's craft, but an ugly rectangular box, had only been fitted out with the pilot's seat and controls, some bamboo and canvas chairs bolted to the floor, bulging nets that held their gear in place, and racks for Aviel's crates of chymicals and equipment. The tiny galley lacked both a bench and a sink.

The cupboards had no doors and neither did the squatting privy, a cramped recess behind the galley with just a square hole in the floor, and lacking even a door. Aviel only used it once, at high altitude and in dire need, but the air that whistled up through the hole was so icy, and her embarrassment so acute, that she neither ate nor drank during each subsequent day's flight to ensure that she never need use it again.

The sky ship, which in defiance of all logic had been named *Hyacinth*, had none of the grace or beauty of the Aachim's vessels and many flaws they did not possess, notably a tendency for the rotors to stop at the most inconvenient moment and a strong disinclination to fly in a straight line. The pilot, Hublees, a fussy little mancer, kept muttering about it being "arse-heavy."

He was a shapeless short-legged fellow with a ridiculous jet-black goatee and white sideburns so long he could have knotted them under his chin. He was said to have special expertise in dealing with ghosts, spectres and similar creatures, though Aviel found it hard to take him seriously.

"Flying experience?" he said in response to her question as *Hyacinth* staggered into the air from the shipyard, lurching and wobbling. Its wooden skids knocked the top off a chimney stack, scattering bricks onto a neighbouring building and smashing through the roof tiles. "I'd never even seen a sky ship until this morning."

People ran out of the building, shouting and brandishing their fists. He smiled amiably and waved. Nothing bothered him.

Everything bothered Aviel. She felt sure he was going to crash the ugly craft into one of the tall buildings along the waterfront, which would see everyone dead in a fiery explosion, or into the icy waters of the River Garr, where they would quickly drown.

Hublees headed out over the river. "But how difficult can flying be?"

He pulled on a black-ended lever and the craft rose sharply, only to drop twenty feet with a jolt that toppled all the packs out of their nets. Aviel's breakfast heaved up to the back of her throat. "Up, down, see." He wiggled a red lever and the sky ship careered sideways towards a bridge. "Left, right." He pushed a green knob in and out. "Stop, go. That's all there is to it, Aviel my dear. I could teach a three-legged dog to fly *Hyacinth* in half an hour—as long as he could channel power to the rotors, of course."

He laughed as though he had made a great joke, swerved wildly, then checked his compass and turned east towards the Sea of Thurkad, rubbing his saggy belly. "Must get on, must get on."

Aviel felt an unpleasant whirling in her head and wanted to throw up. She closed her eyes but that made things worse. She clung to the bamboo frame of her chair, staring wild-eyed out through the boxy front window. They had only been flying for five minutes and the journey to obtain a golden brimstone, some bubble-bark pine colophony and three drams of Archeus of Eidolon would take the best part of a fortnight—assuming they survived the first hour.

They were but five: herself, Hublees and Earnis, who was here to advise Aviel on alchemical methods and make sure the brimstone and colophony were suitable, since she had not seen either before. Osseion was their guard and general assistant.

The fifth member of the team was the squeaky-voiced young Aachim, Nimil, with the metal slit in his throat. He had brought one of Xarah's scrying boards, perhaps to spy on Aviel and report back to Malien, though his main job was cutting a cavity into a priceless plum-sized yellow diamond to make the diamond phial.

Aviel had naively hoped to set up a small bench and work during the journey, but the sky ship lurched, rocked, bounced and tilted constantly. Often it dropped precipitously without warning or shot up at frightening speeds in sudden updraughts; it was never stable for more than a few minutes. She would have to sleep during the flight, then set up her workshop tent at each campsite and work all night.

Hublees flew east to the coast near Vilikshathûr, then across the Sea of Thurkad, here a hundred miles wide. The lumbering flight took most of the day and Aviel was so miserably airsick that she barely managed an hour's sleep.

They landed on the eastern side of the sea, a couple of miles from the coast, by a creek dried to a few muddy waterholes in an empty landscape. The low brown hills were scattered with tussocks of grey grass and withered little bushes; the grey soil was powdery and there was a haze of dust in the air.

"Doesn't look as though it's rained in years," said Aviel, peering out the door.

"The drought is everywhere," Earnis said gloomily.

Aviel picked up a crate of beakers and carried it to the cabin door, then hesitated, wondering how to get it down the six-foot ladder.

"We'll do that," said Earnis. "Find a good spot for your workshop."

He carried the tent poles and rolls of canvas to the door and Osseion heaved them over his shoulder. Aviel went down the ladder and surveyed the site.

"Will there be snakes?" she said warily.

"I dare say," said Osseion. "Scorpions and spiders too. Where do you want it?"

She picked out a flat area, not too close to any bushes where venomous creatures might lurk. "Here. Um . . . do you know how to put up a tent?" She had never seen one before, and this one had dozens of poles, ropes and pegs.

Osseion ruffled her silky hair as he went past. "I've put up thousands of tents. We'll have it done in no time."

The workshop tent was fourteen feet long and eight wide, with a canvas floor to keep the dirt and dust down and a flap that could be opened in the far end to let fumes out. A short bench at the end of the tent and a longer one on the right side were made from canvas stretched drum-tight across wooden frames. Three rectangular metal plates were set on top, one for her charcoal brazier and the other two to provide stable work surfaces. She also had a cauldron for boiling water and washing her equipment, though due to the risk of fire she kept it outside.

Aviel went back and forth, unpacking her crates of equipment and racks of chymicals. It would take at least an hour to set out everything she needed for the night's work and another hour to pack everything away at dawn. It was going to be a very long night and every succeeding night would be the same.

"Anything I can help you with?" said Earnis, putting his head through the flap.

She needed to focus on the unfamiliar methods she had to carry out perfectly, otherwise things would go wrong and she would have to do it all again.

"No, I need to think," she said absently.

He looked disappointed but turned away.

Aviel was assembling a glass still when a low voice behind her said, "Where are you up to?"

She jumped. "Shand?" He appeared slowly, feet first. "Wh-what are you doing here?"

"You're not the only one who needs exotic ingredients."

Her eyes narrowed. "So that's why the sky ship is 'arse-heavy.' You're hiding up the back."

"There's an empty space inside the rotor cowling, and very cold and uncomfortable and noisy it is too. My ears are still ringing."

She checked outside in case anyone was close enough to hear her talking to a traitor, but saw no one. "What do you want?" she whispered.

He studied the layout of the workshop. "Space to finish my scent potion, of course."

She pulled the tent flap closed. "What?"

"To finish the Afflatus Effluvium I have to extract and carefully blend four odorous oils, all related to death, decay and darkness and loss."

How dare he! "You can't use my tent. There's no room."

"The small bench on the end will do me."

This could not be happening. "Someone's bound to see or hear you, and then I'll be hanged."

"Not as high as I will be. You *owe* me, Aviel."

She thought about being condemned to slave in Magsie's disgusting tannery, then about her own lovely little workshop in Shand's back garden. She did owe him. "What have you got to do?" she said dully. "Will it take long?"

"A few hours a night. I have to extract four odours: the essential oil taken from a plant at the moment it goes extinct, smoke from the desiccated corpse of a woman murdered long ago, an exhalation from the ancient past, rising from deep in the bowels of the earth—and the last breath of an undead killer."

The dark was rising up to choke her. "Why do you have to do it in my tent?"

He moved the equipment she had laid out so carefully on the end bench, set up the apparatus he needed for scent potion work and went invisible. She knew he was still there, though; sometimes she caught an unpleasant whiff, or saw phials or flasks moving by themselves. It was impossible to focus on her own work and, until the others went to bed, she lived in dread that they would discover her aiding a traitor.

The following morning they flew south over lands as dry and drab as their campsite, heading for Grund. Aviel saw little of it; after working all night she was so exhausted that she curled up in a corner of the cabin, tied a safety rope around her middle and plunged into sleep.

The days fell into a pattern: land, put up the tent and set out her equipment, work all night, interrupted periodically by an increasingly fractious Shand, whose own work clearly was not going well, then crate her gear up and sleep the day's flight away.

Two days later, after half a dozen near-death experiences due to Hublees' cheerful incompetence, the ramshackle sky ship plunged out of the clouds in mid-morning and Aviel saw, far below, a stone-capped hill, one of a number that stuck up like pimples on the otherwise flat land. The craft lurched in an updraught then dropped with a crash that rattled her glassware in its crates.

"Where are we?" said Aviel.

"The bitumen seeps of Grund."

"What a hideous place," said Earnis.

The land beyond the hill was utterly barren: there was not a tree, bush or tussock of grass to be seen for miles and the ground might have been burrowed by gigantic moles.

Bitumen had been mined here for centuries, and thousands of ragged pits, most only a few yards across, had been dug out as the miners followed the veins and slowly upwelling springs down until the air became too poisonous for them to work. The ground was covered with black castings, heaps of bitumen-coated waste rock. It was a windswept, sterile wasteland—sweltering in summer and miserably exposed to the icy southerlies of winter, as now.

The sky ship passed into another cloud and jerked up and down, making her stomach churn and her head spin. Sometimes she still felt disoriented an hour after they landed.

"Where do we find a perfect crystal of golden brimstone?" she said dully.

"We'll see if we can buy one first," said Earnis.

"Or failing that," Hublees grinned, "take it by force."

"No we won't! That could contaminate its alchemical essence," countered Earnis.

"Without the crystal, we fail. There's no room for your philosophical scruples now."

"You don't know what you're talking about," snapped Earnis. "Alchemy—"

He had touched a nerve, for Hublees was swelling like an inflated bladder. His soft round face twisted and he leapt up from the controls. "You don't know anything about me, you arrogant little pup."

Earnis took an involuntary step back, then stopped, fists clenched by his sides. Aviel, shocked at this violent transformation of a man she had thought to be an amiable buffoon, saw that Earnis was preparing to take him on.

Osseion sprang up, his weight rocking the sky ship, and stepped between them. "My job is to protect Aviel," he rumbled, "and yours is to fly this box of canvas and string. Sit down!"

For a few seconds Aviel thought Hublees was going to thump Osseion, which could not have ended well, then the fury rushed out of him and he deflated and sat down. "Never call me ignorant," he said softly. "Never say that again."

"I'm sorry," said Earnis. "But my job is to make sure Aviel gets the ingredients she needs. Not approximately, not second best, not contaminated by an improper collection method—but *exactly* what she needs."

Hublees, staring straight ahead, nodded stiffly. "But if you can't, any golden brimstone is better than none."

"In alchemy, noble failure is safer than success by unsound means."

Aviel thought so too, though since she was a novice in the art it was not up to her. She had to follow the method on the parchment, precisely.

"When you're fighting the Merdrun there is no noble failure," said

Hublees, jerking the controls in his agitation. "If Aviel fails we'll be annihilated, and not even an alchemist can find nobility in that."

"Are you going to land or not?" said Earnis.

"Can't risk it here," said Hublees, heading east out of the clouds, over a long ridge then down. "The ship is too vulnerable. We'll have to walk in."

The land here was equally barren: every tree had been felled for miles to feed the fires needed to purify the bitumen and distil off naphtha and other valuable products. There were no pits on this side of the ridge though—the land was unscarred and empty save for a herd of grazing animals, unidentifiable from this distance, further north.

Hublees set down in an eroded gully that concealed the sky ship from every direction but the north, where the ridge overlooked it. A heavy frost lay on the pebbles. Earnis and Osseion erected Aviel's tent and carried in her crates.

Nimil, a quiet, solitary fellow, put up his own tent fifty feet away, set up a small table inside, clamped the yellow diamond to a stand and put a magnifying band over his eyes. Then he closed the tent flap and continued the painstaking work of cutting out the centre to make the diamond phial. Given that diamond was far harder than any other substance, Aviel could not imagine how he was doing it, nor was she going to find out. The Aachim were unsurpassed craftsmen and they guarded their secrets jealously.

Osseion, his enormous sword strapped across his back, climbed to the top of a twenty-foot high outcrop of orange sandstone to keep watch. Earnis and Hublees donned their packs and Aviel gathered her own.

"It's too far for you," said Earnis.

The long walk across broken ground would be agonising, and the return journey worse, but she had to do it. "I've got to be there when the brimstone is collected."

"You'll only slow us down," said Hublees.

"If you're caught," said Earnis, "the whole mission fails. I know what to look for." He heaved his pack higher. "Don't expect us until tomorrow. Golden brimstones are only found on the southern side of the Grund seeps, in a bitumen-filled fissure called the Tagly Artery, and it may be guarded."

"If it is, how will you get some?" said Aviel.

"Don't ask," said Hublees.

They set off. Irritable now, Aviel lit a brazier and put a pot of water on to boil for tea. The prepared chymicals Earnis had bought in Sith had saved months of work, and in the past nights she had finished all but the last three steps. They had to be done in a single sequence after she obtained the three final ingredients, one mineral, one vegetable and one animal: the perfect golden brimstone, a lemon-sized lump of bubble-bark pine colophony and finally, to create and activate the nivol, three drams of Archeus of Eidolon.

Aviel had just perched on her stool when Shand popped into visibility in the corner where her crates were stacked. She jumped, spilling hot tea on her knees. "What are you up to?" she snapped.

He selected a small hand pump, a piece of rubber tubing, and a flask and stopper. "Collecting."

"What?"

"*An exhalation from the ancient past, rising from deep in the bowels of the earth*," he said, quoting what he had said previously.

"I don't understand."

"The bitumen seeps of Grund, like the great tar pits of Snizort further west, have welled up from a source deep underground, all that remains of ancient lake life that died and decayed in the mud aeons ago."

"How do you know?"

"I know!" he said forbiddingly, and vanished.

She hurried out, trying to see where he had gone. Invisible people could still leave footprints. Osseion fell in beside her. "Mind if I walk with you?"

"Umm," said Aviel, looking for tracks but not seeing any.

"My job is to guard you, day and night," he rumbled. "From dangers seen *and unseen*."

Heat rose up her face. Did he know about Shand? She looked away, not knowing what to do or say.

Osseion chuckled. "I guarded Mendark for many years," he said quietly. "Nothing about the doings of mancers can surprise me, even them turning invisible."

"But Shand is accused of betraying us to the enemy. Are you going to turn him in?" *And me?*

"I haven't set eyes on Shand, and my full-time job is guarding you. Besides, I've known him for a long time. I trust him—as mancers go."

"*Unwittingly* betraying us. What if the magiz's link is still in him?"

"If you believed it was, would you be aiding him?"

"How do you—? What makes you think I am?"

Osseion's enormous shoulders heaved in silent mirth. "I watch, I listen, I add things up."

"Does everyone know then?" she said, dismayed.

"Nimil is totally absorbed in crafting the diamond phial, and Earnis sleeps like the dead. But less gets past Hublees than you might think. Be careful, Aviel."

31

WE CAME TO YOU IN FRIENDSHIP

Only one lyrinx was still alive: the huge male, Ghyll. He wore body armour, and the Whelm's poisoned missiles had not been able to touch him, while with hammer and enchanted flail he had struck down at least ten of them.

Sulien, shocked by the Whelm's savagery to the injured lyrinx, kept low and looked for a hiding place. But there were too many Whelm; they would soon find her here. Outside was a frozen wilderness where she would be lucky to survive an hour, yet it was better than here. She ran for the exit but three Whelm raced to cut her off.

"Ghyll!" she shrieked. "Help!"

He sought her out among the illusions and looked into her eyes.

"We came to you in friendship, and your people slaughtered us from ambush."

"They're not my people!" she cried. "They're *Whelm*!"

"They're old human, child, just as you are."

She reached out to him. "But they're hunting me."

"Your kind won't get the chance to betray us twice." His voice grated like rock being ground to paste under the weight of a glacier. "One day, when we have the numbers and we finally emerge from our hiding places, Santhenar will endure a war to end all wars. We will grind you down; we will crush you and smash you and put an end to the most treacherous species that ever lived."

He whirled, swinging his flail, and green lightning seared out from each of its seven spiky tips, hurling Whelm to left and right, as dead as stones. He gave Sulien a last contemptuous stare, then ran into one of the tunnels and disappeared.

"*Suliennnnn?*"

Sulien whirled, staring around her. "Mummy?"

No reply. She was sure it had been Karan's voice but it was hard to make anything out through the thick layer of smoke that hung low above the floor. People were shouting, screaming and groaning, and to her left a chunk of the roof fell with an almighty crash that shook the floor and hurled shattered rock everywhere. She caught a fleeting glimpse of tall old Yggur, racing across the cavern sword in hand, and yelled his name but he did not hear.

Had he and Karan come alone? The Whelm would butcher them, just like the lyrinx. She was creeping around in the smoke, trying to find them, when a crook-nosed Whelm grabbed her.

"Got her!" he yelled. "Retreat, retreat!"

Sulien kneed him in the belly. His arm crushed her chest until she could not breathe, he ran a few steps then, *thud*. His blood sprayed her; it was unnaturally cool and had a rank tang, and he fell half on top of her. Sulien prised herself from his dead grip.

"Mummy?" she screamed, looking around frantically. "Yggur?"

There he was. "Yggur! Yggur!"

She could see him searching for her in the smoke, but as she ran his way another Whelm cut in diagonally and grabbed her. It was Yetchah, the Whelm who had saved Sulien's life the day she was born. Yetchah, who had always been kind to her. Yetchah who now planned to betray her.

"You have no honour!" cried Sulien. "Everything you ever said to me was a stinking lie!" She struck at Yetchah with her fists.

"The master comes first, always!" Yetchah hissed.

She held Sulien out at arm's length in one hand, backhanded her hard across the face with the other then bolted into a dark tunnel, where she jerked a sacking bag over Sulien's head and chest and pulled a cord tight around it at waist level, binding her arms to her side. Sulien kicked her. Yetchah struck Sulien in the belly and she doubled over, gasping, her last hope gone.

More Whelm joined Yetchah though no one spoke. All Sulien could hear was their panting and the rustle of soft soles on stone as they raced down the tunnel. They were not wearing their iron-soled boots and would be difficult to track—if anyone lived to track them.

The bag must have been used to store root vegetables—she could smell starch and dusty earth. The coarse sacking rasped at her cheeks and nose with every movement. Suddenly the warmth of the underground was replaced by biting cold—they were outside and, she deduced, hurrying down a mountain path.

They had already been running for an hour but did not stop for a moment's rest. Yetchah handed Sulien to another Whelm, a male whose dry skin rustled as he moved. An hour or two later he gave her to a third Whelm. Later still, after they had been heading down for many hours, she was passed back to Yetchah.

Why are they in such a hurry? Sulien wondered. *Could Yggur and Karan be hunting them?* She prayed for it as she had never prayed before.

Yetchah ran with Sulien for another half-hour, then staggered and nearly fell. "Can't . . . go . . . on," she gasped.

"If we're to gain our master the sacrifice must be today," grated a man's voice. "We cannot stop."

Sulien plunged into despair. The Whelm weren't running from anyone—they were running towards their future master.

Yetchah set off again, stumbling. "I'll take the sacrifice," said the man.

"No!" said Yetchah.

She bent down and threw up, then ran on. Sulien, who had barely slept in days, sank into an uneasy doze troubled by nightmares about the triplets. It now felt as though Yetchah had been climbing an enormous staircase for hours. She was gasping and so were the Whelm behind her.

Yetchah scrambled up a rough, winding path and across a broad ridge top, then onto something smooth, a wooden bridge that quivered underfoot. She ran along it and onto a solid structure exposed to the cold wind. She dropped Sulien onto boards, untied the cords around the sacking and heaved it over her head. Sulien's ears and the tip of her nose stung; the rough sacking had rasped skin off.

It was still night, though she had no idea of the hour, and it was raining gently—it was always raining in Salliban. She was on a vast wooden platform, high in the air, with branches rising up here and there through it. The platform was fixed to the upper trunk of an enormous tree. No, to five enormous trees. Wind swayed their tops and shook the platform, making its beams squeal and groan.

Yetchah threw up again, then wiped her mouth on her sleeve. "Ready?" she called hoarsely.

Voices shouted assent from the edges of the platform and with a series of *whooshes* five pairs of columns, each twenty feet high and thickly coated with pitch or tar, were lit. Flames ran from three feet above the base of each column to the top, lighting the treetops with a wavering yellow glow.

The platform, which was hexagonal and maybe sixty yards across, stood above a slot-like gorge which lay in darkness. Wooden bridges—the one Yetchah had carried her across and another just like it on the far side—linked the platform to the rocky landscape on either side of the gorge.

"Hurry!" said a sallow-faced, pea-eyed Whelm.

Yetchah picked Sulien up by the waist and raised her high so the yellow light from the flares shone on her face and her red hair.

"Make a link!" said Yetchah.

And the moment she linked to the triplets, or to Gergrig, he would order her killed. "Can't," said Sulien. "Losing my gift."

"Liar! Your psychic gift has grown tremendously—that's how the winged beast found you."

Resistance was bound to be painful but it was all Sulien could do. She shook her head.

"We hold your mother. Make the link or she dies."

Her knees gave. They could well have caught Karan, and if they did they *would* kill her to force Sulien to link. What was she supposed to do? She knew what Karan would say—*Don't link!*—but that would condemn her and how could Sulien do that?

"I don't believe you," she said, her voice squeaky.

Yetchah gestured to the pea-eyed Whelm. "Bring the man who caught Karan."

He darted away, shortly returning with a stocky Whelm whose face was blistered and burned, the skin weeping and his swollen, bloodshot eyes streaming.

"Dipl," said Yetchah, "tell Sulien how you caught her mother in the caverns."

"The tall sorcerer was attacking us," said Dipl in a slow, crackling voice, as if he had breathed in the fire that had burned his face. "We took his sword but he blasted fire at us. Azyl burned . . ." His awful eyes flicked to the blazing columns. "Burned like a candle. Her screams still ring in my ears."

"Dipl!" Yetchah said sharply.

"Most of the sorcerous fire missed me. I fell down and pretended to be dying, and when he turned to attack the others I shot him with a poisoned bolt, right through the ear."

Sulien's heart turned upside-down. Yggur, dead?

"And Karan?" said Yetchah.

"All the fight went out of her when I killed him. She whined and whimpered and put her hands up, and we took her."

"I don't believe you," Sulien said scornfully. "Mummy *never* whines, and never gives up. She . . ." If Karan *had* surrendered, it would be with a plan in mind and she, Sulien, must not do anything to arouse their suspicions. "Where is she, then?"

Yetchah stared at her, but Sulien could not read anything in the Whelm's black eyes.

"Make the link," said Yetchah, "or I'll give the order for Karan to be killed."

Sulien could feel the pressure of their combined wills; they were trying to force her to obey. She had to resist them. "I'm not making a link until I see that Mummy is all right."

"Dipl, go to the place where Karan has been hidden. She is to be killed at once." Her eyes met Sulien's in challenge.

Sulien cracked. "Wait!"

Yetchah held up a hand, and Dipl stopped.

"I'll make a link," said Sulien. "But . . . it takes a lot of preparation." Whatever Karan's plan was—if she had one—Sulien had to give her every chance.

"A link can be made in an instant," said Yetchah.

"Some links are really hard. It took Mummy days to make a link to Malien, to get her to come—"

Yetchah's head shot round. "The Aachim are coming?" she hissed.

Had Sulien just revealed something that should have been kept secret? Too late now. "Hundreds and hundreds of them," she lied. She knew that the Whelm and the Aachim had been enemies for ever.

Yetchah's gaunt face went hard. "Then our quest is all the more urgent. Make the link!" She met Dipl's eyes. He was waiting for the order to kill Karan.

Sulien dared not delay any longer. "All right," she said dully, as though they had broken her. She put a whining tone into her voice. "Please don't hurt Mummy."

Was there a way to cheat them? The Merdrun had already invaded Santhenar so how could she make things worse by putting the Whelm in touch with them? It could not be long before the Whelm located the Merdrun anyway, and then they could contact them by skeet, a huge carrier bird, within days.

However a link would reveal her to Gergrig, who wanted her dead to protect the Merdrun's secret. She had no idea what the secret was because she could not recover the nightmare in which it had been revealed. Could she convince him of that?

And why would he take the risk when her death would solve the problem?

32

YOUR EDUCATION HAS BEEN DEFICIENT

Karan was trying to locate Yetchah when Yggur came running. "To the exit, now!"

She was still carrying the crossbow. She snatched up a bag of bolts from a dead Whelm. "Yetchah's got Sulien. They must have gone out that tunnel." She pointed. "We've got to follow them."

"No, there's too many of them. If they fired salvoes of poisoned bolts back up the tunnel they'd be bound to hit us."

"Then how will we know where they've taken her?"

"We can't talk about it here."

He ran lightly down the tunnel by which they had entered. Karan followed, sick with fear. The Whelm had been too violent, too focused. Clearly they had a plan and it could not be far from completion.

"Hingis?" Yggur said softly.

"Here!"

"Damn fine illusion—while it lasted." Yggur clapped him on the shoulder. "Get moving; there are more Whelm and they'll come after us. I'm going to bring the tunnel down behind us or we'll never get out."

He thrust a small lightglass into Karan's hand. "I may be a while. Go!"

Karan felt numb. The Whelm would force Sulien to link to the Merdrun and then they would kill her. It might be over before they even got back to the glacier. She trudged down the tunnel.

"You didn't find her?" said Hingis.

She told him what had happened.

"I'm sorry," he said. "That must be unbearable."

Why, after all it had taken to find Sulien, had Karan hesitated to shoot Yetchah? Had she doomed Sulien? Gergrig was a cruel and vindictive man who had no compunction about killing children—in the Merdrun's attacks on Cinnabar he had tortured every prisoner, old and young, before killing them. He would want Sulien to suffer before the mad triplets drank her life.

She plodded down the tunnel, sinking deeper into despair. Sulien lost, Llian probably dead, Gothryme abandoned, Santhenar soon to be conquered and everyone put to the sword; what was left to live for?

A series of thunderous crashes shook the tunnel then a wind-blast drove her to her knees. She dropped the lightglass and the light went out. Hingis groaned. Karan groped for the lightglass and shook it until it began to glow again. Hingis was crumpled against the wall, his ugly face even more warped than usual.

"It's nothing," he muttered. "Wrenched my back again."

He seemed more like his old self. Had his contribution to the rescue attempt highlighted his own worth? She helped him up, feeling a surge of affection for the twisted little man.

Yggur came running, carrying a Whelm crossbow. He was coated in dust and sweat had carved runnels through it down his face.

"Rock's a bit unstable," he said with a shaky laugh. "Brought down ten times as much as I'd planned. Maybe too much."

"How do you mean?" said Hingis.

"Might have opened up a new path for the Whelm. Let's get going."

"This is the end," said Karan in a dead voice. "They'll force Sulien to link to the Merdrun any minute, and—"

"Not here!" Yggur said roughly. He thrust her down the tunnel. "Move!"

She hurried on. He fell in beside her and Hingis lurched along behind them.

"Why not here?" she said.

"The armoured lyrinx who got away may come back with reinforcements, burning for revenge," said Yggur. "Besides, Gergrig will want to interrogate Sulien."

"Why?"

"She's a clever child and she's met many of our great leaders. She could reveal information of great strategic importance."

"But—"

"To defeat your enemy, first you must know them, but the Merdrun know little about us. Besides, taking a new master is the culmination of a great yearning for the Whelm—they'll want to do so at a place of special significance to them."

"How can you know that?"

"They served me for centuries; I know more about them than anyone alive. They'll be heading to a special place, close by."

"They might be taking Sulien halfway across Shazabba for all you know."

"Their most special places are in the forests and mountains of Salliban. They'll make for the closest one, then force Sulien to make the link at once. Hurry!"

Two exhausting hours later, during which time Karan's sensitive's gift had explored every possible disaster, they reached the sky ship without further sign of either Whelm or lyrinx. It was still dark. Yggur climbed to a high altitude then cut the rotors and allowed the vessel to drift south with the wind. Karan scanned the shadowy peaks and forests below with a pair of night glasses.

"Nothing," she said dully. "But we could be looking in the wrong place."

"From this height we can see every place they can reach within three days' march."

After they had been drifting for half an hour, and Karan had seen nothing but wilderness, Yggur said, "They couldn't have gone this far

south." He turned the sky ship north and, when they were a few miles
west of the glacier, allowed it to drift south again.

"Nothing," said Karan after another five fruitless minutes.

"Fire in the forest," cried Hingis, who was watching out the side
window. "There, *there*!"

Karan saw a flat space among the treetops, lit by flares. Little dots
were moving around on it. She strained until her eyes ached but the
glasses were not strong enough to identify anyone. It had to be the
Whelm's special place, but could Sulien still be alive? Karan was afraid
to hope.

"What is it?" said Yggur.

"A treetop platform above a narrow gorge." She described it. "But
why the flares? Why advertise their position?"

"They're appealing to a great man to be their master; they've got to
look strong and confident." He thought for a moment. "They're getting
ready to force the link." He turned the sky ship away. "Only an hour
'til dawn; we've got to attack now."

She studied the dots in bleak despair. "How? There's dozens of them."

Yggur did not speak for several minutes. The sky ship dived towards
a bare, rocky slope, out of sight of the platform. "I'll drop you down
there, then go up and hover above the platform, out of their crossbow
range—but not ours—and attack them from the darkness."

"The moment you try to land they'll take the sky ship," said Karan
hopelessly.

"I'm not going to land. We're just making a diversion so you can
rescue Sulien."

She laughed hollowly. "How?"

"That's up to you. Have you got a better idea?"

"No."

"Better get ready, then." Yggur turned to Hingis. "Ever used a
crossbow?"

"I've never used any kind of weapon, save my illusions."

"Your education has been deficient." Yggur frowned. "Prepare an
illusion that'll help Karan get onto the platform unseen, and make it
a good one."

Yggur ghosted the sky ship down the rocky valley and landed. "Can't be positive they don't have guards out this far," he said quietly, "but there's no time to look for them. Got your crossbow?"

Karan raised it then went down the ladder. It was raining, the steep slope running with little cascades.

"Dawn is in forty-five minutes," said Yggur.

"I know!" The sky ship lifted. "Wait!" she hissed, waving furiously.

Yggur settled again and looked at her enquiringly.

"How will you know when to pick me up?"

He frowned, then tossed a dull yellow bar, the length of her hand and the thickness of her thumb, to her. She caught it.

"What am I supposed—"

"It's a lightstick. Bend it double, then hurl it high into the air—*right away.*"

The sky ship climbed into the darkness and disappeared. Karan pocketed the lightstick and made her way up the ridge, keeping a careful lookout for sentries. But how, even if Yggur's distraction succeeded, could one person hope to rescue Sulien from dozens of Whelm? It was hopeless; they were all going to die, for nothing.

As she approached the top of the ridge she made out the tips of the tall flares. The platform was only a hundred and fifty yards away now, though she wasn't sure how she was going to get to it. The broken ridge top offered some cover; if she kept low she might be able to reach the wooden bridge, which was sixty yards long and had no side rails, but she would be exposed from the moment she tried to cross it. Yggur's diversion had better be a good one.

She crept across the crest and hunkered down a few yards from the beginning of the bridge. The towering flares lit the centre of the platform brightly but also cast wavering bands of light and shadow outwards, and one of them lay partly across the bridge. It was no help—a Whelm guard stood in the shadow, at the centre of the bridge.

The rest of the Whelm were gathered in a scrying circle at the centre of the platform; she could hear their crow-like chanting. They would keep it up until Sulien was forced to link to the triplets.

Where was she? With the rain and the shifting shadows it was hard to make things out; even the Whelm and the flares were blurry now. Was that due to Hingis's illusion? If so, it wasn't helping.

The figures in the scrying circle separated, and there she was, a small figure at the very centre of the platform, on a short bench with every Whelm staring at her—all their hopes and dreams focused on the master Sulien alone could bring them. She looked tiny and terrified, and Karan's heart broke for her. There had to be a way to save her, but how?

Ten minutes had passed; only thirty-five till dawn, but Karan dared not move until Yggur started his diversion. What was keeping him?

She blocked the worry off; she had to plan her raid. Karan loaded a bolt into her crossbow and thrust the rest into her belt. The moment Yggur acted she would shoot the guard on the bridge, race across and fire at anyone in her way. If she could free Sulien she would send her back across the bridge and retreat after her, trying to hold the Whelm off. It was a feeble plan; Sulien might get away but the Whelm would certainly shoot Karan down. And the sky ship too, when Yggur approached to pick Sulien up.

A large flask fell from the sky, trailing a burning rag, and smashed on the far side of the deck, spreading blazing oil across the boards. Another flask followed, and another, the last landing perilously close to Sulien.

The circle of Whelm broke apart and ran back and forth, shouting and firing crossbows up into the darkness. Karan fired at the bridge guard, hitting him in the thigh; he convulsed and toppled sideways off the narrow bridge. As she ran across, crouched low, she made out the dark outline of the sky ship a couple of hundred feet up.

One of the Whelm at the centre of the platform fell, clutching at the top of his head. Another spun round with a red patch on his left shoulder—Yggur must be firing at them. A barrel tumbled down and burst open on the boards, spraying brown liquid everywhere. It looked like dark ale but wherever it touched the boards sticky foam boiled up like miniature storm clouds for six or eight feet and gummed together everything it touched.

Now a blast of white fire sizzled down into the paired flares on the far side of the deck, toppling the left-hand one onto the head of a Whelm who was aiming his crossbow up at the sky ship. As he fell, his bolt discharged in Karan's direction and whistled past her right hip. She yelped and leapt aside, nearly going over the edge of the bridge herself.

Go! she thought. *This is the best diversion you'll ever get.*

She hurtled onto the weathered platform, which was now burning in three places. It would take a lot of heat to set fire to the heavy framing timbers underneath, but the little blazes were slowly spreading across the boards.

She ducked behind one of the brown foaming messes, which had a strong smell of beer, and tried to work out a plan. Several of the Whelm were running for the far bridge, while others were helping the wounded, avoiding the muck and the burning areas, towards the bridge she had crossed. But they weren't all panicking. Two Whelm were beating out the fires and another half-dozen had surrounded Sulien. Yggur could not shoot at them because they were too close to her.

Karan crept from one brown foam cloud to another. She was only fifteen feet from Sulien but could get no closer. The Whelm bound her to a high stool, facing away from Karan, and five of them formed a smaller scrying circle around her. Yetchah stood in front of Sulien, eyes blazing fanatically.

"The link!" she cried, striking Sulien on the top of her head, then on her right and left cheeks, with a thin blue baton.

"The link," chanted the Whelm. "Or Karan dies!"

What was going on? Had they convinced Sulien that they held Karan captive? Dare she call out that she was free? Then the inside of her skull tingled as Sulien's link sprang to life.

"Master!" cried the Whelm, raising their thin arms high.

Karan caught the link and sent to Sulien from behind the foam cloud. *I'm safe! Cut the link.*

Too late. The triplets had taken command of it, and an image burned itself into Karan's mind—a large white stone bowl half full of red water, with the triplets standing in it up to their knees. Gergrig stood on the wide outer edge of the bowl, watching them.

We have her, hissed Jaguly.

Cast her image on the waters, said Gergrig.

The image of Sulien's face appeared on the red water, hugely magnified, white-faced and trembling. There were small welts on her cheeks and tears on her lashes, though Karan could tell that Sulien was trying to control herself. Had the message got through? Did Sulien know she was close by?

Her lips were moving; was she trying to break the link? There was no hope of her doing so; Karan had struggled to break it when the old magiz had taken hold of her, and the triplets were far stronger.

Is the link embedded? said Gergrig. *So she can be killed at any time I choose?*

His words were like a hammer blow to the head. Even if Karan got Sulien away, which seemed impossible, how could she save her if Gergrig could kill her at any time?

It is, said Jaguly, Unbuly and Empuly in one voice.

Has she told anyone about our weakness? said Gergrig.

Have you revealed our secret? said Jaguly, pointing at Sulien's face on the red water.

The water steamed with the force of Jaguly's command. From the way Sulien's features distorted, Karan could tell she was fighting it. *Don't waste your strength,* she thought, but there was no way to communicate with her without alerting the Whelm that she was close by.

Sulien tried to say *Yes* but the compulsion would not allow her to lie. "No," she whispered. "I don't remember it."

Is that the truth? said Gergrig.

It is, said Empuly.

Gergrig whooped. *Then the moment she dies, our secret is safe.*

Karan peered around the brown foam cloud, which was shrinking as its little bubbles popped. Soon it would not be enough to hide her. Further on, two of the small fires the Whelm had beaten out were burning again, drying out the rain-saturated boards and spreading. The centre of one fire collapsed, raining coals down into the tree canopy and leaving a ragged hole through the deck.

It seemed Yggur had done all he could; high above, the rotors ticked softly as he circled, waiting for Karan's signal. But she still had no idea how to effect a rescue.

The five Whelm in the circle, and Yetchah, stared raptly up as if seeing Gergrig through Sulien's link. Sulien twisted around on her stool, searching the platform. Karan waved, then pointed at herself as if to say, *Get ready.* Sulien gave a stiff little nod.

Compel her to locate the summon stone, said Gergrig.

Find the stone, brat! said Jaguly.

Karan rocked back on her heels. Had the stone *moved*?

Again Sulien tried to resist the compulsion, and again she failed. *It . . . went . . . west,* she said.

What direction, and how far? snapped Gergrig.

A . . . bit . . . north of west. Maybe . . . two hundred . . . miles. Maybe . . . six . . . hundred.

North-western Meldorin? Or beyond?

Yes.

Which, you stupid little girl?

I . . . don't . . . know.

Was Sulien being deliberately obtuse? Karan would not have put it past her, though it was a deadly game to play with Gergrig.

This is taking too long, Gergrig said to the triplets. *Find a way to burn the truth out of her.*

We have invented new tortures, said Jaguly. Unbuly giggled. Empuly let out an eager little squeak.

Use them! But don't break her until you've rebuilt the connection to the stone. Begin!

Sulien doubled up against her bonds and screamed.

33

THE MOMENT IT GOES EXTINCT

"Faster, you old fool!" roared Earnis from the darkness.

"Never—call me—fool!" gasped Hublees.

Aviel's gear was aboard. Osseion shoved the rolled tent in through the door and spun around as Earnis and Hublees raced up. Hublees was red in the face and looked about to burst an artery. He doubled over beside the ladder, gasping. The shouting and yelling behind them grew louder.

"Get in, quick!" cried Earnis, holding the golden brimstones box across his chest. "They're after us." He scrambled up the ladder, one-handed.

Through the nearest window, Aviel saw a band of people pounding towards the sky ship, waving blazing brands and roaring threats. Osseion heaved Hublees in and followed. Hublees staggered to his seat, snatched at the controls and the rotors began to turn.

"Go, go!" yelled Earnis.

The sky ship lifted, tilted sideways, crashed down again, and Aviel was sure it was going to topple onto its side, but Hublees, flying even more recklessly than usual, managed to tilt it the other way and accelerated without taking off. The sky ship spun around and roared forward, its skids ploughing the bare earth as it bounced and hurtled towards the furious people with the torches. They dived to either side, all save one burly fellow who hurled his torch at the sky ship. Hublees jerked on a lever, the craft rocketed into the air and the spinning torch bounced off the left-hand skid in a shower of sparks and fell away.

"What's happened?" said Aviel.

Earnis looked furious. "We couldn't get into the Tagly Artery to look for the brimstones, and the villagers wouldn't sell us any . . ." He flushed and looked away.

"Then why are they so angry?"

"Hublees robbed the village chief of his personal collection."

"The best golden brimstones ever found," said Hublees, grinning.

"But . . . stealing them could contaminate their alchemical *essence*," said Aviel. "They might not work properly." She also felt that this crime reflected on her.

"It was stolen brimstones or none. And none means no nivol."

"We were lucky to get away at all," said Earnis. "I don't understand how we did."

"I *am* a considerable mancer," said Hublees smugly.

Aviel sat back in her seat, dismayed. Golden brimstones were one of the three key ingredients and now their essence was tainted. How would it change things? Would the method fail, or would the nivol, assuming she managed to produce any, also be tainted?

Hublees flew north by north-east for three hundred miles to a windswept sandstone plateau at the centre of the great old forest called Wyrm Wood, reaching it a day and a half later. He circled while Earnis looked down, checking his notebook. Aviel had no idea what he was looking for, since his notes were written in alchemical symbols he had not taught her.

"The location is secret," he had said, "and I may not tell anyone who doesn't need to know."

He was looking for a deep, narrow gorge called the Slot, one of hundreds of similar gorges carved into the otherwise featureless plateau. It took a full day of circling and checking before he was sure that he had found the right gorge, though then he discovered that there was no easy way in; the sides of the gorge were sheer for the top sixty feet.

Osseion lowered Earnis and Nimil on ropes onto a ledge below the cliff. Again Aviel was left behind; the climb down and up was so difficult that only the able-bodied could have attempted it. Hublees did not volunteer either and kept well away from the edge, looking sick. The dumpy little mancer had a terror of falling.

Aviel watched anxiously as Earnis and Nimil headed down from the ledge to the floor of the gorge hundreds of feet below, where they would walk its length searching for a stand of bubble-bark pines. She soon lost sight of them and went back to her workshop. If they found the trees they would collect a bucket of resin according to her instructions.

Seven hours later, after sunset, Osseion called. Aviel went back to the edge.

"They've signalled to haul them up," he said.

"Did you find the stand?" Aviel yelled down.

"Not exactly," came Earnis's echoing reply.

Osseion wound the crank handle to haul Nimil up, then Earnis. They were exhausted and covered in red welts from swarms of orange gorge flies, but triumphant. Earnis carried a sealed bucket of green resin, which he opened in Aviel's workshop. It filled the tent with a clean, aromatic odour like a mixture of camphor, pine and eucalyptus.

"I thought you said—" began Aviel.

"There was no stand," said Earnis. "Just a single, ancient tree, and not long for the world, by the look of it. Taking all this resin has probably hastened its demise."

"Then you should not have taken so much."

"The colophony will be all the more powerful," Hublees said indifferently.

Earnis and Nimil went to scrub the sticky resin from their hands, and Hublees returned to the sky ship. Aviel was fretting about Hublees' words when Osseion's winch shook. She looked over the edge. She could not see anything but had no doubt Shand was on the rope, coming up. Had he collected *the essential oil taken from a plant at the moment it goes extinct*—the second of the four special odours he required to complete his scent potion.

She could not stop thinking about that as she heated the resin to drive off its volatiles and produce colophony. Had Shand killed the last bubble-bark pine to get its essential oil? And had she, by using this nivol-making method, helped to render them extinct? Was this another step down her personal dark path? It seemed so.

From the Slot they flew north half that night and all the following day, over forested hills then past a series of great peaks, the tallest of which Earnis said was the famous Burning Mountain, Booreah Ngurle. All Aviel saw was a haze of brown smoke. They continued across plains and hills towards a long narrow lake that ran north-west in a cliff-bounded gash across the landscape for the best part of three hundred miles.

"Warde Yallock," said Hublees in the late afternoon, gazing down at it from a great height.

"Looks like the earth has torn apart," said Osseion.

"Perhaps it has," said Hublees.

The following day, after a long diagonal crossing of the lake, they passed over grassland and savannah that slowly ramped up to the land called Grossular, a chilly windswept plateau three quarters of a mile high, well grassed and surprisingly green, save on the eastern side.

There a ring of worn-down hills formed a circle a few miles across, and at its centre a scatter of black boulders stood as much as twenty-five feet above the plain. The ground around the rocks was rust-red. Half a mile away a series of broken walls marked the remains of a cluster of buildings. There were white heaps all around it, and even from the sky ship Aviel's keen nose caught an ancient foulness that made her shudder. Thus far the journey had been uneventful, but that would change tonight.

Tonight they had to find the ghost vampire, Lumillal, somehow capture that ferociously deadly spirit and attempt to distil the spectral blood—his Archeus—from him while he was still "alive." But this time it would not be done for her; she had to be present when the Archeus was taken.

"Near the black rocks will be safest," said Hublees, pointing the nose of the sky ship down. It was close to sunset.

Aviel looked blearily ahead. She had laboured in her workshop all last night, rechecking her work and her preparations, then had not slept a wink during the long day's flight. She could not stop worrying about what had to be done tonight, and how unlikely it was that the unluckiest girl in the world would survive it.

"What are those rocks?" she wondered.

"All that's left of a great meteor that crashed here an aeon ago." Hublees swept a stubby arm around the horizon. "See how its impact heaved the ground up into the ring of hills?"

"And the ruins?"

He hesitated, then shook his head.

"Rogues Render," said Earnis in a whisper, as if afraid to speak the name aloud.

"But what *is* Rogues Render? Why won't anyone say?"

Hublees and Earnis exchanged glances. Hublees' face was oddly blank, and Earnis's wavy hair was standing up. Even Nimil looked unnerved; his oval Aachim eyes had a glassy stare and the breath whistled in and out through the slit in his throat.

"Later," said Hublees, heading down towards a flat grassy area to the left of the boulders.

Aviel heard a faint humming sound and felt a brief sharp pain in her temples. As they landed the pain passed; the humming did not.

There were seven large boulders between fifteen and twenty-five feet in height, plus a scatter of smaller ones. Up close they were dark grey or black, but shiny and metallic, and their outsides appeared to have bubbled and melted and flowed. The ground here had a rusty red crust, the air had a metallic tang and a cold south wind howled between the rocks.

The most sheltered place was a patch of bare ground about thirty feet by twenty, between the three largest boulders. Osseion carried the tent canvases to the space and opened them out, and Aviel drove the tent pegs through a hard ironstone crust into the red earth. It was very cold at this altitude and the hard labour warmed her.

Nimil climbed the tallest of the boulders and perched on top, his coat wrapped around him, and stared towards the broken walls of Rogues Render. Aviel was glad the boulders blocked her view.

"What's that humming noise? Can anyone else hear it?" She looked around. Nimil had his palms pressed to his ears and Earnis's face was screwed up.

Hublees laid his plump fingers on the nearest boulder but jerked away as if he had been stung. "This place must have a most powerful presence if even ungifted people can detect it. It must be a mighty place for working the Secret Art."

"I'll need all the help I can get," muttered Aviel.

Osseion had lit the campfire and was preparing dinner. Earnis was studying a scroll in the firelight and scrawling alchemical symbols in a little book. Hublees lay on the ground on his back, his coat wrapped around him, staring up at the sky.

Darkness fell swiftly. After dinner Aviel was staring towards Rogues Render, invisible in the darkness, when a wind-shift brought her that faint unpleasant odour again, as of something that had died a very long time ago. She shuddered and turned her back.

The wind bit like icy iron, stinging the tips of her ears and nose. She returned to the fire and stood downwind where the clean smell of wood smoke blocked out the foulness, then with a sigh she headed through the boulders to begin the night's work.

"Close the flap," Shand said quietly as she entered the tent.

As she did so he appeared slowly, hands and boots first, face last. "You want to know about Rogues Render."

"No," said Aviel. "I *need* to know."

"This ancient crater is called Bundash, and one of Mendark's greatest failures as Magister occurred here—though few would blame him; the Magister's writ never extended into this part of the world." Shand paused as if recalling obscure facts to mind. "He came here . . . ninety-seven years ago, looking for the source of a faint beating sound associated with a series of violent yet inexplicable crimes."

"But I thought the summon stone only woke a few months ago."

"Apparently it *woke again* a few months ago. It first woke more than a century ago, and Mendark spent a good part of his final two lives trying to find out what was going on."

"Did he?"

"Not entirely. At the end, knowing he had failed, he used the great power released by his own death to put the summon stone to sleep, but a few months ago it woke again—or the magiz woke it—and started to do what the Merdrun had ensorcelled it to do an aeon ago: corrupt and kill people, and suck power from them to open the gate from Cinnabar to Santhenar."

"What was Mendark's 'greatest failure'?" said Aviel.

"He ended up in the middle of a massacre and could not stop it; he was lucky to escape with his own life."

"Got to get some work done," she said hastily. She did not want to know about massacres. She had already experienced enough horrors for a lifetime.

"Rogues Render was a rendering plant," said Shand.

There had been one at Magsie Murg's tannery in Casyme. They boiled animal bones there to recover the fat.

At the end bench, Shand checked the odours of a line of labelled phials. "There was a monstrous betrayal on the floor of this crater a century ago—and the doomed last stand of a small, proud nation."

Dread overwhelmed her; she could *feel* the tragedy in her skin and bones.

"A powerful man turned on his lifelong friend," Shand went on. "Each was the leader of a nation, one small, one large. The small nation was Tindule, led by Jussell, the large nation Grossular, ruled by Hudigarde, and the two friends had married twin sisters. Hudigarde wed the beautiful but unstable sorceress Lablag, who came to realise that he despised her and coveted her homely twin, a master brewer, philosopher and composer called Tissany. In his lifetime Hudigarde had always got what he wanted, but not this time—neither Tissany, Jussell or Lablag would countenance the idea of divorce."

"If you swear to someone," Aviel said primly, "you should keep your word no matter what."

Shand heaved a heartfelt sigh, and she remembered that he had been rejected by Yalkara, the great love of his life. She flushed; she had been doing that a lot lately.

"Lablag must have been one of the first people to be corrupted by the summon stone," Shand mused. He sniffed a phial half full of a gluggy brown sludge covered in a layer of grey oil, gagged and hastily capped it. "Embittered by Hudigarde's contempt, she delved into dark sorceries and was ensnared by the stone. I suspect the magiz of that time was able to link to Lablag through the stone, because she saw a threat in Tindule."

"What threat?" said Aviel.

"I don't know, but the magiz ordered Lablag to destroy Tindule. Lablag assumed that meant the people and told her husband that she would give him Tissany if he erased Tindule from the map. And eventually, being greedy, weak and inflamed by her sorcery, and utterly obsessed with Tissany, Hudigarde agreed.

"He challenged Jussell to war games in the crater. Tissany warned him not to go, but Jussell, a pig-headed, trusting man, would hear nothing against his friend. Thinking the idea of war games a great lark he took his entire army, twenty thousand men, armed with wooden weapons so no one would be killed."

"What happened?" she cried when he did not go on.

Shand took a jar of green sap from his pocket and drained it into a flask which he put on a ring over a spirit burner then connected to a distillation apparatus. He was distilling off the essential oil of the bubble-bark pine from sap collected as the species went extinct—no, as he'd *rendered* it extinct. Aviel glared at him; he was a lot further down the dark path than she was. He met her eyes coolly, showing no remorse.

"Hudigarde's much larger army attacked with real weapons," he said. "They wiped out Jussell's army to the last man and killed him too."

"Twenty thousand soldiers were slaughtered here?" she whispered.

"And it gets worse. Acting on Lablag's instructions, Hudigarde invaded Tindule, slew every man and boy and male baby, sold its women and girls into slavery to a neighbouring country and incorporated Tindule into Grossular. What's the matter?"

"The wickedness," gasped Aviel. "The . . . the infamy! What an evil man."

"But Lablag had betrayed him; she had already spirited her sister far away and sold her too. Hudigarde had killed his friend and destroyed a country he loved, for nothing. He divorced Lablag and spent his days searching for Tissany, to no avail, and soon his great kingdom fell apart in civil war."

"I still don't—"

Watching the green vapour creeping up from his flask, Shand talked over her. "Tindule's women did not stay slaves for long. Some married into great families; others became scholars, mancers and teachers, and within a generation their children were free. For the bravest of them, Rogues Render became a place of pilgrimage, though a dangerous one—the battlefield is still drenched in the psychic agony of the soldiers who died here . . . and those who wept over their bones."

"But why is it called *Rogues* Render?"

"Sometimes on battlefields the dead are treated as barbarously as the living."

"What are you talking about?"

"To the most depraved people of all—carrion predators—even corpses have some value. They tore every tooth out of the jaws of the dead soldiers and shipped barrels of teeth to Thurkad, there to be made into dentures for city dandies. But that wasn't the worst. The carrion predators dragged the bodies to huge cauldrons and rendered them down. Boiled the fat out of them to make corpse candles."

"C-corpse candles!" Aviel's skin crawled. "Why?"

"Necromancers and other practitioners of the dark arts will pay a high price for genuine corpse candles. And the more violent the death, and the fouler the treachery that led to it, the more valuable those corpse candles are. Rogues Render is a dark and dangerous place, Aviel, and it'll be far more deadly when the ghost vampire rises."

She opened the flap of the tent and stepped out into a night blacker than the bitumen seeps of Grund. "Then how can we hope to beat it?"

Shand did not reply.

"The method says the Archeus must be collected at midnight," said Aviel.

"Which gives you four hours to make everything ready, so you can leave here by eleven."

The wind dropped, and for a minute or two there was absolute silence. Then, at the very edge of hearing, Aviel heard female voices singing. No, chanting, though it was not a happy sound.

"Lamentations for the dead," Shand said quietly from a few feet in front of her.

She started; he had turned invisible again and she had not realised he had left the tent. "I didn't know there were other people there."

"There aren't; it's just echoes from the past."

The chanting was replaced by an eerie wailing that rose and fell, rose and fell, and she knew instinctively what it was—a whole nation of women and girls wailing for their slaughtered men and boys.

"I hate this place!" she cried.

"This crater is one of the most psychically active spots in the west—even the ground we stand on, half a mile from Rogues Render, is saturated with treachery, agony and grief. It's why the battlefield is such a lure to ghost vampires."

Aviel felt a pang of terror so overwhelming that she could hardly breathe. Why, why had she agreed to this? Lumillal was going to get her; he—or *it*—would suck her spirit out of her living body and . . . She could not bear to think about it.

34

WHY WOULD I BE INTERESTED IN *LOVE*?

"I don't want you to use *this* terrible procedure," said Earnis, holding the scroll at arm's length.

"So you keep saying," Aviel said irritably as she rinsed her powdered charcoal for the required fifth time. "I don't have any choice."

"The Ombley Parchment sets out a far safer method."

"And it takes *three months* to make nivol. We don't have the time."

"What if I combined the Ombley method and the one you're using?"

She gaped at him. "You've told me a dozen times that alchemical procedures must be followed exactly as written. Two different methods can't be lumped together higgledy-piggledy."

"I've spend twelve years studying the theory and philosophy of alchemy," he said coldly. "I wasn't planning to *lump anything together*."

"But you haven't studied the *practice* of alchemy. You've never had to follow a method."

"I'm really worried about you," he said, staring at her. There was a strange yearning expression on his handsome face, and his eyes were shiny. He took a step towards her, reaching out with both arms.

And it struck her. Earnis was falling in love with her—or thought he was. She took a hasty step back. "Now you're being silly," she said briskly. "Can you fill the cauldron? I'm out of hot water."

His face fell, then he nodded. "Of course."

As he turned away, Nimil entered, carrying a little curved object carved from the silky brown and gold burl of a leopardwood tree. Holding it in both hands, he bowed then held it out to Aviel.

She bowed back and took the object, which was coiled like a snail's shell. It was beautifully carved. "Thank you," she said. "What is it?"

He turned it round on her palm, pressed the right side, and a small drawer, so perfectly made that the edges were invisible, slid open. Inside, on a purple-black velvet lining, sat the plum-sized yellow diamond.

"I don't understand," said Aviel. "I thought you were going to—"

Nimil flicked the top of the diamond, and it rose fractionally. He caught it with a fingernail, pulled gently and withdrew a tapering conical stopper.

"It's . . . beautiful. Perfect!" said Aviel.

"Nothing less than perfection would do." Nimil slid the stopper in, put the phial back in the drawer, closed it, nodded and turned away, then swung back, taking a scrap of papyrus from his scrip. "I finally got through to Malien."

He stood there, staring at it. The papyrus was pale brown with a thin darker border and a few lines of writing on it in the Aachim script, which Aviel could not read. His breath whistled through the metal slit in his throat; he was agitated.

"Is something wrong?" said Aviel.

"The flow from the stone is rising again and Malien fears the Merdrun are preparing to reopen the gate. She says you must make the nivol with the utmost urgency and bring it directly to Zile."

"Why Zile?"

"That's where everyone is now." He went out.

Earnis reappeared. "How else can I help you?"

Aviel watched him warily, praying he had got over his romantic fit. She didn't have time for such nonsense. "You can't. Get some sleep. We have to leave at eleven."

"All right," he said reluctantly. "You should also—"

"I need to think." She shooed him out. "Go!"

His liquid, yearning eyes rested on her, then he climbed the ladder to the sky ship. A lightglass glowed through one of the round windows at the rear, then went out. She went back to her bench, irritably.

"Stupid man!" she muttered.

"For falling for you?" smirked Shand, turning visible knees first this time. He was in her canvas chair, and that annoyed her too. Her ankle was throbbing and she wanted to put her feet up, but there was too much to check and recheck. "The hide of the fellow!"

"I'm only sixteen! Why would I be interested in *love*?"

"I can't imagine," Shand said drily. He took the little box from her hand, opened the drawer and stroked the diamond phial. "Nimil has surpassed himself."

Handing it back, he went to the end bench, opened Radizer's grimoire, which he had taken back before Aviel left Sith, and checked the procedure.

"How's it going?" She wished she were working on a fragrant scent potion, not this infernal alchemy.

Shand grunted. Clearly he knew far more about scent potions than he should. He had said he'd been an apprentice when Radizer had blown himself to bits, but Shand carried out the difficult procedures so quickly and effortlessly he must have been a master. Why had he lied about it? And what was he really doing? Could he be trusted?

He cracked the wax around the lid of a small silver-green earthenware pot, prised it up and wafted the air towards his nose, then grimaced. The smell, both pungent and foul, made Aviel's eyes water and burned her nose like hot mustard.

"What's *that*?" she gasped.

"Swamp horseradish, sealed and allowed to rot for ten or fifteen years." He scooped out two slimy grey lumps with a silver spatula, weighed them on her scrupulously clean scales, added another small scoop and scraped the muck into a distillation flask.

Aviel's stomach heaved. She wiped her eyes and walked out into the darkness, the frosty grass crunching underfoot. As she looked between the boulders towards Rogues Render, again she caught that faint charnel odour. Jussell's army had been slaughtered there, and the soldiers' bodies ill used almost a hundred years ago, yet still the stench lingered. It was a very bad place.

When she returned to the tent, her clenched fingers so cold that she had to prise each one open, Shand had distilled the rotten horseradish and was capping a phial of straw-coloured fluid. He labelled it and lined it up alongside all his other phials. She counted them absently. Seventeen. And nineteen scents were blended to make the Afflatus Effluvium.

"Are you nearly done?" she said, warming her hands over the brazier. He shrugged.

"You work like a master. You must be more skilled at scent potion making than you let on."

Shand's green eyes fixed on her, coldly. "It's after eight. Shouldn't you be making your final preparations?"

Aviel lit a spirit burner and adjusted the flame until it was as low as it would go. She clamped a beaker to a stand, moved it over the flame and, with a pair of unused golden tongs, put a piece of bubble-bark pine colophony in to melt, then brought in a small potter's wheel she had left outside. The wheel, which was of thick steel and had a steel ring a handspan across in the middle, was so cold her fingers stuck to it. It would warm a little by the time the colophony was ready, but would the temperature be right?

Aviel turned to ask Shand but he was gone. He was never around when she needed advice. She opened a narrow blackwood box inside which, nestled in a bed of white wool, was the best of the golden brim-stones. It was perfect, yet delicate—the warmth of a human hand might be enough to shatter it. She put it aside.

She caught the cleansing scent of bubble-bark pine; the colophony had melted. She readied her equipment, spun the frigid steel wheel and in one swift movement poured the colophony into the ring at the centre. Taking a little gold bowl, she gently pressed it into the colophony, just deep enough to form the surface into a shallow dish as the wheel spun.

She checked the shape. Not perfect. She pressed the bowl into the colophony again. It was setting from the base upwards. She pressed harder, checked again, went to press it a third time then stopped, afraid of cracking the dish. She braked the wheel.

The dish had some minor imperfections but the method did not require it to be perfect. When the colophony had set hard she gave the steel ring a gentle sideways tap to free it and lifted it away. The colophony dish came free as well. With a gloved hand she laid it carefully on the bottom of a bronze crucible.

The lid of the crucible had a small hole into which, when it was time for the final step, she would insert a glass tube. Vapours from the burning brimstone and colophony would pass along it then through the multilayered filter cake of magnesia, powdered quartz and quintuple-washed char that had been so difficult to make.

The filter cake would strip the vapours of both chymical and arcane impurities, and the refined essence would condense and drip into the diamond phial, where, in the presence of a piece of sintered platinum and three drams of the Archeus—in the unlikely event that she survived the attempt to get it from Lumillal—it would be alchemically transformed into the Universal Dissoluent, nivol. If she had done everything perfectly. And if, she thought with a shiver, her congenital bad luck did not ruin everything, as it had so many times.

The wind had risen and was shaking the tent, twanging the taut mooring lines of the sky ship and whistling between the meteoritic iron boulders that were so powerfully magical that even people lacking the Secret Art could sense it. Was that why the massacre had taken place nearby?

Again she caught the reek from Rogues Render. Again the ghostly chanting rose above the wind. After a few minutes it cut off, and she heard a woman's voice raised in song. It too was cut short and a plangent wailing from thousands of female voices—a lamentation for their dead—raised every hair on the back of Aviel's neck.

Could she, an unskilled girl, possibly make this most difficult of all alchemical substances, one that had defeated the greatest alchemists in the land? Not unless she could somehow trap and immobilise a deadly ghost vampire.

If that could be done at all.

35

WE WILL TELL YOU RULKE'S GREATEST SECRETS

Sulien screamed and screamed, and every time she opened her mouth steam wisped out. The moving images kept flowing through Karan's inner eye, burning her. To save Sulien, she had to break the link, perilous though that would be. But how?

Don't damage her, I said, growled Gergrig. He was still standing on the broad edge of the white stone bowl. The triplets remained in the red water, watching Sulien's reflection on the surface.

Her screams cut off. *Where . . . is . . . the . . . stone?* said Jaguly.

Sulien shook her head. "I don't know."

But you can find it, said Empuly. *I'll show you what it's like.*

Karan's mind was flooded by such festering corruption that her insides crawled. She had to block it out; it was the only way to protect herself. Was that what the summon stone had done to Unick, to turn him into such a monster?

"Ugh!" gasped Sulien. She tore her hands free and clawed at the top of her head as if to rid herself of something clinging there, trying to burrow inside. "Ugh, yuk, blurrgh!" She doubled over and threw up on Yetchah's long bony feet.

That's just a hint, Empuly said gleefully. *The true stone is a thousand times stronger and darker. You'll never forget that, will you, brat?*

"No," whispered Sulien.

Sense . . . it . . . out!

"Can't!" Sulien moaned.

You're a far greater sensitive than that bitch, your mother. You could find the stone even if it was on the other side of the world.

"No, no, no."

This will encourage you. Find it, NOW!

Sulien screamed, but still shook her head, denying Empuly and Gergrig.

Stop! snapped Gergrig. *You'll damage her.*

Not much, Empuly said sullenly.

It's not working. She's stronger than I would have thought possible. Braver too. Use the other way.

Yes, cried Unbuly. *Yes, yes!*

Again that festering corruption flooded Karan. Again Sulien's face twisted in horror and revulsion and she clawed at her skull.

Harder, said Gergrig.

The corruption grew more sickening. Sulien was moaning and thrashing. In her hiding place behind the dwindling foam cloud, Karan gagged.

Harder, said Gergrig.

The foulness washing through Karan's mind was unbearable; it was every monstrous thing the dregs of humanity was capable of, and more. If she were being tortured, by now she would have revealed every secret she knew. How could Sulien hold out?

Then she broke. "I can see it!" gasped Sulien.

An image exploded into Karan's mind, displacing Gergrig and the triplets—an island clad in forest with a tall conical peak in the middle topped by a cliff-bound tooth of yellow rock. A monstrous purple and black thunderstorm coiled up above it, and lightning struck at the peak, over and again. The forest glowed the hideous yellow-green of muck oozing from a rotting corpse.

Aaahhh! sighed Gergrig. *Magiz?*

The summon stone, said Jaguly, Unbuly and Empuly in awestruck tones.

Sulien doubled over, head in hands, her wet hair falling in a curly red stream to her knees. She was still shuddering and as tense as wire. What would Gergrig do now she had no more value for him? Order her killed?

Karan struggled to breathe. She could no longer see or hear the sky ship. It was up to her now. She had to save Sulien. She was going to do whatever it took—and pay the price later.

What is that place, Whelm? said Gergrig.

Yetchah consulted the other Whelm for a minute or two, then said, "Demondifang. A small island off the north-western tip of Meldorin."

Do you have enough, magiz?

It'll be quicker if we force the brat to link to the stone, said Jaguly.

No outsider gets that close to us, he said sharply. *You can do it, can't you?*

Of course, she said resentfully. *But it'll take longer.*

Kill the brat, then work on the link to the stone.

Pain stabbed through Karan. She loaded the crossbow, her hands shaking, then laid it down. How could she stop the triplets from so far away?

"Lord Gergrig!" Yetchah cried, raising her bony arms high. "Lord Gergrig!"

What do you want, Whelm?

"We gave you the child, and she gave you what you needed. Will you take us for your faithful servants?"

Merdrun have no need of servants, he growled.

"We accept no recompense; all we ask of you is shelter and protection. In return we will be your perfect servants—whatever you order we will do it without question or qualification."

Is that so? he said in a breathy voice. *Tell me, what happened to your previous master?*

"He . . . was . . . killed."

Not through your disobedience or negligence, I trust?

"Through treachery, none of our doing."

And the name of this sad failure of a master? Karan could tell that Gergrig was smiling, having a joke at their expense.

"Rulke!" said Yetchah, and there was a thrill of longing in her voice. "Our perfect master's name was Rulke, the greatest of the Charon."

Rulke! As Gergrig hissed the name, Karan heard the fear in his voice. But he recovered and said, very softly, *If I became your master, and you swore to serve me and obey my every command . . .*

"Yes?" Yetchah said eagerly.

What if I commanded you to reveal your dead master's greatest and most perilous secrets? And the greatest secrets of the Charon?

Yetchah reeled, her arms waving, and Karan could see the conflict on her face, her desperation for a strong master warring with the duty she owed to her late master. Karan also knew, because she had overheard Gergrig say it months ago, that Rulke was the only man he had ever feared.

"We swore to serve Rulke," said Yetchah, "and serve him we did, faithfully and long . . . but no oath to the dead can bind the living. If we swear to you," she gulped, but went on, "we will tell you Rulke's greatest and most perilous secrets, and all the secrets of the Charon he revealed to us."

Instantly Gergrig said, in a roar that echoed through Karan's head, *Then swear to me, faithful Whelm, for I will take you for my servants.*

Yetchah laid her hand on Sulien's bent head. "By the power vested in me when my people voted me leader of the hunt for this girl child, I swear that we, who call ourselves Whelm, now take you Gergrig for our master, and that in return for your shelter and protection we will serve you in all ways and all matters, and obey your every command, and tell you all the secrets of our previous master, Rulke, and every secret of his people, the Charon, that he revealed to us, this oath to be binding on every member of the Whelm nation, woman, man and child, for as long as you shall live."

Arise, my faithful servants.

Yetchah cried out joyfully, then puffs of smoke issued from the centre of her forehead. The Merdrun glyph had been burned there, though smaller than on the Merdrun themselves, and it lay on its side rather than upright.

The foreheads of the other Whelm were smoking too; they all bore the glyph. And, though clearly it had been agonising, their craggy faces glowed; they rejoiced in the pain that bound them to their new master. Their shoulders were squarer, their backs straighter, and they held themselves proudly now. The Whelm were complete at last.

And Karan had never been more afraid. Then it got worse.

I had thought to allow my magiz to kill the child who threatens us all, said Gergrig, *yet—*

But Gergrig! whined Unbuly. *You promised.*

In the coming weeks you will drink more lives than you could ever have hoped for. Faithful servant, he said to Yetchah, *kill the child! Then find the mother and kill her too.*

Yetchah looked shocked. Perhaps she had not yet come to terms with the gaining of her greatest desire. She licked her cracked lips. And perhaps, now that the moment was here, she was having second thoughts about murdering an innocent girl she had saved and protected, and yearned for at times. But she had sworn to obey without question, and Karan knew she would.

Karan made sure that the poisoned bolt was properly seated in the crossbow and others were close to hand. To have any chance, she must time her attack perfectly.

"Yes, Master," said Yetchah.

She drew a long knife and went slowly towards Sulien's stool. Karan had lost the image of the white bowl and red pool but she sensed Gergrig watching, his grim face expressionless. The triplets too, each according to their nature: Jaguly eager for the terror of a helpless victim as her life was torn out of her; Unbuly apathetic but aching to experience a death that would make her feel alive for a few precious moments; Empuly cringing away from the horror, yet longing to drink the victim's pain.

The other Whelm were still. The brown foam mounds squelched and popped as they shrank. The fires crackled and spread. Burned boards collapsed in showers of orange coals. The rain poured down, hissing on the embers but not quenching them. In the distance, the mountains were faintly outlined by pale grey sky, the first hint of dawn.

Everyone was staring at Yetchah as she approached Sulien from behind. Karan dared not try and shoot her but, as Yetchah raised the knife, Karan shot the closest Whelm in the thigh. He clawed at the wound, trying to tear the stinging, burning bolt out, but his leg collapsed and he fell.

Yetchah whirled, trying to locate their enemy. Karan loaded and fired again, hitting a female Whelm in the hip, and she too went down. But Karan had been seen behind her dwindling foam cloud and three Whelm flung themselves at her.

She shot the first in the ribs and heard a hiss as his lung collapsed. He lurched around, gasping, but the other two were still coming. Karan ducked around the other side of the foam, knowing she could not escape them both.

With a splintery crash the leading Whelm disappeared in a burst of brown spray and a clatter of staves; Yggur had dropped another little barrel and it had landed on his head. The last Whelm tripped over him and went skidding across the platform, his arms out before him. He got up, wincing; the weathered boards had embedded dozens of huge splinters into his palms and blood was pouring from his hands.

Karan shot him in the shoulder. He lurched around, clawing at himself, trod on a section where the boards had burned to charcoal and fell through into the gorge.

But Yetchah was still behind Sulien, shouting for reinforcements, and the Whelm who had retreated to the ridge were storming back towards the bridge. The platform was burning in half a dozen places now but the rain was not heavy enough to put these fires out.

Karan dropped the crossbow, ran to Sulien, reached into her mind and took hold of the psychic link from the triplets—a silver-grey cord like a length of silken yarn—and tore it out by the roots. Sulien gasped and doubled over, and her stool toppled to the deck. The unravelled end of the link became visible, several feet of it thrashing in Karan's grip, the rest of the silvery cord fading into nothingness.

She heard a psychic scream, loud and shrill, as the triplets tried to force the link back into Sulien. They were stronger than the previous magiz had been and far stronger than Karan. Inch by inch they dragged the flailing end of the link back. Karan fought for the life of her daughter with all the strength she had, but it wasn't enough.

"Get . . . away!" she gasped, trying to push Sulien away with one foot.

Yetchah swooped on Sulien and held her by the shoulders, her face almost as eager now as it had been when she swore to Gergrig. The triplets forced harder, pulling Karan's hands and the end of the link down towards Sulien. It was only a foot from her now and Karan could sense their sick glee.

Stop! said Gergrig. *Yetchah must do it to seal the contract.*

The triplets weren't listening. They wanted Sulien's death too badly and they wanted it this way, through Karan. The moment the link bonded to her they would send a killing pulse down it, then drink both their lives.

Karan's arms were shaking all the way to her shoulders as she fought the force that was dragging her hands and the link back to Sulien. Karan's fingertips were only inches from Sulien's forehead now. An unravelled thread of the link struck her there, leaving a curving red welt across her pale skin, and tried to dig itself in. Karan jerked back desperately but knew she could not do so again.

She had only one hope left. *Duck!* she mouthed to Sulien.

Sulien ducked, and in that instant Karan threw the last of her strength into a desperate attack. She thrust forward and up towards the Whelm who had saved her life in childbirth, praying that the triplets could not react in time to stop her.

Her fists struck Yetchah's forehead and the incomplete link, unable to return to the mind it had been torn from, sought the next closest one. It speared through the Merdrun glyph burned into Yetchah's forehead and into her skull, and Karan sensed it burying itself deep in her mind. At the same instant, the triplets directed all their hate and madness into a killing impulse down the link.

A stray thread of the link, still clinging to Karan's left palm, burned white hot. She gasped, thrashed and it tore away.

Then Yetchah screamed in the uttermost agony of one who had just gained her life's desire only to be robbed of it, and *everything*.

The triplets screamed too, for the killing impulse has to be tailored to each victim, and one designed for Sulien was utterly wrong for Yetchah. It killed her and surged back across the link, rebounding on them agonisingly.

And on Gergrig, who roared and collapsed. Karan caught a fleeting glimpse of him, and the triplets howling and thrashing in the reflective red water, then the link vanished.

"Mummy!" cried Sulien.

The remaining Whelm were storming across the bridge, only fifty yards away, furious that Karan had attacked their new master. There was no escape that way.

The link had utterly drained her but she had to keep going. She slashed Sulien's bonds and peered through the smoke. Could they make it to the other bridge? A quarter of the platform was covered by the creeping fires and another half was blocked by mounds and clots of gluey foam; if they tried to run through it they would stick fast.

Three winding paths were still open to the far bridge, though some of the Whelm were running to block two of them. However if Karan and Sulien went out to the left, then around the left-hand edge of the platform, they might get to the bridge first. But what then?

The signal! Karan twisted Yggur's yellow lightstick hard. It did not light. She bent it double and was staring at it, wondering what was wrong, when she remembered his injunction to throw it at once. She hurled the lightstick straight up as far as she could, took Sulien's hand and they ran.

The lightstick burst with a flash like the sun rising, and fiery flares radiated out in a dozen directions. One shot up towards the sky ship, lighting it from underneath like a looming monster. The Whelm, who could not have seen anything like it before, cried out in fear.

Karan held her breath. If the flare touched the air bag, the sky ship would explode and that would be the end. The flare speared up, up, up, but stopped a few yards short and went out.

The sky ship rocked from the force of the air blast and started to turn. But it was a lumbering craft, difficult to control in the windy conditions that prevailed here, and slow to accelerate. Minutes would pass before it could get to a safe landing place on the far side and, if a Whelm came within range, one bolt from a crossbow could tear the airbag and trap the sky ship on the ground.

"Faster!" said Karan, though clearly Sulien could go no faster. Whatever she had endured over the past week, more than any child should ever have to suffer, had utterly worn her out.

The smoke stung Karan's eyes, making it difficult to see. She considered carrying Sulien, but it would be too dangerous on the edge of the platform; they had to be able to hang on. They headed for the rim, then Karan stopped dead. Three Whelm blocked the way. It was over.

The rotors of the sky ship roared; it hurtled down, wove between two pairs of guttering flares, and the front of the cabin slammed into the Whelm, hurling two over the side into the treetops. The third, struck a glancing blow, lay on his back several yards away, cradling a broken leg.

Karan felt a surge of hope, but it swiftly faded. The sky ship could not land on the burning platform, and another band of Whelm had reached the far end of the bridge. The rain stopped suddenly, and flames, fanned by the wind, spread across the platform. The only path open now was the one around the rim, but not for much longer.

Sulien bent double, coughing. Karan took her hand. "We've got to go around there." Karan pointed. "Can you manage it?" Sulien did not have her head for heights.

"I . . . think so." She looked up at Karan, her lower lip trembling, then gave her a watery smile. "Thank you, Mummy. I knew you'd come."

"Nothing could have stopped me." Karan squeezed her hand. Her eyes stung and the suppressed emotions almost overcame her. *Not yet; not until we're safe* . . .

They were far from safe, for the Whelm with the broken leg had been armed with a crossbow and he was dragging himself towards it. The other Whelm were leaping from one charred patch of the deck to another as if they had no fear for their own lives. No—having a master at last, and obeying his wishes, *was* their lives, and they would gladly sacrifice themselves for him.

Karan and Sulien made their way around the edge, Karan on the outside. The platform must have been built decades ago, and some of the exposed timbers at the edge were rotten, crumbling under hand and foot.

"What's that . . . thing up there?" said Sulien.

"Malien's sky ship."

Sulien's face brightened. "Is Malien here?"

"No. I—I stole it. With Yggur. She's furious; she may never forgive me."

"Oh!"

"But it was worth it." Karan hugged her again.

She could hear the rotors but it was so smoky now that she could not see the sky ship; she could only see a few yards ahead and behind. They crept around the crumbling rim to the end of the second bridge. Its deck was also burning slowly and many of the boards had fallen in, though the heavier framing timbers seemed sound.

Karan swallowed. Could they cross on the framing timbers? It would be very dangerous but there was no choice.

She was about to boost Sulien up onto the remains of the bridge when Idlis stepped into their path. He was a wreck. His face was battered and bruised, his left eye black and completely closed, and his right eye was so bloodshot it appeared to be weeping blood. The Merdrun glyph burned into his forehead was incomplete—the slash on the right side was not there at all.

"Idlis!" Karan said coldly.

"Please don't hurt him, Mummy," said Sulien. "Idlis saved me, and look what they've done to him."

Karan eyed the Whelm, who had proved more true to his word than some of her friends and allies. He looked tormented.

"You killed Yetchah," he said thickly.

"No, the triplets did."

"*You made it happen.* You knew they would attack Yetchah in the heat of the moment, thinking she was Sulien."

"Yes," said Karan.

"Yetchah saved your life! And Sulien's!"

"And I owed her—until she betrayed Sulien to Gergrig."

"She . . . did not know what she was doing."

"Yes she did! She chose to sacrifice Sulien, just to gain a new master."

"Not just for herself," said Idlis. "She did it so the whole Whelm nation could gain that which we longed for so desperately."

"She *chose*," said Karan, glancing over her shoulder at the approaching Whelm. "And in choosing to betray Sulien, Yetchah cancelled the debt."

A gluggy choking sound issued from his upper chest. "All her life she loved me, and I could not return her love. I did not know what love was." His bloody eye looked down at Sulien, then up into Karan's eyes. "But now," he howled, "now she's dead at your hand, *I know.*"

Karan swallowed. She felt for him, but if she did not get past him quickly it would be all over.

"It was the hardest thing I've ever had to do," she said quietly.

"Then why, *why?*"

"For love of the only child I can ever have. Yetchah was good to us both, and I honour her for it, but after she saw Gergrig nothing mattered—not her given word to me, not the life of a child she cared deeply for, *nor even you.*"

"You know it, Idlis," said Sulien, and to Karan's amazement she took his bony hand and clutched it between her own. "You went against your people to be true to your oath. You even denied the thing you wanted most of all." She bent her small head to him. "You are the most honourable man in the world, and I'm sorry you lost Yetchah."

Idlis looked down at her, at her small, smooth hands holding his thin, scarred hand, and the most remarkable expression crossed his face, awestruck joy. "I'm glad I've known you, little one," he said hoarsely. "You are the best of your kind."

He let go of her hand and turned to Karan. "Mine was a life thrice-owed, and I swore to serve you in return, but your ill deed has broken the bond. Will you release me from my oath?"

Behind Karan a large section of the platform fell with a crash that shook the rest. Smoke gushed out in all directions. Idlis was blocking their way and she owed him more than she could ever repay, but what would he do if she did release him?

"Sulien," she said. "Go across."

"But Mummy—"

"Now, please."

Sulien swallowed, then crept onto the beams, which were smoulder-ing in many places and had flames licking out of them here and there. She teetered, threw her arms out wide and cried out, but continued. Karan could not bear to watch.

"Let me past," said Karan to Idlis.

"Release me."

"If I do, the oath Yetchah swore to Gergrig, the oath that binds the whole Whelm nation, will take effect and you will have to kill Sulien. And me."

"Please release me," he croaked.

"I can't."

"Why not? Yetchah's oath to Gergrig cannot bind me."

"Why not?"

"I am no longer Whelm. My people cast me out for helping Sulien to escape. I have nothing now. Indeed, without a master or a people, I *am* nothing."

"But you ache to be Whelm again, and to have a master. If I released you from your oath, how do I know you wouldn't do Gergrig's bidding so the Whelm would take you back?"

Utter outrage showed on his bruised face. "After all I've done for you and your daughter," he choked, "and all I've suffered, *you still don't trust me?*"

Karan went cold inside. Had she made a terrible mistake? But how could she take the risk?

"I trust the man who held to his oath no matter what," she said softly. "But not the man without the oath."

"I am ... the ... same ... man!"

"I'm sorry," said Karan, and she was. Deeply sorry, but Sulien had to come first.

He might have been hewn from obsidian, so hard did his face go. "So be it," he said and stepped aside. "My oath holds and I cannot harm Sulien in any way, thus I must let you go so you can protect her in this accursed place. Yet I remain an outcast, and from this moment forth I am your most bitter enemy *until either you or I are dead*! Go! I will give you until Sulien reaches the far side of the bridge, and not a second longer."

Karan, sick with dread that she had made things worse, stepped up onto one of the smouldering beams of the bridge and went gingerly across. Ahead the beam was burning for a good ten yards, but she had to cross it. She walked into the flames, which licked a foot high around her calves, praying that her sodden boots and trousers did not dry out before she got to the other side.

Sulien was halfway across, out of the fire zone, her green eyes staring out of her pale face. Karan hurried on and reached her, and went to take her hand.

"No, Mummy," said Sulien. "It's safer by myself."

Karan went behind her, which was even worse. Sulien made her halting way across and in another minute they reached the other side. They looked back. The smoke had cleared to reveal most of the boards of the platform gone. The remaining Whelm were creeping across one of the main beams, approaching Idlis. Someone called to him, and he flung out an arm, pointing to Karan and Sulien.

The Whelm ran for the bridge.

"Come on!" said Karan, turning away, and they raced across the top of the ridge to the flattest part, a hundred yards away. She prayed that it was out of crossbow range.

The sky ship swooped down, its skids striking the rock ahead of them with a crash and a trail of yellow sparks. The Whelm, who were creeping across the burning support beams of the platform, fired their crossbows. The bolts fell short, though not by much.

Hingis threw the ladder out. Sulien went up it, Karan followed, Yggur jerked the levers and the craft shot upwards out of reach.

"Thank you," Karan said to Yggur and Hingis. "Thank you."

She threw her arms around Sulien and wept.

36

I'LL FEED ON THEM TOO

"Ghost vampires aren't like ordinary ghosts," said Hublees late that evening. "Ghost vampires have to feed, and that's how we'll trap Lumillal."

He had called her into the sky ship and closed the door so they could make plans without having to worry about being spied upon.

"What do they feed on?" said Aviel, her skin crawling. Outside she could hear the steady crunch of Osseion's footsteps on the frosty grass.

"Other ghosts, mostly. But there are no other ghosts at Rogues Render."

"I'd have thought there'd be thousands," said Aviel.

"All consumed," said Nimil, making a rare interjection. "Or fled."

Judging by the look in his eyes, he wanted to flee too, and Aviel could not blame him.

"I read the records before I agreed to accompany you," said Hublees. "And I have much experience in dealing with ghosts, spirits and spectres, among other creatures."

"What about ghost vampires?"

"No one has experience in dealing with ghost vampires."

"Why not?"

Hublees did not reply.

"No one has lived to talk about it . . ." said Earnis, the last words dying away. His tanned face was waxen, his eyes darting.

"Until now," said Hublees crisply. "After Lumillal appeared here, more than ninety years ago, he consumed hundreds of the ghosts haunting Rogues Render. The rest fled or faded to nothingness or . . . did whatever dying ghosts do."

"I'd have thought you'd know," said Aviel, "since you're so experienced."

Hublees gave her a very cold look. "Terror of a ghost vampire is one of the few ways the thread binding a ghost to a particular place can be broken."

"Then how does Lumillal survive?"

"As the enslaved womenfolk and their children gained their freedom, many of them came on pilgrimage here, and all who were foolish enough to enter Rogues Render after dark he drained to husks. Soon the reputation of the place was so dire that few dared come here."

"He must be starving."

"I dare say, though ghost vampires can go for years without feeding."

Hublees' chilly eyes were fixed on Aviel as if assessing her and finding her wanting. "Lumillal will know we're here by now, though surely he can't imagine *why* we're here."

Aviel let out an involuntary squeak. Air whistled through Nimil's throat slit.

"What if he's after us now?" said Earnis.

"He's bound to the ruins of the rendering works," said Hublees. "In any case, when he has a choice he'll avoid mancers like myself and Nimil, and big strong men like Earnis and Osseion . . ."

"You mean he'll go for me," said Aviel, "because I'm young and small and crippled."

"And because you're gifted."

"What difference does that make?"

"He means Lumillal will get much more out of consuming your life force," cried Earnis. "Hublees, you can't use her as the bait in the trap. I won't allow it. She's so . . ."

"Pretty?" said Hublees with a knowing leer.

Earnis flushed. "Inexperienced, I meant. Helpless. She has to be . . ."

"Protected?" Aviel said coldly.

"Aviel flushed out a murderer when she was thirteen," said Hublees. "He died, she survived. And a couple of months back she was taken by Gurgito Unick, one of the most vicious brutes in the west. He was planning to kill her and feed her to the summon stone, but instead the stone fed on him and Aviel poisoned it at the critical moment. I understand that you're *infatuated* with her—" the mocking way Hublees said this, staring into Earnis's eyes, made him flush and look away "—but she doesn't need to be protected."

"She's still *bait*," Earnis said in a racked tone. "And if something goes wrong—if something prevents us from getting to her in time . . ."

"Bait?" she whispered. "Are you saying I've got to go up there by myself?"

"If we go together, he'll know we're trying to trap him," said Hublees. He raked stubby fingers through his ridiculous goatee. "Lumillal likes to toy with his living victims; he's been known to terrorise them for hours. It helps him to extract every last scrap of their life force and—"

"And you're happy for little Aviel to be terrorised for hours?" Earnis bellowed.

"Don't call me *little Aviel*," she snapped. She had to stay angry; it was the only way to stop herself from screaming. If she went to Rogues Render, she would die there.

"I am a mancer of considerable power," said Hublees, knotting his long white sideburns into his black goatee with jerky, agitated movements. "Lumillal isn't a mancer; he can't defend himself against my spells."

"How do you know he's not a mancer?" said Aviel.

The absurd little man opened his mouth but closed it without speaking. *He doesn't know!* she thought. *He's making it up.*

Earnis's face looked as if he had been scalded. He wrenched the cabin door open and leaped to the ground, then let out a roar of fury: "*Aaarrrgggh!*"

There was a long silence. Nimil was absently moving one of the brass pointers on his scrying board. "It's nearly eleven," he said, rising. "We'd better get ready."

"But what am I supposed to do?" said Aviel. "Just walk over to the ruins and . . . wait for him to find me?"

"Yes," said Hublees. "Pretend you're there to mourn your ancient dead. And don't take any alchemical gear; if Lumillal sees it, it'll give the game away. Once we approach he'll sense us, so he's got to . . . have his hooks in you first."

A scream was building up, louder and shriller than Earnis's. Aviel fought it down. "You mean his teeth."

"What?"

"He's a *vampire*!" she choked.

"I meant his metaphorical hooks."

"I have no idea what you're talking about."

"Lumillal is both greedy and ravenous, and your great gift makes your life force a prize he won't be able to resist. Once he begins to torment you he won't be able to let go, and that's when I'll attack. I'll trap him in one of the old rendering cauldrons. Earnis and Osseion will bang the lid down and we'll distil every drop of Archeus out of the bastard."

The flaws in his plan were a mile wide. *I can't do this*, she thought. *I want to go home.* But the fate of the world depended on nivol, and only she could make it in time. She swallowed. "I'll be ready in five minutes."

"Better dress for the cold."

She returned to the workshop and put on a woollen vest, a heavy coat and gloves. She was breathing so fast that she felt light-headed, and her heart was fluttering like a trapped moth. She recited a list of bitter herbs backwards in a futile attempt to calm herself, then emptied her pockets of everything alchemical.

Shand popped into visibility. "Are you sure you're up to this?"

"No."

"I'll be there, invisibly, as soon as—"

"He's got his hooks into me," she said sarcastically.

"Precisely." He held out a gnarled hand. "Good luck, Aviel." He headed for the opening, then stopped. "Best go unarmed, eh? Do nothing that could damage the Archeus." He turned invisible and went out.

Aviel slumped on her chair, breathing heavily again, trying to find her courage. Damn Hublees! Damn the Archeus and damn Shand! She wasn't taking advice from a traitor.

She withdrew Wilm's black sword from its copper sheath. It was said to be enchanted but what did that mean? It was very sharp and surprisingly light—light enough for her to swing one-handed. She wound strips of rag around the blade, tied a loop onto the hilt, slid the sword into her voluminous skirts and fixed it to her belt under her coat. It would be awkward to draw and unfasten the sword, and almost certainly useless against a ghost, though she felt better for having it.

Aviel crept out between the uncanny boulders and turned towards Rogues Render. The distant wailing rose and fell, but now she saw a greenish glimmer in the direction of the ruins. She stopped, her stomach throbbing. Why was it up to her? Hadn't she done enough?

With a special gift comes great responsibility, she told herself. *And to defeat the great enemy we must all do our utmost.* The little lecture was no help at all, but she went on.

Before she was halfway she sensed something sniffing, as if trying to locate her. Aviel froze, shudders creeping up her back. Could she do this? She took another step forward, but a small rock moved underfoot, jarring her bad ankle. She stifled a cry, waited until the pain eased and hobbled on.

The cold was awful. The tip of her nose was stinging, her eyes were watering in the wind and the tears were freezing on her cheeks. Such cold should have reduced the smell of Rogues Render to an occasional whiff but the disgusting reek grew stronger until it was almost unbearable. How could those carrion hunters have rendered thousands of dead soldiers, just to make corpse candles? Her innards churned.

It reminded her of her first real crime—robbing a grave and disturbing the sacred rest of someone dead. Was distilling the spectral blood from a ghost vampire also a crime? It was certainly a huge stride down the dark path, no matter how noble her motives for attempting it.

This train of thought was undermining what little confidence she had left. She had to focus on getting to Rogues Render, finding a way to trap Lumillal, *and surviving it.*

The eerie wailing died away and was replaced by faint, faded screams, echoes from the past as the betrayed soldiers were cut down. The yellow-green glimmer from the ruins started to waver up and down like the southern aurora she had seen one winter's night as a little girl. It was bright enough, as she approached, to light up the ruins: the stumps of fallen chimneys, lines of brickwork, scattered stone blocks, roof beams and broken slates. To her left, four rusting iron cauldrons stood in a row, each big enough to have contained a couple of oxen.

Not oxen, though . . .

She suppressed the ghastly thought. Further on was a tangle of pipework, rusted through, and three lines of rotting wooden vats. The iron hoops had come away and the staves stuck up like angled teeth.

And everywhere—*everywhere!*—were the great bone middens the human predators had left behind, sometimes round piles, sometimes walls of bones as much as six feet high, ten feet across and twenty feet long. It was the most awful sight she had ever seen—all that remained of twenty thousand soldiers, betrayed and slaughtered because of one man's insane lust for another man's wife.

And driven by the Merdrun's summon stone. Never forget that.

Aviel's right ankle was throbbing and her right knee and hip ached; the long walk over rough ground had shifted her joints out of alignment.

Sssssss. Somewhere behind her.

Aviel spun round, staring into the green-tinged darkness, her heart thundering.

My, you are a pretty one!

"Where are you?" she gasped. "What do you want?"

Gifted too. You'll give me back years and years. Ssssssss.

Now she saw him, a dark outline against the green glow. Lumillal must have been a tall man once, and perhaps a handsome one too, though he was shrunken and stooped as if his desiccated flesh had pulled his frame out of shape and compressed him sideways. His skull was long and very narrow, his teeth large and pointed and slightly luminous. His eyes were black rimmed, deeply sunken and huge, and lit from within by the same oily yellow-green glow that bathed the ruins. Did it come from him?

He drifted towards her, making the hissing sound as if with each breath, *ssssssss, ssssssss, ssssssss.* But ghosts did not breathe; were they even alive?

Aviel backed away and darted down between two of the long bone middens. At the end she turned left and ducked in behind one of the rotting vats. The staves still had a faint fatty odour from the corpse candles that had been made there.

Sssssssss.

She crept out the other way, careful not to tread on the scattered bones, slipped through a small gap between two more vats, then down behind a soot-stained length of wall towards the cauldrons.

Sssssssss.

He was coming straight for her. Perhaps, as a former vampire, he could smell her blood or see her life force. Panic overwhelmed her and she had to fight down a scream, fight the urge to run too. She had a job to do and no one else could do it—get Lumillal into one of the cauldrons so the others could trap him there.

She now saw that there were six cauldrons, not four, though the one closest to her lay on its side and she could see through its rusted-out base to the white midden behind. The cauldron next to it was also on its side. It may have been whole but it would be harder to seal Lumillal in. She scurried through the base of the rusted-out cauldron and out the other side, catching her skirts on jagged edges of metal, and on to the cauldrons beyond. They were all upright.

Sssssssss. Ssssssss.

He was right behind her; how was she to do it? She must not make it too obvious. She hobbled behind the next cauldron, out of sight, then climbed up onto the broken brick wall behind it. She could not see Lumillal from here though the glow from his awful eyes was brightening.

She caught the rim of the middle cauldron, sprang up and, with much scrabbling and gasping, heaved herself onto it. Where was he? She could not tell. She lowered herself into the cauldron but her boots could not grip the steep sides; the rusty scale on the iron was flaking off under the pressure. When she reached the limit of her arms she had no choice but to let go and fall, a foot and a half onto inch-thick ice in the bottom of the cauldron.

It broke with a loud *crack*, the shards stabbing her ankles and shins, and she plunged another six inches into freezing water which flooded in over the tops of her boots and burned all the way down to her toes. She could not get out of it; there was no way to climb the sides of the cauldron. She had trapped herself.

She huddled in the icy water, her feet slowly going numb, now praying that Lumillal would not find her. The thought of being trapped in the cauldron with him, and tortured by him, almost stopped her heart. She prayed that Hublees would catch him first, though she could not imagine how.

All was silent now, as silent as the dead. The wailing and the faded screams had stopped the moment she entered the ruins.

Sssssssss.

Lumillal's hideously elongated head crept above the rim. His green-glowing eyes looked down and fixed on her, then he drifted ever so slowly upwards until he hung in the air above her. His mouth cracked open in a predatory leer. *Sssssssss.*

Aviel let out a screech and sprang up, scrabbling for the rim, but did not even get close.

You can't escape, hissed Lumillal. *And your allies can't save you either. You're all mine now, until you die.*

"What are you talking about?" she blustered, a sickening dread creeping over her.

Do you think I don't know why you're here? You're not the first to come for my Archeus, but I'm still here, and they're in here.

He pointed to his middle, then raised one spectral arm, bared his pointed teeth and strained. Brilliant green light shot up from his fingers for hundreds of feet then split into dozens of rays that curved down over Rogues Render like a protective shield.

"What's *that*?" she gasped. Her heart was now thundering so loudly that he must have been able to hear it.

My terror barrier. A sorcerous spell that renders everyone nearby paralysed by a dread so powerful that they're incapable of thought. Your so-called friends won't come to your rescue; they can't move. And when I'm finished with you I'll feed on them too.

Aviel was incapable of replying. Not because of his terror barrier, which did not affect those at its centre, but because she had been thrown to a wolf and was desperately trying to find a way to save herself.

You fool, Hublees! she thought. *You just assumed Lumillal wasn't a mancer—and you were wrong. He's a powerful sorcerer. We're all going to die and this monster will end up even stronger.*

Your life force is very rich, said Lumillal, eyeing her with such lust that he was drooling strands of glowing plasm. *It might even be enough to bring me back to life as a real vampire. If it does I'll drain you to a husk, break free of Rogues Render and stalk the land for the ninety years' worth of victims I've missed out on.*

"How can you do spells? Were you a sorcerer in life?"

"Aviel?" shrieked Earnis. "Where are you? Are you all right?"

He must have broken free of the terror barrier; she could hear him scrabbling across the bone stacks. Should she call out? Or pray that he never found her and got away to safety?

Then she saw the predatory hunger on Lumillal's face and knew how wrong she was. Earnis hadn't broken free; Lumillal had allowed him to escape so he could run to her—and to his death.

"Earnis," she screamed. "You've done exactly what he wanted. Run!"

With a gesture of his bony left hand, Lumillal raised her in the air until her head was five feet above the top of the cauldron. Aviel dared not struggle; if she broke free she would hit the bottom of the cauldron hard enough to break her ankles. She watched helplessly as Earnis raced along between two bone middens. He saw her suspended there and skidded to a stop.

"Let her go!" he roared.

"Earnis, he's a great sorcerer," cried Aviel. "There's nothing you can do."

Earnis drew a silver throwing knife from a pouch, drew back his arm and hurled it at Lumillal.

Silver can't harm me! Lumillal laughed as it passed harmlessly through him. Earnis drew another knife.

Aviel choked back a sob. Lumillal was going to kill Earnis solely because he cared for her. "Earnis, run!"

Lumillal lowered her onto the broad rim of the cauldron, then drifted slowly towards Earnis, who thrust out his silver knife, but there was nothing he could do to harm a ghost vampire. Lumillal swirled his right hand, and a pale yellow radiance rose like misty tendrils from Earnis's head and chest.

It was his life force. As Aviel watched in horror, Lumillal drifted down and gathered the yellow tendrils in, winding then back and forth between a hand and an crooked elbow like freshly spun thread. Earnis slumped to his knees, gasping.

"Earnis, he wants to kill you. Run!"

"What kind . . . a man . . . abandon you?"

"A live one!"

But Earnis—brave, loyal, gentle—shook his head. Even knowing he was going to die, he would not turn his back on a girl he had come to love. Even knowing that she did not love him.

"Might . . . give you . . . chance," said Earnis.

It won't, said Lumillal, *but I thank you for the donation. The life force of a noble sacrifice is particularly nourishing.*

There was nothing she could do; Lumillal was beyond her reach. He gathered in more and more tendrils until there were barely any left and Earnis was swaying on his knees. His mouth hung open and his eyes were as dull as the eyes of a fish on a monger's slab.

Lumillal gathered the last tendrils and wrenched them out. Earnis collapsed. Lumillal wadded all the threads into a ball, tossed it high and, with a single gleeful movement, swallowed it.

Earnis jerked, then fell on his face. He was dead.

Aviel screamed and screamed.

37

YOU KILLED HER, DIDN'T YOU?

Karan gazed at Sulien in wonder. She was scratched and battered and bruised, thinner and paler than before, and a much older girl looked out of her nine-and-a-half-year-old eyes. She was quivering like a small creature that had to be wary of predators every moment of its life or be eaten.

Then the older girl vanished, and the child threw herself into Karan's arms, hugging her so tightly that the breath was squeezed out of her.

"I knew you'd come for me," Sulien whispered. "I always knew . . . deep down."

Karan's eyes watered. She knew Sulien was thinking of all those times in the past weeks when Karan had not dared to answer for fear the magiz would find her. And those times since Karan had regained some mancery but at the cost of her ability to link.

"Sith?" said Yggur.

"Fast as you can," said Karan.

As the sky ship turned north and climbed, Sulien pulled away. Her eyes roved around the inside of the sky ship, looking at the strangely beautiful Aachim craftsmanship. Every cupboard, every knob, every seat, strut and ceiling panel was beautifully carved and decorated with inlaid woods of many colours, or precious minerals. She turned to Yggur, who was at the controls, staring out the front window.

She took a deep, shivery breath and went up to him, swaying as the craft rocked in the air. She bowed and said gravely, "Thank you, Mister Yggur."

Karan suppressed a snort. Mister Yggur indeed!

Yggur inclined his head to her gravely. "I'm glad you're safe, Sulien. You're braver than any child—and most adults—I've ever met."

After a long pause Sulien came back to Karan, then started. She had just seen Hingis scrunched into a seat down the back. She went down to him and stood there, gazing at his ruined face and sad, twisted body.

"You helped me too," she said. "Thank you." She extended her hand, and, after a long pause, Hingis shook it.

"I didn't help that much," he said and turned away.

The confidence and sense of purpose he had shown after their attack on the lyrinx's cavern was gone. He was a broken man again.

"What happened to you?" said Sulien.

"Sulien!" hissed Karan. "Don't ask personal questions."

"When I was seven, my twin sister dared me to ride a dangerous mule," said Hingis breathlessly, his withered lung crackling with each breath. "She's brave and she loves danger; she had already done it easily. But I'm . . . *not brave*. I was terrified and the mule knew. It threw me off then kicked me when I was down, and kept kicking. I should have died. I wish I had. But Esea ran in and dragged me to safety and . . . I ended up like this. A monster, inside and out."

"I saw you at the door of the sky ship," said Sulien. "You were very brave."

"It's not brave when you don't care if you live or die." He rose, climbed into the hammock furthest away at the back and pulled a blanket over his head.

Sulien took a lurching step back, staring at the desolate shape, then hurried back to Karan, and they sat down side by side. Sulien's hand crept out and found Karan's. Karan sighed and drew her close.

"Mummy, where's Daddy?"

Karan had been dreading the question. "I don't know." She summarised what had happened since Sulien left with the Whelm more than a month ago, then told her how Karan and Llian had finally met at Carcharon and what had happened there and at Alcifer.

"After I got back from . . . *dealing with* the first magiz—"

"You killed her, didn't you?" said Sulien, wide-eyed.

Karan did not want to relive that desperate time up on the ice-covered plateau, on her back with her belly bared to the magiz's knife, but Sulien needed to know.

"She was about to kill me and drink my life, to open the Crimson Gate. I cast the only spell I could, a simple freezing charm inside her open mouth and . . . it killed her. But she used her own death to open the gate, and the Merdrun started to come through. Then something strange happened."

"They ended up on an island a long way away," said Sulien. "But they're trying to escape."

"After I came back from Cinnabar Llian had disappeared. I knew he was in danger but so were you. I saw Yetchah *see* Gergrig, and I heard her vow to take him for their master. I . . . I had to choose between looking for Llian and trying to find you."

"Poor Mummy!"

"I had to choose you. Llian would have done the same, but . . ."

"It must have been horrible."

"Yes. There was only one way to get here quickly enough, so Yggur helped me steal Malien's sky ship."

Sulien turned to Yggur, who was staring ahead, then back to Karan. Sulien must have known there was more to the story but did not ask.

"What happened to you?" said Karan.

Sulien related how she had escaped the Whelm and how good Idlis had been to her. She told of her capture by Ghyll the lyrinx on the arch in Hessular and the bargain he had wanted to offer humanity until the Whelm slaughtered his people, and then his threat of undying war.

"The Whelm are a pox on Santhenar!" cried Yggur. "How could I have ever seen otherwise?"

"And now they've betrayed us to the enemy," said Karan. "For nothing! Gergrig will put them down the moment he has no further use for them." She closed her eyes and leaned back in her seat, and suddenly the force that had driven her all these days drained away. She was so exhausted she could barely hold her head up. "Yggur," she said slowly, "what do you make of the lyrinx's threat?"

"It's an empty one—there can't be a hundred of them in all Santhenar."

Sulien reached over and took Karan's hand. She seemed anxious. She did not speak for some time, though she kept leaning towards Karan as if she wanted to say something.

"What is it, darling?" said Karan.

"Idlis said my gift was growing. He said it was so strong he could sense it . . . and so did Ghyll, but . . ."

"Stands to reason," said Yggur. "A natural gift like yours, an *untrained* gift, could grow to protect you."

"But it feels like I'm *losing* it," said Sulien. "Whenever I've tried to defend myself with it, like I did against Julken, it just . . . fails." She turned to Karan. "Mummy, can you teach me how to use my gift?"

Karan had been dreading that question as well. "No!" she said sharply.

Yggur turned from the controls and gave her a hard stare but did not speak.

"Why not?" said Sulien.

"I wouldn't know how," Karan said hastily. "My own gift was blocked when I was young and now it's too late to learn it properly."

"You have a physical gift for mancery, and a psychic gift," said Yggur to Sulien. "Is it your physical gift that's failing, or both?"

"Physical," said Sulien. "I can't defend myself by touching people any more."

"What about the psychic? Have you had any seeings lately?"

"No . . . but Ghyll said he found me through my gift—*a unique, strong gift*, he said. But Mummy, you can do seeings and sendings and make links. You must be able to teach me about them."

"Your gift is far stronger than mine."

"But—"

"We'll talk about it another time," Karan said firmly. "You need to rest. Come up the back."

She removed Sulien's ruined boots, helped her into a hammock and tucked blankets around her. "Go to sleep." Karan stroked her forehead and Sulien closed her eyes. Karan returned to the seat beside Yggur and gazed out the window at the racing clouds.

After a long silence Yggur said, "Ignored problems don't go away."

"Mind your own business."

"Sulien's gift holds the key to defeating the Merdrun, which makes it my business."

"She's too young."

"The only way to protect her is to extract the enemy's secret from her."

"Even if it breaks her? No!"

"You're following a dangerous course."

Every option Karan could think of was dangerous and she did not know how to choose between them. She went to her own hammock, expecting to lie awake, but Sulien sighed softly beside her and the relief was so overwhelming that Karan tumbled into sleep.

Sulien's hammock rocked with every motion of the racing sky ship. At first it was soothing, but as the day passed the wind became gustier and their passage bumpier, and she woke with her head spinning and her stomach churning.

She sank into sleep again, but the dream of being safe in Karan's arms gave way to an alarming series of silent images: slaves being flogged, Gergrig bellowing at a shaven-headed boy not much older than herself who was dragging a mutilated body to a pit, a burning field of grain, Merdrun soldiers tearing down an ancient temple and smashing its treasures to powder.

Sulien whimpered in her sleep, half-woke but sank again.

Gergrig bellowed, *Drum boy! Did you check on the triplets?*

The boy, who was not much older than herself, came running. He was a stocky lad with large staring indigo eyes and a fist-shaped bruise on his left cheek, and the Merdrun glyph on his forehead wasn't black but scintillating silver. He stopped, looked up at Gergrig then down again.

A scarred fist struck the boy on his bruised cheek, knocking him down. He made no sound, but Sulien felt the pain in her own cheek.

Never show fear, drum boy, and look every man in the eye. Merdrun fear nothing!

The boy rose, touched his swollen cheek but instantly pulled his hand away. He looked up into Gergrig's eyes, and this time managed to hold his gaze.

The triplets are . . . better, the boy said.

About time! They have much to learn and much work to do. Have you finished hauling the bodies to the pit?

No, Gergrig. But why me? Sulien detected a quaver in the boy's voice. *Why not give the job to the slaves?*

You need toughening up, drum boy. You know what happens to Merdrun who recoil from blood and savagery and death? Merdrun who are kind? *Merdrun who allow* emotions *to rule them?* Gergrig emphasised the words as if listing crimes.

You cut them down, whispered the boy. *Because they're weak, they're not true Merdrun.*

Are you *true Merdrun, drum boy?*

Yes! the boy cried. *I'll do anything you say.* But he struggled to look Gergrig in the face this time.

Get the corpses to the pit. And remember you're on a warning. How many warnings do weak people get, drum boy, before I cut them down and throw their bodies to the dogs?

One, choked the boy.

There you are then, Uigg my lad, said Gergrig, cuffing him lightly over the side of the head. *Go!*

Uigg stumbled away to the pile of tangled bodies, natives of Gwine, and heaved at the nearest, a man twice his size. As he looked down at the tormented face and hacked body, shuddering and retching and trying desperately to control the emotions that if revealed would doom him, a disgusting stench of blood, death and decay boiled up Sulien's nose.

She woke abruptly, upright in the wildly swaying hammock, gagging and crying out, "No, no!" then threw up on the floor of the sky ship.

Karan came running. "What's the matter? Are the triplets attacking?"

Sulien was shaking. She wiped her mouth on her blanket. "I *smelled* them, Mummy."

"Smelled *what*?" Yggur yelled over his shoulder.

"The bodies."

"Was it a nightmare or a seeing?"

"A seeing, I think. But I could see and hear, and *smell* them—and that's never happened before. I even felt it when Gergrig hit Uigg on the cheek."

After Sulien finished and was back in her hammock, Yggur said quietly, "The gift for far-seeing is a rare one, Karan, and few who have it can far-hear as well. But *far-smelling* and *far-feeling* into the bargain—I've never heard of such a gift. It troubles me, and you'd better do something about it."

Karan did not reply, though Sulien could sense her rampaging emotions—anger, self-doubt and an all-consuming fear.

The trip north, though otherwise uneventful, was slow. The journey was plagued by bad weather and such wild winds that they twice had to land and tie the craft down in the most sheltered spot they could find, on one occasion for three cold and miserable days. It took them ten days to reach Sith, and the further north they went the more Karan's fear grew that she was taking Sulien into danger rather than away from it. Was Yggur right? Should she be taught her gift? No, she was too young.

Yggur circled over Sith late in the afternoon, looking for a landing place, and Karan saw half a dozen sky ships under construction in one of the shipyards along the southern shore of the River Garr. He landed in the middle of the shipyard late in the afternoon. Workers came from everywhere to stare at the sleek craft, so different from the crude, boxy vessels they were building.

They disembarked and Karan studied the busy yard. She had thought no further than getting here and trying to make peace with Malien and Tallia, but first she had to find them.

A burly officer appeared, a very square man whose blocky head sat directly on shoulders twice as broad as Karan's. His boots were the size and shape of bricks. Yggur introduced himself, then Karan.

"I know who you are," the officer said in a surprisingly high voice.

"Where's Tallia?" said Karan.

"Gone."

"Malien?"

"Gone."

"Where?"

"That's secret."

"Is there any news of Daddy?" said Sulien. "His name is Llian."

"No," the officer said forbiddingly.

She gave a small cry and clutched Karan's hand.

"How's the war going?" said Yggur.

"That's secret." The officer looked longingly at the sky ship. "I'll take charge of this now."

Yggur stood up. "Want to bet?" he said with quiet menace.

"It's army property."

"It belongs to Malien, and unless you want to explain to the Aachim, our allies, how it and half this shipyard was destroyed in a battle with me . . ."

The officer backed off, scowling.

"Karan and Sulien will be going into town now," said Yggur. "They won't be hindered, will they?"

"Not today," the officer snapped, and clumped away.

"You'll need to buy clothes, boots and the like," said Yggur, handing Karan a bag of coin. "I'll stay here; I daren't leave the sky ship unguarded. Don't be long." He lowered his voice. "And see if you can find out what's going on."

Karan took Sulien to the best source of information she knew,

Osseion's tavern, Ninefingers, but it was closed and spiders had made webs in the corners of the front door.

Karan stood on the veranda, wondering what to do. "I haven't been to Sith in years," she said. "I don't know anyone else."

Sulien knocked on the door, and to Karan's surprise someone stumped across the boards inside and opened it.

Ussarine, who was supporting herself on crutches and had lost weight, gave her a wan smile. "Come in." She peered past Karan and her face lit up. "Is this . . . ? Of course it is. You found her! Come in."

Ussarine, hopping on her crutches, led them into the kitchen, where they sat at a well-scrubbed table that bore the marks of a hundred years of chopping and slicing. Ussarine made tea for Karan and a thick yellow brew for Sulien, the consistency of custard, which she sweetened with honey. Sulien's eyes lit up as she tasted it.

"Your legs are healing quickly," said Karan. Ussarine still wore casts though she was taking some weight on her right foot.

"One of Malien's healers cast a charm on the bones," said Ussarine. "She said they'd be fully healed at the end of a month. I hope we get that long . . ."

"What's going on? We haven't heard any news since I left . . . um, two and a half weeks ago."

"I don't know. Everything is secret now. And with two broken legs I'm no use to anyone." There was an edge to her voice.

"That must be hard," said Karan, "after all you've done for us."

"It's the way of war. Oh, Tallia left a message in case you turned up: you and Yggur are to fly to Zile *immediately*."

"We'd better let him know right away," said Karan.

"It's all right, I'll send a messenger. Where is he?"

"The Thorst Shipyards."

Ussarine hopped out, returning shortly. "However I can tell you this—many more Aachim have come west in the past week, in two more sky ships, and another six are on the way. We've got three of our own built and eight more under construction in two shipyards, though they're rickety crates compared to the one . . ."

"That I stole," said Karan. "Why Zile?"

"I don't know."

"What about Daddy?" said Sulien, trembling.

"No one knows," said Ussarine. She leaned forward across the table. "I'm sorry. He just vanished after Snoat was killed."

"Oh!" said Karan, crushed. Sulien's hand crept out and took hers, and they sat in aching silence. Karan pulled herself together. "Ussarine, good news. Hingis is with us. He'd hidden in Malien's sky ship."

Pain flashed in Ussarine's eyes, then she leaned back and folded her arms across her chest. "I have very bad news for him. Esea is dead."

After lunch, Karan said, "We'd better do our shopping and get back. I expect Yggur will want to leave at dawn."

"Do you mind if I come to Zile with you?" said Ussarine."

"You're most welcome."

Karan and Sulien returned to the sky ship after dark, wearing new clothes and boots and laden with bags, to discover that everything had been cleared out of the cabin and Yggur had a crew of cleaners in.

"Malien would want it returned in perfect condition," he said, frowning at one of the twisted skids. "I've arranged for you to sleep in the shipyard's rooming house." He indicated a large, shabby three-storey building on the riverbank.

They left their bags and headed to the rooming house. Their room, on the top floor, was large but low-ceilinged, and everything smelled dank and mouldy. They got into bed but Sulien lay in the gloom, staring up at the water-stained ceiling and trembling.

"What is it?" Karan said tiredly.

"I'm *feeling* people."

"What people?"

"I don't know. People suffering; people hurting; people *hating*."

"You're sensing people's *emotions*? The Merdrun? The triplets?"

Sulien shuddered. "No, just people, near and far."

"What do you mean, *hating*? Hating us?"

"I don't think so. They don't know I'm hearing them. It makes my head ache."

Karan drew Sulien to her. "Close your mind to them; go to sleep now."

What was happening to Sulien? Was this part of her psychic gift of far-sensing?

She slept poorly—each time she drifted off the same nightmare jerked her awake: Sulien was tied to a chair on the burning platform, coughing from the smoke, the triplets were fastening the killing link to her forehead, and Karan could not get to her in time.

"Mummy, *get up!*"

Sulien was shaking her. Karan fought her way out of a deep sleep, her brain leaden and her limbs paralysed. Sulien's blurred face appeared; she was coughing and holding a candle with haloes around it.

"There's smoke everywhere," she said. "I think the place is on fire."

Karan groped for the clothes she had laid out and yanked them on. Sulien opened the door. In the corridor people were shouting and screaming. Karan pushed past Sulien and turned right towards the stairs thirty yards away.

"Not that way, Mummy!" hissed Sulien.

"Why not?"

"Bad, angry, hating people."

"It's the only way down. Come on, or we'll be trapped here."

Sulien bit her lip, then said, "All right."

Three men and a woman, all clad in black, burst up the stairs, holding blazing brands out in front of them. Two of the men went left; the third man and the woman turned right towards Karan and Sulien. An old man opened his door and stepped into the corridor, looking around in confusion. The woman stabbed him in the neck and shoved him aside.

"There they are!" she cried, pointing at Karan and Sulien.

"Back inside!" said Karan. Sulien was frozen in horror, staring at the old man bleeding on the floor and perhaps overwhelmed with his raw emotions. Karan dragged her in and banged the door. "Open the window."

She locked the door and dragged the bed against it. *Crash, crash!* It shuddered under the force of the assassins' assault. Sulien was struggling with the window, which did not appear to have been opened in years. Karan prised at it with her knife, snapping the tip off the blade. She swore, prised again and it groaned open.

She looked out. Sith was a small island with a large population and no space was wasted. The outside of the building rose straight up from the stone wall that formed the edge of the shipyard's dock.

"What are we doing?" cried Sulien.

"Jumping into the water."

They climbed onto the sill and Karan clutched Sulien's hands tightly. "When I say *three*. One, two . . ."

The lock was smashed in and the door heaved so hard that the bed skidded two feet across the floor. The man burst in, followed by the woman, who shouted, "Kill them!" and drew back her right arm to throw her knife.

"*Three!*" said Karan, and they jumped.

Almost anything could be floating in the water of a busy shipyard, and as they fell she prayed they did not hit anything solid. They landed in icy water and went under, the impact pulling them apart. Karan groped around desperately as she rose to the surface but could not feel or see Sulien.

Faces appeared at the window. The man held his torch high; the light fell on Karan's face, and the woman hurled her knife with deadly accuracy. Karan swayed out of the way but not in time, and the knife, slowed only a little by its passage through six inches of water, buried itself in her left shoulder. She gasped.

"You got the bitch," said the man. "Kill her!"

"Damn her!" said the woman. "Where's the kid?"

Flames leaped up at the other end of the long building, casting slanting beams of light across the dock. People were screaming. "Sulien?" whispered Karan.

"Here!" she hissed.

She was clinging to a mooring ring bolted to the wall of the dock. Karan swam awkwardly to her, the knife in her shoulder grating on bone. "You all right?"

"Yes."

They had to find shelter, fast. Several boats were moored fifty yards further along but she did not see how they could get to them—these assassins were experts. The woman was leaning right out of the window, knife in hand, trying to locate them. If she stood on the windowsill it would not be a difficult throw.

The other two assassins appeared at the next window, holding lanterns high.

"If we dive . . ." said Karan.

"They'll have a perfect shot when we come up," said Sulien, her teeth chattering.

The two men heaved a small barrel onto the sill. The bigger man thrust a torch at it and flames leaped up, then they pushed it out. It tumbled over and over, a thick rag stuffed into the bunghole trailing red flame, then struck the water and the rag fell out. Burning oil spread across the water towards them.

The female assassin hurled another knife, which missed Karan by less than a foot. The assassin cursed, climbed onto the windowsill, swayed then pressed her back against the wall and took aim with a third knife.

"You're . . . not . . . touching . . . Mummy," shrilled Sulien.

She yanked the knife from Karan's shoulder, pointed it at the woman's weapon and said something Karan did not catch over the hissing of the flames on the water and the screams coming from the burning building.

The assassin swung her arm back, and Karan knew the knife was aimed perfectly—at Sulien. She tried to shove her aside but too late, too slow.

Then something very strange happened. The assassin's right hand whipped down but she did not release the knife—no, she *could not*. The full length of the blade slammed down into her upper thigh and right kneecap, *crack*.

Blood poured down her thigh; her knee gave and she slowly toppled outwards and fell head first into the water. She went under, there was an explosion of bubbles a long way down, and after a minute she bobbed to the surface halfway between Karan and the blazing barrel, face down.

The man holding the torch let out an anguished cry: "Saley, Saley?" He leaped into the water and thrashed towards her.

Karan pulled Sulien away and they swam towards the moored boats. Sulien was making little whimpering sounds. The man lifted Saley's head out of the water and held her up, then let out an awful moan.

"The stupid slukk *failed*," bellowed one of the men at the next window, using a foul swear word. "Get after them, fool!"

The man in the water looked around dazedly. Karan drew Sulien deeper into the shadows.

"That way!" roared the man at the window, pointing. "Go, go!"

He turned away, and Karan swam quietly off, using only one arm, Sulien by her side. The shoulder wound would continue to bleed while they remained in the water, and she was already faint from shock or blood loss. Sulien's teeth were chattering, and Karan could feel the cold creeping into her own core. The River Garr flowed out of the high mountains west of Sith and the water was icy; they could not endure it much longer. But the moment they tried to climb out, the assassins would find them. They were running this way along the side of the dock.

"There they are!" someone bellowed.

It was a struggle to stay afloat now, she felt so very weak. There was a furious clash of blades, a lot of yelling and screaming and grunting, then silence and a listless peace stole over her. It didn't matter any more.

"Mummy!" Sulien said in her ear. She slapped Karan across the face, hard. "Wake up!"

Cold water rushed up Karan's nose and she roused herself, gasping, her nose burning.

Someone pounded along the dock, holding a lightglass. "Karan?"

"Here," said Sulien. "Mummy's hurt."

Yggur crouched down and extended his long arms.

"Mummy first," said Sulien.

He heaved Karan out and laid her on the rough ironwood of the dock. He lifted Sulien with one hand then knelt beside Karan.

"They got her in the left shoulder," said Sulien.

Yggur checked the wound, put his hand across it and subvocalised a charm. Karan's shoulder steamed and the blood flow stopped.

"Who . . . were . . . they?" she said dully.

He turned to study the burning rooming house. Flames had spread along the roof from one end to the other. "We don't know yet."

"I'll bet the triplets sent them," said Sulien, shivering violently.

Yggur pulled off his coat and wrapped it around her. "Why do you say that?"

"I dreamed them just before I woke up. I'd know Jaguly's laugh anywhere."

"How d-did they know we were h-here?" said Karan.

"That's the question," he said grimly. He picked her up. "Back to the sky ship."

There were lights around it, and guards. Yggur lifted Karan into the cabin, bared her shoulder and studied the wound, frowning.

"You know how to clean wounds?" he said to Sulien.

"Yes," she said softly.

"Get . . . wet clothes off . . . first," said Karan.

Yggur opened a compartment and handed Sulien the healer's bag. "I'll be gone some time. We leave at sunrise."

Sulien stripped off her wet clothes and replaced them with new ones, then dressed Karan's shoulder and helped her into her own new clothes. Karan lay on the floor, enduring the throbbing.

"What did you do back there?" she said. "You saved my life."

"And killed the assassin," said Sulien wanly.

"You didn't kill her; she drowned. How did you make the knife stick to her hand?"

"Once, when you were telling me about the principles of the Secret Art, you said *Like calls to like.*"

"Didn't think you were paying attention," Karan muttered.

"Oh Mummy!" Sulien sighed.

"So your physical gift isn't completely gone, then."

"I couldn't have done it to save myself. Only you."

"How?"

"I took the assassin's knife from your shoulder, *commanded* it to stick to my hand, then pointed it at her knife and spoke the command again."

"And because the two knives were identical," said Karan, "she couldn't let go." She hugged Sulien. "You bother me sometimes."

"Not as much as you bother me," Sulien said sternly. "I've never known anyone to get in as much trouble as you."

"Except Llian," Karan said absently, but regretted it the moment she spoke the words.

Sulien's face crumpled. "Can't you sense Daddy at all?" She had asked that question a dozen times on the way back from Shazabba. "I know you linked to him years ago."

"Before you were born. I've hardly ever been able to do it again. I've tried and tried, Sulien, but I can't sense him at all."

"Me neither," Sulien whispered. "Not even with my empathy gift." She went very quiet and curled up in a corner and did not move, though whenever Karan looked her way she saw the faint light reflected in Sulien's eyes.

Yggur returned not long before dawn. "What did you discover?" Karan said sleepily.

"A well organised attack, ten of them. At three in the morning they slew the guards on the gate and headed straight for the rooming house, killing everyone they met and setting fires to create as much chaos as they could."

Sulien sat up, rubbing her eyes. "Do you think they'll come back?"

"Not in this world, child," said Yggur. "I've led armies. I know what to do in an emergency. I had the gate blocked within a minute and the shipyard guards on the hunt. We got them all."

"Did they reveal anything?" said Karan.

"Only the fellow in the water. All the others fought to the death. Unfortunately he was the least of them and could not tell us who sent them."

"Sulien thought the triplets."

"But they can't be powerful enough to control a squad directly from so far away. They've got to be working through a traitor, someone clever enough to know where to find skilled assassins and employ them . . ." His jaw muscles knotted.

"Not Shand," said Karan.

"I wouldn't have thought it possible either a few weeks ago. But he's bitter and resentful, he can turn himself invisible, and no one has seen him in a fortnight." Yggur looked up. "Who's that?"

"Hello?" called Ussarine from the bottom of the ladder.

"I said she could come with us," said Karan, remembering.

"Does Hingis know?" Yggur said quietly.

"I haven't seen him since we got to Sith."

Yggur called to the guards to let Ussarine through. She tossed up her pack, sword and scabbard and crutches, then he helped to heave her in. She worked her way up to the back, put her gear in one of the racks and sat in the corner.

"Five minutes to dawn," said Yggur a few minutes later. Then, quietly to Karan, "Where the hell is he?"

Ten minutes later she heard footsteps on the paving stones, then the craft shook as Hingis made his slow way up the ladder. He nodded to Yggur, then Karan, then saw Ussarine's glowing face up the back. His twisted features froze and he began to go back down.

Yggur was out of his seat in an instant. He leaped to the doorway and caught the little man by the shoulder. "In!" he growled.

Hingis tried to jump off the ladder. Yggur held him and after a short struggle Hingis evidently decided it was a battle that could not be won. He climbed in and headed for the closest seat.

"Down there!" said Yggur coldly, pointing to the seat next to Ussarine's. "Sort it out!"

Hingis sat next to Ussarine, glowering the other way. Yggur had the stay ropes released, worked his levers, and the sky ship lifted sharply, turned and headed towards the high mountains.

"What's the matter with Ussarine?" said Sulien, looking from her to Hingis.

Karan poked Sulien in the ribs with an elbow. "Don't stare. It's rude."

"But what's the matter?"

Karan lowered her voice and attempted to explain. "Ussarine loves Hingis, and he loves—*used* to love her. But his twin sister, Esea, who was very beautiful, felt threatened. They were very close and she was afraid that Hingis would choose Ussarine and abandon her. Eventually she forced him to choose between them, and he chose Ussarine. Esea, perhaps affected by the drumming from the summon stone, went mad with grief and brought down a stone pavilion on them, breaking both Ussarine's legs, then fled thinking she'd killed them both. Later she transformed the Command device, causing it to explode, and it killed her. And Snoat and his evil mancer, Scorbic Vyl."

Yggur chose that moment to throttle back. The roar of the rotors died away to a distant ticking, and Sulien's high voice soared into the silence.

"Does Hingis know his sister is dead?"

38

IT ACHES TO *POSSESS*

How could gentle, clever Earnis be gone from the world, just like that?

Lumillal looked fuller now, more solid and real. He stroked an elongated hand in Aviel's direction and chills trailed down her front. She sank into the cauldron until she was calf deep in icy water again—freezing, helpless and shattered. First she had lost Wilm—she dared not hope he was still alive for fear her bad luck would jinx him. Now Earnis, and soon Hublees, Osseion, Nimil, and even Shand would be killed. Invisibility was no protection against a ghost vampire who could see a person's life force and smell their blood.

And then *her*.

After feeding on so many gifted people, Lumillal would come back to life as a sorcerer vampire, no longer bound to Rogues Render. He would stalk the land, drinking blood and bringing death—or undeath—to hundreds, all because of her stupidity in coming here. How could she have thought to take on a ghost vampire when everyone else had failed?

Lumillal followed her down. *Afraid?* he hissed. *You will be before I'm done.*

Hublees had told her how it worked. Lumillal wanted to draw her terror out, both for his sadistic satisfaction and because he could extract more of her life force that way. That was why he had murdered Earnis in front of her.

He swirled his right hand at her, as he had done to Earnis. *I won't let you*, she thought, but within seconds the inside of the rusty cauldron was lit by a faint yellow radiance, a streamer of her own life force.

Lumillal swept a claw-like hand through it, scattering it, and the top of her head stung. He held his fingers up to his face; they were covered in little yellow speckles.

A seventh sister, he said as if reading her life in the pattern. *A twist-foot who dreams of being a perfumer.* He laughed mockingly. *A crippled little bastard who doesn't even know her own father. How sad, how pathetic your dreams are.* He turned his hideous hand over and read the back. *You accidentally made a scent potion*, he sneered, *and now you think you have the gift, yet you're terrified of the dark side. I've got news for you, twist-foot—this* is *the dark side, and it's going to get darker than you can ever imagine.*

She whimpered and he laughed mockingly. *Pathetic little fool!*

Aviel took a whisper of comfort from this. It was good to be underestimated.

He made the swirling gesture again; the yellow light brightened and he gathered in the threads and tendrils of her life force as he had done with Earnis, though far more slowly now—only one thread at a time and showing his pointed yellow-green teeth as he drew each thread towards her, luxuriating in her terror.

But Aviel had gone beyond terror to a white-hot, vengeful rage. He was not going to beat her; he was not going to win; she *would not* let him kill her allies. She pretended to cower away from him and, while he wound the silken threads from hand to elbow, she slipped her hands inside her waistband, untied the cord around the hilt of the black sword and slid it out.

He saw it and laughed again, high and cold, and continued his winding. *Do your worst! No blade can harm me.*

Aviel was sure he was right, but, acting on instinct, she pulled off the wrappings and thrust the black sword up between his ribs, into the space where his heart had been—assuming he'd ever had one—when he was alive. Llian had told Wilm that the sword was enchanted, and though she had seen no sign of any enchantment she prayed that he was right. She rotated the sword between Lumillal's ribs for good measure, then wrenched it out.

He reached out, flicked the tip of the sword, *ting*, and smiled. *Like I said.*

She had nothing left. She was lowering the black sword, her arm shaking, when she felt a faint exhalation and a breathy little sigh.

What was that? said a dry, scratchy voice. *Mendark, what's going on? Where am I?*

Lumillal's great luminous eyes blinked three times and he took a small step back through the air.

Hudigarde? said the scratchy voice.

It was coming from the sword! "No," said Aviel. "That's Lumillal, a ghost vampire."

Who the hell are you? the sword said querulously. *Put me down at once. Mendark?*

It felt different now—*alive*. "I'm Aviel. Mendark was killed by a lorrsk in Shazmak ten years ago."

Mendark lived for eleven hundred years. He renewed his life thirteen times. He can't be dead.

"It's in the Histories," said Aviel. "Why did you call Lumillal Hudigarde?"

What right have you got to question me, you little twerp?

Lumillal reached out with those awful elongated fingers, grey bone and sinew tinged with green, as if to draw another thread of life force from Aviel, but the sword rose of its own accord and he drew back, ravenous but frustrated.

"We're continuing Mendark's work," said Aviel. "We're trying to find the summon stone and destroy it."

Who's we?

"Malien, Nadiril, Shand, Tallia, Yggur—"

Never liked Yggur, it muttered. *Cold, arrogant, damaged, unreliable—*

"Mendark didn't like him either," she said boldly, "but he worked with all kinds of people when the need arose."

Presumptuous little chit! said the sword. *What are you doing here?*

She told it. The sword's tip circled the air before Lumillal's chest.

Ah, I remember now, it said. *The former queen, Tissany, being both clever and likeable, soon gained her freedom in the land where the women of Tindule were enslaved. She began plotting retribution on Hudigarde and on her sister, Lablag.*

Tissany allowed herself to be bitten by a vampire so she would become one, then hunted Lablag and Hudigarde down. She brought them in chains to Rogues Render, turned them into vampires and killed them so their ghost vampires would for ever be bound to this terrible place. The sword described another tight circle. *Where's Lablag?*

Lumillal swallowed. *She went mad and starved herself into a wisp.*

The sword prodded his breastbone, releasing a faint acid-green aura. *And then you consumed her—your own wife!*

"So that's how he became a sorcerer," said Aviel.

Not as stupid as you look, said the sword. *And you linger on, Hudigarde*, it said to Lumillal, *tormented by guilt yet unable to accept responsibility for either your crimes or your ruin. Your living death, poetic justice though it is, must be agonising.*

And you're a pissy little persona, snapped Lumillal, *trapped in a worthless old sword that I'm about to destroy—and you with it!* He swirled his hand a third time. Aviel felt an agonising pain in the top of her head, and the cauldron glowed like a yellow searchlight. *I'm taking my freedom now!*

He lunged at Aviel with open hands, ripped bundles of her life force from her and wound them furiously. Instantly the strength drained out of her; she staggered and nearly fell. The tip of the sword grounded on the bottom of the cauldron then jerked back in her hand so hard that she was forced upright. Her back struck the side of the cauldron and her sword hand rose of its own volition.

You can't touch me. Lumillal grinned.

But I can. The sword lunged up towards Lumillal's right eye.

"No!" she cried.

The sword froze in her hand. *You dare command me?*

"You might have destroyed the Archeus."

You should not have stopped it, twist-foot. Too late now. Lumillal began winding her threads again.

But the sword lunged again, this time lower, passing through Lumillal's ghostly neck, striking his equally ethereal backbone and, with a bright blue flash, neatly severing it. The ghost vampire froze, hanging in the air, glaring at her but unable to move anything below the neck.

Best gather your life force and pop it back in, girlie, said the sword gruffly. *Just in case.*

"How?" said Aviel. "I can't touch it."

The sword's black tip prised the yellow threads away from Lumillal and held them under Aviel's nose. *Deep breath!*

She sucked in a breath. The threads shot up her nose with a stinging tingle; her head spun and the last of her strength drained away. The sword fell from her hand, *clang*, into the icy muck at the bottom of the cauldron.

Watch my edges, girlie! Yuk! And when you're done I'll need a thorough cleaning.

Aviel felt so ill that she did not even find it strange to be abused by an inanimate object. She was on her knees, groping in the freezing sludge for the hilt when a pair of big dark hands, one with a missing middle finger, caught the rim of the cauldron and Osseion's dark face appeared. He grunted, heaved himself up, then reached down and hauled dumpy little Hublees up beside him, gasping. Judging by the expression on their faces they had been expecting the worst.

He looked from Aviel to the paralysed ghost vampire and back again. "How?" he said quietly.

Aviel was too weak and ill and cold to speak; she simply held up the sword.

Wouldn't linger if I were you, said the sword. *He's a sorcerer; he might repair himself.*

Lumillal's terror barrier must have collapsed the moment he was paralysed. Osseion lifted Aviel onto the rim and lowered her down. Nimil, who was waiting below, looked shocked. Aviel took stock of herself: her silvery hair was tangled and hard with mucky ice, her nose was bleeding all down her face and front, and she was covered to the knees in stinking sludge.

She cleaned the black sword on her skirts, took a step and fell over; she could not feel her half frozen feet. Osseion dropped to the ground. Hublees, who was perched on the cauldron's rim, uttered a command. Red light flashed; he extended his hand and the paralysed ghost vampire was forced down into the water at the bottom of the cauldron. *Boom, thud.* Muddy ice exploded from the top.

Hublees jumped down. "Put the lid on," he said hoarsely. "*Now!*"

Osseion clambered onto a nearby stack of bones, heaved the heavy hinged lid of the cauldron up to near vertical and held it, straining, while Hublees positioned a half-rotten timber beam to support it. Osseion fetched another beam and, heaving with all their strength, they raised the lid past vertical, and it fell, closing the cauldron with an almighty clang.

Osseion helped Hublees up to the rim then passed him a length of lead pipe. Nimil went up as well and, working swiftly with the Aachim's near-magical ability to shape metal, made a hole in the cauldron lid and fitted the lead pipe into it.

They jumped down, and Nimil fitted the other end into a large lead crystal bottle. Hublees held it in place while Nimil kindled a fire under the cauldron with liquid from a barrel they had obtained at Grund.

"It's naphtha," said Hublees. "Also known as subterranean fire. Just the thing for distilling the Archeus out of a stinking sorcerer ghost vampire. I can't wait to hear the swine scream."

Aviel turned away hastily. Hudigarde had been one of the most genocidal monsters in all the Histories, and as Lumillal he was no better, but Aviel did not want to witness his torment.

"I'll take her back," said Osseion.

He offered her his big warm hand, and she was glad to take it.

Horror had frozen her to the core and he seemed the only normal person among them. Then she looked down the alley of bones to where Earnis lay on the cold, foul ground—handsome, kindly and dead.

She closed his eyes and sat beside him, stroking his hair. He had loved her and, though it had been entirely unrequited, had sacrificed himself to try and save her. No small thing, that.

"We can't leave him in this awful place," she said, not bothering to wipe her flowing eyes. "But . . ." She could not have moved him an inch, and that felt like a betrayal of everything he had stood for and all he had done for her. Not for the first time she cursed being born so small, crippled and weak.

"We'll bring him back," said Osseion, "and give him a decent burial among the great boulders. He'd like that, it being such a magical place."

"Thank you," she said faintly.

Before they had gone fifty yards a naphtha-fuelled fire was roaring behind them, beneath the cauldron where Lumillal was trapped. Immediately the shrieking began, so shrill and penetrating and awful that, even with her fingers in her ears, she could not block it out.

She did not speak again on the painful half-mile back to the sky ship; she lacked the strength, and had it not been for Osseion she might have lain down and never got up again. She felt utterly drained. She *had* been drained and, though the missing part of her life force was back, she wasn't sure it was quite where it belonged. She felt fractured.

"I'll get the water boiling," said Osseion. "You'll want a good warm-up and scrub-down, I expect."

She dragged herself into her workshop tent and slumped in the canvas chair, but got up again, raised the black sword to her lips and kissed it. "Thank you."

More than I ever got from Mendark, it muttered. *The thanks I meant*, it added hastily.

Aviel slid the sword into its sheath and, if it said anything else, she did not hear. She hobbled along her workbench, checking her apparatus. All was as she had left it. She flopped into her chair again, longing for sleep, though there was no chance of that. The moment Hublees and Nimil returned with the Archeus, if they did, she had to carry out the final step in the procedure, perfectly.

"Water's hot," said Osseion cheerfully, carrying in a big canvas bucket in each hand. "Enough for a quick bath."

He set them down, returned with a small tub and poured the water in, then went out, pulling the flaps of the tent closed behind him.

Aviel stripped off her filthy boots and clothes, washed the worst of the muck off with a cloth then sank gratefully into the steaming water. It was only four inches deep but oh how beautiful it was, how warming, how cleansing, how *normal*.

When she tingled all over from scrubbing she dressed in her warmest clothes, dragged the bath outside and overturned it, and returned to her chair. She had planned to rehearse the final alchemical step but sleep overwhelmed her and the next she knew Hublees was shaking her awake. A long time must have passed for he looked exhausted. Even his absurd goatee was bedraggled, but there was a triumphant light in his little squinty eyes.

"Got it!" He set the lead crystal bottle down on Aviel's bench next to the layered filters and the colophony dish.

The bottle was half full of an oily, sluggish, yellow-green fluid, the colour of the light from Lumillal's eyes. She wondered about the process of distilling the fluid, which was clearly real, from a ghost vampire that had been pure spirit. Her head throbbed and she gave the thought up. Either mancery or sorcery had been involved, and as long as it had been done properly that was all that mattered.

"Look out!" Hublees leaped across the workshop, grabbed the bottle and twisted the stopper in hard.

"What's the matter?" she said dazedly.

"The Archeus was oozing out around the stopper."

"What would happen then?"

"I can't bear to imagine, but it's perilous stuff, Aviel. It aches to *possess*. Use only the required amount, keep it tightly stoppered, and if you spill any on yourself, clean it off instantly."

Aviel wired the stopper in as tightly as it would go. "I'd better get started."

She put a low-sided ceramic bowl in a large glass flask and set the colophony dish in the bowl to protect the glass from the fire. Then, taking exquisite care with her golden tongs, she set the best golden brimstone in the centre of the dish, poured in a tiny amount of quadruple-distilled spirits of wine, ignited it and put the top on the flask. It had a glass stopcock in the side, which she opened to allow a small flow of air, and a cooling coil running from the top of the flask then down through a glass pipe containing her multilayered filter, though it was not yet connected.

When the spirits of wine had burned away and the colophony and golden brimstone had caught, she allowed the condensate to run into a waste beaker, then connected the first of her layered filters.

Hublees, Osseion and Nimil had gathered inside the doorway and were watching her intently. Aviel sensed that Shand was also in the workshop, keeping well out of the way so no one would bump into him. She wondered how his own work had gone at Rogues Render. He had still needed two odours to complete his scent potion: *the smoke from the desiccated corpse of a woman murdered long ago* and *the last breath of an undead killer*. Lumillal had consumed many mourning pilgrims before they stopped coming, and Shand could have obtained both odours there.

Aviel put a little flask under the outlet and checked the condensate. When it turned from clear to the palest pink she swiftly connected a different filter after the first and allowed it to drip into a second flask until the pink drops changed to brown, then red-brown. She connected her third and last layered filter and let the condensate drip into a third flask. Then waited. And waited, but the drips remained a stubborn red-brown.

It was hard to see through the fumes in the container though it looked as though the colophony and brimstone were rapidly burning away. Then, suddenly, the drips went a shimmering silvery white.

This was it! With shaking hands she put a fourth flask under the outlet and perched in front of it, watching the drops one by one. When about a teaspoon of the silvery liquid had accumulated she saw that the condensate in the tube was turning pale blue. She pulled the precious flask out of the way and stuck a beaker under the outlet to collect what was left, which was now waste, as were the contents of the first three flasks.

Aviel carried the little flask of silvery liquid down to the far end of the bench, holding it in both hands, and set it down. She took the diamond phial from its leopardwood case, clamped it to a stand and, with a pair of unused golden tweezers, took a small piece of sintered platinum out of a jar and weighed it. It was slightly too heavy so she took a smaller piece and, taking exquisite care, eased it into the diamond phial, where it lodged just above the curved base.

Now with one of her eyedroppers she drew up a quantity of the shimmering silvery white condensate and dripped precisely seventeen drops onto the sintered platinum. The shimmer disappeared though the fluid remained the same colour.

Her heart was crashing about in her chest. Now for the final step. If it failed, or she did something wrong, she would have wasted weeks of work, countless thousands of gold tells, a diamond fit for a princess's tiara and, most important of all, Earnis's life.

She laid out another eyedropper but, in putting it down, crushed its finely drawn tip against the bench. She pushed it aside and took another. Her hands were shaking so badly that she dared not open the lead crystal bottle by herself.

"Need help," she croaked, turning to Hublees. "Can you open the bottle and seal it again the moment I take the Archeus?"

He nodded. "It might be better if you instruct Nimil how much to take and how to use it."

"In this kind of alchemy the whole procedure must be done by the one person."

She walked back and forth, reciting her herbal mantras until her hands were steady again, then took a deep breath and flashed the watchers a feeble smile.

"I'm ready. This is the final step—if I get it right."

She took up the new eyedropper, a large one. Hublees unwired the stopper and lifted it out. Tendrils of yellow-green Archeus oozed out and he grimaced. Aviel inserted her eyedropper and drew some up, then discharged it into a measuring cylinder until it contained exactly three drams. She dribbled it into the diamond phial, giving it a shake on its stand after each half-dram. Hublees put the stopper in the lead crystal bottle and wired it on again, then stepped back.

Aviel stoppered the diamond phial, removed it from the clamp and inverted it three times. The liquid in the bottom of the phial, which had been a muddy brown, went clear. She inverted it again so it flowed through the sintered platinum and it changed to a mustard yellow. After the next inversion it turned blue, then pale grey. She inverted it for the final time and the liquid, now resting on the base of the diamond stopper, set to a pale azure jelly.

"All's well so far," she said with a weak smile. Her heart was thundering again and the shake in her arm was back.

She turned the phial upright, and a small quantity of liquid oozed down the sides, through the sintered platinum and collected in the bottom. It was a brilliant green, though there wasn't much of it. Aviel removed the stopper and the plug of azure jelly came with it. She scraped it into a waste jar and wiped the diamond stopper, then, with a pair of tweezers, picked out the piece of sintered platinum, rinsed it and put it back in the jar with the other pieces.

She replaced the diamond stopper in the phial and held it up. "The colour's perfect—just as the method describes. The whole sequence of colours went right. It's nivol! We've done it!"

Hublees was beaming. He shook her free hand. "I never would have believed it. Very well done, Aviel."

Nimil's oval eyes shone for a moment, then he turned away. A feeling of great exhilaration surged through her. She had done well. No, she had done the impossible. She let out a great sigh. But then she looked into the phial again and her smile faded.

"What's the matter?" said Hublees.

"All that labour, pain and danger, and Earnis's life, and all we've got is one lousy drop of nivol."

39

I SHOULD HANG YOU FROM
THE PORTICO

For a man so crippled, Hingis could move very quickly when he was desperate. Before Karan realised what was happening he had scuttled up to the cabin door and wrenched it open. A blast of freezing air thrust him back several steps. He leaned forward, fighting against it, clearly planning to hurl himself out to his death.

Behind Karan, Ussarine let out a despairing cry, and there was a clatter as she knocked over her crutches. Karan tried to push herself to her feet but a piercing pain shot through the knife wound in her left shoulder and she fell back again.

Sulien dived and caught Hingis around the ankles. "Don't do it!" she gasped.

But he was insane with despair. He lunged forward, one dragging step, then another. He was going to jump.

"Let him go, Sulien," cried Karan, making another attempt to get up. Hingis was at the door now. "He'll carry you with him." She came to her feet but felt very weak; her head was spinning, the cabin wavering.

"Enough!" roared Yggur.

Abandoning the controls, he leaped across the cabin, hauled Hingis back from the door and, with a punch to the jaw, knocked him down. He crashed down on his back beside Karan's seat and lay there, moaning and twitching. Sulien came to her hands and knees by the door, her eyes wide and her mouth open, and her red hair slowly whitened with frost in the icy blast.

Yggur closed the door and locked it, picked her up and said, "There's such a thing as too much courage, child," and put her in her seat.

The sky ship lurched. He took the controls long enough to steady it, then bound Hingis's hands behind his back, cast an enchantment on the bonds so they could only be undone by himself and tied him to a seat as far from Ussarine as possible.

"It's obvious that they're in love," said Sulien in a low voice, "so why doesn't he make it up with her?"

"Every time Hingis looks at Ussarine he sees his dead sister," said Karan, "and he blames himself for her death."

"Well, I think he's stupid!"

Hingis hunched in his seat unmoving for the rest of that eternal and utterly miserable day, refusing food and drink, just staring straight ahead, his jaw tight and his face frozen in despair. A hurt and uncomprehending Ussarine approached him half a dozen times, trying to comfort him, but he would not even look at her.

Sulien went quiet after that, and Karan could get nothing out of her, though surely she was agonising about how close the attack at the rooming house had been to succeeding, and worrying how the triplets would attack next.

In the evening of the following day Yggur flew over the desert lands surrounding the River Zur, heading for Zile. The once vast network of irrigation canals was dry, crusted with salt and partly filled with windblown sand, and the industrious people who had farmed here were long gone.

"Look, there's Zile," Karan said to Sulien. "Which was—"

"Built by Daddy's people, the Zain, thousands of years ago. It was once the most important city in the west, until they fell out with everyone."

"And made a pact with Rulke, and were banished."

The broad avenues of Zile were lined with massive granite columns that had stood for millennia. Behind the columns stood the ruins of many other great buildings, now slowly being overwhelmed by the drifting sand. The only one that remained intact, set on a rise a mile from the city, was the Great Library, that wonder of the ancient world. It was a vast rectangle of red marble with colonnaded walks on all four sides, four storeys high and, Karan knew, with many levels below ground.

Yggur brought the sky ship in to land on the western end of the library's flat roof. Three elegantly curved Aachim sky ships, each different, were tied down in the middle of the roof a hundred yards away. Two more sky ships were moored at the eastern end, though these had the crude rectangular box cabins of the vessels made in the Thorst Shipyards. Soldiers stood guard by each vessel. There were boxes and bags by the ladder of the furthest sky ship, and its rotors were turning slowly.

Someone burst up a set of stairs in the nearest corner and came stalking across the roof in the bright moonlight. Malien! Tallia followed, along with a well-fed officer whom Karan assumed to be Commander Dedulus Janck, and a slender young man in an adjutant's uniform. Tallia looked furious, Malien grim. Janck's face was expressionless. Karan waited for Yggur to disembark, quaking. She had been dreading this moment.

"The music!" said Yggur theatrically, gesturing to the door. "Best you face it, Karan."

Her wounded shoulder throbbed. Her heart was racing and her palms were sweaty. She had let Malien down badly. What would she do?

"Do you want me to come with you?" Sulien said anxiously.

"Stay here for a bit." Karan tossed out the ladder and went down.

"Well?" said Malien, whose face was so brittle it looked about to crack. "Did . . . did you find her?"

"Yes."

"And?"

"We got her back."

Malien shoved past her, sending pain spearing through Karan's shoulder, ran up the ladder and hurled herself in through the door. Inside the cabin, Karan saw her dancing round and round, holding Sulien in her arms. Karan's eyes prickled.

"Lucky for you," Tallia said coldly. "You cost us dear, Karan."

"What happened?" Karan said defensively.

"Dedulus Janck," the commander said, holding out his hand. She shook it warily.

"For want of a sky ship we lost most of Snoat's men," said Janck. "His other armies disbanded before we could take control of them, and the officers stole the army war chests. It was a grievous blow."

Karan had given little thought to what the loss of the sky ship would mean to Malien or the allies; she had been utterly focused on Sulien. She looked up into Janck's penetrating gaze.

"I'm sorry," she said quietly, "but I had to save my daughter."

"Stealing a vital resource in wartime is a capital offence. I should hang you from the portico at the front of the library."

Cold sweat formed on her back. In wartime the commander-in-chief held power of life or death over everyone. If he decided to condemn her, not even her former friends could save her.

Tallia stirred, made as if to say something but did not speak.

"Hmm," said Janck. "But . . . all things considered, and bearing in mind your achievements and your daughter's, that might be counter-productive. Besides, I'm told you can spy on the enemy in ways no one else can."

He paced in a circle. "Hmn, hmn. When you stole the sky ship, it was not *known* that the Merdrun had invaded; we were not offi-cially at war, so the theft, grand larceny though it was, is a matter between you and the Aachim. But take heed, Karan Melluselde Elienor Fyrn—we are in the fight of our very lives and there will be *no more chances.*"

"Thank you," she whispered.

"Hmn, hmn. We have a number of sky ships now, and we've recov-ered some of the war chests and many of Snoat's men. Even so, you've got a lot to make up for."

Malien came down the ladder, followed by Sulien and Yggur, who carried Ussarine's crutches. As she appeared in the doorway, Janck held up his hand and she stopped.

"I'm sorry for all I've cost you," said Karan to Malien. "But I'm not sorry I stole the sky ship. I'd do it again, if—"

"I wouldn't finish that sentence if I were you," said Malien coldly. She turned to Yggur. "I trust *my* craft is in good order?"

"The chief shipwright at Thorst checked it the day before yesterday."

Malien gave a dismissive sniff. "Cack-handed blacksmith!" She turned back to Karan, looking a little more kindly than before.

"What's going on with the war?" said Karan, though right now there was only one thing she cared about. "Is there any news of Llian?"

"Careless tongues cost lives," snapped Janck. "If there's anything you need to know, you'll be told."

"But—"

"The enemy has spies, even here."

"We know," said Yggur. "Karan and Sulien were attacked in the Thorst Shipyards two nights ago by ten assassins. A well-planned attack that nearly succeeded."

Malien rocked back on her heels. "Who dared? And how?"

"We don't know." Karan clutched at Sulien's hand as the memories flooded back.

Yggur told the story. Janck questioned Karan and Sulien, then led Malien and Tallia away. Tallia spoke a command, and a pale green secrecy bubble formed around the three of them. Malien was speaking urgently, Tallia shaking her head. Janck had his arms folded and wore an implacable expression. After several minutes Tallia popped the bubble with a snap of her fingers and they came back.

"Security must be tightened again," said Janck. "And the penalties for loose tongues increased tenfold. Our only recourse is absolute secrecy."

"Karan needs to know," said Malien.

"Karan has a reputation for putting her own wants ahead of ours."

Janck gave Karan a very cold stare and she knew that this was her punishment.

"But surely—" said Tallia.

"No!" snapped Janck. "From this moment on all war councils will be held inside secrecy bubbles, and only those who need to know will attend. No one who doesn't need to know will be told *anything*, and those who do need to know will only be told *when* they need to know." He turned to his adjutant. "Got that, Nizzily?"

"Yes sir," he said. "I'll post the order."

Malien's face set hard. The Aachim were a proud species and did not take kindly to being ordered about. For a moment Karan thought she was going to challenge Janck, then Malien's eye fell on Sulien and softened. She kissed Sulien on the forehead, avoided Karan's eye, and headed towards the pair of Aachim sky ships at a fast walk. Janck headed diagonally across the roof to the vessel whose rotors were turning.

Ussarine lowered herself down the ladder, took her crutches from Yggur and hopped across to Tallia. "I'll be walking in a week and as good as ever a week after that. What can I do?"

Tallia smiled. "Get fit and help with training. If you go to Lilis's room—you know where it is—she'll show you to your quarters."

"Is my father here?"

"Osseion's away on a—" She broke off. "I can't tell you."

Ussarine headed for the stairs and did not look back. After she was gone Hingis crabbed his way down the ladder, lurched across to Tallia and said, "I wish to join the army as a front-line battle illusionist."

Tallia studied him for a good thirty seconds, shaking her head.

"It's all I'm good for now," he said, "and I'm very good at my art. I want to go as soon as possible."

"All right. That sky ship is leaving within the hour." She pointed to the one. "I'll make the arrangements."

"Thank you," he said and headed towards it, his breathing more laboured than ever.

Malien reappeared out of the darkness with two Aachim Karan had not seen before. They went inside her sky ship and banged the door. Karan sighed; she would not be forgiven in a hurry.

"There's a council in half an hour," Tallia said to Yggur. "And I need to speak to you privately before then."

"Very well," said Yggur and also headed for the stairs.

Tallia, Karan and Sulien were alone.

"Well," said Tallia.

Karan swallowed. "You look . . . better."

It was a lie. Tallia's face bore lines that had not been there two months ago. She looked older, almost middle-aged, and rather sad. When the troubles began she had been on the verge of resigning as Magister to sail home to Crandor. Tallia wanted children and was almost out of time to have them.

Maybe it's for the best, Karan thought. In another month we might all be slaves, or ... But she must not think that way. They had to defeat the Merdrun; the alternative was unthinkable.

She realised Tallia was staring at her. "I'm sorry for taking the sky ship," Karan said. "What can I do to help?"

"Come into a bubble," said Tallia. She conjured one to Karan's left and stepped into it.

As Karan and Sulien followed, Tallia held up her hand, pointed at Karan and mouthed, *Just you.*

Karan stopped dead. "But—"

Tallia stepped out. "You heard Janck. *No one who doesn't need to know will be told* anything, *and those who do need to know will only be told* when *they need to know.*"

"Sulien *does* need to know."

"The triplets *linked* to her, Karan."

"It's all right, Mummy," said Sulien, doing her best to avoid conflict as usual. She gave Karan a secret smile which she interpreted as, *I can find out anyway.*

Tallia stepped back into the bubble and Karan followed. "What?" she snapped.

"The enemy are spying on us, corrupting good people and bad to serve as assassins and saboteurs. They've attacked in four places in the past week, not counting the attack on you. They know who to kill and what to destroy to do the most damage to our plans. Clearly they have a spy, or spies, at the highest level, and—"

"Not Shand? Is he here?"

Tallia's face twisted. "We don't know where he is. He disappeared weeks ago ..." She paused, perhaps wondering how much she could reveal. "He's up to something and we don't know whether it's for us or against us. Of all the people to lose ..."

It was almost unthinkable that Shand would betray them, and yet he had, if unwittingly. If the triplets rebuilt the dead magiz's link and forced him to betray them *willingly*, he could do untold damage.

"What do you want of me?"

"Two things. You're the only one who can get near the Merdrun: both those who came through the gate, *and* those we believe are still stuck on Cinnabar—"

Outside the bubble Sulien let out a great cry. Karan could not hear her but her face was easy to read. Sulien had shouted, *No!*

"How can she know?" said Tallia, looking disturbed.

Karan shrugged, turned her back to Sulien and added, "Spying on the Merdrun is too risky. Gergrig has a new magiz, the union of three very strong and nasty triplets."

In the distance soldiers were marching towards the sky ship whose rotors were turning. The bags and boxes were loaded in, they went aboard and it lifted off and disappeared in the darkness, leaving that corner of the roof empty but for the sky ship Hingis had gone to. People went back and forth, carrying supplies, and soon it was gone as well.

Karan told Tallia about rescuing Sulien on the platform over the gorge, and all they had seen and heard. Sulien pressed her face and hands to the outside of the green bubble, watching intently.

"How can we deal with three of them working as one?" said Tallia.

"I hurt them badly," said Karan. "If you send me to spy on the Merdrun again, they'll be waiting."

Tallia met Karan's eyes, bleakly. "Once I give Janck the go-ahead, I'll be sending tens of thousands of men and women to war, probably to their deaths, and many will go unwillingly. Intelligence only you can bring us could save thousands of lives, including your daughter's. How can I treat you differently, Karan?"

And how could Karan expect special consideration from her allies after showing them none? "All right, I'll be your spy. What's the second thing?"

"Keep watch for Shand. Xarah is trying pinpoint his location and, if she does, I want you to track him down, find out what he's up to and . . ."

"You want me to spy on Shand?"

"Yes. He's a condemned traitor now. And when you find him . . ."

"You want me to betray my old friend—to a death sentence."

Tallia's racked face said it all.

40

CLAWS SCREECHING DOWN
THE GLASS

Sulien prowled the bedchamber she and Karan had been assigned. It was a perfect cube twelve feet long and wide and high, with bare walls made from polished yellow-brown conglomerate, a narrow recessed bed shelf on either side and a window that looked south over the moonlit desert landscape.

The room was unfurnished except for a small table, also square, two wooden chairs and a black iron lamp shaped like a lizard up on its back legs. It reminded her of Gothryme and lizard-spotting expeditions to the dried-up River Ryme. And poor old Rachis, abandoned to look after the estate yet again.

She swallowed the lump in her throat. If she stood on tiptoe and craned her neck she could make out the edge of a range of worn-down mountains to the right. Beyond them the Western Ocean was thousands of miles across. Beyond, it was said, were unknown lands where everything was strange.

She sat on one of the beds, swinging her legs. Despite the attack in Sith and many pointed remarks from Yggur about teaching Sulien to use her gift, Karan was still avoiding the issue. But Sulien had to learn fast or neither she nor Karan would survive, and that meant going behind her back to find a teacher.

Who, though? Yggur had responded to Sulien's oblique questions with a knowing smile, then said he knew nothing about the far-seeing or far-sensing arts, and even less about empathic mancery. Not Malien; she was bound to tell Karan. Tallia? But she was working night and day on war business and would not have the time. That only left old Nadiril. He was a clever, stern man she had only met handful of times, though he had always seemed kindly.

After a long search through corridors which all looked the same, she knocked on his door. Shuffling and wheezing sounds went on for a couple of minutes, then the door was heaved open.

"What *now*?" Nadiril said hoarsely.

The scrawny old librarian wore a grey and white striped nightgown, frayed green slippers and a blue cap pulled down over his sagging ears. He peered out a foot above Sulien's head, scowled, then looked down. His eyebrows climbed his forehead in a series of twitches.

"Strange hour for a child to come calling," he said sternly.

"Please Mister Nadiril," Sulien cried, fearing he would send her away. She hopped from one foot to the other. "My gift is growing stronger, and Yggur said it's strange and rare and dangerous. He said I've got to be taught but Mummy won't teach me, and I'm afraid . . ."

Nadiril stooped, his joints cracking like brittle bones, and studied her intently. Sulien flushed under his stare.

"You'd better come in. Leave the door open."

She followed him into a room identical to her own, save that books and other objects were stacked neatly on the second bed shelf. He sat on a hard wooden chair and gestured to her to perch on the bed shelf.

"What does your gift have to do with me?" said Nadiril.

"Can you teach me to use it properly? Please?"

He considered the question. "I know something of the psychic arts. More than something. I probably *could* teach you, but I won't."

"Oh!" she said, crushed. She sat there, staring at her toes, then slipped off the bed shelf. "Thank you anyway, Mister Nadiril."

He smiled. "Aren't you going to ask why?"

"I—that would be rude. You're too . . . important."

"I was important once, a very long time ago. But not any more; I'm just eking out my remaining days, doing the same things I've always done and making no difference at all."

"That's not true!" she cried. "You took charge when Daddy was trapped in Pem-Y-Rum and Snoat was going to kill him."

He favoured her with a snaggle-toothed smile. "Why, so I did. But you're far more important than I am, child. Your memories hold the key to our survival and you need a far better teacher than I could ever be."

"There's no one left to ask. Mummy won't do it and Yggur doesn't know this art. And Tallia is far too busy and Malien would only tell on me."

"What makes you think I won't?" Nadiril said mildly.

Sulien looked up into his clouded eyes, half covered by sagging, wrinkled eyelids, and set her empathic gift loose. "You're not waiting to die. You love Santhenar, and you're terrified of what the Merdrun will do to the world if we can't beat them. And you really care about helping young people like Lilis make the best of their lives."

He stared at her, astonished. "Quite a gift! How do you know what I've done for Lilis?"

"Daddy told me. You took a little street girl who couldn't even read and turned her into the librarian who's going to take over after you're . . . um . . . gone."

"I didn't turn Lilis into anything; I merely guided her to use her own great talents."

"Then guide me!" she cried. "Please."

Nadiril sighed, reached over and took her hands. "You need a far better teacher than I am."

"Who?"

He hesitated, then said, "The one great mancer you know but haven't thought of." He released her and rose with a gasp and a groan. "Off you go now, or your mother will be worried." He ushered her to the door.

As Sulien climbed the many sets of stairs to her room, she pondered who he meant. The only other great mancer she knew was old Shand, but everyone believed him a traitor and no one knew where he was.

He was a brilliant mancer, one of the few people alive who could create portals, and Yalkara had given him part of her own incomparable gift before she left him. If anyone could teach her, surely Shand could, but first she had to find him and convince him to help, without either of them being caught.

The punishment for working with a traitor would be severe.

"Doesn't *anyone* know anything about Daddy?" Sulien asked plaintively as she was getting ready for bed in their little room the following night.

Karan felt sure Janck knew plenty, but he wasn't saying, presumably to punish her for taking the sky ship. "I'm sorry," she said, wiping her eyes. "But I'm sure he's all right," she added with false brightness.

"Yes, Mummy," said Sulien, a desolate look in her eyes.

She was putting on an act for Karan, just as Karan was for her. But Karan felt sure that Llian, the brilliant, frustrating, irritating, wonderful love of her life, was dead.

"Hop into bed now," she said dully.

Sulien climbed the five-rung ladder and slid under the covers. "Brrrr!" she said, though it was nothing like the cold she had experienced in Salliban.

Karan gazed at Sulien, eyes misty, then extinguished the lamp. Even now, a fortnight after the miraculous rescue, it seemed like a dream that she had Sulien back.

She went to the window, which was the same cubic shape as the room—four feet wide, four feet deep through the massive wall of conglomerate, and four feet high. The glass was on the outside, and the deep recess served as a window seat, though not a comfortable one. She took the top blanket off her bed, folded it to make a cushion, wrapped the other one around her, climbed into the recess and sat there, gazing out into the darkness.

Frost was forming little feathery patterns on the outside of the window, growing and spreading as she watched. She leaned her throbbing left shoulder against the glass and the cold dulled the pain, though not enough. Nothing had changed; Gergrig still wanted Sulien dead. How could Karan protect her?

A shadow passed across the window and she groped for her knife, imagining that an assassin had swung down from the roof on a rope.

But it was just a night bird wheeling around the eaves of the Great Library. She squinted between the frost fronds; no, it was a large black bat.

She opened the window a crack. Hundreds, no, thousands of bats were wheeling in the moonlight, issuing like smoke from one of the derelict buildings of Zile. Out hunting.

Several bats flew her way. Karan banged the window shut and twisted the catch. *Thump!* The leading bat struck the window so hard that its bulging eyes flattened against the thick glass. Its eyes were fixed on her and its leathery wings thrashed as if it were trying to get through, then it fell away, leaving streaks of blood and mucus down the pane.

Thump! Thump! Two more bats slammed into the glass and fell. A fourth bat landed on the stone ridge above the window and hung there upside down, glaring at her, its clawed feet screeching down the glass.

"Aaahh!" cried Sulien, jerking upright. "Mummy, what's going on?"

Karan slid out of the window recess. "Just bats," she said, taking Sulien's hands. "Out hunting."

The clinging bat was joined by three more, the dim lamplight reflecting from their unblinking eyes.

"What are they hunting?" said Sulien.

Thoroughly unnerved, Karan gathered her blankets and climbed onto her bed shelf. The bat was only a black outline now but she knew it was watching her, and her sensitive's inner ear picked up its high-pitched call. Was it spying on her? Had the triplets' power grown so enormously that they could even control animals now?

Sulien had gone back to sleep. Karan sealed off the window by propping the table against it and stuffing her blankets around the edges, then went looking for Tallia. After an hour of asking, Karan tracked her to one of the archive rooms three levels below ground. The guards would not allow her through, though one grudgingly agreed to take a message to Tallia.

He returned a few minutes later. "You may enter."

It was after two in the morning. Karan followed him into a large room with benches piled with books, maps and papers on all four sides, and a long table in the centre, empty apart from a large map on beige canvas. As she entered, Janck turned it upside down. Tallia, who was seated at the far end of the table, looked exhausted. Janck was on her left and Malien and Yggur on the right.

Tallia looked up but it was Janck who spoke. "Well?"

"I need to speak to Aviel."

"Why?" said Janck.

"Before I go spying on the triplets, I've got to know where the Merdrun are, who the local people are and what the land is like. She's the only one who's seen it."

Tallia and Janck exchanged glances, then he nodded.

"She's not here," said Tallia.

"When will she be back?" said Karan.

"We . . . don't know."

"What do you know?"

"Xarah has done some scrying," said Malien. "She believes the Merdrun are on the Isle of Gwine—an island about fifteen miles by ten—in the Western Ocean a long way west of Banthey."

"Ah!" said Karan. She had seen Gwine on the map but had never been near it. "How did they end up there?"

"We think Aviel's attack on the summon stone cut the flow of power to the Crimson Gate and made it go wrong, then close prematurely, fortunately for us."

"Why?"

"Large ships seldom go anywhere near Gwine; the Merdrun can't escape save by reopening the Crimson Gate, and that could take a long time, and great power—"

Janck cleared his throat and Malien did not go on, but Karan did not need her to. Clearly, he was hoping to mount an attack before they could reopen the gate.

"It'd be helpful if you could assassinate Gergrig . . . and the triplets," said Janck.

The gall of the man! "You want someone assassinated, do it yourself," she said coldly.

His eyes glittered. "You will go without delay. We—need—that—intelligence."

Karan did not want to go at all, but since she must, she hoped to delay it as long as possible. "I'll need Malien's help and mancery to prepare. I'll go tomorrow . . . evening."

"Make it sooner."

Karan looked to Malien pleadingly and saw a grim smile flicker there, as if she were thinking, *You stole my sky ship and now you want me to help you?* But Malien said, "The preparations are complex and difficult; it can be no earlier than Karan says."

Janck grunted and waved a dismissing hand. "Get going, then."

Karan did not move. "There's something else."

"Another favour?"

"No, another security risk."

He sat up abruptly. "Go on."

She related the incident of the bats attacking her window, and her fear that the triplets were using them.

Janck swore fluently. "Has their power grown so great that every bird and beast can spy on us?"

"I hardly think so," said Malien. "To be useful spies or attackers they would have to be individually controlled. It can only be a few individual bats, chosen from susceptible ones close by. Even so, if a swarm of bats attacked when Karan or Sulien were outside . . ."

"I'll add this threat to the list," he said wearily.

As Karan rose to go he said, "Wait! Your daughter."

"What about her?" Karan said warily.

"I'm advised that her gifts for the Secret Art are remarkable and grow-ing rapidly, and that this is unprecedented in an untaught child her age."

Karan gulped. "I couldn't say."

"Where do her gifts come from?"

"I don't know, precisely."

"Indulge me with your best guess."

"I'm triune, and so is Sulien. I expect her gifts come from our ancestry."

"But Llian has no gift for the Secret Art, and Sulien is only half as much a triune as you. Surely her gift should be weaker, not stronger, and slower to develop."

Karan could see where this was leading but did not know how to divert him. "I don't know enough to say."

"You don't seem to know much at all, yet you refuse to allow her to be taught."

"I haven't refused; I just . . . haven't found the right teacher."

"If it's not Sulien's triune heritage, what is so special about her?"

"It *might* be due to the hrux I was given to ease the agony of her birth."

"How so?"

"Hrux is an aid to far-seeing and other such senses—" Why, why had she said that?

Janck pounced. "Really? Then if we dosed Sulien with hrux she might relive the nightmare in which she saw the enemy's secret."

"It's too dangerous!" Karan cried. "Too high a dose can kill."

"The Merdrun *will* kill all of us if we can't stop them. What have you done to extract the secret?"

"I tried to find it after Sulien first had the nightmares. I found nothing."

"Months ago! What have you done since you took her back from the Whelm?"

"I . . . She was too traumatised. It wasn't the right time."

"But surely," Janck said frostily, "you realise it's not just the key to Santhenar's survival, *but hers as well*?"

Karan could see she was losing. "I . . . I'll have another look in the morning."

"No, you'll bring her here in the morning, eight o'clock, and the best mancers I can gather will examine her."

"Be damned!"

"It's an order, Karan, and if you don't want to see the war out from a prison cell and your daughter in my custody and care, you'll obey! There will be guards outside your door in any case. Now get out of my sight!"

Karan returned to her room, sick with fear. Sulien was still asleep. Karan removed the blankets and table from the window recess to find the bat still staring in. She opened the catch and thrust the window up, dislodging the bat, then closed the window and went to bed. But every time she woke in the night the creature was there, or another like it, motionless save for its orb-like eyes. It was definitely spying on her and Sulien. How had it known they were in this room? Could the triplets see them through its eyes?

Karan put back the table and the blankets, then got into Sulien's bed and held her tightly. She hardly slept a wink that night and woke at dawn feeling more tired than when she had gone to bed. It was small consolation that the bat was gone.

41

YOU'LL BE RID OF ME SOON ENOUGH

"It's quite a *large* drop of nivol," said Hublees.

Stupid, stupid man! thought Aviel. *How can one drop be enough?*

She put the diamond phial in its leopardwood box, cleaned her gear and was packing it when Nimil burst in.

"Malien says fly to Zile with all possible speed, not stopping day or night."

"Why?" said Hublees, frowning.

"She wouldn't say—afraid of being overheard. But the summon stone is more powerful than before and the Merdrun are drawing from it; it can't be too long before they reopen the gate. The entire Whelm nation is racing north to join them, and Tallia needs the nivol desperately."

Nimil ran out and Hublees followed. When everyone had gone Aviel whispered, "Shand? Are you there?"

There was no answer. Had he gone off by himself, seeking ingredients for his scent potion? If he wasn't back soon he would be left behind.

Osseion put his head in through the door. "We're ready for the burial."

He had cut a grave through the ironstone crust into the soft red earth below it, at the far end of the gap between the stones. Earnis's frost-covered body lay beside the grave.

Aviel knelt beside him, took his icy hands and laid a kiss on his forehead. "Thank you for caring," she said softly. "And for being a better friend to me than I could be to you."

Osseion and Hublees lowered Earnis into the earth. She wished she had something to put in his grave but her pockets were empty and her possessions meagre.

Osseion picked up his spade. "I'll cover him now."

"No, wait."

Aviel ran back to her bench, rifled through her phials and found a new perfume she had made recently, based on the cleansing scent of lemon verbena, with hints of citrus and mint. It was not a subtle perfume but it would cut through any drifting foul influence from Rogues Render.

She put a drop on a fingertip, reached down and touched it to Earnis's forehead, his lips and his heart, and tucked the phial into his pocket. "He's ready now."

They buried him, Osseion covering the loose earth with rocks, then went back to their packing. After they had gone Aviel stood in the darkness by the grave. Earnis had been good and kind and gentle; he had helped her even at the cost of being ostracised by his fellows; he had risked his life for her, and lost it, and it was a tragic waste.

Within half an hour they were gone, Hublees flying as high and fast as the sky ship would go. Aviel had no idea if Shand had made it back to his hiding place, and there was no way to check.

They flew night and day for two whole days, crossing the Sea of Thurkad north of the fishing town of Ganport, then the mountains beyond, and halfway across the vast grasslands of the Plains of Folc, a land with few rivers and even fewer towns, occupied mostly by nomadic herders.

"Can't go any further without sleep," Hublees said late on the second afternoon. He headed down towards a hilly area where scattered green patches suggested seeping water.

Osseion put up Aviel's tent and everyone went to their hammocks except Aviel, who had slept all the previous night and dozed half the day. She gathered armloads of a low-growing fragrant mint bush, took them to her workshop and was immersed in the pleasurably repetitive task of extracting the scented oils when Shand appeared.

"Thought you'd leave me behind, did you?" he grated.

Having survived Lumillal, she wasn't going to be bullied by anyone. "Was I supposed to tell Hublees to wait for a traitor?" she said coldly.

He winced. "You're safe enough, having just done the impossible," he said sourly, as if he resented her success.

"I only made one drop."

"Then they'll need you to make more, won't they?"

"I'm not going through all that again."

Shand shrugged. He didn't care. How changed he was, and not in a good way. He looked older, thinner and more gaunt each time he appeared. This trip had forced him to use the dangerous invisibility spell for long periods at a time, and it seemed to be eating him away.

He scraped some foul-smelling gunge—brown streaked with red and acid green—from a jar into a small distillation flask.

"Is that from *the desiccated corpse of a woman murdered long ago*," said Aviel, "or *the last breath of an undead killer?*"

"Fat lot of help you've been."

He added a weighed amount of bright orange powder and clamped the flask over a burner. The lingering stink interfered with her own work but she continued shredding her herbs and spreading them on dishes of white fat, extracting the essential oils to make a balm for dry skin, watching him out of the corner of an eye.

He kept glancing at the opening of the tent as if afraid someone was spying on him. Did Hublees know Shand was aboard? If he did he would report them both the moment he got to Zile.

"Are you nearly done?" she said quietly.

"You'll be rid of me soon enough," Shand said curtly. "This is the last one."

Shand opened the scent potion grimoire to the marked place and ran a gnarled forefinger down the right-hand page. His lips moved, stopped, moved again as if he were repeating lines to memorise them, then he closed the grimoire.

He never left it open, for which she was grateful. All the Great Potions were dark and deadly; she had felt befouled just glancing at them. When all this was over—assuming she survived—she planned to make her own grimoire, only containing scent potions that were good or neutral.

Shand muttered an oath and vanished. A few seconds later Osseion looked in. "Still working?"

"Making perfume helps me to relax."

He wrinkled his nose. "Horrible smell for a perfume."

It was the lingering reek from Shand's muck. "Some of the most beautiful perfumes have unpleasant ingredients," she dissembled. "Just tiny amounts."

"Really?" Osseion scratched his head. "Well, what would I know?" He came in.

Behind her, Aviel sensed the invisible Shand's annoyance. He wanted rid of Osseion. Well, damn him!

"Would you like some tea?" she said. "You must be cold out there on watch."

"Don't feel the cold much," said Osseion, "but tea and company would be welcome."

She made two mugs of mint-bush tea and sweetened his with honey since she knew he liked it that way. She indicated the second canvas chair, near the door.

"Can't sit when I'm on duty," he said, slurping his tea.

His eyes were always on duty, constantly roving over the benches and the tent, and every minute he put his head out through the entrance, watching and listening.

"How are you doing?" he said quietly. "Don't think I could have survived what you went through."

"Work keeps the memories at bay—most of the time."

"And when you're not working?"

"I see Lumillal killing Earnis, over and over." Shudders racked her. "And sometimes I'm drawn back to Carcharon, when Unick held me prisoner."

"The memories fade in time," said Osseion. "But they never go away."

"You must have seen some terrible things."

"Awful things," he said, staring into the middle distance. "In battle, and while I was Mendark's bodyguard. Sights that have broken many a man." He turned back to her. "It's inner strength that really counts, and you have it." He drained his tea, put a heavy arm across her shoulder, then said, "Better get back to it." He went out, and she heard his footsteps moving away.

The grimoire opened as if by itself, then Shand reappeared. "He's suspicious."

Chills touched her back. "He was just being friendly, wasn't he?"

"Bodyguards to the best have to *be* the best, and Osseion was. He misses nothing. Now be quiet; I've got to think."

She worked in silence, watching him from the corner of an eye. Shand distilled the stench, absorbed it in a small quantity of a pale orange fluid that she could not identify, sniffed, made a face, then distilled it once more. His movements were deft and automatic, as if he had used these techniques ten thousand times.

Suddenly her make-work seemed pointless. She went into the darkened sky ship, climbed into her hammock fully dressed and fell asleep, but was jerked awake an hour later as a leering Lumillal wound the threads of her life around his hand. She forced the nightmare away, went out and found Osseion in the darkness.

"I'm afraid to sleep," she said. "Mind if I join you?"

"Your company is always welcome."

They paced around the campsite for a couple of hours. Osseion was the perfect companion: he did not talk for the sake of it and she felt no need to. The night was mild here and absolutely still, and with his massive presence beside her she felt safe for the first time since Tallia, badly injured, had appeared at Shand's house in Casyme more than two months ago and warned him about the summon stone and the Merdrun.

A light appeared in a forward window of the sky ship. "Hublees is up," said Osseion. "Better get packed."

When she entered the workshop Shand had twenty little phials lined up on the rear bench and the grimoire open before him, and was adding drops of each scented oil to a small flat-bottomed flask. It bothered her a little, though she could not work out why.

She packed all her ingredients, including the priceless bottle of Archeus in its own padded box, and was putting the last of the wrapped glassware into its crate when Hublees bellowed, "Aviel! Time to go!"

"One minute!" she yelled.

Shand drew up a small quantity of a yellow-green oil from the last of his phials and discharged it drop by drop into the flask, which was half full of a deep violet fluid. He swirled it, it turned amber and he took a careful sniff. His eyes revolved in their sockets and he let out a strangled grunt, then hissed, "Yes!"

Aviel hauled her crates to the foot of the ladder and went back for the boxes. When she returned with the second-last box Hublees was standing at the door of the sky ship and its rotors were turning gently.

"Get the damned tent down!" he snapped.

"Yes," she squeaked and hurried inside to fold the benches.

"Osseion," he yelled, "give her a hand."

Osseion replied from some distance away. Shand swore, swept his phials into a leather pouch, folded it over and tied the strings, then slipped the little flask into a wooden case half filled with rags. He wrapped them around the flask, closed the case and thrust it and the pouch into his pockets, and vanished a second before Osseion came in.

Osseion slipped Shand's marker in the open grimoire, closed it and handed it to Aviel. She put it in its case and carried it out. He folded the benches, carried them out and began to take down the tent. Aviel grabbed the last box, which was just inside the tent opening. Five minutes later they were in the air and racing for Zile.

Later that day Aviel was listening to Nimil work his scrying board when he let out a small cry, then said, "I'll tell her."

Aviel turned around in her seat. "Is there a message for me?"

"Yes," said Nimil, frowning at the instrument. "You are to present yourself to Tallia the instant you return."

"Did . . . did she say why?"

"Grand Master Tule is dead."

Had her scent potion killed him? She felt sure it had. She slumped in her seat, feeling sick. She had killed an old man and Tallia might not see it as self-defence. To her the scent potion, which Aviel had made specifically to deal with Tule, might be evidence of a far worse crime—premediated murder.

A guilt-ridden eternity later the battered, rattling sky ship settled on the sandy ground outside the gigantic front doors of the Great Library. Aviel, who had not slept since hearing Nimil's message, looked out and let out an involuntary squeak.

Tallia stood just twenty feet away, her arms folded across her breast. Malien was with her, plus the stout figure of Dedulus Janck, and Xarah. Aviel eyed them out the round window, her throat so tight that she could hardly breathe and a hot, churning sickness in the pit of her stomach.

Had Tallia's forensic mancers already identified traces of the scent potion Aviel had tossed in Tule's face, overdosing him so badly that he had never recovered? Surely they would have. Once she gave Tallia the nivol they would hang her from the nearest gibbet. Aviel imagined her sad little body dangling there by the neck, her tongue protruding, the lumpy ankle she had always kept hidden exposed to the world's cruel view.

Osseion threw the door open and the ladder out. She did not move.

"After you," said Hublees. "You're the one everyone wants to see."

Even Nimil was smiling, but Aviel took no comfort from her achievement. *I killed Grand Master Tule, a sick old man, and now I'm going to pay.*

She got up and put on the little pack containing the diamond phial, her phials of scent potions and various other necessaries. Her knees were shaking. She was a fraud and a killer and she had helped a known traitor. As she put her right foot on the ground a sharp pain speared through her bad ankle and she gasped.

Osseion sprang down beside her and gave her his arm. "Off you go," he said, urging her forward. "They're waiting."

She hobbled across. Janck studied her bruised face. "Clearly you have much to tell us."

"But first," said Tallia, "the nivol."

Aviel opened the drawer of the leopardwood box and took out the diamond phial. Its myriad of faces winked in the bright sunlight.

Tallia let out her breath in a long sigh. "The most expensive container in the history of Santhenar."

"A diamond worth fifty thousand gold tells, ruined to make a tiny bottle," said Janck. "Hold it up."

Aviel did so, and the sunlight shone through the drop in the bottom, releasing a narrow, brilliantly green beam.

"Ahhhh!" sighed Tallia. "But . . . are you sure that's nivol?"

"I can show you the method I used. Every transformation and colour change was exactly as the parchment said. Hublees saw it and so did Nimil."

"It looks as I would expect it to," said Malien slowly. "But is one large drop of nivol enough?"

"It should be," said Tallia. "Assuming we can deliver it to precisely the right place on the summon stone. But it'd be better if we had more." She peered into Aviel's eyes. "I assume you can make more?"

Aviel looked down at her boots. Every step of the method would trigger flashbacks about Earnis's life and death, the horror of Rogues Render, and Lumillal. "We have more golden brimstones, more colophony and more Archeus," she said. "The final step only takes a few hours, but . . ."

"Nadiril has equipped a workshop for you upstairs. Lilis will show you there. How quickly can you make more?"

"It takes a lot of work to make all the different kinds of layered filters. I'd say . . . five days."

Tallia looked at Malien, who conferred with Xarah. Xarah shook her head.

"I don't think we can wait five days," said Malien.

"We can't even afford *three* days," said Janck. "The attack force will have to fly out as soon—" He broke off. "Forgetting myself. Secrecy!" He nodded to Aviel, then drew Hublees away. "Got an urgent job for you. Tallia?"

They walked away a dozen yards and Tallia conjured a green secrecy bubble around the three of them. Janck spoke for several minutes.

Hublees did not look pleased, but finally he nodded and Tallia extinguished the bubble. Hublees picked up his pack, looking grim, and went back inside the sky ship.

Tallia and Janck returned. "You look like death," he said to Aviel.

"I keep seeing the way Lumillal murdered Earnis. Over and over."

"Get some rest. There's a banquet tonight and you'll be on my table. Then, first thing in the morning, back to work."

"What about . . . Grand Master Tule?"

"We'll deal with that issue later," Tallia said coldly and walked away.

42

HOW COULD I HAVE TRUSTED YOU?

Aviel did not enjoy one moment of the banquet, and the honour of being on the head table next to Janck was a burden. Because her mission had been top secret, few people knew about her brilliant achievement, and she did not know how to make small talk. The eyes of the room were on her and she felt sure everyone was judging her, saying knowingly that she did not belong there, mocking her. As soon as she finished the first course she slipped away and went to the room she was sharing with Lilis, to bed.

Aviel woke the moment Lilis came in and knew she would not get back to sleep. She lay still until she could tell, by Lilis's steady breathing in the bed on the other side of the room, that she was asleep.

Aviel lit a candle and was looking through the grimoire for a scent potion that could only be used for good purposes when she noticed the marker Osseion had inserted before closing it yesterday. It marked Shand's scent potion, the Afflatus Effluvium, and as she glanced at it she remembered something curious.

Shand had told her that his scent potion required nineteen different scents, smells and reeks, yet when he'd blended the potion there had been *twenty* phials lined up on the bench. Had he made a mistake? It seemed unlikely. Or added an extra scent to the recipe? Not even a master would make such a dangerous change without careful testing.

He had lied! But why would he deceive her about a scent potion she had no interest in ever making? She moved the grimoire so her candle light fell on it. The method was hard to read, the pages stained as if someone had spilled dark tea or black beer on them, and here and there were unidentifiable crusts the colour of porridge. She scanned the list of ingredients. Nineteen.

No, a twentieth ingredient was almost completely obscured by one of the crusted blobs. She poked at it with the tip of her knife and discovered that the crust was only stuck to the page on its right-hand side. Shand must have lifted it to read what was underneath then pressed it down again.

And the twentieth ingredient was Archeus of Eidolon! She let out an involuntary cry.

Lilis stirred. "Something the matter?" she said sleepily.

"Just read something I didn't like."

Lilis's eyes fixed on her until Aviel felt the heat rising up her face. "That's what happens when you pursue the dark side," Lilis said jokingly, then closed her eyes.

Aviel did not smile; it cut too close. She reopened the grimoire and read the last ingredient again. Archeus of Eidolon. And Shand's twentieth phial of scented oil had been a similar yellow-green colour.

She shot up in bed. *You unutterable bastard.*

Had Shand known from the beginning that he needed the Archeus to make his scent potion? She felt sure he had. He must have put the nivol method that used Archeus in with her other parchments because it was the only way to get some for himself. He had been so desperate to get it that he risked her life and everyone else's. And Earnis had been killed for it.

You betrayed us to the magiz, and now you've betrayed us again. How could I have trusted you?

Her heart gave a leaden thud as an even worse thought struck her. What if Shand had made up that recipe for nivol? He'd had time to read the papers and parchments Tallia had given her, and he certainly had the alchemical knowledge to write a fake but convincing recipe, one that added the Archeus at the end.

If Shand *had* invented the recipe she probably hadn't made nivol at all. Had the past weeks, the staggering cost, the trials and torments and Earnis's death, all been wasted?

Aviel groaned. How could she tell? There was no way to test her nivol since she only had one drop of it. But she could not allow Janck to send people off on a doomed mission to destroy the summon stone with fake nivol. She had no choice but to own up to her treacherous collaboration with Shand, that she had kept his secret and allowed him to use her equipment, and that he had betrayed her too.

And in wartime, when they faced such an overwhelming threat, her crime warranted a public, gruesome execution.

She rose and dressed and, taking the grimoire with her, went up to the little cramped workshop. It contained a selection of equipment and chymicals brought from her workshop in Sith, plus the gear from the sky ship, still in its crates. She unpacked it and set it on the benches in the order she would need to use it in the morning.

Tallia had put the drop of nivol in a much smaller diamond phial and given Aviel back the large yellow phial. She clamped it to a stand, pushed it to the back of the bench then lined up the thirty-six ingredients. It took five days of painstaking alchemy to make her layered filters and she was not looking forward to it.

Something was missing. She studied the line of bottles and jars and boxes, then ticked the ingredients off on her list, last of all the box of golden brimstones and the jar containing several pounds of bubble bark pine colophony. She removed the lid and sniffed its cleansing scent.

The sintered platinum! Strictly speaking it was not an ingredient, since it was unchanged by the process. Aviel rooted around in the boxes and found the heavy jar at the back, behind some empty flasks. She reached down to pick it up, but her hand froze just inches from it.

The black cap, carved from ironwood, was half eaten away. But what could eat away ironwood? She shone a lantern on the jar. There were holes in the sides too, as if grubs had chewed through the thick glass, and half the platinum, one of the most resistant of all metals, was gone, leaving a grey sludge in the bottom of the jar.

What could have happened to it? After making the drop of nivol she had picked out the sintered platinum with her tweezers and rinsed it before replacing it in the jar with the rest. There must have been a film of nivol inside the sintered metal and it had eaten the ironwood, platinum and glass away.

Her pulse rose. She checked the little golden pair of tweezers. They were also eaten away; all that remained was the thick end where the two tweezers joined.

Aviel had to sit down; she was shaking. Then it *was* true nivol—and if a tiny film on the tweezers and the platinum could do such damage, the large drop in the diamond phial surely must be enough to eat the heart out of the summon stone. She was saved! She would not have to confess after all.

Now she felt guilty. How could she have so misjudged Shand? He was one of the great figures in the past few hundred years of the Histories, and always he had worked for the good of his friends and allies, and Santhenar. True, he had given her that nivol method to get the Archeus *he* needed, but the method had worked.

Her weary eye wandered along the benches. Thirty-six ingredients; one to go. Aviel opened the small padded crate in which she had packed the lead crystal bottle of Archeus of Eidolon. The crate was empty. She went through all the other crates and boxes. The bottle was not in them either. She scanned the benches and the floor, then checked all the rags she had used to wrap her glassware. No bottle, no Archeus.

She slumped onto a stool, an awful pain in the centre of her chest. She jumped up and went through everything again, then searched every bench, cupboard and drawer in the workshop, even places into which the lead crystal bottle could not possibly have fitted. It was not there.

But it had to be there; she remembered packing it into that very box, the smallest of them, and leaving it inside the opening of the tent only minutes before they departed the campsite on the Plains of Folc. The boxes had travelled in the sky ship all the way to Zile, then had been unloaded under Osseion's watch. He had escorted her precious gear up to the workshop and locked it afterwards, and a pair of guards stood watch outside day and night.

Despair settled over her as she searched again and again. The bottle of Archeus was gone. Had it ever been here? Could a resourceful thief have gained entry to the workshop and stolen it?

No! The bottle must have been taken from the box before it left the tent. She had left it there while she carried her gear across to the sky ship, and there had been ample time for Shand to take the bottle. She had been right the first time; he *was* a despicable traitor.

And she was ruined. She had to confess at once, while there was a hope that he was still in Zile. Assuming he had not slipped away from the campsite on the Plains of Folc.

She put the grimoire in its box and pushed it to the back of the bench, then crept out, her heart thudding dully, and locked the door behind her. Osseion was there, talking to the two guards.

He took one look at her face and said, "Something bad's happened?" She nodded.

He jerked his head sideways, and she followed him around the corner. "What is it?" said Osseion.

"The bottle of Archeus is gone. Stolen! Shand must have taken it."

Osseion asked no questions. "I'll wake Commander Janck—he's got to know right away."

"Janck?" she said in dismay. "I was going to tell Tallia."

"She left after the dinner with Malien and Nadiril, and they won't be back until the morning. Besides, Janck is my commander now. This way."

Aviel was doomed. The three people who might, just possibly, have intervened on her behalf were gone. Santhenar was in desperate peril and her folly had made it worse. Janck would have to make an example of her. They did not need her any more. Now they knew that the method worked, they must be able to find someone who could follow it.

Osseion strode off. Aviel limped after him, knowing there was nothing she could do to save herself. She could not run and she had nowhere to hide. All she could do was ease her conscience by confessing everything she had done, then taking her punishment.

He had stopped and was studying her anxiously. "You all right?"

"No," she whispered.

"It's not your fault. You've always done your very best."

No, I haven't. Osseion's kindness was unbearable.

"Well, the sooner it's out in the open the sooner Commander Janck can deal with it."

And me.

By the time they reached his quarters, after hobbling along endless corridors and up several long flights of stone steps, the bones in Aviel's ankle were grating on one another. But the storm raging inside her was worse. She had done her best to balance her obligation to Shand and her war work, but she had failed.

Two uniformed guards, one on either side of a broad pair of carved wooden doors, moved forward to block Osseion's path.

"Commander can't be disturbed," said the fellow on the left, officiously. He was as tall as Osseion and even wider, with a round, moon-like face, blank of expression.

"Wake him!" Osseion said with an authority that made the fellow step back, blinking at him.

Aviel had no idea how one gained such authority, so simply and quietly.

The guard glanced down at Aviel, pale and trembling and looking like death. "Is she the girl who—"

"Yes," said Osseion.

The guard slipped inside and reappeared shortly to say, in an astonished voice, that Commander Janck would be pleased to see Osseion and Aviel at once. They went in through a wide, plain foyer, down a hall, crossed a long room with six tables in it, all covered in maps, nautical charts and stacks of papers, and then entered another large room with a small, cot-like bed, a table and four chairs, three armchairs and a pair of tall narrow small-paned windows that appeared not to have been washed since the founding of the Great Library three thousand years ago.

Dedulus Janck was at the far end of the table, wearing a yellow and black dressing gown. His commander's uniform hung from a coat stand. A pair of tall black boots stood beside the foot of the bed and a sword in a silver and black scabbard lay across the blue quilt.

"A fine piece of work," he said gruffly, "even if it did only result in one drop of the stuff."

Aviel did not reply. He had said the same thing at dinner, the only words he had spoken to her. He indicated the chairs.

Aviel's ankle was as painful as she had ever known it but she said, "I must stand, sir."

Janck picked up a round bottle and poured a tot of green spirit into a glass. He frowned at it, filled the glass and quaffed half of it, then sat down, staring at her. "Well?"

Aviel gasped out the dreadful story. "Shand kept coming to my workshop, in Sith and on our journey, turned invisible. I . . . I owe him, and he demanded I let him use my equipment—"

"Why?" grated Janck.

"So he could make a powerful dark scent potion, but he was lying to me all along, and now he's stolen the bottle of Archeus, and without it I can't make any more nivol. I'm really, really sorry, sir."

She swayed on her feet, unable to meet his eyes. She lowered her head, half expecting him to fly into a rage, draw the sword and cut off her head. She had heard stories about generals who did that kind of thing.

Osseion stiffened then took hold of her left shoulder, steadying her. Or making sure she did not run for it.

"When did he steal the Archeus?" said Janck, his voice very low.

"I think just before we left the Plains of Folc. But I only discovered it was gone a few minutes ago."

"Did Shand come to Zile in the sky ship?"

"I don't know."

Janck sat down with a thump and drank the rest of the green spirit. He wrote several lines on a piece of paper, folded it three times and sealed it with wax, then wrote a name Aviel could not read on the outside. "Guard!" he shouted.

The enormous guard ran in. "Take this to Captain Jutt, on the double," snapped Janck.

The guard took the paper, saluted and ran out. Janck followed him to the doors and Aviel heard the key turn in the lock. He came back and sat down again, filling his glass and taking another gulp. "Sit! And that's an order."

Aviel sat. Osseion remained standing, still gripping her shoulder.

"How did Shand make you collaborate?" he said in a steely voice.

"I owe him a great debt, sir. Had he not saved me I would have been an indentured slave in Magsie Murg's tannery in Casyme, starved and flogged and worked to death."

"Then he didn't *force* you to collaborate. You *chose* to collaborate with a known traitor because of your obligation to him, despite knowing that collaborating with Shand was treachery, punishable by death."

There was no point making excuses or trying to mitigate her crime. Besides, she had always been painfully honest and could not change, even if she was about to be executed.

"Yes," she whispered. "I chose to collaborate with him."

"Tell me the story, *briefly*. Leave out nothing of importance."

"The moment I arrived in Sith, weeks ago, Shand hauled me into an empty room, locked the door and reminded me of my debt to him. He was furious—"

"Why would he be furious with you, after all you've done for us?"

"I . . . I took his scent potion grimoire while he was in Chanthed, a couple of months ago. That's how I located the summon stone, sir."

He waved a hand to indicate he knew that story. "So you're a thief as well as an enemy collaborator?"

"Yes, sir," she said faintly.

"Go on."

"He said I owed him and I had to pay."

"But when you agreed to aid him, surely you weren't aware that he was a condemned traitor?"

Aviel could not meet his eyes. She felt sick with shame. "Yes, he told me."

"And you still agreed?"

"You don't know what it was like," she said, then realised how feeble that sounded.

"I'm trying to. Tell me exactly what he said."

"*I am a traitor!* he said. *The magiz got to me when I was weak and vulnerable, and embedded a secret link in me, and via that link I unwittingly betrayed our plans to her. How could I have allowed it to happen? How did I not realise? The shame is unbearable! I have to restore my good name.*"

"Shand still believes he has a good name?" said Janck incredulously. "Extraordinary fellow! What's he up to?"

"He's got Unick's Identity device," said Aviel. "And he took the remains of the Origin device I used to poison the summon stone."

Janck leaned forward, and there was a light in his eyes. "Why did he take it?"

"He never said. But he told me I had to repay him by letting him use my workshop to make one of the Great Potions in his grimoire; one of the seven forbidden scent potions."

"Name?" he rapped.

"The Afflatus Effluvium."

"Purpose?"

"He said, *If it works I'll be able to recover brilliant spells, long lost, and make them even more powerful.*"

"Why did Shand want to do that?"

"He didn't say," said Aviel.

"But you gained an impression. An idea?"

"I think he was hoping to make a . . . a master device, like Unick's Command device, only better."

"To what purpose?"

"I don't know. Though he often talked about making up for his unwitting betrayal."

Janck gave a dubious sniff. "Did you believe him?"

"Yes. He's a good man."

"Whatever he *was*, Shand is now a traitor and a thief whose theft may have ruined our best hope. Did he succeed with his scent potion?"

"I think so. Just before we left our last campsite he blended the twenty smells and took a very careful sniff of the scent potion, then said, *Yes!* He sounded . . . triumphant. Then Hublees yelled that we had to go and Shand vanished; I haven't seen him since."

"I'll have the sky ship searched. If he did come back . . ." He scowled, then looked into her eyes again. "Anything else you want to confess while you have the chance?"

Did he mean before she was executed? "Yes," whispered Aviel.

She told him about the parchment Shand had slipped in among the others, containing the simpler and quicker method that required Archeus of Eidolon. And how betrayed and used she had felt when she discovered, only hours ago, that he had risked everyone's lives, and caused Earnis's death, because he needed the Archeus for his scent potion.

"Why didn't Shand take the grimoire?" said Janck.

"There wasn't time. He'd just finished making the scent potion when he heard Osseion coming to the tent."

Aviel could not get over his betrayal. What could have changed him so radically? She could only think of one thing—that he was still under the influence of the Merdrun, or even that they were controlling him. And she had helped him!

The blood drained from Janck's face. "Are you telling me that the drop of nivol, which cost a sizeable part of our war chest to make, could be *useless*?"

"No, it's good."

"How do you know? There isn't enough to test it."

She explained about the eaten-away jar, platinum and golden tweezers.

Janck heaved his bulky body out of the chair, sat on the bed and pulled his boots on. "This has come at a very bad time; we were about to send—" Whatever he had been going to say, he thought better of it. "I've got to be sure. Come!"

He went out in his boots and dressing gown. Aviel followed with Osseion. In the workshop Janck checked the jar of sintered platinum and the golden tweezers, grunted, then said, "Show me the method he used in the grimoire."

Aviel drew its case across from the back of the bench and flipped up the lid. The box was empty. She stared at it, felt around inside, then her knees gave. Osseion caught her as she fell, lifted her onto a stool and held her upright.

She felt faint, hot and cold and shivery. "I put it in this box half an hour ago," she whispered. "I closed the lid and went out and locked the door. Osseion was outside with the two guards. How could it be gone?"

"That bloody bastard Shand!" Janck said savagely. "He must be in the library!"

He strode to the door, dressing gown flapping around his hairless calves, and gave swift orders to one of the guards outside, who sped off. They all left the room. Janck locked the door with Aviel's key, pocketed it and turned to the remaining guard.

"You useless, incompetent prick!" He thumped the guard in the chest. "I should have you hanged."

"Sir?" said the guard, his face turning chalk white.

"Someone got in!"

"But we've been here all the time. We would have seen—"

"The bastard's invisible! Stand here with your back to the door and don't allow anyone in. Don't move for *any reason*—not even if you have to piss your trews."

"Yes, Commander," whispered the guard.

"Come!" Janck said to Aviel. "You too, Sergeant," he said to Osseion.

They returned to Janck's quarters and he sat at the table. Despite the agony in her ankle, Aviel remained on her feet. Whatever her fate was to be, she would face it standing up.

"Is there anything else you want to confess?" said Janck. "Before I deal with you."

"Yes?"

"What?"

"Grand Master Tule is dead." The guilt was sickening. "And it's my fault."

"You'd been away for a fortnight when he died," said Janck.

"But I'm responsible."

"You'd better explain."

She gabbled it out. "Master Tule refused to teach me anything about alchemy; he wouldn't even explain what the words and symbols meant.

He just kept calling me a little bastard and a twist-foot, and telling me to wash all the equipment again and again and again, and hitting me and holding my head under hot water!"

She ran out of air, took a couple of gasping breaths and continued. "Everyone kept saying that I had to find a way to deal with him, so I made a mild little scent potion, Essence of Ague, to defend myself . . . just in case. Master Tule came back and flew into a rage and knocked me down and he was going to stamp on my face, so I hurled the potion at him and it went up his nose and in his mouth, a much stronger dose than I'd planned." She paused, but it had to be said. "And it killed him. *I* killed him."

Janck's eyes slid sideways and up, to Osseion. "Have you something to say on the matter, Sergeant?"

"I saw how he beat her," said Osseion, "and I told her she was entitled to defend herself." He paused, frowning as if trying to recall something to mind, then added, "I also said that our survival relied on Aviel's work and she had to find the best and quickest way to get it done. I told her that nothing else mattered—not the law, nor friendship, nor loyalty. Just the work."

"Did you now?" said Janck. "You take a lot on yourself, Sergeant."

"Yes, Commander."

Janck steepled his pudgy hands in front of him and stared at Aviel. "I told you what a difficult man your master was and advised you to find a way to work with him."

Chills swept over her head and back. This was it—he was going to condemn her. An odd thought struck her: how her sisters would crow. They would tell everyone in Casyme that they had always known she was rotten and would come to a bad end, and now she had got the punishment she deserved. It hurt, for she had always tried to treat people the way she wanted to be treated.

"However, it's clear to me that your way was the only way," Janck added deliberately. "You disabled Torsion Tule so you could do the work we needed urgently, but you did not kill him. He was old and ailing, a choleric man quite unable to restrain his passions, and that's what brought about his end."

Aviel realised that she had been holding her breath. Now she let it out with a little sigh, though her trial was not over yet. Far from it. Janck looked up sharply, then slowly rose, staring at her.

"Aviel Foyl," he said in a cold and formal voice, "you have admitted that you willingly and without coercion assisted the condemned traitor known as Shand, Golias and the Recorder to make a forbidden and possibly sorcerous scent potion, for purposes unknown but very likely inimical to the war effort. You have also admitted that you failed to inform on him, despite many opportunities to do so, thus allowing him to remain at liberty and continue his betrayals. You have also admitted that your culpability in this matter allowed him to steal a priceless bottle of Archeus of Eidolon that is essential to our defence against the enemy." He looked directly into her eyes, and his were as hard and cold as frozen agate. "Do you deny any of these admissions?"

"No," she croaked.

"Each of these offences carries the death penalty," said Janck. "To be carried out publicly by cruel and barbarous means, as a lesson to all."

She looked down at the floor. There was nothing to say.

"Had you attained the age of sixteen," he went on, "I would not have had the slightest hesitation in sending you for public execution in the forecourt of the Great Library, at dawn. However, as you are not—"

"But I *am* sixteen," she gasped. "I turned—"

"How dare you interrupt me! Be silent!" He scowled at her. "Since you are not of age, I cannot accept anything you say on this matter." He looked up. "Sergeant Osseion, you know this girl. What age is she?"

"Not yet sixteen," Osseion said at once. "Possibly only fourteen."

"Fourteen," Janck said ruminatively. "Could I execute a girl of fourteen, Sergeant? There are precedents, certainly, in cases of the most diabolical treachery. But a *small* girl of fourteen? A girl who has not once, but *twice*, despite her handicap, proved to be of the greatest courage and ingenuity. A girl to whom we owe our freedom, if not our lives?"

"In this war of all wars we need heroes to look up to and heroes to inspire us, Commander Janck."

"If I execute the girl it will be disastrous for morale; people will believe that no one is safe from the enemy's corruptions, and they will despair.

While if the tale of Aviel's heroism at Rogues Render is—in due course—added to the other stories about her, people will be inspired."

"Also," said Osseion, "once Shand is captured and the Archeus regained, her gifts will be needed again."

"Indeed," said Janck and again looked into Aviel's eyes. "Aviel Foyl, because you are not of age the charges against you are dismissed, with this warning: by using you so shabbily and involving you in his own treacherous conspiracies, Shand has cancelled your debt to him. You owe him nothing now, and if you ever assist him again your life is *immediately* forfeit."

All the strength drained from Aviel's limbs and she had to sit down. "Thank you," she said in a tiny voice. "Thank you."

Janck stood up. "Sergeant Osseion, did this discussion ever take place?"

"No, Commander," said Osseion.

"Aviel Foyl, you have not seen or heard or spoken to Shand in months. *Have you?*"

"No, Commander," said Aviel. The lie hardly counted beside all her other crimes.

"You are dismissed. Sergeant, escort Aviel to her room and see no one disturbs her sleep. She will have much to do the moment the traitor is found and the Archeus taken back."

"Yes, sir," said Osseion.

"I've given orders for my entire army here in Zile to search for the scoundrel, and I expect he'll be found very soon. And then Shand will hang by his own entrails."

43

I'VE GOT TO REDEEM MYSELF

Zile was not completely empty. A few hundred people still dwelt in the magnificent ruins, eking out an existence by barter, or supplying the necessities of civilisation to those who still lived a largely nomadic existence in the surrounding desert lands, or catering to the needs of the Great Library, or in other less reputable pursuits.

Shand was trudging through the sand-swept back streets to one of those places now, a bar of sorts in what had once been the reception room of a small palace. But not to drink, his all-too-frequent refuge lately. His situation was so desperate that he had sworn off alcohol.

The bar was gloomy, the broken windows having been boarded up long ago, and sand squeaked on the scored marble tiles. There were no customers at the counter. He cocked his head at the barman, Gride, a stringy, desiccated fellow he had known on and off for more than a decade. Gride jerked his head towards a booth at the rear. Shand spotted his quarry, a dark-haired woman bent over a glass, made sure there was no one in any of the other booths and squeezed into the bench opposite her.

Ifoli's head jerked up and for an instant he saw fear in her eyes, until she realised who he was. "C-can I help you?" she said warily, her voice slurred by drink.

So her famed self-control wasn't perfect. He took a grim pleasure in the discovery, though hers was a damn sight better than his own. "We can help each other," he said, longingly eyeing the bottle of white liquor, which was more than half empty. "You come here often, don't you? To drink your guilt away."

"What's it to you?" she snapped.

"We have the same trouble, you and I."

She looked at him in astonishment. No, incredulity! What could a brilliant and beautiful young woman with the world at her feet have in common with a grizzled old fool crushed by bitterness, rejection and folly?

"What?" she snapped.

"Guilt, shame and the need for redemption," said Shand.

"Go away." Ifoli reached for the bottle.

"Will you allow me to unburden myself?"

"To me? Why me?"

"Because you're practically a stranger," said Shand. "It's ... less mortifying."

"All right."

"I was used by the Merdrun's first magiz—the one Karan killed on Cinnabar. The magiz secretly embedded a mind link in me and employed it to spy on my friends and allies, then conveyed their plans to your former master, Snoat. Who used that information to attack us."

She put the bottle down with more care than necessary. "Go on."

"Snoat didn't know the true source of the priceless intelligence he was getting. But many of our allies, and many innocent people, died because of it. The magiz used me!" he cried. "Unwittingly, I betrayed my friends, my allies and my world. Unwittingly but blindly. I was too proud; I ignored signs that should have told me what was happening and abused my friends when they tried to tell me. The shame is unbearable . . . and I think you know something about that."

Ifoli took a swig from her glass. "I thought I was being so clever," she said softly. "serving Snoat while spying for Nadiril. But I tried too hard to be the perfect spy—I stepped over the line and collaborated with Snoat. I did shameful things in order to maintain my cover, Shand, and I allowed him to commit terrible evils." She looked up at him, a trifle blearily. "But I don't see—"

"As with me. My good name, no, my very identity, is under threat. I've got to redeem myself."

"I don't see how I can help you."

Shand checked the room and lowered his voice. "I'm terrified the magiz's link is still buried in me. What if the enemy's new magiz wakes it and forces me to betray us again? I've got to get rid of the link, but I can't do that by myself."

"I don't know anything about such things," said Ifoli.

"I do. I've made a dark scent potion—the Afflatus Effluvium. It's one of the Great Potions and it can be used for a number of purposes, such as finding deeply embedded mind links."

Now she looked interested. "And tearing them out?"

Shand shook his head. "For that I need a special kind of magical device. A Command device, in fact, but a much better one than the one Unick made for Snoat."

"What was wrong with his?"

"By the time Unick made it he had been ensnared by the summon stone, and it made him modify the Command device for its own benefit."

"Ahhh!" sighed Ifoli. "That explains—"

"Whenever the Command device was used, it strengthened the stone. And it could never be used against it."

"And that's why you need me. Because I understand the workings of Unick's three enchanted devices."

"And the theory behind them. Llian once mentioned that you'd made many working drawings."

"Unick didn't use them."

"But if you were to combine your subtle approach with Unick's sledgehammer method to make . . ."

"A device to remove a mind link," said Ifoli.

"Such a powerful yet subtle device could be used for many purposes. It could be of great benefit in the war."

"It would take a long time to make. The components of such a device will be very specific, and few of them will be available in Zile."

"I have Unick's Origin and Identity devices," said Shand, "apart from the flask of quicksilver, and I've just obtained the fragments of the Command device, plus the core Llian recovered. If they were all taken apart . . ."

"It would make the task much easier." Ifoli leaned across the table, her eyes hard. "But I'd have to be sure of you first. Sure that you weren't still under the magiz's control."

"Yes," said Shand. "You would."

44

TAKE HIM DOWNSTAIRS!

Karan, escorted by six of Janck's finest, delivered Sulien for interrogation at eight the following morning, then sweated outside while Tallia, Malien and three unnamed mancers probed the depths of Sulien's mind with every spell they could think of. Mind searches were fraught; they were painful and could cause memory loss, mental damage and occasionally madness.

"Are you all right?" Karan cried when Malien finally escorted Sulien out after a four-hour probing. She was unnaturally pale and unsteady on her feet.

"Head's aching," said Sulien. "Going to bed." She lurched away, looking as though she was going to vomit.

"Well?" Karan said coldly to Malien. "Was it worth her torment?"

"Don't be like that, Karan; it had to be done."

"And?"

"We established beyond doubt that Sulien *did* see the Merdrun's secret in a nightmare."

"You thought she'd made it up?" Karan said incredulously.

"The question had to be asked, but we could not recover a single second of the nightmare. The old magiz must have blocked it, though there's no trace as to how. There's nothing more *we* can do."

"Does that mean it's irrecoverable?"

"Theoretically, any spell one great mancer can devise, another equally experienced should be able to undo." But she did not sound hopeful.

Karan was on the library roof with Malien, preparing with great reluctance for her spying mission to the Isle of Gwine. Sulien, who was still wan, looked on anxiously.

"The way you went to Cinnabar the first time would be best," said Malien, whose hostility was greatly diminished now that Karan was about to risk her life on everyone's behalf. "Via my incantation of disembodiment."

"The triplets will be expecting me," said Karan.

"Avoid them. You can do vital work without going near them."

"Such as?"

"The Merdrun spent the past year on Cinnabar conquering city after city and fortress after fortress; no one could resist them. But the moment they entered the Crimson Gate everything went wrong. Now they're trapped on an island far from anywhere important, and for the first time they're on the defensive. What would they do?"

Before Karan could answer Sulien said, "Build a fortress."

"Precisely," said Malien. "Find out what kind of defences they have, and where, and their strengths and weaknesses."

"Why does Mummy always have to go?" Sulien's face was pale, and no wonder.

"Because no one else can do it," said Malien.

"If anything happens . . ." said Karan. "If I don't come back, Malien will look after you." She turned to Malien. "You will, won't you? And be kind to her."

"Kinder than Tensor was to you when you ended up with us at the age of twelve."

Sulien gave a little shudder, then stood up straight and looked into Karan's eyes. "It can't be nearly as bad as being a little Whelm."

"It's difficult for Aachim to have children," said Malien, "and we love them all the more for it. It's a hard world, and children must be prepared, but you will never be treated badly in the care of Clan Elienor."

It was all Karan could ask for. She checked that she had her hat, knife, water bottle and everything else she would need if forced to materialise, and was focusing on the only clear mental image she had of Gwine—the hill with the white stone bowl and red reflective pool from which the triplets had attacked Sulien—when there came a rattle and a clatter from the north and a very battered sky ship separated from the bright ball of the sun and wobbled down towards the far end of the roof.

She took no notice; sky ships were constantly coming and going on secret war business.

"Mummy!" said Sulien, clutching at her hand.

Karan hugged her tightly, lingeringly, then pulled away. "I have to go."

"No, wait!"

They had scarcely been separated since Sulien's rescue from the Whelm, and she was still clingy. Her safe world had been torn apart; it was a wonder she was coping at all.

The sky ship came in far faster than Yggur would ever have landed his craft. Its skids hit the roof, *crash*, bounced, came down again, *crash*, *crash*, and slewed sideways, metal screeching on stone, then it came to rest canted over to the left. The rotors died.

"Mummy, come on!" cried Sulien, heaving on Karan's hand.

Sulien's eyes were blazing, her whole face glowing, and suddenly Karan's skin rose in goose pimples. She fought down hope; she'd given way to it too many times, and it had failed her again and again.

Sulien persisted and Karan allowed herself to be dragged along. The door of the sky ship opened with a groan, as if the hinges had been forced out of shape. The box-shaped cabin looked as though something had taken hold of it and twisted. A man forced the door the rest of the way and jumped down six feet to the roof, looking around wildly. He stumbled towards the troops guarding the other sky ships, shouting, though Karan could not make out what he was saying.

Another man followed, tall, dark-haired and unmistakeably Aachim. He looked to the main stairs. People were hurrying up—Tallia, Janck and a pair of guards. The tall Aachim ran that way.

A third man appeared, much older than the others, wearing a dark blue cape over a grey shirt and pantaloons, and carrying a short, gnarled black staff. He tossed the end of the boarding ladder down, climbed down it and stood there for a moment, shivering. He was short and plump and rather old, with little feet and hands, a bald head, white sideburns that extended down to his shoulders and an absurd goatee beard dyed soot-black.

"Battle Mancer Hublees," he said, bowing to Sulien and Karan. "A bad business." He headed towards the stairs without waiting for a response.

Sulien faltered, staring at the sky ship. A fourth man disembarked and, moving slowly and wearily, tied the craft down to rings anchored in the roof. The familiar desolation flashed across her face; she gave a little sob but shook it off and kept going.

A few feet from the foot of the ladder she stopped, looking up. "Daddy?"

Karan could not bear it, could not bear for her hopes to be so crushed.

"*Daddy!*" Sulien shrieked.

Karan was shivering and tingling all over. And then he appeared in the doorway. Llian's eyes were bloodshot, his face was purple with bruises, a grubby bandage encircled his left wrist and he was limping badly. But he was alive! Her eyes filled with hot, stinging tears.

"Sulien?" he whispered. "You're safe? And Karan too?"

He scrambled down the ladder, caught a foot in the second-bottom rung and fell flat on his face on the roof.

Sulien threw herself at him and wrapped her arms around him. "Daddy, we've been *so* worried. Where have you been?"

Llian hugged her until she squeaked, then kissed her on the forehead. "It's a long story, though not as long as yours, I'll bet." He hugged her again. "I can't believe it. How did you get here? *When* did you get here?"

"The night before last," said Sulien, letting go and helping him up.

Llian got up, frowning. "But I was—"

Karan could not speak; she was too overwhelmed. She hugged them both. He winced, then looked down at her. "I never thought . . . I barely hoped . . ."

Her relief was so overwhelming Karan felt giddy and had to cling to him. "Are you all right? What's happened?"

Llian's eyes flicked to Janck and Tallia. They had stopped to confer with Hublees, but Janck was now running across the roof towards them. Llian grimaced.

"Silence!" bellowed Janck. "Say nothing, Llian, on pain of death. Guards, take charge of him."

Janck's guards ran ahead, shoved Karan and Sulien out of the way and took Llian by the arms, one on each side.

"This way, if you please," said the first guard, a burly fellow with a broken nose and a gap where his two top front teeth should have been.

"Daddy?" wailed Sulien. "What's the matter?"

"Nothing," said Llian. "They just—"

"Say *nothing*!" roared Janck, who was purple in the face and gasping.

"You're not taking Daddy away," cried Sulien to the guards. "Leave . . . him . . . alone."

"Out of the way, you absurd little brat," said Janck. Then, to the guards, "Take him downstairs."

Sulien reached out towards the burly guard, who was four times her weight. He swatted at her with the back of his free hand, lazily. She ducked then prodded him in the belly with the stiff fingers of her right hand and he was hurled backwards for ten feet, landing with a thump on his broad back. A shock passed through Llian to the second guard, who slipped to one knee, holding his belly and gasping as if all the air had been driven from him.

Karan gaped. Where had that come from?

"Guards?" cried Janck as Sulien advanced on him. "Here, now!"

"Sulien!" Karan said sharply.

Sulien stopped. "I *won't* let them hurt Daddy."

Tallia raced up. "No one is going to hurt Llian. We just need to talk to him about what he—"

"Not here!" hissed Janck. "Spies in the sky, you fool, spies *everywhere*." He scowled at his guards. "Get up, you incompetent fools! Take Llian to my war room and let no one speak to him on the way." He turned to Karan, and there was none of the amiability she had previously seen in his eyes. He looked hard, angry and more than a little afraid. "You can speak to him after you get back."

"What do you mean, *get back*?" said Llian. "Karan, where are you going?"

"Not here!" bellowed Janck. "Guards, clear everyone off the roof, *now*. Karan, get going."

Karan did not move. Nothing added up, but a dreadful suspicion was forming, and she felt her fury rising until it was almost uncontrollable.

"I'm not going anywhere until I get answers," she said coldly. "Llian, when Sulien said we got here the night before last, you said, *But I was . . .* What were you going to say?"

"Guards!" cried Janck. The two guards scrambled to their feet, wincing.

Tallia laid a hand on his right arm. "This is counterproductive, Commander. How can she do her job with this hanging over her?"

"All right!" hissed Janck. "But not here." He held up his hand to the guards and they stopped.

"I was *here* then," Llian said under his breath. "I'd been here almost a week. We left that night; we must have just missed you."

A week! Karan wanted to draw her knife and stab Janck, the scheming, lying bastard, through the heart. With an effort she restrained herself. "We didn't miss you," she said softly. "You left in the sky ship that was moored way over there, didn't you?" She pointed to the far right. "We saw it go! If I'd known you were on it—"

"Yes, we—"

"Not another word," snapped Janck. "Guards, take Karan and Sulien to their quarters and lock the door."

The guards took hold of Karan and Sulien.

"You absolute swine!" Karan ground out. "And you're just as bad," she said to Tallia and Malien. "You all knew Llian was alive, *and you didn't tell us?* Or tell him that we were alive?"

Tallia looked ashamed. Even Malien, who did not take kindly to being lectured by anyone, seemed uncomfortable.

"I ordered them to say nothing," said Janck. "The enemy is trying kill you and Sulien—your identities and locations must be kept secret."

"Though they're known to every bat, beetle and blowfly in Zile," Karan sneered.

"Guards, take them down."

As the guards came forward, Malien took a deep breath then stepped between them and Karan. "This farce has to end now, Janck," she said. "No one has done more to hinder the Merdrun than Karan, Sulien and Llian. I insist that they be included in our councils."

"Or what?" snapped Janck.

"Or I take my people and my sky ships—the three we have here, the six that have just reached Sith and the other fourteen on their way—and go home."

Janck shook with fury, and for a few seconds Karan thought he was going to defy Malien. Karan fought an urge to punch him in the eye. Then his stout figure sagged. "All right, but if it goes wrong it'll be on your head."

"If this goes wrong, none of us will *have* a head," Tallia said sombrely and led the way down.

"Mummy, stop it," whispered Sulien. "We've got Daddy back. That's all that matters."

Karan's fists were clenched so tightly that her knuckles hurt. Sulien was right—she must not allow this shabby deception to ruin a reunion that had, for the past few weeks, seemed beyond hope.

She took Llian's left hand and Sulien took his right, and they followed the others. But as they reached the stairs an uneasy feeling drew her eyes up to a white hawk wheeling high in the air. Had it been watching them?

In the war room Llian summarised his recent mission. Janck had sent them north to see how Demondifang had changed in the time since he, Ifoli and Regg had escaped so narrowly. Hublees had carried various uncanny instruments with which to study the summon stone, though Janck made it clear that only those who needed to know would hear his report.

"Demondifang is much worse now," said Llian. "The entire island is an unreality zone teeming with chimaeras—blendings of all manner of impossible creatures—often insane and all tearing at one another. The forest is tortured and tangled; it's a festering stain all the way down to the sea."

"What about the top of the peak?"

"We didn't lay eyes on the stone; we couldn't get within a mile of it. The storm is huge now; the winds are savage and lightning is striking in all directions." He probed his bruised face with his fingertips. "A gust hurled me from one end of the cabin to the other, and I was lucky not to break my neck. I don't see how we can mount—"

"Just tell us what you saw," said Janck.

"The corruption has spread across the gravel bar to Mollymoot."

"Already?" said Tallia.

"The island looks abandoned." Llian rubbed his stubbly jaw. "I hope Dilly and Regg are all right."

"Very well, you may go," said Janck. "I dare say you've got stuff to do before Karan leaves."

"Where are you going?" said Llian.

She told him about her planned spying mission to Gwine. His jaw tightened though he did not say anything; perhaps he felt he did not have the right.

"When?" he said after a long pause.

"I was getting ready to go when you arrived." The thought of going had been bad enough before. It was utterly unbearable now. She looked up at Janck, expecting him to order her to go at once.

"It can wait," said Janck. "I need to talk to Hublees before you go. Tell the guards to send him in. And don't talk about war business, *anywhere.*"

Karan got a basket of food from the kitchens, and they went back to the roof and found a corner, far from the stairs and the sky ships, where they would not be overheard. She looked over the wall for clinging bats, and up at the sky for birds, but saw none.

They put their backs to the wall and sat there with Sulien between them, soaking up the slanting afternoon sun, nibbling on dried figs and nuts and blurting out fragments of their stories. None of them had the energy for anything more.

Karan leaned against Llian's shoulder, closed her eyes, and a great lassitude crept over her. She tried to imagine that the rest of the world had vanished and all their troubles with it.

The mission to Gwine intruded but she forced it into the background. It intruded again. "Go away!" she said aloud.

"Something the matter?" said Llian tiredly.

"For the next twenty-four hours," she said drowsily, "*nothing* is going to be the matter."

They must have dozed off, for Karan was woken by Sulien crying out in fright: "What's that?"

Karan looked up at the sound, a hissing whine. "Just a sky ship coming in. One of Malien's."

It was late afternoon; the sun was gone and it was windy and rather chilly. Karan packed the remaining food into the basket and shook Llian awake. He stood up, yawning and rubbing his bloodshot eyes.

The sky ship landed in the middle of the roof, and Nadiril came slowly down the ladder, then a tall young man in librarians' robes. He reached up to another man, who slid out a heavy black chest. The young librarian and Nadiril caught it and lowered it to the ground.

"What's *she* doing here?" said Sulien.

"Who?" said Karan, for the only people visible at the sky ship were men.

The second man and the young librarian carried the chest towards the stairs. Nadiril looked around the roof, saw Karan, Llian and Sulien and came tottering towards them, calling the men with the chest to follow.

"Llian," he said in a wispy old voice. "Glad you're back. Got a job for you."

"Not today," said Llian.

The two men set the chest down with a small clicking sound. It was undecorated, made from the immensely hard and durable black metal titane, and Karan recognised it.

So, judging by the look in his eyes—half-astonished, half greedy—did Llian. "Rulke's Histories! Where did you get them?"

"My spy network is almost the equal of the late Wistan's," said Nadiril. "The translation key is inside. If Rulke knew the Merdrun's secret weakness it will be in there somewhere—and how to attack it. You'll start first thing in the morning."

"Yes," Llian said dazedly. "But how—"

"My assistants will take the chest to a secure, guarded workroom. You will work there, and the door will be enchanted to make sure none of the documents or your papers can be removed."

As Nadiril headed towards the stairs, a tall buxom woman leaped out of the sky ship. Her dark hair was long and curly, her face flushed. She stormed across.

"You!" she cried, slapping Llian across the face so hard the blow knocked him sideways. "I should have known you'd be behind it, stealing my precious papers."

"Leave Daddy alone!" cried Sulien, scrambling to her feet.

Karan studied Llian for signs that he felt any affection for Thandiwe. She felt bad about it, but this was also war.

"You stole them first," said Llian to Thandiwe, "and the translation key Rulke gave to me."

"Maigraith gave them to me."

"They weren't hers to give. Besides, you've had them for weeks. Surely you've got what you want from them now."

"I haven't had time to translate a tithe of them yet."

"If I discover anything meaningful I'll make sure to tell you," Llian said nastily, "so you can use it in your *Great Tale*." It was a calculated insult—no teller of integrity would use a secret imparted to them by another teller in their own tale.

Thandiwe raised a fist. Karan hastily stepped between them and pushed her back. "If you ever touch Llian again . . ."

Thandiwe looked down at her. "There's nothing *you* can do to stop me." Then, perhaps to reinforce her message, she thrust her heaving bosom in Llian's direction.

"Go to hell," Llian muttered.

"If I do," said Thandiwe, "I'll drag you down with me. I've got the goods on you, Llian."

"What are you talking about?"

"You'll find out, Llian the Liar." Thandiwe strode away, shoulders back and chest out.

Karan had a very bad feeling, but there was nothing she could do about it.

45

WHOSE BRILLIANT IDEA WAS THAT?

"Llian. *Llian!* Get up."

It was Yggur's voice. Llian groaned. It was pitch-dark and it felt as though he had only been asleep a few minutes. Sulien had stayed with Lilis last night so Karan and Llian could be alone, and they had stayed

up until three in the morning, talking and catching up on all they had
missed about each other.

"What's he doing here?" Karan said sleepily.

"No idea," said Llian.

Yggur conjured light from his fingertips. "Hurry up. We've got to
be gone before dawn."

Karan shot upright. She had always been quicker to rouse than he
was.

"Llian's not moving until you tell us what's going on," said Karan.

Yggur pointed his left hand at the window, and it went black, then
at the door, which set solid. "A vital . . . *substance* has been stolen from
Aviel's locked workshop, and we believe Shand took it. He may have
betrayed us to the enemy already. On the other hand, he may not have
had the chance yet, and if he hasn't—"

"What's that got to do with me?"

"We're flying to Demondifang."

"Llian's just come back from there."

"That was a reconnaissance. This is to attack the stone, and we've got
to leave in darkness so the enemy's spies won't know where we're going."

"Nadiril's just asked him to—" said Karan.

Yggur talked over her. "Llian's the only one with first-hand knowledge
of Demondifang and the summon stone."

"What about Ifoli?" said Llian.

"She's . . . disappeared."

So many secrets, thought Llian. *And so many intrigues.* He rose and
dressed.

"Be on the roof in ten minutes." Yggur unblocked the window and
door, and withdrew.

Karan started to get up. "Stay in bed," said Llian, pulling the covers
up. "I'd sooner think of you here in the warm."

"I'm afraid." The bed was cold now, all the joy of the previous night
gone. "Don't do anything rash."

"You know me."

"Yes," she said softly, "I do."

He hugged her and went out. The roof was dark, for it was a cloudy night, and the sky ship was just a slightly darker shadow as he made his way towards it. It had been loaded in silence, and the moment he went up the ladder it was hauled in and Yggur, at the controls, lifted off.

The cabin was also in darkness though Llian made out the shapes of another eight people at the rear. "No talking until we're well away," said Yggur.

Llian groped his way to an empty seat, settled his head against the side of the cabin and, since it was an eight-hour flight to Demondifang and Yggur wasn't going to tell him anything, tried to sleep. It proved impossible: he was too afraid of going back. This attack was a stupid idea and could not hope to succeed.

A loud exclamation roused him from his fears, then a thump on the side of the head. It was the middle of the day. The sky ship was bouncing around in a stormy sky and he had slammed against the wall of the cabin hard enough to hurt.

The round little mancer Llian knew as Hublees sat to his left, and six soldiers, clad in hardened leather armour, occupied the seats at the back. They were weathered outdoorsmen, many of them missing fingers, teeth or ears.

Their captain, whose name was Blappey, lacked both teeth and ears. His left arm, which had been amputated at the wrist, ended in a spring-loaded spike a foot long. He kept pulling it back to cock the spring and discharging it with a thud into the back of the empty seat in front of him, then baring his black, eroded gums at anyone foolish enough to meet his eye. The spike went right through the wooden seat and would have killed anyone sitting there, and Llian wondered if Blappey was sane. Was that why he had been chosen? Because no one in their right mind would have gone near an unreality zone?

The soldiers were gaping out the front window. The slopes of Demondifang were a couple of miles ahead, and the once-pristine forest was now a tangled riot of yellow, green and brown. But that was not what drew Llian's attention, nor the mountain, the top of which was obscured by low cloud. The storm was massively larger and taller than before, a vast slowly revolving purple monstrosity riven by constant flashes of blue-green lightning, most of them striking the top of the peak.

"That's where the stone was," he said, pointing to the eastern end. "It seemed as though the lightning was transferring power to the stone."

"The strikes are every few seconds," said Yggur. "If that is happening, and I've never heard of such a thing, it's a staggering amount of power."

"I didn't know objects could be empowered that way," said Mancer Hublees, tugging at his stupid little goatee.

"Where's the other sky ship?" said Yggur, turning the craft.

"What other sky ship?" said Llian.

Yggur smiled thinly. "Janck felt our chances would be better if he sent two. Ah, there it is." The second ship, painted cloudy blue in a feeble attempt at camouflage, was half a mile back.

"I thought there was only one drop of nivol?"

"There is."

"Do we have it or do they?"

After some hesitation Yggur said, "They do."

"Then why are we here?" said Llian.

"To make a diversion while they attack."

"How? No sky ship could get within a mile of the mountaintop—the storm would tear it apart."

"The other craft is going to land a squad on the south flank of the mountain, as high as possible, and they're going to race up to the summon stone and hurl the nivol at it."

"Whose brilliant idea was that?" said Llian.

Yggur said, in a voice only Llian could hear, "Not mine."

"How many of them?"

"Twelve of the toughest and most experienced fighters Janck has."

"To have a hope of getting anyone through an unreality zone you'd need hundreds, and most of them would die."

"Keep your voice down. Morale!"

Llian tried again. "This is the dumbest plan of all time. There isn't the faintest hope of it succeeding."

"That's what I told Janck. But he was desperate to do something."

"We're making a diversion on the north-west side," said the captain, discharging his spike again. He favoured Llian with a gummy black grin.

A green light flashed from the other ship, twice in quick succession then three times, slowly. "They're going in," said Yggur. "And so are we."

His sky ship rounded Demondifang to the north-west and headed towards an egg-shaped clearing halfway up the slope of the mountain. "We'll drop you in the centre," Yggur said to the captain, "then climb and keep watch. You know the signals, Captain?"

Blappey grunted.

"If there's trouble, head for that rock and I'll try to pick you up." Yggur indicated a shelf-like rock platform extending five or six yards out from the side of a nearby ridge.

Blappey nodded. His troops had their packs on and their weapons to hand.

"Otherwise," said Yggur, his outstretched finger tracing a line up through the forest, "that looks like the best route up." He turned to Llian. "That's the way you went up, isn't it?"

"More that way," said Llian, pointing out the path he, Ifoli and Regg had taken on the western side. "Though I don't think—"

Yggur's sky ship swooped over the tops of the trees then dived for the clearing. The troops were moving towards the cabin door when he pulled up sharply, tossing them off their feet.

"Something moved! Llian, see what it is."

Llian opened the cabin door, took a tight grip on the rail inside and leaned out as they circled the clearing. "It's an unreality zone, no question."

There were huge, distorted toadstools, mushrooms and bracket fungi everywhere, and writhing and coiling ferns, their wiry fronds questing out in all directions as if seeking victims to strangle. The trees had lurid red and orange bark covered in jagged blades and spikes, and oozed yellow and green sap that foamed and bubbled and consumed whatever it touched.

Llian scanned a cluster of boulders, searching for whatever had moved, and saw, protruding from the rock, a woman's face twisted in silent agony. A gaunt face with black streaming eyes framed by lank hair. Her body could not be seen.

"Yggur, that's a Whelm! *Embedded* in the rock."

Another Whelm, a stocky fellow, lay half buried in the short grass. He was alive too, though grass grew out of his nostrils, mouth and ears, and even over the sound of the rotors Llian could hear him gagging and choking.

The lower bodies of two more Whelm were embedded in living trees, only their heads and torsos sticking out. The first, a small skinny woman, was dead and had been partly eaten by something, but the second, an older man, was still alive. Blood oozed down the trunk from his desperate attempts to escape.

The sky ship tilted. The soldiers had gathered behind Llian and were staring out at the trapped Whelm.

"Sit down!" Yggur snapped. "You're unbalancing the ship."

They hauled themselves back to their seats and the craft steadied. Yggur did a full circuit of the clearing, and another, then climbed back above the trees.

"Well?" he said to Llian.

"I saw twelve Whelm," he said hoarsely. "Though I dare say there's more. All trapped in quickrock or quickearth or quickwood, and most still alive."

Yggur, who must have seen any number of uncanny things in his long life, looked uncomfortable. Blappey was breathing in tearing gasps, and one of his men had thrown up on the floor.

"What are they doing here?" said Llian.

"Perhaps they thought they could aid their new master." Yggur did another circle and looked back at Blappey, whose weathered face had gone a sickly grey-green. "Well?"

"Not goin' down there," he gasped. "Happy to take on any number of ordinary fighters, but not goin' down there."

"No, it's far too dangerous," said Yggur.

Llian was delighted to hear it. "We'd better let the other ship know."

Yggur headed along the shoreline, keeping well away from the forest. As they reached the southern side, keeping seaward of the glowing mangroves, Llian saw the blue sky ship edging along the base of the yellow cliffs at the top of the mountain.

"What's he doing up there? There's nowhere to land."

"He's flying too low," said Yggur, and headed up to pass above the other craft.

The blue sky ship was approaching a steep-sided ridge where the forest thinned; here and there the rocky ground was exposed. A big-bodied, shaggy creature bounded up the ridge, stood on its back legs and hurled a crudely made spear at the sky ship. The pilot turned away but not in time; the spear passed between the whirling blades of the right-hand rotor, shattering them, and the blue sky ship veered right, towards the cliff.

"Cut the power!" said Yggur to himself. "Left rudder, then reverse the rotor."

The pilot was not experienced enough to know what to do. The blue sky ship continued its stately path towards the cliff and struck it full on. Llian expected an explosion to incinerate everything, but the airbag only deflated. The cabin plunged between the treetops, somehow missing every branch, hit the ground and skidded down the steep slope until the skids struck a log, which tore them off, and finally settled with a thump onto the ground.

"That was well done," said Yggur. "Or incredibly lucky. They might not be badly hurt." He headed towards the crash site. "Llian, stick your head out the door. Tell them to run down to the bare ground next to the salt marsh; we might be able to pick them up from there. It's only a mile."

A mile too far, in Llian's opinion.

Yggur drifted across the ridge, keeping out of spear range, and as they passed over the sky ship Llian leaned out. On the ground the hatch of the cabin had been forced out and a soldier stood framed in the doorway, checking all around.

"Hoy!" Llian yelled. "Run down the ridge to the scalded land next to the salt marsh."

The soldier raised a hand in acknowledgement, loosened his sword in its scabbard and went down the ladder. As he reached the bottom

the shaggy creature, or another like it, swung out from a branch overhanging the sky ship.

"It's a chimaera," said Yggur. "A blend of two different creatures."

Short thick legs carried a heavy bear-like body, though the fur was
very long, reddish and tangled, and the head did not match at all; it was
long, scaly and reptilian, not unlike the head of a chacalot, a ferocious
water-dwelling predator that Llian had only encountered in the tropics.

"Look out!" he bellowed.

As the soldier looked up, the chimaera sprang, and before he could
draw his sword it landed on him, crushing him to the ground. Its two-
foot-long jaws closed around his neck and he went limp. More chimaera
appeared from the trees, some racing towards the kill, others going
for the open hatch. Someone inside tried to pull it shut, but a small
chimaera, whose fur was redder than the others, sprang and caught the
door and, using its weight, pulled it open.

It leaped up through the hatch and inside, and two others followed
it. There was a furious roaring and a chilling series of screams, soon cut
short. The windows went red and blood ran from the hatch.

Yggur circled again. No one emerged from the cabin, though
shortly one of the chimaeras jumped down, its fur red. Another chimaera hurled a spear up at the sky ship. It struck one of the skids
and fell back.

"Too close," said Yggur. "We'd better go."

The small chimaera, a female, swung out of the cabin and clambered
onto the roof, holding up something small that shone in the light.

"What's that?" Llian grabbed a pair of field glasses and focused them
on the object in her hand. "Yggur, she's got the small diamond phial.
Can we get it back?"

"Don't see how," said Yggur.

The chimaera tapped the phial on the roof of the cabin, then tested
it with her teeth. She turned it over in her paw-like hands as if curious about the way the light reflected from it, then drew the diamond
stopper with her chacalot teeth. She sniffed the phial, frowned, then
emptied the drop of nivol onto her tongue.

She let out a ghastly shriek. Smoke gushed from her mouth then brown foam bubbled out, and slimy muck. The diamond phial fell from her hand and disappeared. Her lips vanished, then her teeth, and her long snout crumpled like a deflating balloon. Her head caved in, and the remains toppled off the roof and landed with a soggy thud. The dissolution continued along the chimaera's body.

"One single drop of nivol and it's eating her away," Llian said in horrified awe.

"Good riddance!" Blappey fired his spike through the seat again. "Disgusting beasts."

The other chimaera backed away, then bolted.

"That's that then," said Yggur. "We're going home."

It was a crushing failure and Llian was not looking forward to explaining it to Janck. But why, after all it had taken to create that drop of nivol, had he wasted it on such an ill-advised attack? Was Janck reckless, incompetent, or just desperate for any kind of victory? Gloom settled over Llian at the thought. They didn't have a hope.

"We can't give up," said Tallia at the emergency council called within minutes of their arrival in Zile next morning. "We've got to try again. If they reopen the gate and bring the rest of the Merdrun through, we face oblivion."

"Can we *sleep* the summon stone, as Mendark did ten years ago?"

"We don't know how he put it to sleep . . . and he used the vast power released by his own death to do so. Any volunteers?"

No one spoke. They were meeting in Nadiril's private sanctuary, the Rare Books section of the library, which few people knew existed and even fewer had ever been allowed to enter. It was a beautiful chamber full of scrolls and codexes and records on wax tablets, baked clay, tree bark and every other material that had been used in the eight thousand years since writing had been invented on Santhenar. Every book there was priceless, including—Llian was pleased to see—the manuscripts of the twenty-two Great Tales. Lilis had rescued them after Snoat's death and brought them here for safekeeping, along with the charred remains of the twenty-third. He now regretted the mad impulse to burn his manuscript of the *Tale of the Mirror.*

Janck was not there; he had flown north to Framan, the port city at the mouth of the River Zur. In his absence Tallia had relaxed the edict on secrecy and called everyone to the council, even Sulien.

"How long to make some more nivol, Aviel?" said Malien.

"Without any Archeus?"

"Yes."

"A year."

"What?" cried Tallia.

"All the other methods are really complicated and some of the steps take months each."

"Is there any way the time can be shortened?"

"Maybe, by a master alchemist. I wouldn't know where to begin."

"We had a master alchemist, and now he's dead," said Tallia coldly.

"Then you should have ordered him to make the stuff," said Yggur. "Since you chose to use Aviel, and she got it right the first time, better listen to her."

"A year—or even a month—is out of the question. We keep getting hints—" Tallia broke off.

"There's such a thing as too much secrecy," said Yggur.

"—from various endeavours of ours, which I won't detail," said Tallia, "we feel sure the Merdrun will soon be able to escape from Gwine. We've got to act fast. Aviel, how much nivol could you make at a time if you had enough Archeus?"

"Eight to ten drops," said Aviel.

"How long would it take?"

"Five days, since I have all the other ingredients."

"Then get started."

"I don't have any Archeus."

"Shand does," said Malien, "and I don't think he's far away. Yggur, you've known him longest. Hunt him down and get the Archeus."

"By *hunt him down*, you mean . . . ?"

"I'd prefer the traitor was taken alive, so he can be interrogated, but if there's no other way but fatal force to get the Archeus back, do it."

Yggur sat in silence for a minute or two, then said, "Very well."

"Given our failure with the summon stone," Tallia went on, "and our utter inability to do anything about it in the next week, it's all the more urgent that we find out what stage the Merdrun are up to. Karan, you've got to go to Gwine at once."

46

I'VE GOT TO HELP HIM

"You will look for Wilm, won't you?" said Aviel, clutching Karan's hands. Colour tinged her cheeks; she pulled away as if regretting the impulse and looked down at the bench. "He's the only friend I've got, and . . ."

"I'll try," said Karan, who had come to the workshop to hear, first-hand, everything Aviel could remember about Gwine. Karan felt sick; spying on the Merdrun again was reckless and surely doomed to failure.

Aviel's eyes were wet. She turned away to a wooden rack of cork-stoppered tubes, taking them out one by one, holding each up to the light and putting it back. She drew the bung from a tube half full of a thick pale orange oil, and a powerful fragrance made Karan's nostrils tingle; it was like a mixture of cloves and mandarin, though sharp, almost biting. Aviel stoppered the tube, put it back, glanced sideways at Karan then away. She started to say something, but stopped, again flushing a delicate pink.

"Is there a message you'd like me to give to Wilm, if I find him?" said Karan.

Aviel looked pathetically grateful. "He saved me in Carcharon, and on Gwine he sacrificed himself to protect me. That's the kind of man he is . . . and they'll make him pay. You know how cruel they are. Do you think there's any hope?"

"There's always hope," Karan lied.

The words were meaningless, but Aviel seemed to draw comfort from them. "I've got to help him, Karan."

She crossed the workshop to an end bench and drew another rack towards her, a small one containing about thirty little glass phials. Using a series of eyedroppers she drew up small quantities of selected oils, sniffed each one, then blended them in another phial. She stoppered it, shook it twenty times to the right, four times in an up and down motion and eleven times to the left, then removed the stopper and sniffed it again. She frowned, added another drop of a tea-coloured oil and repeated the shaking procedure. This time she was satisfied. She wired on the stopper, wrote WILM on a label and stuck it to the phial.

"Will you give this to him?" she said tentatively, as if afraid Karan would refuse.

Karan took the phial and tucked it away. "Of course. What's it for?"

"It's a scent potion to strengthen his belief in himself. I'm sure they've tortured him and tried to break him. Wilm is brave and strong and true-hearted, but sometimes he lacks confidence. He's . . . had a hard life."

Aviel had too, though one thing she did not lack was confidence.

"To get to Gwine," said Karan, "I'll need the best picture you can give me of the place. I was going to use a mental image from the time when I fought the triplets, but it's too dangerous."

Aviel described it: the brilliantly green grass, the exotic flowers, the forest of gigantic trees whose trunks flared out into buttresses many yards through. The brown river winding across a fertile plain and the town on its further bank, its streets a series of sinuous curves. The smaller town below the hill where the gate had opened, its streets barricaded, its buildings burning, its dark-skinned valiant people doomed.

Karan tried to create the scene in her inner eye but it wasn't clear enough to take her there in spirit form; it was just a description. "What else do you remember?"

"We weren't there long when Gergrig saw us. I mainly remember the attack on the town."

"That won't help," Karan said hastily. The last thing she wanted was an image that might take her to him.

"Well," said Aviel, tapping her fingertips on the bench, "I remember the smell perfectly."

And smells could create very clear pictures. A particular smell could take Karan back to her childhood, to the best times of her life—and to the worst. But could a smell Aviel remembered take Karan to the place? "What did it smell like? Can you describe it?"

"I can *make* it."

Aviel drew her rack of scented oils towards her and chose three phials, which she lined up on the bench. She sniffed them, then went down to the other end of the workshop, opened a cupboard and took out a much longer rack which must have contained a hundred phials.

"My reference collection," she said. "I keep it in the dark; the scents last longer."

She selected another five phials, sniffing each one carefully then putting two back and taking others. Karan caught hints of woodsmoke, grass, flowers and freshly ploughed earth, and a thick, humid, organic odour, not unpleasant, that she associated with visits to the tropical north many years ago. Finally Aviel seemed satisfied. She added the seven phials before her to the three lined up on the other bench and began to blend them.

"Is this another scent potion?" said Karan warily. "I'm not sure any form of mancery would be a good idea . . ."

Aviel's laughter was like the tinkling of little bells. "It's just a simple perfume."

"I heard you once made a scent potion by accident. Are you sure?"

Aviel was still smiling. "I was only thirteen and had no idea what I was doing. I made a laxative scent potion; Shand had the runs for a week." The smile faded. "How could he betray us so, Karan?"

She had often wondered the same thing. She had travelled across the Dry Sea with Shand and would have said he was one of the most reliable people in the world. How could the enemy have corrupted him so quickly?

Aviel completed the blending, capped the phial and shook it, and handed it to Karan. "A little sniff should be enough, but take it with you just in case."

Karan took the cap off and walked away, mentally rehearsing the next step. Sniff the perfume, visualise the destination and trigger the dematerialisation spell the way Malien had taught her. She raised the phial to her nose and sniffed but caught only faint odours of smoke and grass.

"It's thick," said Aviel. "Allow it to warm in your hand, then sniff."

Karan closed her fingers around the phial, held it tightly for a minute and took a deep sniff. She saw the image—her sensitive's gift must have picked it up from Aviel—of a grassy hilltop, but the moment she thought about the triggering spell—

Bang!

Pain flared as her spirit was wrenched from her body. Karan felt her empty body crumpling to the floor of the workshop and saw the shock on Aviel's face, then her spirit was hurled two thousand miles north-north-west to a grassy hilltop with a forest in the background and a river floodplain ahead and below her.

It was a hot, sunny afternoon, around four, with storm clouds building out to sea. But the Isle of Gwine was no longer the pretty, peaceful backwater Aviel had seen weeks ago. The town that had stood a quarter of a mile away had been razed; even the building stones were gone. Karan drifted up a few feet, the better to see.

Great swathes of the forest had been felled and other parts burned. What she could see of the once-beautiful island had been ravaged even more thoroughly than the towns the Merdrun had taken on Cinnabar. Why did they hate everyone so desperately? Did they resent other peoples having a world and an existence they, who had been exiled in the barren and pitiless void for tens of thousands of years, could only yearn for?

Not far from the town she saw an ugly scar on the landscape, a large rectangular enclosure surrounded by a crude palisade made from pointed split logs driven vertically into the ground, with a double wall at the gate.

Lines of laden wagons were heading east, carrying stone taken from the homes and public buildings of the old town, but where were they going? She drifted that way and saw another, far bigger scar on the land several miles away.

A curving ridge dominated by three cliff-bounded hills each half

a mile apart fell steeply away to the north, forming a natural fortress
on the northern and eastern sides of a small valley. The Merdrun,
presumably using thousands of slaves, had built low walls along the
ridge top linking the three hills, and timber watchtowers on top. They
were now enclosing the western and southern sides of the valley with a
much higher wall to form an encampment a mile from north to south
and rather more than a mile east to west. It dropped several hundred
feet from south-west to north-east, and a stream running in the same
direction had been dammed not far inside the gate.

Karan dared not go too close; the triplets were bound to have traps.
From half a mile away and a few hundred feet up she studied the layout
of the fortifications, the height and thickness of the walls and the
strengths and weaknesses of the place, creating mental pictures so she
could report back as accurately as possible. If Janck planned to attack,
thousands of lives would depend on the quality of her information.

Now to estimate the enemy numbers. The only buildings were on
the western side, north of the camp gates, and they were crude wooden
structures built from split logs—cookhouses, storerooms and the like.
The Merdrun were used to living in tents as they moved from one siege
to the next and would not waste time building permanent structures.

The soldiers' tents were erected in lines on the low south-eastern
side of the encampment. She counted twenty-five rows of forty tents,
a thousand in all, so if each tent slept ten men they could have ten
thousand troops, plus more elsewhere on the island, guarding the slave
camp and controlling farms, roads and bridges. Their total numbers
could be twelve thousand. Twelve thousand of the greatest warriors in
the void, capable of beating an army at least four times that number.
Karan had seen them do it on Cinnabar.

She was drifting higher, to make sure that there were no other
camps or fortifications on the island, when she sensed a faint, distant
alertness. She plunged to ground level at once. Could the triplets have
detected her from so far away? She had to assume so and she could not
risk staying much longer.

She floated down to the palisade wall, which turned out to be the
slave camp, a foul, inhuman place. The thousands of slaves had worn

the earth bare and it was now a sea of mud. The buildings were mere shanties, mostly wall-less, made from logs and roofed with palm fronds.

Presumably the slaves slept in the mud, and even in this warm climate that would be a miserable existence. The Merdrun probably planned to kill them before they left and would not give a damn about their health or comfort as long as there were enough of them to complete the fortress and harvest their food.

The sun was plunging rapidly towards the horizon. Darkness would come quickly here, and enemies must be securely locked in beforehand. Yes, in the distance she saw a column of slaves marching along a muddy track, roped together.

Karan headed towards them, keeping high enough to see the whole column, though not so high that she risked being detected. The triplets must not discover where she was going, or that she hoped to make contact with a certain slave. If they did, he would not last a minute.

Wilm's tall figure would stand out among the smaller, darker Gwinians, but she did not find him in the first column of slaves, or the second. He could well be dead. Suddenly her sensitive's gift picked up a series of tingling alerts that made her phantom pulse race. The triplets were looking for her. It was time to go.

Then she saw him, stumbling along near the back of the third column. His back was bent and his face downcast. Had they broken his spirit? She went lower, closer. There were Merdrun guards at the front and back of the column, and midway along either side, though they were just ordinary soldiers.

Nonetheless she kept well back, and only after the slave columns had been marched into the camp, the great gates were swung shut and barred, and the guards took up their positions outside, did she float over the wall and search the camp for Wilm.

The exhausted slaves were untied and fed slops and bread from open troughs as if they were animals. Perhaps the Merdrun thought of them as animals. Afterwards, many simply flopped down where they were and slept. Others wandered about, talking or playing games or, in many cases, staring listlessly into space.

Wilm had shuffled away into a gap between the back of one of the few walled shanties and the palisade wall. It was gloomy there, though not yet completely dark. Wondering what he was up to, she floated over the roof of the shanty and hovered, watching him.

He was as filthy as all the other slaves but his back wasn't bent now. Standing straight and proud, he checked behind him then removed a carved length of wood concealed between two poles of the palisade and, holding it out like a sword, practised fighting strokes. His thin face bore the evidence of many beatings, and he must have been worn out after a day of labour, but he went through his strokes one after another, over and over.

After Dajaes was killed by Unick, Wilm had taught himself to use a sword from Llian's pamphlet, practising every waking hour afterwards. Karan had seen Wilm in action at Carcharon and he had been astoundingly skilled—despite his impoverished background, or perhaps because of it, he was a remarkable young man. He had worn down and killed Snoat's most experienced assassin, Jundelix Rasper.

She drifted down. Dare she risk materialising? She had to; there was no other way she could talk to him. She landed in front of Wilm and triggered Malien's materialisation spell.

Her knees gave way. She had been so focused on getting here that she had forgotten how draining the materialisation spell was, and how weak she would be after several hours' separation from her body. She fell towards him, right into the path of a savage, slashing blow.

47

NO ONE IS SAFE FROM THEM

Wilm halted the blow inches from her face, gaping at her, then lowered the weapon. "You're . . . Karan!"

"Don't have much time." She could not get up; the mere act of breathing was exhausting her. She fumbled in a pocket and brought out the phial of perfume. "Aviel sent this. Said it'll help you."

His long face lit from within. "She's alive? She's *well*?"

"Yes. She's in—" She must not reveal anything that could be tortured from him. "Aviel's with us, doing good work."

He sniffed the scent. Tears ran down his dirty face and for a few seconds he was overcome, then he stoppered the phial, put it away and wiped his eyes.

"Have you come to get me out?" Wilm studied her, on her knees and gasping. "No, you can't. What's happening?"

"Can't tell you anything; I daren't stay long. But if there's anything you can tell me—anything at all."

Wilm lifted Karan to her feet and drew her back where the shadows were deepest. "The Merdrun are a cruel people; I've seen them cut down slaves just for looking at them. They rule by terror. It's all they know."

"How many are there?"

"I don't know. Many thousands, certainly, though . . ."

"What?" said Karan. "Even the smallest bit of information can help us."

"I don't think their numbers are as big as they want us to think."

"Why do you say that?"

"It's just a feeling, from watching them."

It wasn't much help; all armies want to appear stronger than they actually are.

"Their fortifications look strong. Do you know of any weak points?"

"No," said Wilm. "Everything is supervised by their engineers and artificers, and warfare is their life. They know everything about it."

Karan's hyper-alert senses picked up another tingle, a warning that the triplets were on the hunt. "Got to go. The enemy knows I'm on Gwine."

"You know they have a new magiz? Triplets?" Wilm shuddered.

"Yes."

"They come here sometimes, to drink lives and strengthen themselves. It's horrible. They're mad, and no one is safe from them. I could be next." He checked both ends of the alley again.

Karan felt a urgent tingle. "Got to go. *Dematerialise!*"

She was falling, falling . . . *thump*. She landed beside a rack of upside-down flasks, sending them flying off the bench and smashing on the floor.

Aviel let out a shriek. Karan could not raise her head. "Call . . . Tallia."

Aviel went out. After lying still for ten minutes, Karan had regained enough strength to clamber down off the bench, though not to stand up. She perched on a stool, supporting herself against the wall, alternately freezing and sweating. If the triplets found out she had spoken to Wilm they would drink his life in a heartbeat.

She felt an odd tickling sensation in her head, as if they were searching for her. Could they track her this far away? Not that they needed to—the bats they controlled had already told them that she and Sulien were here.

Aviel came back with Janck, who listened in silence to her report, then snapped, "Is that all?"

"I'm sorry?" said Karan.

"That doesn't tell us anything. You'll have to go back."

"It was too risky to go anywhere near the Merdrun camp. The magiz had detected me."

"I need hard facts," said Janck wildly. He stalked back and forth. "What are their true numbers? Are they all based in the one place? What do they know about our plans? What are their weaknesses? Is there a way to attack them in their camp? How many slaves are there and can we use them? Can we cut off their supplies, block their escape routes or poison their water supply? That's the kind of information a *competent* spy would have brought back."

She had never seen him like this. Had something happened while she was away? Or was it the loss of their nivol in that disastrous attack on the stone? "There could be as many as ten thousand in the camp, and more elsewhere, though Wilm had a feeling they were fewer."

"A *feeling!*" sneered Janck.

"As far as I could tell that was their only fortress." Karan felt another of those twinges that she interpreted to be the triplets searching for her.

Mummy, Mummy? sent Sulien.

BOOM!

The workshop shook, then there came a great crashing and rumbling that shook the whole library. Janck drew his sabre, ran for the door and wrenched it open.

"What was that?" he cried to the guards outside.

Karan, who had staggered after him, did not hear their reply, which was drowned by a second *BOOM!* Then three more, each shaking the Great Library to its foundations.

Then, horrifyingly in her inner ear, a high, nerve-jangling giggle that she recognised as Empuly. "It's the triplets!" yelled Karan. "They're attacking."

"That was up near the roof," said one of the guards. "South side, I'd say."

Karan choked. "Our room's up there." *Sulien?*

No answer. She forced herself to overcome her exhaustion and took off along the corridor, then up the stairs at the end, up and up. Janck overtook her halfway and disappeared into a cloud of dust belching down the stairwell.

She heard him coughing as he climbed. Karan was struggling now; she scrambled up the last flight of steps on her hands and knees. At the top everything was so dark and dusty that she did not know which way to turn, though she sensed that the destruction had been to the right. Holding her sleeve over her nose, she stumbled along a hall littered with chunks of rubble, then stopped abruptly.

Ahead the dust was thinning, a chilly wind blowing it into her face. There was no sign of Janck; he must have gone the other way. She looked down and choked; a few feet ahead the hall floor was gone and so were the walls and ceiling and the rooms to the right, plus part of the floor below. The attack had blasted a great hole in the southern side of the Great Library.

She was looking across a fifty-foot gap to the corner of the building. The three or four rooms that had once occupied the space on this level were gone, including the room she shared with Sulien and Llian. If either of them had been inside they could not have survived.

"Sulien?" she panted. "Llian?"

Malien and Nadiril appeared, the latter's cheeks covered in grey dust. "How dare they!" he wheezed. His eyes moved across the gap, and his lips moved as if he were counting the rooms. He noticed Karan. "Was anyone . . . ?"

"I just got back from Gwine. The triplets detected me; I think this attack is intended as a lesson to us. I sensed Empuly laughing."

"And all for nothing," Janck said bitterly, appearing out of the dust behind them. "Karan didn't learn anything."

"But Gergrig has learned a lot to his discomfort," said Nadiril. "He knows we know they're stuck on Gwine, and we can spy on them at will. The Merdrun are used to controlling and dominating; it must be galling to be so helpless."

"But Llian, Sulien . . ." Karan said helplessly.

"They're safe; they're outside with Lilis."

The relief was so overwhelming that she staggered and nearly went over the edge. "What about the other people?" She swept an arm out to indicate the missing rooms.

"All empty so no one could spy on you." Nadiril sighed. "Most of our guest rooms are empty these days. Fewer scholars make the long journey to Zile every year, and every year our funds decline. I fear for the place after I'm gone. Who could possibly take on such a thankless calling?" No one replied, and he went on. "There's another possibility—that Gergrig did not order the attack at all."

"Who else would dare?" said Janck.

"If the triplets did it for the joy of destruction, I doubt Gergrig would be best pleased."

"Why not?" said Karan. "He wants us dead."

"Such an attack from so great a distance must have come at a huge cost in power. Power that's been utterly wasted, and they don't have any to waste—they need an enormous amount to reopen the Crimson Gate and escape."

"But the summon stone seems to be drawing prodigious amounts of power from the storm above Demondifang. It must be far more powerful than the original summon stone by now."

"It'll need to be," said Malien. "Reopening the Crimson Gate on Cinnabar from as far away as Gwine, then drawing it to Gwine so they can escape, will be no easy thing. It will be many times harder than opening it from Cinnabar the first time."

"Why can't the Merdrun on Cinnabar reopen it?" said Janck.

"Karan killed their magiz."

"Then maybe the Merdrun on Gwine aren't as strong as fear made them out to be," said Nadiril.

"If they're only half as strong as we fear," Janck said grimly, "it's all over."

48

THE KILL-SPELL WILL GET YOU TOO

Using her empathic gift, Sulien discovered that Shand was hiding in Zile, and tracked him and Ifoli to a small pyramid-roofed cupola at the top of what had once been the governor's palace. Most of it lay in ruins but the cupola and the section of roof under it had been built so solidly that it had endured the aeons.

Its green copper roof was held up on four columns of pink- and black-flecked granite. It was empty inside save for two stone benches, cleaned of their dust, and mounds of bird droppings. A lead crystal bottle sat on the further bench, light reflecting off its myriad facets as if it were a cut diamond. Beside it stood a small redwood rack containing phials, eyedroppers, a tall measuring cylinder and sundry other pieces of equipment Shand must have pilfered from Aviel's workshop.

Shand and Ifoli went to the bench. What were they up to? Sulien knew Ifoli had worked for the evil Cumulus Snoat for years—were they both traitors? Sulien slipped into the shadow cast by a pile of rubble next to the cupola, uncertain now. She had to have a teacher, but how could Shand be trusted after all the bad things he had done?

"Are you sure this is safe?" said Ifoli, holding a phial between finger and thumb and eyeing it uneasily.

"It's very unsafe," said Shand. "The Afflatus Effluvium is one of the Great Potions, and one of the forbidden ones."

A forbidden potion, thought Sulien with a shudder. *What for?* She wanted to run but dared not move. If they *were* traitors they might kill her or betray her to the enemy.

Ifoli held it further away. "Why forbidden?" she said hoarsely.

"No one knows—that list was made fifteen hundred years ago. Possibly because it's so dangerous to obtain certain ingredients." His gaze slid to the crystal bottle of Archeus and he grimaced. "Or because it's so deadly to make."

"But you made it successfully."

"I'd already seen how to make it *unsuccessfully*," said Shand. "My late master, Radizer, blew himself to bits trying to make this very scent potion a couple of hundred years ago. I've been thinking about what he did wrong ever since, on and off. However I believe it's safe to use, in small doses."

"How can you possibly know?" said Ifoli.

"Because I've already used it twice."

"Searching for the magiz's link?"

"I can't do that on myself—you'll have to. But the scent potion can also enhance creativity in the Secret Art."

"What for?"

"Making our new Command device better and stronger."

Shand picked the device up and turned it in his hands. The inner ends of six narrow copper tubes had been embedded in a hexagonal block of shiny black graphite, one to each side, to form a flat star. There was an opal-lined cavity on the underside of the block and a compartment with a silver lid on top. Sulien wondered what it was for.

"Tell me," said Ifoli thoughtfully. "Why did you steal the Archeus?"

Shand looked towards the lead crystal bottle, uneasily. "How could I do it to her?"

"What are you talking about?"

"Long ago the woman I loved—Yalkara, the great Charon who bore me a daughter then rejected me—murdered a crippled girl to cover up a crime. That's why I took pity on one of the myriad of unfortunates in this land and took Aviel in. I thought I was compensating in a tiny way for Yalkara's wickedness, but three years later, corrupted by the magiz's link, I recklessly risked Aviel's life to get that bottle of Archeus. Not to aid her noble project, but for my own shabby needs. I, who had always thought myself above base motives, stood revealed as low as any."

"You needed the Archeus to make your scent potion," said Ifoli, "but why steal the whole bottle after the potion was done?"

"In case I needed to increase the strength of my potion—to see deeper."

"Wouldn't that be dangerous?"

"Exceedingly."

"How much stronger did you need the scent potion to be?"

"Triple strength required another six drams of Archeus."

"And Aviel can't make more nivol without it," said Ifoli. "Today, after this, you will give it back."

"But I might need—"

Ifoli leaped to her feet, shaking with fury. "You stupid old fool!" she raged. "You're not atoning for your folly—you're compounding your crime. Give it back or you'll get no aid from me."

Shand retreated, swallowing hard. "All right, tonight."

"Lie down."

"What?"

Ifoli yanked the stopper out of the scent potion. "I'm looking for the magiz's link, right now."

Was she planning to remove it by herself? Sulien had a very bad feeling about that but dared not show herself.

"I'm not ready," said Shand.

"Too bad," snarled Ifoli.

She wafted the scent potion towards her nose, and her eyes wobbled in their sockets. She took a deeper sniff then sprang at him. Shand, off balance, lurched back. Ifoli shoved him down onto the empty bench, snatched up the Command device and jammed the leading copper tube so hard against his forehead that it broke the skin.

Via the empathic gift, Sulien felt an awful pain spike through Shand's skull, then, like a black leech standing on its tail and questing around for the scent of blood, something slid into his head, and lunged. She gasped, though it was drowned out by Shand's shrieks.

His fists were drumming on the floor, his feet kicking, head banging, nose belching blood. He kicked over the redwood rack on the other bench, the phial of deadly scent potion fell to the floor and the stopper came out. Yellow-brown fumes oozed from it and trailed up in a dozen places.

Ifoli spun the tube on Shand's forehead as if winding thread onto a reel then jerked the device back. He screamed and fainted. Sulien rose from behind the rubble pile. The referred pain was gone, but her skin was creeping.

Shand groaned, opened his eyes and looked up at Ifoli. "Find . . . the . . . link?" he croaked.

"Yes."

"Tear it out?"

"Yes."

"Thank you," he whispered. "I can't tell you what it's been like with that malevolent presence embedded in my mind all this time."

He let out a great sigh, but then his eyes bulged and went red, and he began to choke and gasp.

"Shand!" cried Ifoli.

"It's *still there*! Can't save me. Run! It'll jump to you."

Ifoli grabbed the Command device. "I'll try again."

"No. Link's got deep roots, well hidden. Can't remove them; can't see where they are."

As Ifoli put the copper tip of the device to Shand's forehead, she choked and began to shudder uncontrollably.

"Link must have a kill spell," gasped Shand. "Go!"

"Can't . . . move." Pink foam was oozing from her mouth.

They were both going to die. Sulien ran to Shand and reached out with her hands cupped to the shape of his head, close but not touching.

"Go . . . away!" moaned Shand.

"I can see it," said Sulien. "Black tendrils, creeping in all directions. Ifoli, can you see them?"

"The kill spell will get you too," gasped Shand.

"Not if we're quick. Ifoli, now!"

But Ifoli was still choking, the foam gushing from her mouth now, and the tip of the Command device was battering at Shand, making red circles on his forehead.

Sulien saw, in her mind's eye, the malevolent black tendrils buried in Shand's psyche. She tore the device from Ifoli's fingers, spun the copper tube on his forehead, then jerked it backwards. Again he shrieked but this time the black tendrils stretched to three times their length, twanged, then came free and vanished.

Ifoli fell over and landed on her back, her fingers clenching and unclenching.

Shand came to his knees, panting. "Thank you," he whispered. He focused on Sulien and scowled. "*What are you doing here?* If Karan finds out she'll have my guts—"

"I . . . My gift is growing fast," said Sulien. "I've got to have a teacher. And Nadiril hinted . . ."

"Did he now, the villain?" Shand said darkly. He looked Sulien up and down. "Are you all right?"

"I know about buried links. It didn't get me."

Ifoli had not moved, but now she sat up slowly. "You saved us both, child." She reached out with both arms. "Come here."

Sulien took two steps and passed through a faint yellow plume rising from the spilled scent potion. Some went up her nose, her eyes crossed, then she sat down hard on the empty section of the bench.

"I saw it!" she whispered.

Shand pushed himself upright, alarmed. "Saw what?"

"A long line of power . . . cutting across the land west of Zile."

He was staring at her as if she had gone mad. "What kind of power?"

"The power of mancery."

"That's impossible. Power can only be drawn from within a mancer or from an object enchanted by a mancer. It's a fundamental limitation on the Secret Art."

"It . . . can't be," said Ifoli. "I'm sure the summon stone was drawing power from the storm above Demondifang."

"Then some great mancer enchanted it to do so." Shand turned to Sulien. "Can you send me a link showing what you saw?"

Sulien did so. It was a long but very narrow oval of shimmering power, running across the land for miles.

Shand scratched the shape, a long curve, across the roof with the tip of his knife, then studied it, frowning. "I don't understand . . . Wait! There's a geological fault there—you can see it where it cuts through the rocks."

"So what?" said Ifoli.

"I don't know, but it could be big."

"You owe me a favour," said Sulien boldly, though she was quaking inside. "Teach me how to use my gift."

"I will," said Shand. "The moment I'm cleared of being a traitor."

49

WE CAN'T WAIT TWO MONTHS

Karan, Llian and Sulien had been on a picnic down by the River Zur, but their peaceful afternoon was shattered the moment they returned.

As they reached the front doors of the library, Lilis, who was standing outside, called, "*There* you are. Down to the war room, quick!"

"What's the matter?" said Llian.

"Can't talk about it here. Go!"

They ran down to the war room and two wild-eyed guards ushered them inside. The door was closed and Yggur pointed at it, sealing it. Tallia, Malien, Yggur, Nadiril, Aviel and Janck were seated around the long table, watching Xarah, who was at the end, studying her scrying device.

"Continue," said Janck.

Xarah's device now resembled an astronomical armillary, having a number of brass rings that could be moved in three dimensions independently of each other. She edged several of the little crystal pointers along their rings, moved one ring to the vertical and another at right angles to it, then nudged a pointer this way, another that way. She was staring intently at the device, though Karan could not imagine what she expected to see.

No one spoke. Beside Karan, Sulien was shivering. The crystal Xarah had just moved along the vertical hoop emitted a dark red flash. She exhaled in a great sigh and thrust the hoops out of alignment.

"Well?" Janck said roughly.

"In the past hour the flow from the summon stone has trebled," said Xarah.

"And?"

"It appears—as far as I can tell—to be flowing out of the world to Cinnabar."

"To the Crimson Gate," said Karan.

"I assume so."

"Once the Merdrun reopen the gate," said Malien, "their army will be able to move in minutes to any place on Santhenar, and bring the rest of their army here from Cinnabar. They'll be able to attack Thurkad from *inside* its walls, or any other target they want."

"On Cinnabar they were invincible when attacking mighty fortresses from outside," said Llian. "If they got into Thurkad, or Roros, or any other great city . . ."

"How are we going to stop them?" said Malien. "We have to decide right now."

"We can't let them complete the gate," said Janck. "We've got to attack Gwine."

"How?" said Tallia. "The Merdrun number ten to twelve thousand there. To invade the island and attack any normal army that size, behind strong fortifications, we'd need an advantage of at least four to one—an army of fifty thousand, say. But the Merdrun are not a normal army. Each soldier is the equal of three or four or five normal fighters."

"In another month I'll have an army of sixty thousand," said Janck. "And a fleet to carry them."

"But it's another month's sailing to Gwine, assuming the winds are favourable and the winter storms allow it. We can't wait two months, Commander, or even two weeks, or the Merdrun will be gone and the war lost."

Janck stood up suddenly. "There's too many people here who don't need to know. Out, everyone! Those who need to be here will be called within the hour."

Karan was heading towards the door when she realised Sulien was still sitting at the table, head in hands, staring at the polished surface. Karan touched her on the shoulder.

Sulien did not move. Karan gave her a little shake. "It's time to go."

Sulien's head slumped forward. Now alarmed, Karan raised Sulien's head and looked into her eyes. The pupils were dilated so widely that hardly any of the iris could be seen; her mouth was open, her jaw slack and her breath was hissing in and out.

"Sulien, what's the matter? *Llian?*"

She heard him running back and the others speaking urgently among themselves. Sulien gave a great start and a choking gasp, then shoved herself away from the table with such force that her chair fell over backwards. Llian caught her and lifted her up.

"The triplets," whispered Sulien, her pupils slowly returning to normal. "I saw them drinking lives, dozens of lives." She took another gasping breath; her eyes widened and flicked from side to side, then she howled, "The gate! The gate!"

Janck, Yggur and Malien pushed through the throng. "What about it?" said Janck.

"Saw its shadow," said Sulien. "Red as blood."

"What the hell does that mean?"

Malien shoved him aside, took Sulien's hand and said gently, "How did you see all this, Sulien?"

"It was . . . a *seeing.*"

"Was the shadow of the gate on Cinnabar? Was it the great Crimson Gate Karan saw there?"

"It was like the Crimson Gate, but it was in a hot place, not a cold one."

"On Gwine?"

"I . . . think so."

"But a shadow, you said. Not solid stone. Not real."

"I could see right through it," said Sulien.

"Was it getting more solid?"

"Not really."

"That's something," Malien said to the others. "So it's not forming quickly. It could take days."

"It'd better," Janck said grimly. "What else does she know?"

"What can you can tell us about the triplets?" said Malien.

Sulien squirmed. "They're much worse than before, and stronger. I don't want to think about them; I'm scared they'll get me."

"Do you know why they're worse?"

"Yes," said Sulien.

"Why, damn it?" said Janck.

"Leave her alone!" said Karan, shoving him aside. She took Sulien's hands, then said quietly, "Is there anything you can tell us about them? Any tiny little thing you noticed?"

"They're worse because they're taking power from the summon stone, and it's *really* foul now." Her voice dropped to a whisper. "It's making them worse . . . *and they're making it worse.*"

Yggur leaned across and said quietly to Janck, "We can't let them open the gate."

"In another week and a half—"

"We can't wait! This is an emergency, Janck. We've got to strike now, ready or not."

PART THREE

BATTLE

50

I'M BEING SENT TO *GWINE*?

"Well?" said Janck coldly, the moment the guards escorted Llian into the oppressive subterranean chamber known as the Tomb. Janck, who was even more paranoid about secrecy than before, had moved his war room there immediately after the last meeting. The guards went out and closed the door.

"You've had Rulke's papers for days," Janck went on. "What have you discovered?"

Llian sat down at the other end of the twenty-foot-long table. He had no idea what was being planned, when or where. Everyone was doing sixteen-hour days and no one was allowed to talk about their work.

"I've translated the most important papers and scanned the rest. The Histories of the Charon in the void are ... incredible. Someone will make a Great Tale out of them one day."

"I couldn't give a damn about *tales*," snarled Janck. "What does he say about the Merdrun's weaknesses?"

"Nothing."

Janck's voice rose. "But the Charon fought a civil war with the Merdrun right across the void. Rulke must know their weaknesses."

"They come from the same stock," Llian pointed out. "And the Charon were surrounded by far more numerous enemies: the Aachim, Faellem and us. Maybe Rulke removed anything that could have been used against his own people."

"You've got nothing for me," Janck said disgustedly. "This has been an utter waste of time."

Llian, who had a chronicler's thick skin, did not react. "There was one intriguing thing though."

Janck brightened. "Go on."

"While Rulke was imprisoned in the Nightland he designed a virtual construct that could fly and create portals from one place to another."

"And after he escaped he built it," growled Janck. "Everyone knows that. So what?"

"Rulke talks about using his virtual construct to move *forwards in time*—and he may even have done so."

"Bloody nonsense," Janck said coldly. "Get back to work. You've got half a day to find the Merdrun's weaknesses— Forget I said that."

"You never mentioned it," said Llian, rising.

But he could not stop thinking about it as he returned to the locked room where Rulke's Histories were stored. Why only half a day?

As he turned the key, Aviel limped up, walking oddly. "Hello," said Llian.

"Can I talk to you?" she said softly. "In private."

"Come in."

She followed him into the little room and he closed the door. "What is it?"

Her cheeks went a delicate shade of pink, then she said, "Wait a minute." She turned away, fumbled with her skirts, then turned back and laid the black sword in its copper sheath on the table.

"What's that for?" said Llian.

"Can you give it to Wilm?"

He gaped at her. "He's a prisoner. On Gwine."

"Yes."

It hit him like a punch in the mouth. "I'm being *sent* to Gwine?" She did not reply, though he could read it in her eyes. "How do you know?"

"I . . . overheard something," said Aviel. "Llian, I've got to help him. Will you give him the sword? It saved me from Lumillal, and it's the only thing that can save Wilm now." Her eyes were dripping. "Please."

"I'll do everything I can."

After she left he sat at the table stroking the embossed sheath. This was it. He, who was useless with weapons of any kind, was being sent to war. To his death.

"Why would they send *you?*" said Karan when, in defiance of the edict on secrecy, he told her later that night.

"I keep asking myself the same question."

"You've got to say no."

"None of us has a choice any more."

It was a grim night, probably their last together, and neither of them slept well. Whenever he woke Karan was lying rigidly beside him, staring at the dark ceiling. He finally got to sleep around four in the morning, but again had the unpleasant experience of being woken by Yggur an hour before dawn.

"Get up," said Yggur.

"What the hell for?" said Karan.

"We're under sealed orders," Yggur said unhelpfully.

Everyone had been ordered to pack days ago, though no one had been told why. Was Janck sending Llian to punish him? It was the only explanation that made any sense.

In a desperate silence he dressed, gathered his gear and strapped on the black sword. Karan rose, her hair a wild tangle across her shoulders, clung desperately to him for a minute, then shoved him away.

"I hate goodbyes," she said. "Especially . . ." She threw herself at him and hugged him again. "Just go!"

The thought was unbearable. Would he ever see her again? Or Sulien? Llian stood there gazing at his precious daughter, asleep on her bed shelf. What would become of her if Janck's plan failed?

Karan put her arms around him from behind. "You're going for her," she said quietly. "Whatever you have to face, no matter how bad it is, you're doing it because it's the only way to save her. And when my time comes, whatever they ask of me, I'll do the same. It's why we keep going, Llian."

It helped. "Thank you."

She pulled free. He kissed Sulien, who stirred uneasily in her sleep, and followed Yggur out and up. The roof lay in darkness, though starlight showed it crowded with dozens of sky ships. He counted fifteen sleek Aachim craft, most of which had only arrived recently, plus many boxy vessels, much larger than the ones he had seen before, made in the shipyards of Sith.

Llian followed Yggur to a marshalling point where their names were taken and they were ordered to one of the huge sky ships on the western side of the roof. Their names were checked again and they were ordered aboard.

"What's this all about?" said Llian to the bearded thickset fellow at the foot of the ladder.

"No questions!"

Llian clambered in, staying behind Yggur so he could whisper to him when no one was listening, "Can *you* tell me?"

"I know no more than you."

"I find that hard to believe."

"I'm here solely because of my flying ability. No non-Aachim has more experience than me. Or a greater ability to channel the power needed to make a sky ship fly."

"But you know where we're going?"

"I will when I open my sealed orders."

"Don't suppose you could leave them lying around where I could have a peek?"

Yggur gave him a cold stare. "You and I are not friends, Llian, nor are we ever likely to be."

True enough. Llian looked around. The boxy interior, lit faintly by glowing strips along the roof, was spartan. There were no fitted cupboards, just racks of gear covered by nets, and only one seat, for the pilot.

"Are we supposed to sit on the floor?" said Llian.

"By stripping out unnecessary weight, the craft can carry another six men. There are loops fixed to the floor. Put your legs through that one." Yggur pointed to a loop next to his seat.

Llian did so. The floor was hard, cold and uncomfortable. "How long do we have to put up with this?"

"How long do I have to put up with your whining?"

Soldiers climbed aboard and trooped up to the back. Llian counted forty of them. An officer followed, a massive fellow with a square head, a severe deficit of neck and boots like rectangular slabs. In a surprisingly high and nervous voice he directed his troops to put their packs behind the cargo nets and sit down.

"Anything you say, Cubo," sang out a soldier up the back.

"Who said that?" he cried.

No one answered. "The name is Cubbers," he said coldly. "Captain Cubbers." When he sat down on the bare floor the whole cabin shook.

A thin, nervous man entered. "Healer Lukey," he said almost inaudibly. Hingis clambered in, nodded to Llian and sat behind him, looking serene. He had wanted to go to war for ages; he wanted to die and would soon get his wish.

Last of all to board was a young Faellem male. Llian stared at him; he had not seen a Faellem in a dozen years. He was small, slender and golden-skinned, like most of his people, and very handsome. He nodded to Yggur and Llian, then took the last loop, beside Hingis.

When everyone was aboard and the hatch had been closed, Yggur extinguished the lighted strips along the ceiling, took off smoothly and turned west.

"If there are spies about," said Llian, "the moment they see all these sky ships take off they'll guess what we're up to."

"Who said everyone is taking off at the same time?" said Yggur. "Or heading in the same direction?"

He opened a sealed envelope, holding the contents in his lap while he read using a glimmer from a fingertip, then tore the slip of paper to pieces and put them in his mouth. Yggur flew into cloud then turned, watching a small compass strapped to his wrist. He kept turning until Llian was completely disoriented, then straightened up and headed on, the great rotors going *ticker-tick*.

"Can we have some light?" said Llian, getting out his journal.

"No."

It was going to be a very long flight.

51

DON'T MENTION
THAT TRAITOR'S NAME

"Where's Daddy gone?" said Sulien in the morning.

"I don't know," said Karan. "And if I did, I wouldn't be allowed to tell you."

"Stupid secrets! I'm going to find out."

"Yes, darling."

Two agonising days passed without a scrap of news, then in the following afternoon Karan was ordered to the Tomb. The usual people were there: Nadiril, Malien, Tallia, Janck and Xarah, plus Hublees and two men she had not seen before.

The first was a big, grizzled old officer, Juto Clept. A dip halfway down his broad nose looked as if it had been hacked out with a blade, and a scar ran from his left cheek to his ear, which had been split in two horizontally. His bare arms were deeply tanned, heavily scarred and sparsely covered in coarse yellow hairs. The other man was small and slender, with short black hair and a shark-belly complexion, as if he never went outside in daytime. His arms were hairless.

"The attack is on," said Janck. "Twenty-eight sky ships left two and a half days ago, heading in all directions, though most went to a secret location on the north coast. There, twelve hundred troops and thirty officers embarked in the dead of night and flew north—to Gwine."

"And you sent Llian with them," said Karan. "Why would you send *him* to war?"

Janck gave her a very cold look. "The Merdrun share many characteristics with the Charon, and Llian knows more about the Charon than anyone alive."

"Except Shand."

Janck went an unhealthy shade of purple. "Never mention that traitor's name!" He controlled himself with great difficulty. "Llian's advice, if he succeeds in finding the enemy's secret weakness, could prove crucial—since you and Sulien have signally failed in this endeavour."

When Karan did not reply, he went on. "But once there, Llian will have to fight like everyone else. There's no room for baggage on this mission."

Fight and die. An image flashed into her mind: Llian lying in the bloody mud of a sweltering tropical battlefield, dying, flies swarming— She choked down a scream.

Janck was still talking " . . . and our troops include ninety Aachim and fifty-five Faellem."

"I didn't know any Faellem had come," Nadiril said interestedly.

"They only arrived three days ago."

"Good. The Merdrun will see that all three human species on Santh are united against them."

"That remains to be seen," Janck said ominously.

"But only twelve hundred. How can it be enough?"

"It's not. There's a second prong to my plan, one I dared not even whisper until we were sure it would work, a couple of hours ago. I'm sending a larger force through a gate made by Malien and her Aachim mancers."

"You're daring to direct a gate to Gwine," said Nadiril, "knowing they're trying to open their own gate there?"

"I'm desperate."

"The enemy will detect it the moment it opens."

"If Malien can open it inside the enemy camp, in the middle of the night, we can take them by surprise."

Tallia grimaced. Karan felt sick. Gergrig had fought hundreds of battles and won them all; they would never take him by surprise.

"How many troops?" said the scar-faced general.

"Two thousand, eight hundred," said Janck. "Plus the twelve hundred on the sky ships makes four thousand."

"Against ten thousand."

"Our forces are just there to make a diversion while Hissper's assassins—" He indicated the pale black-haired man. "—hunt the triplets down and cut their throats."

"It can't work," Karan said flatly.

"Why not?" Janck seemed amused.

"The sky ships could be delayed by days. How can you coordinate their attack—to the second—with the attack from the gate?"

He smiled coldly. "That's why you're here."

It hit her like a brick in the eye. Why else would Janck have ordered her to one of his secret councils? "What for?"

"If all goes well, the sky ships can reach Gwine in three days, flying non-stop over the ocean."

"What if some of them break down? Or crash?"

"Everyone on board will drown."

He said it so casually that Karan wanted to jump onto the table, run down and kick his big square teeth in.

"I've allowed an extra two days in case of bad weather and . . . other eventualities," Janck went on. "The attack is planned for half past one in the morning of the sixth day, counting from when they left. That's two and a half days from now."

"And me?"

"You'll return to Gwine in spirit form on the afternoon of the fifth day. You'll stay well away from anywhere the magiz could detect you, and hide. You'll keep watch with a spyglass and, when you see the sky ship fleet approaching from the south, you'll link to Malien."

"I can't link any more. I've lost the gift. Why don't you use Nadiril's farspeaking devices?"

"They don't work at such long distances," said Nadiril.

Janck scowled at Malien. "Is there any way she can get back the ability to link?"

"I don't know," said Malien.

"But this undermines the whole plan. There's no other way to coordinate the attacks."

It was Karan's way out. "Then there's no point me going."

"You're not weaselling out. Malien?"

She thought for a moment. "Sulien can make a link to Karan before she goes. Karan will block it until she sees the fleet, then unblock the link and tell Sulien the fleet has arrived. Sulien will tell me and we'll open the prepared gate and send the troops through."

It was a stupid plan with far too many holes. "What if you can't send the gate to the right place?" said Karan. "Or the enemy have defences against gates? Or they're waiting when the sky ships land? Or the Crimson Gate they're trying to open interferes with your gate?"

"Just worry about doing your own job," Janck said savagely.

"What then?"

"I don't follow."

"You said everyone has to fight. What are my orders after the invasion begins."

"Assassinate Gergrig."

Karan reeled. It was a death sentence. "I'm not an assassin."

"You've killed before."

"Not in cold blood."

"Not even to protect your daughter?"

"If I go near Gergrig the triplets will detect me."

"If the triplets are dead, and Gergrig is dead, your daughter is safe. If we allow him to live he'll soon create another magiz and it'll start all over again. *Gergrig has to die.*"

"I'll ... try," said Karan numbly.

"No one has asked the obvious question," said Nadiril. "How are the survivors supposed to get away?"

"Back through the gate," said Janck.

"It won't be there."

"Why the hell not?" Janck's purple face started to turn crimson.

"It's hard enough to hold a gate open for a few minutes; no one can do so for hours. Besides, we daren't risk leaving the gate open in case the Merdrun take control of it."

"Then the survivors will come back on the sky ships."

"The Merdrun won't let them land a second time."

Janck did not reply.

"Given that it's a suicide mission," said Nadiril, "and clearly it is, you might have had the decency to tell your troops before they left."

"I'll be telling them when I get there."

"You're going?" Nadiril said in astonishment.

"I know what you think of me," said Janck. "But I'll be leading my troops from the front."

"Glad to hear it," said Nadiril. "And I have some good news."

"What's that?"

"The stolen bottle of Archeus has turned up."

52

THE FLIMSIEST OF PLANS

"Take no unnecessary risks before the sky ships appear," said Janck as Karan prepared to dematerialise. "If you're caught, Gergrig will torture the plan out of you and the whole mission will fail."

You don't give a damn about any of us, she thought. *Just your precious plan.* "I've been on a damn sight more covert missions than you have," she said coldly.

He studied her with active dislike. "Then get going."

She was lying on a pallet this time; she could not risk injuring her abandoned body. Saying goodbye to Sulien had been agonising. She had been unbearably formal, then had disappeared, and Karan felt sure she would never see her again. She blocked the unbearable emotions, focused on a safe part of Gwine and, without a word, triggered the spell.

Pain tore through her from throat to groin as her spirit was ripped from her body; she felt a painful stretching as if she were made of elastic, a rushing sound, a cold wind, then with a *boingg* and a popping of her ears her spirit materialised on the island.

But she was miles away from the treeless hill she had intended to use as a lookout. She was inside the enemy camp, between two rows of soldiers' tents. It was ten in the evening and there were Merdrun everywhere.

Panic overwhelmed her. She should not be here. The triplets would trap her and force her to materialise. They would torture her, or Gergrig would, until she broke and betrayed Janck's plan. Then the triplets would unblock the link to Sulien and kill them both.

She forced herself to think calmly. Being stuck in the middle of all these tents raised a question she had not previously thought about—where the rest of the Merdrun lived. They must have a safe refuge for the mothers, children and the folk, and the people who taught, trained and guarded the children.

In Sulien's first nightmare, months ago, Gergrig had talked about gaining a world of their own, and his yearning had been palpable. Clearly he had not thought barren Cinnabar a world worth having; they were only there for the Crimson Gate and because they *needed practice in killing*.

Where then was the Merdrun's home? Was it some desolate rock drifting through the eternal void? Was that the secret weakness they were so desperate to protect? Could she find out?

She drifted through the shadows. This place was unlike any other army camp she had ever seen. There were no camp followers and no one sat around drinking, dicing or playing cards. The tents were either empty or occupied by sleeping soldiers. Those outside were all practising combat with manic intensity. Were they obsessed with war? Or were they afraid to stop training in case they were judged unworthy and killed, as Gergrig had threatened to do to his drum-boy, Uigg?

Karan also noticed that they were slower than they had been on Cinnabar. There they had bounded effortlessly up the steep slopes; their attacks had been unstoppable. Here they just seemed normal.

She tucked the thought away and looked for signs of the Crimson Gate they were trying to open. At all costs, Malien's gate had to avoid any other gate, complete or partial, because the consequences of two gates trying to occupy the same place would be cataclysmic.

There was no sign of a gate. Karan was drifting upslope when the back of her neck tingled. A robed acolyte was staring in her direction. The young woman, who had shining black hair and a heart-shaped face that would have been beautiful had it not been marred by the ugly black glyph burned into her forehead, appeared to be straining to see something—her jaw was set and the tendons stood out in her neck.

She's straining to see me! *She's sensed me.*

Karan's instinct was to flee, though moving rapidly took energy that she could not spare. At this distance from her comatose body in Zile she could only draw a trickle. Afraid to fly in case it exposed her to the triplets, Karan drifted down until the soles of her boots touched the hard-packed ground. She felt the tiniest impact, then kept sinking.

It took more of her precious strength than she had expected and the earth rasped at her, inside and out, as her spirit slid into it and came to rest at eye level. It was a most peculiar feeling: she felt thicker and denser, like a bag that had been filled with hard-packed dirt.

The ground was an uncertain refuge, though; if she were detected, she could easily be trapped. She waited, every nerve singing, while the acolyte frowned and walked back and forth. If she called the triplets they would find her in seconds.

The acolyte came forward, head cocked, and reached out to feel the air where Karan's spirit had been. Could the acolyte see her? She had undoubtedly detected something. Karan dared not move or do anything to attract attention.

A minute passed, then another. The tension slowly faded from the acolyte's eyes and she shook her head and walked away. Earth could defeat many spells, Karan knew; perhaps it had been enough to hide her.

She eased herself out of the ground and drifted down the slope, over the fifteen-foot-high southern wall and south for several miles until she reached a steep rocky hill near the south coast. The grey limestone was sheer on the southern side and pitted with shallow caves.

From the top she could see the wooden watchtowers on three sides of the fortress, a fourth watchtower at the gates and a muddy cart track winding up to it. A mile to the west was the palisade wall of the slave camp, and the ruined towns and devastated lands lay beyond.

Karan settled into a cave halfway down the cliff. Even if she were detected, the Merdrun could not attack her here without descending from the peak on ropes. Judging by the stars it was 11 p.m. Not long to go now.

The sky-ship squadron was to rendezvous at an uninhabited island thirty miles south-west of Gwine and wait. If the journey had gone well they would have been there two days ago, and even if some craft had been delayed, all twenty-eight ships should have reached there by this morning. They would have left by now, so as to reach Gwine by 1.30 a.m.

She took a small night glass out of her pack. It was just a tenuous shadow of its real self and she prayed that it would still work—she had little experience of using objects while in spirit form. Karan aimed it south-west and scanned the horizon but there was nothing to see.

Her empty stomach clenched painfully. She had used more energy than she had expected and there was no way to eat while in spirit form. She had to ignore it and pray that the squadron was on time. After they arrived she would head back to the fortress, materialise in some out-of-the-way spot, then begin the deadly hunt for Gergrig.

What must Llian be thinking at this moment? That even if he sur-vived the landing and the Merdrun's furious counterattack, he would be slaughtered on the battlefield? How long could the small attack force hold out against so many Merdrun? Perhaps only minutes. What a stupid, tragic waste.

Sulien, with nothing to do but wait for the worst news, must be in torment. How would she fare under the Aachim's care? Clan Elienor was kinder than most Aachim clans but they were a proud, remote folk, not given much to levity or life's simple pleasures, and the Aachim looked down on outsiders. Sulien, only one quarter Aachim, would always be an outcast among them.

Karan knew she had failed her.

Only an hour before the gate was due to be opened, Sulien finally found a way through the barrier around Gergrig and sensed out his drum boy. That did not take long; Uigg radiated both the frozen outward calm that was his mask, and the inner anguish he denied even to himself. The mix of emotions was unmistakeable. He stood straight-backed between the rows of tents, Gergrig's empty command tent behind him, staring straight ahead and playing his drums with manic fury as if trying to beat them to death.

Uigg? she whispered. *Are you all right?*

His head shot round and he stared at the place from which her voice issued, then looked straight ahead. *I am Merdrun*, he said in a dead voice. *I am not troubled by feelings. I simply serve and obey.*

Of course you feel, said Sulien. *How could you not after all the terrible things Gergrig has made you do?*

I'm on a warning. If I display forbidden emotions I will be killed in front of our army as an example to all. I . . . will . . . not . . . feel!

She moved closer. *But you do feel, because you're good and decent and kind.*

I'm . . . not . . . kind! he choked. *Kindness is weakness and weakness is failure.*

I think you are kind. I know you care.

Stop it! he moaned. *You'll be my death.*

She had pushed him too far. *I'm sorry. I would not hurt you for anything, but . . .*

He froze, looked around jerkily, and she saw the treacherous tears in his eyes. Uigg wiped them away furiously. *Why are you being nice to me?*

I can feel your pain. Are you getting ready for battle?

Why do you ask? he said between his teeth.

She had made a big mistake. Merdrun would never reveal their plans to outsiders. *You just . . . look as though you're getting ready for something.*

Just training. Sulien knew he was lying. *Who are you?* he said suspiciously.

No one important.

Only two people from Santhenar have been able to come to us this way, said Uigg, quivering. *The mother and the daughter. You're Sulien, our most deadly enemy!*

There was no point denying it, so she projected an image of herself. *Yes, I am.*

It shocked him. *But you're just a little kid! How can someone so small be our worst enemy?*

Are you going to call Gergrig?

Uigg was shaking. It was his duty to denounce her, and he would be guilty of the worst treason if he did not, yet she was the only person who had ever spoken kindly to him. Denouncing her would be a personal betrayal.

His eyes were bulging and his breath came in gasps. He was trying to speak but unable to get the words out. A lifetime of brutality had left him emotionally stunted.

Fly! he choked. *I give you . . . one minute.*

As Sulien retreated, footsteps came towards the tent and she expected psychic nets to fall on her. But a minute passed, and another, and still Uigg kept silent. Why hadn't he informed on her?

What's the matter with you now, drum boy? snapped Gergrig. Clearly he knew something was wrong. Would he tear the truth out of Uigg, then kill him?

I . . . I'm afraid I won't do you proud, said Uigg, *when battle comes.*

I fear that too, my son. But you won't have long to wait. The fools think they can take me by surprise. Me! *Go and fill your belly; it won't be long now.*

Yes, Father.

Sulien withdrew. This was bad. The enemy were expecting an attack in the night. She had to find Janck and convince him to call it off, but if he did, it would surely doom Karan and the fleet of sky ships that had left days ago. What was she to do?

And how could any father treat his son so cruelly?

Karan swept the southern horizon with her night glass once more. Finally the appointed hour came, 1.30 a.m. The squadron would appear in the next few minutes, and it would be on.

She swept the horizon again and again, but it remained empty save for a scatter of streaky clouds. What if they were coming in from the west? No, that quadrant of the sky was just as empty.

Five minutes passed, then ten. Then twenty and there was still no sign of a single sky ship. Why not? They'd had over five days, two more than needed. Something was wrong, and Sulien knew it too; even over the blocked link Karan could sense her anxiety.

Had Gergrig's spies been watching as the squadron took off? Or had Shand? The loading and departure of so many sky ships must have been detected, and once Gergrig knew about it he would jump to the obvious conclusion.

Could the triplets have located the squadron out over the ocean and attacked it? There was no way of knowing. *Llian!* she sent fruitlessly. *Where are you?*

Or was Gergrig waiting for the sky ships to come sweeping in, planning to shoot them down before they could land to disembark their troops? A spear or heavy arrow could tear open an airbag and send a sky ship plunging uncontrollably to the ground, while a blast of mancery or a fire arrow would blow it to bits and possibly the sky ships on either side as well.

An hour passed, minute by agonising minute. Then two hours. Three. Four, and the southern sky remained empty. Sulien's anxiety was now a mind-shriek but Karan dared not relax the block.

It was not long until dawn. The squadron would not come now; it would not approach the island in daylight. It had either been lost on the long, hazardous trip from Zile, or been delayed and hopefully would come tonight.

But Karan could not last that long without food. She was already weak from hunger and by the end of the day she would be useless. Remaining here was tremendously draining on her body back home, but nothing could be done about it.

Should she return to Zile and come back tonight? No, too risky— both her departure and return could be detected. She would have to wait it out.

By dawn the hunger was unbearable. She would have expected it to be far less apparent in spirit form but her stomach ached constantly. Should she go down to the shore, materialise and try to find food?

But materialisation also created traces that the triplets could detect, and it was so exhausting that she might lapse into unconsciousness. She had to conserve her remaining energy for tonight. Karan lay down at the back of the cave. She did not need to, being weightless, but taking up the usual position would make it easier to get to sleep. If she slept the day away the trickle of energy flowing from her body might be enough to keep her going until 1.30 tomorrow morning.

She did not sleep well; she kept jerking awake with her heart pounding and sweat prickling all over her at the thought that the fleet was lost, Llian dead, and the mission already a failure.

That afternoon she heard the echo of voices far below her. A heavily armed party of ten Merdrun, accompanied by an acolyte, was moving purposefully across the rocky shore below the cliff as if searching for something. Chills spiralled down her back.

Not something, someone. Her.

53

FIND GERGRIG AND KILL HIM

The acolyte looked up at the cliff. If anything aroused her suspicions the Merdrun would soon hunt Karan down.

Finally they moved off to the east and she lost sight of them, but an hour later she saw another search party to the west. The enemy were on high alert; had they got wind of the attack? If they had it could not succeed. Should she contact Malien and tell her not to open the gate? But that would doom everyone on the sky ships.

The sun set; the eternal day dragged on and she felt weaker than ever, but she had to stay until 1.30 a.m., the next rendezvous. Then, if the squadron had not arrived she must return to Zile. If the spirit link broke, she would die.

By 1.30 she could barely hold up the weightless night glass. She propped it on a rock and directed it along the south-western horizon, which was completely empty. What to do? She would risk another quarter of an hour.

Another minute passed. Two. Five. Then fifteen.

Just a few minutes more, she thought desperately. Just five minutes.

She scanned the horizon one final time, hopelessly. Nothing, nothing, noth—

Were those tiny spots specks before her eyes, or was it the squadron? Her heart thumped and she struggled to her feet and focused the night glass. The spots were in one place, clustered together a little west of south.

As she watched they resolved into pairs of round dots, heading directly for Gwine. The squadron had made it after all. At least, part of it. Karan only counted sixteen sky ships. She checked the horizon east and west, then the sky above, but there were no more.

Sixteen out of twenty-eight. Had the rest turned back or had they been lost? As they crept on, keeping low over the water, she saw strips of fabric fluttering behind the leading ship. The other vessels also looked battered, as if they been through a terrible storm.

If nearly half had been lost, she thought with a stabbing pang, the chances were high that Llian was dead. She doubled over, keening softly. But he could also be on one of the surviving craft, and they were waiting for her signal.

She reversed the night glass, aimed its smaller end at the leading craft and pressed the little yellow hump to turn it into a signalling torch. The signal that meant she was in place and everything was ready was two long flashes, four short, a pause then two more long flashes. If it did not come the squadron would know that something had gone wrong, but would they turn back or attack on their own?

They did not signal back; they could not do so without the flashes being seen by the Merdrun's lookouts. Then suddenly the sky ships blurred and disappeared. The Faellem on board, all master illusionists, had hidden the fleet, though the enemy's mancers might be able to see through the illusions.

Karan felt extraordinarily weak now, but her most important job was still to be done. It was 1.50 a.m., twenty minutes later than the rendezvous time. She reached deep into her mind to Sulien's link and released the block.

Mummy, what's going on? Are you all right? Mummy, what about Daddy? Mummy! Mummy! Mummy!

I'm all right, Karan gasped, then, *Now!*

But before she could re-block the link a blinding pain flowered in the centre of her head and raced to the top of her skull. The triplets had detected the link and were attacking through it. Sulien screamed. Karan fought the attack, re-blocked the link, and the scream cut off. The pain in her head died away though the top of her skull felt hot and blistered.

Was Sulien all right? Had she got the message to Malien to open the gate? If she had not the sky ships were doomed, but Karan dared not reopen the link to find out. The triplets would attack instantly and they might be able to get to Malien as well.

And they could have located Karan, so she had to act fast. She stuffed the night glass into her pack and dived out of the cave, down the cliff and along the wave-washed rocks for as far as she could go, a quarter of a mile. She settled to the ground and triggered the materialisation spell that would bring her body all the way here from Zile and unite it with her spirit.

It was excruciating and took all the strength she had left. Karan collapsed on her back on the sharp rocks. She could smell the sea, hear the waves crashing on the broken shore, feel the salt spray raining down on her and taste it on her dry lips, but she could not move.

After a few minutes enough strength returned for her to sit up. She crawled along the wet rocks towards the water's edge, feeling for anything to eat. Her fingers identified seaweed, the kind like a string of beads. She tore off a few strands and stuffed them in her mouth, but they were chewy and flavourless, and would not give her the energy she needed.

Karan cut a fingertip on a sharp oyster shell. With the point of her knife she levered it open, scooped the oyster out and swallowed it whole. Though it was a small one, it did her more good than half a bucket of seaweed would have. She groped along the rocks to a patch with dozens of oysters and ate until her belly was taut and the desperate hunger had been replaced by a throbbing ache.

The squadron was still concealed by illusion though soon it would be close enough for the rotors to be heard, and when the sky ships passed overhead no illusion would be able to conceal them from the Merdrun's guards.

Karan scrambled across the rocks and headed inland to a path that ran up the side of the hill; there a ridge offered an easy climb to the top. As she got there, with a hissing of wind through cables and the beating of its twin rotors, the leading sky ship passed overhead.

It raced across the mile and a half towards the Merdrun's camp, closely followed by three more craft, passed over the southern wall and dropped abruptly. Had they shot it down? Karan climbed onto a boulder that offered a better view. No, it had disgorged its troops inside the mile-long camp and shot up like a cork from a bottle. The three craft behind it hurtled in as well, then more. The attack was on.

Karan turned away. Now her orders were to go after Gergrig, which meant returning to the disembodied state, and it was going to hurt a lot more the second time.

Her stomach was churning. Had one of the oysters been bad? She climbed thirty feet up a tree to a three-way fork where she would not be visible from the ground and where, she hoped, no local predator would find her, then tied herself on. She hoped the sickness would go away when she dematerialised. It was all she could do to stop herself from throwing up.

The pain of returning to spirit form made the churning in her stomach worse. As she floated towards the camp, sick with terror that Llian was dead and the magiz's attack had killed or injured Sulien, Karan knew she had never been less ready to take on the most powerful man on Santhenar.

Where was Malien's gate? A good dozen minutes had passed since the sky ships had landed, yet there was no sign of the gate. The unsupported troops must be dying by the hundred. Was there anything she could do to help them?

Only find Gergrig and kill him.

54

LUCKY TO LAST TEN MINUTES

Tarstang Dunt, despite his great height and confident manner, was little more than a boy, full of romantic notions about becoming a great hero and routing the evil Merdrun. But his stomach proved sensitive to motion sickness, and when the great storm struck, hurling Yggur's sky ship up and down and across the heavens, Tarstang had spewed on the floor until he brought up blood.

Almost out of his wits and desperate for fresh air, he staggered to the cabin door.

"Leave that alone!" Yggur roared, struggling to control the craft in the wild winds.

But Tarstang opened the door. He was clinging to the rail, gasping, when another lurch tossed him out. He caught the rungs of the ladder and clung there in the pouring rain and flashing lightning, desperation written across his young face.

Llian was hauling himself towards the open door, praying he could save the lad, when Yggur bellowed, "Sit ... down ... *now!*"

After an agonised hesitation Llian retreated. Tarstang, with almost superhuman strength, hauled himself up until his white face appeared in the doorway, but as he tried to take hold of the rail a vicious down-blast tore his other hand free and he fell into the night.

Llian looked around at the silent, staring troops, shocked as he was at the suddenness of Tarstang's death. The lad had been popular; his naïve enthusiasm had helped them overcome their own fears. No one spoke for several minutes while Yggur fought the controls. When the sky ship was steady again he pointed a finger at the door and it slammed.

"He didn't suffer," said Yggur softly. "Impact with the water would have killed him instantly."

"But it's such a *waste*," said Llian.

"Few know more about how war wastes lives than I do."

That reminded Llian of two stories about Yggur from a dozen years ago, when he had waged war on Iagador and captured it. Yggur had been a hard and remorseless man in those days; he had once decimated an army for failing him. Another time he had lost an entire army when Faelamor's incomparable illusions led a thousand men over a cliff in the fog. That disaster, that failure, had shaken Yggur to the core, and he had not been the same man since.

Llian expected to die a dozen times that night, and more the following day as the sky ship fought the endless storms. His only consolation was that Karan and Sulien were safe in Zile.

Two days later, when they finally cleared the seven-hundred-mile-wide band of storms and rotored into clear skies only an hour south-west of Gwine, the sky ship stank of piss and vomit, and groaning soldiers, some with broken bones and one with a cracked skull, lay everywhere. Even Yggur, whose toughness and stoicism were legendary, was swaying in his seat, his sunken eyes black-rimmed and his skin a waxen grey.

During the ghastly six-day flight he had barely managed as many hours of sleep, and his arms had cramped so badly that Llian, less affected by airsickness than most of the troops, had been forced to massage Yggur's forearms for hours on end so he could keep the craft in the air.

"*That* was a storm," Yggur murmured. "If it hadn't been for you, Llian . . ."

"Or you," Llian said quietly. "I don't know how you brought us through it."

He had gained a new respect for Yggur, a mancer he had known for a dozen years and cordially disliked for most of that time. He was a complex, brilliant, difficult man, hard to like, but without him they would have been dead a dozen times.

"I don't see how any lesser pilot could have done it," Llian said wearily. "Are we the only ones . . . ?"

"We were well ahead of the others. They may have been able to go around the storm front." He rubbed his eyes and peered to the west. "I can see them—at least, some of them. How many ships are there? Can you count them?"

"Nine," said Llian grimly. He was exhausted too, though he had managed to sleep every night but the last one. "Only nine. No, there's another one. Does that mean we've lost—"

"Doesn't mean anything yet," said Yggur. "Let's give them another hour before we write anyone off. What's the damage here?"

"Two men with broken arms, three with broken or sprained wrists and one with a broken leg—caught it behind a stay just before that last vicious updraught and it snapped like a carrot. Plus various other injuries, including smashed teeth and broken noses. And Thurn with the cracked skull, of course. Healer says he won't be any use for days."

"How many fit to fight?"

"If I'm honest, none. Half of them have been throwing up for the past two days, and no one has had enough sleep. But since we have to fight—those of us who can stand up—I'd say thirty-one of the forty we took on board."

"Don't forget Tarstang."

"I never will," said Llian.

Shortly Yggur was circling over a small sandy island inside the western arc of a large teardrop-shaped coral reef. Five sky ships had beaten them there and were lined up on a dazzlingly white beach, their troops and crew scattered along the beach or swimming in the water. Llian wished he was; in the tropical heat the cabin was stifling and the reek unbearable.

"That makes sixteen," he said. "Out of twenty-eight."

Yggur scanned the sky in every direction but saw no more. "And given we're so late, I wouldn't expect any more. I fear the other twelve ships are lost."

"Along with the five hundred people they were carrying," Llian said bleakly.

It was 3.30 p.m. when Yggur set the sky ship down on the sand, ten hours until the second rendezvous on Gwine. The other sky ships settled further along the beach and the troops exploded out of the cabins, staggered into the water, then lay on the sand in whatever shade they could find.

Llian could not blame them. He helped Yggur and Healer Lukey wash the vomit out of the door. Llian found his own shady spot and, despite his overwhelming fear of what was to come tonight and how unequipped he was to deal with it, fell asleep and did not wake until he heard the officers calling their troops to order eight hours later.

They gathered on the sand at midnight. He expected that the sealed orders would be opened and they would be told their mission, but they were ordered aboard in silence. No one was in any doubt about their destination, but there was considerable speculation about what they would face when they got there. Most of the soldiers thought, as Llian did, that they were on a suicide mission.

An hour and a half later, soon after they sighted the Isle of Gwine, a small light blinked in the distance.

"That's Karan's signal," Yggur said quietly. "All is ready."

It was a blow right over Llian's heart. "Karan's *there?*" he cried. "On Gwine, *all alone?*"

"There was no other way to synchronise the attacks," said Yggur.

Llian sat in the dark, fear alternating with fury. It made things a hundred times worse. Every time Karan had spied on the Merdrun they had detected her; the triplets would be hunting her with all their terrible power, and when they caught her they would torture her until she revealed everything, then force her to link to Sulien and kill them both.

He could not focus on anything save Karan, only miles away yet beyond reach, beyond helping. He was staring blindly out the window when everything went out of focus. The soldiers cried out.

"Yggur, what's happening?" Llian hissed. "Are the triplets—"

"Don't panic," Yggur said calmly. "Our mancers have worked a mass illusion to hide us." He tore the seal off his envelope and scanned the contents. "As we fly over the southern wall of the Merdrun's camp the illusion will fade. Fix the layout of the camp in your minds."

He handed the square-headed Captain Cubbers, whom everyone now called Cubo, a copy of the sketch map Karan had made after her spying mission.

"Timdey's squad will attack the enemy in their tents with fire and alchemical smoke blasters," said Cubo. "The Faellem and Hingis will create illusions to further confuse the enemy. My squad will secure the camp gates in case the enemy have reinforcements outside. Everyone else, do your best to create chaos so the troops who come through Malien's gate can carry out their appointed tasks."

Yggur turned to Llian. "I assume you know the layout of the camp?"

"I've seen Karan's map."

"Good. Janck thought you should fight 'like any proper man'—" Yggur grimaced. "—but I'm giving you a job more suited to your talents. Wilm's black sword may be some protection to you on the battlefield, but don't rely on it."

Llian nodded absently, unable to focus on anything but Karan being hunted by the triplets.

"You're to sneak away to the slave camp, find a way in and use your teller's voice to incite the slaves to rebellion."

They might have taken Karan already, might be torturing her right now . . .

"Llian!" Yggur said sharply. "Did you hear me?"

"Sneak away to the slave camp," Llian recited in a dead voice. "Find a way in and use your teller's voice to incite the slaves to rebellion."

"A slave revolt could mean the difference between some of the attack force surviving, and none."

"I'll do my best," he said dully.

"Don't do anything foolhardy."

The next ten minutes passed swiftly. Suddenly they were over the island, then swooping low over the massive southern wall of the enemy camp. It was lit by blazing columns, and Llian saw shocked guards on the wall dive to right and left as the sky ships burst out of the Faellem's mass illusion only yards above their heads.

The vessel to the right of Yggur's hurtled in even lower, accidentally impaling one of the wall guards on its left skid. It carried him, open-mouthed and thrashing, for twenty yards before he slipped off and fell out of sight.

Yggur's ship swooped low over rows of tents, then landed on a flat area with a crash that rattled Llian's teeth. Another sky ship landed on the left and a third on the right, and more beside them. Yggur pointed at the door and it popped open.

Cubo yelled, "Go, go!"

They leaped through the door and within seconds Llian heard the clash of sword on sword and the ululating scream of a man dying in agony. He prayed it was one of the enemy though that seemed unlikely.

Hingis lurched down the ladder, then the small, golden-skinned Faellem he had spent the flight talking to. They turned towards the southern wall, raised their arms together and most of the flares went out.

"Get moving!" said Yggur, and Llian caught a hint of fear in his voice. "The next flight of sky ships is coming in fast."

Llian's knees were shaking. He half-climbed, half-fell down the ladder, then stood at the bottom, having no idea what to do.

"Take this, you bloody fool! Then get out of the way."

Something struck him in the chest, hard—the black sword in its copper sheath. He buckled it on. Yggur's sky ship shot up.

The other vessels were gone, and soldiers were running in all directions, though in this light it was difficult to tell friend from foe. The next flight was racing over the southern wall; he had to get out of the way. He ducked low and ran south towards the tents, then crouched down and turned to check his surroundings.

The landing area had been paved with flat stones and might have been a parade ground. It was dimly lit by flares on poles a couple of hundred yards apart, though as he watched they both went out. Two sky ships were still on the ground, one apparently in the hands of the enemy. Another was slowly rising with several Merdrun swinging from its mooring ropes, trying to hold it down. And there was a great convulsion over to the left: hundreds of allied troops in a chaotic melee with the enemy.

To the south, more allied soldiers had attacked the tents, but they were empty. Llian's blood froze for it could only mean one thing—the Merdrun had been expecting them. But did they know about Malien's gate? If they did, there was no hope.

The last sky ship rose, but as it reached a hundred feet it intersected with a blazing lance hurled up in a fiery arc.

BOOM!

The airbag exploded, lighting up the camp like a summer's day. Pieces of metal, timber and blazing fabric spun through the air. Remarkably, the sky ship low in the air remained undamaged, but a spinning rotor struck the one captured by the Merdrun and it exploded even more catastrophically.

The searing blast hurled Llian backwards, knocking the wind out of him and ruining his night vision. He got up shakily and turned round and round, trying to get his bearings, but there was smoke everywhere and he could not tell which way he was facing. He tried to bring Karan's sketch map to mind, to find some reference point. It should have been for ever imprinted on his memory, but he could not recover it.

Downhill, he thought dazedly. *The camp gates are downhill and to the right.* He stumbled down a gentle slope, praying he was going the right way. Dimly, through the smoke, he glimpsed pieces of burning wreckage, blazing tents and groups of men fighting and dying, though with the Faellem's illusions warping everything around him it was impossible to know if what he was seeing was real.

He was creeping through sticky mud, thinking he must be close to the dam, when an awful thought stopped him in his tracks. Where was Malien's gate? Yggur had said it would open within minutes of the landing, bringing a larger force of soldiers, but there was no sign of it. They were needed desperately; without them, the troops from the sky ships would be lucky to last another ten minutes.

The noise of battle died away, then rose to a clamour and the thundering of hundreds of boots. He looked back. A mass of soldiers was pounding his way, pursued by a second group, though he could not tell which was friend and which was enemy.

In an instant they were on him, his own people, knocking him down without realising he was there and trampling him into the mud. There was a moment's respite, though not enough for him to get away. The pursuing Merdrun were coming fast.

He lay still, clutching the hilt of the black sword and praying its protective enchantment would do some good, then the Merdrun were there. Most of them leapt over his prone body but one, a big, heavy fellow, planted one booted foot on Llian's backside and the other on his head. The weight pushed his face into the mud until his nose struck something hard and he felt it break.

He must have gasped or choked, for the soldier skidded to a stop, then came back. Llian clutched the sword desperately. Could he stab the fellow? Not with the sword in its scabbard; if he showed signs of life the Merdrun would hack him in two. He might anyway; he could hear the soldier's heavy breathing.

"He's maggot food," said a voice close by. "Come on, there's killing to be done."

The first soldier kicked Llian in the side of the head and turned away. The blow dazed him and he lay still, blood pouring from his nose into the mud. The enemy ran on, and soon he heard the sounds of battle again, though it sounded more like slaughter.

He lurched to his feet, head and nose throbbing, and staggered the other way, keeping low. The Faellem's illusions weren't so strong down here, and Karan's map came back to mind. The camp gates were only a hundred yards further down, though how was he supposed to get through them?

As he approached he heard fighting ahead of him as well, then remembered that a squad had been ordered to take the gates and hold them. He went forward gingerly—covered in mud as he was, he could have been friend or foe, and in this bloody madness he might be cut down by his own people, unrecognised.

He scrubbed the mud off his forehead—absence of the black Merdrun glyph was his best protection from his own side—and looked back. Some of the flares on the walls had been relit, though they revealed little through the smoke. Fires blazed in half a dozen places on the western side, where the storerooms and other buildings had been. There was still no sign of Malien's gate.

Only a single lantern burned at the camp gates, and as he approached he saw bodies everywhere, Merdrun as well as his own people. The gates were closed and unguarded. Every man was dead including Captain

Cubo, and as Llian made his way through the bodies old nightmares rose to the surface. He wished he were a thousand miles away.

But Karan was here somewhere, and Sulien was in danger, and if he did not succeed, this battle would be the prelude to the end of his world. He turned the great timber wheel that lifted the bar to open the gates and was about to slip through when he realised that they could easily be barred again against the slaves—assuming he could free them.

He hacked the lifting rope off the wheel, cut it to pieces and chopped through the wheel as well. The black sword cut through the wood as if it were kindling. It was unlike any weapon he'd ever held—light but strong and its edge as sharp as the day he had dug it up from Mendark's hoard two months ago.

The enemy could still bar the gate manually, though it would take half a dozen people to heave the bar—a massive slab cut from a tree trunk—back in place. He went through, then stopped. A slave rebellion would fail instantly if none of them was armed. He collected knives from the dead and shoved them in his pack, then gathered all their swords, save one that was broken a third of the way from the tip, and warily headed down the rutted road into the darkness. He encountered no one and, following his mental image of Karan's Gwine map, headed towards the slave camp. It was not hard to find; the palisade wall must have required the felling of a small forest.

The gates were guarded, though only by four Merdrun, and they looked jumpy. No wonder, with flames and smoke gushing up from inside the army camp a mile away, and the sounds of fighting audible even from this distance. There could be more guards inside and others patrolling outside the walls, but he would have to risk that. There was no time to waste.

Llian crept around the back of the camp, listened for pacing guards and heard none, then found a place where the palisade felt flimsiest and thrust the tip of his sword into the timber. Any ordinary blade would only have penetrated an inch but the black sword went in three. He thrust again and again and finally it passed right through.

After ten minutes' heavy work he thrust with his right foot, and a section of the palisade a foot and a half square fell in. He shoved his armload of weapons through and wriggled into the camp, which was inches deep in mud and stank like the foulest privy in the slums of old Thurkad.

There was only a couple of feet between the palisade and the rear wall of a building with four solid walls, presumably a storeroom for food or supplies. From what Karan had told him, the slaves' sleeping shelters had roofs but no walls. He gathered his weapons and crept around the side, then stopped.

The open area ahead was crammed with thousands of slaves, all milling about excitedly. Clearly, the clamour at the camp had reached them. Hundreds had their eyes pressed to chinks in the palisade and were reporting to the others. Llian saw no evidence of guards inside; perhaps they had been called up to the battle.

He strode out into the middle, tossed the ten swords and eleven knives down in a clanking heap and yelled, "Wilm?"

The slaves stared at him, and Llian realised that he must be a sight; he was saturated in mud and the lower half of his face and chest were covered in blood. They looked hungrily at the weapons though no one made a move towards them. They were cowed by the Merdrun's brutality and perhaps suspected a trick.

He wiped his forehead again and pointed to it. "I'm not one of them. *Wilm!*"

A minute passed, then Wilm emerged from among them. He was filthy and his skin was the colour of mud, as if he had not bathed in the five weeks he had been held here. He looked thinner than before, yet harder and older—no longer a boy who had not yet grown into his body but a thin, intense and determined young man.

"Llian?" he whispered. "Can it really be you?"

He ran to Llian and embraced him, then stepped back, looking him up and down, and shook his hand. His grip was crushing, his bony hand callused.

"Aviel asked me to bring you your sword." Llian unbuckled the sheath and handed it to him.

"Aviel," Wilm said in a choked voice. "And you. Yet again you've come to save me. I have the best friends in the world."

"I think we're even on that score."

Tears formed in Wilm's eyes and Llian knew he was thinking about Dajaes. Wilm buckled on the black sword, then picked up the rest of the weapons.

"I'm going to address them," said Llian. "We've brought nearly four thousand troops—" assuming the gate had got there "—and if I can incite them to rebel—"

Wilm shook his head. "No need."

"But with my teller's voice . . ."

Wilm got out a wrapped phial and took a sniff of the contents. His shoulders went back, he stood straighter and taller, and the weariness fell from him.

"I'm one of them, Llian," he said quietly. "It's up to me now."

He headed towards the nearest slaves, carrying the weapons like the precious gifts they were. He held them out, and a number came forward, each taking a sword or a knife. There was no rush, no fighting; everyone seemed unnaturally calm.

Wilm addressed them softly and simply—he would not want to alert the guards outside. "We have to kill the Merdrun," he said, "or they'll kill us, then destroy Santh the way they've ruined your beautiful island. Will you follow me? But not as slaves—never again as slaves. Will you follow me as proud Gwinians, to take your country back?"

A stir passed through the Gwinians, and Llian knew that no speech he could have given, even in his most compelling teller's voice, could have moved them more than those simple words by a fellow slave. It was staggering how the awkward youth Llian had met at Shand's house in Casyme three months ago had transformed himself.

"Wait by the gate," said Wilm to the gathering. He went forward and spoke softly to the leaders. "This many minutes," he said, holding up five fingers. "How many guards are outside, Llian?"

"Four."

Wilm smiled grimly. "How did you get in?"

"Cut a hole." Llian pointed.

Wilm led half a dozen of the armed Gwinians back to the hole

Llian had come through, and outside. He followed in silence, clutching his own knife. There was little he could do to help, given that he was useless as a fighter, but the slave camp unnerved him and he could not bear to spend another minute inside it.

Wilm and his men crept around the palisade wall towards the front. Llian followed, keeping out of the way and counting the seconds. What was Wilm's plan? The Merdrun were brilliant fighters; how could he hope to overcome them with half a dozen poorly armed Gwinians?

Smoke had drifted down from the Merdrun's encampment and there were haloes around the twin lights over the gates to the slave camp. They only lit the area immediately outside the gates; thirty feet away in the darkness, Wilm and the Gwinians were invisible.

Wilm waited, tense as wire. Llian's thoughts drifted back to the battle up the hill. The fighting had died down. Were all the soldiers from the sky ships dead? If Malien's gate had failed, they soon would be. And what about Karan?

He heard a distant boom and flames climbed a hundred feet in the sky. Another sky ship destroyed? The sounds of fighting grew again. The Merdrun guarding the gates of the slave camp moved closer together and stared up at the fortress, whispering among themselves. They looked unnerved; they had never experienced anything except swift victory.

The five minutes were up. Inside the slave camp someone cried out, then four thousand throats roared defiance and the gates shook as if they had been struck by hundreds of shoulders at once. The guards spun round, staring at the gates. There came another roar, another blow that shook the gates. And another.

"Now!" Wilm said softly.

His band crept forward until they were only twenty feet away then, as the Gwinians roared and shook the gates again, they rushed the distracted guards, who had their backs to them. The Merdrun whirled and one struck at Wilm, but the black sword sheared straight through the lesser weapon, leaving the man holding a useless hilt. Wilm cut him down and stabbed a second Merdrun in the thigh. He lurched sideways and Wilm's second blow killed him.

The Gwinians had not done so well—the third guard had killed one of them and, with a savage sweeping blow, had cut both hands off another as he wielded his sword two-handed. The third guard went for the next Gwinian, who hurled his knife. It went through the guard's throat and pinned him to the planks of the gate.

The other Gwinians surrounded the fourth guard and killed him, then dispatched the third man. Wilm went through the guards' pockets, found a long iron key and unlocked the gates.

The Gwinians surged through, some arming themselves with the weapons of the dead guards, then followed Wilm up the track towards the Merdrun's camp.

Llian watched them go. Against the odds he had succeeded, though he did not see how Wilm or the allies could prevail. If Karan's numbers were correct there were at least ten thousand Merdrun up there, the toughest and most experienced fighters in the void. The Merdrun had never been defeated, so how could a few thousand troops, plus four thousand inexperienced and mostly unarmed Gwinians succeed against an army forewarned of the attack?

They could not.

55

I'VE COME HERE TO DIE

As Hingis lurched down the ladder onto the paved ground of the fortress, for the first time in twenty years he was free of pain and almost happy. He had made a friend!

He had spent all his waking hours on the long, wild journey from Zile talking about the art of illusion with Culligon, a young Faellem from the icy forests of Mirrilladell. Culligon, like Hingis, felt sure he was going to die on Gwine, and it had relaxed the chilly reserve the Faellem normally showed towards the other human species.

"It's forbidden to speak about our arts to outsiders," Culligon said after they had been in the air for an hour or two. His voice was high and melodious, and Hingis could have listened to him all night just for the beauty and purity of his speech. Even more marvellous, Culligon gave no indication that Hingis's hideous face and body mattered to him.

"But in this case ..." Culligon had continued, "... since we're going to be killed, yet by our deaths we might save many others and possibly this world we've come to love almost as much as our beautiful Tallallame ..." Tears formed in his eyes and he fell silent.

"Your people were exiled from Tallallame long ago, weren't they?" said Hingis. He did not know the ancient Histories well.

"Not exiled, just unable to return. And not me—I was born here. My ancestors came to Santhenar almost four thousand years ago in the hunt for Shuthdar, after he stole Rulke's Golden Flute and broke open the Way Between the Worlds for the first time. It exposed the Three Worlds to the deadly void and the savage creatures that dwelt there, and every human species was desperate to close the Way again."

"I barely know that story," Hingis prompted.

"Shuthdar, who had been hunted for an aeon, was finally trapped. The enchanted flute had drawn out his life by a thousand years, though by then he was decrepit beyond imagining, yet he was determined to never give up his most precious possession. He destroyed the Golden Flute, but that brought down the Forbidding that sealed the Three Worlds off from each other, and from the void. It trapped many Aachim here, and my people, and also the three most powerful Charon: Rulke, Yalkara and Kandor."

"It must have been a terrible thing," reflected Hingis, "to have lived on the most beautiful world of all, and to for ever be cut off from it."

"We had a saying to describe it," said Culligon. "*The loneliness of Faelamor.* She was the greatest and most long-lived of us all, and she suffered for every one of those four thousand years. But enough of the Histories; tell me about your arts of illusion. They must be utterly different from our own, and I'm eager to learn new ways in the time I have left."

"Me too," Hingis said. "Because I've come here to die."

"You look like a man with the best of his life before him."

Hingis told the story of his love for Ussarine, his bitter choice and his twin sister's death, briefly and baldly and without self-pity.

Culligon considered his words for a long time. "Choices make our lives, and can break them and perhaps make them anew. As I said, it is utterly forbidden for us to speak of our arts, and yet, in the cause of freedom . . . I will tell you what I may."

What I may, over the eternal, brutal flight, turned out to be a remarkable amount about the art of illusion. It had opened Hingis's eyes. He had tried a few of Culligon's suggestions and found that they transformed his art, lifting it to a higher plane.

Now, as he reached the paved ground and scanned the Merdrun's vast camp, he was excited about the possibilities and about working with Culligon on collaborative illusions which could be so much greater than either of them could do individually.

As he turned to ask which illusion Culligon planned to use first, the Faellem sighed and crumpled to the ground, a Merdrun throwing spike embedded in his heart. He was dead without ever knowing that he had been hit.

Tears pricked Hingis's eyes, the pain he had forgotten on the turbulent journey flooded back, and a titanic rage overwhelmed him. He was cursed! He was destined to never have a sister, a lover or a friend. Life was determined to rob him of every good thing he had ever gained for himself.

So be it! He no longer cared because his life would soon be over, and that was good. He would gladly sacrifice himself to aid his people and his world—it was the best thing he could possibly do.

He traced the trajectory of the throwing spike back to its source, a squad of Merdrun on a mound fifty yards away. Hingis focused his wits and his art as he had never done before and walked out into the open, facing them and daring them to attack him. But before they could, he thrust both arms out towards the squad and its scarred leader, summoned all the power stored in his twisted and throbbing bones and conjured his most terrifying illusion—a rampaging lyrinx.

He combined it with an illusion Culligon had taught him that induced witless convulsions, then with a roar of fury cast it at the Merdrun.

The illusion sighed away towards them and disappeared. The Merdrun stared at Hingis in astonishment, then started mocking him for a monster, a hideous little cripple. He was sure the illusion had failed, that he had got the combination wrong. The scarred leader took out another throwing spike, kissed it and drew back his arm. Hingis did not move; whichever way he tried to run, the spike would impale him.

"I'll show you a monster!" cried Hingis and worked the illusion again.

The scarred leader let out a shriek of terror and began flailing about with his sword in one hand and the spike in the other, striking at the sky, the ground and his own subordinates. His men were shrieking and convulsing, attacking the ground and the grass, the stone bastion behind them and each other, and even their own arms and legs, as if everything they saw was a beast about to tear their limbs from their bodies. Within minutes they had cut one another down, but still they thrashed on the bloody ground until every one of them was dead.

Hingis looked upon his work and found it good. The pain of his twisted bones was utterly gone. Nothing could touch him now.

He turned, seeking his next target. He felt serene.

56

YOU'RE GOING TO DIE

Malien had chosen the most imposing place in Zile to create her gate— the broad granite-column-lined central boulevard that stretched a mile from one part of the abandoned city to the other. The rotors of Aachim sky ships had been used to blast the drifted sand away for several hundred yards and lay bare the ancient paving slabs, then blazing torches had been fixed to the tops of the columns. To either side, the beautiful ruins stood like shadowy sentinels.

In this tranquil place Janck stalked back and forth before his assembled forces, cursing everyone and everything. Sulien had never seen him so rattled. She had to tell him what Gergrig had said, but his guards would not let her near.

"What the blazes is the matter *now?*" he bellowed at Malien.

She scowled but did not reply. Sulien did not think she had the strength. Her people had made all the preparations twenty-four hours ago, but Karan's call had not come, and today they'd had to do it all again. Malien and four of her most skilled Aachim mancers, all males, had been preparing the massive gate for hours and they were all exhausted.

Nausea washed back and forth through Sulien's belly. Something was terribly wrong. And where was Llian? He'd been sent away days ago and she knew he was in terrible danger.

"This gate will be bigger than any that has ever been made on Santhenar," said Tallia, "and it's got to last far longer. It's taking everything Malien has, and more."

"Why does it have to be bigger?" said Janck.

Tallia rolled her eyes. "Because you're sending a hundred cavalry through, and an armoured warhorse weighs ten times as much as the soldier riding it. The loading on the gate, and on the people powering and controlling it, is enormous, and if Malien gets anything wrong bad things can happen."

"Like what?"

"Like none of the cavalry ever being seen again. Or the gate and everything inside it exploding so catastrophically that it would level Zile and melt the ruins for a mile around in all directions."

Janck rubbed his ample belly and took several steps backwards. "Why does it have to last longer?"

"I should have thought that was obvious," she said with stinging sarcasm. "If five troops can pass through abreast every second, which is optimistic, it'll take nine and a third minutes for twenty-eight hundred to go through the gate to Gwine. Realistically it'll be more like twelve minutes, and that's an awfully long time to hold open a gate—even a normal-sized gate. The strain will be enormous; I'll be surprised if Malien and her mancers can manage it."

"I'm not interested in excuses," barked Janck. "Tell her to make it happen."

"You don't know what you're talking about," Malien said coldly.

"I give the orders around here."

"You can't order Malien to defy the laws of mancery," said Tallia, "any more than you can order your troops to swim up into the sky. If the gate fails before everyone has gone through, the very best that will happen is that everyone still inside it will die."

"And the worst?"

"I already told you that."

"Without the gate, the mission to kill the triplets fails," said Janck. "If they live, they'll soon reopen the Crimson Gate and that will begin the end of the world. Malien has to find a way and she's got to do it quick." He checked a pocket chronometer the size of a small cauliflower. "It's 1.22 a.m. If all goes well *this time*, Karan will call in eight minutes, and the sky ships will land their troops ten minutes later. Once she gives the word I can't call them back. The gate must be ready in eight minutes, so *see to it*!" He stalked away.

Tallia went across to Malien. Sulien followed, trying to look inconspicuous. She had to find out what was really going on before it was too late.

"I heard," said Malien. Her face was pinched, her lips white and her breathing ragged.

"Is there anything more—"

"No!" she snapped. "Move! You're within the gate space."

Tallia moved away and checked the gear in her battle pack. She had done so three times in the last hour. Behind her, Janck was loudly counting down the minutes. She ground her teeth.

Sulien crept across and caught her by the arm. "Tallia," she said in a desolate voice, "where did Daddy really go?"

Tallia glanced at Janck. He shook his head. "It's a secret," she said unhappily.

Sulien looked from Janck to Tallia, then back to Janck, and the blood drained from her face. "You sent *Daddy* to Gwine with the sky ships?" she cried.

"Shut her up!" snapped Janck. "There could be spies, even here."

Sulien ran at Janck, lowered her head and butted him in his great round belly. He stumbled back, tripped and fell. "You sent Daddy to Gwine to be killed! And Mummy!" she screamed. "You foul, stinking *monster.*"

Janck rose, his face the colour of a storm cloud. "Get the brat out of my sight."

"The enemy know the attack is coming!" cried Sulien. "I heard Gergrig say so."

"What?" he cried, staggering back. "No, that's impossible. Take her away."

Tallia took Sulien's hand and squeezed it hard. "She's got to relay Karan's call. No one else can do it."

"Then stop her mouth!"

"Sulien has a great gift," said Tallia, "and I want to know what she heard."

"As do I," said Malien. "Quickly, child!"

Sulien told them how she had found and befriended the drum boy Uigg, Gergrig's son, how Uigg had realised who she was, and his and Gergrig's final words.

I . . . I'm afraid I won't do you proud, Uigg had said, *when battle comes.*

I fear that too, son, said Gergrig. *But you won't have long to wait. The fools think they can take me by surprise.* Me! *Go and fill your belly; it won't be long now.*

"Gergrig can't know," said Janck in hopeless denial. "He detected you and fed you lies."

"If he'd detected Sulien," said Malien, "he would have killed her."

"Get rid of her!" he bellowed. "How can I think with her nonsense in my ears?"

Sulien pulled free, pointed a finger at Janck and spoke without thinking. "You're going to die," she whispered. "As soon as you go through the gate."

"Sulien!" cried Tallia. "Never say such things."

Sulien flushed scarlet. "Sorry." She did not know why she had said it.

Janck reeled, then walked in a tight circle, rubbing his face and shooting her desperate glances. "Nonsense," he repeated. "It's all nonsense."

One-thirty passed, and Karan did not call. One-forty passed. Janck was pallid and sweating. Tallia went back to Malien. "Have you heard?"

"No! Go away!"

Sulien stumbled back and forth, trying to think. Karan and Llian were in desperate danger, though if things got really bad she could dematerialise. But Llian was clumsy, accident-prone and not a fighter; he would be lucky to survive a minute on the battlefield. Was there any way she could use her gift to help him? Sulien could think of nothing.

One-forty-five. One-fifty.

A sharp pain struck behind Sulien's eyes and the block on the link gave. *Mummy, what's going on?* she cried across the link. *Are you all right? Mummy, what about Daddy? Mummy! Mummy!*

I'm all right, Karan gasped. *Now!*

The pain spread and burned, and Sulien heard sick laughter. The triplets were attacking through the link. She clapped her hands to the sides of her head and screamed. Malien snatched at her but missed. Sulien reeled around in a circle, fell to her knees, still screaming, then the pain and the laughter were cut off. Karan had re-blocked the link.

Sulien turned to Malien and gasped, "Mummy said *now*!" She got up shakily, her head throbbing again. "The sky ships are there."

Malien issued swift orders to the four male Aachim, and they began to work. "You have ten minutes," she said to Janck.

He made a choking sound in his throat, as if he had not thought the gate would actually succeed, then took an envelope from his pocket, called his officers to him and tore the seal off. Sulien crouched and watched him suspiciously.

"W-we're taking the gate to the Isle of Gwine," said Janck. "Our cavalry will storm through the moment it opens. They'll be followed by your company, Clabb," he said to the thin, twitching officer on his left.

"You'll poison the enemy's water cisterns, then attack their armoury and food stores with fire barrels, burning everything you find and creating as much chaos as you can.

"Thix," he said to the next officer, a dark fellow with black eyebrows the size of drowned rats, shading tiny eyes, "your company will burn the soldiers' tents, hopefully with them inside. Gunce—" (a small, delicately boned officer whose veins could be seen through the skin of his forehead) "—go for the Merdrun's command post, kill every officer you see and disrupt their battlefield communications. And your company, Pikell—" (a massive, troll-like, slab-faced fellow) "—will take their key defensive positions and hold them at all costs. Got it, everyone?"

"Yes, Commander," they said.

"We're going to Gwine for a single reason," Janck went on. "So Hissper and his squad can hunt down the triplets and kill them. They're the key; only the triplets can reopen the Crimson Gate, and that must be prevented at all costs."

The pallid, hairless Hissper, whose black eyes were mere slits, nodded, a sinuously reptilian movement that made the skin on the back of Sulien's neck crawl.

"Once the triplets are dead the job is done," said Janck. "On the signal, fight your way to the rendezvous point and we'll try to bring everyone back, either via the sky ships or, if it proves impossible for them to land, the gate. But it will only open fleetingly the second time, and anyone who can't get to it will be left to their fate. A fate that, in the Merdrun's hands, will be most unpleasant."

He checked his chronometer again. "One-fifty-five. Where's the damned gate?"

"Still not ready," Tallia said quietly.

"When . . . will . . . it . . . be . . . ready?" he said through his teeth.

Tallia glanced at Malien, who was sighting through some incomprehensible Aachim instrument made of the soft iridescent metal bismuth, with oval opal inserts along the sides and quartz lenses. "A few minutes, I'd say."

Sulien's throat had clamped so tight she could hardly breathe. Why was it taking so long? Could Llian be . . . ? No, she dared not even think it.

Janck paced, scowled, paced then came back. "Three minutes! What the hell's wrong?"

The Aachim were making slow movements in a trance-like state. "Are you asking me to interrupt them to find out?" Tallia said in a deadly voice.

Janck seemed close to breaking point. "Damn it, Magister, my sky-ship troops are dying through lack of the support I promised them. It's unbearable."

"My friends and allies are there too, Commander. And plenty of Malien's people."

And Mummy and Daddy, thought Sulien, her heart aching.

Five minutes passed, then ten. She could almost smell the blood being shed on Gwine. Fourteen minutes . . .

The air shimmered before them, then pale yellow lightning crackled and entwined and twisted to form an egg-shaped circlet, the bottom half wider than the top. It was fifteen feet wide and twenty feet tall, and a milky swirling grey inside. A hot, humid wind gushed out of it, carrying the odour of spicy plants, the moisture condensing in the wintry air of Zile to form billows of mist.

Sulien crept forward, peered through the gate and saw a high stone wall in the distance, running along the crest of a ridge between two small cliff-bounded hills, each topped by a wooden watchtower. It was just as Karan had described it.

"It's opened inside the fortress," said Tallia. "Malien, is it ready?"

"Yes," gasped Malien. "Go! Can't hold it long."

Janck signalled to his cavalry. The horsemen trotted down the boulevard in pairs, leapt into the gate and disappeared. It took a minute and a half for the hundred to pass through. Clabb's company followed, then Thix's. Another three minutes.

"Hissper, get going," said Janck.

Hissper's black-clad band of ten assassins glided into the gate and vanished. Sulien was glad to see them go. They were horrible, but she prayed they succeeded.

"Can't hold it," gasped Malien. "Anyone who *must* go, go now."

Gunce's and Pikell's companies went through. Six minutes had passed but over a thousand troops still waited for their turn at the gate and it was starting to look ragged. Sulien did not see how the Aachim could hold it long enough. If she were to do anything for Llian, she had to go now. Dare she? She must. She ran forward and sprang into the gate.

"Sulien, stop!" shrieked Malien.

As Sulien looked back the egg-shaped circlet wobbled; the yellow lightning forming it went dull, and for an awful few seconds she thought the gate was going to collapse, then Malien regained control and shot Tallia an imploring look.

Janck was no longer pale, no longer sweating. He drew his sabre, squared his shoulders and strode into the gate. Tallia raced after him. Sulien, fearing they would stop her, bolted ahead and disappeared.

Tallia hurtled after Sulien. The gate picked her up and spun her, tumbled her head over heels and hung her upside down while a hot wind roared in her ears, then after a minute or two spat her out at the other end, dizzy and disoriented.

She took three steps and stumbled over a body, a rotund man in a commander's uniform. A huge gash in his chest was making gurgling sounds, but Janck was dead, just as Sulien had predicted. It was a chilling start, the worst.

As she came to her feet a stocky Merdrun warrior came at her, swinging a serrated double-edged sword in a vertical stroke intended to cleave her head in two. But Tallia was vastly experienced in combat with and without weapons and had been training solidly for the past five weeks. She sidestepped then kicked him under the jaw so hard that his neck snapped; he fell back, alive but paralysed.

She looked around frantically. Behind her the gate was disgorging troops like a catapult, sometimes one at a time, sometimes in clumps of three or four. To the left Clabb's company was racing down to its target. The other companies were spreading out in all directions through the smoke. She could not see Hissper's assassins; they had already vanished on their murderous business.

Neither could Tallia see any of the green-uniformed troops who had come in on the sky ships. Were they all dead?

Most vitally, where was Sulien, and what on earth had possessed her to come through the gate to such a deadly place? The revelation about Llian being here, of course. She was nowhere in sight. Now Tallia thought of it, Sulien had been showing signs of distress for days. And no wonder.

Another Merdrun attacked. Tallia fought him absently, killed him and was moving on when the gate spat out two halves of a man—one of Captain Gunce's group—belched a spray of blood and vanished.

It had been open for eight or nine minutes but the passage had been much slower than expected; no more than sixteen hundred of the twenty-eight hundred had passed through, and Malien would not reopen the gate to send them. They had agreed that in advance, otherwise she and her Aachim would be too exhausted to recreate the gate for the retreat.

But sixteen hundred was not enough.

57

IT VANISHED

As Sulien tumbled head over heels through the gate, the inside of her skull still felt as if it had been burned. If Karan had taken a few seconds longer to block the link, Sulien knew she would be dead.

And Llian was in terrible danger. He was the cleverest and most wonderful teller in the world, but he was useless at most other things. He was always falling out of the fruit trees in the orchard and once he had nearly amputated his toes digging out carrots. She had to save him.

But when the gate tossed her out onto the bloody, corpse-strewn ground of the Merdrun's fortress, she saw that she had made a terrible mistake. How could she even find Llian in this chaos? She scuttled under the blackened wreckage of a sky ship cabin and hid. It looked as though it had been blown in two, then partly burned, though the pilot's seat and levers were intact and thankfully there were no bodies inside.

Twenty yards away, a Merdrun warrior hacked down a skinny nervous officer, poor Captain Clabb, and looked around for someone else to attack. Sulien squeezed under the tilted cabin where the firelight did not reach. The wreckage was still hot, and smoke stung her eyes and nose, but it was better than smelling the blood.

She closed her eyes but could not stop reliving Clabb's death or imagining Llian being killed the same way. How could she have imagined she could help him? She had made things much worse—delivered herself to an enemy who wanted her dead.

Sulien was checking that all was clear between her hideout and Malien's gate so she could scuttle back to it when, with an unpleasant belch, it sprayed blood everywhere and vanished.

Now she had no way of escape. She poked her head out, looking for familiar faces, but did not see any. What was she to do? If she left her hiding place she was bound to be caught. Could the triplets detect her presence? They had sensed Karan every time she had spied on them so they would probably realise Sulien was here before long. She looked out from under the other side of the cabin and saw thousands of enemy reserves waiting in formation on the north-eastern and eastern hills. The Merdrun were so confident of victory that they had not bothered to send them down.

It was hopeless. The allies would all be killed, and the Merdrun would take Santhenar and ruin it just like they had ruined Gwine.

"Daddy, Daddy," she whispered, "where are you?"

No answer. Only one chance remained—the triplets. Their spells, based on power gained from drinking the lives of innocent people, made the Merdrun stronger and Gergrig much stronger. And Sulien knew the triplets better than anyone. She had to locate them and find a way to break their power—quickly. If she succeeded it would give the army, and Karan and Llian, a chance. If she failed, it would be hideous.

She dared not use her far-sensing gift. The triplets would recognise her immediately and hunt her down. She would use the new, untaught gift that allowed her to sense feelings and emotions from afar.

It did not take long; the triplets' emotions were so strong and strange and sick that they shone like mud-brown beacons. Sulien peered out, plotted the safest path to them and, so afraid that she was fighting not to throw up, began to crawl across the corpse-strewn battlefield.

58

THEY LOVE DRINKING LIVES

Where was the gate? It should have opened ten minutes ago. Had Malien failed? Without the rest of the troops the battle would be over in minutes. Without the gate and Hissper's assassins, there was no point being here.

In spirit form again, Karan made her way across the series of little battlefields within the walls encircling the great Merdrun camp, searching for Gergrig. She did not see him, nor anyone else she recognised, but there were many bodies, and few of them were the enemy. The troops from the sky ships had taken terrible casualties and the odds were high that Llian was one of them.

She dared not pursue that thought; it would only undermine her when she needed all her wits about her. The huge walled camp was now a maze of smoking pieces of sky ship, dead soldiers, broken weapons, burning buildings and blasted cisterns whose tops had fallen in, turning them into pits of unknown depth that it would be easy to fall into in the smoky dark and impossible to get out of.

And the night was thick with illusions that Karan, who had much experience of the incomparable arts of the Faellem, recognised at once. Without their illusions, carefully tailored to confuse the Merdrun but not the allies, every one of their troops would now be dead.

Boom!

Several hundred yards away, near the smoking rags of the soldiers' tents, the air was hissing into a luminous oval halo—the gate. A pair of horsemen burst out, their mounts bucking and whinnying in their terror. Gates were bad enough for people, who at least knew what to expect. How much more terrifying would the passage be for an animal?

The cavalry poured forth, a company of about a hundred. Janck's dumb idea, she presumed. On an open battlefield in daytime armoured horsemen might have decimated the Merdrun, who surely had not fought cavalry before, but in this dark, crowded camp there were too many obstacles to fall over or into, too many places where a horse might break a leg or its rider his neck. It was unlikely any of them would survive the next hour. Karan turned away, disgusted. She cared more for horses than for most of the people she knew.

She searched for signs of the Faellem but did not see them; they were too well hidden. Their arts, honed over more than fifty thousand years, were uncanny.

Nor was there any sign of the triplets. The previous magiz had been easy to find; she had always been close to the greatest mayhem, drinking the lives of the dying. But perhaps, with the summon stone now so mighty, they could obtain the power they needed elsewhere.

No! Karan remembered their greedy lust as they had drained the first group of acolytes. *They love drinking lives; they crave having power over the powerless.*

"Karan?" said a low voice behind her. Tallia.

"Yes?" She was behind Karan, looking all around. Tallia's art was sufficient to tell that Karan was nearby, though not enough to see her in the disembodied state.

"Embody yourself? We need to talk."

Why? Pain speared through Karan. Was Llian dead?

She triggered the spell that dematerialised her body from the tree fork several miles away and, with even more pain than usual, materialised it here. Instantly the churning in her belly was back; she was sure she had eaten a bad oyster. She threw up violently.

Tallia, who was almost a head taller than Karan, effortlessly scooped her up. "Can't talk in the open." She carried her past a line of shredded tents to the smoking ruins of a storeroom.

"What is it?" Karan's teeth were chattering, for Tallia had the sick look of someone bearing awful news. "Is . . . it Llian?"

"I don't know anything about him."

Relief flooded Karan. "Did he even get here?"

"Yes, he was on Yggur's sky ship."

"He's hopeless at fighting," Karan said frantically. "Why did Janck send him anyway?"

"I have no idea, but Janck's dead. Karan, it's Sulien," said Tallia, then stopped.

Karan clutched at her heart. "The triplets got to her, didn't they? I was too slow to block the link; I heard her scream." She grabbed Tallia's hands. "Is she . . . ?" She could not say it. Just thinking it was unbearable.

"Sulien was all right, last I saw." Tallia looked even sicker. "Karan, she came through the gate."

"*What?*" Karan shrieked.

Tallia shoved a hand across her mouth. "Shh!" She checked outside, then came back and said in a rush, "No one had the faintest idea what she was planning. She just ran into the gate. Janck and I went after her but there was no sign of her."

Karan had no strength left. She slumped to the ashy floor of the storeroom. "Why would she come to the most dangerous place in the world," she said dazedly, "after all we've done to protect her?"

"She spied on Uigg and heard Gergrig was expecting an attack," said Tallia. "And then she discovered Llian was here, and walking into a trap . . ."

"The triplets must have lured her here," said Karan, getting up. "We've got to find her before they do."

"How?" said Tallia. "Anyone out in the open will be killed in seconds."

"We've got to find her," Karan said implacably.

"What if she's safer where she is?"

"What the hell are you talking about?"

"She's a clever, sensible girl."

"Really sensible," Karan snarled, "coming to the enemy's camp."

"You once told me Sulien is good at hiding and not being seen. If you go looking for her you'll attract attention to her, and if you're caught—"

"So now I'm a danger to my own daughter, am I?" Karan snapped.

"Yes, you are. I think—"

Tallia broke off as a squad of black-clad men and women went by so stealthily that they appeared to be gliding. Karan shuddered.

"Is that . . . ?" she whispered.

"Hissper and his assassination squad, hunting the magiz."

The assassins crept from one patch of darkness to another, making their way up the slope in the direction of a small cliff-bound hill due north. But as they crossed a rivulet the ground erupted, then dozens of Merdrun encircled the assassins. They fought desperately but the Merdrun's numbers were too great, and one by one the assassins were cut down until all were dead.

"That's it," said Tallia in a deathly voice. "The mission has failed. It's all been for nothing."

59

SO WE'RE TRAPPED

"There's nothing more we can do here," Tallia said grimly. "I'd better signal a retreat and call the sky ships down."

"The Merdrun will shoot them out of the air," said Karan.

"Then it'll have to be the gate, assuming Malien's people have the strength to reopen it."

"The enemy will be expecting that too."

"We've no choice. Call Malien—"

"*I can't link!* I can only contact her through Sulien."

"Are you saying," said Tallia with an uncharacteristic shiver, "that there's no way to contact Malien?"

"Yes."

"Why can't one of the Aachim do it?"

"Mind linking is a very rare gift."

Tallia swallowed. "Then call Sulien."

"The moment I unblocked her link last time, the triplets attacked her. If I do it again, they'll find her long before Malien can reopen the gate, and Gergrig will know where it's going to open. He'd take the gate and send his army through to attack Zile."

"Then we're trapped and we're all going to die," said Tallia. "Unless . . ."

"What?"

"Unless you can find the triplets and kill them."

60

THEY'RE KILLING MUMMY!

Llian caught up with the freed Gwinians as they followed Wilm up to the Merdrun camp, though he did not plan to fight with them. Karan was somewhere in this chaos and he had to find her.

After the Gwinians attacked, he slipped up the splintery wooden stairs to the top of the watchtower. A short distance to the north, in the smaller western half of the camp, there had been a number of rude wooden buildings—storehouses, cookhouses, eating halls and all the other structures required in a semi-permanent camp—though these had been targeted in the early attacks and most had been burned.

On the left side of the stream, further up the slope, stood a cluster of large tents, mostly blue and one red, which probably belonged to Gergrig and his officers. Further on a group of yellow tents would be for the triplets and their acolytes.

North-east of the gates the ground was bare for half a mile. More than a thousand orange tents had stood there for the common soldiers, though they had also been burned. North of them was the paved parade ground where the sky ships had landed. Half a mile further on the ground rose to a gentle mound where a battle was raging.

Karan would not go near Gergrig—he was too dangerous—but she might go after the triplets to eliminate the threat to Sulien and to prevent the Crimson Gate being opened. Where would they be?

He climbed down and headed up towards the burned buildings. The smoke was thick there and reeked of charred meat and grain. There were bodies outside several of the buildings and more inside. Llian did not go in—the past hour had given him memories for a whole year of nightmares—but he had to be armed.

The Gwinians had taken all the fallen weapons, though beneath a corpse he found a badly notched sword with the tip broken off—better than nothing. He buckled it on and headed up to the officers' tents, which were unguarded. Each held no more than spare clothes, eating and drinking utensils and other sundry items. The largest blue tent, which he assumed to be Gergrig's, contained a number of locked metal chests, but at the entrance Llian felt an overwhelming premonition of danger and went no further. Mancers knew how to protect their treasures.

The yellow tents must have belonged to the young female acolytes, judging by the clothing. There were also several small books written in Merdrun glyphs and a large chart on grey leather containing rows of symbols in various colours. They meant nothing to him either.

The last tent stood by itself and was red with a green rope down the ridgeline. The triplets' tent, he assumed; Karan had seen the old magiz working in such a tent on one of her visits to Cinnabar. This one was larger than all the others except Gergrig's—it had to accommodate three large women. He was hesitating outside when Sulien's terrified voice rang through his mind.

Daddy, help! They're killing Mummy!

His heart gave the desperate lurch of a fish trying to free itself from a hook. "Who?" he gasped. "Who's got her?"

No answer, of course. Sendings could sometimes reach him, if the sender was gifted enough, but he had no way of answering.

They're killing Mummy! That could mean the triplets, but it could also mean Gergrig and his soldiers.

"Where is she, Sulien?" he said uselessly.

He stepped out from between the tents and scanned the camp. The fire near the top of the northern hill burned as white and bright as before. The battle against the north-western wall continued, now lit by bonfires lit on top of the wall. Despite the intervention of close to two thousand Gwinians the Merdrun still had the upper hand and were slowly squeezing the trapped soldiers into a tighter space.

The battle around the north-eastern mound had broken up into a series of smaller conflicts, but these were too far away for Llian to tell who was winning. The Merdrun, he thought gloomily. They always won and, though Wilm had led the rest of the Gwinians that way, what could they do?

The triplets could be anywhere, and so could Gergrig, though Llian imagined he would be in the thick of the fighting. It was more probable that the triplets had Karan, but where?

Their tent was a mess of clothes and robes, half-eaten meals, discarded underwear and boots, and various items that might have been pieces of strange jewellery or for ritual use. He hurled the clothes about, searching for anything that might give him a clue to their whereabouts.

After several minutes' searching he found, beneath a pile of underwear, several scraps of paper. One contained a crudely drawn torus, apparently carved from stone, which had been coloured red with a fingertip dipped in blood. It must have been done some time ago for the blood was flaking and had gone a red-brown colour. It had to signify the blood torus, a chilling symbol but no use in finding Karan, and time was running out. *They're killing Mummy!*

He looked down at the second scrap of paper. It depicted what he first thought to be an eye with something inside it, though he subsequently realised that it was more likely to represent a cave containing a tall vase— or a high, narrow altar—with rays or tongues of fire rising from the top.

It did not help at all.

61

IT BARELY HURT AT ALL

Karan had scoured the camp for Sulien and the triplets but had found neither, though Sulien was exceptionally good at hiding.

But Karan could not stop sensing the triplets. They were capering around a fire, gleefully drinking lives and sending surges of power to Gergrig to maintain his invincibility in battle.

To do their foul business they had to be close to the dying, though she did not think they would be on the defensive walls among the patrolling guards. Unlikely they would be on the battlefield either— Gergrig would not risk them in such chaos. They must be on one of the three hills, and the northern one was highest and had the best view of the camp.

She closed her eyes and rotated slowly, trying to sense them out. Their presence was in her mind whichever way she faced, though it was overwhelmingly strong when she was looking north. They had to be somewhere on that hill.

No time to waste. She found a hiding place for her physical body between a cluster of boulders in the centre of the camp, near where two rivulets became one and the ground was boggy. It wasn't very safe but it was the best she could do, and she used the disembodiment spell at once. Instantly she detected an eager alertness, a salivating greed and a sick hunger. The triplets knew she was in the camp.

There was no time to plan—in spirit form she raced north, then up the steep slope of the hill, up a thirty-foot cliff and onto the crest. All vegetation had been cleared from the top and it was now a bare dome of rock with a crudely built wooden watchtower, twenty feet high, at the highest point. A rickety ladder led to a platform at the top, barely large enough for two guards to stand there.

Where were the triplets? As she drifted across the hilltop she caught a whiff of scalding air and the smell of hot metal issuing from a crack in the rocks. There must be a considerable fire somewhere below. At the left-hand side of the hill, where it met the ridge, a narrow ledge ran halfway across the face of the cliff to the lens-shaped mouth of a cave partly concealed by an overhang. The triplets had to be inside. But did they know she was coming?

As tense as wire, Karan floated along the ledge to the corner of the cave mouth and peered in. The interior was partly concealed by a screen made from woven strips of green leather, behind which a fire in a tall brazier of dark blue metal burned so intensely that the roof, around the wide crack that served as a flue, had softened until the rock flowed like toffee.

The triplets were inside, dressed only in shifts and running with sweat, and no wonder: the heat flooding from the cave was the temperature of Karan's bread oven at Gothryme. But evidently it was not hot enough, for Jaguly scooped what appeared to be powdered iron from a barrel and tossed it onto the centre of the fire. It blazed blue-white, the flames doubling in height and lapping at the ceiling, and the soft rock around the crack sagged and dripped.

They must be working some terrible form of mancery, either to strengthen the Merdrun army and weaken the allies, or to open the Crimson Gate. Or both. Karan ducked back out of sight. She had known the triplets were big women, but not how big. They were over six feet tall, strong and fleshy and twice her weight. And being Merdrun they would be highly skilled in all forms of combat. It was highly unlikely that she could beat one of them; taking on three was out of the question.

Then it got terrifyingly worse. The middle triplet, Unbuly, picked up the blood torus and licked it, then crooned, "Sulien, Sulien?"

Karan managed to stifle a cry but was less successful at controlling her terror and rage. The emotions flooded out of her, and she knew at once that the empath, Empuly, had detected her.

Karan darted away but Jaguly hurled herself out of the cave onto the narrow ledge, pointed her meaty hand and hissed, "Paralyse!"

Karan lost all control of her spirit form. She could not move or speak, rise in the air or sink. She simply floated there, sick with dread, as Jaguly moved under her, touched the ghostly outline of her left calf and said, "Materialise!"

Karan's body and spirit reunited and she fell into Jaguly's arms, still paralysed. Jaguly carried her into the cave and dropped her on the floor. The back of her head slammed into hard stone and pain shrieked through her skull—she could still feel.

Unbuly took a thick-bladed knife from a sheath and showed it to her sisters.

"Too thick," said Jaguly and produced her own, a much longer knife, very thin but with a tapered blade two inches wide at the hilt.

"Too wide," said Empuly. She drew her own knife and held it up. It was a stiletto, and the blade was only half an inch from one side to the other.

"Just right," said Jaguly and Unbuly together.

"Stab her," Unbuly added. She tore Karan's shirt open and prodded her belly with a thick forefinger. "There!"

"Too quick," said Empuly. "Do it there." Her finger pressed lower.

"Too slow," said Jaguly. "Here is best." She put her finger a little higher and to the left.

"Just right," said Unbuly and Empuly.

And Jaguly stabbed Karan so hard that she felt the tip of the stiletto come out her back and snap off on the stone floor.

Surprisingly, it barely hurt at all, and when Jaguly withdrew the knife the little slit closed over with just a small welling of blood, though Karan knew it was intended to be a fatal wound. They wanted her to bleed to death internally, but not too quickly. When drinking the life of a dying victim, they could take more power if she died slowly.

This was it. She had been in many dangerous situations in the past but there had always been a way out. Not this time.

How long did she have? Belly wounds were unpredictable. She might last as little as five minutes or as long as a few hours, though Karan already felt fuzzy in the head. Half an hour would probably end her.

Then Empuly raised that same thick finger and said, "Ah!"

"What have you sensed?" said Unbuly eagerly. "Is it . . . ?"

"It's the *prize*," said Empuly. "Hush, she's just outside."

No pain, not even the agony of birthing Sulien through the badly healed bones of her shattered pelvis, had been as bad as this. It was so bad that it broke through the paralysis spell. She jerked herself upright, blood pulsing from the wound, and shrieked, "Sulien, run!"

There was no more she could do. She fell back and the spell tightened around her again until every muscle in her body was locked.

Jaguly hurled herself through the mouth of the cave, skidded on the ledge, lunged and caught Sulien by the wrist. She swung her by the arm out over the cliff, and Karan was sure she was going to hurl her to her death or dash her small body against the rock.

But that would have been too quick and painless. Jaguly sent her spinning into the cave, tumbling head over feet. Unbuly swung a massive fist at her, but Sulien ducked, darted away around the metal-burning brazier, then saw Karan on the floor with blood on her belly.

She froze, her pretty face twisting in the most awful agony, then screamed out a sending so powerful that the flame from the brazier was blown sideways and started to melt the wall of the cave.

"Daddy, help! They're killing Mummy!"

The sending burned a track through Karan's mind, blasting away the shock from the belly wound. Empuly let out a cracked shriek, then doubled up and dug her fists deep into her ample belly as if trying to prise out something gnawing at her insides. Jaguly toppled to the stone floor, breaking her nose.

But the sociopath Unbuly merely smiled, picked up the thick-bladed knife and licked her full black lips. "Just right!" She giggled and went after Sulien.

Jaguly rose, wiped the blood off her face and flicked it into the fire, then began to hum a ragged tune. Shortly Empuly joined in, an octave higher, then Unbuly, higher still.

Sulien was backing away around the brazier. Karan tried to sit up again, tried to tell Sulien to run, but the paralysis spell was much tighter now and she could not even twitch a lip.

Still humming, the triplets spread out, Unbuly covering the mouth of the cave, Jaguly moving towards Sulien from the left and Empuly from the right. As she passed the bag of powdered iron Jaguly scooped out a handful and tossed it onto the fire, which roared even higher.

Suddenly Sulien stopped, thrust both arms out at Empuly, strained, then gasped, "Sever!"

The humming broke off and Empuly let out a thin scream. Jaguly stopped as if she had run into a wall; her face lost all expression and she looked around at her sisters as if she did not know who they were or why they were here. Unbuly, whose face seldom wore any expression, looked utterly lost; she gave a choked sob, ran to Jaguly and tried to embrace her. Jaguly shoved her away like an unwanted stranger.

But Empuly regained control and extended an arm towards each of her sisters, saying, "Bind! Bind *for ever*!"

Jaguly shivered and shuddered, wiped her bleeding nose on the back of her hand, then smiled cruelly. Unbuly, who was still clutching the thick-bladed knife, said, "Just right, just right, just right!" and lunged at Sulien.

Sulien struck at her, and in a lucky blow knocked the knife from her hand, sending it soaring high to land in the brazier. Again the triplets froze, staring at the fire. Molten metal had begun to drip from the brazier, splashing on the floor and setting to black iron there.

"Unlucky," whispered Jaguly. "Very, very unlucky. We'll have to bind her."

"Sever!" cried Sulien. "Sever, sever, *sever*!"

But the spell, presumably one she had made up, did not work this time. Unbuly lunged at Sulien. She backpedalled, but Jaguly flung a long muscular arm around Sulien's middle, crushing her to her own massive chest. Empuly then came at her with a thin diamond-patterned rope that appeared to be made from snakeskin, tied Sulien's wrists together, then her ankles, and threw her down beside Karan.

Unbuly studied the knife with the tapered blade. Karan exerted every ounce of will in a desperate attempt to move, but could not. Her bare belly was bloated now from internal bleeding.

"Too wide!" cried Empuly.

Unbuly fetched the broken-tipped stiletto with which Jaguly had stabbed Karan.

"Too narrow and incomplete," hissed Unbuly.

The triplets looked at the red-hot metal dribbling from the brazier, all that remained of the third knife.

"Can it be reforged?" said Empuly.

"No," said Jaguly. "You'll have to strangle her." She was humming again, though this time she could not get the tune right.

"Not me."

"Nor me," said Jaguly.

"*I'll* strangle her," said Unbuly with another trilling giggle.

She reached for a red stone torus leaning against the rear wall of the cave. The blood torus must have been very heavy for she strained to lift it. She held it out to her sisters and they licked it one after another. They clicked their red teeth and licked their black lips with eroded tongues, then linked arms and cavorted around the brazier.

It's carved from the mineral cinnabar, Karan realised. *The ore of quicksilver.* She had seen great outcrops and ridges of it on the little world of Cinnabar. And quicksilver was deadly—it could drive you slowly mad or kill you quickly, according to the form and the dose.

"Mummy?" whispered Sulien. "Are you all right?"

Karan could not turn her head or speak. She tried desperately to think of a way to save Sulien, but there was none. A mother's greatest duty was to protect her child and she had failed, and that failure would allow Gergrig to destroy her world.

"Sorry, Mummy. I wish—"

Just then a great roar erupted from one of the battles down below. The triplets separated and ran to the mouth of the cave.

Jaguly held up an object that resembled a magnifying glass, though the glass within was not shaped like a lens, but rather a prism. She peered through it. "The enemy have had a small victory. Gergrig needs more power."

"Gergrig's not hurt, is he?" quavered Empuly. "He's not going to—"

"Don't be ridiculous," Jaguly said scornfully. "While we strengthen him he cannot be defeated, much less killed. But the enemy have proved surprisingly determined. Bring the blood torus."

Unbuly passed it back and forth through the blistering flame, three times, until quicksilver droplets formed on it, then carried it outside. The others went with her and the triplets stood side by side, Empuly in the middle. Unbuly laid the blood torus on top of her head like a heavy red crown then touched the left side with the fingertips of one hand. Jaguly touched the right side of the blood torus and, with her free hand, held up the object that resembled a magnifying glass and moved it carefully, as if aiming one side of the glass prism. The triplets started chanting in a harsh language Karan did not know.

"Jung sither garg, jung sither garg, jung sither GARG!"

On the final word an intense blue-white ray shot from the metal-fuelled fire to the prism, then burst out the other side in a narrow ribbon containing all the colours of the rainbow and streaked down towards the battlefield.

"To Gergrig!" sighed Empuly.

Suddenly the darkness outside was lit by an ominous scarlet glow, all too familiar to Karan, because she had seen it on Cinnabar when the Crimson Gate had been opening. So that's what the triplets were really up to. They were close to opening the gate, and that would spell the end.

They were humming now. For a few seconds the clamour of fighting, always in the background, ceased, and there was silence apart from the hissing roar of the brazier and Karan's laboured breathing. She was not in pain though she felt very weak now. Even if the paralysis spell had been lifted she would have struggled to move.

Dying, she thought. *Might only have minutes left.* Was there anything she could do for Sulien, anything at all?

She did not think so. She could not link or send, so there was no way to call for help. The Merdrun had won.

62

A MUD-SHOVELLING HICK!

Wilm led the freed Gwinians up the track, trying to put on an air of confidence. But how could he feel confident when the odds were so against them?

The Merdrun, Llian had told him, numbered more than ten thousand, and Wilm led four thousand Gwinians, though only twenty were armed with proper weapons. The rest carried cudgels, sharpened sticks and rocks, though few had any fighting experience. They would be outnumbered and outmatched, and he had a sick feeling that he was leading these gentle people to their deaths.

He almost turned back more than once, but each time reminded himself that he had been in hopeless situations before and had prevailed through ingenuity and a determination never to give up. For the sake of the world and his friends and allies, he had to fight on. And for Aviel, who had never lost faith in him or stopped thinking about him.

He unstoppered the phial of scent potion she had sent him via Karan, and the familiar bouquet of the flowers and herbs of home stiffened his heart. He would fight to the bitter end and, if there was any justice at all in this world, he would prevail.

They reached the great wooden gates of the enemy camp, which Llian had left unbarred, to discover that someone had re-barred them. Wilm scanned the wall to either side but saw no guards, which was surprising.

How to get in? The gates were made of six-inch-thick timber slabs reinforced with another layer of slabs at right angles. Not even the black sword could cut through them in time.

"We'll make a human ladder," he said, instructing the Gwinians to form a pyramid by standing on each others' backs.

When it was six feet high he climbed up, reached up for the top of the gate and felt along it carefully in case shards or spikes had been embedded there. He found none, heaved himself up, scanned the camp—darkness, smoke, fire and confusion—then dropped to the ground inside. After checking for guards—none—he called more Gwinians up and over. It took six of them to heave the bar up, then the gate swung open and they flowed in, looking at him expectantly.

Wilm had a sudden crisis of self-confidence. He had never led men before; what was he supposed to do now?

"Tell them to keep to the shadows," he whispered to his captains, the Gwinians he had been able to arm, "while we climb the watchtower."

They gave the orders and followed him up the back-and-forth wooden staircase to the top. The stairs were rudely built and creaked with every step. Thirty feet above the entrance they stood shoulder to shoulder and studied the camp. There was fighting in two places. High on the north-western side, several hundred Merdrun had pinned a larger number of allied fighters against the curtain wall and were slowly closing around them. On the eastern side, a little lower, as many as eight hundred invaders had been trapped on a small mound and were encircled by Merdrun. Wilm could not tell how many, though it could have been five hundred. Given that one Merdrun fighter was the equal of three or four ordinary soldiers, the odds were poor. In both places the invaders were likely to be wiped out within half an hour.

Unless he attacked, though what strategy could a lad of seventeen possibly come up with? Until three months ago he had done nothing but dig gardens and muck out stables.

"Go down," he said to his captains. "I just . . . need to think things through."

They obeyed at once as if he were a real leader. How could they have such faith in him? He took another sniff of Aviel's perfume, which strengthened him more than he would have expected, then drew the black sword. Llian had once told him that it was enchanted to protect its previous owner, Mendark, and Wilm imagined that he could sense that enchantment now. If only he could get it to help him, somehow . . .

But Mendark was ten years dead, his guts opened by a lorrsk when he had not been wearing the sword, and why would it want to protect Wilm?

Indeed. Why would we?

The thin, scratchy voice was in his head, and he answered without thinking. "Because I'm fighting for the same cause Mendark was for the last hundred years of his final life. I'm fighting for the world I love."

Thousands of people fight for such things, but few ever make a difference.

"Who are you? What do you want anyway?"

A worthy partner.

"I'm not worthy," said Wilm, since he'd been brought up honest and could not think of any lie that wouldn't immediately reveal itself. "But I am determined."

To do what?

"To fight. To do whatever it takes to beat the enemy. To win!"

You can't win. Mendark said the Merdrun had never been beaten.

"Yet! We've got a chance, if you help me the way you helped him."

I would have helped him, sniffed the sword, *had he not lost faith in me and buried me in a rusty box in the desert.*

Wilm sensed a chance. "Why did he lose faith?"

I . . . became distracted.

"Why?"

A private matter. No organism could ever understand.

"Please help me," said Wilm. "I—"

Never beg! It's demeaning.

"I'm determined to save our beautiful world, and surely you feel the same."

I'm a persona enchanted into a length of hand-forged metal. Why would I care about this or any world?

Wilm was getting nowhere. How could he be talking to his sword anyway? Was he losing his mind? No, the blade was definitely enchanted . . . and it had already given him the key. It wanted *a worthy partner.*

"I could be a worthy partner to you," he said softly.

A barnyard boy! it sneered. *A muck-shovelling hick!*

"A great man taught me how to use a sword."

Who?

When Llian had copied out the booklet describing the seven basic strokes of sword fighting, he had written the author's name at the end. Wilm had no idea who he was, though he must have been a great swordsman or a great teacher. "Fratince Loode, the author of *The Seven Basic Strokes.* They're burned into my sword arm."

I knew Loode, though lewd *would be a better name for the villain. But have you ever used me in combat?*

"Surely you know when you've been used?"

I've only just woken from a very long sleep. I remember nothing lately.

"I duelled Jundelix Rasper, an assassin sent by—"

I met Rasper when he was young. You duelled him and lived?

It was wrong to boast about killing another man, even such a wicked one as Rasper who had made his living from death; Wilm's mother would have been ashamed of him. But he sensed he was close to the key now. The enchanted sword wanted a strong, determined master, one it could respect, and in the strange world it inhabited a strong man did not hide his achievements out of modesty.

"I fought him to a standstill," said Wilm, not boastfully. "Rasper was better than me—much better—but I held him off with the seven basic strokes until he weakened. I'd practised so much that my sword arm knew what to do. I suppose that was your doing."

Flatterer, said the sword, though Wilm did not sense that it was displeased.

"He was better, but I was much fitter and stronger and younger, and in the end when his strength was failing, he panicked and I held firm."

The kill, was it clean? The sword sounded eager now.

It wasn't easy to think about. Killing a man had not hardened Wilm; on the contrary it had reminded him, not that he needed the reminder, how fragile life was and how easily ended. *Dajaes, Dajaes, how I miss you.*

"Straight through the heart. He died instantly. Then I bent my head over him." It was important to Wilm that he say this. "Rasper had been an evil man, but a human being nonetheless, and I honoured him for the life I had taken."

Nobly done, said the black sword. *Tell me, Wilm—*

"I don't have time," Wilm said firmly. "Less than a mile away my people are outnumbered and surrounded; they can't hold out much longer. Will you help me?"

What good can four thousand unarmed Gwinians do?

"I don't know, but we're determined to fight for all we hold dear."

Wilm sensed eagerness. It was a sword after all, and presumably it yearned to be used.

And die for it?

"If necessary." Then, risking everything on intuition, he added, "Will you help me to win a fabulous victory, or should I prop you up in some dusty corner to be forgotten and find a more willing weapon on the battlefield?"

Oh, all right! I'll cast my protection over you and aid your sword arm—if I think you deserve it. But consider yourself on probation until you've proved yourself worthy.

"Does your protection mean I can't be harmed? Or killed?"

Of course not, the black sword sneered. *You can be killed in a hundred ways, in a deliberate attack or by accident. My protection gives you a small advantage—it's up to you how you use it.*

"I'll take it." Wilm realised that he had been up here far too long and his men must be wondering about him. If they'd heard him talking they might think he was mad.

He ran down the steps and stopped in front of his captains. Behind them, the great mass of the Gwinians was spread out along the wall, keeping to the shadows. Wilm drew the black sword and raised it high.

"This is a famous blade, an enchanted blade that once belonged to the great Magister, Mendark, and now is mine. I've bargained with the sword, and it has offered me its protection in the coming battle."

Don't get ahead of yourself, boy, said the sword. *My protection is provisional.*

"We're going to fight the Merdrun," said Wilm, "and with our own strong hearts and unquenchable wills, and the aid of this mighty sword, we ... will ... win!"

A sigh ran through the Gwinians. Wilm split them into two groups, one to attack the Merdrun up on the western side of the great camp, the other to the battle in the east, and swiftly gave his orders.

"On the way you will come across many abandoned weapons," he said. "Arm yourselves with whatever you can find."

He led the larger force, which consisted of more than two thousand Gwinians, mostly men but also a few hundred young women, up the slope and to the right towards the mound where the allied force had been encircled by the Merdrun. Above the smoking remains of the tents they passed through a battle zone littered with hundreds of bodies, and the smell of death—of blood and guts, meat and ordure—was so strong in the hot, humid night that he had to turn aside and throw up.

He wiped his mouth and stood there in the dark, shivering while his Gwinians armed themselves with whatever weapons they could find. *This will be us in a few minutes*, he thought. *Hacked, brutalised, dying in agony, hundreds of young lives wasted. Possibly all of us.*

Not as easy as you thought, said the sword.

"I never thought it would be easy," Wilm muttered. "What kind of a man thinks war is easy, good or noble?"

A Merdrun man. Merdrun women too.

Wilm led them up the slope, across boggy ground on either side of a stream flowing from the easternmost hill, then towards a low rise. The Gwinians' dark skins made them almost invisible in the night, and he was so covered in mud and filth that he also blended into the darkness.

He stopped a hundred yards down from the rear of the Merdrun force. He could hear the clash of weapons and smell the blood; his heart was thundering and he was breathing heavily. Panic swelled. How could they hope to beat the greatest fighters in the void?

Stop it! He took a series of deep breaths. *We'll win because the alternative is unthinkable.*

"They don't know we're here," he whispered to his captains. "We'll creep to within twenty yards if we can, then charge."

As he headed up, Wilm realised that he had not seen Llian since killing the guards outside the gate of the slave camp, but he could not think about him now. They were only twenty yards from the rear of the encircling Merdrun.

He drew the black sword and charged, felt a moment of panic when he thought he was on his own, then the Gwinians were behind him and he felt a surge of exhilaration. In a minute he might be dead but he would have done his best.

He raised his sword and twenty-two hundred Gwinians roared as with one throat, their cry echoing back from the high stone wall a few hundred yards to the right. As the shocked Merdrun turned to face this new enemy, the charging Gwinians drove deep into the enemy formation.

Then everything was a chaos of hand-to-hand fighting, with enemy coming at Wilm from all directions, hacking and thrusting. They were easily identifiable—both the men and women were bulkier than the slender Gwinians, and the glyph burned into every Merdrun forehead glowed a luminous silver in the semi-darkness.

Wilm cut a man down, then another Merdrun who could have been man or woman—it was impossible to tell in the smoky gloom—without knowing where the sword had struck either time. An empty-handed Gwinian dived for the Merdrun's fallen sword, came up with it in two hands but was killed before he could use it. Beside Wilm a second Gwinian died, spraying warm blood all over his left shoulder.

Behind him someone was screaming, "My leg, my leg! Help me."

But there was no helping anyone. Wilm thrust, killed, thrust again. More Merdrun came at him, and he felt sure he was going to be slain a dozen times. He had taken four wounds already though none serious; he was even able to evade the most furious killing blows. He wasn't such a fool as to think it was his doing—the sword was aiding him—and if someone came at him from behind, unseen, or several of them at once, he would die as easily as the man to his left had just done.

There was death everywhere Wilm looked, and it was awful, but there was no time to think about it, no time to think about anything save kill or be killed.

Up on the fortress wall to his right someone set fire to a pile of oil-soaked timber and flames shot twenty feet into the air. He cast a quick glance over his shoulder and saw a wedge of bodies behind him, dead and dying. Most were Gwinians, though this part of the attack had killed at least a dozen Merdrun.

"Forward!" he bellowed, and the couple of hundred Gwinians behind him charged again, driving through the Merdrun's lines. Their circle was thinning now; could he break through to the trapped allies?

A black-bearded fellow hacked at him. Wilm ducked just in time, struck back, and the man parried. They exchanged a dozen furious blows without penetrating the other's defences. The Merdrun thrust; Wilm diverted the blow aside, putting his attacker off balance, but the Merdrun had been faking it. He struck hard, not at Wilm but at the blade of the black sword. Wilm, unable to get it out of the way in time, was sure his own blade would shatter, but the hilt twisted in his sweaty grip, turning the blade edge on to the Merdrun's blow, and the black sword sheared through the enemy's steel weapon in a shower of stinging sparks.

The Merdrun dropped the hilt and his hand flashed for a knife in his belt, but the sword, moving of its own volition this time, delicately opened the jugular vein in his neck.

So it went on, the blood, the screams, the horror that edged weapons can make of a human being, and the killing, the endless killing. Wilm had no idea how long he had been fighting. It might only have been ten minutes though it felt like a day, as though there had been nothing else in his life. He was utterly exhausted.

Then the wedge of Gwinians cleaved through the last line of Merdrun to the trapped soldiers on the mound. The encirclement was broken. The Merdrun drew back and regrouped a hundred yards away across the slope.

Wilm took stock. At least a hundred Gwinians had died behind him, and many times that number around the other parts of the circle, and he knew dozens of them; he had slaved beside them for weeks, heaving the massive stones of the fortress wall into place. They had been good people, people he had liked, now dead in an instant of violence. And he had led them to war, led them to their deaths. That was the hardest part of all.

He guessed that a hundred Merdrun had died in the attack on the mound, though their reserves, waiting in their shadowed ranks on the two eastern hills, numbered so many that the losses were insignificant. Still, a hundred was more than he had expected, given their reputation for invincibility. They were supposed to be as tough and strong as Charon, and a hundred Charon—Rulke's famous Hundred—had taken the world of Aachan.

These Merdrun weren't as fast as Wilm had been led to believe. He had killed a number of them, and he did not think it was all to do with the sword. There were times when it had definitely helped him, and other times when it had seemed like a lifeless piece of metal in his hands. It was . . . odd.

He stretched and winced. He had taken a shallow gash in his left side, between the lower ribs, without realising it. His left shoulder was sore too—a small deep wound made by the tip of a sword. He had no memory of that either.

The best of his strength was gone, and his empty belly was rattling, but he had no food, and there was no way out save by winning or dying.

63

NO MAN CAN BEAT GERGRIG

Leaving Karan to locate the triplets, Tallia crept out across the camp, hoping to rally the allies' remaining troops. Most of Janck's senior officers were also dead because the Merdrun had targeted them from the beginning, and only Tallia's mancery and the Faellem's illusions had kept her alive.

She heard renewed fighting to the right, up near the mound—the Merdrun's encirclement had been broken! Through her night glasses she saw that they had been attacked by a silent horde of Gwinians. Llian must have got through to the slave camp after all.

Karan would be desperate to hear this news but Tallia could not go back. She had to know the Gwinians' numbers and their plans. She scurried up towards the mound. "Llian?" she yelled. "Are you here?"

"I don't know where he is," said a tall, filthy, blood-covered young man Tallia had not seen before, though the black sword was identification enough. "I'm Wilm. I'm leading the Gwinians."

"Very well done," said Tallia, shaking his hand. "Without you we could not have lasted this long, but the mission has failed." She told him about the loss of the assassins, and her inability to contact Malien and get her to reopen the gate.

"As a slave I learned to live minute by minute," said Wilm. "I never expected to survive another day. Over the past couple of months every cause I've fought has seemed hopeless. I expect nothing, but I'll keep hoping we can beat them."

"Good on you," said Tallia, though she had no hope left. "Where's Llian?"

"Haven't seen him since we escaped the slave camp." Wilm reached out for the pair of night glasses she still held, forgotten, in her hand. "May I?"

She gave them to him and he studied the conflict against the western wall, the silent formation of Merdrun a couple of hundred yards away, then the rest of the camp. He handed the glasses back.

"Gergrig is the key," he said. "If he can be killed . . ."

"Surely you don't think you can beat *him*," said Tallia, unable to keep incredulity out of her voice.

"I wouldn't have a hope against so great a warrior, normally . . ."

"But?" said Tallia.

"Mendark's enchanted sword protects me as long as I prove myself worthy . . ." Wilm paused, head cocked as if listening to a voice only he could hear.

"No man can beat Gergrig in single combat," said Tallia.

"Why not?"

"I've been studying the way he fights. He's always in the thickest fighting but few blows ever touch him. I think he's protected too."

"By his sword?"

"No, by the triplets. I believe they're channelling power to him to make him seem invincible. If you attack him, it'll be suicide."

"I've got to," said Wilm, "because no one else has any chance. But I'm not planning to attack him on my own." He checked on the enemy again. "I'm going back. Good luck."

"Good luck," Tallia echoed. *You'll need it.*

64

BRING THE BLOOD TORUS

Llian was looking desperately around the camp when he noticed the fire coming from the northern hill. But it was no ordinary fire; it was a searing blue-white glow, shaped like the pupil of an eye. He looked down at the scrap of paper in his hand, then up again. Definitely not an eye. A cave with a magical fire inside.

It was half a mile away. He raced up a muddy slope where all the grass had been worn away, passing in the darkness a couple of hundred yards to the right of the vicious battle raging against the north-western section of the wall, then splashing across a little stream, his boots sinking into spongy earth on the other side, then on and up the slope where it ramped up to the ridge on his left and the hill straight ahead. This part of the camp was empty, and the sounds of battle were just a distant clamour over the pounding of his boots and the thundering of his heart.

His legs were going wobbly and there was a stitch in his left side but he could not stop. Sulien's cry had been at least ten minutes ago. Karan might be dead already.

The base of the cliff suddenly loomed up out of the darkness. Llian flung his arms forward to protect himself and thudded into the rock. He searched desperately to left and right and found a track leading up to the left, near the point where the stone wall of the camp met the cliff. He staggered up the steep, narrow path, slipping and skidding, until he must have been sixty feet above the floor of the camp. More than high enough to die if he fell.

Where was the cave? The mouth must be well across the cliff to his right, though from this angle it would be hard to see. He stood there for a second, gasping, then made out a blue-white reflected glimmer forty or fifty feet away.

A crumbling two-foot-wide ledge was the only way to get to it. He had never been good with heights but there was no time to worry about that now. He freed his notched sword in its sheath and was about to head across when someone spoke inside the cave.

"Mummy? Are you all right?"

Llian staggered and almost fell. What was Sulien doing here? Was she all right? If the triplets were killing Karan, or had already killed her, Sulien would be next.

Karan did not answer. She must be dead. He was Sulien's only hope; he had to save her. He had to be careful but he also had to be quick.

He was about to creep across the ledge and attack with his broken sword when a many-throated roar sounded from the battlefield below and a mile to the east. The triplets appeared at the mouth of the cave and one of them held up a small glassy object in one hand.

"Gergrig's not hurt, is he?" one of the triplets said in a ragged voice. "He's not going to—"

"Don't be ridiculous," said the triplet holding the device. "While we strengthen him he cannot be defeated, much less killed. But the enemy have proved surprisingly determined. Bring the blood torus."

Llian crouched down in the shadows. He did not think they could see him here, and since he could not do mancery they probably could not sense him. But how was he supposed to take on three of them, all trained fighters as well as overwhelmingly powerful mancers?

The middle of the three triplets now had the blood torus on her head. They chanted. *"Jung sither garg, jung sither garg, jung sither GARG!"*

A narrow, rainbow-coloured ribbon of light burst forth from the object the end triplet held above her head, streaked across to the eastern side of the battlefield without spreading appreciably and touched someone there.

"Gergrig!" said one of the triplets in a breathy sigh.

Then, to Llian's horror, the red outline of a huge trilithon appeared in the centre of the camp. So that's what the triplets were up to in the cave—diverting power from the summon stone to reopen the gate from Cinnabar to Gwine and bring the rest of the Merdrun through. And by their satisfied looks, it was nearly done.

The whole camp had fallen silent, though Llian could imagine the despair of his own people, and the joy of the enemy.

The triplets stood there, gazing down at the camp for a few seconds, then went inside, humming in unison. Were they singing the life out of Karan? Or had they done so and were about to start on Sulien?

His heart was beating so wildly that he felt dizzy, and sweat was running down his back and chest. He drew the sword and crept along the ledge. How was he to take on three mancers with a sword that did not even have a point? It was hopeless but he had no choice. He had to save Sulien and Karan, and stop the triplets completing the gate.

He reached the left side of the cave mouth. The heat gushing out was incredible; the cave must be like the inside of a stove. What were they doing in there? He peered in.

The triplets were capering around a tall brazier made from bluish metal. They were humming, and every so often one of them fed the fire with a handful of black powder from a bag. Iron dust, he assumed.

He knew about metal-fuelled fires; the Aachim sometimes used them. The powder was hard to set alight but once it caught it burned twice as hot as ordinary fuel—hot enough to burn through rock.

He leaned forward and saw Karan and Sulien on the floor, shaded from the glare of the fire and laid out side by side. Karan's bare middle was covered in red-brown, flaking blood that had dried in the heat. Her belly was swollen, and there was a small patch of fresh red blood on the right side. Her eyes were open, glassy. She looked dead.

A pang of unbearable loss tore through him, but he had to put it aside because Sulien was still alive. She lay a couple of feet away, her hands and feet tied. Her jaw was set, her fingers moving in patterns, though he could not guess what she was trying to do.

The humming rose in pitch; the triplets held the blood torus high, licking it ecstatically, then the one with the blank face flexed her fleshy fingers and said eagerly, "Is it strangling time?"

"It's *slow* strangling time," said another, and they continued to hum while the blank-faced triplet headed for Sulien.

Llian let out a great roaring battle cry, reinforced with his teller's voice to make him seem far more fearsome than he could ever be, and leapt into the cave, swinging the notched sword at the blank-faced triplet.

She did not move; she wasn't the least bit afraid. Before he came within two yards of her the other two triplets moved in from either side. A massive fist struck him in the right temple and another over the left ear, which felt as though it had burst like a squashed peach. He collapsed, his head ringing and his vision going in and out of focus.

The blank-faced triplet kicked him in the ribs.

"The chronicler and teller," said the triplet with the most mobile face. "His creative life force will be very strong. We'll do him next."

"How?" said the third triplet.

"Boil his sword down and make him drink it."

65

HE'S THE ONE!

Since they now had no way of contacting Malien to reopen the gate, Tallia knew she was going to die here, along with the rest of the invasion force. She had been fighting for half an hour now and was flagging rapidly, but she was not going to die easily.

She had gone to the aid of the troops trapped against the northwestern wall. Barely a hundred of them survived, and they were surrounded by about three hundred Merdrun. The smaller group of Gwinians, numbering well over a thousand, had attacked the Merdrun from the rear, but few had been armed with anything but sticks and stones, and the Merdrun had turned on them so ferociously, slaughtering them by the hundreds, that they had broken and many had fled.

Ahead of Tallia a small band of Gwinians, no more than a dozen, had been trapped against the circular walls of a pair of above-ground water cisterns and were under attack by three Merdrun warriors, who despite their disadvantage in numbers, were mercilessly cutting the Gwinians down. Five fell in a furious onslaught, then two more.

Tallia ran in and, with a savage blast of mancery, knocked the feet out from under the closest of the enemy. He bounced upright and came at her, but with a delicate stroke that took him by surprise she glided the tip of her blade past his and into the base of his throat.

As he fell she went after the second Merdrun, who had just struck down another of the Gwinians. The wounded man let out a cry which resonated through her in a way that the agony of hundreds of other victims had not.

She went at the Merdrun as he turned to face her and with a horizontal slash sent his head flying from his shoulders. The third Merdrun, who looked even more exhausted than Tallia felt, took one look at her grim face, another at his two dead comrades, and did what few other Merdrun had done anywhere on the battlefield that day. He ran.

Of the dozen Gwinians, only three were still on their feet. They grabbed the weapons of the fallen enemy and bolted, and Tallia could hardly blame them. She looked down at the injured man, a tall dark fellow whose black hair, unlike the curly-haired natives of Gwine, was as straight as her own.

She could not see his face, for his right arm was crooked across it as if to ward off a blow. He had been struck in the left thigh, a long deep gash that was pouring blood. The femoral artery had been severed, and if she could not stop it he would bleed to death in minutes.

Was there any point in trying to save him when they were all going to die anyway? He was not armed, nor did he look like a soldier, yet he had come up here to face the enemy and do his best. Tallia could do no less for him.

She tore away his trouser leg, mopped the eight-inch gash with a rag until she could see inside and identified the severed artery. With a focused blast from her bloody right forefinger she sealed it, then did the same for several smaller arteries and veins. That was the easy part.

In the right circumstances she might have attempted a healing charm, but that was not possible here; she did not have the strength or time for such delicate and subtle work. In any case, the wound must first be cleaned of all the mud and muck, otherwise it would turn septic and he would lose the leg to gangrene, and probably his life.

Having dealt with many a battlefield injury, Tallia had brought balms and bandages, stitching needles and thread. She got them out of her pack and tore his trouser leg off.

"Handsome thigh you've got there," she said. "It'd be a pity to lose it."

His arm still lay across his face and he did not answer.

She supposed he was in shock. She cleaned the wound, spread balm over it and pushed the sides of the gash together as neatly as she could. "Put your hands here and here."

He did so. She moved his fingers. "Push down on either side of the gash. Not too hard."

When the lips of the gash were pressed together to Tallia's satisfaction she put forty-five stitches through it, then bandaged the wound tightly and sat back.

"Nice job," he said.

She looked at his face for the first time, then into his warm brown eyes, and felt a sudden shock, a recognition of what—or who—she had been searching for all this time. *He's the one!*

"Who are you?" she said. Despite the heat she had goose pimples all up her arms. "You're not from Gwine, are you?"

Though he must have been in considerable pain, he managed a smile as he looked into her eyes. "I'm Zanser, master healer. Crandor born, as, I'm sure, are you."

"My family dwells near Roros," said Tallia. "Cocoa plantations. But I haven't been home for many years. I'm—"

"I know who you must be," said Zanser. "The Magister, Tallia bel Soon. And I thank you for saving my life."

"Don't thank me yet." With an effort, for he was a tall man, she picked him up and carried him to a spot between the cisterns where he would not be readily seen. "We're probably going to die, but if we don't—if we can get the gate back—I'll come back for you."

"That would be risking your life, and you've already done that once."

"I'll risk my life for you whenever I feel the need," she said tartly, "and no mere man is going to tell me otherwise."

Zanser laughed and extended his hand. "Likewise!"

66

I'VE SEEN MANY A WORSE DEATH

Hingis would not have said that he was happy.

No one with a shred of humanity could have smiled in the midst of such bloodshed, brutality and carnage, yet he felt a sort of grim satisfaction at his achievements. His illusions, bolstered by the arts Culligon had taught him, were far more powerful than before, yet incomparably more subtle, and he could either target a whole army or one individual in an army of thousands. He had struck at Gergrig on four occasions, confusing and weakening him, and that alone had saved a hundred lives. His other illusions might have saved a thousand.

Hingis's twisted bones ached unbearably, each in a different way. He could have identified every bone in his skeleton from the unique character of the pain it gave him, but right now it did not matter a damn. He had repaid Culligon, and he almost felt—almost but not quite—that he had atoned for the wrong he'd done his beautiful, tragic sister. Esea was at peace now, and since he had done the very best he could, he was ready to join her.

The battlefield, which was wreathed in drifting smoke illuminated by dozens of fires, looked like a vision of damnation. There were bodies everywhere, dead or dying or longing for death but unable to find it, silent or groaning, begging for help or to be put out of their misery.

He was lurching along, looking for another opportunity to use his illusions, when a familiar face, as black as coal, appeared before him.

"Osseion!" said Hingis. "I didn't know you were here."

"Couldn't keep me out of it," said Osseion with a painful smile. He was slumped on the ground, leaning against a boulder, and blood soaked the front of his shirt and trousers.

"Can I help you?"

"Seen enough wounds to know no one can help me. Blade to the belly. Won't be long now."

"I'm sorry," said Hingis and was. He had always liked Osseion, even after the unbridgeable schism—all his own fault—that had separated himself and Ussarine.

"When you're a soldier you expect it to end this way. Never thought I'd live to see twenty, much less fifty." Osseion paused, panting, then went on, "But there is one thing you can do for me."

"Name it."

"Ussarine?" Osseion called.

"She's *here*?" said Hingis, shocked and dismayed. He had done everything possible to keep her at a distance since his sister's death.

"And not too good. Ussarine, where are you?"

"Here, Father."

Ussarine staggered out of the smoke to Hingis's left, carrying a gigantic broadsword. There was a bloody gash on her upper left arm, another on her left hip and a third on her right thigh. And her left hand was gone. The arm ended at the wrist and was wrapped in a bloody bandage. She looked down at her father and tears appeared in her eyes, then at Hingis, and her face took on the lost look he remembered from their last awful meeting.

She turned away abruptly and knelt before Osseion. "How is it, Father?"

"I've seen many a worse death, and delivered a few such deaths myself. It's not so bad."

"You've got to hold on. If I can find a healer, a good one . . ."

Osseion shook his head. "It was a fatal wound from the moment I took it. I'm sorry to leave you, Ussarine. I could not have wished for a better child."

"Not even a son?" she said teasingly, though with an ancient sadness.

"Not even a son," he said firmly. He moved sideways as if to ease his pain, and blood surged from the wound in his belly.

"Don't move," she begged.

"It's time to go," he said quietly. "But first one last thing."

"Yes, Father. Anything."

"Give me your hand."

She put her large well-shaped right hand in his three-fingered paw.

"Hingis!" said Osseion in a tone that did not admit of refusal. "Come here."

"I don't—"

"I asked you for a favour and you said, *Name it*. This is it. No man of honour can refuse a dying man."

Hingis very reluctantly knelt beside Ussarine and took Osseion's other hand.

Osseion pressed Hingis's hand into Ussarine's, then, as they tried to pull apart, enclosed both in his own enormous hand and gripped them so tightly that Hingis could not move.

"You'll make an odd couple," Osseion said, "though I dare say there have been odder. More importantly, you were made for each other. I can see that even if you can't. And you *need* each other. Don't you, Ussarine?"

"Yes, Father," she said meekly.

"Don't you, Hingis?"

"Yes, I do," said Hingis, and at last he knew it to be true.

"Despite the loss of her left hand?" Osseion said in a hard voice.

Hingis had betrayed his sister by showing his revulsion after she had lost two toes trying to save him from the mancer Scorbic Vyl. To Hingis that small imperfection in Esea's otherwise flawless beauty had been unbearable—it had made his own hideousness so much harder to endure. But now he gazed at Ussarine's big, strong arm, which would forever end in a stump, and realised that it did not matter one iota.

"I love her just as she is," said Hingis, "and ever will."

67

SMASH IT, DADDY!

Llian lay on his back on the floor of the sweltering cave, bitterly regretting his stupidity.

Why had he attacked the triplets when any one of them was his match, either with a blade or unarmed? Why hadn't he kicked over the brazier and its metal-fuelled fire, which was clearly so important to the mancery they were doing here to reopen the gate? It would have given him the chance to grab Sulien and run, and could even have delayed the gate. But he had not thought clearly enough or acted quickly enough. He was brilliant writing about conflict, but when it came to action he was a dunce and a duffer.

The triplet he now knew to be Jaguly held up a heavy, broad-bladed knife. "Is it too wide?"

"The teller's got no mancery," sneered Unbuly. "*Any* blade will do for him."

"Melt it and make him drink it," said Empuly eagerly.

Jaguly looked out the cave mouth, frowning. "That'd take too long; Gergrig needs more power."

"Stab him. Do it now."

Jaguly knelt between Llian and Sulien, facing him. Unbuly and Empuly took their places to either side. "Quick or slow?" said Jaguly.

"Quick!" cried Unbuly, licking her black lips.

"Forehead or chest or belly?"

"Forehead!" Empuly and Unbuly said together. "All the way through."

A few feet away, Karan moaned, faint and quivering. She was still alive! He struggled desperately.

"Kill the teller!" shrieked Unbuly.

Jaguly raised the knife, and the other triplets clamped their hands around hers, over the hilt. Llian flinched. Between them, from a corner of an eye, he saw Sulien's fingers working above the knots, though not touching them. They smoked, charred and fell away. She sprang to her feet, caught Unbuly's head from behind in one hand and Empuly's in the other, then slammed them against Jaguly's head. For a few seconds the triplets were dazed.

"Unbuly to Empuly!" Sulien shrieked, pressing the triplets' heads together. "Empuly to Jaguly, Jaguly to Unbuly, *flood, flood, FLOOD!*"

A pale green nimbus formed around the triplets' heads, ran up

Sulien's arms and vanished. The triplets fell back, thrashing and screaming incoherently, and Jaguly's heavy knife went flying. As Llian rolled over a big foot caught him under the ribs, knocking the wind out of him. Sulien grabbed the knife and hacked through the ropes biding his wrists, removing a long strip of skin in the process, then freed his legs.

"Smash it, Daddy, smash it!"

"Smash what?" He looked around and saw, placed lovingly on a golden stand, the blood torus. He staggered across and kicked it off the stand, then looked around for something that could break it.

"The sword!" cried Sulien, dancing from one foot to the other and holding Jaguly's knife out in both hands.

Llian slammed the notched sword down onto the blood torus. Chips of red cinnabar flew off, but it remained unbroken. And now the triplets were recovering, coming to their hands and knees, preparing to spring.

"Harder!" said Sulien. "Quick, Daddy!"

He raised the sword as high as he could reach, its broken tip scraping the ceiling, then brought it down with all his strength, cleaving the blood torus in two.

"Smash it to bits, Daddy."

Jaguly, the first to recover, dived for the blood torus. Llian kicked the two halves apart. She shrieked then hit the floor hard, screaming and thrashing. She staggered to her feet, cursing and kicking her sisters, and battering the walls with her fists. Unbuly and Empuly attacked her and each other, each trying to gouge her sister's eyes out.

Llian hacked the halves of the blood torus into pieces and heaved them into the brazier, then tossed in another scoop of powdered iron. The fire blazed high, crackled and sparked, then began to vomit choking clouds of white smoke.

"It's poison," sobbed Sulien. "Get Mummy out, quick!"

She tossed the device Jaguly had used to strengthen Gergrig into the fire. The prism burst, showering hot glass everywhere. Llian picked Karan up. Her belly was as swollen as when she had been four months pregnant; she must have lost pints of blood.

There came a mighty boom from outside. Was he too late? Had the Crimson Gate opened? He ran for the entrance and edged along the ledge, sick with terror. Karan's skin was cold and clammy. She was dying, almost dead. Behind him the mouth of the cave billowed white and brown fumes, and the triplets' shrieks became more incoherent.

He could not see the shadowy Crimson Gate and thought no more about it. Sulien was ahead of him, though he had no idea how she had got there. He was incapable of thought. His entire being was reduced to the dying woman in his arms and a loss that would be unendurable, that would break him. Sulien was standing with her hands up around her mouth, and Llian realised that the whole camp had gone silent.

"Tallia!" Sulien shrieked, her high voice echoing across and back between the walls of the camp. "Mummy's dying."

Llian saw Merdrun running along the northern wall in their direction. He headed down. Sulien repeated her cry three more times, then came after him.

"What did you do to the triplets?" he said.

"When I got there, I tried to sever the bond that binds them together and makes them magiz, but it didn't work . . . so I did the opposite. I flooded them with each other's feelings, and because they're all so different and horrible, they couldn't cope."

"And when I chopped up the blood torus?"

"It *did* sever the bond, and that was even worse. It drove them mad . . . or madder." She looked at Karan's blanched face. "Is Mummy going to be all right?"

"I don't know." Llian stopped to adjust her position in his arms, then awkwardly hugged Sulien to him. "I think—we'd better prepare for the worst."

"I'm never giving up on Mummy," said Sulien. She shouted, "Tallia!" again and again.

There was no fighting against the western wall now. Battle had resumed on the eastern side with renewed fury; how long until the last of the allied troops, and Wilm's Gwinians, were dead? It was hopeless. It had always been hopeless.

As they reached the floor of the camp, Tallia came running, her eyes shining with some emotion Llian could not begin to imagine. He felt only despair. He stood there numbly, holding Karan in his arms, while Sulien told Tallia what had happened.

Tallia put her hands on Karan's swollen belly and worked a lengthy healing charm. When Tallia finished she crouched head-down, gasping. Then she checked Karan's pulse and eyes, and felt her forehead, frowning.

"Mummy's going to be all right, isn't she?" said Sulien.

"She needs a far better healer than I am," Tallia said grimly. She rubbed her forehead, smearing it with Karan's blood. "Take her down there." She pointed to a pair of walled cisterns. "An injured man, Zanser, is hidden between those two cisterns. He's a master healer from Crandor, and they're the best in the world. If anyone can save her ..."

"You've got to come too," said Sulien. "Mummy needs you."

"I have to make sure of the triplets."

Llian carried Karan down to the cisterns at the upper side of the smoking storerooms and cookhouse. Sulien went with him, then ran ahead into the dark gap between the cisterns.

"Careful," said Llian, nearly choking with despair. "There could be Merdrun anywhere round here."

"Master Zanser?" she called. "Master Zanser?"

Llian did not hear any reply, but Sulien darted forward. "It's Mummy," she said. "The evil triplets stabbed her in the stomach and she's dying. Can you help her?" She raced out. "Daddy, in here!"

He carried Karan in. Zanser was just a shadow among shadows.

"Lay her down here," he said in a lilting Crandorian accent. "Injured leg. I can't get up." Llian did so.

"I can make light with my fingers," said Sulien.

"Can you really? A very small light would be welcome," said Zanser. "Block the gap," he said to Llian. "No one else must see the light."

Sulien conjured a warm yellowish glow from a fingertip and held it over Karan's face. Zanser checked her pupils and her pulse, then said, "Lower down."

In the light from Sulien's fingertip he probed Karan's swollen belly, identified the small slit the knife had made, then felt all around her middle. "With a wound there she should be dead," he said, "but she clings to life. It's almost inexplicable."

"Mummy's a triune," said Sulien. "And so am I. We have Aachim blood, and a little Faellem blood too."

"A triune!" Zanser whistled between his teeth. "That might explain it. The internal organs of the other human species are arranged differently. And their constitutions are stronger."

He put both hands on Karan's belly and closed his eyes.

"What are you doing?" said Sulien curiously.

"Sensing out the damage so I can work out how best to heal it. It's a delicate business that can easily go wrong."

"But Mummy will be all right, won't she?"

"I hope so. But sometimes—if too much blood has been lost . . . Put out the light and hush now. I've got to concentrate."

It did not feel secure here, with the battle less than a mile away. The Merdrun would never give up; they could be hunting Sulien even now. Llian walked twenty yards to a small rise. Nothing felt real; nothing made sense any more.

Up at the cave, thick white smoke had reduced the metal-fuelled fire to a dull bluish glow. Could the triplets be dead? He dared not think so. *Crack-crack-crash!* The glow went out. Chills spiralled down his back. What if they had recovered and were on their way down?

There came another great roar from the battlefield, as if from hundreds of throats, then the fighting stopped. The Merdrun must have finished the job, and he saw that the reserves on the north-eastern hill were gone. Were they after Sulien too?

He ran into the gap between the cisterns. "Is Karan . . . ?"

"No better," said Zanser. "But no worse."

"The battle's over, and I think we've lost. Sulien, can you . . . ?"

"I linked to Malien," said Sulien. "She's trying to reopen the gate."

"At the same place?" said Llian.

"It's easier there."

He had little hope that they could reach the gate before the enemy found them, but he had to go on. "We'd better get down there. Will Karan be all right if I carry her?"

"I hope so," said Zanser sombrely.

Llian lifted Karan in his arms. She moaned and her hand rose and caught his shirtfront, but fell back. She did not have the strength to hold it.

Zanser forced himself to his feet, shuddering with the pain.

"You can lean on me," said Sulien.

He put a hand on her small shoulder and took a hobbling step. Llian headed south, bypassing the officers' and acolytes' tents. Before they had gone far, Tallia came running.

"Couldn't get inside the cave," she panted. "Full of poisonous fumes. But I brought the roof down. If the triplets were still inside, they're dead."

"If," said Llian.

68

YOU INSOLENT LITTLE PUP!

The great red-tinged shadow gate loomed over the camp, a threat Wilm could do nothing about, though neither could he dismiss it from mind. All he could do was fight on. He hacked his opponent down and staggered forward, gasping. He was desperately sick of the killing and the dying.

The ground was clear for twenty yards ahead so he stopped to survey the battlefield. It must have been four in the morning. Most of the wall bonfires had burned out and it was impossible to know the true state of the battle, though he thought the enemy had lost seven hundred dead or badly wounded. The allied casualties were more than twice that number, including almost all their officers, and at least half of the four thousand Gwinians were dead. An unknown number had fled and he could not blame them.

Given that the enemy had vast reserves there was no hope of victory, but no point in surrendering either—the Merdrun either tortured their prisoners to death or killed them out of hand. Before he died, Wilm hope to take down the master, the superhuman and invincible Gergrig. But not by himself; he wasn't that much of a fool.

Wilm had discussed his plan with his three most experienced fighters, men who had fought in battles far from Gwine. They were ready to go for Gergrig as soon as Wilm gave the signal, along with another nine Gwinians who would surround Gergrig and prevent any other Merdrun coming to his aid.

And there he was, only forty yards away, his domed, shaven head reflecting the light from a dying bonfire on the eastern wall. His right arm, his killing arm, was red all the way to the shoulder. He ran after a staggering Gwinian and slew him with a thrust to the back, then cut down a second man with a sideways slash. He was a tireless killing machine, dealing death as if it was the only pleasure in his life. He had to be stopped.

"Are we ready?" said Wilm, raising the black sword.

"Sooner die on my feet than chained to one of that bastard's flogging racks," said Yuun, a slim Gwinian who looked no older than Wilm but was almost as good with a sword.

"Then we rush him," said Wilm. "Now!"

He ran, and the twelve went with him, angling across the slope of the hill to cut Gergrig off in a small depression around a cluster of boulders where, with a lot of luck, they might be able to finish him off before anyone realised he was under attack.

Wilm's long legs took him out ahead of the others—or perhaps they, having seen the fate of many of their fellow Gwinians, hung back. In any event he reached Gergrig a good ten yards ahead of his companions. He hurled himself at the Merdrun, who was staring up at the northern hill, where bright white light glowed in a cave.

Gergrig whirled and produced a flurry of blows, cutting Wilm shallowly across the chest and then piercing him under the left arm. Wilm threw himself back, each breath tearing at his throat, and his legs suddenly feeling weak. *The legs are always the first to go.*

Panic almost overwhelmed him, for the three-second exchange had

shown him that he was utterly outmatched; only the enchantments of
the black sword had kept him alive. Gergrig wasn't just brilliant, he
was superlative, head and shoulders above every other Merdrun Wilm
had seen on the battlefield this night.

But there was more to it. The other Merdrun were slower than Wilm
had expected, given what he'd heard of their prowess on Cinnabar.
There they had seemed superhuman; here they fought like experienced
but normal fighters.

Not Gergrig though. He was a big man, but so light on his feet that
at times he appeared to be floating, and so quick that he could parry any
stroke, no matter how unexpected. He *was* being protected by mancery,
and he was being strengthened by it too. The triplets' mancery, surely.

He had not come after Wilm; he was standing with his sword raised,
alternately watching the slowly advancing Gwinians, the steadily brightening shadow of the Crimson Gate, and the glowing cave on the hill.

Wilm groped in a pocket for Aviel's scent potion, desperately need-
ing the strength and self-confidence it could give him, but pricked his
fingers on shards of glass. Sometime during the dozens of battles he'd
fought tonight the phial had been broken and the contents were gone.
He sniffed his fingers but smelled only blood and mud, an unhappy
omen.

But he had to fight and he had to win. "Come on!" he roared.

The other Gwinians charged with him but Gergrig sprang away and
set his back against the tallest boulder, which was higher than his head
and slightly concave. No one could get behind him, or come at him
from the sides without interfering with Wilm's blows.

He went at Gergrig again, and again failed to land a single blow,
though with his third thrust Wilm's sword tip almost touched
Gergrig's windpipe. Gergrig struck back, a thrust that passed through
Wilm's guard and snapped a rib halfway down his left side. The pain
was awful but he had to ignore it. He attacked again and again, and
his seventh stroke cut Gergrig across the back of his right hand. It was
no more than a scratch, yet Gergrig looked down at it in astonishment.

"You touched me," he breathed. "You actually *touched* me."

Again he glanced at the shadow gate, and then at the northern hill. Something had definitely changed: he seemed less in control than before.

Wilm struck again and cut an inch-long slice from the side of Gergrig's right ear.

He slapped a hand to his ear, stared at the blood and then at Wilm, and his eyes narrowed. "You don't have the skill to touch me. It's the damnable sword!"

"You don't have the skill either, *old man*," Wilm sneered. "The moment the triplets stop channelling power to you, you die!"

"Not at your hands, you insolent little pup!"

Gergrig lunged, faster than before, and Wilm would have been impaled had the black sword not jerked back, the hilt slamming into his chest so hard that he was hurled six feet backwards into the mud.

Gergrig started to advance from his niche, but the twelve Gwinians stood resolute, their weapons out, while Wilm climbed to his feet, his chest aching. Gergrig smiled grimly. "One at a time then."

He now fought harder and faster than ever. Wilm's broken rib and gashed side were so painful that it was a struggle to fight on, and his knees were shaking. He had not had a decent meal since the gate brought him to Gwine five weeks ago and he was rapidly burning what little energy he had left. He could not win.

Gergrig struck a series of blows which the sword just managed to parry. He wasn't attacking Wilm any more; he was targeting the black blade. He struck a mighty blow, and the black sword flew from Wilm's sweaty hand and landed in the mud a couple of yards away.

He staggered and fell to one knee, unable to get up. Gergrig raised his sword for a blow that would take Wilm's head off. But then he gasped as if he'd been kicked in the belly and froze in mid-stroke, shooting a desperate glance towards the northern hill.

White smoke was belching from the glowing cave. Then, with a colossal, rolling *BOOM*, the outline of the Crimson Gate vanished. Something had gone wrong for Gergrig and Wilm knew this was his last chance.

He dived for his sword, rolled over and came up with it in his hand, barely avoiding a blow that buried the blade of Gergrig's weapon a foot in the soft ground. Gergrig wrenched it out, but before he could strike again Wilm's upthrust struck his breastbone and went in for a good half-inch. Gergrig reeled back to his niche, shocked and shaken—an inch to either side and he would have been dead.

He attacked again, but now he was no longer superhuman; he was just a normal Merdrun warrior, experienced and quick, but desperately tired after hours of fighting. He could be beaten.

"Merdrun!" Gergrig bellowed. "To me, to me!"

But he had moved out of the shelter of the boulder, and Wilm's companions rushed him from all sides. Gergrig cut one down, then another, then a third, but Yuun drove his blade three inches into Gergrig's upper thigh just below the hip bone. The blow roused Gergrig to greater fury and he killed two more Gwinians with blows that hinted at his earlier mastery. But only hinted.

Another Gwinian had taken his boots off and was climbing the boulder. He reached the top and launched himself at Gergrig, landing with all his weight on his head and shoulders and driving him into the ground. Gergrig shook off the Gwinian and slew him with a slash to the neck, but as Gergrig rose, Wilm and the other Gwinians all attacked at once.

"Merdrun!" Gergrig roared, desperately this time. "To me!"

Crack-crack-crash! The roof of the glowing cave had fallen in. Gergrig reeled as if he'd been stabbed in the back.

Fighting despairingly now, he killed another Gwinian then put his sword through the muscle of Wilm's left upper arm. Wilm had to finish it before the Merdrun came to his rescue. He thrust again, and this time the black sword slipped between two ribs into the outer side of his right lung.

Gergrig looked stunned, disbelieving. Had he believed he could never be defeated?

Holding Wilm at bay with his sword, he put his free hand inside his shirt, jerked out a small red cube that might have been cut from the Crimson Gate, and pressed it to the glyph on his forehead. A wisp of smoke rose from it and Gergrig raised the cube to the sky, crying, "Merdrax! *Merdrax?*"

Gergrig cocked his head as if listening, nodded then rapped out orders in a harsh language Wilm did not know. Was he calling for help? Three Merdrun were racing across. Wilm had to finish him.

He ran in and swung hard at Gergrig's neck. Gergrig parried the blow absently, still giving orders. Wilm struck again and again, moving a little further to the right each time, but Gergrig parried every blow. He seemed desperate to convey his message, whatever it was.

While he was distracted Yuun moved in from the left, spat on Gergrig's boots and contemptuously glided the blade of his sword across Gergrig's throat. It was not a deep wound but deep enough. Blood sprayed out.

Gergrig tried to finish his message but could not. He turned to Yuun, his wide eyes conveying some private horror, then slowly crumpled. He hit the ground, one foot kicking and the breath bubbling in his severed windpipe, then his head flopped into the mud.

"He's dead," said Wilm, then raised the black sword as high as he could and let out a ringing cry that no one could have failed to hear: "GERGRIG IS DEAD!"

The three Merdrun turned and ran, but the Gwinians went after them and cut them down, and several others they came to.

Silence fell. Absolute silence.

Wilm looked around. Something had definitely changed: the mental pressure he had been under ever since the battle began had gone. The reserves on the wall had gone too. Were they coming down to attack? Despite the hot night and his exertions, he shivered.

"We've beaten the bastards!" someone shouted in a Thurkad accent from further across the battlefield. "We've won!"

Silence again.

"We've won, you morons!" the same voice bellowed. "Let's hear you say it."

"We've won!" roared a hundred throats, then more and more. "We've won, we've won, we've won!"

"We can't have won," said Wilm. "They've got thousands of reserves."

"They're running like the cowardly dogs they are," said someone behind him.

"Whatever the Merdrun are, they're not cowards."

"Then where have they gone?"

An awful thought struck him. "That glow up on the hill—did the triplets open the Crimson Gate somewhere else, to attack Thurkad or some other place?"

No one answered. Suddenly Wilm felt cold and afraid. Had it all been for nothing?

Tallia came running. "What's going on?" said Wilm. "I don't understand what just happened."

"Llian and Sulien severed the link between the triplets, destroying them as magiz," said Tallia. "And they died when I pulled the roof down. It's over."

"How can it be over? They had more than ten thousand troops, ten thousand of the best fighters in the void. Where are the rest?"

"They never got here."

"But they had all those reserves."

"Xarah has finally tracked the full path of the Crimson Gate," said Tallia. "Only a thousand Merdrun came through before it closed. We have you and Aviel to thank for that."

"Only a thousand," Wilm said dazedly. "But—"

"The reserves on the hill were just illusions created by the triplets' mancery, using the immense power they could draw from the summon stone. That's why they never moved. They were good enough to fool us from a distance, but not up close."

"And when the triplets died, they vanished. So it really *is* over."

"It'll only be over when the summon stone has been destroyed."

"But we've won." Wilm could not take it in.

"At a terrible cost," Tallia said quietly.

"How bad?"

"Of our twenty-three hundred troops, two thousand are dead, including almost all our officers."

"And more than two thousand of my Gwinians."

"Four of our troops died for every Merdrun, and even then we had it easier than we should have," said Tallia

"What are you talking about?"

"Karan said that on Cinnabar they were almost superhuman. They could fight for hours without tiring and they didn't so much run as bound. But they weren't bounding here. They tired just as quickly as our best."

"I did wonder about that," said Wilm. "But why?"

"Cinnabar is a small world, and the Merdrun's muscles gave them extra strength there. But Santhenar is a much bigger world and they weren't here long enough to adapt to it. Everything felt heavier and every movement was harder."

"Are you saying that if the Merdrun had adapted, we wouldn't have won?"

"It might have taken ten thousand of us to beat their one thousand."

"Then we'd better pray they never find a way to reopen the Crimson Gate."

69

THEY'RE RAISING A NEW MAGIZ

An hour before dawn Karan was still barely alive, and Sulien could not stand it any longer. She kissed her on the forehead and walked away across the camp, sick with guilt. Was it her fault Karan was dying? It must be. According to Tallia, Karan had panicked on hearing that Sulien had come through the gate, and the triplets had then drawn her into their trap.

Sulien was trudging across the muddy ground near the stream, keeping well away from the battlefields to east and west, when her gift picked up a familiar, anguished mental outburst.

"Uigg?" she said softly.

He groaned, not far away. She squelched through the mud and found him huddled behind a clump of reeds. She hesitated for a moment—he was Merdrun after all—but he was also a confused and terrified boy not much older than herself.

She knelt beside him. His chest was wet with blood. "Uigg, what happened?"

His voice was feeble, thread-like. "I betrayed my people."

"By not telling your father about me?"

"I did a terrible wrong. I had to confess it and take my punishment."

"What . . . happened?"

"Father had no choice. He had to kill me; that's our way."

"It's a terrible way!" she cried.

"I know that now," he said, voice gurgling in his throat. "You taught me the meaning of kindness."

"There's a great healer close by. I'll bring him."

"Too late. Soon be gone." His mud-covered hand gripped hers. "My people are bad people. It isn't right that they want to steal Santhenar from you."

"But what can we do?" said Sulien.

"We . . . have one . . . weakness. And . . . and . . . I'm your best clue to it."

Uigg's hand fell away, his throat gave a final gurgle, and he was dead. Sulien remained beside him, kneeling in the mud. Had he been killed because she had been kind to him? She had certainly brought conflicts to the surface that he had been struggling with for some time. If she had never contacted him, would he still be alive?

The question was unanswerable. She closed Uigg's eyes and with a heavy heart stumbled back to the barely living.

"Is she any better?" said Llian in a leaden voice.

Dawn had broken. He was sitting on the paved parade ground, well away from the grim evidence of the first battle, still holding Karan in his arms. She had not moved since he'd picked her up, and he felt sure she was slipping away. Sulien had come back and, judging by the desperate look on her face, she thought so too.

Zanser sat beside Llian, his bloody sewn-together thigh stretched out, periodically checking Karan's vital signs. Her pale skin was cool and waxen, her pulse weak, her belly still swollen and her breathing slow and shallow.

"The same," said Zanser, who was clearly in great pain.

The Merdrun were dead and Sulien was safe at last—one small joy in a sea of torment. Tallia had signalled to the sky ships, then had gone to round up their surviving troops. Various people Llian knew straggled in, including Ussarine and Hingis. Neither spoke, though they stood very close. Llian did not have the strength to wonder what had happened between them.

Wilm appeared, his ragged clothes dripping and his skin so vigorously scrubbed that it was glowing. He must have bathed in the dam further down the hill.

He crouched beside Llian, wincing. "How is she?"

"Not good." Llian could not focus on anything save the cool weight in his arms and the piercing throbbing in the nose he had broken soon after arriving on Gwine.

Wilm rose slowly, letting out an involuntary groan and clutching at his side.

"Let me see that," said Zanser.

"You've got Karan to look after. It can wait."

"Show me!"

Wilm drew up his shirt, revealing a two-inch wound and a broken rib. Zanser put his palm over it and held it there for a minute.

"You're lucky," he said. "No serious damage, but another couple of inches . . ."

A sky ship settled a quarter of a mile away, and shortly Yggur's tall figure appeared. He stopped by Ussarine and Hingis for some time. Llian assumed they were giving him the news. Yggur's eyes flicked towards Llian and Sulien, then settled on Karan.

He strode across, crouched down wearily and laid two long fingers across her brow. Yggur frowned and turned to Zanser. "And you are?" he said.

"Zanser, master healer from Roros."

"Then you're more use than I am." Yggur got up. "Where's Tallia?"

Wilm pointed west. "She went to search Gergrig's tent."

In the distance squads were burying the bodies. They would want to get as many underground as possible before the sun, the flies and the heat of the day made the job intolerable. Llian looked down at Karan and a choking sob burst out of him, then suddenly he was bawling and Sulien was too, hugging them both and clinging as if she never wanted to let go.

Suddenly she pulled away. "The gate's coming."

Half a mile to the south yellow lightning fizzed and crackled, then formed a neat egg-shaped oval, much smaller than before. When Malien emerged Tallia and Yggur brought her across, along with Xarah and three other Aachim Llian had not seen before.

Malien also checked Karan, then said, "I'll send—"

Sulien was staring up into the sky, her green eyes wide. She rotated three times, then stopped, staring in the same direction.

"They're raising a new magiz," she said in a low, moaning voice.

Llian held Karan more tightly and rocked back and forth. Sulien's words held no meaning for him; nothing did.

Malien put an arm around Sulien. "All the Merdrun are dead. You don't have to worry about them any more."

Sulien pulled away. "It's the ones on Cinnabar. Their new magiz is an old man. A very bad man, and he's right next to the Crimson Gate. He's reaching out to it, and there's lightning spiking up from the top."

"How do you know?"

Sulien hesitated. "When I banged the triplets' heads together I *got something* from them."

"What?" Malien said sharply.

"I don't know."

"What else can you see?" rapped Yggur.

"A gigantic army on the ice, all around the gate. It's much bigger than the army they had there before." Her lips moved; she appeared to be counting. "It covers the whole top of the mountain."

The voices briefly broke through Llian's agony. *What were they talking about?*

"The army they had there before was at least ten thousand," Malien said to Tallia and Yggur. "And if this one is much bigger—"

"It's ten times bigger," said Sulien. "The soldiers have blocks of stone on their backs and iron weights on their legs, and they're running round and round."

"Before Gergrig died, he told them what had happened here," said Tallia. "They're training to be fit to attack again. Malien, we've got to attack the summon stone right away. Send someone back to Zile. We've got to have the nivol, if Aviel has finished making it."

"And if she hasn't?"

"All is lost."

Llian struggled to his feet with Karan in his arms. This could not be happening; how could victory, agonising though it had been, turn in an instant to defeat?

Malien called two Aachim across. "Return through the gate to Zile. Collect Aviel and all the gear she needs, and Nadiril. Load our last three sky ships and all the supplies we'll need for an attack on the stone, then fly to . . ."

"Healer's Isle," said Yggur. "The Isle of Qwale. It's got the best healers this side of Crandor, and it's only a five-hour flight west to Demondifang. We'll take Karan and as many other injured as we can carry there."

"Whereabouts on Qwale? It's a big island."

He crouched down and with the point of his knife scratched a triangular outline on the paving stones, then marked a point on the south-western side. "Nukkilick. The central square of the healery."

"Have you been there?" said Malien.

"Many times," said Yggur, "during my . . . troubles."

"You can direct the gate." Malien turned to her two Aachim. "Bring the sky ships to Nukkilick on Qwale. Run!"

They ran for the gate.

Malien, Tallia and Yggur squatted down and conferred for ten or fifteen minutes. Yggur sketched a number of maps or diagrams on the ground with the point of his knife, and they studied them, talking in low voices. Llian paid no attention. He did not care.

Then, with considerable effort, Malien and Yggur diverted the gate to Nukkilick.

"It's ready," she called.

Tallia lifted Zanser to his feet, and they gazed into each other's eyes, then she helped him across to the gate. Llian took a firm grip on Karan and, with Sulien beside him, walked into the gate. He did not look back; he never wanted to see Gwine again.

The passage was an unusually smooth one; Llian supposed that was Malien's doing. A minute later, with a reverberating *crack-crack*, they exited into a small square paved with black hexagonal slabs and surrounded on four sides by low buildings built from the local stone, a magnificent patterned marble with swirls of red, yellow and blue. Dawn was just breaking this far south and it was very cold; the humid air gushing through the gate condensed to fog.

Two stocky female healers who looked like sisters bustled out with a canvas stretcher. They took Karan from Llian's arms and laid her down on the canvas.

"I've been attending her," said Zanser, still leaning on Tallia and clearly in a lot of pain. "Stabbed in the belly three hours ago. Lost a lot of blood, internally. I'm a master healer—Crandor."

One of the healers frowned. Her sister said something in a low voice, though all Llian heard was, "That's the Magister."

The first healer looked Zanser up and down, focused on his bare, bloody thigh and the many stitches down it, then nodded. "Come with us."

They carried Karan under a marble portico and in through double doors. Llian made to follow, but the first healer said, "You'll be sent for when we have something to tell you."

Sulien squeezed Llian's hand. "Mummy will be all right now." She followed the healers, trying to look inconspicuous. Another healer came out, gave Zanser his shoulder, and they also went in.

Cold fear washed over Llian. They'd got here too late; Karan's wound had been bleeding for so long not even the best healers in the world could save her. He would never see her again.

"Come with me," said Tallia. "We need to go through the plan in detail."

"What plan?" he said dully.

"The one Yggur, Malien and I worked out half an hour ago—right next to you."

"Wasn't listening," said Llian. "Don't care."

"I need you for the attack on the summon stone."

"Not as much as Karan and Sulien do. Haven't we done enough?"

"If we stop before the job's done we'll soon be fighting the Merdrun again, and they'll be a hell of a lot stronger next time."

"I'm not up to it."

"Llian," she said coldly, "You've just seen what a thousand unfit Merdrun could do. What will a hundred thousand of them be like after they've trained for Santhenar? An army of half a million would not be able to stop them."

Sulien peeped out the front doors of the healery at Llian, then disappeared inside. He could not speak. If he went on this mad mission, would he ever see either of them again?

70

THE GREATEST TREACHERY OF ALL

After a tormented night in the visitors' dormitory beside the healery, his dreams haunted by blood, violence and utter despair, Llian was shaken awake by Tallia.

"Get up. We've got him, and you're wanted at the trial."

"Got who? What trial?"

"Shand."

"He's here?"

"We set a trap and he walked off the sky ship, still invisible, right into it."

Llian followed her across the courtyard to another imposing building and into a large square room lined with slabs of superlative red- and blue-veined marble. It would have graced the reception rooms of a palace anywhere else, but on Qwale it was just the local stone used everywhere.

A square table made from a pale yellow hardwood had a dozen chairs around it though only half were occupied. Tallia, Malien, Yggur and Nadiril sat along one side. Nadiril gestured Llian to the seat beside him. Shand and Ifoli stood by the other side of the table, wearing hand manacles. What had Ifoli done?

"We'll try Shand first," said Tallia. "Briefly. There's no time to waste."

Shand put his square hands on the table. A dark silvery chain ran in a spiral around his wrist manacles. Some kind of mancery blocker, Llian assumed. He looked haggard and much thinner than when Llian had last seen him at Alcifer five weeks ago.

"Shand, you are charged with treachery, punishable by death," said Tallia. "You betrayed our secrets to the Merdrun, and—"

"I *betrayed* no secrets to the Merdrun," snapped Shand, "or to anyone else."

"You revealed our secrets to the magiz on Cinnabar, allowing her to whisper them to Snoat, who blocked us at every turn."

"*I* revealed nothing. She put some kind of link in me when I was searching for Maigraith two months ago. I never knew anything about it, so how can I be accused—"

"Ignorance is no excuse. Karan told you the magiz was boasting about her *pet spy*, but did you examine yourself to see if that spy could be you? You did not! You blamed Karan and Yggur to divert attention from yourself."

"At my first examination," said Malien, "you refused to consider that Karan's accusation could be true, then used an illegal invisibility spell to escape justice. But did you use your freedom to help us in our great need?"

"I did, actually," Shand said coldly.

"Liar!" said Nadiril. "You coerced and threatened Aviel, *a child*. With utter recklessness and callous disregard for her life you used her equipment to prepare the Afflatus Effluvium, a forbidden, flawed and highly danger-ous scent potion that killed your own master, Radizer, and could have killed her. You used her very badly, Shand; you gave her an alchemical formula that's also forbidden and even more dangerous, not to help her—"

"The method I gave Aviel was the only one that could create nivol in time."

"But you gave it to her because it was the only way you could get Archeus for your own potion. You risked everyone's lives to get it, Shand, utterly indifferent to their fate."

The defiance faded from Shand face. "Not indifferent," he said softly. "But you're right: I was unforgivably reckless."

His old face cracked, and for an awful moment Llian thought Shand was going to cry.

"I'd planned it so there would be no danger to anyone but myself," he went on. "I planned to capture Lumillal before anyone could come to harm, but I failed; I didn't know he'd consumed the spirit of a considerable sorcerer—his own wife!—and gained her gift for the black art. Because of my folly Aviel was almost consumed by a ghost vampire, and Earnis was, and it will haunt me all my remaining days."

"Which will be numbered on the fingers of a leper's hand unless you can satisfy us about the greatest treachery of all," said Tallia. "Even knowing that Aviel had to make as much nivol as possible, you stole the one essential ingredient—the Archeus."

"You got it back in time," said Ifoli.

Tallia gave her a very cold stare. "Why, Shand?"

"Ifoli and I have been working on a vital project," said Shand. "One that could save us. The proof is in the device you took from me."

"Ah, yes." Tallia put a battered red leather bag on the table and withdrew an object a handspan across made of six short copper tubes sticking out of a central graphite hub like the spokes of a small wheel. "This . . . *conglomeration*. What is it, pray?"

"It's a greatly improved version of Unick's Command device. Ifoli and I saw that if it were made properly it would be the most powerful device ever built on Santhenar. It would allow a mancer—assuming he had the strength and the skill—to find, control and use all other sources of power, even great natural sources of power that are presently not known to us."

"What on earth are you talking about?" said Nadiril.

"Coming to that," said Shand. "The device would also allow us to *block* sources of power, including the summon stone."

"Ah!" said Yggur.

"That's why I needed the Archeus," Shand went on. "To make the Afflatus Effluvium."

"To what purpose?"

"It gave us the insights to work out what was wrong with the Command device, and how to improve it. Ifoli was the only one who understood Unick's original design."

"That would be the same Ifoli who served Snoat faithfully for two years," Yggur said coldly. "She was so keen to be the perfect servant that she even served him in bed."

Ifoli put her head in her hands. Nadiril looked away.

"We might have overlooked all those crimes," Tallia said relentlessly, "had your device actually worked. But this ... monstrosity—" she nudged it with the back of her hand "—isn't even as strong as Unick's."

"Of course it isn't," said Shand. "We never found the black crystal from the original device, so we don't yet know what it was."

Ifoli raised her head. Her eyes were red. "With the right crystal our device will be many times more powerful—and it can draw on an entirely new source of power that—"

"Sulien was the first person to see," said Shand.

"What the hell have you been up to?" cried Llian, leaping to his feet. "How dare you use my daughter in your corrupt schemes?"

"I didn't," Shand said wearily. "She was spying on us in the ruins of Zile. We got into trouble and she saved our lives, and then, quite by accident, she saw this new source of power ..."

Llian was shaking. How could this have happened, right under his nose? "Why don't I know anything about this?"

"You'd have to ask her." Shand explained what had happened. "And it's the most important breakthrough in mancery in a thousand years."

He had everyone's attention now.

"Go on," said Tallia, leaning forward eagerly. "But this had better be good."

"Until now," said Ifoli, "mancers have only been able to get their power from three places: their own frail bodies, or via the necromantic arts from the bodies of others, or from artefacts that have been painstakingly enchanted. But Sulien saw an entirely new source of power, a natural source far greater than anything we've been able to use before . . ."

"Continue," said Yggur.

"We call this source a field, and it's formed around a natural node— the great fault line west of Zile."

"How is it formed?" said Tallia, frowning.

"I don't know, but we suspect there may be other nodes and other fields—almost certainly there's one at Demondifang. With our new Command device we've been able to draw tiny amounts of power from the fault-line field. And when we discover the right black crystal—"

Yggur held up a hand and conferred briefly with Nadiril, Malien and Tallia. "You've bought yourselves a reprieve," he said, "though only because we're desperate."

"We've got to attack the summon stone right away," said Malien.

"So we're prepared to give you two a chance," said Tallia. "We're sending three sky ships to Demondifang at first light and you'll both be on them. Yggur will take charge of the Command device."

Yggur rose, locked a metal collar around Shand neck before he could move, then another around Ifoli's.

"What are they for?" snarled Shand.

"If there's any further evidence of treachery," said Yggur, "I trigger the collars."

71

IT WOULD HAVE BEEN A DISASTER

Yggur climbed aboard the first sky ship. Llian, white-faced and blank-eyed, went next, stumbling on the ladder and nearly falling. Aviel felt for him. Karan was hovering between life and death; he was in agony and clearly could not comprehend why he had been sent on this desperate mission.

Ifoli and Shand followed in silence, then fourteen soldiers and their baby-faced captain. Aviel waited until everyone was in their seats then climbed the ladder and heaved herself in, limping more than usual. She had overstrained her ankle on the walk to Rogues Render and back, and none of the scent potions she had made in increasingly desperate attempts to heal it had made any difference.

Now this madness. The previous attack on the summon stone had been a disaster, and the stories she had heard about Whelm trapped in the unreality zone, embedded in trees or rocks while still alive, gave her the horrors. Would that be her fate, as punishment for her ventures to the dark side?

The captain of the squad, a slim young fellow who did not look much older than herself, pulled a grey curtain across the rear half of the cabin, hiding the soldiers from view. The sky ship, with Yggur at the helm, lifted off and headed west across forested hills for Demondifang.

Aviel sat with her fingers writhing in her lap and a painful knot in her belly. There had not been time to finish making the second batch of nivol. The final stage of preparation remained, though she did not see how it could be done in an unsteady sky ship. Everything—all these people's lives, the lives of everyone back on Healer's Isle and the fate of the world—depended on her now. What if she mucked it up? It was easy to get things wrong in alchemy; if one tiny step was done imperfectly the whole procedure would fail, and it would be her fault.

"Once we're out over the sea we'll have clear air for an hour or two," said Yggur to Aviel. "It'll be your best chance. If you need a hand, Llian can help."

She glanced sideways at Llian. He was a famous man, a good man too. He had freed Wilm from the slave camp, and that had meant the difference between victory and defeat, but she did not see how he could help her now. He looked . . . broken.

"Alchemy requires delicate hands," said Shand, "and Llian is a clodhopper."

"His calligraphy in the *Tale of the Mirror* was almost perfect," said Yggur coldly. "It can't be you or Ifoli, for the obvious reason—"

"That you don't trust us not to bugger it up."

"Good of you to be so understanding."

Aviel glanced at Ifoli, whose only reaction had been to hunch even further down in her seat. Aviel had heard so much about her: how extraordinarily beautiful she was, how brilliant, how accomplished in a dozen separate fields, how quick thinking.

This Ifoli was undoubtedly beautiful but looked tormented. Had she, in her desperation to be the perfect spy and gain the respect of her famous great-grandfather, also gone too far down the dark path? It was a warning Aviel must not ignore.

When they were out over the Sea of Qwale, in steady air, she went to the workbench the Aachim had installed against the left side of the cabin. They had carved recesses to hold the bases of every piece of equipment she needed to use, and had fixed her apparatus stands to the bench top.

Llian rose. "What do you want me to do?" he said dully.

"Nothing yet."

Aviel was used to working by herself at her own pace, and having the clumsy Llian as her assistant made her feel self-conscious and irritable. She could feel the sequence of procedures, which she had done perfectly after Rogues Render and had fixed carefully in her mind again, slipping away.

She imagined that she was in her beloved workshop in Casyme, with the door closed to keep the outside world at bay. Slowly the tension eased, and the other people in the sky ship faded into the background. It was not a bumpy flight so far, though the gentle rocking of the sky ship required her to constantly adjust her balance, and soon her bad ankle was throbbing.

She put a colophony disc in a flask and set a golden brimstone in the middle, dribbled spirits of wine around it as before, ignited it, put the top on and opened the glass stopcock.

Llian hovered irritatingly. She wanted him to go away, but how could she say so when he had done so much for Wilm? And when Llian was in such agony?

Once the initial condensate had been discarded she connected the first of her layered filters, waited until the condensate had passed through, and checked the colour, which was the palest pink. She connected the next filter, continued the process, then the one after, making sure the sequence of colour changes was exactly as the procedure stated. Finally, after more than an hour, the drips went a shimmering silvery white.

Over the next twenty minutes, drip by careful drip, she collected a fifth of a cup of the silvery liquid into a flask before the condensate in the tube took on a pale blue hue. Aviel carried the precious flask down to a small stand to which the diamond phial was clamped, placed the flask in its carved recess and slipped a pre-weighed piece of sintered platinum into the phial. She then dripped a hundred and thirty-six drops of the shimmering condensate onto the sintered platinum and checked the colour. It was still silvery white, though no longer shimmering. Now for the final, exceedingly dangerous step. Every eye in the cabin was on her. Her hands were shaking, her heart pounding and sweat was running down her forehead.

"Llian!" she snapped. "Sweat's getting in my eyes."

He wiped her forehead with a rag and stood by.

"Wash your hands and dry them."

He scrubbed them in the bowl at the far end of the bench and wiped them on a pure-white towel.

"See that bottle," she said, indicating the one clamped into a deep recess near the end of the bench. It was a quarter full of the thick oily yellow-green fluid. When she had last seen it, it had been half full— Shand must have used the rest. "Take the wire off the stopper but don't open it until I say so."

"Why not?"

"It contains the Archeus distilled from a deadly ghost vampire called Lumillal, and it's very, very dangerous. Hold the stopper in."

A spark lit in Llian's eyes for the first time. "I'd love to hear that tale."

Aviel noticed Shand's smouldering eyes on her. What was he thinking about? She took a small measuring cylinder, put a glass funnel on top and limped down to Llian; she didn't trust him not to trip over if he brought the bottle to her.

"Lift the stopper out, very carefully."

His hands were steadier than hers. When he lifted the stopper out, wisps of yellow-green Archeus trailed up as if, even after all this time, Lumillal's spirit essence was still trying to escape. Aviel took the bottle, her hands shaking, poured twenty-four drams into the measuring cylinder and rapped, "Stopper it and wire the stopper down."

He did so, then put the bottle back in its recess and clamped it down. She dribbled the Archeus in, following the steps as before, removed the plug of azure jelly and the sintered platinum and rinsed them three times, then checked the colour of the liquid at the bottom of the diamond phial. It was a brilliant green, just as it should be.

She felt exceedingly weary. The process had taken almost three hours; they were three quarters of the way to Demondifang, and she had been on her feet the whole time.

"It's done," she said hoarsely, holding up the phial so Yggur could see it. "Eight drops of nivol."

The sky ship lurched. Pain shrieked through her right ankle and she fell sideways. The diamond phial hit the side of the bench, and for an awful moment she thought the nivol was going to spill. Llian caught her by the waist with strong hands, steadying her.

"Thank you," she whispered, shivering.

Had even a single drop of nivol spilled it would have been a disaster. There was no way to clean it up, and even washed down with water it would eat through the floor of the sky ship within minutes. She stoppered the phial carefully, snapped a band tightly from stopper to base to hold it on, then put it away.

"Well done," said Yggur.

Aviel lurched across to her seat and collapsed into it. She could not have stood up any longer. She closed her eyes, trying to hold back tears of pain, then rubbed her throbbing ankle. That did not help, and it was bound to get a lot worse before they returned to Qwale.

If they ever did.

72

GIVE THE NIVOL TO LLIAN

Working with Aviel had drawn Llian out of his endless agonising about Karan, but now, as the sky ships approached Demondifang from the east, the pain returned redoubled.

What if she had come to, calling for him, and he was not there? What if she had died and Sulien was having to carry the burden all alone? She did not even know where he was—he had not been permitted to tell her. Sulien would only know that in their greatest need he was not there—again! Curse the war, curse the summon stone and curse Yggur, Malien, Nadiril, Tallia and Shand!

"The other two sky ships are decoys," said Yggur. "The first one carries spring-fired harpoons with square ends made from hardened steel."

"Won't work," said Shand quietly, rubbing the metal collar around his neck.

"Maybe you don't want it to work. The Aachim who made the harpoons believe that, fired with great force, they'll smash the summon stone to bits."

"It won't let them get near."

Llian listened to this exchange with increasing alarm. With Shand and Yggur constantly at each other's throats and Aviel in constant pain, how could they hope to succeed?

Especially if Shand was, as clearly Tallia and Malien feared, still a traitor. Could the first magiz's link have survived her death? Might the triplets have reactivated it? Could the new magiz on Cinnabar take him over again? Why had Shand been sent anyway, when the new Command device was so weak?

"Quiet," said Yggur, jerking his head towards the grey curtain. Behind it, the baby-faced captain was briefing his troops: "The second sky ship is loaded with barrels of blasting powder. It'll attack the stone from another direction at the same time."

"Just as useless," muttered Shand, "and a damn sight more dangerous."

Yggur shrugged. "They're just here to make a diversion so we can sneak in from the west and put down at the very edge of the peak."

"Same plan that failed last time," Llian muttered. "Anyway, the great storm won't let us get near the peak."

"Xarah says the summon stone has been weaker since Gergrig and the triplets were killed; the storm too. I'm hoping to set down at the western end in an area concealed from the stone by a rocky ridge."

"The summon stone doesn't *see*," said Ifoli softly. "It senses."

"Best we can do. That's the peak on the horizon—we'll be there within the hour."

Aviel whimpered. Was she reliving the terrors at Carcharon, when Unick had tried to feed her to the summon stone? Llian took her hands. She clung to him desperately, her eyes closed, her whole body trembling.

He swallowed. *And it already knows we're coming.*

Yggur turned hard to the right to stay well to the north of the island, and accelerated. Llian, looking out the window, saw the other two sky ships continuing slowly on, a couple of hundred yards apart. How could their diversion work when the stone knew three ships were coming?

"It's changed again," said Ifoli forty minutes later, after they had gone past the island, turned south and were now heading back towards it from the west. She kept pressing her fingertips to the shiny collar around her slender neck. If things went wrong, or Yggur saw evidence of treachery, would he hesitate or would he just trigger the collars? Llian could not bear to think about that.

The monstrous thunderhead that had hung above the peak for more than a month was gone. The sky was clear in all directions, though every so often a flash of blue lightning burst up or out from the peak where the summon stone stood.

"It's damaged and uncontrolled," said Yggur. "Spraying power in all directions."

"The more power it discharges," said Shand, "the weaker it'll become."

"If one of those lightning bolts hits us . . ." whispered Aviel.

"We'll die without knowing what happened," said Shand with a grim chuckle.

"Why is that amusing?" said Yggur coldly.

"It's the perfect death. In a single flash, all our worries about friends or family, even the future of Santhenar in the hands of the Merdrun, become irrelevant."

"Only a traitor would find that comforting."

Shand closed his mouth with a snap. Llian, now thoroughly unnerved, went to the large window at the front of the cabin and looked out. "There's smoke everywhere. Most of the forest has burned."

"I dare say the lightning—" began Yggur.

"It looks like the fires were deliberately lit. Everything's been burned from the edge of the mangroves up to the yellow cliffs."

"Deliberately?" Yggur descended and raced across the smoking forest a few hundred feet up.

Llian peered down. The lower and middle sections of the island had been burned some time ago, and parts of the upper slopes; most of the forest had been reduced to ash and smoking stumps. Then a long, gaunt face looked up, and another. They were everywhere.

"Whelm!" cried Llian. "Thousands of them. They must have burned the forest to kill the chimaera and all the other mad stuff in the unreality zones. But why?"

"The Whelm's motives are simple and never change," said Yggur. "Gergrig's death and the defeat of the Merdrun on Gwine would have been an awful blow. The master they'd yearned for all these years, and a month ago swore to serve, is gone."

"It would have strengthened their resolve to take charge of the stone," said Shand.

"Why?" said Aviel.

"To protect it until the Merdrun's new magiz on Cinnabar can reopen the Crimson Gate. If the Whelm can aid them in that, it'll prove how worthy they are to serve the Merdrun's next leader— Merdrax, presumably."

"Then we've got to get to the stone before the Whelm do," said Llian.

Yggur banked the sky ship around and raced back to the west. "The other ships are going in. Aviel, tell the troops to get ready."

As they shot past the western end of the peak Llian saw that the summon stone had turned the brown of a scab on an old wound. The trilithon was eroded, cracked and tilted so crazily to the left that it was a wonder it was still standing.

Before Aviel could move, the grey curtain was wrenched back. The captain stood there, swaying on his small feet as the sky ship lurched and bounced in the smoky air. "We're ready!"

"Better tell us the plan," said Shand, green eyes glinting.

Yet again Llian's doubts surfaced. If Shand betrayed them now . . . *No! I know the man better than that . . . don't I?*

Did Yggur and the others have a solid reason for their suspicions? Did they think Shand had craved the summon stone's power all this time, as he had at Carcharon? Was that what he had really been doing with the Archeus and his six-spoked Command device—crafting something that would allow him to control the stone?

"The moment the other sky ships attack," said Yggur, "I'll dive to the sheltered area behind the western ridge and land. Shand, Llian, Ifoli and six of the soldiers will take the nivol and head for the summon stone."

"Why only six?" said Shand.

"The Whelm know we're here now and they can't let us destroy the stone. The only quick way up onto the peak is via the path at the western end. We'll hold them back while you do the job."

"Thousands of Whelm?" Shand said sceptically.

"They can only come up in single file." Yggur looked up. "That's Hublees firing!"

Hublees' ramshackle sky ship hurtled in from the east, and Llian saw it shudder each time one of the heavy harpoons was discharged. He could not see them in flight, but a churning ball of orange fire formed a few yards in front of the trilithon, then a second ball and a third. They coalesced into a fiery orange spear that shot back towards the sky ship's airbag. It exploded in a fireball that rained blazing debris and bodies down on the eastern side of Demondifang. The comical little mancer was dead, and everyone in his sky ship.

Aviel gasped and snatched at Llian's hand. "Those poor people."

It had been so quick, so final and so *easy* that Llian knew they had no hope of succeeding. "We'll be lucky if we even make it onto the peak," he said to no one in particular.

"Lucky!" Ifoli said shrilly.

Another orange fire spear sizzled up towards their own sky ship, but Yggur dived and it passed harmlessly overhead. He raced down towards the landing place, a patch of broken rock not much bigger than the vessel.

The third sky ship roared in from the north and hurled two barrels of blasting powder from a spring-loaded catapult. Llian saw them arcing towards the summon stone one after the other, but both barrels exploded long before they got near. Working furiously, the catapult crew slammed in a third barrel; the sky ship was so close now that Llian saw it clearly.

The top of the barrel came off, spilling black powder everywhere. A spark ignited it, and the contents of the barrel flared like a monstrous skyrocket. The sky ship disappeared behind the peak, there was a small *boom* and a fireball appeared above the mountain.

"And they were dead," Llian said quietly. *And we'll be next.* Beside him Aviel had gone as white as a boiled egg.

Yggur's sky ship landed on the bare yellow rock with a crash. A ridge of yellow rock with a cleft running through it concealed them from the summon stone, which was a few hundred yards to their right. The path down the western cliff was on their left.

"Out!" he bellowed.

"Wait!" cried Llian, for already he could feel the corrupt emanations from the stone probing at him, trying to find a way in. "The stone will try to lure us to it—to feed on us—and some of us will find it irresistible. Keep a close watch on each other. If anyone is drawn to it, stop them."

"How?" said the baby-faced captain.

"Knock them out if there's no other way."

The captain thrust the door open and leaped down. It was windy. Two soldiers tied the sky ship down fore and aft, and half a dozen more took up positions to guard the top of the steep, narrow path that was the only way the Whelm could come up. Yggur, Shand and Ifoli disembarked. Ifoli's face was even more drawn than before and she was holding her back. Llian got out and Aviel struggled after him, carrying the diamond phial.

"Stay with me, Aviel," said Yggur. Then, as Shand reached out for the phial and she was about to hand it to him, Yggur added, "Give the nivol to Llian."

Shand froze, and a terrible sadness crossed his weathered features, though it was quickly replaced by the cold rage Llian had seen so often in the past months. "Even now, even *here*, you don't trust me."

"Trust has to be earned, Shand. It can't be manufactured on demand." Yggur turned to the captain. "Go with Llian, Shand and Ifoli. Make sure their way to the stone is clear."

"Be careful," Llian reminded the captain. "The summon stone will promise you your greatest desire."

He rolled his eyes. "We're trained soldiers!"

He led the other eight soldiers into the cleft. Llian waited, his heart thundering and his knees weak. He could hear the harsh cries of the Whelm as they came scrabbling up the steep track. Having lost their master they would be desperate, and determined to kill everyone between them and the summon stone.

"Take this, Llian," said Yggur. "Just in case." He met Shand's eyes then handed Llian a little yellow rod that appeared to have been carved from a tusk of some sort.

"What is it?" said Llian.

"In case of treachery, you hold one end of the rod and twist the other. It triggers the collars."

Llian's eyes were drawn to Shand's neck, then Ifoli's. "What, both of them?"

"Yes."

Llian gulped. Could he do it? He did not think so. He put the rod away, secured the diamond phial in his pocket and followed Shand and Ifoli into the cleft. The soldiers were going out the other end.

Llian looked out, carefully. There had once been a ring of wiry bushes around the rim of the peak but everything had been burned or blasted by lightning. The soldiers were creeping across uneven rock in the direction of the summon stone.

Suddenly the captain let out a quivering cry of yearning, then yelled, "I'm coming!"

"Stop, you bloody fools!" roared another man.

"Captain, no!" screamed a third.

There came a sizzling sound, then a horrible series of *splats*, moans and screams. One of the soldiers hurled himself back into the cleft, scrambling across the sharp rocks on torn hands and bloody knees.

Shand hauled him upright. Blood was splattered across the soldier from head to foot, though it did not appear to be his own.

"Gone!" he gasped. "Blown to bits, just like that."

"The captain?" said Shand.

"And the four men who went with him. It called them, sir; it wouldn't let them go."

"What about the others?"

"Don't know."

"Go and find out."

The soldier looked Shand in the eyes, shuddered and said, "I'd sooner you killed me, sir."

Shand cursed. "Go and join Yggur's men. Clean yourself up first."

Shand went forward, beckoning Llian and Ifoli to follow, and peered around the edge of the cleft. Llian went too. Ten yards ahead, five pairs of boots, some containing ankles, others nothing but blood, stood on the stony ground. The rocks around had been sprayed with blood but there was no other sign of the captain or the four soldiers who had died with him.

The other three were huddled behind rocks, too afraid to move. Llian could not blame them; their training was no use here. The emanations from the stone were beating at him like the heat from a furnace.

Shand drew Llian back into the cleft. "Going to be a bastard to get to the stone."

"We could have told everyone that a month ago," said Llian. "No, wait," he added sourly. "We did."

Shand looked back at Ifoli, who was on her knees, throwing up. "What's the matter with you?"

She wiped her mouth and looked up, still retching. Her face was flushed and her eyes shiny; she looked as if she had a high fever.

"Just like last time," she said, pressing her hand against her back. "Only worse."

"What the hell are you talking about?"

"Is the lump back?" said Llian.

Ifoli nodded. "It's so hot it's burning me."

"What lump?" said Shand.

"In my back," said Ifoli. "First felt it after the gate brought us from Alcifer. It was really bad as we climbed Demondifang, but as we headed back down it stopped hurting."

"We all felt safe for a while," Llian remembered. "Even Regg, and he had been badly affected by the stone. It was as if we were protected from it."

"Where was this?" said Shand.

"About where Yggur is now."

"Wait here." Shand ran back towards the sky ship, but reappeared a couple of minutes later, shaking his head. "It doesn't feel any different over there, with *any* of my senses. Did you do anything that could have protected you? Think! It could be vital."

"Not that I remember," said Ifoli. "We were just going down as fast as we could."

"I gave you my manuscript bag," said Llian, "so I could hang on to Regg—the stone was trying to lure him back. You put the bag over your shoulder . . . and not long afterwards we felt protected."

"It may not mean anything," said Shand to Llian. Then to Ifoli, "Let me see."

He drew her shirt up. Her pale amber back was flawless save for a plum-sized black lump halfway down on the left side. He probed it with thick fingers, and she gasped.

"It's hot," he said, "really hot, and it seems to be pulsing. Why the hell didn't you tell me about this before?"

73

I CAN'T DO IT ON MY OWN

From below and behind them, Llian heard a harsh Whelm cry and the sound of metal hitting stone, then a blast and iron-shod boots scrabbling on gravel.

"The Whelm are attacking."

"Yggur will have to deal with them," said Shand, still studying the lump in Ifoli's back. "Why didn't you tell me?"

"I told Tallia after Llian and I first reached Zile, but it had disappeared by then," said Ifoli. "And I'm afraid of surgery so I . . . ignored it."

"Incredible!" said Shand, shaking his head in disgust. "Better conquer that fear, Ifoli, because I'm going to cut the lump out."

"No!" she gasped. She tried to run but only got a few yards before doubling over again, moaning. "Not here, of all places."

"Llian, hold her down."

Llian, not without reservations, did so. Ifoli struggled for a few seconds, then went still, shuddering.

Shand drew his knife, made a small slit in Ifoli's skin, a third the length of the black lump, then shoved on one end. The lump rotated and something dark slid from the slit. He pushed harder and it fell into his cupped hand.

"Clean that up," he said, handing it to Llian.

Llian rinsed it in rainwater from a depression in the rocks. Shand was smearing balm on Ifoli's back. The two sides of the slit had pulled together, and it was now just a small coin-shaped red swelling.

"Doesn't even need stitching," said Shand. "How does it feel now?"

"As though you've worked a miracle," said Ifoli, wiping tears from her eyes and sweat from her brow. "The pain, the churning in my stomach, the sick whirling in my head, it's all gone."

"What is it?" Shand said to Llian.

"I'd say," Llian said slowly, looking down at the black object, "it's the crystal from Snoat's Command device. When Esea reshaped the device and it exploded, its core became embedded in my manuscript bag."

"And the crystal buried itself in Ifoli's back. How come you didn't notice, Ifoli?"

"We were carried away in a gate, and it was very painful."

Shand took the crystal, which was an inch long and half an inch wide, stubby and black, with striations down the long sides. "It's *schorl*," he said. "A black form of the mineral tourmaline. And schorl has unusual properties."

"Why did it protect us from the summon stone?" said Llian.

"When I put your manuscript bag over my shoulder," said Ifoli, "the core embedded in the base must have been close enough to the crystal to activate the device."

Shand took the rebuilt Command device from his pack, prised up the silver lid on top of the graphite hub, withdrew a small black crystal and thrust the schorl crystal inside. Instantly Llian felt the corrupting emanations from the summon stone, which had been beating at him all this time, ease.

"I'd say it's created a kind of *force cage*," said Shand. "A protection of some sort from the stone's emanations. Run and tell Yggur. And tell him we're attacking now."

Ifoli darted away and shortly reappeared. The pain lines were gone and she was utterly transformed: she looked just like the remarkable young woman Llian had known at Pem-Y-Rum.

"Got your precious nivol ready?" said Shand.

Llian nodded and took it out of his pocket, though he did not remove the elastic band holding the diamond stopper in the phial. Having seen what one drop had done to a chimaera last time, he was not anxious to open it. Even a smear could eat away half his body, and it would be a hideous way to die.

Shand's green eyes flashed. "And your triggering rod, in case I turn out to be a traitor?"

"Yes," Llian whispered. He gestured to the six-spoked Command device. "Are you sure the protection will be enough, up close?"

"I'm not sure about anything."

Neither was Llian, and he feared to go near the summon stone again. It had almost got him last time; how could he resist it again? Why was it up to him to chuck the nivol on it, anyway? Shand was far better equipped to attack it, in all kinds of ways.

"Ifoli?" said Shand. "Llian still isn't sure of me—and neither am I. You'll have to do it again."

"Do what?"

"The scent potion and the device." He pointed to a small round scar on his forehead.

"What, here?"

"Do it here and you'll *know*." Shand handed her the Command device.

Ifoli drew a phial from her pocket, unstoppered it and took the device.

What were they up to? Was this the betrayal Yggur feared? Llian's hand involuntarily slipped to the triggering rod in his pocket. Could he use it? He'd better be sure. His fingers touched it then he pulled away. Shand's gave him another of those sour, knowing smiles.

Ifoli sniffed deeply from the phial, jammed the end of the device against Shand forehead and pressed hard. There came a dull black flash, his arms flapped like wings and he went, "Nnnnnnnnn!"

Again Llian's fingers crept to the triggering rod. Ifoli spun the Command device on Shand's forehead, tearing the skin. Blood flowed, then she tensed and gave an almighty heave. A single black wispy thread clung to the end of the tube, then evaporated into the air.

"Again!" croaked Shand.

She sniffed the scent potion and repeated the process, with no result this time.

"Again!" Shand said with a groan.

She did it again. "Nothing! It's all gone this time."

"You sure?" Shand said weakly.

"The scent potion lets me see everything in your head." She managed a smirk.

"Poor you!" He rubbed his forehead, smearing blood across it, then stood up straight, and the strain faded from his old face. "Yes," he said. "I can feel the difference. Let's get it done."

Llian let his breath out with a hiss. Shand led them out of the cleft. The rocks the three soldiers had been cowering behind were melted and they were dead. They passed the five pairs of army boots, some with bloody ankles in them and some without. Llian tried not to look at them.

Suddenly the summon stone went wild, blasting lightning in every direction save one—the direction they were coming from. The force cage was working so far, but for how long?

They advanced across lightning-shattered rocks. A film of grey ash and scattered lumps of charcoal were all that remained of the ferns and mosses that had once flourished here. Lightning sizzled and dazzled, thunder cracked and boomed.

Now they were only thirty feet from the summon stone. Llian's ears throbbed from the cataclysmic racket, and every hair on his body was standing on end.

Abruptly the lightning and thunder stopped, and in the sudden silence he heard the harsh cries of the Whelm as they hurled themselves up the steep cleft at Yggur and his soldiers again and again. They sounded desperate.

Llian went forward a few feet, then a few feet more. He was only fifteen feet away from the stone when he realised that Shand and Ifoli had not come with him. Ahead, the tilted summon stone was quivering, and he could smell the corruption emanating from it, a festering rottenness that reminded him of the triplets. Had they corrupted the stone as much as it had warped them?

His knees were trembling and his stomach was empty; he felt hollowed out inside, or eaten away.

"Can't . . . do it on my own," he croaked. "Not . . . strong enough."

"I daren't take the Command device any closer," said Shand.

"What . . . do I do?"

"Get as close as you can. I'll release the force cage so you can throw the nivol, but you'll only have a second. Hang on to the phial and flick the nivol. If you let go, none of it might end up on the stone."

Llian's bowels clenched painfully. He'd seen what the stone had done to Unick, and the myriad ways it could attack and kill. And it was fast—when Shand released the force cage the stone might get Llian before he could throw the nivol. Assuming Shand could be trusted at all. What if his intention was to command the stone for himself?

And even if he *was* on their side, he could be ruthless when it suited him. He had risked everyone's lives hunting the ghost vampire at Rogues Render, and there was no saying he wouldn't risk Llian's if it suited him.

"The longer you hesitate, the worse it gets," said Shand.

Llian did not move. This was suicide.

"Dozens of people died today to get us here," said Shand hoarsely. "Get moving!"

Llian crept forward, step by fearful step, until he was only three feet away from the right-hand stone and could have touched its decayed surface, which stank like rotten cheese. He could feel the pressure again, the loathing and corruption. It *burned* to consume him.

He removed the stopper, careful not to touch the part that had been inside the diamond phial, and drew back his arm.

"Now!" cried Shand.

As the protection vanished, Llian felt an overwhelming compulsion to throw his arms around the stone. He fought it and jerked his arm forward to flick the nivol onto the face of the stone.

Nothing happened. The thick green fluid was stuck in the narrow opening. What was he supposed to do now?

"Throw it!" shrieked Shand.

"It won't come out."

The summon stone shimmered, and Llian felt a humming in his ears. He dived to his left as lightning blasted where he had been standing, scattering blistering-hot chips of stone everywhere. He rolled over, came to his feet and, as the stone started to shimmer again, he spat into the phial, put the stopper back in and shook it, then flung the slightly diluted nivol out onto the left upright, then the right, and up onto the capstone.

"Back!" roared Shand as the stone blasted again, and he jammed the schorl crystal back into the Command Device.

In another second Llian would have been burned to charcoal, but the blast was diverted past his left ear. He stumbled back to Shand and the three of them stood there in the force cage, waiting.

The bright green drops were oozing down the three stones but weren't affecting them in any way.

"It's doing nothing," said Llian. Had he made a colossal blunder by spitting in the phial? But how else was he supposed to get the nivol out?

Then the stones themselves started to fade.

"Is that the nivol?" said Ifoli.

"No," Shand said grimly. "The stone's trying to move to a safer home, as it did after it was poisoned at Carcharon. And we've got nothing left."

But the fading stopped and Llian saw that the nivol that had reached the ground was dissolving both the rock the stone stood on and the silver that had solidified between the uprights.

"How can a few drops of nivol dissolve cubic yards of rock?" said Llian.

"It's an alchemical fluid," said Ifoli absently. "It's both chymical and magical."

Within minutes the rock and silver had dissolved for yards around the uprights, and suddenly they teetered. The whole of Demondifang shook wildly. Boulders toppled and went crashing down the sides of the peak.

"Out of the way!" cried Shand and sprang forward.

What was he doing? Llian's mistrust surfaced again. Was this the moment Shand had been waiting for?

Shand shut off the force cage, pointed the Command device at the stone and recreated the force cage around it. It stopped shuddering and its emanations cut off. It had gone perfectly still. Then, still in the form of a teetering trilithon, the two uprights slid down into the pool of dissolved rock and silver until they and the slab of stone that formed the capstone disappeared. The pool swirled for a minute or two, slowly went still, then set like quickrock in an unreality zone.

"Cover it, quick!" said Shand urgently.

Llian did not ask why. They kicked dirt, loose rocks, ash and charcoal across the surface until it looked like the rest of the mountain top.

"Yggur?" Shand yelled.

The sounds of fighting from the western side of the peak had stopped.

"Lost all my men," called Yggur. "Can't do any more."

"Let the Whelm leaders through."

There was a long silence. "Are you—"

"Just do it," yelled Llian.

Shortly Yggur and Aviel appeared. Yggur studied Shand suspiciously.

"It's over," said Llian. "We've done it." He stoppered the diamond phial and gave it back to Aviel.

Yggur went back through the cleft. Shortly half a dozen Whelm appeared, two women and four men. They were panting, bloody and exhausted, their faces hooded against the bright sunlight and their black eyes glinting behind slitted bone eye covers.

"The summon stone has been destroyed by our nivol," said Yggur. "The Merdrun can never draw power from it again. Satisfy yourselves on that point, then go home and never come here again."

The Whelm, several of whom were masters of their own strange branch of the Secret Art, directed their staves at the place where the summon stone had stood and carried out various tests incomprehensible to Llian. After ten minutes their gaunt faces sagged, then they turned and stumbled away, calling out to their people. Yet again the Whelm were masterless, broken and bereft.

Yggur made sure they were all heading down the mountain, then Shand and Llian explained what they had done.

"But what good is it?" said Yggur. "One day, perhaps not that long from now, the force cage will fade, and—"

"We're going to make it permanent," said Shand.

"How?" said Yggur cheerfully, as if the enmity between them was long forgotten.

"The silver lode here has been so charged up by all the lightning strikes that it's a mighty source of power," said Ifoli. "A node of power, in fact."

"Another one?" said Yggur.

"Yes," said Shand. "And if we bury the Command device here, concealed by an illusion and powered by the node, it'll prevent the summon stone from drawing or using power, or sending it anywhere else. That'll block the Crimson Gate from reopening into Santhenar."

"For how long?"

"I believe the node contains so much power that our mancery could never exhaust it," said Ifoli.

"Never say never. Let's do it. But first . . ." Yggur touched a fingertip to Shand's collar, then Ifoli's, and they fell off.

"Thank you," said Ifoli, rubbing her chafed neck.

When they had powered the Command device from the node, buried it and concealed it with a mighty illusion, they returned to the sky ship and Yggur lifted off. Far below, thousands of Whelm were streaming across the gravel bar that linked Demondifang and Mollymoot, heading south to Shazabba.

And may they rot there, Llian thought, *masterless and bereft, until the very sun ices over.*

When the sky ship was well out over the sea on the way back to Qwale, and Demondifang had blurred into the haze, Shand said, "None of this can ever be mentioned. It never happened."

"What are you talking about?" Llian said irritably, for he was already spinning the tale in his head.

"It can't be included in the Histories," said Shand, "because the summon stone still exists. Its summoning sequence may be frozen, but if it's ever woken again it'll be as deadly as ever. Besides, it would be an irresistible magnet for the greedy, the power-hungry and the corrupt."

"We'll spread a story that we blasted it to dust," said Yggur. "Since you've got nothing to do, Llian, you can compose the tale while we fly home."

"You want me to craft an *untrue story*?" cried Llian, shocked. "That's a violation of one of the chroniclers' fundamental commandments."

"From what I hear," Yggur said pointedly, "it wouldn't be the first time. Shand, one of us will come back once a year to make sure the

Command device is still doing its job, and to renew the illusion." Yggur
yawned, then rose from his seat. "I'm a tad worn out. Take over the
controls, there's a good chap."

"You trust *me* to fly this sky ship?" said Shand, goggling at him.

"Never doubted you for an instant." Yggur grinned. "I'm going to
have a nap."

He slipped into a vacant seat at the back, leaned back and tipped
his hat over his eyes.

PART FOUR

REVELATION

74

YOU'VE GOT TO ADMIRE HER GALL

"How are you feeling today, Mummy?" said Sulien.

Karan struggled to open her eyes; she felt utterly drained. "Much better, darling. How long have I been here?"

"Six days."

"I dreamed I was being looked after by a tall dark man with a limp. A very kind man."

"That's Master Healer Zanser." Sulien leaned in and said in a theatrical whisper, "He's Tallia's *boyfriend*."

"Really?" Karan struggled into an upright position, not without some stabbing pains in her belly. "Tell me more."

Sulien propped her up with pillows. "They met on the battlefield. He's from Crandor, just like her. Tallia saved his life, and it was love at first sight." Sulien's eyes were huge; she seemed awed by the thought.

"I'm glad. No one deserves it more."

"Was it the same with you and Daddy?"

"Not . . . exactly. Though we made quite an impression on each other. And an even stronger second impression. Llian was being all arrogant and patronising, then he fell down and knocked himself out at my feet." Karan chuckled. "Are we going home soon? I'm worried about Gothryme and poor old Rachis. How long have we been away?"

"Months and months. Last night I heard Nadiril asking Shand and Malien about making a final gate so everyone can go to Chanthed."

"Why a final gate?"

"They're the only people who can make them, and they said they're not doing it any more. Malien is going home to Tirthrax soon, and Shand says every gate takes five years off his life, and if people want to go somewhere they can bollocking-well walk. Sorry," Sulien said unapologetically, "but that's what he said."

"What's Nadiril want to go to Chanthed for?"

In the olden days Karan had loved her annual trips there to hear the Great Tales told, but Llian's relentless pursuit by Thandiwe, the false accusation that he had murdered the previous master, Wistan, and Llian's incarceration and near death at the hands of Snoat in Pem-Y-Rum had tarnished the place in her eyes.

"Nadiril says we need a party before we all split up—to celebrate our great victory—and I think so too."

Karan just wanted to go home but said, "Who am I to argue with Nadiril?"

Someone knocked on the door, and Tallia came in, looking years younger, accompanied by Zanser, who wore grey robes edged with scarlet and blue and walked with the aid of an amber and black barleycorn-twist cane. Their shoulders touched as they walked, for they were the same height, and they kept turning to look into each other's eyes. It was a side of Tallia Karan had not seen before, but long overdue. She had given so much for so long; it was time for her to live.

"Sit down." Karan gestured to the bench beside the bed. "Tell me everything."

"We came to say goodbye," said Tallia.

"You're not coming to Chanthed for the celebrations?"

"There's a ship leaving port on the next tide, heading north all the way to Crandor. If we catch it, we can be home a month sooner than I'd hoped."

There was such eagerness on her face, such longing in her eyes, that Karan suppressed her own disappointment. "You've wanted to go home for a very long time."

"Almost from the moment I got to Thurkad." Tallia sighed. "Twenty years ago."

"I'll miss you. It's such a long way away, and I don't suppose we'll see each other again ... but I'm glad for you. And I hope you get your wish."

"What wish is that?" said Zanser.

"For a child," said Karan, hugging Sulien to her.

"There's no time to waste," Tallia said impishly. "We'll be practising all the way home."

Karan laughed. "Good for you. And Llian and I—"

"Mumm*ee*!" said Sulien, scandalised.

Three days later Karan, walking with the aid of her own stick, hobbled from the gate in Chanthed, with Sulien on her left and Llian to her right, into an oval courtyard paved in pale blue stone.

"What is this place?" she wondered.

The courtyard was surrounded by a wide cloister with slender columns of darker blue stone set on purple-black plinths. The great house, of two storeys, was also of blue stone, with dark red window surrounds, silver slates on the roof and very tall, slender, intricately decorated chimneys that must have been a nightmare to sweep.

"Belongs to a friend of Nadiril's," said Llian. "A spice merchant, away in the east."

"Do you suppose it's got hot water? Healer's Isle was all very well, and the next time I'm dancing on death's trapdoor I'll go straight back, but—"

"You'd eat your own left arm for a hot bath." Sulien, who had heard it many times before, grinned.

"Haven't had one since we left Gothryme," Karan muttered. "Haven't had many cold baths, for that matter. You could scrape the grime off me with a trowel."

"What are we really doing here, Nadiril?" she said the following morning. Having had a lingering hot bath, a massage, a ten-hour sleep and an enormous breakfast, she felt at peace with the world. All that mattered now was going home, the sooner the better.

"What I said in Qwale, mainly," said the old man. "Great victories must be celebrated, the lost mourned and heroes duly honoured."

"I don't want to be honoured; I just want to go home."

"Honours aren't for the heroes who earned them. They're for we humble, ordinary folk who aren't heroes."

"I've never thought of you as humble," said Karan cheekily. "Or ordinary."

He continued as if she had not spoken. "Honours highlight that, even in the darkest of times, the actions of small, quiet, reluctant or even badly flawed people really matter."

"I still think you're up to something."

"I don't know that I am," said Nadiril, smiling faintly. "We've also had the original manuscripts of the first twenty-two Great Tales in safekeeping ever since Snoat was killed. They're the greatest treasure of the college, and now that his pet master, Basible Norp, has fled and the war is over, it's time to hand them back."

He paused. "Finally, as part of the celebrations, we're going to hear a brand new tale in two nights' time. We know the ending, and some people know the beginning, but no one has heard the rest of the tale."

Llian, who was eating his fourth slice of toast with chunky gellon marmalade, said sharply, "What tale is that?"

"The *Tale of Rulke*."

Karan set her lips in a hard line. "Not written by that thieving bitch Thandiwe, by any chance?"

"As it happens," said Nadiril.

Llian let out a mirthless bark of laughter. "You've got to admire her gall."

"No . . . we . . . don't," said Karan through gritted teeth.

"How could she have done it so quickly?" said Llian. "Even with Rulke's key, which I've got, it'd take a year and a half to translate all those papers and another year to put a competent tale together." He turned to Nadiril. "But Thandiwe would never be satisfied with a *competent* tale; she wants a Great Tale to her name. She's burned for one since the day I was awarded mine."

"She's a greedy woman and she's spotted an opportunity," said Nadiril. "I wonder if you've seen it too?"

"Can't say I have, or care." Llian assumed his attack on his toast.

"This is the best marmalade I've ever eaten." He put his sticky fingers in his mouth and sucked noisily.

"Daddy!" hissed Sulien. "Manners!" But when Karan only smiled vaguely Sulien licked her own fingers.

"Since Norp is gone," Karan said slowly, "there'll have to be an election for a new master. Is that why you brought us here, Nadiril? To make Llian master of the college, as Wistan intended before Snoat had him murdered?"

Nadiril sighed. "I'm no puppet master, Karan. Nonetheless, the past three months have reinforced the vital role of the Histories, not just as a binding force for the myriad nations and peoples of Santhenar, but also as a true record of deeds done and lessons learned—or not learned and doomed to be repeated. The Histories were of great aid to us in the last conflict and may prove vital in the next."

She sat up straight. "What next conflict?"

"There's always a next conflict. All the more reason for the college to be led by a master who, despite some past, er, misdemeanours, believes absolutely in the Histories as truth, not as propaganda for the victors."

"It won't be me," said Llian. "We're going home." He linked arms with Sulien, who was on his left, and Karan on his right. "I'm going to write the *Tale of the Gates of Good and Evil*. It'll take me at least a year." He grinned at the prospect.

"Are you absolutely sure?" said Karan. "Surely you remember how unhappy you were a few months ago?"

"Because I was forbidden to work at my craft and yearned for something that could never make me happy. Now I know better."

Karan's eyes narrowed. "You'd better not be referring to that bodice-bursting trollop!"

"Don't be silly, Mummy," said Sulien. "Daddy's talking about the college, aren't you?" There was a hint of anxiety in her voice.

"I used to think I wanted it," said Llian, "but I'm not cut out to be a teacher, and I couldn't bear to sit in Wistan's office moving papers from one place to another. I'm going to write the Histories and tell the tales, and that should be enough for any man."

"It should," said Nadiril, "but how are you going to support your family?"

"Live on my wits," Llian said breezily. "They've served me well enough so far."

Karan snorted into her cup, spraying tea across the table. Sulien rolled her green eyes.

"I suppose they have," said Nadiril. He half-rose, found it too much of a struggle and sat down again. "You're entitled to vote on Thandiwe's tale, of course. And whether you do or don't, I'd like your opinion on it."

"As a Great Tale?"

"No, I want your opinion on the *Tale of Rulke* in terms of its historical truth and completeness." He pushed himself up with his hands and succeeded in rising this time. "You can promise me that much?"

"Of course," said Llian. "I'm looking forward to hearing the tale, very much."

"I'm not," said Karan.

75

IS THERE NO END TO YOUR CUNNING?

They assembled in the Great Hall of the College of the Histories two nights later. It was a small but lovely theatre that dated back to the founding of the college almost three thousand years ago, and the Great Tales had been told there ever since, apart from a long hiatus during the bloody chaos of the Clysm, when the tales had been kept alive in caves and forest clearings and even in private homes with the blinds down and the lamps out.

Llian gazed around him. The hall had a high triple-vaulted timber ceiling supported on intricately carved beams, and the walls were clad in carved panels depicting scenes from the Great Tales and the Histories. It was not nearly large enough these days, and every aisle was packed.

As the only living creator of a Great Tale he was entitled to sit at the dignitaries' table on the left-hand side of the stage, but he had chosen the front row of seats with Karan and Sulien, Yggur, Shand and Ifoli, and Wilm and Aviel.

Thandiwe was a fine teller, one of the best the college had produced in decades, and Llian had been looking forward to hearing her tale, though from the beginning he felt disappointed. This was not due to the facts of the tale. Rulke's life had been one of such towering courage, brilliance, achievement and cunning that even a teller of modest means could have made a lesser Great Tale from it. So what was it? Thandiwe's telling was flat and dull, and a Great Tale must not be either.

"Well?" Nadiril said after she finished and the masters and dignitaries had withdrawn to a cramped side room, where they stood elbow to elbow, jostling each others' cups of overly sweet yellow wine before the judging.

"A marvellous story . . ." Llian said ruminatively. "It could not be otherwise . . ."

"But?"

"How could Thandiwe write a Great Tale in a few weeks?"

"It's been done before."

"Only with short tales. Never about such a towering and long-lived figure as Rulke. Besides, Thandiwe can't have translated a tenth of Rulke's papers. I took a few key ones with me, and the rest I left at the Great Library."

"I have them in my baggage, as it happens," said Nadiril with a ghostly smile. "Didn't want to leave them in the library where they . . ."

"Might fall into the wrong hands," said Llian. "Is there no end to your cunning?"

"I carried them to Healer's Isle but never got the chance to give them to you. Come and see me in the morning. But going back to Thandiwe's tale, it does seem . . . hasty."

"And far too short, barely two hours! Written out, it can't be more than sixty pages. It's just a summary with most of the drama left out."

"Whereas the *Tale of the Mirror?*"

Llian felt sure Nadiril knew as well as he did. "The Great Tale, as I presented it here ten years ago, is four hundred pages long, and it took me four nights to tell it."

"Four great nights. All right, what about historical truth?"

"I didn't hear anything I knew to be wrong, or slanted to make Rulke greater than he was. If anything, by condensing the story so much she's made him seem less extraordinary."

"And completeness?" said Nadiril.

"She's left too much out, much of it vital to understanding the Charon and why Rulke was so driven to save them."

"For instance?"

"She skipped over Stermin's crafting of the Crimson and Azure Gates, then ordering his people to choose one or the other and banishing everyone who chose the Crimson Gate. And she hardly mentioned the Merdrun, even though their 'civil war' with the Charon defined both peoples and Rulke."

"Why do you think she downplayed them?"

"In the early days Thandiwe denied that the Merdrun existed. She kept parroting Snoat's line that our leaders had invented them as a diversion from their own failures. I suppose the denial made it easier for her to justify stealing Rulke's papers, and perhaps she discounted everything he wrote about the Merdrun—or simply didn't read it."

Nadiril's clouded eyes roved over the throng while he considered that. "Anything else?"

"Only what I warned Thandiwe about in Alcifer before she fled with Rulke's papers, and it's the biggest flaw of all.

"*Every tale is also a performance, and a Great Tale has to be a towering performance, but you must believe in your heart that, before everything else, you are that great teller. If you don't believe it, your teller's voice will show it. It can't be faked. If you steal the tale or kill for it, in your own mind that's what your real identity will be when you tell your tale to the masters: not a teller,*

*but a thief or a murderer. You can't be both. In reaching for the prize, you will
have put it for ever beyond your reach."*

Llian met Nadiril's eyes. "Thandiwe lied and cheated and stole for
the tale, again and again, and that's what she's become in her own
mind—not a teller but a thief. That's why her tale feels so flat."

A bell rang in the distance.

"Very perceptive," said Nadiril sadly. "Though it doesn't mean she
won't get her Great Tale. That's the bell for the voting. You'd better
go in."

Llian went up onto the stage with all the other masters. There were
sixty-four masters' positions, though four were vacant due to death or
incapacity, while Basible Norp had fled and Thandiwe could not vote.

Candela Twism ambled up. A short, square, heavily built woman
with massive jowls and an untameable mass of grey ringlets, she had
become acting master of the college after Norp's flight.

She counted the masters. "Fifty-seven." She frowned then said, "Ah!
Plus me, of course."

She sat in the vacant seat and turned to stare at Thandiwe, who stood
exposed in the centre of the stage. She looked nervous, even terrified,
and Llian knew how she felt. He had felt that way himself after telling
the *Tale of the Mirror.*

Candela rose again. "Who would not want to be college master on
such an historic occasion?" she said. "The reading of a new Great Tale—"

"We . . . haven't . . . voted!" grated Limmy Tuul, a cold, hard-faced
master, the black wen on his right eyelid fluttering. He had been a
strong supporter of Thandiwe's push to become master of the college
several months ago and presumably supported her tale, but no master
could endure having his vote taken for granted.

"Of . . . of course we haven't," Candela said at once, now flustered and
smiling vaguely. She went to the front of the stage, turning her back
to Thandiwe to show that her destiny was in the masters' hands, and
faced the audience. "How does it go?" she muttered, looking down at
her plump fingers.

"My fellow masters, distinguished visitors, students," hissed Master
Laarni, the small, dark master at the end.

"Ah!" said Candela. "My fellow masters, distinguished visitors, students, I hereby nominate Thandiwe Moorn's *Tale of Rulke* to be a Great Tale. The master chroniclers have all read the supporting documents and checked the facts. What say you? Is it a Great Tale? Yea or nay? Answer one by one and the recorder will register your vote."

"Yea," said Limmy Tuul.

"Yea," said Master Cherith beside him. She favoured both Llian and Thandiwe with her enchanting smile.

"Yea," said Master Laarni over-loudly, as if to emphasise his importance in the vote.

That was the way it went, the college masters saying *Yea* one by one, until only Candela was left.

"Yea!" she cried. "A Great Tale, a very Great Tale, the twenty-fourth."

"Not yet," grated Tuul. "There's one vote to be counted. Llian's."

He had waited to vote last, as required, because though he was a master of the college, he did not hold a position at the college.

"What say you, Llian?" said Candela. There was nothing vague about her smile now. She was quivering with eagerness. Few college masters ever saw a Great Tale proclaimed; before Llian's there had not been a new one in hundreds of years.

Thandiwe was quivering too, though Llian imagined it was with dread. The vote had to be unanimous; if he said *Nay* her tale would not become a Great Tale. She was staring at him, her lips slightly parted. Was she remembering the words he had quoted to Nadiril half an hour ago? Or running through the litany of crimes she had committed against Llian and the many threats she had made to destroy him, terrified that he would treat her with the malice she had shown him?

After a long pause, during which even Llian did not know how he was going to vote, he said, "I abstain."

"What?" cried Thandiwe, shooting him a look of such hatred that he quailed.

There was a great stir in the audience. A third of the people were on their feet, staring at the masters, at Thandiwe and at himself. Llian looked down at the row of seats where he had been sitting previously, at the pale faces and long red hair of Karan and Sulien. Their eyes were on him but he could not read what they were thinking.

"You can't abstain, Master Llian," said Candela. "You have to vote Yea or Nay."

"Yes, he can," Limmy Tuul said in his grating voice. "But Llian must give a sound reason for doing so. He can't abstain just because he finds the decision too hard."

"Well, Master Llian?" said Candela.

Llian had not expected to have to justify himself. "I abstain," he said, "because Rulke gifted his papers to me. *We are extinct, chronicler,* he said just before he died. *The Charon will live on only in your tales. Will you take them on for me?* It would not be fair for me to vote Yea or Nay on the *Tale of Rulke.* I could not eliminate my bias."

"But you did nothing about the papers," said Candela. "In nine and a half years you never even went looking for them."

"I . . . was . . . under . . . a . . . ban," Llian said through his teeth.

"Even so, you can't possibly begrudge Thandiwe her tale, not after all this time."

"I don't," Llian lied. He did begrudge her a Great Tale, though not out of malice. Her tale was rushed, oversimplified and utterly failed to convey the sweep, grandeur, passion and drama of Rulke's life. It wasn't worthy. "In any case, an abstention doesn't change the vote."

"It has to be unanimous," said Candela. "Doesn't it, Master Tuul?"

"An abstention is a null vote," said Limmy Tuul. "It doesn't count for and it doesn't count against. Therefore the vote is unanimous—fifty-seven for the Yea, and none for the Nay."

Candela's lips moved. She nodded then stood there, rocking on her feet as if she did not know what to do next.

Master Laarni stood up. "Acting Master Twism," he roared, "you have heard the vote for the *Tale of Rulke,* and it is unanimous. What do you say to Master Thandiwe Moorn?"

Candela Twism swallowed, cleared her throat, beamed at the audience then at Thandiwe. "The *Tale of Rulke* is a Great Tale, the twenty-fourth."

76

ENJOY YOUR LAST MONTH!

The audience roared, but Thandiwe stood there for a full minute, staring vacantly into the audience as if she had not taken it in. Then she turned to the masters and her face lit up. Briefly she was the young, beautiful and passionate student Llian had known, lived with and even briefly loved before his Graduation Telling twelve years ago, and in the instant of her triumph he did not begrudge her the Great Tale one iota.

Then she looked him in the eyes and hers were so hard with malice that he jerked backwards in his seat. He did not know what she had wanted of him, though after blocking the overturning of his ban for nine years, betraying him to Snoat, stealing his gold and his papers and almost choking Karan to death on Maigraith's orders, she could hardly have expected his vote.

But Thandiwe was a strange, unpredictable woman—though she had many times declared herself to be his enemy, she always expected his unwavering support and saw every denial of it as another betrayal. Tonight would be the same. She would view his abstention as a calculated insult intended to undermine the greatest night of her life and the Great Tale she so richly deserved.

Someone cleared their throat and Llian realised that Candela was talking again.

"The vacant mastership will now be decided," she said. "In the previous election Master Thandiwe was the runner-up, and I hereby nominate her for the post of master of the college. Do you accept the nomination, Master Thandiwe?"

"Yes," she said softly, eagerly. "Oh yes."

"Are there any other nominations?"

More than half the masters turned to look at Llian, and it occurred to him that if he were to accept nomination he would probably win the mastership. He briefly considered it, then shook his head. He had other priorities now. Karan, who had gone rigid in her seat, slowly relaxed.

"Are there any other nominations?" Candela repeated.

None were made. Again she looked confused. She consulted Limmy Tuul, then said, "As Master Thandiwe Moorn is the only candidate, she is declared elected as the seventy-sixth master of the College of the Histories."

Tuul whispered to Candela again, then took something from a blue velvet bag and handed it to her. It was an engraved brass disc on a white gold chain. Candela stood up on tiptoes, put the chain over Thandiwe's head and settled the brass disc below her throat.

"The seal of office of the seventy-sixth master," said Candela. "May you endure as long as it does."

There was a great cheer from the audience, and all the masters rose to congratulate her. Llian was tempted to slip away and prevail on Karan to leave Chanthed immediately, but resisted the notion. Failing to congratulate Thandiwe would seem both petty and churlish.

He gestured to Karan and Sulien to come up: he never wanted to be alone with Thandiwe again, not even in such a public place. They climbed the steps to the stage, Karan wincing and pressing her hand to her belly where Jaguly had stabbed her.

She gave him a hug. "Well done, my love. Can we go home now?"

"Right now?"

She smiled. "Tomorrow or the next day, I meant. Once we've said our farewells."

"Yes," said Llian. "I'd like that."

The line of masters congratulating Thandiwe was short now; it was almost his turn. He waited until Master Cherith had shaken Thandiwe's hand, then stepped forward.

"Congratulations," he said sincerely. "You've long wanted to be Master of the College and I wish you joy of it." He held out his hand.

Thandiwe's smile disappeared. She did not take his hand. "Why didn't you stay away? You came so you could publicly abstain, didn't you?"

"How could I stay away? You're a great teller and I wanted to hear your tale." *The tale you stole from me.*

"No, you came so you could ruin my great night—yet again."

"But you've got everything you ever wanted," he said, bewildered.

"And you're going to get what you deserve," she hissed. Her gaze swept across Karan to Sulien, who was halfway across the stage, talking to Lilis. "All three of you."

The temperature on the stage seemed to drop by ten degrees. "What do you mean by that?"

Thandiwe lowered her voice. She was smiling now, though with a grim and malicious vindication. "Maigraith never went to the void in search of Rulke's *mythical* brother Kalke."

"What?" gasped Karan.

Thandiwe gave Karan her sweetest smile. "Something about Llian's *story* in Alcifer aroused her suspicions and she came after me, but I'd ridden off in great haste and she had no horses. It took her more than a month to track me down to Zile, and the first thing she did was ask me about Kalke. I told her there was no Kalke. Rulke never had a brother, much less a twin. Llian, the master chronicler and teller who had sworn a solemn oath to always put truth first, tried to send Maigraith to her death in the void with a tale that was a blatant lie."

She prodded Llian in the chest with a hard finger. "You falsified the Histories for your own gain, and wouldn't the masters love to know that?"

Llian could not breathe. Many times she had threatened to ruin him, only to try and win him over again as if nothing had happened. Now she could destroy him, and there was nothing he could do about it. But why was she doing this?

Clearly, Thandiwe knew her *Tale of Rulke* was an unworthy one and feared he would expose her, both for the many crimes she'd committed getting Rulke's papers and the hasty way she had written her Great Tale without translating most of them. Exposure would mean the loss of her Great Tale and perhaps the mastership as well, but the truth about Llian's lie would destroy his career as a chronicler and teller for life.

"What do you plan to do about it?" he said.

"What do *you* plan to do?" she said sweetly. "That's what really matters."

"Nothing. I'm going home with my family. Goodbye, Thandiwe. I hope I never see you again."

He turned away, linking arms with Karan to reinforce the point.

But Thandiwe always had to have the last word. "She's coming after you."

"What did you say?" cried Karan, tearing free and confronting the much taller woman so fiercely that Thandiwe took a step back.

"A message came by skeet from Maigraith this morning. She was leaving Zile and heading for Gothryme to fulfil the promise she made before she left Alcifer."

It took a few seconds for Llian to work out what she was talking about, then Maigraith's final words rang through his mind like a graveyard bell.

Your man has earned you and Sulien a reprieve. Use it well, for if he has deceived me you will pay a hundredfold.

"She's coming for Sulien," Thandiwe added in a low voice, her voice dripping malice.

"Why are you being like this?" said Llian, utterly bewildered.

"Because you chose *me* over her," said Karan. "And when she tried to get you back, again and again you chose me."

"You've been the one since the first time I set eyes on you. Isn't it obvious?"

"Not to Thandiwe. She's as much a narcissist as Snoat ever was— surely you realise that? She wanted you because you were the only teller in the world with a Great Tale to your name, and she has to get what she wants—it's the only way she can feel complete. She felt she was doing you a favour, anyway. She never understood what you saw in me, or why you'd hide away in rustic Chanthed, allowing your career to wither and die."

"A career she'd deliberately blocked."

"She expected you to leave me and go back to Chanthed and her. Had you done so, she would have had the ban overturned in weeks."

"How can you possibly know that?" said Llian.

"I'm a sensitive; I read people the way you read books. For a narcissist like Thandiwe, any stain on her partner's career would have been unbearable. She would have raised you up for her own glory."

"Very clever," sneered Thandiwe. "But I don't want him now and I certainly don't need him."

"We feel the same way then," Llian said wearily and turned towards Sulien, who was now standing by herself, looking anxious. She was a sensitive too, a far stronger one, and she knew something was wrong.

"It'll take Maigraith a month to ride from Zile to Gothryme," said Thandiwe, following him. "If she doesn't hurry, and why would she? I imagine she wants to draw out the anticipation before she abducts Sulien and takes her to live with herself and Julken."

"Mummy?" cried Sulien. "What's she talking about?"

"Rulke failed, the Charon are gone and Julken is all that's left of him," said Karan, quoting Maigraith's terrifying words at Black Lake after Karan had foolishly dosed her with hrux, and the drug, plus the nearby summon stone, had turned Maigraith's silly idea into an obsession. *Karan, please listen. All their greatness and all their promise can't be lost. Julken and Sulien could found an entirely new line of people. Their children would be tetrarchs—four-bloods!"*

"Enjoy your last month with your pathetic little family, Llian," Thandiwe said spitefully and walked off.

Karan just stood there, her face chalk-white, her hand pressed to her belly. She tried to speak but could not get the words out.

Sulien let out a cry of fury and pointed at Thandiwe's back as she went down the steps. Her gown split from front to back, fell down around her ankles, and she tripped and fell flat on her face. There came a metallic crack. A quarter of the audience laughed and, to Llian's surprise given that they had just voted for her tale, more than a few masters laughed as well.

Thandiwe got up, her face scarlet, hauled her gown up and clutched it around her, then let out a cry of dismay and snatched at her seal of office. It was broken in half. The brass seal, freshly cast for the seventy-sixth master, must have had a flaw in it, for it had snapped when it hit the floor.

"Not the best of omens for the new master," Llian said quietly. He gave Karan his arm. "Come on; we'll go out the back way."

"What are we going to do?" Karan whispered as they were walking back to their room through streets crowded with people all talking about the new Great Tale. "Llian, I can't think. My mind's spinning round and round. I've got nothing left."

"I don't know." Llian was fretting about Sulien, who had not said a word and was trembling. "But we can't talk about it here. We'll say our farewells in the morning and ride home, and decide what to do on the way."

77

ARE YOU GOING TO RETIRE?

"Ride home in your condition?" said Malien at a dawn breakfast. "Don't be ridiculous. I'm taking you in my sky ship."

"I didn't know you had one here," said Karan.

"I was in a hurry to go home so I sent it ahead from Qwale. It arrived last night." She leaned forward and looked into Karan's eyes. "You don't look well; the healers shouldn't have let you leave so soon."

"It's not the knife wound; it's healing well."

"Then what is it?"

Karan told her about Maigraith's threat, relayed by Thandiwe.

"And nothing can be done to dissuade Maigraith?" said Malien.

"She's always been obsessive and manipulative, but after Carcharon she became utterly implacable. No force on Santhenar can turn her from her course now."

"Not even Shand, her grandfather?"

"He has no influence over her any more." She paused. "Malien, can Maigraith make gates?"

"Possibly . . . though Shand and I plan to make it far more difficult for anyone else to make a gate on Santhenar—an extra precaution against the Merdrun trying again." Malien rose. "I'll be ready to leave in half an hour. Better get ready."

Karan had not expected the gathering to break up so quickly. As the sun was rising, she, Sulien and Llian collected their gear and carried it out to Malien's sky ship, which stood in the oval courtyard where the gate had opened. Heavy frost covered the blue paving stones and a fountain on the far side of the courtyard had frozen. The black chest containing Rulke's papers stood by the ladder, and Nadiril was there, talking to Lilis and Ifoli. The rest of their allies were gathered round, stamping their feet to ward off the cold and breathing out clouds of steam.

"We'll say goodbye," wheezed Nadiril, always a bit chesty on cold mornings. "We're flying back to the Great Library soon." He looked very gloomy.

"How are you going to repair all the damage?" said Karan.

"I don't know. It may be beyond me."

"We'll find a way," said Lilis stoutly.

Karan embraced them, then Ussarine and Hingis, who stood quietly together at the rear of the sky ship. "What are your plans?"

"We're going riding," said Hingis.

"Nowhere in particular," said Ussarine, "but together."

"I hope you have a wonderful time," said Karan. "Thank you for everything."

Behind them, the rotors started to turn.

"Time to go," called Malien.

Shand, Aviel, Wilm and Yggur were coming with them, plus half a dozen of Malien's people, who were already inside. Aviel, Wilm and Shand were going back to Casyme, while Yggur was heading on to Thurkad, a city he had ruled until a year ago. He had not said what he was going to do there and Karan did not ask. She had no energy for anything but the insoluble problem of Maigraith.

When she climbed in, Llian and Sulien were already in their places. She took a seat in front of them.

"We're going home!" said Sulien. "I can't wait to see Rachis again, and the swans, and my little garden." She sniffled.

Karan's eyes watered. She had longed for this day for many months, without daring to hope it would ever come. Now their whole future was clouded. How long did they have? A lot less than a month, she felt sure.

The hop over the mountains from Chanthed to Casyme was a hundred miles in a straight line, though with a blustery south-westerly wind behind them it would to be a quick trip. It proved a cold and bumpy one at the altitude they had to fly to cross the peaks north of Shazmak, and by the time the sky ship corkscrewed down out of the overcast at Casyme it was snowing heavily and Karan was airsick and utterly miserable.

"We won't stop," Malien said firmly after a dangerous landing behind Aviel's workshop at half past two in the afternoon. Shand's big house was just a shadow in the distance. "I want Karan tucked up in her own bed before dark."

The sky ship was being buffeted by the wind so they said hasty farewells.

"What are your plans now, Shand?" said Karan.

"He promised to teach me to use my gift," said Sulien.

"Really?" Karan said coolly. "First I've heard of it."

"I was waiting until you were better," Sulien said deceitfully.

"Well, you've got to be taught, and Shand's a great teacher so . . . I'll think about it. And after that," she said to Shand, "are you going to retire?"

"Certainly not! I've got unfinished business here, and then I'm heading back to the Great Library."

"What for?"

His eyes glowed. "Ifoli and I are working on something . . . big."

"Care to tell me?"

"No." He turned away, but swung back and said quietly, "I did a lot of damage, both unwittingly and when I was in hiding. Aviel, Earnis . . . I've got to make up for it, insofar as I can."

The sky ship heeled over in a gust of wind. "Hurry up!" said Malien.

But Karan also needed to make amends. "Shand, I'm sorry," she said quickly. "About Maigraith . . . and about what I said to you at Alcifer."

"Ah well," said Shand, "neither of us were quite ourselves. We got through it; that's the main thing."

"But will we get through the next month?"

His mouth set in a grim line and he turned away. Karan's heart sank; Maigraith, his granddaughter, must always come first. In a daze she shook hands with Wilm, marvelling at how changed he was. A few months ago he had left Casyme a clumsy, painfully shy boy; now he was returning a man, a hero and a leader.

"Thank you for everything you did for Llian," said Karan.

"No more than he did for me." They shook hands.

Karan embraced Aviel. "You must be glad to be home. What's the first thing you're going to do?"

"Light the braziers in my workshop and get to work."

"In this weather?" Karan could not think of anything worse. "It'll be like an ice box."

"I've missed it so. Making perfumes and scent potions is everything to me."

"Everything?" said Karan, watching Wilm climb down the ladder into the snowy gloom.

"Almost everything," said Aviel, flushing. "He's my dearest friend, but my place is here . . . and Wilm's isn't."

The flight along the eastern flank of the range was only twenty-five miles but took a frightening hour and a half. The wind had turned around to the south-east, the snow had become rain, and it grew heavier the further they went north.

When they finally landed in comparative shelter between the two wings of Gothryme Manor it was after four and the short winter's day was almost done. The rain was lashing down, the gutters were over-flowing and the paved courtyard was awash.

"There's not a light on anywhere," said Karan, studying the windows of her beloved, dilapidated manor. "Something's wrong. Llian." She grabbed his arm. "Do you think Snoat's army . . ."

"There's no sign of damage," said Llian.

"I've never seen rain like this in my life," said Sulien, her eyes alight. "Daddy, did you see the swan pond? It's overflowing!"

The sky ship was blown sideways by a gust of wind. "Get it tied down and get inside," yelled Malien over the thunder of rain on the cabin roof.

Yggur and the Aachim jumped out and tied the sky ship down. Karan was saturated before she got to the bottom of the ladder. She lurched to the door of the old keep and heaved it open. It was dark inside.

"It's freezing! Doesn't feel as though the fires have been lit in weeks."

"We'll get everything sorted," said Malien, holding up a lightglass. "Go to bed."

"I'm not going to bloody bed," Karan snapped. "Sulien, help me look for Rachis." She stopped, overcome by an unhappy thought. "No, help Llian."

"Daddy doesn't need help," said Sulien, "and if something's happened to Rachis I want to know."

"I don't think—"

"I saw awful things when the Whelm hunted me, and on Gwine. If dear old Rachis is dead . . ."

Her eyes filled with tears. She took Karan's hand and they searched the keep but found no sign that anyone had been inside it in weeks. "There's dust on the table," said Karan. "He must be . . . gone."

"Rachis hardly ever comes in here when you're away," said Sulien. "He keeps to his room and his office."

He wasn't in his room either, which was tidy and spare, as always. What if he'd fallen down outside and broken a leg? He was a frail old man; the cold would carry him off quickly.

"Mummy!" yelled Sulien. "He's in here."

Karan stumbled into the estate office with its two desks, a wall of pigeonholes containing rolled documents, all neatly labelled, and shelves of massive ledgers detailing every aspect of life and work on the estate for more than a hundred and fifty years.

Rachis was slumped in his old straight-backed chair with a blanket wrapped around him, so still that Karan was sure he was dead. Then his eyes moved and he managed the faintest of smiles. "Welcome home," he said, his voice wispy as a breeze blowing through spider webs. "Hope I . . . didn't give you a fright."

Sulien threw her arms around him. "Of course not. I knew you would be here." She gestured to the window. "Just look at the rain! You said it would rain, and it has."

"The best we've had since the great floods of forty-three years ago. The flowers we planted on poor Piffle's grave are two feet high." Rachis looked up at Karan. "I've heard news of your doings, and Llian's. And yours too," he said to Sulien. "Would you run and get me a drink? I'm a trifle dry—haven't moved for a day and a half."

Sulien ran out.

"Why not?" said Karan.

"Can't get out of my chair."

Her eyes watered. He was dying.

"My time was up long ago," said Rachis. "I only hung around in the hope that you three would come home safe and sound."

"And now we have, and you're coming in to sit by the fire."

Sulien came back with a cup of water, then they helped Rachis to the armchair closest to the great granite fireplace, where a fire now blazed, and arranged cushions around him.

"You must be starving," said Karan. "I'll make you some supper."

"Just a bit of bread and cheese," said Rachis. "And, Sulien . . ."

"Yes?" she said.

He reached out a withered claw and she took it. "Save the sadness until I'm gone. A happy, laughing home is the best send-off you can give me."

In the kitchen Sulien said, "He's dying." Tears shone in her eyes.

"Yes, and we won't say anything about Maigraith."

The Aachim, who generally preferred their own company, had taken over the empty North Wing, though Malien came across after dinner. Karan, Llian, Sulien, Rachis and Yggur sat by the fire, not talking much. There was no wine left in the cellar worth drinking, but Malien produced a squat black bottle. It was a beautiful object in itself, the glass intricately etched down to a white under-layer depicting a clump of the luminous bog blossoms of upland Aachan. It was sealed with green wax.

She broke away the wax and poured small measures of the scintillating blue liquid for the adults. "This is Thousand-Year Lisk, distilled aeons ago by the elders of Clan Elienor from the nectar of these night blossoms. Have any of you tried it?"

No one had even heard of it.

"I didn't think so," she went on. "This bottle is far older than a thousand years now; it was brought here by my ancestors when they came. It's probably the only bottle on Santhenar and it's said to be . . . memorable." She paused. "It's fitting that we toast our impossible victory with it, and give thanks to the three people who, almost single-handedly, made it possible."

Llian, who had been staring into the fire for ages, his arm around Sulien, who was almost asleep in his lap, said, "Many people made it possible, and most didn't live to see the victory."

"If victory it is," rumbled Yggur, "given that the Merdrun are more numerous than ever on Cinnabar and the summon stone still exists."

"That's a deadly secret," said Malien with a glance at Rachis.

His chuckle was like knuckle bones rattling in a cup. "One I'll be taking to my grave any day now."

Sulien sat up and glared at Yggur. "We're supposed to be having a nice evening where we don't talk about all the bad stuff."

Yggur bent his long head to hers. "I'm suitably chastened." He raised his goblet. "To a thousand heroes, both recognised and unknown, and a victory no one ever thought possible."

"And long years of peace and good harvests to follow," said Rachis, taking a tiny sip of Thousand-Year Lisk. His eyes watered, and Karan fancied she saw a trickle of steam come from his beak of a nose.

"To heroes recognised and unknown," she said, raising her own goblet. "And the breaking of the longest drought in four decades."

Llian echoed her but made no toast of his own, which was almost unprecedented. He had barely said a word since Thandiwe dropped her malicious bombshells. Knowing him, she was sure he was blaming himself, though Llian was no more to blame than anyone else.

The Thousand-Year Lisk was silky smooth, aromatic, slightly bitter, and had a blistering spicy heat that burned all the way down to the pit of Karan's stomach. "Aah!" she gasped, tossing half a mug of water down her throat. "It's certainly memorable. I'll be remembering it internally for a fortnight."

"An acquired taste, they say," said Malien, sipping her own.

Karan settled back in her favourite saggy old armchair, enjoying the sound of the teeming rain. She felt no need for conversation and evidently neither did anyone else. Rachis was nodding in his chair, Sulien asleep in Llian's lap. He was staring into the fire, his Thousand-Year Lisk untouched—and that *was* unprecedented.

"Are you going home tomorrow?" Karan said to Malien.

"No, I'm taking Yggur to Thurkad."

"What for?"

"Things to do."

Karan raised her eyebrows. Malien and Yggur had never been friends; the idea of them working together was hard to take in. But the past three months had changed everything. "I thought you were in a hurry to get home to Tirthrax?"

"Things have changed."

"The world will be really different when there are sky ships everywhere," Karan mused. "Wicked old Thurkad will only be two hours away. I'm not sure I like the idea of that."

"You don't need to worry," said Malien.

"Why not?"

"The device that allows a strong mancer to channel power to a sky ship's rotor depends on a very rare mineral—so rare that only fifty suitable crystals are known to exist. We brought them all with us, but thirty-two have been destroyed in crashes and explosions, another nine are in our remaining sky ships, and by now we will have taken the other nine back."

"Why?" said Karan.

"We don't feel the time is right for old humans to fly."

"That's pretty damn arrogant!"

Malien shrugged. "The crystals were only ever on loan for the duration of the war. If old humans really want to fly they can find their own way."

This illustrated, not that Karan needed reminding, how different the Aachim were from her own kind, and the belief in their own superiority that they never tried to hide.

The conversation petered out. Llian carried Sulien up to her bed and came down again. "Think I'll have an early night. Rachis, can I help you to bed?"

"Won't be as warm or as comfortable as where I am now," said Rachis sleepily.

"I'm going too," said Karan.

All she wanted was her big old box bed and Llian beside her. At the turn of the stairs she looked down. Rachis was asleep. Malien and Yggur had drawn their chairs together and were deep in conversation. Extraordinary!

She undressed and got into bed. Llian was staring at the ceiling. "Do you want me to blow out the lamp?" she said, snuggling up to him.

He put an arm around her. "I don't mind."

"Want to talk about things?"

"Not tonight. Tomorrow, when everyone else is gone."

When Karan went down in the morning Rachis was dead in his chair. She stood there, frozen, staring at him. She had been expecting him to die for years, but now it had happened she could not take it in.

"Mummy?" said Sulien anxiously from the doorway. "Are you all right?"

"Rachis is—"

"I know, I came down early. I . . . I sat with him for an hour. He looks so peaceful."

"All his troubles are over. Dear old Rachis. He was an old, old man, more than eighty, but still . . ."

"Yes." Sulien stroked her hand.

"He's been the mainstay of my life. All my life he's been here, always reliable when . . . when Mother and Father were not."

Karan sat beside her old friend, keeping him company and remembering all the times, good and bad, when he had just been there. He had never asked for anything save his modest salary, and there had been times when he had slipped it back into her money box, unspent. As a younger man, she knew, he had wanted a family, but it had never happened and, without complaining, he had become part of her family.

When the rain eased an hour later they buried him in the garden next to Piffle. Karan, Llian and Sulien filled in the grave with earth that was rapidly turning to mud. Yggur, Malien and the Aachim stood there for a few minutes, heads bowed, then set off in the sky ship for Thurkad.

It was overcast and very cold, and soon it began to rain again. Llian tamped down the mound over the grave and they spent a few minutes more by it in the teeming rain, then ran inside and stood by the fire, muddy and dripping.

"It all seems a bit . . . hasty," said Karan. "Our farewell should have taken longer."

"I'm sure it's what Rachis would have wanted," said Llian. "He hated to be fussed over, and he did love the rain."

"I suppose so," she said mournfully. She shivered in her sodden clothes. "I need a nice hot bath."

"But there's no hot water," said Llian, moving closer to the fire until his clothes steamed. The vast old stove Karan's father had built to heat water for the household had failed a year ago, and Karan could not afford to get it fixed.

"Yes, there is," said Sulien smugly. "The Aachim can fix anything made of metal. They took the stove apart in the middle of the night and made it better than ever."

78

MY PEOPLE WOULD FORBID IT

"I dreamed about Maigraith last night," said Sulien in a hollow voice at breakfast the following morning. "And that evil Julken. She's coming to take me away. Coming fast."

Karan started and knocked the teapot over. Tea flooded across the old pine kitchen table towards the pile of estate papers she had been going through last night. She blocked it with her forearm.

"She's not taking you!" Llian said explosively. He moved the papers onto a bench and mopped up the tea with a frayed towel.

"It'd be worse than being a little Whelm," said Sulien. "I still feel like a little Whelm, sometimes."

"This is all my fault. If I hadn't made up that tale—"

"Either I'd be dead, or you would be," said Karan wearily. "In which case Maigraith would have taken Sulien long ago, and the Merdrun would have escaped from Gwine, reopened the Crimson Gate and conquered the world. It's nobody's fault—or maybe it's mine. If I hadn't dosed Maigraith with hrux—"

Sulien clapped her hands over her ears. "It's *Maigraith's* fault!" she said through her teeth. Then, in the stern parental tone that Karan sometimes used to her, "Maigraith's doing this and you're not helping by arguing about it."

"But what are we going to do?" said Llian.

"Whichever way Maigraith comes," said Karan, "she can be here in under three weeks, if she hurries."

"Then we've got to be gone in two weeks. At the latest."

"But there's nowhere in the world where she won't hunt us down," said Karan. "Unless . . . I ask Malien to take us in."

"Do you want me to link to her?" said Sulien.

"I don't see as we have any choice."

Sulien made a link to Malien far more easily than Karan had ever done, then included her in it.

Sulien? said Malien and paused. Karan sensed that she was eating. *Is something the matter?*

Mummy wants to ask you a favour.

Yes?

I dreamed about Maigraith coming to take me away. Sulien paused but Malien did not speak. *Mummy wants to ask you to please take us in and hide us.*

The silence stretched until it became uncomfortable, then continued for a minute longer. Karan's pulse was pounding in her ears and she felt a sick dread that Malien was going to say no. Llian was staring at her. Although he could not be included in the link, he was adept at reading faces.

It's the first thing Maigraith would expect, said Malien. *And . . . she's too powerful now and a bad enemy. I'm sorry, Sulien, but my people would forbid it. Taking you in, I mean. The best I can do is take the three of you east or wherever you want to go.*

"Oh!" said Sulien aloud. *Th-thank you.* She broke the link, cutting Malien off as she started to apologise again.

We're kin! Karan thought furiously. *How can you turn us away?* The rejection was crushing. "That's that then," she said heavily. "Get everything packed and ready. The moment Malien comes back I'll get her to take us east . . . somewhere. Long before Maigraith gets here we've got to disappear. There's no other solution."

After another very long silence, Llian said, "Maybe there is."

"What, Daddy?" said Sulien, gazing at him in wonder.

"Remember what I told you about Rulke when he was a prisoner in the Nightland?"

"No," said Karan numbly.

"He wrote about using his virtual construct to travel to the future, to ease the unendurable burden of his sentence."

"Doesn't ring a bell."

"He never mentioned it again, but the next nine hundred years of his time in the Nightland are unrecorded, and that doesn't make sense. Why would he say nothing about his life for nine centuries?"

"What if he did go to the future?" she said irritably. "We've got no way of getting to the Nightland. And supposing we could, and his construct could go forward in time, we'd still be stuck there."

He looked sheepish, but said, "I'm going to follow it up. I've still got the bulk of Rulke's papers to translate."

"I thought you handed them in to the college library so Thandiwe could write his Histories."

"Only the ones she translated, and I'd already memorised them."

"Why not the rest?" said Karan.

"Must've slipped my mind," he said blandly.

"Daddy!" whispered Sulien, scandalised but admiring.

"Now you're being a bad influence on your daughter," said Karan, but she was smiling. "Sulien, link to Malien and tell her we'll be ready when she gets here."

"All right. Do you want to talk to her?"

"No."

The rain stopped for a day, then started again, though gently now. The River Ryme was still in flood and spreading a thick layer of fertile silt over the fields. Gothryme would have wonderful harvests for years to come, but Karan would not be here to see them. She gazed out the window at her unfamiliarly green estate, then wiped her eyes and got on with her work.

"Can we finish sorting out all the old stuff?" asked Sulien three days after their return. They were in the library, and she was at the table with Karan. She was still clingy, and no wonder.

"I thought we had," Karan said absently. Why was Malien taking so long? Maigraith was getting closer every day. Karan could sense her, a great knot of vindictiveness and implacability.

"There's still that old box of Faelamor's in the secret passage. Where did you get it, anyway?"

"At the end of the Time of the Mirror she felt guilty about all the wrongs she'd done me, and she left me the contents of her cave in Dunnet as reparation."

"What was in it?"

"Just Faellem stuff, none of it worth much to anyone else. I sold most of it years ago to keep Gothryme going through the drought." Karan frowned at Sulien. "How did you know about the secret passage, anyway?"

Sulien rolled her eyes.

"I can't keep anything secret from you, can I?" said Karan.

"No you can't, Mummy. Can I get it?"

"All right. Do you need me to show you . . ."

Sulien was up in a flash and had opened the passage before Karan could finish speaking. After some minutes she came out bearing a beautifully made box, a foot square and high, made from silkwood aged to the colour of amber.

"What's this?" she said when they had taken everything out. Sulien held up a dirty wooden ball the size of a small orange. It was rather knobbly.

Karan took it. It felt rather too heavy to be solid wood. "It's called a mimemule."

"What's it for?"

"No idea."

"Can I have it?"

Karan felt reluctant, but then, it was just a carved piece of wood. "Yes, but be careful. It belonged to Faelamor and it could be enchanted."

"I thought the Faellem were forbidden to use enchanted objects."

"They were. And she broke the prohibition more than once."

Karan saw much less of Sulien after that, and when she did, her daughter was always playing with the mimemule. She had scraped the layers of compacted grime away to discover that it was actually made of four interlocking wooden spheres, red-gold in colour. Like all Faellem artefacts it was beautifully made, but what was it for?

The next morning Karan turned over in bed and Sulien was standing beside it, her teeth chattering.

"I saw Maigraith again."

Karan shot upright. "Where?"

"Galloping along a dusty road. Then she came to a town where everything was made from blue stone and all the roofs were green."

"Dark blue stone?" said Llian.

"Yes, except the town hall. It was yellow and had a tower at each end."

"Shantin," said Karan. "It's about a week north-west of Chanthed."

"It's easy riding from Shantin to Chanthed. At this rate Maigraith could be here in . . ."

"Thirteen days," said Llian. "Five days earlier than our worst fears. She must be riding half the night."

Karan got up and busied herself with her final preparations. She was almost ready to leave; Sulien and Llian had their bags packed and were ready to go at a moment's notice. Karan had found a few more items to sell to add to her small emergency stock of gold tells and silver tars. She had written to everyone who needed to be notified that she was leaving Gothryme indefinitely, though she had not yet sent the letters, and she had written out deeds giving her farmers the land they worked.

It had proved surprisingly easy to set her affairs in order; she had little left of value save the estate itself. Her family had lived here for almost a thousand years, and soon it would be gone. Since a distant cousin would take over the manor and the bulk of the estate when she was gone, she had to put Gothryme out of her mind.

Llian was working furiously on his pointless project of translating Rulke's papers and crafting his tale of *The Gates of Good and Evil*, focusing on his work as he had not for years. She envied his ability to escape their overwhelming troubles. Annoying man!

She had to focus on where to go and how to hide. They had to leave Meldorin, but going south was out—Shazabba was the realm of the Whelm, and the lands further east were equally bleak and inhospitable. The few Faellem who still lived on Santhenar could be found in the endless forests of Mirrilladell, south of the Great Mountains, though they were not a welcoming folk.

North was also problematic. The huge island of Faranda was mostly sweltering desert and she did not know how they could survive there. The north-east was possible—it had vast rainforests, though it was also unbearably hot and humid and neither she nor Sulien were comfortable in such climes.

It had better be the east then. Malien would take them there in her sky ship, and they could lose themselves for a while in the endless forests and mountains of the east coast, though when their money ran out they would be indigent foreigners in a land none of them knew. What then?

A huge shadow passed across the window, and Malien's sky ship settled next to the swan pond, sending them flapping in all directions, hissing and trumpeting.

She and Yggur had come alone; the other Aachim had stayed in Thurkad. After a cool and reserved early dinner, Karan hardly saying a word to Malien and a frosty Sulien steadfastly playing with the mimemule and ignoring Malien's every approach, Llian returned to the ridiculous idea he had mentioned the other day.

"Rulke definitely did go forward in time," he said, holding up a piece of paper. "I have the translation here, and it says how he did it too, though it didn't help him escape the Nightland."

Yggur took the paper, scanned it without comment and handed it to Malien.

When she had read it he said, "He's careful not to say anything that another mancer could use to reconstruct what he did."

"You wouldn't need to," said Llian. "All you'd have to do is study the settings of the virtual construct."

"A truly great mancer *might* succeed, assuming he could get to the Nightland, understand the controls and mechanisms of Rulke's virtual construct—if it still exists—and had the power to use it, but it would be fiendishly dangerous. What works in the strange reality of the Nightland might go dangerously wrong in the real world. But, lacking any way to get to the Nightland anyway, I'm sure it's impossible."

"I'm not," Llian said. He poured the last dribble from a bottle of miserably bad wine into Yggur's goblet. "Sorry. All the drinkable stuff went years ago." He took on a dreamy expression. "Remember the bottle Nadiril shared with us the night before Thandiwe's Great Tale?" He sighed heavily. "I can recall every sip. The Uncibular '81, if I'm not mistaken."

"Are you ever mistaken about wine?" Karan said tartly.

Clunk. A freshly uncorked bottle of Uncibular '81 appeared in the middle of the table. Llian started, gaped, then reached out suspiciously and sniffed the bottle. A dreamy look appeared on his face.

"Thanks, Malien," he said, pouring a measure and tasting it. And sighing.

Malien was staring at the bottle. "That was beautifully conjured, but I didn't do it."

"Neither did I," said Yggur.

"Then who did?" said Llian.

79

OUR FRIENDS DON'T GIVE
A DAMN ABOUT US

Sulien was twirling the mimemule on her palm. "Umm . . . it was me."

"Can I see that?" said Yggur, plucking it away. He wrapped his big hands around it, closed his eyes and appeared to be concentrating hard. "Where did you get it?"

"Faelamor left it to Mummy, ages ago. It's called a mim—a mimemule."

"I've never heard of such a thing. Where did you conjure the wine from, Sulien?"

"I didn't conjure it. Daddy wanted some, so I made it for him."

Yggur stared at her. "How do you mean, *made* it?"

"I imagined the wine Nadiril had really clearly, turned the mimemule in my hands, and the wine was there."

"Have you made anything else?"

"Umm . . ." Sulien shot a nervous glance at Karan. "Just some . . . little things I wanted."

Yggur handed it back. "Well, I dare say you can't do any harm with it." He poured a goblet, quaffed it, sighed then rose. "If we're going to get to Casyme at a civilised hour, we should go."

"You're going to *Casyme* now?" said Karan.

"News to discuss," said Malien, "and plans to make."

"You promised to take us east."

"And I will."

"When? Sulien had a seeing about Maigraith this morning," said Llian. "She was in Shantin. She'll be here in under a fortnight."

Yggur and Malien exchanged glances. "That's not good," said Yggur, "but the sooner we go to Casyme—"

"What's the hurry?"

"The town was sacked by one of Snoat's armies a couple of months ago, and Wilm's mother was killed."

"Oh, poor Wilm," said Sulien. "I can't imagine . . ." She pressed up against Karan, who put an arm around her.

"And Aviel's workshop was robbed and most of Shand's house destroyed. They've lost everything."

"But we landed there!" said Karan. "How come Shand didn't say?"

"The snow was so thick we couldn't see the house," said Llian.

"Well, they can live here," she said bitterly. "We'll never see Gothryme again."

"Shand's planning on going west," said Yggur. "He's working on something mysterious with Ifoli. We'd better go."

"When will you be back?" Karan cried, her voice cracking.

"Soon."

After they had gone, Karan and Llian went back to the table. Sulien had sneaked upstairs, presumably to avoid interrogation about what else she had made with the mimemule, and Karan did not have the energy to follow her. She stared at the bottle. Llian poured hefty measures of Uncibular '81 into their goblets.

"Our so-called friends don't give a damn about us," he muttered.

"Apparently," said Karan.

"We can't leave it to the last minute. Maigraith can travel faster than we can."

"Let's give Malien a week. If she's not back by then, we ride east."

"Yes," said Llian. He sipped his wine. "I wonder if Sulien could make a case of this?"

80

HAND YGGUR THE MIMEMULE

A week went by with no word from Malien, then another eternal day, and Sulien's premonitions about Maigraith grew stronger and more vivid by the hour. Karan was frantic and Llian was increasingly worried

that she was going to crack up. She kept running backwards and forwards, stuffing items into her pack then taking them out again and
flinging them about.

"Karan, stop!" cried Llian. "You're not helping."

She drew back her small fist and for several awful seconds he thought
she was going to punch him. "Aaarrgh!" she shrieked.

She hefted a plaster bust of Tudup, one of her most unpleasant
ancestors, and hurled it through the kitchen window. *Crash!* Glass went
everywhere and pieces of plaster scattered across the terrace outside.
She spun round, reached for a cast-iron frying pan and was about to
hurl it through what remained of the window when Sulien caught her
by the arm.

"No, Mummy!" she said sharply.

Karan came to her senses and dropped the frying pan on the table.
"I'm sorry. I . . . I can't take much more of this."

"We can't wait for Malien any longer," said Llian.

"No. We'll leave at dawn."

The following morning they were saddled up and about to ride out
when the sky ship came racing in, landing so fast that it slid across the
icy snow and skidded around to face back the way it had come.

Wilm jumped out and stood by the ladder while Aviel came down,
then Shand and Malien climbed out, and Yggur last. Wilm's eyes were
red and he kept rubbing them, not looking at anyone.

"I'm really sorry to hear about your mother," said Llian.

"Yes," Wilm said vaguely. "Thank you, Llian."

Aviel, who was staring at her boots, seemed lost. She put a hand on
Wilm's arm and he looked down at her gratefully. She stared at her
boots again.

"I heard your workshop was robbed," said Llian. "I'm sorry. There's
plenty of room here, and you're welcome—"

"They took everything I had," Aviel whispered. "I've got nothing to
work with. How am I going to survive?"

Llian did not know what to say. "Shand, I'm sorry you've lost your
house."

"Ugly place," said Shand indifferently. "Can't think why I moved there. Are you going somewhere?" He seemed better than he had in a long time; the haunted look he had worn for months was gone.

"In another minute we would have," Llian said coolly. He felt very let down by Malien.

"No need now. Let's go inside."

"What for?"

"We can't talk out here."

"Why the hell not?"

"My granddaughter is a most formidable mancer," Shand said quietly. "One whose skills even *I* don't fully understand. We can't take *any* chances."

They all went into the old keep, and Llian headed for the big fireplace. "No," said Shand. "Best we do this in the library."

"Do what?"

Shand frowned at a small device partly concealed in his cupped right hand. In the library he closed the shutters, drew the heavy curtains and walked around, passing the device over the walls and floors. He climbed onto the library table and raised the device towards the ceiling. He jumped down, moved it back and forth across the section of wall beside the window, said, "Ah!" and pushed the concealed catch.

"How come everyone knew about the secret passage except me?" said Llian.

Shand said, "It's safe," and gestured to the library table. They sat. "This is the plan."

"You mean, 'We have a suggestion,'" said Karan tartly.

"No, I don't. Maigraith's power has grown tremendously since you dosed her with hrux, Karan. She spent weeks at Carcharon fighting the influence of the summon stone, and it almost overcame her; being that close to it for that long, it would have overcome anyone else.

"But she spent most of her life fighting the influence of Faelamor, who was the greatest manipulator of all, and Maigraith is stronger mentally than anyone I've ever met. She overcame the influence of the summon stone by focusing, no, *obsessing* on her own most earnest desire—to create a living monument to Rulke by uniting two triunes, Julken and Sulien.

"That obsession both corrupted and saved her, and she can't give it up. And because of other powers Rulke gifted her before his death, powers Maigraith is only now learning to use, there's *nowhere* you can go on Santhenar where she can't find you."

"Then what's the point?" said Karan.

"Yggur and I believe there may be a *nowhen* where she can't find you."

"Going to the future!" said Llian. "Yes!"

"Does anyone else know that Rulke wrote about it?" said Shand. "Thandiwe for instance?"

"No, she never translated his Nightland papers. I only told Janck, and he's dead."

"What did he say?"

"He told me not to waste his time with such utter nonsense."

"Then no one else knows about it," said Shand, "and it's unlikely Maigraith can find out. Let's proceed. Sulien, would you hand Yggur the mimemule?"

Reluctantly, she passed it to him. Yggur closed his hand loosely around it, his eyes went out of focus, then a miniature stone cottage appeared in the middle of the table. His eyes misted; he shook the mimemule and the cottage faded away.

"An easy test," he said but did not explain. "Let's try it with one of the hardest."

He strained until sweat ran down his forehead, until his knuckles went white and his eyes bulged. A sheet of black metal the size of a small book slowly formed in the centre of the library table. A metal mirror.

The edges of the sheet were raised to form a frame, and inside it a reflecting material like jellied mercury shimmered and ghosted with phosphorescence. The frame was scribed with the finest silver glyphs, and a symbol was impressed in the top right-hand corner. It was like three golden bubbles grown together, enclosed by touching crescent moons in scarlet set within a platinum circle, the circle infilled with fine silver lines twining and intertwining.

"No!" cried Karan, shoving her chair back and leaping to her feet.

"How dare you!" said Shand, his breath hissing between his teeth.

Yggur slumped forward, breathing heavily. "Takes a lot out of you."

Malien was staring at the mirror with a mixture of fear and longing. "The Mirror of Aachan! Stolen from us in the deeps of time."

"And utterly corrupted," said Llian, "long before Karan stole it from Yggur."

Yggur came to his senses. "Not *the* mirror, but a copy perfect in every detail." He shook the mimemule again and the mirror vanished, though the phosphorescence lingered in the air for several seconds. He stared at it regretfully, then laid the mimemule on the table.

"I had to put it to the sternest test I could think of," he said. "I had to be sure before we began."

"What happened to the mirror?" said Karan.

"As it was made, so was it unmade. It no longer exists."

Sulien reached for the mimemule.

"Don't touch it!" Karan said sharply. She swivelled towards Yggur. "Are you saying that the mimemule can copy *anything*?"

"Not at all. But I held the Mirror of Aachan for many years and I know it inside and out. No one else could have recreated it without knowing it equally well, the good and the bad."

"And your plan is?"

"To copy the virtual construct you and Llian saw in the Nightland, but make it real."

"You don't know the construct inside and out, and I don't remember it that clearly."

"Llian does," said Yggur. "A master chronicler can remember things he's seen and heard perfectly—both words and images."

Karan turned and stared at the fire. "But Llian isn't a mancer's bootlace."

Llian was used to Karan saying things like that and no longer took offence. At least, not much.

"We've learned a lot about memories since we tried to recover Sulien's nightmare. Malien and I have created a . . . a *spell* I suppose you'd call it," said Yggur, sounding remarkably hesitant, "to extract Llian's perfect memory of the virtual construct. Once I have it, I'll use it to recreate the construct the way Rulke used it in the Nightland—but I'm going to make it real. In Shazmak."

"Why Shazmak?" Karan's voice shook.

"Travelling to the future will require monumental power, and far more in the real world than Rulke would have required in the Nightland. Such a gate can't be made with my innate power, or even mine plus Shand's and Malien's."

"It can only be made at a powerful natural place," said Shand. "A place Ifoli calls a node of power. And we believe the most powerful node in Meldorin is at Shazmak."

"Once we've extracted Llian's perfect memory of the virtual construct," said Malien, "Shazmak is the one place powerful enough for the mimemule to make the construct. So, Llian, while Yggur readies his spell, tell us what you saw."

"All right," said Llian, still shocked that they believed his mad idea could work. He collected his thoughts. "This is how I saw it, and what I thought *when* I saw it.

"Even from the outside the construct was a big, complex device, about six yards long and three yards wide and high. It was shaped in strange alien curves made from a blue-black metal. There were bulges all around and curious levers and projections on top. It looked as solid as everything around us now, but when I touched it my hand went straight through the side. Rulke had made it, complete in his mind, but he hadn't given it physical form."

Llian looked around the table. Everyone was staring at him. "Curiosity is one of my little weaknesses."

"One of your major character flaws, I would have said," said Shand.

"I had to know what it was like inside, so I put my head and shoulders in. The interior was lit by an unnerving dark-red light . . ."

"What did you see?" said Yggur.

"There were two oddly curved seats, and in front of them a variety of levers, knobs and glassy plates with coloured lines and moving patterns—and everywhere I looked there were more incomprehensible devices."

"If he didn't understand it," said Malien, "how can he describe it so perfectly that it can be made?"

"Ah, but then Rulke found me," said Llian. "I was terrified; I was sure he was going to punish me. But instead—he was never predictable—he linked his arm through mine as if we were brothers and led me around the construct, telling me all about it and explaining everything. I gathered that it was a device for making gates from one place to another—and for other greater purposes."

"Why did he explain everything?" Malien said suspiciously. No Aachim could ever trust a Charon's word.

"He told me that. Once I returned to Santhenar, Rulke wanted me to spread the story far and wide, to show how unsurpassed his own power was and to undermine his enemies. I don't understand how the construct worked, but his description of it is burned into my memories."

"Then as soon as Shand can make a gate to Shazmak—" said Yggur.

"I thought you weren't making any more gates," said Karan to Shand. "You said each gate took five years off your life."

"Getting you three away will *add* five years to my life," muttered Shand. "I made most of the preparations before we got here. It'll only take an hour to finish the gate."

"Then, once we're in Shazmak . . ." said Yggur. "Malien, where would be best?"

"The top of the highest tower. It's where Tensor used to go when he wanted to work a particularly challenging piece of mancery."

"It must lie right over the node. All right; once we get to the top of the tower I'll use the spell to extract Llian's perfect memory of the virtual construct, and then the mimemule—I hope—will make it real."

"Lot of *ifs* in the plan," said Shand.

"Let's assume it works and you can recreate the construct, perfectly," said Karan. "How do we go to the future?"

"I'll make sure of the settings," said Yggur.

"But how do we know where to go—and when?"

"Ah!" Shand smiled. "I gave Aviel my grimoire and she's crafted a scent potion from it—a damned dark potion, as it happens."

"I thought her workshop was destroyed?" said Karan.

"I flew her down to the one she used in Sith," said Malien. "That's why we were gone so long. Karan, the scent potion will allow you to visualise where you want to go, and the year—more or less—you want to end up in."

"It all seems a bit . . . thrown together," said Karan.

"There's a risk," said Yggur. "Quite a big risk, actually. So if it's too big for you—"

"*She's coming!*" moaned Sulien.

81

SHE'S ONLY MINUTES AWAY

"She's just left Tolryme," said Sulien, huge-eyed.

The shock ran though Karan like a knife to the belly. How could Maigraith have made up so much time? She must be travelling day and night, riding horses into the ground.

Everyone scrambled up from the table. "She could be here in fifteen minutes," said Karan. "Possibly ten. Can you make the gate any quicker?"

"At a very heavy cost," said Shand. "But not in ten minutes. You'll have to delay her." He ran out.

How? thought Karan, mentally frozen. Ten minutes wasn't nearly enough time to implement this absurd plan that was their only hope. "Llian, Sulien, get your gear." They raced off. "What about you, Malien?"

"My sky ship's ready to cast off."

"Don't leave yet. If Shand can't make the gate in time we'll have to go with you."

"I'll give him a hand; that'll save a few minutes."

Llian came in, a heavy pack on his back and his journal bag slung over his shoulder. He was wearing a sword, which looked so wrong; he hadn't strapped the scabbard on properly and it swung between his legs as he moved, threatening to trip him. "Are we going?"

"One way or another," Karan said grimly.

She heaved on her own pack, made sure her knife was secure in its sheath and a second one hidden in an ankle sheath, and took a last look around the family home she would never see again. Memories surged, both wonderful and terrible, but there was no time for them, nor her tears. She wiped them away and went to the front door. Was that a cloud of dust along the cart track to Tolryme? It was.

Awful fear shivered through her. Maigraith always exceeded their direst forecasts. What would she do next? Could she blast the sky ship out of the sky? Possibly, though she would only do so if she knew Sulien wasn't on it.

A minute hurtled by. Karan ran to the library, the pack banging against her back. "If the gate's not ready, it's too late. She's only minutes away. We'll have to go on the sky—"

Shand was doubled over to the left of the table, gasping, his face crimson.

Malien stood beside him, blanched and trembling. "It's—"

Craaack! A black cavity rimmed with wildly flapping streamers of white and silver formed in the centre of the library. The gate was open. A wind from nowhere slammed the library door, then sucked books and papers from the shelves and hurled them into the gate. The huge canvas map was torn off the wall and blasted against the entrance, temporarily blocking it. The centre of the map bulged further and further into the gate, tore in a star pattern, and the map was sucked through.

"It's ready," Shand said redundantly.

Karan heaved the library door open. Yggur, Llian and Sulien were outside, along with Wilm and Aviel. "Malien, go!"

"Fare well," said Malien. She hastily embraced Sulien, then Karan and Llian, and ran out.

"Go through the gate," Karan said to Llian and Sulien. "Wilm, Aviel, you can't stay here. Go with Malien."

Aviel shook her head. "I've got to tell you exactly how to use the scent potion. It's complicated."

"All right, go after Llian," said Yggur. "You too, Karan."

As Karan went in, Llian was standing beside the gate, white-faced, holding Sulien's hand. The wind was tugging at them, almost lifting her off her feet.

"Get going!" Karan yelled.

"Keep your heads down," said Shand.

Llian and Sulien, heads lowered, stepped in front of the gate. As the wind took hold of them and hurled them through, *boom-boom*, a pang pierced Karan where Jaguly had stabbed her in the belly. There had been so little time, and the gate felt too wild. What if they hadn't made it properly?

She ran after them, forgetting to lower her head. *Boom!* The wind lifted her off her feet, cracked the side of her head against something hard, then hurled her down a pitch-black passage that reminded her unnervingly of the Nightland.

Boom-boom behind her. That would be Wilm and Aviel.

The gate belched her out into a vast tiled chamber and she skidded across the floor on her bottom for twenty feet. This hall had once been the grandest space in the whole of Shazmak, but the city had been badly damaged in the Whelm's attack eleven years ago, when they had killed many Aachim and driven out the rest, and parts had been vandalised during the Whelm's brief occupation.

Now, having lain empty for a decade, everything was layered in dust, which the humid gale howling through the gate lifted into mud-coloured clouds. The floor was littered with shredded books and papers and the rags of Karan's magnificent old canvas map. Did they symbolise her own life, her own future?

Llian, Sulien, Wilm and Aviel were ten yards away, picking themselves up. Llian was kneading his shoulder and wincing; the others did not seem to be hurt.

Boom! Boom! Yggur came through, skidding on the soles of his boots, then Shand sliding on his knees. He lurched to his feet, wincing, and pointed at the gate. It closed, then vanished.

Yggur and Shand stood side by side, Shand the best part of a foot shorter, and worked some incomprehensible mancery. Karan assumed they were erasing all trace of the gate's path.

"Can that really hide us from her?" said Yggur.

"I don't know," said Shand. The knees had been torn out of his trousers and his own knees were bloody.

"Where to?" said Llian.

Karan pointed to the staircase, the most magnificent ever built on Santhenar, that coiled gently around the walls of the huge hall, then spiralled up the mighty tower above it for a good seven hundred feet.

His eyes followed her finger up. "Hell of a climb."

"She's coming," whispered Sulien. "Mummy, *she's coming.*"

"How has she traced the gate so quickly?" said Yggur.

"I'd say she's come into the powers Rulke gifted her," said Shand.

"Go up, Sulien," said Karan. "Don't run; you'll exhaust yourself."

"I guess I won't be teaching you how to use your gift," Shand said to Sulien. "And I was looking forward to it."

Sulien and Llian began the ascent, Llian labouring under his heavy pack, which was no doubt half full of Rulke's papers. Karan sighed. Stupid, impractical man!

"You'd better tell me how to use the scent potion," said Karan to Aviel.

"Not here!" hissed Yggur. "Don't talk about anything until we get to the top and I've put up a secrecy barrier."

Aviel headed for the staircase, limping, with Wilm and Yggur beside her. It would take four full circuits of the great hall before they were up in the tower out of sight. If Maigraith reopened the gate before then they would be clearly visible.

"Get moving," Shand said to Karan. "My work is done now, and if Maigraith does reopen the gate I might be able to delay her."

I wouldn't bet on it, Karan thought. "Thank you. If this works I'll never see you again."

"The past twelve years have been . . . interesting." Shand took her hands in his and she thought he was going to embrace her, but he just squeezed her hands and pushed her away. "Go!"

"I'll miss you, Shand."

She hurried after the others, her mind whirling. So many farewells, so many old friends she would never see again. So uncertain a future— assuming they had one.

Above her Aviel was hobbling and wincing with every step. She said something to Wilm, who nodded, heaved her over his shoulder and, taking three steps at a time, soon left Karan behind.

The healed knife wound in her belly throbbed with every step. After five minutes of interminable climbing she entered the tower. The diameter of the spiralling stairs was much narrower here and finally she felt that she was making good progress, though she still had five hundred painful feet to go.

Then, when she was halfway up, from one or two floors above her came a thick, glutinous voice that froze her marrow. She could not make out what he had said but Sulien's voice was clear. "I'm waiting for Mummy."

"So am I," said Idlis.

Her legs were aching, but Karan raced up, fighting a stitch in her side and the stabbing pains in her belly. The others were out of sight. Idlis, who was even thinner and more battered than the last time she had seen him, stood on the landing between Sulien and the next flight, blocking her way.

"What are you doing here?" Karan gasped.

"Cast out by my people," he said thickly. "Nowhere else to go."

"Let Sulien past."

"I swore to protect her, and I always will," said Idlis. "But my obligation to you is cancelled, Karan, and now you will die."

82

NO ESCAPE SAVE IN DEATH

"Please don't hurt Mummy," said Sulien .

"I am truly sorry, little one, but her betrayal cut too deep. She has to pay the price."

BOOOOOOOM! echoed up the tower, and three puffs of wind, one after another, lifted Sulien's unbraided red hair.

"She's coming!" she moaned. She reached out to Idlis pleadingly. "Maigraith is coming for me. She's going to take me away to live with her and her evil son, Julken."

Idlis's black eyes flicked from her face to Karan's. "Is this so?"

"Yes," Karan croaked. "It's as I told you when we met near Chanthed, months ago."

"When I saved you from Ragred. Another debt you refuse to acknowledge."

"I acknowledge it. Please, Idlis."

"No."

Shouting echoed up the tower, Shand's deep voice and Maigraith's reply, though the words were so distorted as to be unintelligible. Karan felt a sharp pain in her chest.

"Let her pass," she said.

Idlis moved aside, then drew a wavy-bladed knife. "Go up, child. I would not have you see this."

Sulien did not move. "If you kill Mummy you'll be dooming me too."

He turned slowly, studying her then Karan. "You have powerful friends here, little one. Yggur and Shand, and the young man with the enchanted sword. They will protect you."

"Maigraith will hunt me to the ends of the world. There's only one way to escape."

"From the top of the tower there is no escape save death," said Idlis.

"Yes, there is," Sulien said desperately, "but only Mummy can do it."

"Don't say any more!" said Karan.

Far below, she could hear feet on the stairs. Light feet, not Shand's heavy tread.

"Why can only Karan do it?" said Idlis.

"Say nothing!" said Karan.

"I trust Idlis with my life!" Sulien lowered her voice. "We're going to the future, and only Mummy is sensitive enough and experienced enough to *see* where to go. Without Mummy we'll all die."

Karan groaned. Idlis would betray them to Maigraith. They were utterly lost now.

"How?" he said, his close-cropped hair standing up.

Sulien explained briefly.

He considered her words for at least a minute. The sound of feet on the stairs grew louder.

"You speak the truth," he said, "and my oath holds. Go!"

"Not without Mummy."

"Go, both of you."

Sulien ran to the strange, gaunt, unlikeable man, reached up and hugged him. "You are the noblest Whelm in the world."

An unfathomable expression crossed Idlis's hideous face—awe, per-haps—and his eyes went a shiny black.

Karan stared into his eyes. "Thank you."

"I don't like you, Karan, and never will," he said. "But you and your daughter are the bravest people I've ever known. I hope you succeed." He bowed, turned the other way and stood looking down the stair. Waiting.

Karan adjusted her pack and went up, Sulien by her side. Up and up and up. Sulien did not speak. Would Idlis keep to his oath? How could he? If Maigraith suspected anything she would tear the secret out of him, and neither Sulien, Llian nor herself would ever be safe. Maigraith would find a way to pursue them, even to the future.

"Is it much further?" said Sulien five minutes later.

"Hope . . . not," Karan gasped. Her belly was agony, and her knees felt as though they were on fire. "Can't go much further."

"I'll run up." Sulien dropped her pack and raced away around the curve of the stairs.

Karan picked it up and laboured on. She could not hear Maigraith now, which was worse.

Wilm came running down. "Give me your pack."

Karan was so exhausted that it was a struggle to get it off. Wilm slipped it on effortlessly, and Sulien's as well. She supposed that, after five weeks hauling heavy stones for the Merdrun, the weight of two packs was insignificant.

"Take my hand," he said.

She gripped it. It was hard, callused. Wilm ran up, hauling her behind him. One flight, two, three, four, five, then they were up on the top of the tallest tower of Shazmak. It was fifty feet across, circular, paved in dark, red-flecked greenstone, with a chest-high wall of carved black basalt around the rim. Karan pushed through a bubble-like membrane, Yggur's secrecy barrier, and looked around her.

At this altitude, high in the mountains, it was bitterly cold. The day was overcast, the cloud base not far above the top of the tower, and huge flakes of snow were drifting in the wind. Llian was to her left, keeping well away from the wall; he had a tremendous fear of heights. Aviel sat with her back to the wall. She had taken off her belt, which held dozens of little scent phials in loops, and was sniffing them one by one. Yggur had both hands on the wall and was looking at the jagged mountains beyond. Their tops were concealed by clouds.

Karan stumbled to the parapet and looked over. The walls of the tower fell almost sheer for seven hundred feet to the level of Shazmak, then another three hundred feet into the great River Garr, a monumental torrent that hurled itself downstream as if determined to destroy everything in its path. She could not see the water, for mist filled the river gorge, but she could hear its roar and the sounds of boulders grinding against one another.

The scene reminded her of her dear friend Rael, Malien's only child, who had helped her and Llian escape from Shazmak twelve years ago. This place had cost him his life; he had drowned just down there.

A distant cry, muffled by the secrecy barrier, echoed up the stair. There was no time for memories. "Maigraith must have got past Shand."

"What took you so long?" said Yggur, who had the mimemule in his left hand and was running his fingers over the interlocking wooden spheres.

"Idlis."

"Oh! How long do we have?"

"I don't know. Not long."

"I'm not sure we can . . ." Whatever he had been going to say, Yggur thought better of it. "Aviel, give Karan the scent potion and tell her how to use it. Llian, come here. I've got to extract that memory, and it's going to hurt."

Karan crouched beside Aviel. "What do I do?"

Aviel handed her a glass phial the length of her little finger. The outside of the glass was bubbly. Through it Karan saw a thin yellow oil with bluish streaks in it.

"It's called Balsam of Hereafter and—"

"Where did it come from?"

"Radizer's grimoire, but Shand had to change the method a bit . . ."

Aviel seemed uneasy, and that did not inspire confidence. "Does it work?"

"There's no safe way to test the Great Potions."

So the scent potion might not work at all. Or it might go disastrously wrong. Even if it did work there was no certainty Yggur could extract Llian's memory of the virtual construct in time. And if he did, the mimemule might not be able to recreate such a powerful and complicated device. There were so many ways that this could end up a disaster.

But there was no choice—Maigraith had made sure of that.

"Keep the phial in your hand," said Aviel. "If the potion gets cold you won't be able to smell it. Take the stopper out but don't sniff it directly; waft the scent towards your nose."

"Now?" said Karan.

"Yes. It takes a few minutes to work and doesn't last long. You'll have to sniff it at least two more times before you go, and a few more times on the way to the future, depending how long you take to get there."

"Why so many times?"

"You have to hold on to your vision of where you're going, otherwise you could end up anywhere—or *nowhere*."

"How can I see the future anyway? How can I possibly know where to go? And when?"

"I didn't invent the potion," said Aviel. "I just made it."

Was attempting to reach an unknown but undoubtedly dangerous future really better than the alternative? When the alternative was Maigraith killing Llian and abducting Sulien, the answer had to be yes.

Karan wafted the scent potion towards her nose and took a tentative sniff. It was neither fragrant nor foul, herbal nor mineral. There were hints of warm iron, many unidentifiable floral and spicy scents, and cold sweat. No, that last odour came from herself.

"Deeper sniff," said Aviel.

Karan wafted it from a closer distance, closed her eyes and sniffed hard. She caught the previous odours plus two others: almonds baking and hot rock. Her head whirled gently, the *here and now* blurred out, and she saw a battlefield littered with dead in strange uniforms, wild dogs tearing at the bodies and crows pecking.

"Shand said you have to focus on both *where* you want to go to, and *when*," said Aviel.

Karan had not thought much about *when*. Maigraith, being a triune, could not expect to live nearly as long as her Charon or Faellem ancestors, but she could easily live another hundred years. Maybe a hundred and fifty, and, being implacable and obsessive, she would not give up her quest. Karan would have to go forward in time at least two hundred years.

It was a frightening prospect. Santhenar had changed greatly in the ten years since the Way Between the Worlds was opened; in two hundred years it might be unrecognisable. She tried to imagine the sequence of years, each winter and summer flickering by in a second, but lost count and there wasn't time to start again.

From the other side of the tower Llian gasped and fell to his knees. His hands were pressed to the sides of his head and he was shaking it from side to side. Yggur stood above him, right hand on the back of Llian's neck.

"More," said Yggur.

Llian threw his head back. His eyes were wide and staring, his mouth open. It snapped closed, and he strained until the tendons on his neck stood out.

"More!" said Yggur.

Llian rocked forward. His forehead touched the icy floor and the breath escaped from between his clenched teeth with a hiss, forming frost on the greenstone.

"More!" said Yggur.

Llian toppled onto his side, fists clenched, his lower legs swinging backwards and forwards. Yggur bent to stay in contact, held it for another half-minute then stood upright, made a double swirling motion with his free hand and turned away.

"Aaahh!" said Llian weakly. "That was . . ."

"Are you all right, Daddy?" said Sulien.

He came to his knees again, swaying from side to side. "Not the most pleasant experience I've ever had. And . . . the memory is gone completely."

"Because I've got it," said Yggur, tapping his forehead.

Sulien's face twisted. "Shand must have come up after Maigraith and tried to stop her. She's knocked him down, her own grandfather!" she cried, outraged. "She's racing up the stairs."

"Where is she?"

"Past halfway."

"Five or six minutes then," Yggur said thickly. "Not sure I can do it in time."

He put both hands on the wall, wiped sweat off his face then took the mimemule out of his pocket and reached over the parapet.

"What are you doing?" said Karan.

"Maigraith must never know the construct exists; she must believe you've thrown Llian and Sulien over the edge, then jumped after them."

"What?" cried Karan.

Llian spun round, gaping.

"It's the only way," said Yggur.

"You want the whole world to believe I went mad, killed my family and committed suicide?" Karan grated.

"By jumping into the Garr, where the three of you would have vanished without trace."

"You might have discussed this with us first."

"We were planning to but Maigraith got to Gothryme far too quickly. I'm going to materialise the construct ten feet down the side of the tower and set it to hover there. You'll have to jump in."

"Over a thousand-foot drop?" croaked Llian.

"Yes. Get ready."

They heaved their packs on. On the far side of the secrecy bubble Wilm had drawn the black sword and was looking down the stairs.

"Karan," said Aviel, "you need to smell the potion again."

It was hard to concentrate but she must. Karan wafted the Balsam of Hereafter towards her nose, closed her eyes and took a big sniff. She saw a yellow waterfall, a plain covered in what appeared to be armoured tortoises though they had twice the normal number of legs, then a spiky tower made of blue-white ice in a snow-covered landscape. The look of it, and the sense of it, made her shudder. *No*, she said to herself. *As far away from there as possible. Somewhere safe.*

She saw a steep hillside running with water, surrounded by rainforest, but it did not feel right either. *Not there.*

A rugged, empty coastline appeared, one she recognised, a few days' walk south of Alcifer. It would do. At the same time she could feel the years racing by, flipping summer to winter, summer to winter, though again she lost track of them. Then the image of the coastline and her sense of the racing years faded.

"Uuuugghhhh!" grunted Yggur, who was leaning over the wall, holding the mimemule with both hands. "Uuuugghhhh! Uuuugghhhh! *Uuuugghhhh!*"

Crack!

Karan stumbled on wobbling legs to the wall and looked over. And there it was—Rulke's construct, hovering in the air and looking exactly as she had seen it all those years ago.

It was made of metal so black it would have stood out against darkness, and it hung in the air like a soap bubble though it must have weighed tons. Its sides were scooped in and bulged out in perfect, complex curves no human smith could have duplicated. The long front soared up to a flaring binnacle crammed with knobs and wheels, behind which was a thicket of levers, a place to stand and a high seat carved from green serpentinite. A round hatch beside it led down to the red-lit interior.

"But is it real?" she said. "Is it solid? We walked right through the one in the Nightland."

Yggur took a gold tell from his pocket, considered it for a moment and tossed it down onto the hatch. *Clink!* "It's real. I'm going in."

"What for?"

"To make sure it's set right so you can jump to the future, otherwise it might take you anywhere."

He climbed onto the wall, balanced there for a few seconds in the wind, then dropped. Karan held her breath, but he landed square in front of the binnacle, pulled up the hatch and went down.

"Maigraith's coming fast," said Sulien. "She'll get here before we're ready."

"Stay near the wall," said Karan. She ran across to Wilm. "When Maigraith comes—"

"I'll hold her off as long as I can," said Wilm.

"Don't take any risks. I don't want you to get hurt."

"The black sword will give me some protection."

Karan did not see how an enchanted blade could delay Maigraith for more than a few seconds but did not say so. She raced back to the far side. "Is Yggur done yet?"

"No," said Sulien. "There seems to be some problem."

Karan groaned. The plan was absurd, outlandish; it couldn't work.

"Smell the potion again," said Aviel. "Focus as hard as you can on *exactly* where you want to go, and when—to the nearest year or two, Shand said."

It was hard to get rid of a host of intruding images—a wingless lyrinx stalking someone across broken black rock, a vast sky ship with three or four airbags, the redly dripping skin of a corpulent man hanging from a tree—yuk! A crystal glowing blue in a mine, a tunnel being filled in by a creeping bulge of liquid tar . . .

Of all the places she had seen so far, there was only one she would be happy to go to, the coast of the Sea of Thurkad south of Alcifer. She focused on it, on a long grassy ridge she had seen many years ago and always remembered, a pretty place running all the way down to the sea. The grass was green, so it wasn't winter, and they would be able to fish and forage for shellfish along the shore.

She fixed it in her mind and ran the years, spring and autumn this time, spring and autumn. But again the image and the years slipped from her mind.

"I know where," said Karan. "And I know roughly when. It's—"

"Don't tell us!" cried Aviel. "No one can know."

Karan felt stupid. "Sorry."

Sulien cried out again, and again Karan heard running footsteps on the stairs, distorted by the secrecy bubble. Maigraith was not far below, and Yggur still had not come up from the construct. They were out of time. Karan pushed out through the bubble to Wilm.

"I'll delay her as long as I can," he whispered.

Karan clutched his shoulder. He was brave and generous and good, and Maigraith would probably kill him. Karan should tell him to stand aside; why should he risk his life for them? But she kept silent; Sulien had to come first.

From down the stairs came Maigraith's voice: "What do you think you're doing? Get out of my way."

"You may not pass," said a familiar thick voice. Idlis!

"And you think a pathetic, masterless Whelm can stop me?"

"I do."

"Move or you're dead."

"Go back, triune! I will not let you past."

There came a howling blast, a flash of red and a belch of smoke, then a shrill cry echoed up and down the inside of the tower. A cry that could not have come from the throat of any male Whelm. What had Idlis done, and how could he have hurt Maigraith?

"You will pay for that, Whelm!" she gasped.

Karan glanced over to the parapet. Yggur was heaving himself up onto it. She ran to him.

"It's ready—I hope," said Yggur. "Llian, this is what you must do in the construct." Yggur whispered in his ear. "Got it?"

"Yes," said Llian, whose teller's memory for the spoken word was perfect.

"All right! Llian and Sulien, onto the wall."

They climbed up. The parapet was a foot wide and safe enough, had it not been for the hissing wind and the thousand-foot drop if they missed the top of the construct.

Sulien shot an anxious glance at Karan and an even more troubled one at Llian, who had his arms out and was swaying and sweating; he was almost as green as the stone floor of the tower.

"Go!" Yggur said to Sulien.

She jumped, landed on the construct and slid feet first through the open hatch. Karan saw her stand up, bathed in the eerie dark red light, and look around in awe.

"Llian," said Yggur.

Llian looked as though he was going to have apoplexy. He gasped, swallowed, teetered, his arms windmilling, and tried to jump but could not move. Fear froze him to the spot.

Yggur grimaced, reached out and gave him a measured shove in the back. Llian fell, hit the construct with a thud, slid sideways, gave a convulsive jerk and fell head-first inside, fortunately onto Sulien's pack, which she had just taken off.

"Karan, up on the wall!" said Yggur. "Then wait until Maigraith gets here. She's got to see you jump."

"It's a hell of a risk," said Karan, climbing onto the wall. "If she looks over before the construct leaves . . ."

"Leave me to worry about that," said Yggur.

How? She remembered, oddly, that Yggur and Maigraith had been lovers briefly, twelve years ago, and afterwards he had wanted her back but she had refused him. On the stairs the sound of combat grew louder.

Aviel climbed onto the wall, shivering and not looking down. "Karan?"

"Yes?"

"As soon as you're in the construct, take a huge sniff of the scent potion and fix your destination firmly in mind, then tell Llian to work the mechanism exactly as Yggur showed him. The instant he does, allow the future to run forwards until you reach the year you want to go to, and focus on it with all your wits."

"Yes," said Karan uneasily. It could not work. The idea was ridiculous.

"Shand said if the journey takes more than a couple of minutes, you'll need to take a *small* sniff of the scent potion to maintain the where and the when."

Karan nodded.

"Time to go," said Yggur, and thrust the mimemule into his pocket.

"Can I have that?" said Karan.

"No, it's part of our plan to cover your tracks."

"Wait!" said Wilm. He ran across, clambered onto the wall beside Aviel and unbuckled the copper sheath with the black sword inside. He shouted down to Llian, "Take this, for luck."

"Don't be silly," Llian called up. "I can't."

"You need it more than I do."

Wilm tossed the sheath down to him, but something very strange happened. A clear envelope formed around the sword, bulged upwards until it enclosed Wilm and Aviel, then shrank again and they were inside the construct.

Yggur cursed. "What the hell happened there?"

"The sword pulled us down," whispered Wilm.

"What do we do now?" cried Karan.

From down the stairs there came a thick, clotted scream of agony. A dying scream, surely, and from the sound it had to be Idlis.

"It's too late to get them out," said Yggur. "Put on your most insane and tragic face."

Karan turned to face the stairs and tried to look like a woman who had just pushed her man and daughter to their deaths. Yggur vanished the secrecy bubble and was reaching out to her, a convincing look of horror on his own stern features, when Maigraith burst up the stairs. Her hair was wild, her face crimson and her manner desperate.

"Karan, no!" she shrieked.

"Too late," Karan said with rolling eyes and a mad laugh that was only half-feigned. "You'll never have her! Or Llian! I shoved him over the side and threw Sul—" She choked. It was not an act; the thought was almost too awful to articulate. "I threw my beautiful Sulien after him, down into the River Garr."

Karan turned and jumped, straight down through the hatch and onto the packs. Llian, still white-faced, turned seven calibrated dials the distances he had been instructed, then reached for an inconspicuous lever with a red button on the end.

"Wait," said Karan. "I've got to see the *where* and the *when* first."

She got out the phial, removed the bung and took a deep sniff. Nothing. Her heart gave a single leaden thud. She stared at Aviel frantically.

"The potion must have set in the cold," said Aviel. "Warm it in your hands, quick!"

Karan clenched her fingers around it. From above she could hear shouting and screaming, then Yggur's voice rose above the tumult.

"You drove her to it," he said furiously. "I hope you're happy with the world you've created for yourself."

"It's nothing to the world I'm going to create," Maigraith said poisonously.

The phial was warming. Karan put it to her nose, took a deep sniff, focused on the clearest image of the coast south of Alcifer that she could manage and said to Llian, "Now!"

He depressed the red button and shoved the lever forward to the fifth notch. Karan allowed the future to run, winter and summer and winter and summer, flashing by ever faster.

In absolute silence they vanished.

83

THE SEA MUST HAVE GONE DOWN

All Karan could see was that long grassy ridge running down to the sea, and all she could feel were the seasons flicking by, one cycle every second, hot and cold, bright and dark.

Gates from one place to another were dangerous and sometimes went wrong, leaving their passengers stranded for ever, *between*. How much more perilous must be the passage from the present to an unknown future? What if they ended up not just nowhere, but nowhen?

There was no way of knowing. No one had ever gone into the future from the real world. What if the construct took them to a battlefield, a ruined world or a land in the grip of a vicious narcissist like Snoat? Or a future where they would be regarded as aliens? In addition to Karan's coin they had a small amount of gold, donated by their friends, warm clothing and as much food as they could carry, though now they had to share it with Wilm and Aviel it would not last long.

At a hundred and twenty seconds she sniffed the scent potion again. The years raced by, summer, winter, summer, winter, more than two hundred now. *Stop!*

With a gentle sigh the construct dematerialised and she tumbled five or six feet to the grass. Pain shivered up her right leg, a reminder of old injuries. Karan rolled over and sat up. Sulien and Llian were ten yards up the slope and Aviel and Wilm a few yards higher. They were getting up, rubbing their bruises and looking around.

The ridge ran down to the Sea of Thurkad, just as she had envisaged. The grass was green, the air mild—it felt and looked like spring or early summer. In the distance she could just make out the shore of the dry land of Rencid, sixty miles away across the sea. On this side a succession of ridges, mostly forested, extended north and south.

"Well," she said, walking up to Sulien and Llian, "we're here."

"Where *is* here?" said Wilm.

"The coast about thirty miles south of Alcifer."

"What year is it?"

"It was impossible to keep count. But more than two hundred years later."

"How can Wilm and I get back?" said Aviel in a small, frightened voice.

"You can't. I . . . I don't think the construct exists any more."

"But how will we live?" wailed Aviel, utterly distraught. "We've got *nothing*."

"We'll share what we have."

"You don't have much either."

"But we're safe!" cried Sulien. The stress had gone from her pixyish face, the deep darkness from her green eyes. She ran to Karan and gave her a hug, then Llian. "We're free. Maigraith can't get to us ever again."

"And that's something to celebrate," said Llian.

Clearly Aviel did not think so, but he could think of nothing to say to her.

"Can we go down to the sea?" Sulien's eyes were glowing with excitement. "There might be crabs ... or jellyfish or ... anything."

Karan's thighbone still throbbed from the impact, and momentarily she thought about hrux. But she had lost the little box Idlis had given her long ago, and he had sacrificed his life for Sulien. There would be no more hrux, ever. Better get used to it.

It was about a quarter of a mile down to the sea, and at first it felt like a pleasant stroll, though the further they descended the more strongly Karan felt that something was wrong. Sulien could sense it too; she was gripping Llian's hand tightly, no longer smiling.

Then, when they were about forty feet above sea level, the grassy ground became bare rock which ran all the way down to the water.

"That's odd," said Llian.

The strip of bare rock ran up and down the coast, into each inlet and out along the bottom of each headland, for as far as Karan could see, always at the same height. She looked down at a band of little white bumps. "Barnacles."

"What are barnacles doing up here?" said Llian. "They grow at the edge of the sea."

"They're dead. They look years old." She continued to the water line, where there was another, smaller band of barnacles, live ones. "The sea ... it must have gone down."

"But the Sea of Thurkad is connected to the ocean. What could cause the level of the ocean to fall so far and so quickly?"

"I don't know," Karan said grimly. "But I don't like it."

They ate black bread with cold sausage and blisteringly hot Aachim pickles, had a swim while Sulien searched the rock pools for crabs and, to her delight, found several, then walked back up the ridge until they came to the coast road, which Karan knew to be a mile or two inland in these parts. It was so overgrown that she almost missed it.

She leaned against a tree growing from the middle of the road, trying to work things out. "Llian, what's going on? I've ridden this road several times, and it was always in good condition; you could drive wagons along it."

"Lucky to ride a horse along it now," said Llian, shifting the straps of his heavy pack and rubbing his shoulders.

Serves you right for bringing half a hundredweight of Rulke's papers, she thought, *instead of more food*.

Aviel, who was limping badly, pressed closer to Wilm. She had lost everything and no longer had the means of pursuing the art she loved; she looked utterly desolate. Wilm, who was as brave and resolute as anyone Karan had ever met, seemed unnerved, and she could not blame him.

"There's a town a few miles north," she remembered. "Called Unsted. Come on."

They headed north along the remains of the road, which could not have been used in many years, since mature trees grew all over it. At Aviel's slow pace it took most of the day to reach Unsted, at the end of a long, narrow inlet, but they found it overgrown, the buildings roofless and crumbling.

"Have we come to an empty world?" Karan said quietly to Llian. "Did the Merdrun get through after all and kill everyone?"

"Even if they did," said Llian, "why would the sea have dropped so far?"

Nothing they saw even hinted at what had happened. They camped by the water that night, collected oysters and mussels and caught fish and crabs, which were plentiful. Clearly no one had fished the inlet in a very long time.

In the morning it was raining, and for three more days they continued north, making slow progress. It was a struggle for Aviel to walk even a few miles a day and often Wilm had to carry her on his shoulders. Everywhere they went it was the same: overgrown roads,

abandoned towns and villages, and no sign that anyone had lived there
in a hundred years.

"Tomorrow we should get to Alcifer," said Karan on the fourth
afternoon after their arrival. "Then we'll see."

"See what?" said Sulien.

"I don't know. But it was built to last. If it's gone too . . ." She shivered and did not go on.

They camped on a headland where they had a clear view in all
directions, and were collecting mussels for dinner when Karan heard
a high-pitched humming and a bizarre flying contraption appeared in
the distance.

"What the blazes is that?" said Llian, not realising that his bag was
upside down and orange-lipped mussels were sliding down his pants
onto his boots.

"It's some kind of sky ship," said Karan. "Back into the trees!
Quick!"

They ran up the slope and into shelter, but the craft continued in a
straight line, flying directly towards them.

"Whoever they are," said Llian, "they know we're here."

84

A MOST IMPERTINENT QUESTION

The craft raced up, and it was the weirdest thing Karan had ever seen.
It had the deep keel and curving sides of a seagoing galleon, save that
they were sheathed in brass interleaved with some black metal intricately decorated with silver. Its bow was high and pointed, with flaring
metal shields extending along the sides of the deck in place of rails,
while several white hoop-like structures rose above the deck like the
frames for wagon covers. But it had no airbags, so what was holding
it up?

A big spear-throwing device set in a box-like wooden frame was mounted behind the bow shields, and a catapult on a swivelling mount stood on a platform at the stern. An inscription in flowing writing on the bow read, *Three Reckless Old Ladies*.

"Has the future gone mad?" said Llian.

"Either it has or we have," Karan muttered.

The sky galleon turned so sharply that it slewed sideways through the air, then it hovered, and a skinny, scarred and incredibly ugly man appeared at the bow, looking down at them.

"Is that them?" he said to a small white-haired old lady.

She was staring at them, then she leapt up and down, waving furiously. "It's them. They made it. Karan, Llian, it's *me*!"

"It's . . . Lilis!" cried Sulien.

"How can it be Lilis?" said Llian in alarm. "What year is it?"

Sick horror crept over Karan. Lilis had been twenty-five when they left and she looked in her sixties now. If they'd only gone forty years into the future they would not be safe at all.

"Today is the eighth day of Criffin, 3325," said the ugly man.

"Then . . . two hundred and fourteen years have passed," said Llian. He looked at Lilis. "How have you—"

"Lived so long?" said Lilis, pursing her lips. "A most impertinent question to put to an old lady, Llian." Then she smiled. "When I succeeded Nadiril as librarian he bestowed the Librarian's Gift on me, and it extended my life, as it had done his."

"What are you doing in that . . . contraption?"

"After working day and night with books for a couple of centuries I felt a trifle desiccated. So I threw it in and went adventuring."

She looked sideways at the ugly little man. "This is Xervish Flydd. He was once a mighty scrutator, and one of our leaders in the great war, but you don't know anything about that."

"Great war?" said Llian. "Did the Merdrun get through after all?"

"No, they haven't been seen since we beat them on Gwine."

The sky galleon settled on the ground with a crunch. Lilis introduced everyone to Flydd.

"You look worn out," said Flydd. "Hop in."

Karan did not move. Nothing added up. Was this an elaborate trap? "Why were you looking for us?"

"Your friends told us you were coming two years ago, and we've been keeping watch."

"What friends?" she said warily.

"Yggur and Malien."

Karan's heart leapt. "Are they here, then?"

"Yggur is in Crandor. Roros, I believe," said Flydd. "He doesn't have long to live, I'm afraid. Malien was well when we last saw her. She returned to Aachan two years ago with many of her people. Come aboard."

Karan felt dazed; it was too much to take in. "Why have you been searching for us? What are we to you?"

"Unfinished business."

"What's that supposed to mean?"

"Another time," said Flydd.

"But this land is abandoned, and even the sea has gone down. What's happened? Where have you come from?"

"Most recently, Guffeons."

Karan struggled to remember where Guffeons was. She had to imagine it on her beautiful old map, shredded on the tiles of Shazmak. "But that's on the north-east coast of Lauralin, two thousand miles away. You flew all the way across Lauralin just to find us?"

"Yes," said Flydd, "but it'll soon be dark and we can't talk here. Get in."

"Why can't we talk here?"

"You're in great danger."

"Karan," said Lilis, "we need to hurry."

Karan shivered and rubbed her arms. In this strange and unnerving world their fate depended on what she did now. How could she decide? "What do you say, Sulien? You can always tell if people are good or bad."

Sulien had not spoken all the while. She studied Flydd, her head to one side, her red hair streaming in the wind, then Lilis, then Flydd again.

"He's ... *mostly* good," she said after a long interval. "But he's got some ... dark bits."

Flydd took a step back, staring at her and rubbing his twisted fingers. They looked as though they had all been broken, then healed badly.

"Dark bits!" he said, smiling grimly. "Indeed I have, Sulien, very dark. In my time as scrutator I made some harsh decisions, some bad ones, and some that turned out to be utter disasters. But your mother doesn't trust me as far as she can spit; she needs a clearer answer."

"He's good enough," said Sulien with a look that said, *but I'll be watching you.*

She had been right before, but could Karan really entrust their lives to the intuition of a nine-year-old girl? Yet was staying here any better? Whatever had caused a whole country to be abandoned, she did not want to come face to face with it.

"All right," she said.

Sulien climbed into the sky galleon, and Karan and Llian followed, then Wilm and Aviel.

"There's something about you," said Flydd, studying Aviel, his head to one side.

"Aviel made the scent potion that allowed Karan to ... find this future," said Wilm.

"Did she now? And you?" he said to Wilm. "What's special about you, Wilm?"

"Nothing, we only came by accident. The black sword ..."

Flydd held out his hand and, after a slight hesitation, Wilm passed him the weapon. "It was Mendark's."

"Ahh!" sighed Flydd, and pressed his gnarled hands to the blade. "And yet it adopted you. I wonder why."

"Wilm's a hero!" cried Aviel. "He's the bravest man I know ... and the kindest."

"Santhenar has need of brave men, *and* kind ones." Flydd studied Aviel from her shining, flyaway hair to the toes of her battered boots, then his gaze fixed on her lumpy right ankle. She put it behind the left. "I see great courage in you; I think you're also a hero."

"I'm lost," she whispered. "I have nothing left."

"You're the only scent-potion maker in a troubled world—we'll soon find work for you, and a workshop."

Aviel brightened a little. "Thank you."

He turned to Karan and Llian. "Where were you headed?"

"Alcifer," said Llian.

He still seemed dazed; Karan had never known him to be so economical with the words that were his trade, or so uninterested in finding out what had happened here.

"As safe a place to spend the night as any," said Flydd.

"But what's happened to the world?" said Karan.

"We'll talk when we get there."

He signalled to a plump untidy woman with thinning hair who stood in the wheelhouse, holding a knob where the wheel of a ship would normally have been mounted. "This is Mechanician M'Lainte," he said. "She can make *anything.*"

M'Lainte nodded, twisted the knob, and the galleon soared into the sky and raced north, far faster than any sky ship Karan had ever been in. Was it a kind of construct? It had to be, but where had it come from?

Ten minutes later it was hovering over the once magnificent city of Alcifer, between two of its many clusters of slender red or black towers. When Karan had last been here there had been bowl-shaped lakes set on the tops of towers, and tall, narrow spires without windows or stairs, and domes, some hundreds of yards across and roofed with glass, covering wonderful gardens or splendid spaces. The towers had been linked by a variety of aerial walkways, some in red metal and others in black.

But Alcifer, which had endured unchanged for many centuries after Rulke had it built, was decaying. Several of the slender towers had fallen, crashing through domed roofs and smashing what lay beneath, and most of the self-maintaining gardens were withered.

The craft edged through a broken dome that had been whole when Karan and Llian had left Alcifer in Malien's sky ship seventy-two days ago. No, *two hundred and fourteen years* ago. It still seemed impossible.

M'lainte settled the big vessel by a long pool, the very one Karan and Llian had landed in after the gate carried them from Carcharon, though now the water was a greenish-brown. What had changed? And why wouldn't Flydd say?

"Dinner first, then we'll talk." He had taken charge as if born to it. "I'm sure you have many questions."

Karan scowled. How dare he assume that they would meekly follow his orders? But she felt lost, disorientated and very afraid. Before she took him on she had to understand the world they had come to.

"Who's the third lady?" said Sulien.

"What?" said Flydd.

"The ship is called *Three Reckless Old Ladies*. There's only two here."

His snaggle-toothed smile was a fearsome sight. "The third is Yulla Zaeff, but she's too busy to go adventuring right now." He looked up at M'Lainte. "How long will dinner be?"

"Thirty-two minutes." M'Lainte, whose ability to "make *anything*" evidently extended to cooking for a multitude, busied herself in the galley of the sky galleon.

"This way, everyone." Flydd, who clearly knew his way around Alcifer, led them through a bronze door into a circular chamber sixty feet across. Its dome was still intact, as was everything inside. There was a dusty oval blackwood table near the eastern wall, surrounded by sixteen carved blackwood chairs. Doors led out at the four points of the compass.

Flydd and Lilis wiped down the table and chairs. Llian and Wilm carried baskets of crockery and cutlery from the sky galleon and set out plates, bowls and cutlery. When dinner was ready, they sat at the table. M'Lainte had prepared a tureen of spicy yellow chowder, thick with chunks of fish and crab, and a platter of dried meats with cheeses, preserved fruits and vegetables, plus assorted pickles in lurid colours.

"All right," said Llian. "Tell us the Histories. What happened to—"

"The Lyrinx War happened," said Flydd. "You may not know this, but lyrinx got into Santhenar when the Way Between the Worlds was opened back in your time. They hid in the wilderness for many years, increasing their numbers and growing strong—"

"They offered to help us in the war with the Merdrun," cried Sulien. "But the Whelm slaughtered them and they blamed us. That's why the lyrinx hated us."

"What war?" said Flydd, frowning as if trying to remember some minor detail. "Ah, yes, there is something in the old Histories about the Merdrun, though I wouldn't call it a war. There was a skirmish in some out-of-the-way place . . . Gwine, wasn't it? But the Merdrun threat never came to anything."

"How dare you call it a *skirmish?*" cried Karan, leaping to her feet so violently that she knocked her plate of cheese and pickles off the table. "Thousands of good people were killed in that battle, and Sulien and Llian and I nearly died."

"Our war with the lyrinx lasted a hundred and fifty years," said Flydd quietly, "and took at least a *million* of our lives. It utterly transformed Santhenar, and we lost large parts of it, including Meldorin, for a hundred years. And the lyrinx very nearly won."

"So that's why the land is empty," said Karan. "But if they didn't win . . ."

"The war ended twelve years ago, but with so many lives lost and so much ruin there's far more land than there are people to work it. Santhenar is a much poorer place than it was. We don't have the coin to rebuild all the roads and bridges and viaducts, the cities and ports, and all the other things destroyed in the war. It may take a hundred years to get back to where things were before the war began."

"But if the lyrinx are still out there . . ." said Llian.

"They're gone but plenty of other predators remain, two-legged as well as four, which is why we're spending the night in the safety of Alcifer."

"If Meldorin was abandoned and occupied by the lyrinx," Llian said slowly, "what happened to places like Thurkad and Sith? And the Great Library and the College of the Histories. Did the lyrinx destroy everything?"

"What about Gothryme?" said Karan, quivering.

"Thurkad was abandoned and partly burned, and is still largely ruined," said Flydd. "A few thousand people have gone back, but it's now a small town in the ruins of a city that once held a million people. Sith is still largely intact, but also nearly empty. The College of the Histories was abandoned eighty years ago and most of its treasures were lost, though some of them ended up at the Great Library."

"Which still exists," said Lilis. "The lyrinx, unlike the Merdrun, aren't vandals. They have a great love of culture and books; they left the library untouched."

"What about Gothryme?"

"I have no idea."

"You were saying about the Histories?" said Llian.

"Where was I?" said Flydd. "Ah yes. After the Trihorn Peaks blocking the Hornrace were destroyed, and the Dry Sea started to fill again—"

"So that's why the sea level has fallen," said Karan.

"Quite. We managed to turn the tables on the lyrinx and trapped them on the bed of the Dry Sea, robbed of their mancery and unable to fly, as it flooded. Our leaders, in their 'wisdom,' wanted to drown the lot of them, but a number of us rebelled. We could not countenance genocide and reached a secret deal with the lyrinx, then made a gate and offered them Tallallame, the most beautiful of all worlds."

"But it's the Faellem's world," said Karan.

"Not any more. Tallallame was infested by savage creatures from the void when the Way Between the Worlds was opened, and they had hunted the Faellem almost to extinction. The lyrinx, also faced with extinction, were prepared to take on Tallallame, and they've since had some success."

"So they're gone." Karan let out a great sigh. "We're safe at last."

Flydd frowned. "Not exactly."

"Why not?"

Lilis spoke. "Maigraith—now known as the Numinator—is still alive, still vengeful and still determined to complete her plan."

"But she believes we're dead!" said Karan. Chills crackled through her. *Had it all been for nothing?*

"She did for a long time. We—Malien, Yggur, Shand and myself— laid down all manner of false trails and red herrings, and told many outright lies to prevent her discovering the truth. But we think she did. We think she now suspects you went to the future."

Karan choked. "Then she'll hunt us down," she said limply. "She never gives up."

She took Llian's hand. It was as sweaty as her own. Sulien got up from the table, trembling. Her eyes were as big as teacups. She spun on the soles of her boots, the gritty floor squeaking underfoot, then ran out through the eastern door of the circular chamber.

"Where are you going?" yelled Karan, starting after her but falling over her own chair. "Come back!"

"She can't come to any harm down there," said Llian.

"How would you know?" she snapped. "We haven't been here for two hundred and fourteen years."

"If there was danger here, we would know," said Flydd.

Karan picked up her cheese and pickles, which were still scattered across the floor. As she finished, Sulien's voice echoed across the chamber. "Daddy? Mummy? Come here."

"What's the matter?" cried Karan.

"Nothing. Just come."

Karan and Llian went after Sulien, and Flydd followed. They entered a vast white cubic chamber, empty apart from an eighteen-foot-high statue—a male nude carved from a single block of granite—on a broad, stepped platform. The hard, granular stone had been polished to a silky smooth finish and, apart from a little dust, the years had not diminished its perfection. The man's stone eyes were fixed on the opposite wall, which was covered in intricately embossed silver, at the point where Llian had discovered Rulke's Histories last time he was here.

"It's modelled on Rulke," said Llian. "It's a fine likeness."

Sulien was staring up at the carved wound in the man's side. The wound that had killed him.

"What's the matter?" asked Karan.

"There's something inside it," said Sulien.

"How can there be? It's carved from a single block of granite."

Sulien shrugged and walked over to the platform, her unfocused eyes sweeping back and forth. Karan knew that look: Sulien was *seeing*, and no one saw further or deeper. Suddenly Karan felt a shivery premonition. Something was wrong here. Could the statue be a trap?

"Sulien!" she said sharply. "Come away!"

Sulien crouched down. Her small hand appeared to slip right into the stone platform near the base, then she pulled on something.

Crack, crack, crack.

"Look out in front," bellowed Flydd. "And behind!"

They scattered. The statue split from one side to the other, then the front half toppled forward, struck the floor with a shattering impact and broke into pieces. The vast room shook. The back half rocked on its heels, fell the other way and the head came off, though the rest of the half-statue remained intact.

"What's that?" cried Flydd pointing at something shimmering among the rising dust at the centre of the platform. Dust plumes rose like fast-growing mushrooms. "A stasis spell? Why would there be . . ."

The shimmer faded, the dust settled, and Karan's scalp developed goose pimples as the stasis spell died. Shivers spread down her back and all over her, for a huge man lay there. A naked, black-bearded man with a massive scar in his side.

And then he moved.

"But . . . you're dead!" whispered Llian. "We all saw you die."

85

THE BLOCK ON THE STONE
WOULD HAVE FAILED

The black-bearded man sat up slowly and painfully. He had lost a lot of muscle since Karan had last seen him but she did not doubt who he was for a second.

Several seconds passed before he found any words. "Because . . . we were . . . so few," Rulke said haltingly, as if he had forgotten how to talk, "we made plans . . . Yalkara and I . . . in case either . . . took . . . mortal wound." He paused for three rasping breaths. "I cast . . . stasis spell. Mimic . . . signs of death."

"But—" said Llian.

"Maigraith took . . . body to Yalkara," said Rulke. "Yalkara used . . . potent healing spells. Secret. Even from Maigraith. But could not save me . . . hid me until statue . . . prepared. Put me inside . . . reinforced stasis charm . . . so time . . . and body's own healing processes . . . repair . . . damage."

He studied Karan and Llian, looked long at Sulien and favoured her with a ghostly smile. In a stronger voice he said, "I judge . . . ten years have passed. Is Yalkara about?"

"She's two years dead," said Flydd.

Rulke reeled. "Yalkara dead! How?"

"Two hundred and twenty-four years have gone by since you were 'killed'," said Llian. "Just days ago we fled to the future using—"

"My virtual construct!" he said delightedly. "However did you manage it?" His face became grave. "Two hundred and twenty-four years!"

He shook the dust off a pair of trews, then a shirt that would have fitted three of Karan, and socks and boots. Rulke dressed with an effort and got up, but swayed on his feet and had to sit down again.

"Too soon," he said hoarsely. "Need food and drink. Desperately."

"This way," said Flydd, who for the first time since Karan had met him had nothing to say. He looked stunned.

Karan also struggled to take it in. She had liked Rulke at the end; he had been a much-wronged man, a legend whose choices and actions had been shaping the Three Worlds for thousands of years, and now he was back. What would he do? Where would he take them?

Rulke realised that Sulien was staring at him. There was dust in her long red hair and on the tip of her nose. "The black pill I gave you worked, I see," he said to Karan.

"Without Rulke you would not be here," Karan said to Sulien.

"I know, Mummy," sighed Sulien. "You've told me a million times."

He lurched forward, stooped and shook her hand. "Thank you for *seeing* me and freeing me; my flesh was wasting from lack of food and I would soon have died. May I lean on you?"

"Yes," she said in a small, awed voice. "My name is Sulien."

Flydd led the way back to the circular chamber, Rulke walking slowly, supporting himself on Sulien's shoulder. Flydd introduced Lilis, who had met Rulke as a girl and was suitably astonished, M'Lainte, who merely handed him a full bowl and a heaped plate, and Wilm and Aviel, who said nothing at all.

Karan knew how they felt. Too much had changed, too quickly, and she could not see through it to any happy future. Yet with Rulke on their side ...

He ate like a man who had not dined in centuries, gobbling the food and spilling it down his front. M'Lainte, who seemed rather taken with him, replenished his plate.

Llian started. "I've just thought of something. Wait here."

"What are you doing?" Karan said irritably, but he had already run out.

He returned a few minutes later carrying a dusty bag. "Something to celebrate with."

He drew out a cut-crystal decanter, a beautiful object with an extravagant silver stopper and a base of silver basketwork.

Rulke raised a black eyebrow.

"It's Driftmere," said Llian. "The finest brandy ever made, already aged for a hundred and seventy-eight years when I left it here two centuries ago."

"A trifle beyond Gothryme's budget, I would have thought," said Rulke, eyeing Llian's shabby clothing and generally unkempt air. He took the decanter.

"It was my ... um, fee. For a private telling of my Great Tale."

"You got your tale then? Congratulations." Rulke weighed the decanter in his hand. "Unlikely the cork will have survived."

"The stopper is glass."

Rulke drew it out, sniffed, and his face lit up. "Yet again I underestimate you, chronicler." He conjured goblets from somewhere in Alcifer, wiped the dust off and poured a measured amount of the red-gold fluid into each. He raised his goblet and everyone else did too. "To old friendships."

They drank. Karan only took a small sip; she needed a clear head. Sulien merely tasted the brandy with the tip of her tongue, grimaced, said, "Yuk!" and put her goblet down.

Rulke raised his goblet again, to Sulien. "And to brilliant young gifts."

He studied her as if there was something about her he could not fathom. This reminded Karan that she still had to find Sulien a teacher, someone gifted in the art. Rulke? She turned the idea over in her mind.

He turned to Llian. "Chronicler, would you be so good as to fill in the intervening years?"

Llian told him about the ten years after Rulke's "death," focusing on the summon stone and the Merdrun, and the invasion force that had come through the Crimson Gate to Gwine. Rulke's dark eyes showed shock and dismay, and possibly fear at the mention of the Charon's greatest enemy, though he did not comment.

"Why did you flee so far into the future?" he said curiously.

Karan hesitated, for she knew he had loved Maigraith—they had sworn to one another, for ever. But he had to be told.

As she and Llian related Maigraith's obsessive plan to create a living monument to Rulke, and her relentless pursuit of Sulien, his jaw tightened. "You say she bore me twins. What happened to them?"

"Julken was killed before he was eighteen," said Lilis. "Hunted down by a band of men whose daughters he had outraged. He was . . . not a good man."

"Any children?"

"Only one—Gilhaelith, a master geomancer and mathemancer. He died twelve years ago, without issue."

"And the other twin?"

"Illiel took after Maigraith's Faellem side, so she abandoned him to them. I don't think he's still alive but he had a daughter, Liel, now known as Tulitine. She's . . ."

"Now Yggur's partner," said M'Lainte when no one else spoke. "She's been good for him. She's helped him with his troubles."

"Now there's an irony," said Rulke. "My only descendant taking care of the man who was one of my greatest enemies." He sighed wistfully. "But I have a granddaughter; I'm not alone in the world." He stared into the middle distance for a minute or two, then said in a hard voice, "Clearly I was wrong about Maigraith. How could she do such a thing?"

Was he talking about her obsessive pursuit of Sulien, or her abandonment of Illiel?

His plate was empty again. M'Lainte refilled it without being asked and gave him a jug of water. Rulke gulped half of it, gasped and wiped his mouth. He looked stronger now and this time did not touch the food; he was staring at Sulien.

"What's the matter?" said Karan.

"How did you know I was inside the statue?" he said to Sulien.

"I . . . saw you," said Sulien. "With my inner eye. Like I saw the Merdrun way across the void."

"Ah!" he said as though that explained everything.

Karan shivered. What did he know that she did not? "What's going on?"

"Unintended consequences," said Rulke.

"You'd better explain."

"The black pill I gave you when I lay dying was designed to increase the chances of conception—as you know, we Charon are plagued by terribly low fertility—but it was also tailored to heighten the far-seeing gift in any Charon child conceived through it."

"Why?" she snapped. She felt a surge of anger. It was happening again! What had he done to Sulien?

"As an early warning. If the Merdrun ever turned their attention to this world, that child's heightened gift would detect the psychic signal from the enemy, even from across the void. If this happened, my people would be in desperate peril and there would be little time to prepare." He studied Sulien again, as if looking into her mind. "But if Sulien already had the seeing gift from you, the pill may have developed it even more strongly."

Karan thrust back her chair and stood up, knuckles pressed hard against the tabletop. "You used us!" she cried, struggling to hold back her fury. "You planted this gift in Sulien to aid your own people."

"What people?" Rulke said mildly. "I'm the last Charon there is, and I didn't know the black pill would work on you at all, since most triunes are sterile. Besides, I was dying. I wasn't in the right frame of mind to think things through. It was a generous impulse, no more."

It sounded convincing but she refused to believe it. "The moment Sulien saw the Merdrun's vital secret in a nightmare," Karan said furiously, "she was condemned. They hunted her for months, tried to kill her a dozen times . . . and almost did. The gift you heightened in her, the gift she doesn't know how to use properly, could have doomed her."

"I can teach her." Rulke reached out to Sulien.

"Don't touch her!" cried Karan.

Rulke withdrew his hand. "As you wish." He turned back to Llian. "So Shand and Yggur blocked the summon stone. A clever piece of work. And since then?"

Llian explained how they had come to the future, then Flydd related the story of the Lyrinx War and its aftermath, as he had done earlier.

"Mister Flydd, you said there's far less mancery now?" said Sulien. "Why is that?"

"That's a very good question," said Flydd. "The Lyrinx War became like a . . . a magical arms race, with each side developing ever more powerful weapons and drawing more and more power from the fields around nodes."

"Fields that Sulien first saw," said Llian.

"Did she really?" Flydd gazed at her in wonder, then continued. "At the end, Tiaan, one of our most gifted geomancers, was utterly sick of war and all the ruin done to the world. She found a way to destroy every node and field at once, and that almost wiped out the Secret Art."

"But not the two sorcerous quicksilver tears, Gatherer and Reaper, that had accidently formed in an exploded node years before," said M'Lainte. "They now held almost all the magical power left in the world, and Jal-Nish, a vicious ex-scrutator, had them."

"So began the brutal reign of the god-emperor, as he styled himself," said Flydd, "which lasted another dozen years until he was killed two years ago, and Gatherer and Reaper were destroyed. Only in the past two years have people's lives begun to get back to normal—whatever normal is. And some of the fields that were destroyed are slowly regenerating, though—"

Rulke thrust himself to his feet, wild-eyed. "You said Shand's blocking device was powered by a node at Demondifang."

"That's right," said Llian. "Why does that matter?"

"When Tiaan destroyed all the nodes and fields fourteen years ago, the block on the summon stone would have failed."

Karan felt a sharp pain in the top of her head where the old magiz had attacked her months ago. *It can't be happening again.*

"But the Demondifang node would also be dead," said Llian. "There wouldn't be anything for the summon stone to draw power from."

"Until Gatherer and Reaper were destroyed two years ago," said Rulke, "and the fields began to regenerate. The summon stone would have started to draw power straight away, from Demondifang or any other nearby field. Clearly, that's what the Merdrun designed it to do."

"But the block—"

"Wouldn't resume by itself after all that time. The Command device would have to be reset."

Karan felt trapped, helpless, numb with terror. There was nothing she could do this time.

Flydd scrambled to his feet. "M'Lainte, how quickly can we get to Demondifang?"

She rose. "A day. I'll get the sky galleon ready." She headed for the door.

"Wait!" said Rulke. "The stone may not be there any more."

He swept the table clear in front of him, rested his elbows on it and his head on his hands, then stared, eyes unfocused, at the wall. Karan could feel her own leaden heartbeat, *thud-thud, thud-thud.* She was utterly reliant on him and Flydd now, but could she trust either of them?

"I know how the Merdrun's devices work," said Rulke. "I can see the stone, but it's moved." He gestured, and an image appeared on the wall, a steaming blue lake in a shallow crater. The summon stone, a trilithon now standing more than twenty feet high, stood in the middle of the lake, upright again, the decay and corruption gone.

"It's very strong," he added. "I dare say it's been drawing power for years; it must be close to reopening the Crimson Gate. And if the enemy know we're spying they'll redouble their efforts." He snapped finger and thumb, and the image was gone.

"Can we block the stone again?" said Llian.

"I . . . don't see how."

"What about Sulien's nightmare?"

"Ah!" said Rulke. He looked at Karan. "May I try to recover it?"

"No!" Karan snapped. "I don't trust you."

"Then what solution do you offer?" said Flydd.

She had none. "I . . . Very well, ask her!" Karan said furiously.

"I want the nightmare out and gone," said Sulien.

Rulke laid his huge dark hand on top of her head and pressed down the curly red hair until it flattened against her skull. His eyes closed, his lips moved. He did not move for several minutes, then his eyes sprang open and he said, "There's a block, put there by the old magiz I'd say, to prevent you remembering their secret weakness."

"Can you remove the block?" said Sulien.

"Part of it, at least." He murmured words in the Charon tongue then lifted his hand away abruptly. "Speak the nightmare!"

Sulien closed her own eyes. "There's an old blind man . . . so weak he can barely hold his head up. He gets up . . . and he's shaking . . . as if he's going to fall down. His eyes are white and . . . oozing. The old man faces the Merdrun leader, but it's not Gergrig. I think this must be long ago.

"The old man says, *A child of a lesser race can defeat us if her mighty gift is allowed to develop to . . .*" She strained to speak but no more words came.

"What child?" said Flydd when she did not go on. "What gift? Defeat them how?"

"I don't remember the rest," said Sulien. Her eyes had a far-off stare, as if her gift had not fully returned her to Alcifer. "Then the old man falls down and . . . Yuk! Worms swarm all over him as if he has been dead the whole time . . . as if he was *raised* so he could speak the words."

"Look deeper!" Flydd said to Rulke.

"Too risky," said Rulke.

"Perhaps the child will grow up to develop a mighty weapon of war or attack spell," said M'Lainte.

Suddenly Rulke spun round, staring up in wonder as if he'd seen or heard something they had not. "Incarnate?" he said wonderingly. He rubbed a black ring on the smallest finger of his left hand, repeated, "Incarnate," and vanished.

"Where's he gone?" said Flydd. "Has the bastard betrayed us?"

Karan was thinking the same thing. What could *Incarnate* mean?

Sulien, whose eyes were still unfocused, cried, "Mummy, Daddy, they're coming!"

A low rhythmic sound began, like someone tapping a fingertip on a large drum. It quickly swelled until it was like the thundering of a gigantic drum-clock, counting down the seconds towards catastrophe.

"I can *see* them!" cried Sulien. "They're at the Crimson Gate, on Cinnabar."

She broadcast what she was seeing, and Karan viewed it with perfect clarity in her mind's eye, for it was so strong even Llian and Wilm, who lacked any gift, caught glimpses.

The thundering cut off as the Merdrun army began to march through the gigantic Crimson Gate. The gate too was bigger than before; twenty soldiers could pass through side by side. Karan tried to estimate their numbers. The top of the icy plateau was completely covered in troops.

"They've got to be a hundred and fifty thousand strong," said Flydd in a choked voice.

"Last time, with just a thousand," said Llian, "they nearly beat six thousand of us."

"To have a chance against the most deadly fighters in the void we'd need an army of a million men."

"How many do you have?"

"None," Flydd said hopelessly.

"Why the hell not?" cried Llian.

"Jal-Nish's army was disbanded two years ago. After a hundred and sixty years of war and bloodshed the whole world ached for peace."

"Xervish," said M'Lainte, "is there any hope you could divert their gate to the middle of the ocean, and drown the bastards?"

"Right now I couldn't divert a beetle to the other side of a spider web," said Flydd. He grabbed Karan by the arm. "What's happened to your friend Rulke?" he said roughly. "He's the last of his species, and blood will out. Maybe he's decided to join the Charon's mirror selves— the Merdrun. And he knows everything!"

Karan shook his hand off and backed away, towards Sulien.

"Is that what he meant by *Incarnate*?" said Llian. "Bloody war on humanity?"

"Sulien must be the child the seer spoke of," said Flydd. "The key to defeating the Merdrun. We've got to develop her gift—"

Karan swept Sulien behind her. "A room full of brilliant adults," she said contemptuously, "and all you can come up with is using a *child* as a weapon? It's a death sentence."

"Is no one going to ask me what I think?" Sulien said quietly.

"You're only nine!" Karan choked.

"And I'm already under a death sentence. But if I'm our only hope, I've got to try."

The Gates of Good and Evil will continue.

GLOSSARY OF CHARACTERS, NAMES AND PLACES

Aachan: One of the Three Worlds, the realm of the Aachim and, after its conquest, the Charon.

Afflatus Effluvium: A forbidden and highly dangerous scent potion that is reputed to give a mancer new insights into the Secret Art.

Archeus of Eidolon: A deadly necromantic fluid obtained by distilling the spectral blood from a ghost vampire.

Aachim: The human species native to Aachan, who were conquered by the Charon. The Aachim are a clever people, great artisans and engineers, but melancholy and prone to both hubris and indecision.

Aftersickness: Illness that people suffer after using the Secret Art or using a native talent or gift. Sensitives like Karan and Sulien are very prone to it.

Alcifer: The greatest of Rulke's cities, designed by Pitlis the Aachim.

Aviel: A crippled girl, fifteen, who was training herself to become a perfumer until it was discovered that she had a gift for making scent potions.

Bannador: A narrow, poor, hilly land on the western side of Iagador.

Brimstone, Golden: A rare, perfect crystal of sulphur, only found in Grund.

Bubble Bark Pine: An exceedingly rare species of pine tree, only found in one remote gorge in Worm Wood.

Calendar: Santhenar's year is roughly 395.7 days and contains 12 months, each of 33 days. The months are: spring—Thays, Criffin, Bunce; summer—Bolland, Guffins, Thisto; autumn—Mard, Pulin, Ballin; winter—Sord, Galend, Talmard.

Carcharon: A tower built on a rugged ridge high above Gothryme Forest by Karan's mad ancestor Basunez at a node where the Secret Art was especially powerful. The summon stone was drawn to it.

Chacalot: A large water-dwelling reptile, somewhat resembling a crocodile.

Chanthed: A town in northern Meldorin, west of the mountains. The College of the Histories is situated there.

Chard: A kind of tea.

Charon: They fled out of the void to take Aachan from the Aachim long ago but were sterile there. Ten years ago the last of them went back to the void to die.

Chronicler: A graduate in the art and science of recording and maintaining the Histories.

Citadel: A fortified palace in Thurkad.

Clysm: A series of wars between the Charon and the Aachim between 1500 and 1000 years ago, resulting in the almost total devastation of Santhenar.

College of the Histories: The oldest of the colleges for the instruction of those who would be chroniclers, tellers and even lowly bards. It was set up at Chanthed soon after the time of the Forbidding.

Colophony: rosin left behind after distilling off the volatile oils from tree resin.

Construct: A machine at least partly powered by the Secret Art.

Council, also Council of Santhenar, Great Council: An alliance of the most powerful mancers for the protection of Santhenar.

Crandor: A rich tropical land on the north-eastern side of Lauralin. Tallia's homeland.

Demondifang: A little uninhabited island at the north-western tip of Meldorin, connected to Mollymoot by a gravel spit.

Dilly, Aunt: Ifoli's aunt who lives on Mollymoot.

Elienor: A great heroine and subsequently a clan leader of the Aachim from the time when the Charon invaded Aachan.

Empuly: An empathic triplet, sister to Unbuly and Jaguly.

Esea: A beautiful, clever but troubled reshaper. Twin sister to Hingis.

Essence of Ague: A scent potion that induces uncontrollable shaking.

Faelamor: Leader of the Faellem species, who came to Santhenar soon after Rulke to keep watch on the Charon and maintain the balance between the worlds. She led her followers back to Tallallame, and self-immolation, ten years ago.

Faellem: The human species who originated on the lush world of Tallallame. A small dour people who are forbidden to use machines and particularly magical devices but are masters of disguise and illusion. Some still dwell on Santhenar in Mirrilladell.

Fiz Gorgo: A fortress city in Orist, flooded in ancient times, now restored; the stronghold of Yggur.

Flute; also Golden Flute: A device made in Aachan at the behest of Rulke, by the brilliant smith Shuthdar. He subsequently stole it and took it back to Santhenar. When played by one who is sensitive, it could be used to open the Way Between the Worlds. It was destroyed by Shuthdar, and this created the Forbidding.

Forbidding: See *Tale of the Forbidding*.

Galliad: Karan's father, who was half-Aachim but exiled from them. He was killed at Carcharon when Karan was eight.

Gate: A structure controlled by the Secret Art which permits people to move instantly from one place to another. Also called a portal.

Gate, Crimson: One of the Gates of Good and Evil, the evil gate. It had been closed for more than 9000 years, but the Merdrun briefly opened it hoping to invade Santhenar.

Gate, Azure: One of the Gates of Good and Evil, the good gate.

Gates of Good and Evil: A pair of gates created by Stermin long ago and enchanted to sort his people into good (Charon) and evil (Merdrun).

Gellon: A fruit tasting something between a mango and a peach. Shand makes an incomparable gellon liqueur.

Gergrig: Leader of the Merdrun.

Ghâshâd: The ancient mortal enemies of the Aachim. They swore allegiance to Rulke after the Zain rebelled 2000 years ago, but when Rulke was imprisoned in the Nightland 1000 years later they forgot their destiny and went back to their old name, Whelm. Since his death they have been a lost people, constantly seeking a great master to serve and obey.

Ghyll: Joint leader of a band of lyrinx.

Gift of Rulke; also Curse of Rulke: Knowledge given by Rulke to the Zain, enhancing their resistance to the mind-breaking spells of the Aachim. It left a visible stigmata that identified them as Zain.

Gothryme: Karan's impoverished and drought-stricken estate near Tolryme in Bannador.

Great Library: Founded at Zile by the Zain in the time of the empire of Zur. The library was sacked when the Zain were exiled, but was subsequently re-established. Its current librarian is Nadiril the Sage.

Great Mountains: The largest and highest belt of mountains on Santhenar, enclosing the south-eastern part of the continent of Lauralin.

Great Tales: The greatest stories from the Histories of Santhenar, traditionally told at the Festival of Chanthed and on important ceremonial occasions throughout Santhenar. A tale can become a Great Tale only by the unanimous acclamation of the master chroniclers. In 4000 years only 23 Great Tales have ever been created, the most recent being Llian's *Tale of the Mirror.*

Grint: A copper coin of small value.

Grossular: A high plateau east of the great lake Warde Yallock. The scene of a dreadful betrayal and massacre nearly a hundred years ago, and home to the sickening ruins of Rogues Render.

Grund: A barren area of western Taltid, greatly scarred from thousands of little pits from mining the bitumen seeps.

Gwine: A remote tropical island a long way west of Banthey.

Gyllias: See *Shand.*

Hessular: A ruined Whelm city overgrown by forest in the rain-drenched southern land of Salliban.

Hingis: A clever but physically grotesque illusionist, maimed by a kick from a mule as a boy. Twin of Esea.

Histories, the: The collection of records which detail more than 4000 years of recorded history on Santhenar. The Histories consist of historical documents written or held by the chroniclers, as well as the tales, songs, legends and lore of the peoples of Santhenar and the invading peoples from the other worlds, told by the tellers. The culture of Santhenar is interwoven with and inseparable from the Histories and all long to be mentioned in them.

Hrux: A dangerous pain-relieving drug produced by the Whelm. Addictive and can have strange side effects, especially to people with Charon blood.

Hublees: A fussy little mancer.

Hudigarde: The leader of a great nation, Grossular, who betrayed his friend Jussell, the leader of Tindule, because Hudigarde coveted Jussell's wife Tissany. Hudigarde massacred Jussell's army near Rogue's Render, had every male of Tindule slain and every female sold into slavery.

Huling's Tower: The place where Shuthdar destroyed the Golden Flute and Yalkara subsequently murdered the crippled girl.

Human species: There are four distinct human species: the Aachim of Aachan, the Faellem of Tallallame, the old humans of Santhenar, and the Charon, who came out of the void. All but the old humans can be very long-lived—Tensor, Rulke, Yalkara and Faelamor, for instance, all lived for thousands of years. The Merdrun and the Charon were once the same people, but the Merdrun are greatly changed due to selection through the Crimson Gate, and because all those who show human feelings have been expunged from their bloodline.

Hundred, the: The Charon who survived the taking of Aachan. Rulke was the greatest.

Hythe: Midwinter's day, the fourth day of Endre, midwinter week. Hythe is a day of particular ill-omen.

Iagador: The fertile and wealthy land that lies between the eastern mountains of Meldorin and the Sea of Thurkad.

Idlis: Formerly the least of the Whelm, also a healer and long-time hunter of Karan and the Mirror. Karan spared his life three times, a debt that he repaid by healing her bones after she was gravely injured in Shazmak and once a year bringing her a small supply of the pain-relieving compound hrux.

Jaguly: a psychopathic triplet, sister to Unbuly and Empuly.

Janck, Dedulus: Commander of the allied armies.

Karan: A woman of the house of Fyrn, but with blood of the Aachim from her father, Galliad, and old human and Faellem blood from her mother. This makes her triune. She is also a sensitive. Llian's partner; mother of Sulien.

Lauralin: The continent east of the Sea of Thurkad.

League: About 5000 paces, three miles or five kilometres.

Librarian, the: Nadiril the Sage.

Lightglass: A device made of crystal and metal that emits light after being touched.

Lilis: Once a street urchin in Thurkad, rescued by Tallia at the age of twelve and apprenticed to Nadiril, now his anointed successor as Librarian.

Link, linking; also talent of linking: A joining of minds by which thoughts and feelings can be shared and support given. Sometimes used for domination.

Llian: A Zain from Jepperand, partner to Karan and father of Sulien. He is both a master chronicler and a teller, a rare combination. After his *Tale of the Mirror* was voted a Great Tale he was banned from practising, for meddling in the Histories.

Lumillal: A very powerful ghost vampire, bound to Rogues Render.

Magiz, the: The greatest sorcerer among the Merdrun. She (or rarely he) gains power by drinking people's lives.

Magister, the: Mendark, a great mancer, chief of the Council of Santhenar, and Magister for 1000 years, he renewed his body an unprecedented thirteen times. He was killed in Shazmak at the end of the Time of the Mirror (see below).

Maigraith: An obsessive, cold, repressed triune. She is a master of the Secret Art. Mother of non-identical twins Julken and Illiel, nine, fathered by Rulke, though Illiel, who takes after the Faellem, lives far away with them, and Maigraith has nothing to do with him.

Malien: An Aachim of Clan Elienor, now leader of the Aachim.

Mancer: A wizard or sorcerer; someone who is a master of the Secret Art.

Master Chronicler: One who has mastered the study of the Histories and graduated with the highest honours from the College of the Histories.

Meldorin: The large island that lies to the immediate west of the Sea of Thurkad and the continent of Lauralin.

Mendark: See *Magister.*

Mirror of Aachan: A device made by the Aachim in Aachan for seeing things at a distance. In Santhenar it changed and twisted reality and became corrupt, but stored many secrets. Yalkara took it to the void with her.

Mollymoot: A little island at the north-western tip of Meldorin, connected to the mainland by a causeway and to its twin island, Demondifang, by a long spit of gravel. Both causeway and spit are often flooded by the very high tides here.

Moon, the (Santhenar's moon): The moon revolves around Santhenar about every thirty days. One side (the dark face) is blotched red and black, and because the moon rotates on its axis much more slowly, the dark face is fully turned towards Santh only every couple of months. This rarely coincides with a full moon, but when it does it is a time of ill-omen.

Murg, Magsie: The evil old owner of a tannery in Casyme.

Nadiril: The head of the Great Library and the most senior current member of the Great Council.

Nightland: A place, distant from the world of reality, wherein Rulke was kept prisoner for 1000 years.

Nimil: A young Aachim man who has a metal slit in his throat. A gifted artisan.

Nivol: The Universal Dissoluent. An alchemical fluid that can dissolve everything except pure diamond.

Norp, Basible: A self-effacing master at the College of the Histories.

Old human: The original human species on Santhenar and by far the most numerous.

Osseion: A former captain of Mendark's guard, a huge dark man, now the innkeeper of Ninefingers. Father of one child, a grown-up daughter, Ussarine.

Portal: See gate.

Persona: A magical presence in an enchanted device. For instance, the presence in Mendark's black sword.

Qwale: Healers' Isle, north of Meldorin.

Rachis: Karan's steward at Gothryme Manor, now an ancient frail man.

Rasper, Jundelix: A master assassin, slain by Wilm at Carcharon.

Recorder: The person who set down the account of the four great battles of Faelamor and Yalkara, among many other tales. His name was Gyllias (see *Shand*).

Regg: Ifoli's fifteen-year-old cousin, who lives with Dilly on Mollymoot island.

Rogues Render: A ruined rendering works in Grossular, where the bodies of dead soldiers were rendered of their fat to make corpse candles.

Rulke: The greatest of the Charon. He enticed Shuthdar to Aachan to make the Golden Flute. After the Clysm Rulke was imprisoned in the Nightland until a way could be found to banish him back to Aachan. When Tensor opened a gate into the Nightland Rulke escaped, later occupying Shazmak and Carcharon. He died in Shazmak at Tensor's hand ten years ago.

Julken: The obnoxious, over-indulged son, aged nine, of Maigraith and Rulke.

Salliban: A wet, forested southern land, west of Shazabba. The Whelm's original homeland.

Santhenar, Santh: The least powerful but most populous of the Three Worlds, home of the old human peoples.

Secret Art: The use of magical or sorcerous powers (mancing). An art that very few can use and then only after extensive training. Notable mancers have included Mendark, Yggur, Maigraith, Rulke, Yalkara, Tensor and Faelamor, and the Merdrun's magiz.

Sending: A message, thoughts or feelings sent from one mind to another.

Sensitive: Someone whose human senses and feelings are far more acute than normal. Sensitives, for instance Karan, may have *seeings* of things happening far away. Rarely they can make mind connections such as one-way *sendings* and two-way *links*. Sensitives can be unstable because they feel things far more strongly than other people.

Shand: A friend of Karan's late father, also known as Gyllias and the Recorder. He had a daughter, Aeolior, with Yalkara. Aeolior, who died young and tragically, also had a daughter, Maigraith.

Shazmak: A great city of the Aachim in the mountains west of Bannador, now abandoned after being sacked by the Ghâshâd twelve years ago.

Shuthdar: An old human of Santhenar, the maker of the Golden Flute. After he destroyed the flute and himself, the Forbidding came down, closing the Way Between the Worlds.

Sith: A free city and trading nation built on an island in the River Garr in southern Iagador. A very law-abiding place.

Sky ship: A craft invented by the Aachim, held aloft by the highly explosive gas protium, and powered by rotors driven by the Secret Art.

Snoat, Cumulus: A wealthy narcissistic power-hungry collector.

Span: The distance spanned by the stretched arms of a tall man. About six feet, or slightly less than two metres.

Stermin: A foolish, moralistic but brilliant mancer who, after his people were exiled into the void many thousand of years ago, created the Gates of Good and Evil to sort them into those who were worthy and those who were not, thus creating the Charon and the Merdrun and putting them forever at war.

Sulien: Karan and Llian's only child, a girl aged nine. She is a powerful sensitive and has other unknown gifts.

Tale of the Forbidding: Greatest of the Great Tales, it tells of the final destruction of the flute by Shuthdar more than 3000 years ago, and how this created a Forbidding which sealed Santhenar off from the other two worlds.

Talent: A native skill or gift, usually honed by extensive training.

Tallallame: One of the Three Worlds, the home of the Faellem. A beautiful mountainous world covered in forest, recently invaded by savage creatures from the void.

Tallia bel Soon: Formerly Mendark's chief lieutenant, and now Magister of the High Council, she is a mancer and a master of combat with and without weapons. Tallia comes from Crandor.

Tar: A silver coin widely used in Meldorin. Enough to keep a family for several weeks.

Tell: A gold coin to the value of twenty silver tars. Enough to keep a family for a year.

Teller: One who has mastered the ritual telling of the tales that form part of the Histories of Santhenar. Great tellers also write their own tales, which must be based on truth; and a rare few of these will become Great Tales.

Tensor: The former leader of the Aachim. He saw it as his destiny to restore the Aachim to finally take their revenge on Rulke, who betrayed and ruined them. He was proud to the point of folly. He died in Shazmak ten years ago.

Thandiwe: Llian's former lover, now a master chronicler desperate to have her own Great Tale.

Three Worlds: Santhenar, Aachan and Tallallame.

Thurkad: An ancient, wealthy and notably corrupt city on the River

Saboth and the Sea of Thurkad. Seat of the council and the Magister.

Time of the Mirror: The period of several years, beginning about twelve years ago, during which the events set down in Llian's *Tale of the Mirror* took place.

Tirthrax: A city of the Aachim in the Great Mountains.

Tolryme: A town in northern Bannador, close to Karan's family seat, Gothryme.

Triplets, the: identical triplets, Jaguly, Empuly and Unbuly, gifted but crazed mancers whom Gergrig makes into the Merdrun's new magiz.

Triune: A double blending—one with the blood of all Three Worlds, three different human species. They are extremely rare, mostly infertile and can be mentally unstable or obsessive. They may have remarkable abilities. Karan is one, Maigraith another.

Tule, Torsion: An aged, ailing master alchemist; a bigoted and choleric man.

Uigg: A Merdrun drum boy.

Unbuly: A sociopathic triplet, sister to Jaguly and Empuly.

Unick, Gurgito: A genius at inventing magical devices, but a sociopathic, depraved drunk.

Unreality zone: A place corrupted by toxic magical wastes.

Ussarine: Osseion's daughter. A huge, kindly warrior.

Voice: The ability of great tellers to move their audience to any emotion they choose by the sheer power of their words.

Void, the: A place where life is more brutal and fleeting than anywhere. The void teems with the most exotic life imaginable, for nothing survives there without remaking itself constantly.

Vyl, Scorbic: A mancer in the service of Snoat.

Way Between the Worlds: The secret, forever-changing and ethereal paths that permit the difficult passage between the Three Worlds. They were closed off by the Forbidding.

Whelm: Former servants of Yggur—his terror-guard—they are now masterless and dwell in the frigid southland of Shazabba.

Wilm: A good-hearted but unself-confident country lad aged seventeen, who after seeing his friend Dajaes murdered by Unick, has transformed himself into a noble warrior.

Xarah: A young Aachim woman in Malien's group, a gifted scrier.

Yalkara: The last of the three Charon who came to Santhenar to find the flute and return it to Aachan. She was Shand's partner for a time. Maigraith is her granddaughter.

Yetchah: A Whelm woman, partner to Idlis.

Yggur: A great, powerful but troubled mancer and warlord, and a former member of the Great Council. Last year he had a relapse and withdrew from all his captured lands, creating a power vacuum that Cumulus Snoat took advantage of.

Zanser: A master healer from Crandor.

Zain: A scholarly race which once dwelt in Zile and founded the Great Library. They made a pact with Rulke. After he was imprisoned in the Nightland most were slaughtered and the remnant exiled. They are still hated.

Zile: A city in the north-west of the island of Meldorin. Once capital of the empire of Zur, now chiefly famous for the Great Library.

GUIDE TO PRONUNCIATION

There are many languages and dialects used on Santhenar by the four human species. While it is impossible to be definitive in such a brief note, the following generalisations normally apply.

There are no silent letters, and double consonants are generally pronounced as two separate letters; for example, *Yggur* is pronounced *Ig-ger*, and Faellem as *Fael-lem*. The letter *c* is usually pronounced as *k*, except in *mancer* and *Alcifer*, where it is pronounced as *s*, as in *manser*, *Alsifer*. The combination *ch* is generally pronounced as in *church*, except in *Aachim* and *Charon*, where it is pronounced as *k*.

Aachim *Ar'-kim*
Chanthed *Chan-thed'*
Charon *Kar'-on*
Faelamor *Fay-el'-amor*
Iagador *Eye-aga'-dor*
Karan *Ka-ran'*
Llian *Lee'-an*
Maigraith *May'-gray-ith*
Shuthdar *Shoo'-th-dar'*
Ussarine *Oos-sar-een*
Whelm *H'-welm*
Yggur *Ig'-ger*
Xarah *Zha´-rah*

ACKNOWLEDGEMENTS

I would like to thank: my editor and publisher Jenni Hill and the great editorial, sales and marketing team in the UK; my Australian publisher, Fiona Hazard and all her friendly and enthusiastic team; and my U.S. publisher Will Hinton and his terrific team. I would especially like to thank Tim Holman for advice, assistance and encouragement since I first became an Orbit author in 1999. To my agent, Selwa Anthony, thank you for your unstinting support and advice over the past twenty years and thirty-two books.

Most of all I would like to thank my family for putting up with me while I write these vast series.

extras

orbit

meet the author

IAN IRVINE, an Australian marine scientist, has also written thirty-two novels. These include his internationally best-selling Three Worlds epic fantasy sequence, comprising the View from the Mirror quartet, the Well of echoes quartet and the Song of the Tears trilogy, and a related fantasy series, the Tainted Realm trilogy.

His other books include an anthology of Three Worlds stories, *A Wizard's War and other Stories*, a trilogy of eco-thrillers, *Human Rites*, set in the near future when the world is undergoing catastrophic climate change, and thirteen novels for younger readers. He is currently writing book three of *The Gates of Good and Evil*.

Ian can be contacted at: https://www.facebook.com/ianirvine .author
Website: http://www.ian-irvine.com
Goodreadspage:https://www.goodreads.com/author/show/153703 .Ian_Irvine

Find out more about Ian Irvine and other orbit authors by registering for the free monthly newsletter at www.orbitbooks.net.

if you enjoyed
THE FATAL GATE
look out for
THE SHADOW OF WHAT WAS LOST
Book One of the Licanius Trilogy
by
James Islington

It has been twenty years since the godlike Augurs were overthrown and killed. Now, those who once served them—the Gifted—are spared only because they have accepted the rebellion's Four Tenets, vastly limiting their powers.

As a Gifted, Davian suffers the consequences of a war lost before he was even born. He and others like him are despised. But when Davian discovers he wields the forbidden power of the Augurs, he sets into motion a chain of events that will change everything.

To the west, a young man whose fate is intertwined with Davian's wakes up in a forest, covered in blood and with no memory of who he is...

And in the far north, an ancient enemy long thought defeated begins to stir.

Chapter 1

The blade traced a slow line of fire down his face.

He desperately tried to cry out, to jerk away, but the hand over his mouth prevented both. Steel filled his vision, gray and dirty. Warm blood trickled down the left side of his face, onto his neck, under his shirt.

There were only fragments after that.

Laughter. The hot stink of wine on his attacker's breath.

A lessening of the pain, and screams—not his own.

Voices, high-pitched with fear, begging.

Then silence. Darkness.

Davian's eyes snapped open.

The young man sat there for some time, heart pounding, breathing deeply to calm himself. Eventually he stirred from where he'd dozed off at his desk and rubbed at his face, absently tracing the raised scar that ran from the corner of his left eye down to his chin. It was pinkish white now, had healed years earlier. It still ached whenever the old memories threatened to surface, though.

He stood, stretching muscles stiff from disuse and grimacing as he looked outside. His small room high in the North Tower overlooked most of the school, and the windows below had all fallen dark. The courtyard torches flared and sputtered in their sockets, too, only barely clinging to life.

Another evening gone, then. He was running out of those much faster than he would like.

extras

Davian sighed, then adjusted his lamp and began sifting through the myriad books that were scattered haphazardly in front of him. He'd read them all, of course, most several times. None had provided him with any answers—but even so he took a seat, selected a tome at random, and tiredly began to thumb through it.

It was some time later that a sharp knock cut through the heavy silence of the night.

Davian flinched, then brushed a stray strand of curly black hair from his eyes and crossed to the door, opening it a sliver.

"Wirr," he said in vague surprise, swinging the door wide enough to let his blond-haired friend's athletic frame through. "What are you doing here?"

Wirr didn't move to enter, his usually cheerful expression uneasy, and Davian's stomach churned as he suddenly understood why the other boy had come.

Wirr gave a rueful nod when he saw Davian's reaction. "They found him, Dav. He's downstairs. They're waiting for us."

Davian swallowed. "They want to do it now?"

Wirr just nodded again.

Davian hesitated, but he knew that there was no point delaying. He took a deep breath, then extinguished his lamp and trailed after Wirr down the spiral staircase.

He shivered in the cool night air as they exited the tower and began crossing the dimly lit cobblestone courtyard. The school was housed in an enormous Darecian-era castle, though the original grandeur of the structure had been lost somewhat to the various motley additions and repairs of the past two thousand years. Davian had lived here all his life and knew every inch of the grounds—from the servants' quarters near the kitchen, to the squat keep where the Elders kept their rooms, to every well-worn step of the four distinctively hexagonal towers that jutted far into the sky.

Tonight that familiarity brought him little comfort. The high outer walls loomed ominously in the darkness.

"Do you know how they caught him?" he asked.

"He used Essence to light his campfire." Wirr shook his head,

581

the motion barely visible against the dying torches on the wall. "Probably wasn't much more than a trickle, but there were Administrators on the road nearby. Their Finders went off, and…" He shrugged. "They turned him over to Talean a couple of hours ago, and Talean didn't want this drawn out any longer than it had to be. For everyone's sake."

"Won't make it any easier to watch," muttered Davian.

Wirr slowed his stride for a moment, glancing across at his friend. "There's still time to take Asha up on her offer to replace you," he observed quietly. "I know it's your turn, but…let's be honest, Administration only forces students to do this because it's a reminder that the same thing could happen to us. And it's not as if anyone thinks that's something you need right now. Nobody would blame you."

"No." Davian shook his head firmly. "I can handle it. And anyway, Leehim's the same age as her—she knows him better than we do. She shouldn't have to go through that."

"None of us should," murmured Wirr, but he nodded his acceptance and picked up the pace again.

They made their way through the eastern wing of the castle and finally came to Administrator Talean's office; the door was already open, lamplight spilling out into the hallway. Davian gave a cautious knock on the door frame as he peered in, and he and Wirr were beckoned inside by a somber-looking Elder Olin.

"Shut the door, boys," said the gray-haired man, forcing what he probably thought was a reassuring smile at them. "Everyone's here now."

Davian glanced around as Wirr closed the door behind them, examining the occupants of the small room. Elder Seandra was there, her diminutive form folded into a chair in the corner; the youngest of the school's teachers was normally all smiles but tonight her expression was weary, resigned.

Administrator Talean was present, too, of course, his blue cloak drawn tightly around his shoulders against the cold. He nodded to the boys in silent acknowledgment, looking grim. Davian nodded back, even after three years still vaguely surprised to see that the Administrator was taking no pleasure in these proceedings. It was sometimes hard to remember that Talean truly didn't hate the Gifted, unlike so many of his counterparts around Andarra.

Last of all, secured to a chair in the center of the room, was Leehim.

The boy was only one year behind Davian at fifteen, but the vulnerability of his position made him look much younger. Leehim's dark-brown hair hung limply over his eyes, and his head was bowed and motionless. At first Davian thought he must be unconscious.

Then he noticed Leehim's hands. Even tied firmly behind his back, they were trembling.

Talean sighed as the door clicked shut. "It seems we're ready, then," he said quietly. He exchanged glances with Elder Olin, then stepped in front of Leehim so that the boy could see him.

Everyone silently turned their attention to Leehim; the boy's gaze was now focused on Talean and though he was doing his best to hide it, Davian could see the abject fear in his eyes.

The Administrator took a deep breath.

"Leehim Perethar. Three nights ago you left the school without a Shackle and unbound by the Fourth Tenet. You violated the Treaty." He said the words formally, but there was compassion in his tone. "As a result, before these witnesses here, you are to be lawfully stripped of your ability to use Essence. After tonight you will not be welcome amongst the Gifted in Andarra—here, or anywhere else—without special dispensation from one of the Tols. Do you understand?"

Leehim nodded, and for a split second Davian thought this might go more easily than it usually did.

Then Leehim spoke, as everyone in his position did eventually.

"Please," he said, his gaze sweeping around the room, eyes pleading. "Please, don't do this. Don't make me a Shadow. I made a mistake. It won't happen again."

Elder Olin looked at him sadly as he stepped forward, a small black disc in his hand. "It's too late, lad."

Leehim stared at him for a moment as if not comprehending,

then shook his head. "No. Wait. Just wait." The tears began to trickle down his cheeks, and he bucked helplessly at his restraints. Davian looked away as he continued imploringly. "Please. Elder Olin. I won't survive as a Shadow. Elder Seandra. Just wait. I—"

From the corner of his eye, Davian saw Elder Olin reach down and press the black disc against the skin on Leehim's neck.

He forced himself to turn back and watch as the boy stopped in midsentence. Only Leehim's eyes moved now; everything else was motionless. Paralyzed.

Elder Olin let go of the disc for a moment; it stuck to Leehim's neck as if affixed with glue. The Elder straightened, then looked over to Talean, who reluctantly nodded his confirmation.

The Elder leaned down again, this time touching a single finger to the disc.

"I'm sorry, Leehim," he murmured, closing his eyes.

A nimbus of light coalesced around Elder Olin's hand; after a moment the glow started inching along his extended finger and draining into the disc.

Leehim's entire body began to shake.

It was just a little at first, barely noticeable, but then suddenly became violent as his muscles started to spasm. Talean gently put his hand on Leehim's shoulder, steadying the boy so his chair didn't topple.

Elder Olin removed his finger from the disc after a few more seconds, but Leehim continued to convulse. Bile rose in Davian's throat as dark lines began to creep outward from Leehim's eyes, ugly black veins crawling across his face and leaching the color from his skin. A disfigurement that would be with Leehim for the rest of his life.

Then the boy went limp, and it was over.

Talean made sure Leehim was breathing, then helped Elder Olin untie him. "Poor lad probably won't even remember getting caught," he said softly. He hesitated, then glanced over at Elder Seandra, who was still staring hollowly at Leehim's slumped form. "I'm sorry it came to this—I know you liked the lad. When he wakes up I'll give him some food and a few coins before I send him on his way."

Seandra was silent for a moment, then nodded. "Thank you, Administrator," she said quietly. "I appreciate that."

Davian looked up as Elder Olin finished what he was doing and came to stand in front of the boys.

"Are you all right?" he asked, the question clearly aimed at Davian more than Wirr.

Davian swallowed, emotions churning, but nodded. "Yes," he lied.

The Elder gave his shoulder a reassuring squeeze. "Thank you for being here tonight. I know it can't have been easy." He nodded to the door. "Now. Both of you should go and get some rest."

Davian and Wirr inclined their heads in assent, giving Leehim's limp form one last glance before exiting the Administrator's office.

Wirr rubbed his forehead tiredly as they walked. "Want some company for a few minutes? There's no chance I'm going straight to sleep after that."

Davian nodded. "You and me both."

They made their way back to the North Tower in thoughtful, troubled silence.

If you enjoyed
THE FATAL GATE
look out for
SOUL OF THE WORLD
by
David Mealing

Three must fight. Three must die. Three must rise.

It is a time of revolution. in the cities, food shortages stir citizens to riots against the crown. In the wilds, new magic threatens the dominance of the tribes. And on the battlefields, even the most brilliant commanders struggle in the shadow of total war. Three lines of magic must be mastered in order to usher in a new age, and three heroes must emerge.

Sarine *is an artist on the streets of New Sarresant whose secret familiar helps her uncover bloodlust and madness where she expected only revolutionary fervor.*

Arak'Jur *wields the power of beasts to keep his people safe, but his strength cannot protect them from war amongst themselves.*

Erris *is a brilliant cavalry officer trying to defend New Sarresant from an enemy general armed with magic she barely understands.*

Each must learn the secrets of their power in time to guide their people through ruin. But a greater evil may be trying to stop them.

587

1

SARINE

Fontcadeu Green
The Royal Palace, Rasailles

Throw!" came the command from the green.

A bushel of fresh-cut blossoms sailed into the air, chased by darts and the tittering laughter of lookers-on throughout the gardens.

It took quick work with her charcoals to capture the flowing lines as they moved, all feathers and flares. Ostentatious dress was the fashion this spring; her drab grays and browns would have stood out as quite peculiar had the young nobles taken notice of her as she worked.

Just as well they didn't. Her leyline connection to a source of *Faith* beneath the palace chapel saw to that.

Sarine smirked, imagining the commotion were she to sever her bindings, to appear plain as day sitting in the middle of the green. Rasailles was a short journey southwest of New Sarresant but may as well have been half a world apart. A public park, but no mistaking for whom among the public the green was intended. The guardsmen ringing the receiving ground made clear the requirement for a certain pedigree, or at least a certain display of wealth, and she fell far short of either.

She gave her leyline tethers a quick mental check, pleased to find them holding strong. No sense being careless. It was a risk coming here, but Zi seemed to relish these trips, and sketches of the nobles were among the easiest to sell. Zi had only just materialized in front of her, stretching like a cat. He made a show of it, arching his back, blue and purple iridescent scales glittering as he twisted in the sun.

She paused midway through reaching into her pack for a fresh sheet of paper, offering him a slow clap. Zi snorted and cozied up to her feet.

It's cold. Zi's voice sounded in her head. *I'll take all the sunlight I can get.*

"Yes, but still, quite a show," she said in a hushed voice, satisfied none of the nobles were close enough to hear.

What game is it today?

"The new one. With the flowers and darts. Difficult to follow, but I believe Lord Revellion is winning."

Mmm.

A warm glow radiated through her mind. Zi was pleased. And so for that matter were the young ladies watching Lord Revellion saunter up to take his turn at the line. She returned to a cross-legged pose, beginning a quick sketch of the nobles' repartee, aiming to capture Lord Revellion's simple confidence as he charmed the ladies on the green. He was the picture of an eligible Sarresant noble: crisp-fitting blue cavalry uniform, free-flowing coal-black hair, and neatly chiseled features, enough to remind her that life was not fair. Not that a child raised on the streets of the Maw needed reminding on that point.

He called to a group of young men nearby, the ones holding the flowers. They gathered their baskets, preparing to heave, and Revellion turned, flourishing the darts he held in each hand, earning himself titters and giggles from the fops on the green. She worked to capture the moment, her charcoal pen tracing the lines of his coat as he stepped forward, ready to throw. Quick strokes for his hair, pushed back by the breeze. One simple line to suggest the concentrated poise in his face.

The crowd gasped and cheered as the flowers were tossed. Lord Revellion sprang like a cat, snapping his darts one by one in quick succession. *Thunk. Thunk. Thunk. Thunk.* More cheering. Even at this distance it was clear he had hit more than he missed, a rare enough feat for this game.

You like this one, the voice in her head sounded. Zi uncoiled, his scales flashing a burnished gold before returning to blue and purple. He cocked his head up toward her with an inquisitive look. *You could help him win, you know.*

"Hush. He does fine without my help."

She darted glances back and forth between her sketch paper and the green, trying to include as much detail as she could. The patterns of the blankets spread for the ladies as they reclined on the grass, the carefree way they laughed. Their practiced movements as they sampled fruits and cheeses, and the bowed heads of servants holding the trays on bended knees. The black charcoal medium wouldn't capture the vibrant colors of the flowers, but she could do their forms justice, soft petals scattering to the wind as they were tossed into the air.

It was more detail than was required to sell her sketches. But details made it real, for her as much as her customers. If she hadn't seen and drawn them from life, she might never have believed such abundance possible: dances in the grass, food and wine at a snap of their fingers, a practiced poise in every movement. She gave a bitter laugh, imagining the absurdity of practicing sipping your wine just so, the better to project the perfect image of a highborn lady.

Zi nibbled her toe, startling her. *They live the only lives they know,* he thought to her. His scales had taken on a deep green hue.

She frowned. She was never quite sure whether he could actually read her thoughts.

"Maybe," she said after a moment. "But it wouldn't kill them to share some of those grapes and cheeses once in a while."

She gave the sketch a last look. A decent likeness; it might fetch a half mark perhaps, to the right buyer. She reached into her pack for a jar of sediment, applying the yellow flakes with care to avoid smudging her work. When it was done she set the paper on the grass, reclining on her hands to watch another round of darts. The next thrower fared poorly, landing only a single *thunk*. Groans from some of the onlookers, but just as many whoops and cheers. It appeared Revellion had won. The young lord pranced forward to take a deep bow, earning polite applause from across the green as servants dashed out to collect the darts and flowers for another round.

She retrieved the sketch, sliding it into her pack and withdrawing a fresh sheet. This time she'd sketch the ladies, perhaps, a show of the latest fashions for—

She froze.

Across the green a trio of men made way toward her, drawing curious eyes from the nobles as they crossed the gardens. The three of them stood out among the nobles' finery as sure as she would have done: two men in the blue and gold leather of the palace guard, one in simple brown robes. A priest.

Not all among the priesthood could touch the leylines, but she wouldn't have wagered a copper against this one having the talent, even if she wasn't close enough to see the scars on the backs of his hands to confirm it. Binder's marks, the by-product of the test administered to every child the crown could get its hands on. If this priest had the gift, he could follow her tethers whether he could see her or no.

She scrambled to return the fresh page and stow her charcoals, slinging the pack on her shoulder and springing to her feet.

Time to go? Zi asked in her thoughts.

She didn't bother to answer. Zi would keep up. At the edge of the green, the guardsmen patrolling the outer gardens turned to watch the priest and his fellows closing in. Damn. Her *Faith* would hold long enough to get her over the wall, but there wouldn't be any stores to draw on once she left the green. She'd been hoping for another hour at least, time for half a dozen more sketches and another round of games. Instead there was a damned priest on watch. She'd be lucky to escape with no more than a chase through the woods, and thank the Gods they didn't seem to have hounds or horses in tow to investigate her errant binding.

Better to move quickly, no?

She slowed mid-stride. "Zi, you know I hate—"

Shh.

Zi appeared a few paces ahead of her, his scales flushed a deep, sour red, the color of bottled wine. Without further warning her heart leapt in her chest, a red haze coloring her vision. Blood seemed to pound in her ears. Her muscles surged with raw energy, carrying her forward with a springing step that left the priest and his guardsmen behind as if they were mired in tar.

Her stomach roiled, but she made for the wall as fast as her feet could carry her. Zi was right, even if his gifts made her want to sick up the bread she'd scrounged for breakfast. The sooner she could get over the wall, the sooner she could drop her *Faith* tether and stop the priest tracking her binding. Maybe he'd think it no more than a curiosity, an errant cloud of ley-energy mistaken for something more.

She reached the vines and propelled herself up the wall in a smooth motion, vaulting the top and landing with a cat's poise on the far side. *Faith* released as soon as she hit the ground, but she kept running until her heartbeat calmed, and the red haze faded from her sight.

The sounds and smells of the city reached her before the trees cleared enough to see it. A minor miracle for there to be trees at all; the northern and southern reaches had been cut to grassland, from the trade roads to the Great Barrier between the colonies and the wildlands beyond. But the Duc-Governor had ordered a wood maintained around the palace at Rasailles, and so the axes looked elsewhere for their fodder. It made for peaceful walks, when she wasn't waiting for priests and guards to swoop down looking for signs she'd been trespassing on the green.

She'd spent the better part of the way back in relative safety. Zi's gifts were strong, and thank the Gods they didn't seem to register on the leylines. The priest gave up the chase with time enough for her to ponder the morning's games: the decadence, a hidden world of wealth and beauty, all of it a stark contrast to the sullen eyes and sunken faces of the cityfolk. Her uncle would tell her it was part of the Gods' plan, all the usual Trithetic dogma. A hard story to swallow, watching the nobles eating, laughing, and playing at their games when half the city couldn't be certain where they'd find tomorrow's meals. This was supposed to be a land of promise, a land of freedom and purpose—a New World. Remembering the opulence of Rasailles palace, it looked a lot like the old one to her.

Not that she'd ever been across the sea, or anywhere in the colonies but here in New Sarresant. Still.

There was a certain allure to it, though.

It kept her coming back, and kept her patrons buying sketches whenever she set up shop in the markets. The fashions, the finery, the dream of something otherworldly almost close enough to touch. And Lord Revellion. She had to admit he was handsome, even far away. He seemed so confident, so prepared for the life he lived. What would he think of her? One thing to use her gifts and skulk her way onto the green, but that was a pale shadow of a real invitation. And that was where she fell short. Her gifts set her apart, but underneath it all she was still *her*. Not for the first time she wondered if that was enough. Could it be? Could it be enough to end up somewhere like Rasailles, with someone like Lord Revellion?

Zi pecked at her neck as he settled onto her shoulder, giving her a start. She smiled when she recovered, flicking his head.

We approach.

"Yes. Though I'm not sure I should take you to the market after you shushed me back there."

Don't sulk. It was for your protection.

"Oh, of course," she said. "Still, Uncle could doubtless use my help in the chapel, and it *is* almost midday…"

Zi raised his head sharply, his eyes flaring like a pair of hot pokers, scales flushed to match.

"Okay, okay, the market it is."

Zi cocked his head as if to confirm she was serious, then nestled down for a nap as she walked. She kept a brisk pace, taking care to avoid prying eyes that might be wondering what a lone girl was doing coming in from the woods. Soon she was back among the crowds of Southgate district, making her way toward the markets at the center of the city. Zi flushed a deep blue as she walked past the bustle of city life, weaving through the press.

Back on the cobblestone streets of New Sarresant, the lush greens and floral brightness of the royal gardens seemed like another world, foreign and strange. This was home: the sullen grays, worn wooden and brick buildings, the downcast eyes of the cityfolk as they went about the day's business. Here a gilded coach drew eyes and whispers, and not always from a place as benign as envy. She knew better than to court the attention of that sort—the hot-eyed men who glared at the nobles' backs, so long as no city watch could see.

She held her pack close, shoving past a pair of rough-looking pedestrians who'd stopped in the middle of the crowd. They gave her a dark look, and Zi raised himself up on her shoulders, giving them a snort. She rolled her eyes, as much for his bravado as theirs. Sometimes it was a good thing she was the only one who could see Zi.

As she approached the city center, she had to shove her way past another pocket of lookers-on, then another. Finally the press became too heavy and she came to a halt just outside the central square. A low rumble of whispers rolled through the crowds ahead, enough for her to know what was going on.

An execution.

She retreated a few paces, listening to the exchanges in the crowd. Not just one execution—three. Deserters from the army, which made them traitors, given the crown had declared war on the Gandsmen two seasons past. A glorious affair, meant to check a tyrant's expansion, or so they'd proclaimed in the colonial papers. All it meant in her quarters of the city was food carts diverted southward, when the Gods knew there was little enough to spare.

Voices buzzed behind her as she ducked down an alley, with a glance up and down the street to ensure she was alone. Zi swelled up, his scales pulsing as his head darted about, eyes wide and hungering.

"What do you think?" she whispered to him. "Want to have a look?"

Yes. The thought dripped with anticipation.

Well, that settled that. But this time it was her choice to empower herself, and she'd do it without Zi making her heart beat in her throat.

She took a deep breath, sliding her eyes shut.

In the darkness behind her eyelids, lines of power emanated from the ground in all directions, a grid of interconnecting strands of light. Colors and shapes surrounded the lines, fed by energy from the shops, the houses, the people of the city. Overwhelmingly she saw the green pods of *Life*, abundant wherever people lived and worked. But at the edge of her vision she saw the red motes of *Body*, a relic of a bar fight or something of that sort. And, in the center of the city square, a shallow pool of *Faith*. Nothing like an execution to bring out belief and hope in the Gods and the unknown.

She opened herself to the leylines, binding strands of light between her body and the sources of the energy she needed.

Her eyes snapped open as *Body* energy surged through her. Her muscles became more responsive, her pack light as a feather. At the same time, she twisted a *Faith* tether around herself, fading from view.

By reflex she checked her stores. Plenty of *Faith*. Not much *Body*. She'd have to be quick. She took a step back, then bounded forward, leaping onto the side of the building. She twisted away as she kicked off the wall, spiraling out toward the roof's overhang. Grabbing hold of the edge, she vaulted herself up onto the top of the tavern in one smooth motion.

Very nice, Zi thought to her. She bowed her head in a flourish, ignoring his sarcasm.

Now, can we go?

Urgency flooded her mind. Best not to keep Zi waiting when he got like this. She let *Body* dissipate but maintained her shroud of *Faith* as she walked along the roof of the tavern. Reaching the edge, she lowered herself to have a seat atop a window's overhang as she looked down into the square. With luck she'd avoid catching the attention of any more priests or other binders in the area, and that meant she'd have the best seat in the house for these grisly proceedings.

She set her pack down beside her and pulled out her sketching materials. Might as well make a few silvers for her time.